lighting down the ra
priest's words were l
another opportunity.

shadows for
atience.

By Anthony Ryan

Raven's Shadow
Blood Song
Tower Lord

TOWER LORD

A RAVEN'S SHADOW NOVEL

ANTHONY RYAN

www.orbitbooks.net

ORBIT

First published in Great Britain in 2014 by Orbit
This paperback edition published in 2015 by Orbit

Interior text design by Tiffany Estreicher
Main map by Steve Karp, based on an original by Anthony Ryan
Two empires map, Asrael & Cumbrael map, the Northern Reaches map, and
Alltor map by Anthony Ryan

A CIP catalogue record for this book
is available from the British Library.

ISBN 978-0-356-50243-4

Printed and bound by CPI Group (UK) Ltd, Croydon CR0 4YY

Papers used by Orbit are from well-managed forests
and other responsible sources.

For my mother, Catherine,
who believed long before I did

PART I

The raven soars on wings of fire
When flames are born
In summer winds.

—SEORDAH POEM, AUTHOR UNKNOWN

Verniers' Account

I was raised in luxury. I make no apologies for this, one cannot influence one's parentage after all. Nor do I find much to regret in a childhood lived amongst opulence with numerous servants and excellent tutors to nurture my ever-curious and talented mind. So there are no tales of hardship from my youth, no epic of struggle against the inequalities and injustices of life. I was born to a family of noble lineage and considerable wealth, received an exceptional education and was thence facilitated into court service via my father's connections, and although loyal readers will be aware that heartbreak and grief were not absent from my life, I had never known a day of physical exertion in the thirty-six years preceding the events detailed in this narrative. Had I known, of course, that the voyage to the Unified Realm, where I would begin my work on a complete and unbiased history of that terrible but fascinating land, would ensure an end to my previous ignorance of labour, degradation, humiliation and torture, please rest assured I would have happily leapt over the side and endeavoured to swim home through countless miles of shark-enriched waters.

You see, by the advent of the day on which I choose to begin this tale, I had learned pain. I had learned the lessons of the whip and the cudgel, the metallic taste of one's own blood as it gushes forth taking teeth and resistance with it. I had learned to be a slave.

That is what they called me, for that is what I was, and despite whatever nonsense you may have heard or read since, I was never, at any point, a hero.

The Volarian general was younger than I'd expected, as was his wife, my new owner. "Doesn't look a scholar, true-heart," he mused, looking me over from the comfort of his couch. "Bit too young." He reclined in silk robes of red and black, long-limbed and athletic as befits a soldier of some renown, and I was struck by the absence of scars on the pale flesh of his legs and arms. Even his face was smooth and completely unmarked. By now I had endured numerous encounters with warriors from several nations, but this was the first to be entirely unscarred.

"Does seem to have a keen eye though," the general went on, seeing my scrutiny. I immediately lowered my gaze, bracing for the inevitable cuff or whip-strike from the overseer. During the first day of my enslavement I had seen a captured Realm Guard sergeant flayed and disembowelled for glaring in the direction of a junior officer in the Free Cavalry. It was a quickly learned lesson.

"Honoured husband," the general's wife said in her strident, cultured voice. "I present Verniers Alishe Someren, Imperial Chronicler to the Court of the Emperor Aluran Maxtor Selsus."

"Can this really be him, true-heart?" The general seemed genuinely interested for the first time since my entrance into this finely appointed cabin. The chamber was huge for a ship-berth, richly decorated in carpets and tapestries, tables generously laden with fruits and wine. But for the gentle sway of the huge warship beneath my feet we could have been in a palace. The general rose and approached me, eyes examining my face closely. "The author of The Cantos of Gold and Dust? Chronicler of the Great War of Salvation?" He stepped closer and sniffed me, nostrils twitching in disgust. "Smells like any other Alpiran dog to me. And his gaze is far too direct."

He moved back, waving idly at the overseer who administered the blow I knew was coming, a single, hard strike to the back with the ivory handle of his whip, delivered with practised economy. I stifled the shout of pain, caged it behind my teeth. Crying out was considered speech, and speaking without consent was a fatal offence.

"Husband, please," the general's wife said with a tinge of annoyance. "He was expensive."

"Oh, I'm sure." The general held out a hand, a slave scurrying over to fill it with a wine cup. "Don't worry, honoured wife. I'll ensure his wits and hands are left intact. Won't be much use without them will he? So, scribbling-slave, how do you come to be here in our newly acquired province, mmm?"

I answered quickly, blinking away agonised tears, hesitation was always punished. "I came to research a new history, Master."

"Oh excellent. I'm a great admirer of your work, aren't I, true-heart?"

"Indeed, husband. You are a scholar yourself." There was something in her voice when she said the word "scholar," faint but present. Scorn, I realised. She doesn't respect this man. And yet she makes him a gift of me.

There was a brief pause before the general spoke again, a slight edge to his voice. He had heard the insult, but chose to tolerate it. Who truly holds power here?

"And what was its subject?" the general enquired. "This new history of yours?"

"The Unified Realm, Master."

"Ah, then we have done you a service, have we not?" He chuckled, delighted with his own humour. "By giving you an ending."

He laughed again, drinking from his wine cup, and raising his eyebrows in appreciation. "Not bad at all. Make a note, Secretary." The bald-headed slave in the corner stepped forward, stylus poised over parchment. "Orders for the scouting parties: the vineyards are to be left untouched, and halve the slave quota in the wine-making regions. The skill set should be maintained in the fief of . . ." He paused, looking at me expectantly.

"Cumbrael, Master," I said.

"Yes, Cumbrael. Can't say it has much of a ring to it. I've a mind to propose a complete renaming of this province to the Council on my return."

"One must be a Council-man to propose to Council, honoured husband," his wife said. There was no scorn this time, but I noted how he hid a glare of fury in his wine cup.

"Where would I be without your readiness to remind me, Fornella?" he muttered. "So, Historian, where did we have occasion to welcome you into our family?"

"I was travelling with the Realm Guard, Master. King Malcius had given me permission to accompany his host on its mission to Cumbrael."

"So you were there? You witnessed my victory?"

I fought down the immediate upsurge of hellish sounds and images that had plagued my dreams ever since that day. "Yes, Master."

"It seems this gift has more value than you realised, Fornella." He snapped his fingers at the secretary. "Pen, parchment and a cabin for the historian. Not too comfortable, don't want him nodding off when he should be writing his, no doubt, eloquent and stirring account of my first major triumph in this campaign." He came close to me again, smiling fondly. The smile of a child with a new toy. "I expect to be reading it by morning. If I'm not, I'll take one of your eyes."

My hands ached, my back strained from hunching over the short-legged table they had given me. Ink was liberally spattered over my mean slave's garb and my vision swam with exhaustion. Never before had I produced so many words in such a short time. Parchment littered the cabin, filled with my often stumbling attempts to craft the lie the general wanted. Glorious victory. There had been no glory on that field, fear, pain and slaughter amidst the stink of death and shit, but no glory. Surely the general knew this, he had been the architect of the Realm Guard's defeat after all, but I had been commanded to produce a lie and, dutiful slave that I was, bent to the task with all the energy I could summon.

Sleep claimed me sometime past the peak of night, dragging me into nightmare freshly stoked by my enforced remembrance of that day . . . The Battle Lord's face when he knew defeat was imminent, the grim determination as he drew his sword and rode straight at the Volarian line, cut down by the Kuritai before he could strike a single blow . . .

I scrambled to wakefulness by a hard rap on the cabin door, stumbling to my feet as it opened. A house slave entered bearing a tray of bread and grapes, plus a small flask of wine. He placed them on the table and left without a word.

"I thought you might be hungry."

My fearful gaze fixed on the sight of the general's wife in the doorway. She wore a gown of red silk embroidered with gold thread. It did much to enhance her figure. I switched my gaze to the floor. "Thank you, Mistress."

She came in, closing the door behind her, taking in the sight of the sheets covered in my feverish script. "Finished then?"

"Yes, Mistress."

She picked up one of the sheets. "This is in Volarian."

"I assumed my master would wish it so, Mistress."

"Your assumption was correct." Her brows furrowed as she read. "Elegantly phrased too. My husband will be envious. He writes poetry, you know. If you are particularly unfortunate, he may recite it for you. It's rather like listening to a duck with an unusually annoying quack. But this." She held up the sheet. "There are Volarian scholars of great reputation who would be shamed in comparison."

"You are kind, Mistress."

"No, I'm truthful. It's my weapon." She paused then began to read aloud. "'Foolishly the Realm Guard commander gravely under-estimated the guile of his enemy, attempting an obvious and mundane strategy of engaging the Volarian centre whilst his cavalry sought to turn their flank. He reckoned without the sublime tactical acumen of the general Reklar Tokrev, who anticipated his every clumsy move.'" She looked at me with a raised eyebrow. "Clearly, you're a man who understands his audience."

"I'm glad it pleases you, Mistress."

"Pleases me? Oh hardly. But it will please my honoured husband, dullard that he is. This doggerel will be on the fastest ship back to the empire by tomorrow evening, no doubt with instructions to produce a thousand copies for immediate distribution." She tossed the sheet aside. "Tell me, and I command you to speak honestly, just how did the Realm Guard come to suffer such a defeat at his hands?"

I swallowed hard. She could command truth from me, but what protection could she offer if she carried such truth back to the marriage bed? "Mistress, I may have used some colourful phrasing . . ."

"The truth, I said!" Strident tones again, full of authority. The voice of a woman who had owned slaves all her life.

"The Realm Guard fell to weight of numbers and betrayal. They fought hard but were too few."

"I see. Did you fight with them?"

Fight? When it became obvious the tide of battle had turned I flogged my horse bloody to escape to the rear, except there was no rear, the Volarians were everywhere, killing everyone. I found a convenient pile of bodies to hide in, emerging in darkness to immediate capture by the slave hunters. They were an efficient lot, keen to assess the value of every captive and my worth had become apparent after the first beating extracted my real name. She had bought me at the camp enclosure, plucked from the shuffling, chained mob. It seemed they had instructions to bring any scholars to her. From the handsome purse she handed the overseer, it seemed I was a considerable prize.

"I am no warrior, Mistress."

"I should hope not, I didn't buy you for your martial prowess." She stood, regarding me in silence for a moment. "You hide it well, but I can see it, Lord Verniers. You hate us. We may have beaten you to obedience but it's still there, like dry tinder waiting for a spark."

My gaze remained firmly on the floor, concentrating on the swirling knots in the planking, fresh sweat beading my palms. Her hand cupped my face, lifting my chin. I closed my eyes, fighting down a fearful whimper as she kissed me, one soft brush of her lips.

"In the morning," she said. "He'll want you to witness the final assault on the city, now the breaches are in place. Make sure your account is sufficiently lurid, won't you? Volarians expect some colour to their tales of slaughter."

"I shall, Mistress."

"Very well." She moved back, opening the door. "With any luck our business in this damp land will be concluded soon. I should like you to see my library in Volar. More than ten thousand volumes, some so old there are none who can translate them. Would you like that?"

"Very much, Mistress."

She sighed a laugh before leaving the cabin without a further word.

I stared at the closed door for a long time, ignoring the food on the table despite the growling emptiness in my stomach. For some reason my hands had stopped sweating. Dry tinder waiting for a spark.

True to her prediction the general had me brought to the foredeck in the morning to watch the Volarians finally take the city of Alltor, under siege now for more than two months. It was an impressive sight, the twin spires of the World Father's Cathedral rising from the closely packed mass of housing within the great walled island, linked to the mainland by a single causeway. I knew from my various researches that this city had never been taken, not by Janus during the Wars of Unification, nor any other previous aspirant to Kingship. Three hundred years of successful resistance to all conquerors, now about to end thanks to the two breaches torn into the walls by the massive ship-borne ballistas barely two hundred yards offshore. They were still at work, casting their great stones at the breaches, though the rents pounded into the walls seemed fairly complete to my unmilitary eye.

"Magnificent, aren't they, Historian?" the general asked. He was dressed in full armour today, a richly adorned red enamel breast-plate and thigh-length cavalry boots, a short sword strapped to his belt, every inch the Volarian commander. I noticed there was another slave seated nearby, a stick-thin old man with unusually bright eyes, a charcoal stub in his hand moving over a broad canvas to capture the general's image. The general pointed at one of the ballistas, holding the pose and glancing over his shoulder at the old slave.

"Only ever used on land before, but I saw their potential for bringing us victory here. A successful marriage of land and sea warfare. Write that down." I wrote it down on the sheaf of parchment I had been given.

The old man stopped sketching and gave the general a grave bow. He relaxed from his pose and went to a nearby map table. "Read your account," he told me. "Clever of you, being so restrained in your flattery."

A fresh spasm of fear lurched in my breast and I briefly wondered if he would let me choose which eye he would pluck out.

"But an overly complimentary account would arouse suspicion amongst those at home keen to read of my exploits," he went on. "They might think I had exaggerated my achievements somewhat. Clever of you to know this."

"Thank you, Master."

"Not a compliment, merely an observation. Look here." He beckoned me closer, gesturing at the map on the table. I knew Volarian cartographers to be renowned for their accuracy but this was an extraordinarily detailed plan of Alltor, each street rendered with a clarity and precision that shamed the best efforts of the Emperor's Guild of Surveyors. It made me wonder just how long the Volarians had been planning their invasion, and how much help had they enjoyed in doing so.

"The breaches are here and here." His finger picked out two charcoal marks on the map, crude slashes through the finely drawn walls. "I will be assaulting both simultaneously. No doubt the Cumbraelins will have prepared all manner of unpleasantness on their side, but their attention will be fixed entirely on the breaches and therefore will not be expecting another assault on the walls." He tapped a point on the western-facing wall marked with a small cross. "A full battalion of Kuritai will scale the wall and take the nearest breach from the rear. Access to the city will be secured and I expect it will be in our hands by nightfall."

I wrote it all down, careful to resist the temptation to slip into Alpiran. Writing in my own language might arouse his suspicion.

He moved away from the map table, speaking with a theatrical air. "I find these god lovers to have been a valiant enemy, the finest archers I've ever faced in the field, truth be told. And this witch of theirs does seem to inspire them to great efforts. You've heard of her, no doubt?"

News had been scant in the slave pens, confined to snatched whispers of overheard gossip from the Free Swords. Mostly it comprised grim tales of yet more defeat and massacre as the Volarian armies ravaged their way through the Realm, but as we were whipped ever southward into Cumbrael the tale of the dread witch of Alltor had come to the fore, the only gleam of hope in a doomed land. "Scant rumour only, Master. She could be merely a figure of legend."

"No, she's real enough. Got the truth of it from the company of Free Swords that fled after the last assault on the walls. She was there, they said, a girl no more than twenty, in the thick of the fight. Killing many men, they said. Had them all strangled, of course. Worthless cowards." He paused for a moment, lost in thought. "Write this down: cowardice is the worst betrayal of the gift of freedom. For a man who runs from battle is a slave to his fear."

"Very profound, honoured husband." The general's wife had elected to join us. She was dressed simply this morning, the glamour of her silk gown exchanged for a plain muslin dress and red woollen shawl. She brushed past me, closer than was seemly, and went to the rail, watching one of the ballista crews working the great windlass that drew the twin arms back for another throw. "Be sure to find room for it in your account of the impending bloodshed, won't you, Verniers?"

"I shall, Mistress." I watched the general's hand twitch on the hilt of his short sword. She baits him at every turn. Yet he holds his anger, this man who has killed thousands. What is her true role here? I wondered.

Fornella's gaze was drawn away from the sight of the ballista by the approach of a small boat, oars dipping in the placid surface of the river at low tide. A man stood at the prow, barely recognisable at this distance but I noticed her stiffen at the sight of him. "Our Ally sends his creature, honoured husband," she said.

The general followed her gaze and something passed across his face, a twitch of anger but also fear. I felt a sudden urge to be away from this scene; whoever approached, I knew I did not want to make his acquaintance if he could arouse fear in the hearts of such as these. But there was no escape, of course. I was a slave and had not been dismissed. So I could only stand and watch as the boat came ever closer, the Volarian slave-sailors catching the ropes as they were tossed to the deck, tying them up with the kind of efficiency that only came from years of fearful servitude.

The man who hauled himself onto the deck was of middle years and stocky build, bearded and balding, his features largely devoid of any emotion. "Welcome," the general said, his tone carefully neutral. No name or greeting, I realised. Who is this man?

"You have more intelligence to share, I assume?" the general went on.

The man ignored the question. "The Alpiran," he said in Volarian tinged with an accent I had come to recognise as coming from the north of this fallen Realm. "Which is he?"

"What do you want of him?" Fornella asked in her strident tone. He didn't even glance at her and my fear found new depths as his gaze scanned the deck until it fixed on me. He strode forward, coming close enough for me to smell the stench of his unwashed body. He stank of death and a complete disregard for any human standard of cleanliness, and his breath was like a gust of vaporous poison as I cowered away.

"Where," he demanded, "is Vaelin Al Sorna?"

CHAPTER ONE
Reva

May the World Father, who sees all and knows all in His love, guide my blade.

She watched the tall man as he made his way down the gangplank and onto the quayside. He was dressed in common sailor's garb, plain, dun-coloured cloth and sturdy but aged boots, a threadbare woollen cloak about his shoulders and, she was surprised to see, no sword at his belt or on his back. He did, however, have a rope-tied canvas bag slung over his shoulder, a bag of sufficient length for a sword.

The tall man turned as someone called to him from the ship, a broad, black-skinned man with a red scarf tied around his neck, marking him as captain of the vessel that had carried such an illustrious passenger to this minor port. The tall man shook his head, a polite but strained smile on his lips, gave a friendly but emphatic wave of farewell and turned his back on the ship. He walked on quickly, drawing the hood of his cloak over his head as he did so. There were a good number of hawkers, troubadours and whores on the quayside, most affording the tall man the barest attention, though he drew a few glances due to his height. A clutch of whores made a half-hearted attempt to entice his custom, clearly he was another salt-dog with little wealth to share, but he just laughed easily, hands spread in a sham of apologetic and reluctant poverty.

Stupid sluts, she thought, crouched in the dank alleyway that had been her home for the past three days. Fish traders occupied the buildings on either side and she was yet to accustom herself to the stench. *He lusts for blood, not flesh.*

The tall man rounded a corner, making for the north gate no doubt. She rose from her hiding place to follow.

"Payment's due, love." It was the fat boy again. He had been plaguing her since her arrival in the alley, extracting payment in coin not to alert the guards to her presence here, the port authorities had little tolerance for vagrants these days, but she knew it wasn't payment in coin that really interested him. He was perhaps sixteen, two years her junior, but an inch or so taller than her and considerably wider. From the look in his eye he had spent much of her coin on wine. "No more pretending," he said. "One more day an' you'd be gone, y'said. An' yer still here. Payment's due."

"Please," she backed away, voice high, fearful. If he had been sober, he might have wondered why she backed away from the street into the shadow, where surely she was more vulnerable. "I've got more, see?" She held out her hand, a copper gleaming dully in the half-light.

"Copper!" He batted it away, as she had assumed he would. "Cumbraelin bitch. I'll take your coppers and more besi—"

Her fist caught him under the nose, fore-knuckles extended, a precise blow to a spot which would cause the most pain and confusion. His head snapped back, a small explosion of blood coming from his nose and mashed upper lip. Her knife came free from the hidden sheath at the small of her back as he staggered, but the killing blow wasn't necessary. The fat boy ran his tongue over his ruined lip, incomprehension lighting his eyes, then collapsed to the alley floor. She took hold of his ankles and dragged him into the shadow. His pockets yielded what remained of her coppers, a small vial of redflower and a half-eaten apple. She took the coppers, left the redflower and walked away munching on the apple. It would likely be hours before anyone found the fat boy and even then they would assume he was the victim of a drunken fight.

The tall man came into sight within the space of a moment, making his way through the gate, giving an affable nod to the guards but keeping his hood in place. She lingered, finishing her apple as he took the north road, letting him get a good half mile ahead before following.

May the World Father, who sees all and knows all in His love, guide my blade.

The tall man kept to the road for the rest of the day, occasionally stopping to check his surroundings, eyes scanning tree-line and horizon. The actions of a careful man, or an experienced warrior. She kept away from the road, staying in the trees that dominated the country north of Warnsclave, just close enough to keep him in sight. He walked at a steady pace with a regular, long-legged stride that ate up the miles with deceptive speed. There were a few other travellers on the road, mostly carts carrying cargo to or from the port, a few lone riders, none of whom stopped to talk to the tall man. With so many outlaws haunting the woods, talking to a stranger was unwise, though he seemed unconcerned at their wary disinterest.

As night fell he left the road, entering the woods to seek out a campsite. She tracked him to a small clearing sheltered beneath the branches of a large yew, hiding herself in a shallow ditch behind a copse of gorse, watching through the weave of ferns as he made his camp. It was all done with an impressive economy, the near-unconscious actions of a practised wilds-man; wood gathered, fire lit, ground cleared and bedroll laid in the space of what seemed mere moments.

The tall man settled himself against the trunk of the yew, ate a supper of dried beef, washed it down with a gulp from his canteen, then sat watching his fire burn down. His expression was oddly intense, almost as if he were listening to a conversation of some import. She tensed, wary of discovery, knife already drawn. *Does he sense me?* she wondered. The priest had warned her he had the Dark in him, that he was the most formidable enemy she was ever likely to face. She had laughed and cast her knife at the target on the wall of the barn where he spent so many years training her. The knife shuddered in the centre of the target, which split and fell apart. "The Father blesses me, remember?" she said. The priest had whipped her, for her pride and the crime of claiming to know the mind of the World Father.

She watched the tall man and his oddly intense expression for another hour before he blinked, cast a final glance around at the forest and huddled in his cloak to sleep. She forced herself to wait another hour, until the night sky was as dark as it would get and the forest was near black as pitch, the only light of substance the lacelike wisps rising from his dead fire.

She rose from her ditch in a crouch, knife reversed, blade flat against the skin of her arm to hide the gleam. She moved towards the tall man's sleeping form with all the stealth the priest had beaten into her since the age of six, as near soundless as any forest predator could be. The tall man lay on his back, head tilted to one side, neck laid bare. It would be so easy to kill him now, but her mission was clear. *The sword*, the priest had told her, over and over. *The sword is all, his death is secondary.*

She switched the grip on her knife, the blade poised, ready. *Most men will talk with a knife at their throat*, the priest had said. *May the World Father, who sees all and knows all in His love, guide your blade.*

She launched herself onto the tall man, knife reaching for his exposed throat . . .

The air whooshed from her lungs in a pained rush as her chest connected with something hard. *His boots*, she realised with a groan. Then she was in the air, launched by the tall man's boot thrust to land on her back a good ten feet away. She scrambled upright, knife slashing into the spot where she knew he would follow up his attack . . . The knife met only air. The tall man was standing next to the yew, regarding her with an expression certain to provoke an upsurge of rage in her breast. Amusement.

She snarled, charging forward, ignoring the caution instilled by the priest's cane. She feinted to the left then leapt, the knife slashing down to pierce the tall man's shoulder . . . The knife met only air. She stumbled, unbalanced by the momentum of her attack. Whirling, seeing him standing close by, still amused.

She lunged, knife moving in a complex series of jabs and slashes, accompanied by a dizzyingly fast array of kicks and punches . . . They all met only air.

She forced herself to stop, drawing breath in ragged gasps, fighting down the rage and hate. *If an attack fails, withdraw.* The priest's words were loud in her head. *Watch from the shadows for another opportunity. The Father will always reward patience.*

She gave the tall man a final snarl of rage and turned away, ready to sprint into the darkness . . .

"You have your father's eyes."

GO! the priest's voice shouted in her mind. But she stopped, turned back slowly. The tall man's expression had changed, the amusement replaced with something like sorrow.

"Where is it?" she demanded. "Where is my father's sword, Darkblade?"

His eyebrows rose. "Darkblade. Haven't heard that one in years." He moved back to the camp, tossing fresh branches on the fire and striking a flint.

She turned back to the forest, then back to the camp, self-hate and frustration burning in her. *Weakling, coward.*

"Stay if you're staying," the Darkblade said. "Or run if you're running."

She drew a deep calming breath, sheathed her knife and went to sit down on the other side of the growing fire. "The Dark saved you," she accused. "Your unholy magics are an affront to the love of the Father."

He gave an amused grunt, still feeding the fire. "You have dung on your shoes from Warnsclave. Town dung has a particular smell. You should have hidden yourself downwind."

She looked at her shoes and gave an inward curse, resisting the urge to scrape it off. "I know your Dark sight gives you knowledge, how else would you know about my father?"

"You have his eyes, as I said." The Darkblade sat, reaching for a leather pouch and tossing it over the fire to her. "Here, you look hungry."

The pouch contained dried beef and a few oatcakes. She ignored the food, and the growl of protest from her stomach. "You should know," she said. "You killed him."

"Actually, I didn't. As for the man who did . . ." He trailed off, expression momentarily sombre. "Well, he's dead too."

"It was at your command, your attack on his holy mission . . ."

"Hentes Mustor was an insane fanatic who killed his own father and plunged this Realm into a needless war."

"The Trueblade brought the Father's justice to a traitor and sought to free us from your Heretic Dominion. His every action was in service to Father's love . . ."

"Really? Did he tell you that?"

She fell silent, head lowered to hide her rage. Her father had told her nothing, she had never met him, as this Dark-afflicted heretic obviously knew. "Just tell me where it is," she grated. "My father's sword. It's mine by right."

"That's your mission? A holy quest for a yard of sharpened steel." He reached for the canvas-bound bundle propped against the yew tree and held it out to her. "Take this one if you want. It's probably forged with greater skill than your father's in any case."

"The sword of the Trueblade is a holy relic, described as such in the Eleventh Book, blessed by the World Father to bring unity to the Loved and an end to the Heretic Dominion."

He seemed to find further amusement in this. "In truth, it was a plain weapon of Renfaelin design, the kind used by a man-at-arms or a knight with scant funds, no gold or jewels in the hilt to make it valuable."

Despite his scorn the words were enticing. "You were there when it was taken from my father's martyred corpse. Tell me where it is or I swear by the Father you will have to kill me for I will plague you all your days, Darkblade."

"Vaelin," he said, putting the bundle aside.

"What?"

"It's my name. Do you think you could use it? Or Lord Al Sorna if you're of a formal inclination."

"I thought it was Brother."

"Not any more."

She drew back in surprise. *He is no longer of the Order?* It was absurd, surely some kind of trick.

"How did you know where to pick up my trail?" he asked.

"The ship put in at South Tower before sailing to Warnsclave. A man as hated as you shouldn't expect to avoid recognition. Word flies quickly among the Loved."

"So, you are not alone in this great endeavour."

She bit down on more anger-stoked words. *Why not tell him all your secrets, you worthless bitch?* She rose, turning her back on him. "This doesn't end here . . ."

"I know where to find it."

She hesitated, glancing over her shoulder. His expression was entirely serious now. "Then tell me."

"I will, but I have conditions."

She crossed her arms tightly, face wrinkled in contempt and disgust. "So the great Vaelin Al Sorna bargains for a woman's flesh like any other man."

"Not that. As you said, I should not expect to go unrecognised. I require a disguise of sorts."

"Disguise?"

"Yes, you will be my disguise. We will travel together, as . . ." He thought for a moment. ". . . brother and sister."

Travel together. Travel with him? The very thought of it was sickening. But the sword . . . *The sword is all. May the Father forgive me.* "How far?" she said.

"To Varinshold."

"That's three weeks from here."

"Longer, I have a stop to make along the way."

"And you will tell me where to find the sword when we get to Varinshold?"

"My word on it."

She sat again, refusing to look at him, hating the ease of his manipulation. "I agree."

"Then you'd best get some sleep." He moved back from the fire to lie down, wrapping his cloak around him. "Oh," he said. "What do I call you?"

What do I call you? Not, what's your name? He expected her to lie to him. She decided to disappoint him. When he died she wanted him to know the name of the woman that killed him. "Reva," she said. *I was named for my mother.*

She awoke with a start, stirred by the sound of his scattering the remains of the fire. "You'd best eat something." He nodded at the leather pouch. "Many miles to cover today."

She ate two of the oatcakes and drank water from his canteen. Hunger was an old friend, she didn't remember a day when it had been absent from her life. *The truly Loved,* the priest had said the first time he left her out in the cold all night, *require only the love of the Father for nourishment.*

They were on the road before the sun had climbed over the trees, Al Sorna setting a punishing pace with his long, even stride. "Why didn't you buy a horse in Warnsclave?" she asked. "Don't nobles always ride everywhere?"

"I have barely enough coin for food never mind a horse," he replied. "Besides, a man on foot attracts less attention."

Why is he so keen to hide from his people? she wondered. *Mere mention of his name in Warnsclave and they'd have laden him with all the gold he could carry and given him the pick of the stables.*

But hide he did, every time a cart trundled past he averted his gaze and tightened his hood. *Whatever he returned for,* she decided, *it wasn't glory.*

"You're quite good with that knife," he commented during a brief rest by a milestone.

"Not good enough," she muttered.

"Skills like that require training."

She ate an oatcake and said nothing.

"When I was your age I wouldn't have failed." It wasn't a taunt, just a statement of fact.

"Because your unholy Order whips you like dogs from child-hood and verses you in death."

To her surprise he laughed. "Quite so. What other weapons can you use?"

She shook her head sullenly, unwilling to give him any more information than was necessary.

"You must know the bow, surely," he persisted. "All Cumbraelins know the bow."

"Well I don't!" she snapped. It was true. The priest had told her the knife would be all she would need, telling her the bow was not for women. He had a bow of his own of course, all Cumbraelin men did, priest or not. The pain of the beating he had given her for trying to teach herself the use of it in secret had been matched by the humiliation that came from the discovery that drawing a longbow required more strength than she had. It was a point of considerable annoyance.

He let the matter drop and they continued on their way, covering another twenty miles by nightfall. He made camp earlier than he had the night before, disappearing into the woods for at least an hour after lighting the fire and telling her to keep it stoked. "Where are you going?" she asked, suspecting he would simply walk away and leave her there.

"To see what gifts this forest can offer us."

He came back as the gloom was beginning to descend in earnest, carrying a long branch of ash. After supper he sat by the fire and began whittling at the branch with a short sailor's knife, stripping away the twigs and bark with accustomed ease. He offered no explanation and she was unable to resist the urge to ask. "What are you making?"

"A bow."

She snorted, her anger rising. "I'll accept no gifts from you, Darkblade."

His eyes didn't rise from his work. "It's for me. We'll need to hunt some meat before long."

He worked on the bow for the next two nights, thinning the ends and shaping the centre into a curve, flat on one side. For a bowstring he flensed a spare boot-lace, tying it to the notches carved into the ends. "Never was much of an archer," he mused, thrumming the string and drawing forth a low note. "My brother Dentos, though, it was like he'd been born with a bow in his hand."

She knew the story of Brother Dentos, it was part of his legend. The famed Brother archer who had saved him when he brought fiery destruction down on the Alpiran siege engines, only to die in a cowardly Alpiran ambush the next day. The tale had it that the Darkblade had turned the sands red with his fury as he cut down the ambushers, though they begged for mercy. She had serious doubts as to the truth of this or any of the other fanciful tales attached to the life of Vaelin Al Sorna, but the effortless ease with which he had defeated her attack that first night made her wonder if there wasn't some truth hidden amongst all the nonsense.

He made arrows from another ash branch, sharpening the points as they had no metal for arrowheads. "Should do for birds," he said. "Couldn't take on a boar with it though, need iron-heads to get through the ribs."

He hefted the bow and walked off into the forest. She waited a full two minutes, cursed and then followed. She found him crouched behind the husk of an ancient oak, an arrow notched to the bowstring. He waited with an absolute stillness, eyes fixed on a patch of tall grass in a small clearing ahead. Reva moved cautiously to his side but contrived to step on a dry twig, the loud crack echoing through the clearing. Three pheasants rose from the grass, wings thundering as they sought the sky. Al Sorna's bowstring snapped and a bird tumbled back to earth, trailing feathers. He gave her a glance of faint reproach and went to fetch the game.

Not much of an archer, she thought. *Liar.*

In the morning she awoke to find herself alone in the camp, the Darkblade no doubt off hunting again, though his bow had been left propped against a fallen tree-trunk. There was a curious feeling in her belly, a strange heaviness and she realised this was the first time she could remember waking with a full stomach. Al Sorna had spitted and roasted the pheasant, seasoning the plucked skin with lemon thyme. The grease had covered her chin as she wolfed down her share. She caught him smiling as she ate, making her scowl and turn away. But she hadn't stopped eating.

Her eyes lingered on the bow for a moment. It was shorter than the longbow that had frustrated her for years, the stave thinner and no doubt easier to draw. She glanced around then picked it up, notching one of the arrows from Al Sorna's makeshift quiver of woven long grass. It felt light in her hands, comfortable. She took aim at the narrow trunk of a silver birch some ten yards away, it seemed the easiest target to hand. The bow was harder to draw than she anticipated, raising memories of hours of fruitless practice with the longbow, but she did at least manage to get the string back to her lips before loosing. The arrow glanced off the edge of the birch and disappeared into a patch of ferns.

"Not bad." Al Sorna was striding through the undergrowth, freshly gathered mushrooms were piled in his cloak.

Reva tossed the bow back to him and slumped down, drawing her knife. "It's unbalanced," she muttered. "Threw my aim off." She took hold of the hair at the nape of her neck and began her twice-weekly ritual of cutting.

"Don't do that," Al Sorna said. "You're supposed to be my sister, and Asraelin women wear their hair long."

"Asraelin women are vain sluts." She pointedly sawed off a chunk of hair and let it fall.

Al Sorna sighed. "I suppose we could say you're simple-minded. Took to cutting your hair as a child. Me old mum could never get her out of the habit."

"You will not!" She glared at him. He smiled back. She gritted her teeth and returned the knife to its sheath.

He placed the bow and quiver of arrows next to her. "Keep it. I'll make myself another."

The next day saw them walking the road again. Al Sorna's pace hadn't slackened at all but she was finding it easier to keep up, no doubt helped by the recent improvement in her diet. They had been going for an hour when Al Sorna came to a halt, his head tilted upwards, nostrils flaring a little. It was a moment before Reva caught it, a scent on the westerly breeze, acrid, corrupt. She had smelt it before, as had he, no doubt on many more occasions.

He said nothing but left the road, walking towards the forest. It was beginning to thin as they travelled north, but there were still patches of thick woodland in which to camp or hunt. She noted a change in his movements as he approached the trees, a slight curve to the shoulders, a looseness to his arms, fingers splayed as if ready to reach for something. She had seen the priest move in a similar way, but never with such unconscious grace and she realised in a rush that the Darkblade was the priest's superior, a thing she always thought impossible. No man could best the priest, his skills were born of the Father's blessing after all. But this heretic, this enemy of the Loved, moved with such predatory grace she knew any contest between them would end only one way. *I was a fool*, she decided. *Trying to take him like that. When the time comes to kill him, I must be more guileful . . . or better trained.*

She followed at a short distance. She still carried the bow and wondered if she should notch an arrow but decided against it, her archery skills were hardly a threat to whatever might await them in the trees. She drew her knife instead, eyes continually seeking movement, finding only the sway of branches in the wind.

They found the bodies about twenty yards in, three of them, man, woman and child. The man had been lashed to a tree and gagged with a hemp rope, dried blood stained his bare chest from neck to waist. The woman was naked and her flesh bore the marks of prolonged torment, bruises and shallow cuts. One of her fingers had been hacked off, whilst she still breathed judging by the amount of blood. The boy could be no more than ten years in age and was also naked and similarly abused.

"Outlaws," Reva said. She peered closer at the man tied to the tree, seeing how the hemp gag gouged into the flesh of his cheeks. "Looks like they made him watch."

Al Sorna's gaze was moving over the scene with an intensity she hadn't seen before, scanning the ground as he moved, tracking. "This happened at least a day and a half ago," Reva said. "Any tracks will be stale. They'll be in the nearest town, drinking and whoring with whatever spoils they got here."

He turned a fierce gaze on her. "Your World Father's love seems to make you cold."

His anger made her take a firmer grip on the knife. "This land is thick with thievery and murder, Darkblade. I've seen death before. We've been lucky not to have drawn any outlaws ourselves."

The fierceness in his gaze faded and he straightened, losing the predatory readiness. "Rhansmill is closest."

"It's out of our way."

"I know." He went to the body of the man and used his sailor's knife to cut the bonds securing him to the tree. "Gather wood," he told her. "A lot of wood."

It took another day to get to Rhansmill, an unimpressive huddle of houses clustered around a water mill on the banks of the Avern

River. They arrived at night, finding the place in the throes of some form of celebration, numerous torches had been lit and the townsfolk thronged around a semicircle of garishly painted wagons.

"Players," Reva said with distaste, seeing the frivolous and occasionally lewd depictions on the sides of the wagons. They made their way slowly through the crowd, Al Sorna's hood drawn close about his face; however, the audience's gaze was fixed on a wooden stage in the centre of the semicircle. The man on stage was narrow of face and dressed in a shirt of bright red silk with tight-fitting trews of yellow and black, he sang and played a mandolin whilst a woman in a chiffon dress danced. The man's playing was expert, his voice melodious and pure, but it was the dance that captured Reva's attention, the grace and precision of the woman's movements drawing her gaze like a flame-entranced moth. Her bare arms seemed to shine in the torchlight, her eyes, bright and blue behind a chiffon veil . . .

Reva looked away and closed her eyes, fingernails digging into her palms. *World Father, I call on your forgiveness once more . . .*

"My lover's hand held soft in mine," the man in the red shirt sang, the final verse of "Across the Valley." "Upon her cheek bright tears do shine, To the Beyond I'll take her smile, Where for her love I'll wait . . ." He stopped, eyes wide as they caught a figure in the crowd. Reva tracked his gaze, finding it directed straight at Al Sorna's hooded face. ". . . a while," the man finished, forcing the words out. The crowd's applause was quick, despite the stumble.

"Thank you, my friends!" The mandolin player bowed deeply, raising a hand to the dancer. "The lovely Ellora and I thank you most humbly. Please show your appreciation in the usual manner." He pointed at the bucket placed at the front of the stage. "And now, dear friends"—the player's voice dropped a little, his expression becoming grave—"prepare yourselves for our final performance of the night. A tale of high adventure and low treachery, of blood spilled and treasure stolen, prepare yourselves for *The Pirate's Revenge!*" He threw his arms wide then took the hand of the girl and rushed from the stage, hampered somewhat by a noticeable limp. Two men promptly strode onto the boards, both dressed in a fanciful approximation of Meldenean sailor's garb.

"I spy a ship, Captain!" the shorter of the men said when the applause had faded, holding a wooden spyglass to his eye to scan an imaginary horizon. "A Realm vessel, if I'm any judge. Rich plunder to be had, by the gods."

"Plunder indeed!" the taller player agreed, a false beard of loose wool covering his chin and a red scarf on his head. "And much blood to spill to sate our gods' thirst."

Al Sorna gave a soft touch to her arm as the two players shared an evil laugh. He inclined his head to the left and she followed as he moved through the crowd, making for a gap between the line of wagons. She was unsurprised to find the mandolin player there, eyes bright in the shadows, drinking in the sight of Al Sorna as he drew back his hood.

"Sergeant Norin," he said.

"My lord," the man breathed. "I had heard . . . there were rumours, but—"

Al Sorna moved forward and embraced the man warmly, Reva noting the player's expression of complete astonishment. "It's very good to see you, Janril," Al Sorna said, drawing back. "Very good indeed."

"There are a thousand tales of your death," the minstrel told Al Sorna over supper. They had been welcomed into the wagon he shared with Ellora. She had exchanged her chiffon dancer's garb for a plain grey dress and cooked them a meal of stew and dumplings. Reva avoided looking in her direction and concentrated on the food. Al Sorna had introduced her as "Reva, my pretend sister for the next few weeks." Janril Norin just nodded and told her she was welcome, any curiosity he might have felt about the nature of their relationship carefully hidden. *Soldiers don't question their commanders,* she thought.

"And a thousand more of your escape," Norin went on. "They say you fashioned a mace from your chains with the aid of the Departed and slew your way out of the Emperor's dungeons. I wrote a song about it, always goes down well."

"Well, I'm afraid you'll have to write another," Al Sorna said. "About how they just let me go."

"I thought you went to the Meldenean Islands first," Reva said, letting her disbelief colour her tone. "Killed the pirates' champion and rescued a princess."

He just shrugged. "All I did in the Isles was take part in a play. Though, I'm not much of a player."

"Player or not, my lord," Norin said. "You know you're welcome in this company. For as long as you wish."

"We're making for Varinshold. If you're heading there, we'll gladly accompany you."

"We're going south," Ellora said. "The Summertide Fair in Mealinscove always reaps a healthy profit." There was a guardedness to her tone and a clear discomfort at the Darkblade's presence. *Smart enough to know he brings death everywhere he goes,* Reva surmised.

"We're going north," Norin told her in a flat tone, then smiled at Al Sorna. "The fair in Varinshold will be just as fruitful, I'm sure."

"We'll pay our way," Vaelin said to Ellora.

"Won't hear of it, my lord," Norin assured him. "Having your sword with us will be payment enough. So many outlaws about these days."

"Talking of which, we found their handiwork a few miles back. A family, robbed and slaughtered. Came here looking to ensure justice, in fact. Notice any candidates tonight?"

Norin thought for a moment. "There was a rowdy bunch in the alehouse this afternoon. Their clothes were mean but they had money for ale. Drew my interest because one of them had a gold ring on a chain about his neck. Too small for a man's ring, if I'm any judge. Caused a bit of a ruckus when the brewer refused to sell them one of his daughters. The guards told them to quiet down or move on. There's a vagrants' camp a mile or so downriver. If they haven't gone back to the forest, likely we'll find them there."

Ellora's gaze turned into a glare at the mention of the word "We."

"If they were drunk they'll be sleeping it off," Al Sorna said. "They'll still be there in the morning, I'm sure. Though, ensuring justice will mean involving the guards, and I was hoping not to draw any attention."

"There are other forms of justice, my lord," Norin pointed out. "Was a time we dealt it to outlaws on a fairly regular basis, as I recall."

Al Sorna glanced at the canvas-wrapped sword in the corner of the wagon. "No, I'm no Lord Marshal these days and no longer exercise the King's Word. Seems it can't be helped. I'll find the guard captain in the morning."

After supper Norin sat on the wagon steps playing his mandolin, singing with Ellora at his side. The other players gathered round to listen and call for him to sing their favourites. Reva and Al Sorna drew a few curious glances and, from the awed expressions of a few, some had clearly divined his identity. However, Norin's statement that she and his old friend from the Wolfrunners were his guests and their privacy was to be respected seemed to be all that was required to ensure no questions were asked.

"Doesn't look a soldier," Reva observed to Al Sorna. They had placed themselves a short distance from the company, lighting a fire against the night's chill.

"He was always more of a minstrel," Al Sorna said. "But a hard fighter when it mattered. I'm glad he took his pension. Seems happy enough with his lot."

Reva shot a quick look at Ellora, her smile as she rested against Norin's knee. *Well he might,* she thought.

The company drifted off to their own wagons as the hour grew late and Norin and Ellora retired to bed. He had provided them with thick blankets and soft furs to lie on and Reva marvelled at the comfort of it. Sleeping on hard ground was all she had known for most of her life. *Comfort is a trap,* the priest had said. *A barrier to the Father's love, for it makes us weak, servile to the Heretic Dominion.* With that he had beaten her for the crime of hiding a sack of straw in the barn to sleep on.

She waited a good two hours. Al Sorna never snored, in fact he barely made a sound or moved at all when sleeping. She watched the gentle rise and fall of his chest beneath the blanket for a while longer to be sure, then slipped from her own coverings, picked up her shoes and made her way barefoot to the river. On the bank she splashed water on her face to banish any lingering tiredness, pulled on her shoes and followed the current downstream.

The vagrants' camp wasn't hard to find, the smell of woodsmoke announced its location before the cluster of shacks and tents came into view. Only one fire burned in the camp, raucous laughter echoing from the few occupants. Four men, passing a bottle around. *Must've scared the rest away,* she thought. She crept closer until their voices became clear.

"You rutted on that bitch when she was dead, Kella!" one of the men laughed. "Fucking a corpse, you filthy animal."

"Least I didn't rut on the boy," the other man shot back. "Against nature that is."

Reva saw little reason for stealth or further delay. This needed doing quickly before Al Sorna missed her.

The four men fell silent as she walked into the camp, surprise soon replaced by drunken lust.

"Looking for somewhere to sleep, lovely?" the largest of the men said. He had an extensive mop of unkempt hair and the gaunt, wasted look of a man who lived from day to day without regular meals or shelter. There was also a gold ring hanging on a string about his neck. *Too small for a man's ring, if I'm any judge.* Reva remembered the sight of the woman in the forest, the finger hacked from her hand.

She said nothing and stared back.

"We've got plenty of room," the man went on, coming closer on unsteady legs. "Everyone else's pissed off. Can't think why."

Reva met his gaze, saying nothing. Drunk as he was, some faint warning must have sounded in his head for he stopped a few feet short of her, eyes narrowing. "What you want here gir—!"

The knife came free of the sheath in a blur, she ducked forward then upwards in a fluid motion, the blade slicing through his neck, then twisted away as he fell, blood spraying through his fingers.

The second one she killed was too shocked to react as she leapt, wrapped her legs about his chest and stabbed deep into his shoulder, once, then twice. She leapt free, darted towards the third man, now fumbling for a cudgel in his belt. He managed a single swing which she ducked with ease, rolling on the ground then slashing back to sever his hamstring. He fell, cursing and screaming. Reva turned to the fourth man. His fevered gaze took in the scene around him as he fidgeted, a long-bladed knife in his hand. He gave Reva a final terror-stricken glance, dropped the knife and fled. He had almost reached the sheltering darkness beyond the firelight before her knife throw took him between the shoulder blades.

Reva went to the large man's body, pushing it over to retrieve the ring from around his neck. There was also a good-quality hunting knife in his belt, Realm Guard issue from the regimental crest on the handle. She took the knife, pocketed the ring and walked to the man with the severed hamstring, now weeping desperate pleas through a cloud of snot and spittle.

"Don't worry, Kella," she said. "I promise I won't fuck your corpse."

Ellora made them a breakfast of eggs and mushrooms fried in butter. *As good a cook as she is a dancer,* Reva thought, tucking in. She waited until Ellora and Norin had gone to tend to the drays that pulled their wagon, then took the ring from her pocket and tossed it to Al Sorna. He looked at it for a long time. "The sun and the moon," he said softly.

Reva frowned. "What?"

He held it up for her to see, an engraving on the inside of the band, two circles, one wreathed in flame. "They were Deniers."

She shrugged and returned to her breakfast.

"The bodies," Al Sorna said.

"Weighted and dumped in the river."

"Very efficient of you."

She looked up at the hardness in his tone, seeing something in his gaze that gave new fire to her anger. Disappointment. "I am not here because I choose to be, Darkblade," she told him. "I am here for the sword of the Trueblade so that I might earn the love of the Father by bringing down your unholy Realm. I am not your friend, your sister or your pupil. And I do not care one whit for your approval."

Janril Norin coughed, breaking the thick silence that reigned in the aftermath of her words. "Best be looking for the guard captain, my lord. If this is to be done today."

"That won't be necessary, Janril." Al Sorna tossed the ring back to Reva. "Keep it, you earned it."

CHAPTER TWO
Frentis

The shaven-headed man coughed blood onto the sand and died with a faint whimper. Frentis dropped his sword next to the body and waited, still and silent but for the harsh rasp of his breathing. This one had been harder than usual, four enemies instead of the usual two or three. Slaves scurried from the dark alcoves in the pit wall to clean up the mess, dragging the bodies away and retrieving his sword. They kept their distance from Frentis. Sometimes the killing rage the overseer instilled in him took a while to fade.

"Remarkable," said a voice from above. There were three spectators today, the overseer joined by the master and a woman Frentis hadn't seen before. "Hard to believe he's actually improved, Vastir," the master went on. "My compliments."

"My only thought is to serve you, Council-man," the overseer said with just the right amount of fawning servility. He was a diligent fellow and never overplayed his part.

"Well?" the master said to the woman at his side. "Does he meet with our Ally's approval?"

"I don't speak for the Ally," the woman said. Her tone, Frentis noted, was free of anything that might be described as servility, or even respect. "Whether he meets with *my* approval, however."

Bound as he was, Frentis could not outwardly express surprise, or any other emotion not permitted him by the overseer, but he did twitch in astonishment as the woman leapt into the pit, landing from the ten-foot drop with practised ease. She was dressed in the formal robes of a Volarian highborn, dark hair was tied back from a face of feline beauty with eyes that gleamed bright with interest as she examined Frentis's naked form from head to toe. "Prettier than I expected," she murmured. She looked up at the overseer, raising her voice. "Why is his face unscarred?"

"He never gets any scars, Honoured Lady," Vastir called back. "A few have come close over the years, but he was already highly skilled when he came to us."

"Highly skilled were you, pretty one?" the woman asked Frentis, then grimaced in annoyance when he didn't respond. "Let him speak," she called to the overseer.

Vastir glanced over the edge of the pit at Frentis, and he felt the slight loosening of the will that bound him. "Well?" the woman demanded.

"I am a brother of the Sixth Order," he said.

She raised an eyebrow at the lack of an honorific.

"My profound apologies, Honoured Lady," Vastir gushed. "However many punishments we administer he refuses to use correct language, and we were cautioned that the only death he should face would be in the pits."

The woman waved a hand in dismissal. "Swords!" she commanded.

There was a moment's confusion above, a whispered discussion between master and overseer from which Frentis discerned the words, "just do it, Vastir!" Another brief delay then two short swords were tossed into the pit, landing in the sand between Frentis and the woman.

"Well then," she said in a brisk tone, shrugging off her robes to stand as naked as he was. Her body was lithe, displaying the finely honed muscle of one who has spent many years in hard training and was, by any standard, quite beautiful. But what interested Frentis was not the curve of her thighs or the fullness of her breasts, but the pattern of whirling scars that covered her from neck to groin, a pattern he knew with intimate precision. They were an exact mirror image of his own, the matrix of damaged tissue One Eye had carved into him in the vaults beneath the western quarter before his brothers came to free him.

"Pretty aren't they?" the woman asked, seeing how his eyes tracked over the scars. She came closer, reaching out to caress the whirling symbol on his chest. "Precious gifts, born in pain." Her hand splayed flat on his chest and he felt warmth emanating from it. She sighed, eyes closed, fingers twitching on his skin. "Strong," she whispered. "Can't be too strong."

She opened her eyes and stepped back, removing her hand, the warmth fading instantly. "Let's see what your Order taught you," she said, crouching to pick up the swords, tossing one to him. "Release him!" she ordered Vastir. "Completely."

Frentis could sense the overseer's hesitation. In the five or more years he had been caged here they had only ever fully released him once, with very unfortunate results.

"Honoured Lady," Vastir began. "Forgive the reluctance of one who only seeks to serve . . ."

"Do as I say, you corpulent pile of dung!" The woman smiled for the first time, her gaze still locked on Frentis. It was a fierce smile, joyful with anticipation.

Then it was gone, the will that bound him lifted like the planks of the stocks he remembered so well from childhood. The sudden rush of freedom was exhilarating, but all too short.

The woman lunged at him, sword extended in a perfectly straight line for his heart, agile, accurate and very fast. His own blade came up to meet hers, deflecting the thrust with scant inches to spare. He whirled away towards the wall of the pit, jumped, rebounded from the rock, back arched as her blade slashed beneath him, landed on his hands in the centre of the pit then bounced to his feet.

The woman gave a laugh of unbridled joy and attacked again with a prepared scale of thrusts and slashes. He recognised it from one of the Kuritai he had killed a few months ago. It was how they taught him, new tricks every time to sharpen his skills to ever greater heights. He parried her every blow and retaliated with a scale of his own, learned under another master he had once thought harsh but now recalled with fond remembrance.

She was unfamiliar with these moves, he could tell, parrying his thrusts with less fluency than she had displayed in her attack. He forced her back to the wall of the pit, completing the scale by feinting a blinding stab at her eyes then bringing the blade up and around to slash into her thigh. Their swords rang as she parried the blow.

Frentis drew back a little, meeting the woman's gaze. She was still smiling. The parry had been too fast. Impossibly fast in fact.

"Now I've got your attention," the woman said.

Frentis smiled back. It was not something he did with any regularity and the muscles of his face ached from the novelty of it. "I've never killed a woman," he said.

She pouted. "Oh don't be like that."

He turned his back on her and walked to the centre of the pit. They had given him a choice for the first time, and he was taking it.

"This could be a problem," the woman said, her voice soft, and he realised she was thinking aloud.

"Honoured Lady?" Vastir called down.

"Throw me a rope!" she called back. "I'm done here." She gestured at Frentis. "You can have this one for the spectacles."

"He'll make fine show at the victory celebrations, no doubt," the master said. Frentis found it strange that he sounded relieved.

"Indeed, most honoured," Vastir agreed, dragging a rope ladder to the edge of the pit, "I should despair if all my efforts were wast—"

Frentis's short sword took him in the neck, slicing through veins and spine to protrude from beneath the base of his skull.

He staggered for a moment, eyes bulging in terror and confusion, blood gushing from mouth and wound, then collapsed forward, landing on the sand of the pit with a soft thump.

Frentis straightened from the throw, turning to the woman. Death would come now, killing an overseer was a crime they could not forgive, whatever his value might be. However, he was dismayed to find her smile had returned.

"You know, Arklev," she said to the master, now staring at Frentis in appalled astonishment. "I think I've changed my mind."

The binding came again when she had climbed out of the pit, clamping down hard with enough force to make him stagger and fall to the sands, his scars burning with an agony as yet unknown. He looked up to see her smiling and twiddling her fingers, remembering the warmth that emanated from her touch. *This is her!* he realised. *She binds me now.*

He watched her laugh and disappear from view, the binding lifting after a few seconds more torment. The master lingered a moment, his lean features regarding Frentis with a mixture of anger and fear, restrained but still palpable to a man well versed in reading the face of his opponents.

"Your Realm will suffer for your failure to die today, slave," the master said. Then he was gone and Frentis experienced a sudden certainty that he would most likely never see him again. It was a shame, he had hoped opportunity might arise when he could send him to join Vastir in the Beyond.

He got to his feet as the alcove doors clattered open to admit the slaves. They were joined by a platoon of Varitai. They circled him with spears levelled as the slaves did their work, dragging away the overseer's bloated corpse, raking the blood from the sand, then disappearing back to wherever it was they went. Frentis had never seen beyond the alcove doors, but from the sounds of pain and toil that echoed through them at night, he doubted there was much he wanted to see.

One of the Varitai, silent as they always were, came forward to place a bundle in the centre of the pit. With that they trooped out in single file, the door slamming shut behind.

Frentis went to the bundle. They always left him food after a fight. Usually a bowl of surprisingly tasty porridge and an occasional serving of well-cooked meat. Starving him would not serve their purpose. In that respect at least, they were just like the Order. Today was different. In addition to the food he had been given clothes, the plain and serviceable tunic and trews of a Volarian freeman, dyed blue to signify his status as a journeyman of some kind, permitted to travel between the provinces. There was also a pair of solid boots, a belt of leather and a cloak of tightly woven cotton.

He fingered the clothing and recalled the burn of his scars. *Where will she take me?* he wondered, a new chill in his heart. *What will she make me do?*

In the morning a rope ladder was lowered into the pit. He had dressed in his new clothes, the feel of cloth on his skin strange after so many years of enforced nakedness. It made his scars itch. He climbed the ladder without hesitation, feeling no need for a final glance at his home of five years. There was nothing here he wanted to remember, but even so he knew every fight, every death, would stay with him forever.

The woman was waiting as he climbed from the pit. There were no guards; she didn't need them. Her fine robes of the previous day had been exchanged for the more modest gown of a mid-status freewoman, dyed grey. His knowledge of this land and its customs was meagre, confined to what he had learned during his journey here after being taken in Untesh, plus whatever scraps of information he had been able to glean from overheard conversations between master and overseer. The colour grey, he knew, signified a person of property, usually slaves but also land and livestock. If a free Volarian acquired sufficient property, one thousand slaves or assets of equivalent value, they were permitted to wear black. Only the richest Volarians wore red, like the master.

"I hope you got some sleep," she said. "We have a long way to go."

The binding was still there, but restrained now, a faint tingle to his scars, enough to prevent him tying his new belt about her neck and strangling her, but with sufficient freedom to allow a survey of the environs. The pits surrounded them on every side, a hundred or more, each thirty feet in diameter and ten feet deep, carved into a broad plateau of bare rock, honeycombed with tunnels and dwellings. From some came the sound of combat, from others torture, screams rising into the morning air, overseers directing the various torments as they strolled the rim of the pits. This was a place of punishment as well as training.

"Sorry to be leaving?" the woman asked.

She had left him enough freedom to speak but he said nothing.

Her gaze darkened and he knew she was considering another punishing burn to his scars. He stared back, still refusing to speak, or beg.

To his surprise she laughed again. "So long since I had something truly interesting to play with. Come along, pretty one." She turned and began walking to the edge of the plateau. It rose from the Vakesh Desert like an island in a sea of sand; when the midday sun ascended to its full height the temperature on the surface was enough to make even the overseers desist from their labours. Caravan routes ran from the north and west. He had memorised all this when they brought him here, back when he still indulged in the dream that he might one day contrive an escape.

She led him to the winding set of steps carved into the western face of the plateau, where it took them the best part of an hour to descend to the desert floor. A slave was waiting with four horses, two saddled for riding, two more bearing packs. She took the reins from the slave and dismissed him with a wave.

"I am a widowed landowner from the province of Eskethia," she informed him. "I have business in Mirtesk. You are my journeyman escort, contracted to see me there safely without injury to body or reputation."

She gave him the care of the packhorses and hauled herself into the saddle of the tallest riding horse, a grey mare which seemed to know her from the way it snorted in pleasure as she patted its neck. Her gown had slits to accommodate riding full saddle and her bare thighs were bronze in the morning sun. He looked away and saw to the pack animals.

Their loads consisted mainly of food and water, sufficient, he assumed, for their journey to Mirtesk. They were well cared for with no signs of infirmity that might lay them low in the desert, hooves shod with broad but thin iron shoes suitable for trekking across the sands. He remembered how the Alpiran desert had taxed his scout troop's mounts to the limit until they copied the smithing tricks used by the Emperor's cavalry. Memories of the Alpiran war came to him constantly and, despite all the blood spilled in their doomed attempt to fulfil the King's mad vision, the months spent with the Wolfrunners, with his brothers, with Vaelin, had been the best days of his life.

His scars gave a short burn as the woman shifted impatiently in her saddle. He tightened the straps on the packs and mounted his own horse, a youthful black stallion. The mount was somewhat feisty, rearing and snorting as he settled onto the saddle. He leaned forward to cup the stallion's ear, whispering softly. Instantly the animal calmed, trotting forward without demur as Frentis nudged his heels to its flanks, the packhorses trailing behind.

"Impressive," the woman said, spurring her own mount into motion. "Only seen it done a few times. Who taught you?"

There was a command to her tone and the binding tightened a little. "A madman," he said, recalling Master Rensial's conspiratorial smirk as he imparted the secret of the whisper, something, Frentis knew, he had never taught any of the other novice brothers. *Looks like the Dark, doesn't it?* he said with one of his high-pitched giggles. *If only they knew. The fools.*

He said no more and the woman let the binding recede to the now-standard tingle. "There will come a time," she said, as they rode towards the west, "when you'll tell me every secret in your heart, and do so willingly."

Frentis's hands clenched on his reins and inside he howled, raging at his prison of scars, for he knew now it was the scars that bound him, the means by which each overseer and master bent him to their will. One Eye's final gift, his ultimate revenge.

They journeyed until noon, resting under small awnings as the sun baked the desert, moving on when the shadows grew long and the heat abated. They stopped at a small oasis, already crowded with caravans setting up camp for the night. Frentis watered the horses and established their camp on the fringes of the temporary community. The caravan folk seemed a cheerful lot, all free citizens, exchanging news with old friends or entertaining each other with songs or stories. Most wore blue, but here and there was a grey-clad veteran with a long beard and a longer string of horses. A few approached them with wares to sell or requests for news from the wider empire. The woman was all charm and affability in refusing the wares and offering minor gossip about the Council's doings or the recent results of the Sword Races, which seemed to be a major preoccupation.

"The Blues lost again?" one older grey-clad said, shaking his head in disappointed wonder. "Followed them all my life, I have. Lost two fortunes in bets."

The woman laughed and popped a date into her mouth. "Should switch to the Greens, grandfather."

He glowered a little. "Man can't change his team any more than he can change his skin."

After a while they were left in peace. Frentis completed the remaining chores then sat by the fire watching the night sky. Master Hutril had taught him to read the stars during his first year in the Order, and he knew that the hilt of the Sword pointed to the north-east. But for the binding he would be following it back to the Realm now, however many miles it took.

"In the Alpiran Empire," the woman said, reclining on a blanket, elbow propped on a silk cushion, "there are men who grow rich telling gullible fools lies about the portents foretold by the stars. Your Faith does not allow such nonsense, I believe."

"The stars are distant suns," he said. "So the Third Order has it anyway. A sun so far away can't have any power here."

"Tell me, why did you kill the overseer and not the master?"

"He was closer, and it was a difficult throw." He turned his gaze on her. "And I knew you could deflect the blade."

She gave a small nod of acknowledgment, lying back onto her pillow and closing her eyes. "There is a man camped next to the water. He's dressed as a journeyman, grey hair and a silver ring in his ear. When the moon's fully risen, go and kill him. There's poison in the packs, the green bottle. Don't leave any marks on the body. Take any letters you find."

She hadn't stopped his speech but he didn't ask for a reason. There was no point.

The Volarians, like the Faithful, gave their dead to the fire. The caravan folk wrapped the grey-haired man in canvas, doused it in lamp oil and set it aflame with a torch. No words were said and there was no display of grief from the onlookers as none seemed to know the man who had died in his sleep, only his name taken from his citizen's tablet: Verkal, common and nondescript. His belongings were being auctioned off as Frentis and the woman continued on their way.

"He was sent to spy on us," the woman said eventually. "In case you were wondering. One of Arklev's, I expect. Seems the Council-man's enthusiasm for our grand project has waned somewhat." This wasn't for his benefit, he knew. Sometimes she liked to voice her thoughts, converse with herself. Something else she had in common with Master Rensial.

Five days' travel brought them in sight of the Jarven Sea, the largest body of inland water in the empire according to the woman. They made for a small ferry port situated in a shallow bay, the terminus of the caravan route, busy with travellers and animals.

The sea was broad and dark beneath the cloudless sky, tall mountains visible in the haze beyond the western shore. The ferry passage cost five squares each plus five circles for the horses. "You are a robber," the woman informed the ferryman as she handed over the coin.

"You're welcome to swim, citizen," he replied with a mocking bow.

She laughed shortly. "I should have my man here kill you, but we're in a hurry." She laughed again and they led the horses aboard.

"When I first took this tub it was one square per man and one circle per horse," she said later, as the slaves worked the oars under the whip of an overseer and the ferry ploughed its way across the sea. "That was over two centuries ago, mind you."

This made him frown. *Centuries? She can't have more than thirty years.*

She grinned at his confusion but said no more.

The crossing took most of the day, the city of Mirtesk coming into view in early evening. Frentis had thought Untesh the largest city he was ever likely to see but Mirtesk made it a village in comparison. It sprawled in a great bowl-like coomb ascending from the shore, countless houses of grey granite stretching away on either side, tall towers rising from the mass, the steady hum of thousands of voices growing to a roar as they reached the dock. A slave was waiting on the quay as they guided the animals ashore. "Mistress," he greeted the woman with a deep bow.

"This is Horvek," she told Frentis. "Ugly, isn't he?"

Horvek's nose looked as if it had been broken and reset several times, most of his left ear was missing and scars covered the muscular flesh of his arms. But it was his bearing that Frentis noticed, the set of his shoulders and the width of his stance. He had seen it many times in the pit. This man was Kuritai, a killer, like him.

"The Messenger is here?" she asked Horvek.

"He arrived two days ago."

"Has he been behaving himself?"

"There have been no reported incidents in the city, Mistress."

"That won't last if he lingers."

Horvek took the packhorses and forced a passage through the dockside throng as they followed, turning down myriad unknowable cobbled streets until they came to a square, rows of three-storey houses forming the four sides. In the centre of the square a large statue of a man on a horse stood in a patch of neatly trimmed grass. The woman dismounted and went to the statue, gazing up at the face of the rider. The figure was dressed in armour Frentis judged as somewhat archaic, the bronze from which he was fashioned liberally streaked with green. He couldn't read Volarian but from the extensive list adorning the plaque on the base of the statue, this had been a man of no small achievement.

"There's gull shit on his head again," the woman observed.

"I'll have the slaves whipped, Mistress," Horvek assured her.

She turned away, walking towards a three-storey house situated directly opposite the statue. The door opened as she mounted the steps, a female slave of middle years bowing deeply. The interior was a picture of elegant marble and gleaming ornamentation, tall canvases on most walls, each depicting a battle of some kind, some showing a figure whose features resembled those of the bronze man outside.

"Do you like my home?" the woman asked Frentis.

Again the binding was loose enough to permit speech, but again he refused to do so. He heard the slave stifle a gasp but the woman just laughed. "Draw a bath," she told the slave, turning to ascend the ornate staircase rising from the marble floor. Her will tugged Frentis along as she climbed the stairs and entered a large room where a man sat at a long table, a grey-clad somewhere past his fiftieth year. He was eating a plate of cured meat, a crystal wineglass at his side, and seemed to recognise Frentis instantly.

"You've put on some muscle, I see," he said in Realm Tongue before taking a long drink from the wineglass.

Frentis searched his face, finding nothing familiar, but there was something in the man's voice. Not the tone, the cadence. Plus he spoke Realm Tongue with no trace of a Volarian accent.

"Our young friend spent five years in the pits," the woman said, keeping to Volarian. She perched herself on the tabletop, pulling off the calf-length boots she had worn in the desert to massage her feet. "Even the Kuritai only have to survive for one."

"They don't have the benefit of a life in the Sixth Order, eh, Frentis?" The man winked at him, provoking another surge of familiarity.

The woman gave the grey-clad a look of close scrutiny. "Older than your last. What's this one's name?"

"Karel Teklar, a wine seller of middling station, with a fat wife and five perfectly horrible children. I've done little else but beat the little beasts for two days."

"The gift?"

The man shrugged. "Some small scrying ability he didn't know he had. Always wondered why he did so well at cards though."

"No great loss then."

"No," the man agreed, getting to his feet and coming closer to Frentis. The angle of his head as he studied him once again maddeningly familiar. "What exactly happened at Untesh, brother? I always wondered."

Frentis remained silent until a flare of the woman's will forced the words out. "Council-man Arklev Entril arrived to treat with Prince Malcius after the Alpirans laid siege, bringing greetings and offers of trade with the Volarian Empire. He shook my hand after I'd searched him for weapons. When the last Alpiran assault hit the walls his will bound me, forced me to abandon the prince. I ran to the docks and came aboard his ship."

"That must've stung a bit," the man said. "Losing the chance for glorious self-sacrifice. Another tale for Master Grealin to tell the novices."

Frentis's confusion deepened. *How can he know so much?*

"Don't fret though." The man moved away, casting his gaze about the room, taking in the racks of weapons lining the walls.

"Malcius survived and returned to rule the Realm, though by all accounts, not remotely so well as his illustrious father."

"Did Malcius see you run?" the woman asked.

Frentis shook his head. "I was commanding the southern section, he was in the centre." *I fled and left two hundred good men to die,* he thought. *They saw me run.*

"So for all he knows," the man said, "brave Brother Frentis, one-time thief raised to great renown by service in the Sixth Order, died heroically in the final attack on the city." He exchanged a glance with the woman. "It'll still work."

She nodded. "The list?"

The man reached into his shirt and tossed a folded piece of parchment to her. "Longer than I expected," she said, reading it.

"Well within your abilities, I'm sure." He picked up the wine-glass and took another large gulp, wincing a little as if he found it sour. "Especially with the help of our deadly urchin here."

Urchin. Nortah used to call him that, Barkus too. But Nortah was dead and Barkus, he hoped, safely back in the Realm.

"Anything else?" the woman asked.

"You need to be at South Tower within a hundred days. Once there, someone will find you. You'll be tempted to kill him. It's important you don't. Tell him the Fief Lord alone won't suffice. The whore must die as well. He should also have some word of our perennial foe, some stratagem to kill him, or at least make him vulnerable, the details are a little vague. Other than that." He drained the wineglass and Frentis noticed a sheen of sweat on his forehead. "Only the usual, eternal pain if you fail, and so on. You've heard it before."

"He never was very original in phrasing his threats." She got down from the table and walked to a rack of thin-bladed swords over the fireplace. "Any preference?"

The man flicked a fingernail against his wineglass, bringing forth a sharp *ping*. He smiled at the woman. "Sorry to disappoint you." He dropped the glass to the floor where it shattered, slumping into the chair at the head of the table, face now bathed in sweat.

His gaze grew unfocused, but brightened momentarily when he saw Frentis. "Give them all my regards, won't you, brother? Especially Vaelin."

Vaelin. Frentis burned as the binding surged, keeping him immobile. He wanted to charge at the man, wring the truth from him, but could only stand in rigid fury as he grinned a final time. "You remember that last fight, that outlaw band the winter before the war?" he asked, voice fading to a whisper. "The blood shone like rubies in the snow. That was a good day . . ."

His eyes closed and his arms dropped, limp, lifeless, the swell of his chest halting shortly after.

"Now," the woman said, shrugging off her clothes. "Time for a bath, don't you think?"

CHAPTER THREE
Vaelin

I should have stopped her.

Reva took aim at the sack of straw they were using as a target, loosing an arrow which caught the edge of the charcoal circle in the centre. He saw her hide a grin of satisfaction. They had purchased a quiver and arrows in Rhansmill, gull-fletched with broad steel-tipped heads best suited to hunting. Every day she rose early to practice, at first scorning his advice but eventually accepting the guidance in sullen silence when she saw the wisdom of it.

"Your bow arm's still too stiff," he said. "Remember, push and pull, don't just pull."

She frowned in annoyance but did as he said, the arrow smacking firmly into the circle. She gave him a smug grimace, the closest she ever came to smiling, and went to retrieve the arrows. Her hair was growing in and she had lost much of the whippetlike leanness he recalled from her abortive attack outside Warnsclave. Ellora's cooking was a considerable help in building muscle.

They hadn't spoken of the outlaws since leaving Rhansmill. He knew it would do little good to lecture her, the strength of her attachment to her god was such that any suggestion she had done wrong would invite only scornful rejection, plus another diatribe on the love of the Father. The men had been an obstacle on her path to the Trueblade's sword, an impediment to the will of the World Father. So she removed them and the burden of killing seemed to weigh on her soul not at all. But he knew she felt it, deep down. The blood-song's music was always sad when his thoughts touched on her, the notes discordant and sombre. She was damaged, twisted by someone into this unhesitating killer. He knew she would feel it eventually, but after how many more years and more deaths he couldn't say.

Then why didn't you stop her? He had lain awake as she rose and stole away, casting the blood-song after her, listening to the rise and fall of the tune, the harsh tumult of sharp notes that always denoted killing. But he hadn't gone after her, the song had warned against it, flaring in alarm as he started to rise intending to follow, disarm the men when they found them and fetch the guards. But the song said no and he had learned to heed its music. The outlaws were scum, deserving of death no doubt, and they were as much an obstacle to his mission as to hers. Recognition now would be a burden, one he had always detested. So he had lain awake, eyes closed when she returned, slipping into her coverings and falling into an untroubled sleep.

"Ready for the off, my lord?" Janril Norin called from his wagon; the rest of the players had packed up and were already trundling off towards the road.

"We'll walk a ways," he called back, waving the minstrel on.

Reva tossed the straw sack onto the back of the wagon and they fell in step behind. "How much longer?" she asked, a question that had become something of a daily ritual.

"Another week at least."

She grunted. "Don't see why you can't just tell me now. This lot offer all the disguise you need."

"We have an agreement. Besides, you haven't mastered the bow yet."

"I'm good enough. Brought down that deer the other night on my own, didn't I?"

"That you did. But there are other weapons than the bow."

Her gaze took on the sullen reluctance he knew signified an internal debate. *She wonders why I train her when she intends to kill me.* It was a question he had also asked himself. With or without his aid her skills would grow, and she was already formidable. But the blood-song's tune was emphatic whenever he trained her: this is necessary.

"The sword," she said after a few moments wrangling her conscience. "You'll teach me the sword?"

"If you like. We'll start tonight."

She gave a small huff of what might have been pleasure and darted forward, leaping onto the back of the wagon and hauling herself up onto the roof, sitting down cross-legged to watch the country go by. *Strange she should have no notion of her own beauty,* he thought, watching her auburn hair shining in the morning sun.

"The first thing to learn," Vaelin told her, touching his ash rod to hers, sweeping it up then around in a blur, twisting it from her grasp to spin in the air. He caught it as it fell and tossed it back to her. "Is the grip."

She learned fast, as he knew she would, mastering the grip and the basics of parry and thrust on the first evening. By the end of the third day she could perform the simplest of Master Sollis's sword scales with near-perfect form, and no small amount of grace.

"When do I get to use that?" she asked at the conclusion of the fourth day's practice, pointing at the roped canvas bundle propped against the wagon wheel. She was sweating a little from the sparring, the part she enjoyed most since it gave her the chance to inflict some pain on him, though as yet all her attempts had been frustrated, not without difficulty.

"You don't." She looked away and he could read her intention without any help from the blood-song. "And if you take it out when I'm sleeping, these lessons will stop. You understand?"

She glowered. "Why do you carry it around if you're never going to use it?"

A fair question, he knew, but not one he wanted to discuss. "Ellora's cooking supper," he said, walking back to the wagon.

The dancer's frostiness had thawed somewhat as they travelled north, but he knew he still made her nervous. Every sixth day she would spend an hour alone beyond the circle of players' wagons, sitting with her eyes closed, lips murmuring a whispered chant. Although he was no longer a brother his story was well-known and those with her beliefs had good reason to fear the Order. Though he had been surprised to see her performing Denier rites so openly.

"Things have changed in the Realm, my lord," Janril explained that evening. "The King abolished the strictures on Denier beliefs a year after ascending the throne. No more tongueless unfortunates hanging in the gibbets, so Ellora can recite her Ascendant creed openly if she wishes. Though it's best not to be too open."

"What made the King do it?"

"Well." Janril's voice dropped into a whisper, even though they were alone. "The King has a queen and she, some say, has more than a passing interest in all things Denier."

The Queen of the Unified Realm is not of the Faith. He wondered at it. *Much can change in five years.* "And the Orders had no objection to this?"

"The Fourth certainly did, Aspect Tendris made speeches aplenty on the matter. There was some grumbling amongst the commons, fearing a return of the Red Hand and such. No more riots though. There was a lot of discord after the war. My last two years in the Wolfrunners were spent putting down riot and rebellion the breadth of Asrael. Since then most people just want a quiet life."

The next day saw them travelling across the flatlands covering the regions south of the Brinewash River, great fields of wheat and goldflower stretching away on either side of the road. Vaelin asked Janril to stop at a crossroads a few miles short of Haeversvale.

"I have business on the east road," he said, climbing down from the wagon. "I'll meet you in the town tonight."

Reva leapt down from the top of the wagon and fell in step alongside as he took the easterly road. "You don't have to come," he told her.

She raised a sardonic eyebrow and gave no reply. *Still expects me to run off leaving her swordless,* he thought, wincing internally at the likely reaction when she heard what he had to say about her father's sword.

A few miles' walk brought them to a small village nestling amongst a copse of willow. The buildings were run-down, window frames empty and doors either vanished or hanging from rusted hinges, rafters showing through thinning thatch. "No-one lives here," Reva said.

"No, not for years." His eyes roamed the village, picking out a small cottage beneath the tallest willow. He went inside, finding bare dust-covered floor, fallen bricks piled into the fireplace. He stood in the centre of the room, eyes closed, and began to sing.

She laughed a lot. Little giggler her father called her. Times were hard, they were often hungry but she always found reason to laugh. She had been happy here. The song changed a little as he went deeper, the tone more ominous. *Blood spattering on the floor, a man screaming, clutching at a wound in his leg. A soldier from the look of him, the crest of an Asraelin noble house on his tunic. A girl of no more than fourteen took a glowing poker from the fire and slapped it to the wound, the soldier screamed and fainted.*

"Got a talent for this girl," another soldier said, a sergeant by his bearing. *He tossed the girl a coin, a silver, more money than she had ever held in her life. "Put even the Fifth Order to shame with skills like that."*

The girl turned to the woman who stood in the corner casting nervous glances at the soldiers. "What's the Fifth Order, Mumma?"

"Vardrian," Reva said, breaking the vision. She was standing by the fireplace reading a wooden plaque nailed to the wall. "The family who lived here maybe?"

"Yes." He went to the plaque, fingers tracing over the letters, finely carved, painted white, the colour peeling away.

"You're bleeding."

It was just a spot on his upper lip. It had happened sometimes back in his cell, when he sang rather than listened. The louder the song the more the blood would flow from his nose, or on one occasion as he had sought to reach across the broad ocean to the Far West, his eyes. *It is the price I pay,* the blind woman said. The truth of it was becoming ever more clear: *We all pay a price for our gifts.*

"It's nothing," he said, wiping the spot of blood away, leaving the plaque in place and going outside.

Two more days and the bridge over the Brinewash came into view. What had once been wood was now stone, broader and sturdier than its predecessor. "The King likes to build," Janril said as the wagon rolled up to the toll-house, tossing the bridgemaster a purse with enough coin for the players' wagons. "Bridges and libraries, healing houses. Tears down the old, builds the new. Some call him Malcius the Bricklayer."

"There are worse names to earn," Vaelin replied. He sat in the wagon's shadowed interior, wary of showing himself even in his hood this close to the capital. *Butcher, madman, schemer, invader. Janus earned them all.*

They made for the great expanse of grass where the Summertide Fair made its home every year. A large number of other player caravans had already gathered, along with numerous hawkers and craftsmen come to sell their wares, and a group of carpenters had begun construction of the wooden arena where the Renfaelin Knights would assail each other in the tourney. Vaelin waited for evening before leaving the wagon. He offered Janril his remaining coin, knowing it would be refused, and embraced the minstrel in farewell.

"You don't need this place, my lord," Janril said. His eyes were bright and his smile forced. "Stay with us. The common folk may sing their songs about you but few nobles will relish the sight of your return. There's only envy and treachery inside those walls."

"There are things I must do here, Janril. But I thank you." He gripped the player's shoulders a final time, hefted his canvas bundle and walked off towards the city gate. Reva quickly appeared at his side.

"Well?" she said.

He kept walking.

"You may have noticed we're at Varinshold," she went on, casting a hand at the city walls. "In accordance with our agreement."

"Soon," he said.

"Now!"

He stopped, meeting her gaze squarely, voice soft but precise. "You will have your answer soon. Now, come with me or stay here. I'm sure Janril can use another dancer."

She eyed the city gate with a mix of distrust and contempt. "Not even inside yet and it stinks like a fat man's outhouse," she grumbled but followed as he walked on.

His father's house had once seemed huge, a mighty castle in his boy's mind as he raced around hallway and grounds in a tireless frenzy of imagined heroism, his wooden sword a terror to servants and livestock alike. The great oak that stretched its branches over the slanted roof had been his arch-enemy, a giant, come to tear down the castle walls. Childhood fickleness sometimes made a friend of the giant, and he would nestle in his thick arms as he watched his father put a warhorse through its paces on the acre and a half of grass between the stables and the riverbank.

It never seemed strange to him that he had no real friends, that the only children he knew were the sons and daughters of the servants with whom he was permitted only the briefest play-time before his mother shooed them away, kind but firm. "Don't bother them, Vaelin. They've better things to do." He realised later she deliberately kept him from other children, forming a true friendship would only make it harder when the time came for him to join the Order.

The house had shrunk in the many years since, and not only to his adult eye. The roof sagged and had sore need of a slater, the walls dull and grey with aged whitewash. At least half the windows were boarded up, and those free of boards lacked more than a few panes. Even the branches of the great oak were drooping, the giant was getting old. He could see a fire burning in one of the windows, just one flicker of warmth in the whole house.

"You grew up here?" Reva asked in surprise. The rain had come in earnest as they made their way through the northern quarter to Watcher's Bend, droplets falling thick from the hem of her hood. "The songs say you are of the common folk, risen from the streets. This is a palace."

"No," he murmured, walking on. "It's a castle."

He stopped in front of the main door. The quality door, one of the maids had called it, a jovial plump woman he was ashamed to find he could no longer name. *Quality door for quality people.* Looking at the bell, tarnished and dull, the rope threadbare, he wondered how many quality people had been through it recently. He watched the rope sway in the rain as Reva gave a loud and deliberate sniff. He drew a breath and pulled the rope.

The echo had died away for a good few minutes before there came a muffled shout from beyond the door. "Go away! I've got another week! The magistrate decreed it! There's a mighty hero of the Alpiran war upstairs who'll hack your hands off in a trice if you don't leave us in peace!"

There was a faint sound of retreating footsteps. Vaelin exchanged a glance with Reva and rang the bell again. This time the wait was shorter.

"Right! You were warned!" The door swung inwards and they were confronted with the sight of a young woman drawing back a bucket, the contents looking both moist and unfragrant. "Week's worth of slops for you l—" She froze when she saw him, the bucket slipping from her hands, eyes wide as she slumped against the wall, hands going to her face.

"Sister," Vaelin said. "May I come in?"

He had to half carry her to the kitchen where it seemed she made her home, judging from the chill emptiness of every room they passed. He sat her on a stool before the range, clasping her trembling hands, finding them cold. Her eyes seemed unable to leave his face. "I thought . . . you were hooded . . . for a moment I thought." She blinked away tears.

"I'm sorry . . ."

"No . . ." Her hands came free of his, reaching up to touch his face, a smile growing as the tears fell. The dark, earnest eyes of the little girl he had met on that distant winter day were still there, but womanhood had given her the kind of comeliness he knew could be dangerous, especially when living alone in a ruined house. "Brother. I always knew . . . I never doubted . . ."

There was a loud clatter as Reva dumped the slop bucket in a corner.

"Alornis, this is Reva. My . . ." He paused as she raised an eyebrow at him from the depths of her hood. ". . . travelling companion."

"Well." Alornis used her apron to wipe away tears and rose from the stool. "Having travelled, you must be hungry."

"Yes," said Reva.

"We're fine," Vaelin insisted.

"Nonsense," Alornis scoffed, bustling off to the larder. "Lord Vaelin Al Sorna welcomed back to his own house by a snivelling girl who can't even offer him a meal. Won't do at all."

The meal was small, bread, cheese and the heavily seasoned remains of what was at most half a chicken.

"I'm a terrible cook," Alornis confessed. Vaelin noted she hadn't eaten anything. "That was mother's skill."

Reva cleared the last crumb from her plate and gave a small burp. "Wasn't so bad."

"Your mother?" Vaelin asked. "She's . . . not here?"

Alornis shook her head. "Just after last Winterfall. The bloody cough. Aspect Elera was very kind, did everything she could, but . . ." She trailed off, eyes downcast.

"I'm sorry, sister."

"You shouldn't call me that. The King's Law says I'm not your sister, that this house isn't mine and every scrap Father owned his by right. I had to beg the magistrate to stay on a month before the bailiffs come for the rest. And he only did that because Master Benril said he'd paint his portrait free of charge."

"Master Benril Lenial, of the Third Order? You know him?"

"I'm his apprentice, well more of an unpaid assistant in truth, but I'm learning a lot." She gestured at the far wall where numerous sheets of parchment were pinned to the plaster. Vaelin got up and went closer, blinking in wonder at the sight of the drawings. The subjects were wide and varied, a horse, a sparrow, the old oak outside, a woman carrying a bread basket, all rendered in charcoal or ink with a clarity that was little short of astounding.

"By the Father." Reva had moved to his side and was staring at the drawings with the kind of wide-eyed admiration he thought beyond her. The gaze she turned on his sister was awed, even a little fearful. "This touches the Dark," she whispered.

Alornis managed to hold her laugh for a second or two before it burst from her. "It's just marks on paper. I've always done it. I'll draw you if you like."

Reva turned away. "No."

"But you're so pretty, you'd make a fine study . . ."

"I said no!" She went to the door, face hard and angry, then paused. Vaelin noted how white her knuckles were on the doorjamb and there was a soft lilting note from the blood-song. He had heard it before, fainter but still there, when they first began travelling with Janril's players and he noticed her watching Ellora as she practised one of her dances. Her gaze had been rapt, fascinated, then suddenly furious. She closed her eyes tight and he saw her murmur one of her prayers to the World Father.

"My apologies," she said, still not looking at Alornis. "This is not my house." She glanced at Vaelin. "This night is for you and your sister. I'll find a room to bed down in." Her tone became harder. "We'll conclude our business in the morning." With that she went into the hallway. There were only faint scuffs as she moved through the house, she had a knack for stealth.

"Your travelling companion?" Alornis asked.

"You meet all kinds on the road." He returned to the table. "My father really left you with nothing?"

"It wasn't his fault." Her tone had an edge to it. "Whatever coin we had went fast when the sickness came. Any lands he held, or rights to pension, disappeared when he stopped being Battle Lord. His friends, men he had been to war with, no longer knew him. It was not an easy time, brother."

He could see the reproach in her gaze, knowing he had earned it. "There was no place for me here," he said. "Or so I thought. You knew him, grew up under his eyes. I did not. If he wasn't at war, he was training his horses or his men, and when he was here . . ." *The tall black-eyed man stared down at the boy with the wooden sword and no smile came to his lips as the boy lunged at him, laughing but also pleading. "Teach me, Father! Teach me! Teach me!" The black-eyed man batted the sword away and commanded a steward to take the boy to the house, turning back to continue grooming his horse . . .*

"He loved you," Alornis told him. "He never lied to me, I always knew who you were, who I was, that we did not share a mother. That every hour of every day he wished with all his heart he hadn't followed your mother's wish. He wanted you to know that. As the sickness grew worse and he couldn't leave his bed, it was all he could talk of."

There was a sudden thump of something heavy hitting the floor above, a man's voice raised in alarm then a snarl. *Reva.*

"Oh no," Alornis groaned. "He doesn't usually wake up until well past the tenth hour."

Vaelin rushed upstairs, finding Reva astride a tall, handsome but unshaven young man, knife held rock-still at his throat. "An outlaw, Darkblade!" she said. "An outlaw in your sister's house."

"Merely a poet, I assure you," the young man said.

Reva loomed over him. "Quiet you! Come into a young maid's house, would you? Itch in your breeches is there?"

"Reva!" Vaelin said. He was wary of touching her. The scene in the kitchen had left her wound tight and in need of release, any touch like to make her snap like a drawn bowstring. He kept his voice calm. "This man is a friend. Let him up, please."

Reva's nostrils flared and she gave a final snarl before rolling away, coming smoothly to her feet as her knife disappeared into its sheath.

"You always did have dangerous pets, my lord," the young man said from the floor.

Reva started forward again but Vaelin put himself between them, offering the young man a hand and hauling him upright in a haze of cheap wine. "You shouldn't bait her, Alucius," he said. "She's a better student than you ever were."

Alucius Al Hestian sat on the red-brick well in the yard, blinking in the morning sun, eyes dark and red, sipping from a flask as Vaelin joined him. The practice with Reva had been more vigorous than usual. She had plenty of anger left over from the night before and seemed more determined than ever to land at least one blow with the ash rod. Defeating her had not been easy and his shirt was damp with sweat.

"Brother's Friend?" he asked, nodding at the flask as he hauled the bucket from the well.

"It's called Wolf's Blood these days," Alucius replied, raising the flask in salute. "Some enterprising former soldiers of yours set themselves up in a distillery with their pensions, started churning out bottles of the regiment's favourite tipple by the thousand. I hear they're rich as Far West Merchants these days."

"Good for them." He settled the bucket on the rim of the well, scooping water to his mouth with the wooden ladle. "Your father is well?"

"Still hates you with a fiery passion, if that's what you mean." Alucius's grin faded. "But he's . . . a quieter man these days. The King has a new Battle Lord now."

"Anyone I know?"

"Indeed, Varius Al Trendil. Hero of the Bloody Hill and the taking of Linesh."

Vaelin remembered a taciturn man biting down angry words born of frustrated greed. "Many victories to his name?"

"There's not been a real battle in the Realm since the Usurper's Revolt. But he was singularly efficient in quelling all those riots and rebellions."

"I see." He took another drink and rested himself next to Alucius. "I find myself compelled to ask an indelicate question."

"Why is a drunken poet sleeping in your sister's house?"

"Quite."

"He thinks he's protecting me," Alornis said from the kitchen doorway. "Breakfast's ready."

Breakfast was a sparse serving of ham and eggs which disappeared almost as soon as it touched Reva's plate. He could see her resisting the impulse to ask for more, but her stomach felt no need to restrain a loud rumble. "Here." Alucius pushed his own untouched plate towards her, his unstoppered flask still in his hand. "Peace offering. Wouldn't want you cutting my throat for a meal."

Reva favoured him with a curled lip but accepted the food readily enough.

"Our father died three years ago," Vaelin said to Alornis. "Why has it taken so long for the King to claim his property?"

She shrugged. "Who can say? The slow wheels of bureaucracy perhaps."

The ship that carried him from the Meldenean Islands had called in at South Tower little over a month ago. Plenty of time for a fast horse to ride to the capital. *A man as hated as you shouldn't expect to avoid recognition.* He suspected the wheels of bureaucracy had ground much faster than she knew.

"I'm glad you're alive by the way, Alucius," he told the poet. "If I didn't say it before."

"You didn't, and thank you."

"You were amongst the party that fought its way to the docks, I assume?"

Alucius looked down at the table, taking another sip of Wolf's Blood. "Stay close to my father, you said. It was good advice."

From the dullness of his tone and the shadow in his eyes, Vaelin judged it best to let the matter drop. "So, what exactly are you protecting my sister from?"

He brightened a little. "Oh the usual, outlaws, vagabonds"—he gave Reva a pointed glance—"wayward Deniers with sharp knives, Ardents seeking to pester the kin of the great Brother Vaelin for words of support."

Vaelin frowned. "Ardents? What's that?"

"Those that are ardent in their Faith. They started appearing after the King's Edict of Toleration. They hold meetings, wave banners, sometimes attack people they suspect of Denier practices. They call themselves the true followers of the Faith, given public support by Aspect Tendris. The rest of the Orders are less enthusiastic." His expression became more serious. "Your return will be a great joy to them. The Faith's greatest champion, betrayed to a Denier dungeon by the Al Nieren dynasty. I'm afraid they will have unrealistic expectations, my lord."

Reva's head rose from her plate, head angled to the broken window in the south-facing wall. "Horse coming."

Vaelin looked at the open door hearing the clatter of hooves on cobble. The blood-song's note was strong with recognition, but also had a faint trill of warning. He suppressed it as well he could and went outside.

Brother Caenis Al Nysa reined his horse to a halt and dismounted in the yard. He stood regarding Vaelin in silence for a moment, then came forward with his arms wide, a bright smile on his lips. They embraced with all the warmth expected of reunited brothers, Caenis's grip fierce, a small shudder escaping his chest. But still the blood-song trilled its warning . . .

His face was leaner, more lines at the corner of his eyes, even some grey in the close-cropped hair on his temples. Life in the Order did not make for a prolonged youth. He seemed as strong as ever though, even a little broader across the shoulders. Never an imposing figure, Caenis was now possessed of a palpable air of authority, perhaps brought on by the red diamond sewn onto the dark blue of his cloak.

"Brother Commander no less?" Vaelin asked. They were strolling on the grass by the riverbank. The Brinewash was in full spate after the night's rain, the water threatening to spill over the earthen dike his father had built to ward against floods.

"I command the regiment now," Caenis replied.

"Which would mean I have the honour of addressing Lord Caenis Al Nysa, Sword of the Realm, would it not?"

"It would." Caenis didn't appear especially proud of his elevation which was at odds with the man he remembered. The younger Caenis had been the most loyal subject the Al Nieren line could ever have desired. But then came Janus's betrayal at Linesh and Vaelin recalled the mystification that shrouded his brother when it became clear the old schemer's dream of a Greater Unified Realm was a broken vision. *He never makes mistakes* . . .

They paused, Caenis regarding the fast-flowing river in silence for a moment. "Barkus," he said eventually. "The captain of the ship taking him home had a tall tale to tell, about how the big brother threatened to hack his head off with an axe if he didn't sail his vessel back to the Alpiran shore. When they got to the shallows he jumped over the side and swam for the beach."

"How much have they told you?"

Caenis turned back from the river, eyes meeting his. "The One Who Waits. It truly was Barkus?"

So they told him. How much more does he know? "No, it was something that lived in his skin. Barkus died during the Test of the Wild."

Caenis closed his eyes, head downcast, voicing a sigh of deep sorrow. After a while he looked up, forcing a smile. "That just leaves the two of us, brother."

Vaelin returned the smile, but it was a small one. "In truth it leaves just the one, brother."

Caenis clasped his hands together, speaking in earnest tones. "Sister Sherin is gone, Vaelin. I have said nothing to the Aspect . . ."

"Sister Sherin and I were in love." He spread his arms wide and shouted it out, the words carrying across the river: "I was in love with Sister Sherin!"

"Brother!" Caenis hissed, looking around in alarm.

"And it was not a transgression," Vaelin went on, voice dropping to an angry rasp. "It was not *wrong*! It was glorious, brother. And I gave her up. I lost her forever in my final service to the Order. And I'm done. Tell the Aspect, tell the whole Realm if you like. I am no longer part of your Order and I no longer follow the Faith."

Caenis became very still, his voice a whisper. "I know the years of imprisonment must have taken a toll on your spirit, but surely it was the guidance of the Departed that brought you back to us."

"It's all a lie, Caenis. All of it. As much a lie as any god. Do you want to know what that thing inside Barkus said before I killed it?"

"Enough!"

"It said a soul without a body is a wretched, wasted thing . . ."

"I said enough!" Caenis was white with fury, stepping back as if disbelief were catching. "You hear bile from a creature of the Dark and take it as truth. My brother was never so trusting, never so easily gulled."

"I can always hear truth, brother. It's my curse."

Caenis turned away, mastering himself with some effort. When he turned back there was a new hardness in his gaze. "Do not call me brother. If you shun the Order and the Faith, you shun me."

"You are my brother, Caenis. You always will be. It was never the Faith that bound us, you know that."

Caenis stared at him, fury and hurt shining in his eyes, then turned to walk away. He halted after a few steps, speaking over his shoulder in a strained tone, "The Aspect wishes to see you. He said to make it clear it was a request, not a command." He resumed walking.

"Frentis!" Vaelin called after him. "Do you have news of him? I know he still lives."

Caenis didn't turn around. "Talk to the Aspect!"

CHAPTER FOUR
Lyrna

Princess Lyrna Al Nieren had never liked riding. She found horses dull company and the hardness of the saddle like to leave her with bruises she couldn't ask her maid to salve. In consequence the many miles her party had covered on its journey north had done nothing to improve her temper. But then that was true of the last five years.

Does the rain ever cease here? she wondered, peering out from the hood of her ermine-trimmed robe at the rain sheeting onto the slate-grey landscape. Five days out from Cardurin and the rain hadn't stopped once.

Lord Marshal Nirka Al Smolen reined in alongside and saluted, rain streaming over his breastplate in a matrix of ever-changing rivulets. "Only five more miles, Highness." His voice had a wariness to it. This endless journey was making her less restrained in voicing rebuke, and she knew her tongue could carry all the sting of an angry wasp when it chose to. Seeing the caution in his face she sighed. *Oh, give the man some respite, you hateful witch.* "Thank you, Lord Marshal."

He saluted again, some small relief colouring his cheeks as he spurred on ahead to scout the route, a troop of five Mounted Guards in close escort. Another fifty closed in around her and the two ladies she had chosen to take north, hardy girls from country manors, of more middling rank than most of her attendants but not given to either giggles or complaints of discomfort. She gave Sable a nudge with her knee and they started forward, ascending the rocky path to the dark narrow slash of the Skellan Pass.

"Highness, if I may," ventured Nersa, the taller of the two ladies. She was braver than Jullsa who was wont to lapse into prolonged silence after Lyrna's more acid rebukes.

"What is it?" Lyrna said, feeling every jab of Sable's hips despite the thickness of the saddle.

"Are we likely to see one today, Highness?"

Nersa had been fascinated by the prospect of laying eyes on a Lonak since leaving Varinshold. Lyrna put it down to the morbid curiosity of youth, like a child who prods at the guts of a dead dog. But so far the fabled wolfmen had been absent from their path, at least as far as they could tell. *None can hide so well as a Lonak, Highness,* the Brother Commander back at Cardurin had warned her, a husky man with bright shrewd eyes. *You won't see them, but by the Departed they'll see you before you're ten miles from this city.*

Watching the pass grow in size as they approached, a shadowed cavern cleaving into the mountain, Lyrna saw the first sign of fortification, a squat tower covering the southern approach, a faint speck of blue on the battlements. Some lonely brother on the morning watch no doubt.

"If not here, then likely not at all," she told Nersa. Despite her brother's assurances she still harboured deep doubts about this whole enterprise. *Can they really want peace after so many centuries?*

The Brother Commander waiting at the tower was somewhere past his fortieth year with cropped silver-grey hair and pale eyes beneath a scarred brow. He voiced his greeting in a harsh, battle-seasoned voice, bowing as low as formality required. "Highness."

"Brother Commander Sollis is it not?" She climbed down from Sable, resisting the urge to rub some feeling into her benumbed rump.

"Yes, Highness." He straightened, gesturing at two more brothers standing nearby. "Brothers Hervil and Ivern will also be accompanying us north."

She arched an eyebrow. "Only three? Your Aspect assured the King of his full support for this mission."

"There are only sixty brothers to hold this pass, Highness. I can spare no more." There was a finality to his tone that told her no amount of regal intimidation, or grace, would change his mind. She had heard of him of course, the famed sword-master of the Sixth Order, scourge of Lonak and outlaw, survivor of the fall of Marbellis . . . Master to Vaelin Al Sorna.

Father, I beg you . . .

"As you will, brother," she said, smiling. It was one of her best, gracious, not overly dazzling, with just the right amount of admiration in her eyes for the dutiful brother. "I would, of course, never question your judgement in such matters."

The dutiful brother stared back with his pale eyes, face betraying no emotion whatsoever.

This one's different, at least. "The guide is here?"

"Yes, Highness." He stepped aside, gesturing at the tower. "I've had food prepared."

"Most kind of you."

The tower interior had seen some recent and vigorous scrubbing but still retained the cloying, sweaty odour of men living in close proximity. She looked at the plain but copious array of food on the table before the fireplace, finding the seats bare of occupants, as was the rest of the chamber. "The guide?" she enquired of Sollis.

"This way, Highness." He moved to a heavy door at the rear of the chamber, working a key in the large padlock on the handle. "We were obliged to quarter her downstairs."

He hauled the door open, revealing a set of descending stone steps, lifting a torch from an iron brace on the wall. "If you would care to follow me."

Lyrna turned back to Nersa and Jullsa. "Ladies, please remain here and partake of the meal the brothers have kindly provided. Lord Marshal, if you could attend me."

She and Smolen followed Sollis down the winding steps to a small chamber, lit only by a narrow window inset with iron bars. A woman sat in shadow at the far end of the chamber, long legs clad in dark red leather protruding into the light, eyes glittering in the gloom. She stirred at the sight of Lyrna, shifting into a crouch, the chain around her ankle jangling on the stone floor.

"This is our guide?" she asked Sollis.

"It is, Highness." The hardness of his expression as he stared at the shadowed woman told her much of his regard for this whole adventure. "Arrived two days ago with a note from the High Priestess herself. We gave her bed and board as ordered and that night she knifed one of my brothers in the thigh. I considered it prudent to confine her here."

"Did she have cause to attack the brother?"

Sollis gave a small sigh of discomfort. "Seems he refused to assuage her . . . appetites. A terrible insult in Lonak society, apparently."

Lyrna moved closer to the Lonak woman, Sollis keeping two paces ahead, hands loose at his sides. "You have a name?" she asked the woman.

"She doesn't know Realm Tongue, Highness," Sollis said. "Hardly any do. Learning our words sullies their soul." He turned to the Lonak woman. "*Esk gorin ser?*"

She ignored him, shuffling forward a little, her face becoming clear. It was smooth and angular with high cheekbones, her head almost entirely bald but for a long black braid protruding from the crown to snake down over her shoulder, a steel band shining on the end of it. She wore a sleeveless jerkin of thin leather, an intricate mazelike tattoo of green and red covering the skin from her left shoulder to her chin. Her gaze scanned Lyrna from head to toe, a slow smile coming to her lips. She said something in a rapid tumble of her own language.

"*Ehkar!*" Sollis barked, stepping closer, glaring a threat.

The woman stared back and smiled wider, showing teeth that gleamed in the gloom.

"What did she say?" Lyrna asked.

Sollis gave another discomforted sigh. "She, erm, wants food, Highness."

Lyrna's Lonak had been learned from a book, the most comprehensive guide she could find in the Great Library. An aged master from the Third Order had tutored her in the various vowel sounds and subtle shifts of emphasis that could change the meaning of a word or a sentence. He had freely admitted his understanding of the wolfmen's tongue was patchy and dulled with the years since he had journeyed north in his youth, gleaning knowledge from a few Lonak captives willing to talk in return for freedom. Nevertheless, Lyrna had sufficient command of the language to produce a rough translation of the woman's words, but decided she would enjoy hearing the dutiful brother say it.

"Tell me exactly what she said, brother," she commanded. "I must insist on it."

Sollis coughed and spoke as tonelessly as possible. "When the men are on the hunt Lonak women look to each other for . . . nightly comforts. If you were of her clan, she'd want them to stay on the hunt for good."

Lyrna turned to the Lonak woman and pursed her lips. "Really?"

"Yes, Highness."

"Kill her."

The Lonak woman jerked back, the chain between her fists, ready to ward off a blow, eyes fixed on Sollis in readiness for combat, even though he hadn't moved.

"It seems she speaks Realm Tongue after all," Lyrna observed. "What's your name?"

The woman scowled at her, then abruptly laughed, rising from her crouch. She was tall, standing an inch or two higher than both Sollis and Smolen in fact. "Davoka," she said, raising her chin.

"Davoka," Lyrna repeated softly. *Spear, in the archaic form.* "What are your instructions from the High Priestess?"

Davoka's accent was thick but the words spoken with enough slow precision to be understood. "Take the Merim Her queen to the Mountain," she said. "See she arrives whole and living."

"I am a princess, not a queen."

"A queen she said. A queen you are." There was a certainty to the woman's words that warned Lyrna further questioning on this point would be unwise. The meagre collection of works on Lonak history and culture in the Great Library had been vague and often contradictory, but they all agreed on one point: the words of the High Priestess were not to be questioned.

"If I release you, are you going to stab any more brothers, or make unseemly suggestions that insult their calling?"

Davoka cast a contemptuous glance at Sollis, muttering in her own language: *Wouldn't sully my nethers with any of these limp-pricks.* "No," she told Lyrna.

"Very well." She nodded at Sollis. "She can join us for dinner."

Davoka sat at Lyrna's side at dinner, having glared at Jullsa to make a space. The lady had blanched and excused herself from table, curtsying to Lyrna before rushing off to the chamber she and Nersa had been given. *I'll send her home in the morning,* Lyrna decided. *Not so hardy as I hoped.* In contrast, Nersa seemed fascinated by Davoka, stealing glances over the table, earning a fierce glower or two in return.

"You serve the High Priestess?" Lyrna asked Davoka as the tall woman ate, slicing pieces of apple into her mouth with a narrow-bladed knife.

"All Lonak serve her," Davoka replied around a mouthful.

"But you are of her household?"

Davoka barked a laugh. "House? Hah!" She finished her apple and tossed the core into the fireplace. "She has a mountain, not a house."

Lyrna smiled and summoned up some patience. "But you have a role there?"

"I guard her. Only women guard her. Only women can be trusted. Men act crazy in her presence."

Lyrna had read fanciful accounts of the supposed powers of the High Priestess. Noble-hearted men driven to insane passions by the merest glimpse, according to a somewhat lurid tome entitled *Blood Rites of the Lonak*. Whatever the truth of it, all the accounts pointed to a strong belief in her Dark powers. In truth, it was this, rather than her brother's entreaties, that had made her agree to this expedition.

Many years of study, quiet investigation, tortuous cross-referencing but still no evidence. *Look in the western quarter for the tale of the one-eyed man,* he said, that day he stole a kiss before the entire Summertide Fair. And she had. The tale, brought to her by the few servants she could trust to seek answers in the capital's poorest quarter, had seemed absurd at first. One Eye was king of the outlaws and could bind men to him by will alone. One Eye drank the blood of his enemies to gain power. One Eye defiled children in dark rites conducted in the catacombs beneath the city. The only certainty to the tale was its end; One Eye had been killed by the Sixth Order, some said by Al Sorna himself. On this all the sources agreed, but on little else.

And so she kept looking, gathering accounts from all over the Realm. A girl who could call the wind in Nilsael, a boy who could talk with dolphins in South Tower, a man seen raising the dead in Cumbrael. A hundred or more fantastical tales, most of which turned out to be exaggeration, misunderstanding, gossip or outright lies on further investigation. No evidence. It maddened her, this absence of clarity, this lack of an answer, spurring her on, making her deepen her research, becoming a burden to the Lord Librarian with her constant demands for older and older books.

She knew much of this interest stemmed from the simple fact that she had little else to do. Her brother's rule left her with no real place at court. He had a queen now, little Janus and Dirna to secure his line and a boundless supply of advisors. Malcius liked advice. The more the better, especially when one advisor contradicted another, which of course would require him to order the matter at hand be subject to further investigation, usually so thorough in nature it was several months before a conclusion had been reached and the matter had resolved itself or been superseded by more pressing affairs. In fact the only advice Malcius wouldn't listen to was that offered by his sister.

Never forget, her father's words, spoken to a little girl many years ago as she pretended to play with her dolls. *A man who asks for advice is either indulging in the pretence of consideration or too weak to know his own mind.*

To be fair, Malcius always knew his own mind when it came to one thing: bricks and mortar. "I will make this a land of wonders, Lyrna," he told her once, laying out his grand plan for a reborn western quarter of Varinshold, broad streets and parks replacing narrow alleys and slums. "This is how we secure the future. Give the people a Realm fit for living, not merely existing."

She loved him, it was true, a fact she had demonstrated in the most terrible manner. But her dearest brother was the most colossal fool.

"How many men do you have, Queen?" Davoka asked her abruptly.

Lyrna blinked in surprise. "I . . . have fifty guardsmen as my escort."

"Not guards. Men . . . Husbands you call them."

"I have no husband."

Davoka squinted at her. "Not one?"

"No." She took a drink of wine. "Not one."

"I have ten." The Lonak woman's voice dripped with pride.

"Ten husbands!" Nersa said in astonishment.

"Yes," Davoka assured her. "None of them with more than one other wife. No need when married to me!" She laughed and thumped the table, making Nersa jump.

"Guard your tongue, woman!" Lord Marshal Al Smolen growled at her. "Such talk is not fit for Her Highness's company."

Davoka rolled her eyes, reaching for a chicken leg. *"Merim Her."* She sighed. *Sea scum, or debris swept onto the shore, depending on the inflection.*

"How many days to the Mountain of the High Priestess?" Lyrna asked her.

Davoka clamped the chicken leg into her mouth and held up all ten fingers then repeated the gesture.

Twenty more days in the saddle. Lyrna suppressed a groan and reminded herself to ask Nersa for some more salve.

Jullsa cried and begged to be allowed to stay. Lyrna gave her one of the bluestone-inlaid silver bracelets she kept for such occasions, a purse of ten golds and thanked her for her service, assuring her she would write to her parents in the most glowing terms and that she was always welcome at court. She walked to Sable as Nersa soothed her weeping friend.

"You do right, Queen," Davoka said from the back of her sturdy pony. She was dressed in a thick wolf fur and carried a long spear with a triangular blade of black iron, the sharpened edges bright in the rising sun. "That one's weak. Her children will perish in their first winter."

"Call me Lyrna." She hauled herself into the saddle. The riding gown was pleated from waist to hem to allow her to ride full saddle but she found it still too constricting for comfort.

"Lerhnah," Davoka repeated carefully. "What does it mean?"

"It means my mother was fond of her grandmother." She smiled at Davoka's confusion. "Asraelin names don't mean anything. We name our children on a whim."

"Lonak children name themselves." Davoka shook her spear. "Named myself when I took this from the man I killed."

"He had wronged you?"

"Many times. He was my father!" She laughed and spurred her pony forward.

The fortifications of the Skellan Pass were a complex maze of walls and towers, each great stone barrier angled so as to funnel any attacking force into a tight killing space. Lyrna admired the intelligence behind the design, the way it allowed for continuous defence even when one part of the fortifications had fallen to an enemy, the towers and walls arranged in ascending heights depending on how deep they were in the pass.

Sollis led them through ten gates, each protected by a thick iron portcullis that had to be hauled up to allow egress. Despite the strength of the defences she could see the truth of his words; there were too few brothers to man the fortifications. She saw Davoka's narrowed gaze as she surveyed the walls and knew she was coming to the same conclusion. *Is this all a ruse?* Lyrna thought. *A design to place a spy here to report on the state of the defences.*

She quickly discounted the thought, recalling the shrewd-eyed brother's warnings about the omniscience of the Lonak this far north. *They know how weak we are here, yet instead of attacking, the High Priestess sends word that she wants to talk peace, but only to me.*

It took over an hour of tortuous winding through pathways between the walls and gates, built so narrow as to allow only one horse to pass at a time, before they finally emerged on the northern side of the pass. The rain had abated today and the sun shafted through the clouds, curtains of light descending on the mountainous dominion of the Lonak. The peaks stretched away into the distance, formidable, blue-grey monsters of granite and ice.

Davoka raised her head to the sky, breathing deep then exhaling in a rush. *Clearing the stench of us from her lungs, no doubt,* Lyrna surmised.

The Lonak woman guided her pony to the head of the column, taking the narrow, rock-strewn path descending to the floor of the valley beyond. She gave no instruction or gesture, beginning the descent without preamble, seemingly expectant that they would follow without question. Lyrna saw the suspicion on Smolen's face and gave him a nod of assent. She could tell he was biting down words of argument as he barked a command to his men.

They journeyed for another four hours, tracking over an array of valley and hillside interspersed with small patches of pine forest. Lyrna found there was a stark beauty to be found this side of the pass, the grey monotony of the country north of Cardurin replaced with a land of shifting hues, ever-changing skies allowing the sunlight to paint the rocky outcrops and heather-clad hills with a varied palette, rich in colour and very pleasing to the eye. *Perhaps this is why they fight so hard to keep it,* she thought. *Because it's beautiful.*

When the Lonak woman finally called a rest, Nersa placed a silken pillow on a patch of heather and presented Lyrna with a luncheon of chicken and raisin bread, together with a goblet of the dry Cumbraelin white she liked so much. Dessert consisted of a selection from their diminishing supply of chocolate fancies.

"Look like rabbit turds," Davoka said, giving one the sweets a suspicious sniff. She had hunkered down to join their lunch without asking permission. It seemed the Lonak shared food without favour or propriety when on the march.

"Try one," Lyrna said, popping a fancy into her mouth. *Rum and vanilla, very nice.* "You'll like it."

Davoka took a cautious bite of the sweet, her eyes widening in instant delight, which she was quick to conceal, muttering a phrase in her own language as she frowned in self-reproach. *Comfort makes you weak.*

"You carry a weapon," she said, pointing to the trinket hanging on a chain around Lyrna's neck. "Can you use it?"

Lyrna held up the trinket. A plain throwing knife of the type commonly used by the Sixth Order, little bigger than an arrowhead. It was the least ornate piece of jewellery in her entire extensive collection, and the only one worn with any regularity, at least when she was safely away from the eyes of the court.

"No," she said. "It's just a keepsake. A gift from . . . an old friend." *Father, I beg you . . .*

"No use carrying a weapon you can't use." Faster than anyone could give thought to stopping her, Davoka leaned forward and hooked the chain and knife over Lyrna's head. "Here, I show you. Come." She rose and walked towards a small pine growing near the edge of the trail.

Nersa rose to her feet in outrage. "You insult Our Highness's person! The Princess of the Unified Realm does not sully herself with martial pursuits."

Davoka gave her a look of total bafflement. "This one speaks words not in my head."

"It's all right, Nersa." Lyrna got to her feet, calming the lady with a touch to the arm, speaking softly. "We need to make all the friends we can here."

She followed Davoka to the pine. The Lonak woman detached the knife from the chain with a sharp tug and held it up to the sunlight. "Sharp, good." She moved in a blur, the knife spinning from her hand to bury itself in the pine trunk.

Lyrna glanced over to where Sollis sat with his two brothers. He watched the scene with no sign of amusement on his face. She noted he had placed his bow within reach, an arrow notched to the string.

"You try, Lerhnah." Davoka returned from the pine having worked the knife loose from the bark.

Lyrna looked at the knife in her hand as if seeing it for the first time. All the years she had owned it she had never once attempted to use it for its true purpose. "How?"

Davoka gestured at the pine. "Look at the tree, throw the knife."

"I've never done this before."

"Then you miss. Throw again and miss. Again and again until you hit. Then you know how."

"It's really that easy?"

Davoka laughed. "No. Really hard. Learning any weapon really hard."

Lyrna looked at the tree, drew her arm back and threw the knife as hard as she could. Nersa and the guards spent a half hour searching before it was found amongst the surrounding heather.

"We try a bigger tree tomorrow," Davoka said.

They covered what felt like a hundred miles by nightfall, but Lyrna knew it was closer to twenty. Davoka chose a campsite atop a rocky rise overlooking a small vale, a position both Sollis and Smolen pronounced defensible on all sides. Smolen organised his men in a perimeter around the camp, with Sollis and his two brothers no more than ten feet from Lyrna's tent. Dinner was roasted pheasant with the last of the raisin bread, a treat Davoka seemed to enjoy greatly, albeit without any words of appreciation.

"So, Lerhnah," she said when the meal was complete, squatting in front of the fire, hands raised to the warmth. "What stories do you offer?"

"Stories?" Lyrna asked.

"Your camp, your stories."

There was a gravity to the Lonak woman's voice as she spoke the word "stories," similar to how some of the more devoted Faithful spoke the word "Departed." Lyrna's researches had contained numerous references to the respect the Lonak had for history, but she hadn't realised it approached religious fervour.

"It's their custom, Highness," Sollis said from the other side of the fire. "Doesn't have to be long, just true."

"Yes," Davoka insisted. "Truth only. None of the lies you write down and call poems."

Truth only. Lyrna concealed a wry smile. *How long since I did that?* "I have a tale," she told Davoka. "It's very strange and, although many swear to its truth, I cannot confirm it. Perhaps if you hear it, you can be the judge."

Davoka sat in silent contemplation for a moment, brow furrowed. This, it seemed, was an important decision. Eventually she nodded. "I'll hear it, Queen. And tell you if I hear truth."

"I'm glad." Lyrna straightened on her pillow, offering Sollis a gracious smile through the flames. "And you, brother. I would greatly appreciate your opinion of this tale, I call it the Legend of the One-Eyed Man."

His pale eyes betrayed nothing. "Of course, Highness."

She paused for a moment to modulate her breathing. She had been trained in oratory, at her own insistence, since her father regarded the art with a measure of disdain; he always did prefer speaking in private. "Over ten years ago," she began, "in the city we call Varinshold, a man rose to claim lordship over all the outlaws in the city."

Davoka squinted at her. "Outlaw?"

"*Varnish*," Sollis said. *Exile, without clan, worthless, thief or scum, depending on the inflection.*

"Ahh." She nodded. "Go on, Queen."

"This man had always been of vicious temperament," Lyrna continued. "Given to foul acts of theft, murder and rape, of both boys and maids it's said. His viciousness was such that all the other outlaws feared him to the extent that they would pay him to be left in peace. But one young thief wouldn't pay, a young thief with a keen eye and a knife, just like mine." She held up the throwing knife, gleaming red in the firelight. "And that young thief put his knife into the lord outlaw's eye. He lingered for days in great pain, thrashing and wailing, and then succumbed to a sleep so deep his minions thought him dead and began to wrap him in canvas in preparation for dumping in the deepest part of the harbour, for such is the resting place of most outlaws in Varinshold. But death hadn't claimed him, he rose again this lord of outlaws, to be known for ever more as One Eye.

"His anger was great, terrible acts were committed in his name as he sought the young thief, finding to his rage the boy had become a brother of the Sixth Order, and therefore beyond his reach, for now. And here is where the story becomes strange, for it's said the loss of his eye had birthed in him a great power, a Dark power."

"Dark?" Davoka asked.

"*Rova kha ertah Mahlessa,*" Sollis told her. *That which is known only to the Mahlessa, the High Priestess.*

The Lonak woman got to her feet. "I can hear no more of this," she stated, avoiding Lyrna's gaze and stalking away into the darkness.

"It's a thing they don't talk of, Highness," Sollis explained. "To voice a thing gives it substance. They prefer the Dark to have no substance."

"I see." Lyrna wrapped her cloak more tightly around her shoulders. "Well, it seems I am left with an audience of one for my story."

"I've heard it before. A one-eyed man with the power to bind others with his will alone. It's nonsense." Sollis got to his feet, hefting his bow. "I have the first watch, by your leave, Highness." He gave a precisely correct bow and walked away.

"How does it end, Highness?" Nersa asked, huddled at the entrance to her own tent, her face a pale oval in fox fur. "What happened to the one-eyed man?"

"Oh, they say he died a predictably ugly death. Slain by the Sixth Order in the bowels of the city." Lyrna went to her own tent. "Best get some rest, Nersa. I doubt tomorrow will be any easier than today."

"Yes, Highness. Sleep well."

Sleep well. Any sleep would have been welcome, troubled, dream-filled, fitful, she didn't care. Any release from this restless squirming in her cage of furs as she stared at the weave of the canvas over her head. A stiff northerly wind was ruffling the tent walls, making them snap and thrum in a most aggravating manner. But it wasn't this that kept her from sleep, nor had it been for the past five years. *Every night!* she raged. *Even here in this chilled waste, after so many miles on that blasted horse.*

It was always the same, every night she would lie abed waiting for sleep, but it wouldn't come, not until she had spent most of the night hours awash in memory and sheer exhaustion dragged her mind into slumber. Despite the nightly trial she never sought out a healer for a sleeping draught, never partook of wine to excess or dulled her senses with redflower. She hated it, this torment, but she accepted it. It was her due after all.

The memory became clearer when her mind had lost enough sensation of the world beyond her body to give its vision clarity, but not enough to bring the gift of sleep. *The old man in the bed, so old, so sunken into age and regret, barely recognisable as her father, barely believable as a king.*

She stood in the doorway to his bedchamber, a scroll clutched in her hand, the seal broken. The Alpiran Emperor had done them the courtesy of having it penned in Realm Tongue. The old man's eyes tracked from her face to the scroll. He waved an irritated hand at the physicians surrounding the bed, a harsh bark coming from his throat, louder than she would have thought him capable. The physicians fled.

The old man's skeletal claw beckoned to her and she came forward to kneel at his bedside. The voice that came from his throat was a dry rasp, but quick, the words clear. "So that's it, is it?"

Lyrna placed the scroll on the bed. "Would you like me to read it?"

"Caahh!" he snarled, hand twitching. "Know what it says. No point. They want the boy. They want the Hope Killer."

She looked down at the scroll, the neat precise text, beautifully scribed. "Yes, in return for Malcius. He's alive, Father."

"'Course he is, curses never die."

Lyrna closed her eyes tight. "Father, please . . ."

"That's all? Just the boy?"

"His men can leave. They ask for no reparations, no tribute. Just him."

There was no sound save for the old man's laboured breathing, like a dry rope dragged through an ungreased block. Lyrna looked up, meeting his eyes, fierce and bright enough to tell her he was still in there, still scheming away in his prison of age and illness. "No," he said.

"Father, I beg you . . ."

"No!" The shout brought a fit of coughing, doubling him over in the bed. He was so thin and wasted she feared he might snap.

"Father . . ." She tried to ease him back onto the pillow but he shrugged her off.

"You tell them no, daughter!" His eyes blazed at her, blood staining his lips and chin as he drew air into his lungs in painful gulps. "I did not do all this . . . to be thwarted now. You will send the Alpiran ambassador home . . . with a refusal and a statement of our rightful claim to the ports . . . Then you will send the remaining fleet . . . to Linesh with orders for Al Sorna to embark himself and his army . . . They are to return to the Realm with all dispatch . . . When I die, as I surely must before long . . . You will wed him as consort and ascend to the throne . . ."

"My brother . . ."

"Your brother is a waste of my blood!" He thrashed at her, lunging across the bed. "Do you think I have worked . . . for all these years to bequeath my Realm . . . to a fool who'll see it in ruins within a decade!" The cough took him again, wracking him, blood misting the bedcovers. Lyrna turned to call for the physicians but his claw-hand snared her wrist. For all his age and infirmity he still had a warrior's grip. "The war, Lyrna . . ." he said, fierce eyes softer now, imploring, ". . . the Realm Guard shattered, the treasury emptied . . . All for you to make it right, rebuild, be the saviour of this Realm. All for you . . ."

Revulsion engulfed her then, making her flesh burn where he touched her. She tore her wrist away, retreating as he continued to beg, blood now streaming from his mouth. "Please, Lyrna . . . all for you."

She stood in silence as he raged and flailed, until it seemed all the blood in him had stained the bedclothes and he lay spent and twitching, no more words coming from his hateful mouth. She swallowed, waited until his eyes were closed, until his chest had slowed to little more than a tremor. "Good sirs!" she called, making her voice as shrill with alarm as she could. "Good sirs, the King!"

The physicians returned in a flurry of robes and panic, flocking around the bed like crows around a perished horse. "Do all you can, good sirs!" she implored them. After another half hour of fussing one of the physicians came forward and bowed.

"Sir?" she enquired, tears streaming from her eyes.

"Highness, he has slipped into the final sleep. He will be with the Departed before the sun rises." He sank to one knee before her, the others following suit.

She closed her eyes, letting the final tear fall, knowing it would be the last she would ever shed for her father. "Thank you, sir. Please see to his comfort."

She retrieved the scroll and walked from the chamber. The Alpiran ambassador was seated where she had left him, on a bench in the main courtyard. It was a full moon and the marble paving stones were painted a pale blue, the pillars casting deep shadows.

"My lord Velsus," she greeted him.

Lord Velsus, a tall black-skinned man in a simple robe of blue and white, returned the bow. "Highness. What word from your father?"

She clutched the scroll tight, feeling the parchment crack, ruining the fine calligraphy it held. "King Janus Al Nieren finds your proposal acceptable."

She knew she was dreaming now, the blue of the moonlight too bright, Lord Velsus's eyes too mocking as he bowed, then lunged forward to clamp his hand over her mouth . . .

She jerked awake, the shout stifled by the hand trapping her lips against her teeth. Davoka's eyes were directly above hers, reflecting the bright gleam of the knife in her hand.

CHAPTER FIVE
Frentis

"You are a free man of little property and I am your recently acquired wife. We are travelling to the Alpiran border where you have secured employment as an apprentice slave breeder." The woman had donned grey clothing of more loosely woven cloth than her previous attire, instructing Frentis to dress himself in similarly mean garb. "We have no children. My mother warned me against you but I didn't listen. If this latest venture of yours is a failure, I'll be seeking a decree of annulment, you mark my words." She shook a finger at him with a shrewish scowl.

They were in her courtyard where a pony and cart had appeared that morning. Horvek had shown her the hidden panel above the axle where a variety of weapons and poisons were concealed. She inspected each dagger, short sword and vial before nodding in satisfaction. "It may be another year before my next visit," she told the Kuritai as she climbed onto the cart. "Be sure to see the general is well cared for."

"I shall, Mistress."

"Let's be off then, you worthless little man," she told Frentis with a laugh. "I think I might enjoy this role."

Frentis took the pony's reins and walked ahead, guiding them from the courtyard and into the square. A group of slaves were busy cleaning the statue of the man on the horse, the woman's gaze lingering on the great bronze until they turned a corner and made for the southern gate. "You want to know, don't you?" she called to him as he tugged the pony onward through the throng. "About the man on the horse."

He glanced at her over his shoulder but said nothing. She had an uncanny ability to read his unspoken moods, though he strove to keep any sign of curiosity or puzzlement from his face. "Don't worry," she assured him. "It's a long story but I don't mind the telling. It'll have to wait till we're on the road though."

The journey to the gate took an age of forcing their way through the bustle, the streets of Mirtesk were thick with slaves and free men all seemingly intent on getting to wherever they were going with as much inconvenience to others as possible.

"Out the way, you beggar!" a fat grey-clad shouted at Frentis, trying to force his way past, aiming a cuff at the nose of their pony. There was a momentary loosening of the binding and Frentis kneed the fat man in the groin, leaving him gasping on the cobbled street.

"I do so hate the ill-mannered," he heard the woman say.

A few streets on his attention was captured by an odd scene. A man stood outside a well-appointed house dressed in the threadbare garb of a slave. He was perhaps forty years old and stood with his head bowed, a placard hung about his neck bearing a single word. Behind him, slaves were carrying furniture and ornaments from the house under the eye of an overseer whilst a woman and two children sat and watched from the small courtyard. Frentis was struck by the glances of sheer hatred the woman directed at the man with the placard, matched by the glare of the elder child, a boy of about fifteen. As they trundled past Frentis saw the overseer hand the woman a scroll as one of his slaves fastened a chain with a heavy lock on the door. He picked up the word "annulment" amongst the babble before the scene was lost from view.

"A man with debts he can't pay," the woman said from the cart. "Deserves neither family, home nor freedom."

They had to pay a gate toll of three circles to exit the city and another one to use the road. Frentis was finding the Volarians were very fond of tolls, although he had to admit the road was worth the price; a smooth-surfaced highway of close-packed bricks broad enough to accommodate two heavy wagons side by side, stretching off into the gathering haze. There were no roads in the Realm to match it and he marvelled at the speed with which an army could move along such a route.

"Impressive, isn't it?" the woman commented, once again reading his mood with maddening ease. "Built by the man on the horse, nearly three centuries ago."

Frentis resisted the urge to glance back at her, although he did want to know more. "Savarek Avantir was his name," she went on as they continued through the neatly ordered orange groves bordering the road on both sides. "Council-man and general, conqueror of the southern provinces and perhaps the greatest military mind the empire, or even the world, has known. But even he knew defeat, husband dear. Like your mad king, he found himself humbled by the Alpirans. For ten years he fought to secure the final province, the last corner of this continent not in our hands. And for ten years the Alpirans spilled an ocean of blood to stop him. Defeat after defeat they suffered, army after army shattered by Avantir's genius, but they always sent more. Numbers are their strength, not their pitiful, imaginary gods. It was a painful lesson to learn, one which in truth drove Avantir to insanity and the assassin's blade when his demands for ever more men made the Council worry if their great military genius was in fact something of a liability. It's always the way with great men, they can't see the knives of those who live in their shadow."

She fell to silence and said no more until evening. They made camp at a rest stop some thirty miles south of Mirtesk where she fell into her role of nagging wife with effortless aplomb, scolding him about the camp as she cooked their meal, demanding more firewood in between lecturing him on his obvious failings as a husband, drawing amused glances or looks of sympathy from the other free travellers. The slaves, of course, went about their chores with eyes averted and faces void of any expression.

"Eat it then, you ungrateful cur," she said, handing him a bowl of goat stew.

His first mouthful convinced him that the woman's skill with a blade was not matched by her ability with the stewpot. He forced it down, his years in the Order having left him with a stomach capable of accepting the most unappetising fare.

The woman kept up the charade until the sky grew dark and the other travellers had retired to their tents. "You're wondering about my connection to him," she said. Frentis sat unmoving on the far side of their fire, saying nothing.

The woman gave a small smile. "An illustrious forebear perhaps? My great-great-great-grandfather?" Her smile faded. "No. He was my father, dear husband. I am the last of the Avantir line, though I no longer have need of that name, or any other."

She's lying, he decided. *Playing some trick.* She liked to toy with him, as she had proved when she forced him to share her bath the first night in her house, pressing herself against him, hands reaching beneath the water, stroking, her lips soft against his ear, whispering, *I can make you . . .* He closed his eyes against the memory and the shame of his body's betrayal.

"It's true, I assure you," she said. "Though I don't expect you to believe it, mired as you are in your superstitions. But you will, dearest." She leaned forward, eyes intent. "Before our journey is done you'll have seen enough to make my story seem a dull tale indeed." She smiled again and rose, moving to the half tent he had secured against the side of the cart. "Time for your husbandly duties, dearest," she said, disappearing into the shadowed interior of the tent. He sat by the fire until she flared the binding with enough agony to make him follow.

They travelled the road for another ten days, orange and lemon groves gradually giving way to ever-thicker forest of unfamiliar trees, growing in height the further south they went. The heat deepened as well, baking the road and making each day a trial of sweaty trudging in front of the cart. He didn't like this forest, it smelt like rot, birthed a million troublesome bugs and made a din like a madhouse in the night hours.

"It's called a jungle," the woman told him. "I expect they don't have them in your land."

The tenth night saw him staring into the jungle, his hand itching for a sword as something large crashed about in the trees, occasionally giving off a deafening crack that could only be a tree snapping in two.

"Ah, so there are still some left this far north," the woman said in mild surprise. "Come on, dearest." Her will tugged him along as she walked into the jungle. "It's a rare sight, one you'll cherish."

His eyes darted about as he followed, searching the blackness for unimaginable horrors. Fear was an old friend, but terror was a stranger. "Look." The woman came to a halt, crouching and pointing. The only light came from the half-moon above the tree canopy, painting the jungle floor a faint blue. It took him some time to fathom what he was seeing, the size and oddness of the thing defeating his comprehension. The beast stood at least ten feet tall, covered in long shaggy fur from tip to tail, moving about on great elongated limbs tipped with vicious-looking hooks. Its head was long and tubular, the narrow mouth giving off a faint hoot as it tore down a sapling, the crack echoing through the jungle.

"He's an old one," the woman said. "Probably been haunting this jungle longer than you've been alive, dearest."

What's it called? he wanted to ask, but didn't. As ever she didn't need to hear him say it. "The great sloth. It's not dangerous, provided you don't get too close. Only eats tree bark."

The beast stopped suddenly, a strip of bark hanging from its mouth, two black eyes staring straight at them. It gave a low, sombre hoot and turned, lumbering away into the depths of the jungle on its impossible limbs.

"I doubt I'll see another," the woman commented as they returned to the road. "Every year the jungle grows smaller and the roads grow longer. Oh well." She settled onto her bedroll. "Perhaps we'll see a tiger tomorrow."

The next day brought them to the great river forming the border with Alpiran territory where a small town of stilted structures waited on the near shore. The river was nearly a mile wide but unlike the lake crossing to Mirtesk, there was no ferry to be seen here. The stilt-town was a series of interlinked platforms at the end of a long jetty, dwellings clustered on each, uniform only in their ramshackle construction. A slave market was in full swing on the largest platform, the overseer's voice a constant chorus of barely intelligible jargon as he took bids from the audience, mostly grey-clads, although a few black robes were also present, sweating in the sun as their slaves wafted stale air over them with palm leaves.

"Lot seventy-three!" the overseer called as a naked girl was dragged onto the platform by a brawny Varitai. Frentis judged her to be no more than thirteen years old. "Fresh from the Twelve Sisters. No skills, no Volarian. Too plain for the pleasure house but trainable as a house-slave or breeding stock. Four circles to start."

Frentis felt his binding flare as he watched the girl stand trembling and weeping on the platform, a stream of urine covering her thigh. "Now, now, dearest," the woman said, clasping his hand, the loving wife replacing the scolding nag. She leaned close to plant a kiss on his cheek, whispering, "Your heroic days are gone. But, if you want to spare this one all that awaits her, I'll buy her and you can kill her. Would you like that?"

It was no empty threat, he knew. She meant to do it, possibly even in kindness rather than cruelty. He was beginning to suspect she barely understood the difference between the two. He shook his head, trembling.

"As you wish."

The girl went for two squares and a circle. She began to scream as they dragged her away, choking into silence as an overseer clamped a gag in her mouth.

"Lot seventy-four," the overseer on the platform intoned as a stocky, broad-shouldered man was brought forward, his back striped red with fresh whip-strokes. "One-time pirate, this one. From some islands in the north. Speaks Alpiran but no Volarian. Bit too spirited for the fields but will make a good show in the spectacles or fetch a decent price if you care to take him to the pits. Six circles to start."

"Come along," the woman said, leading him away from the auction. "I think this is making you a little too nostalgic."

They found a merchant on one of the smaller platforms who took the cart and pony in exchange for two squares. Frentis secured the contents of the hidden compartment in his pack and they made their way to a boardinghouse, renting a room at an exorbitant rate. "Slavers in town," the owner said, spreading his hands. "Should've come tomorrow, citizens."

"I told you, dullard!" the woman snarled at Frentis. "Oh why did I shun my mother's wisdom?"

"This is on the house though, citizen," the owner said, handing Frentis a bottle with an understanding wink. "Might help the night go quicker, eh?"

They waited in their small room until nightfall. This unnamed stilt-town falling to silence as the slavers took their purchases to the road and their various fates.

"You don't have slaves in your realm, do you?" the woman asked.

He stared out of the window at the broad, fast-flowing river and said nothing.

"No, you're all free," she went on. "But still slaves to your various superstitions, of course. Something we divested ourselves of centuries ago. Tell me, do you really think you're going to live forever in some paradise with your dead relatives when you die?"

She flared the binding again when he didn't answer. Tonight, it seemed, she actually wanted a conversation. "'What is death?'" he quoted. "'Death is but a gateway to the Beyond and union with the Departed. It is both ending and beginning. Fear it and welcome it.'"

"What's that? One of your prayers?"

"The Faithful don't pray. Prayers are for god worshippers and Deniers. It's from the Catechism of the Faith."

"And this faith promises eternal life after death?"

"Not life, life is of the body. The Beyond is the realm of the soul."

"The soul?" She shook her head and gave a small laugh. "Well, in that at least, your Faithful seem to know something. A childish conceit, but founded on a grain of truth."

She reached into the pack and extracted a pair of narrow-bladed daggers. "We need a boat." She handed him a dagger which he concealed in the leather sheath strapped to his forearm.

The jetty where the boats were moored was guarded by two Varitai, both armed with the standard-issue broad-bladed spears common to this lowest tier of Volarian soldiery. They were a poorly maintained pair, with badly repaired armour showing numerous gaps and too much dullness in their eyes, bespeaking an overseer with a meagre knowledge of the correct mix of drugs.

"No boats available," the largest of them said, blocking their path, the butt of his spear thumping onto the planks. "Come back in the morning."

Frentis stabbed him in the eye, the narrow blade piercing the orb and the brain beyond in a single thrust. The woman leapt past the falling corpse and ducked under the orthodox but too slow slash of the second soldier to thrust her dagger into a gap between his breastplate and armpit, stepping behind him as he collapsed to his knees, pushing his helmeted head forward and finishing him with a thrust to the base of the skull.

They slipped the bodies into the river feetfirst, slowly so as to avoid any telltale splash. The woman chose a medium-sized boat, a flat-hulled river craft propelled by a single oar in the stern. She undid the mooring rope and let the river take them downstream for a mile or more before instructing Frentis to begin rowing. The current was swift, too swift to allow a straight crossing and he could only keep the prow pointed at the opposite bank with strenuous hauling on the oar.

"Atethia," the woman said as the far bank grew in size, a stretch of marshland peppered with small islets each covered in tall rushes. "Southernmost province of the great Alpiran Empire, where we have much to do, dearest."

The dawn saw him guiding the boat through the marshes amidst an unceasing cloud of midges. The water was dulled brown with silt, the channels through the countless islets narrow and difficult to navigate.

"Awful place, isn't it?" the woman commented. "The graveyard of my father's final invasion in fact. He spent three years building a fleet on the opposite bank. That wretched town was first constructed from wood salvaged from the wrecks. Four hundred warships and a thousand boats carried his great host across the river where they spent a full month slogging through this marsh, hundreds died of disease or drowning but on they went, only for them to die by the thousands in a great and mysterious fire that ravaged the marshes. Most Alpirans believe the gods intervened to destroy the invaders with their divine fury, but Volarian historians insist they simply soaked the fringes of the marsh with naphtha and set it alight with fire arrows. Fifty thousand Free Swords and slaves burned to cinders in the space of a single night. Not my father though. Mad as he was by then, he was still wise enough to remain on the other side of the river." She glanced around at the rushes which grew so high as to obscure any view of the surrounding country. "Even today the Alpirans don't bother to fortify this stretch of bank, for what general would be insane enough to try the same tactic?"

It took another two days before the marsh finally gave way to solid ground, the boat grounding on a silt bank where the rushes were less tall and they could see a stretch of open country beyond. After the monotony of the marsh and the fetid threat of the jungle the green fields ahead were a welcome and inviting reminder of the Realm.

"We'll need new clothes," the woman said, starting forward. "I am the daughter of a wealthy Alpiran merchant from the northern ports, sent to the Twelve Sisters to meet with a prospective husband. You are a runaway slave turned mercenary hired as my bodyguard."

A half-day's walk brought them to a midsize town hugging the banks of one of the tributaries to the great river. There were no defensive walls but from a distance they could see numerous Alpiran soldiers walking the streets. "A little too busy for us, dearest," the woman decided. "There should be a plantation house or two further north."

They stayed off the roads, avoiding occasional Alpiran cavalry patrols by trekking through the fields of cotton that seemed to be the main crop in the region. Before long a plantation house came into view, a wide two-storey complex of interlinked houses and farm buildings, busy with workers. They hid in an irrigation ditch until nightfall when the woman sent him to the house to seek out the laundry. "The finest you can find for me, dearest," she told him. "I have appearances to maintain. Kill anyone who sees you. If it's more than one, kill everyone in the house and burn it down."

He approached from the west, the house having fewer windows on this side, moving from shadow to shadow, hugging the exterior wall. There were no guards, not even a dog to bark at the stranger appearing from the darkness. He made his way to the rear of the house where he assumed the servants' quarters were situated. The house was quiet but for the faint sound of song coming from what he judged to be the kitchen from the rich, savoury aroma emanating from the window.

He stopped at the sound of movement, lying prone beneath a large cart as two women emerged from a doorway to the courtyard. They chatted as they worked, hanging clothes on the lines strung across the yard. Frentis had picked up a little Alpiran during the war but this was an unfamiliar dialect, the accent harsher and more guttural than in the northern ports. He could pick out only one word in ten, but the term "Choosing" was voiced more than once, spoken in a kind of hushed reverence, as was the word "Emperor."

He watched the women complete their task and go back inside, waited the space of a hundred heartbeats then stole from beneath the wagon, pulling clothes from the washing line and wrapping them in a tight bundle. He was no judge of fashion but decided the woman would be content with a finely made robe of cotton with silk sleeves, plus a long cloak of dark blue—he froze at the sound of shuffling feet.

The boy stood in the doorway, playing with a wooden spindle on a string. He was no more than seven years old with a tumble of unkempt dark hair, his eyes rapt on his toy as it spun on the string. *Kill anyone who sees you . . .*

Frentis stood as still as he ever had, more still than the time he brought down his first stag under Master Hutril's guiding eyes, more still than when he hid from One Eye's thugs during his Test of the Wild.

The top spun and spun on the string.

Kill anyone who sees you . . .

Slowly, the binding began to flare. *She knows,* he realised. How did she always know?

It would be easy. Snap his neck then take him to the well. A tragic accident.

The top spun and spun . . . and the binding burned with a new pitch of agony. The damp bundle of clothes in his hands dripped onto the courtyard, a slow steady patter sure to draw a boy's curious eyes.

"Neries!" a woman's voice called from the kitchen window, followed by an insistent string of verbiage carrying a tone of maternal authority. The boy huffed, spun his top a few more times then went back inside.

Frentis fled.

"It'll do, I suppose." The woman discarded her grey attire and dressed in the silk-sleeved robe he had brought her. Frentis had already donned the pale blue trews and shirt he had chosen for himself. "Little loose around the waist though. Do you think me fat, dearest?" She grinned at him. The sun was rising and lit her face with a golden hue. *You would never know,* he thought, studying her feline beauty, the grace with which she moved. *A monster lives behind her face.*

"It was a child, wasn't it?" she said as he hefted the pack onto his shoulder and they made for the road. "Boy or girl?"

Frentis kept walking, saying nothing.

"Doesn't matter," she continued. "But you shouldn't indulge in any delusions. Our list is long and your tiresome notions of morality will no doubt cast every name in the role of innocent victim. But we will strike them through, each and every one, and you *will* do what I require of you, child or no."

They came to another town in late afternoon, the woman seeking out a dressmaker and purchasing something more to her liking, paying with an Alpiran gold from the supply sewn into the lining of the pack he carried. She posed for him in a simple but elegant ensemble of black-and-white silk, saying something in Alpiran, presumably seeking his opinion. The dressmaker had been kind enough to help with her hair, now bound up and braided in the Alpiran style, an ornate comb shining in the lustrous black mass. *You would never know . . .*

One day I will kill you, he thought, wishing he could voice the words. *For everything you've done, everything you're going to do and for everything you will make me do. I will kill you.*

The dressmaker recommended an inn near the market square where they rented two rooms, her new role requiring the appearance of propriety. He had hoped this might give him some respite but she used him again before dismissing him, straddling his naked form on the bed, sweat sheening her skin as she took the pleasure she wanted. When it was done she collapsed against him, breath hot on his cheek, fingers teasing the hair on his chest, making him put his arms around her. She always did this, creating the tableaux of contented lovers, perhaps she even believed it.

"When this is done," she breathed, "I'll have you give me a child." She nuzzled his neck, kissing, caressing. "Our blood will produce the most beautiful offspring, don't you think? In three centuries I've not found a man worthy of the honour. And now I find him in you, a slave from a soon-to-be-conquered land. How strange the world is."

Morning saw them on the road again, riding now, the woman having spent another gold on two horses, a dappled grey mare for herself and a russet-coloured stallion for her bodyguard. They were sturdy enough animals and docile of nature, making him pine for his old warhorse. Master Rensial had chosen the stallion for him, black from head to tail save for a flash of white on his forehead. "Loyal but spirited," the mad master had said handing him the reins. Frentis had named him Sabre and in time came to understand he was probably the finest mount ever ridden by a brother of the Sixth Order, an obvious sign of Rensial's favour. He had last seen Sabre in the stables at the Governor's mansion in Untesh, treating him to a final grooming before going to take his place on the wall, fully expecting death to come within the hour. *Where is he now?* he wondered. *Taken as booty by some Alpiran highborn, probably. Hope he gave him a good life.*

They rode north for another week, sleeping in the many way-stations to be found on this road. It was a poor thing in comparison to the Volarian wonder stretching away from Mirtesk, just a loose gravel track raising dust every time they spurred to a canter. They saw numerous soldiers on the road, all heading south in well-ordered but dusty columns. The basic kit of the Alpiran infantryman hadn't changed since Frentis last faced them in battle, mail shirts reaching down to the knee, a conical helm and a seven-foot spear resting on every shoulder. He recognised these as regulars, with plenty of veterans in the ranks, judging from the scars and age visible on some dusty faces. The Alpirans may not have fortified the bank but the Emperor was clearly diligent in ensuring the security of this province.

"Were they good soldiers?" the woman asked. They had dismounted by the side of the road to allow a column to pass by, a cohort of about a thousand men marching under a green banner emblazoned with a red star. "The Alpirans, did they fight well in that little war of yours?"

The insistent throb of the binding told him she expected an answer. "It was their land," he said. "They fought for it. And they won."

"But I expect you killed quite a few in the process, yes?"

The binding continued to throb. *The battle of the dunes, the arrows loosed at the Bloody Hill, the frantic struggle on the wall . . .* "Yes."

"No guilty feelings, my love? All those sons and fathers taken by your sword for the crime of defending their own land? No twinges of conscience?"

At Untesh he had cut down an Alpiran officer with a slash to the leg as he clambered over the wall. After the assault had been repulsed a Realm Guard healer bent down to staunch the wound and received a dagger through the neck as a reward. The officer was still spitting hatred at them as a half-dozen pole-axes pinned him to the stones. "It was war," he told the woman.

The throb abated and she remounted as the last of the Alpiran column trooped by. "Well, now you have another," she said. "Except this time you get to win."

The evening of the seventh day on the road brought them within sight of a port city and the shimmering blue of an ocean beyond. "Hervellis," the woman said. "Provincial capital of Atethia and home to the first name on our list, an old friend in fact. I'm very keen for you to meet him."

The architecture of Hervellis bore some similarities to the winding streets and tree-garnered squares of Linesh and Untesh, but held considerably more grandeur. They passed several temples as they made their way from the gate towards the main square, impressive marble buildings of pillars and relief carvings, each festooned with numerous statues to the uncountable gods of the empire. The woman maintained an affable mask as they trotted through the streets, but he could see contempt in her eyes as she surveyed the temples. *I pity them their delusion,* he thought. *But she hates them for it.*

They took rooms in a boarding-house on the north side of the square, more expensive than the others but also considerably more comfortable. She didn't use him this night, instead telling him to get some rest, taking the pack and going to her room. He lay on the voluminous bed until darkness, unable to sleep despite the luxuriant softness that engulfed him. *She'll make me kill tonight.*

The binding flared a few hours later and he went to her room, finding her dressed in black silk from head to toe, hair tied back from her face into a tight bun. She wore a dagger on each forearm and a short sword on her back. She nodded at the weapons set out on the bed alongside a silk shirt and trews, black like her own.

"Make no mistake, my love," she said, smearing coal dust on her face. "You are unlikely to meet a being more vile and dangerous than the man you'll meet tonight. I can afford no more nostalgia."

The binding flared, the pain severe but just below the level when it became unbearable. Her control was absolute now, forbidding any hesitation or even thought. She would will it and he would act. He was completely her creature.

She went to the window, pushing open the blinds and clambering out onto the rooftop. She lingered, surveying the street below then ran along the tiles to leap to the rooftop opposite. He followed as she continued to make her way across the city from roof to roof, wall to wall, in a tireless display of athleticism that would have earned his grudging admiration, although the continuous flare of the binding left him incapable of any such feeling.

She led him north, away from the dense streets clustered around the main square, to the broader avenues near the docks. She stopped atop a wall overlooking a square where a small temple sat surrounded by trees. The temple was a rectangle of pillars supporting a flat-topped pyramidal roof crowned with a statue of a woman, her face hidden in her marble cowl. Unlike the other temples Frentis had seen, this one was guarded, two armoured men with spears flanking the entrance. The door was closed but outlined by the glow of a fire within.

The woman rose, sprinting along the wall to launch herself into the nearest tree, catching a branch and hauling herself up with barely a leaf falling as she did so. He watched her crawl along the underside of the branch then drop onto the roof of the temple. Had the binding left any room for consideration, he would have concluded this was a feat he couldn't match, despite all his training and years in the pits. But her will left no room for doubt and he followed without demur, running, leaping, catching the branch and crawling to the roof all as if he had done it a thousand times before.

She led him to the rear of the temple, past the statue, even this close, he could see only shadow in the cowl. The woman peered over the edge of the temple roof, withdrew a dagger from her wrist sheath and stepped out into space, turning in midair. There was a faint sound, only the softest thud. Frentis looked over the edge seeing her sheathing her dagger, standing astride the body of a third guard. He dropped down next to her as she tested the door in the rear wall of the temple. It swung open, smooth and quiet on oiled hinges. He saw her hesitate. This was unexpected.

The interior of the temple was austere, bare walls devoid of mosaics or reliefs, a narrow bed in the corner next to a table holding pen, ink and a few sheets of parchment. The space was dominated by the large fire burning in the centre, a marble basin filled with coals burning hot and bright, the smoke escaping through holes in the ceiling. A man sat in a chair facing the fire, his back to them. Frentis could see only the crown of his grey head and his hands on the armrests, gnarled and spotted with age. The woman stepped into the temple, forsaking stealth with a loud clatter as she shoved the door fully open. Frentis saw the hand on the armrest twitch, but the man in the chair didn't rise.

"A temple to the Nameless Seer," she said in Volarian, striding forward to stand in front of the old man, regarding him with an arched eyebrow. She kept Frentis where he was, dagger drawn, ready to stab through the chair-back at the slightest command. "This is where you choose to seclude yourself these days?"

There was a faint sound from the man in the chair that might have been a laugh. The voice was frail, the words unaccented. "Forgive an old man a small conceit." A pause as the grey head shifted to regard her. "Still clinging to the same shell I see."

"Whilst you have allowed yours to wither." She examined the old man's form with obvious disgust.

"What better protection from the Ally's servile dogs? Why bother taking the body of a man who can't walk more than ten feet without falling to his knees?"

"Why indeed." She glanced around at the temple's unvarnished interior. "I would have thought the Emperor might provide more salubrious accommodation for your dotage. Given the great service you did his forebear."

"Oh he offered me great rewards, fine houses, servants and a sizeable pension. I asked only for this. People come seeking wisdom from the servant of the Nameless Seer and leave happy for the cost of a few coppers. A fitting diversion for a lonely old man."

The woman's lips curled into a small sneer. "I am supposed to believe you have mellowed with age? Don't forget what I've seen, what we did."

"What we were made to do."

"I recall no reluctance on your part."

"Reluctance? Oh there was that, when it was time to leave you, then I was truly reluctant. When your father's army came slogging out of the marshes, even more so. I had changed by then you see, wanting only a quiet life, but the Emperor asked for my aid, *asked*. No commands, no threats . . . No torture. He just asked. It was the last time I used my gift."

The woman stared at him in silence for a moment. "Why was the door unlocked?"

"It's been unlocked for twenty years now. The guards are here at the Emperor's insistence, not mine. In truth, I expected you and your young friend sooner, but my scrying is not what it was. It's the way with stolen gifts, don't you find? They tend to dull with age."

She took a firmer grip on her dagger and he saw her hesitate before forcing out a final question. "Why did you leave . . . me?"

"You know why. You were cruel and fierce and beautiful, but the Ally made you monstrous. It broke my heart."

"You don't know what the Ally made me, Revek. But you'll discover it soon enough."

The binding seared Frentis with an implacable command, spurring him forward, dagger drawn back. The old man surged to his feet, quicker than any old man should, raising his arms, fingers splayed, turning, revealed a face of great age but also profound sadness as he regarded Frentis. His fingers spasmed and fire engulfed his hands, but this was not the illusion conjured by One Eye all those years ago. The blast of heat on his face told him this old man had just brought forth true fire from his hands. He raised them, two flaming fists aimed at Frentis as he charged.

The woman moved in a blur, looping her arm over the old man's head to draw her dagger across his throat, releasing a red rush of blood. The old man's fire died as he stumbled, uncharred hands clutching at his throat.

There was a crash as the front door thrust open, the two guards rushing in, eyes wide in horror as they viewed the scene. The woman killed the one nearest her with a dagger throw to the neck, drawing her short sword and rushing the other. He was quick and well trained, parrying her thrust with his spear blade then jabbing at her face and neck, keeping her at bay. Frentis started forward then stopped as the old man's hand snared his ankle. He tried to pull away but couldn't. *The binding was gone.*

Frentis staggered with the sudden rush of freedom, the pain vanishing in an instant. The old man's mouth was moving in a welter of red spray, his other hand clamped around the gaping wound in his neck. Frentis crouched to hear his words, spoken in Realm Tongue, the faintest whisper, "The seed will grow." Too quick to catch it the old man's hand came away from his neck, clamping onto Frentis's face, smearing, the blood staining his skin, clouding his eyes, seeping into his mouth. He reeled away, the old man's hand coming free of his ankle, the binding returning instantly.

He looked up to see the woman side-step a thrust of the guard's spear, catch hold of the haft and use it to swing a kick into his face. He staggered back, the spear coming loose from his hands, fumbling for the sabre in his belt. He was too slow, her short sword thrusting easily through the mail on his chest, plunging deep to find the heart.

She dragged her blade from the corpse and looked up at Frentis, striding forward, eyes searching his face. "He touched you." She took a wine jug from a nearby table and splashed it onto his face, washing the blood away, then stood back in a fighting stance, sword poised and ready. The binding surged to its greatest severity yet, making him tremble from head to foot, his mind filled with the scream his lips couldn't voice. She held him for what seemed an age, wary eyes searching his face the whole time. Finally she grunted and loosened her grip, letting him fall to the temple floor, gasping and writhing in pain.

Through the shuddering aftermath he saw her move to the old man's body, kicking his lifeless chest, breaking frail ribs with an audible crack. She grasped his grey head in a tight fist, hauling the corpse upright, the short sword coming down once then twice to sever the neck. She lifted the head high, tilting her own back, mouth wide, the rain of blood falling into it as she drank.

The binding was loose enough to allow Frentis to vomit.

"Now," the woman said, tossing the old man's head aside and dragging a sleeve across her mouth, blood and coal dust smearing together in a black paste. "You'll see what the Ally made me, Revek."

She sheathed her sword and raised her hands, eyes closed in

concentration, teeth clenched. For a moment it seemed nothing would happen then fire engulfed her hands and she screamed, both in pain and triumph. She laughed as she sent fire in a stream towards the old man's corpse, leaving it in an instant shroud of flame, then cast fiery whips about the temple, setting light to anything that could burn. Soon the whole place was wreathed in flame and the heat fast becoming unbearable.

She let her arms drop, the fire vanishing from her hands. Her gaze settled on Frentis as the binding forced him to his feet, making him come closer. Great pain dominated her features and fresh blood streamed from her nose and eyes, but still she smiled, fierce and exultant, the flames gleaming red in her eyes. "There's always a price to pay, my love."

CHAPTER SIX
Vaelin

The office of the King's Notary was free of other petitioners on this the first day of the Summertide Fair, but Vaelin was still obliged to wait for almost an hour before the clerk looked up from his ledger book. He was a youngish man with the harassed air of the overworked and underpaid. "My apologies, sir," he said. "We're short-staffed today, what with the fair."

"I fully understand." Vaelin rose from the bench and approached the young clerk's desk, so piled high with papers and ledgers he resembled a badger in an untidy den. "When I was last in the Realm the Fourth Order had charge of the King's records," he said.

"Not these days. These days the brothers of the Fourth Order are more like the Sixth, swaggering about, swords and all." The clerk reclined in his seat, stifling a yawn and giving Vaelin a curious glance. "You've been travelling then, sir?"

"Indeed, far and wide."

"Anywhere exotic?"

"The Meldenean Islands most recently. Before that the Alpiran Empire."

"Didn't think they even allowed our ships to land any more."

"I took a roundabout route."

"I see." The clerk reached for a blank piece of parchment. "So, good sir. What brings you here with the delights of the fair but a short walk away?"

"I require a Warrant of Acknowledgment, for my sister."

"Ah." The clerk dipped his pen in an inkwell and jotted something onto the parchment. "Complicated families are truly the life-blood of this office. Fortunately, the procedure is fairly straightforward. You simply swear to your sister's legitimacy in my presence, I will inscribe the warrant, we both sign and the deed is done. The fee is two silvers."

Two silvers. It was fortunate Reva had agreed to sell the fine Realm Guard knife she acquired on the road. "Very well."

"Excellent. Now, your name sir?"

"Lord Vaelin Al Sorna."

The nib of the clerk's pen made a loud crack as it snapped, ink splattering across the parchment. He stared at the black stain for a moment, swallowed and slowly raised his head. There was no doubt in his expression, just awe.

Pity, Vaelin thought. *I was starting to like him.*

"My lord . . ." The clerk began, rising and bowing, low enough for his forehead to bump the desk.

"Don't do that," Vaelin told him.

"They said you were dead . . ."

"So I heard."

"I knew it was a lie. I knew it!"

Vaelin forced a smile. "The warrant for my sister."

"Oh." The clerk looked down at his desk, then around at the empty office, sweaty hands leaving a stain on his tunic. "I fear this is above my station, my lord."

"I assure you it isn't."

"My apologies, my lord." He backed away from the desk. "If you could wait just one moment." He fled into the shadowy depths of the office. There was the sound of a door being thrust open, a bark of annoyance then a hushed conversation. The clerk soon returned followed by an overweight man somewhere past his fiftieth year. He faltered for a moment at the sight of Vaelin but gathered his composure with admirable speed.

"My lord," the man said with a formal bow. "Gerrish Mertil, formerly of the Fourth Order, now Chief Notary for the City of Varinshold."

Vaelin bowed back. "Sir. I was explaining to this man . . ."

"A Warrant of Acknowledgment, yes. Might I enquire your purpose in seeking this document?"

"No, you might not."

The Chief Notary flushed a little. "Your pardon my lord. But I am aware of the King's Order regarding your late father's property and the Magistrate's judgement in your sister's case. A Warrant of Acknowledgment will negate the judgement but not the King's Word, which as you know, is above the law."

"I am aware of that, thank you." He reached into his purse and extracted two silvers, placing them on the desk. "Nevertheless I wish to acknowledge my sister. I believe I am merely exercising rights enjoyed by all Realm subjects."

Gerrish Mertil nodded at the young clerk who hurried to prepare the documents.

"Would it be presumptuous, Lord Vaelin," the Chief Notary said, "for me to be the first official of the Realm to welcome you home?"

"Not at all. Tell me, how does a former brother become Chief Notary?"

"By the King's grace. When he decreed the crown should resume stewardship of the Realm's records, His Highness was wise enough to recognise the value of skills possessed by so many brothers of my Order."

"You left your Order at the King's command?"

Mertil's expression became sombre. "It was no longer the Order I joined as a boy. The ascension of Aspect Tendris brought many changes. Instead of bookkeeping, novice brothers were being taught sword play. The crossbow instead of the pen. May the Departed forgive me, but I and many of my brothers were glad to leave."

The young clerk hissed an obscenity, crouched over a sheet of velum at a writing desk, the quill shaking in his hand. "Oh give it here." The Chief Notary nudged him aside, blotted away the spilled ink and began to write in smooth-flowing letters. "In my day they used to whip us if the flourishes were not all exactly the same length." It was quickly done, signed by the Chief Notary himself. Vaelin appreciated his silent patience as he laboured over his own signature.

"I hope all is to your satisfaction, my lord." Mertil bowed, handing over the scrolled warrant, tied with a red ribbon.

"My thanks, sirs." Vaelin held out the two silvers but the Chief Notary shook his head.

"I had a nephew in the Blue Jays," he said. "He was with you at Linesh. Thanks to you his mother got to welcome him home."

Vaelin nodded. "Fine regiment, the Blue Jays."

The Chief Notary and the young clerk were both bowing as low as they could as he made for the door, resisting the impulse to run.

He found Alornis and Reva at the crossroads of Gate Lane and Drovers Way. The streets were largely empty thanks to the fair but his experience at the notary's office made him keep his hood in place. A large marble plinth was positioned in the centre of the crossroads, covered in scaffolding from base to top. Alornis was standing on the highest platform, dressed in a mason's apron, holding a rope threaded through a block and then to ground level where Reva placed various implements in the basket it was attached to.

"The big hammer!" Alornis called from the platform. "No the other one."

"Your sister's even more a tyrant than you," Reva grumbled as Vaelin approached.

"Vaelin!" Alornis greeted him with a cheerful wave. "Master, my brother's here!"

After a moment the head of an old man appeared over the

edge of the platform. He was heavily bearded and dressed in the green robe of the Third Order, his brow furrowed like a ploughed field as he regarded Vaelin, grunted something then disappeared. Alornis gave a weak smile of apology.

"What did he say?" Vaelin asked.

"He thought you'd be taller."

Vaelin laughed and held up the scroll. "I have something for you."

She descended to street level by the expedient of taking a tighter hold of the rope and jumping off the platform, the heavy basket of tools acting as a counterweight. The old man's surprisingly muscular arm appeared to haul the basket onto the platform above.

"So," Alornis said after scanning the scroll, "ink and paper make me your sister where blood does not."

"And a fee of two silvers, but they let me off."

"So we can eat tonight?" Reva asked.

"I still need to petition the King," Vaelin told Alornis.

"You really expect him to reverse his Word?"

His efforts will be wasted if he doesn't, though I doubt I'll like the price. "I'm certain he will."

Something fell to the cobbles nearby with a loud clang followed by a bellow from above. "Wrong chisel!"

Alornis sighed. "He's tetchier than usual today." She raised her head to the platform. "Coming Master Benril!" She began to gather tools together from the base of the plinth. "You two should go home. I'll be a few hours yet."

"Actually, sister, I was hoping you could take Reva to the fair. She's never seen it."

Reva gave a quizzical grimace. "Couldn't give a snot for your heathen celebration."

"But my sister does. And I would feel better if she had protection." He tossed her his purse. "And you can choose tonight's dinner."

"I can't," Alornis insisted. "Master Benril needs me . . ."

"I'll help Master Benril." Vaelin undid the ties on her apron and lifted it over her head. "Off with you both."

She gave an uncertain glance at the top of the scaffolding. "Well, he hasn't paid me for weeks."

"Then it's decided." He shooed them away, watching them walk along Gate Lane, the blood-song sounding the same curious lilting note when Alornis took Reva's hand, chatting away at her as if they had known each other since girlhood. He saw Reva flinch, but was surprised when she didn't snatch her hand away.

"Chisel!" came an impatient shout from above.

Vaelin gathered all the chisels he could find into a leather toolbag and clambered up the successive ladders to the top of the scaffold. The old man was crouched against the plinth's summit, hands roving over the marble surface. He didn't turn when Vaelin dumped the tool bag at his side.

"My sister says you haven't paid her," he said.

"Your sister would pay to help me, brother." Master Benril Lenial turned to regard him with the same deeply furrowed brow. "Or is it just my lord these days?"

"I'm no longer of the Sixth Order, if that's your meaning."

Master Benril grunted and turned back to the plinth.

"What will it be?" Vaelin asked.

"The Realm's monument to the greatness of King Janus." The old man's tone said much about his enthusiasm for this project.

"A royal commission then."

"I do this and he promises to leave me alone for two years so I can paint. It's the only true art. This." He smacked a palm against the marble. "This is mere masonry."

"I knew a mason once. I would say he was as much an artist as any man could be."

"And I would say you should stick to swinging your sword about." He glanced back again. "Where is it anyway?"

"I left it at home wrapped in canvas, as it has been since I returned to the Realm."

"So you've given up more than just the Faith, eh?"

"I've gained more than I've given up."

Master Benril shifted about to face him, showing no signs of stiffness in his aged limbs. "What do you want?"

"My sister, I need to take her away from here. I want you to tell her to let me."

Benril raised his extensive eyebrows. "You feel my word carries that much weight with her?"

"I know it. I also know there is no life for her here, not as my father's daughter, or as your pupil."

"Your sister's gift is a great and wonderful thing. To prevent her from nurturing it would be a crime."

"She can nurture it in safety, far from here."

Benril ran a hand through the long grey mass of his beard. "I'll agree not to speak against her leaving, but that's all."

Vaelin inclined his head. "My thanks, Master."

"Don't thank me yet." The old man rose and went to the ladder. "I have a condition."

"Hold still will you!"

Vaelin's back ached and a cramp was starting to build in his neck. Benril had made him hold several poses now, each more theatrical than the last. This latest had him standing, back straight and head raised, staring off into the distance, holding a mop as if it were a sword. The old man had started and discarded numerous sketches already, the chalk never ceasing in his hand, his eyes flicking constantly between Vaelin and the dark brown parchment on his easel.

"You don't hold a sword like this," Vaelin advised.

"It's called artistic licence," Benril snapped back. "Lower your right arm."

It was another half hour before five troopers of the King's Mounted Guard trotted into the crossroads, a riderless horse in tow. The captain in charge dismounted and strode forward to offer a smart salute, his polished breastplate providing Vaelin with a fine reflection of his ridiculous pose. "Lord Vaelin, may I say this is an honour?"

"I was expecting Captain Smolen," Vaelin said.

The captain hesitated. "Lord Marshal Al Smolen is in the North, my lord." He straightened with pride. "I bring warm greetings from His Highness . . ."

"All right." Vaelin abandoned the pose and reached for his cloak. "Master Benril, it appears I'm needed at the palace. We'll have to finish this another time."

"Tell the King I need more coin for the blacksmith," Benril said to the captain. "If he wants his monument before winter sets in that is."

The captain stiffened. "I am not a messenger, brother."

"I'll tell him," Vaelin assured Benril, pulling on his cloak. He paused to look at the master's sketch, frowning in puzzlement. "I'm not that tall."

"On the contrary, my lord." Benril leaned closer to the parchment to add some shading to Vaelin's cheekbones. "I think you stand very tall indeed."

King Malcius Al Nieren wore a more ornate crown than the plain band favoured by his father, a ring of gold inlaid with an intricate floral design and featuring a centre-piece of four different gemstones, each presumably representing the four fiefs of the Realm. The eyes beneath the crown held a wariness not matched by the warm smile he offered Vaelin as he rose from one knee before the throne.

"Record," the King intoned, making the three scribes positioned to the left of the throne dip their pens in readiness. "King Malcius Al Nieren welcomes his most loyal and honoured servant Lord Marshal Vaelin Al Sorna back to the Unified Realm. Be it known that all honours and titles previously his are restored."

He came forward, arms wide, gripping Vaelin by the shoulders. Malcius had always struck Vaelin as a man of considerable vigour, a seasoned warrior possessed of a strong arm and a keen mind. The man who confronted him now was thinner, his complexion sallow beneath a dusting of powder, the hands on his shoulders trembling a little.

"By the Faith it's good to see you, Vaelin!" the King said.

"And you, Highness." He glanced around as the King's hands remained on his shoulders. There were numerous courtiers in attendance, it seemed the King had delayed the royal procession to the fair to honour his unexpected guest. To the right of the throne sat a young woman, hands clasped in her lap, a crown smaller but otherwise identical to the King's on her head. She was handsome and slender, with a keen intelligence shining in her eyes, which were, like her husband's, also wary.

"Rest assured," the King said, dragging Vaelin's attention away from the queen. "This Realm is fully aware of the debt it owes you." His hands clutched Vaelin even tighter.

"Thank you, Highness." He lowered his voice. "I . . . wondered if I may raise a small matter with you, regarding my father's estate."

"Of course, of course!" The King finally released him, drawing back. "But first, I must present you to my queen. She has been looking forward to meeting you since word reached us of your return."

The queen rose as Vaelin went to one knee before her.

"Lord Vaelin," the King said. "I present Queen Ordella Al Nieren. Please pledge your loyalty to her as you would me."

Vaelin glanced up at him, finding his smile had faded somewhat. "Merely a formality," Malcius said. "Required of all Swords of the Realm these past four years."

Vaelin turned back to the queen, head lowered. "I, Lord Vaelin Al Sorna, hereby pledge my loyal service to Queen Ordella Al Nieren of the Unified Realm."

"I thank you, my lord," the queen said. She had a cultured voice with the soft vowels of southern Asrael, but there was something of an edge to it as she continued. "Do you pledge to follow my commands as you would your King?"

"I do, my Queen."

"Do you pledge to protect me and my children as you would your King? To lay down your life in our defence should it be necessary? And to do so regardless of what lies or deceits are voiced against us?"

Vaelin became aware of how silent the court had become, feeling the weight of so many eyes on his kneeling form. *This is not for me,* he decided. *This is for them.* "I do, my Queen."

"You honour me, my lord." She held out her hand, which Vaelin duly kissed, finding her skin icy on his lips.

"Excellent!" Malcius clapped his hands together. "My love, be so good as to proceed to the fair with the court. I shall be along directly, once Lord Vaelin and I have concluded our business."

Alone with Vaelin save for two guards at the door, Malcius took off his crown, hanging it on the arm of his throne with a weary sigh. "Sorry about all that," he said. "A necessary piece of theatre, I'm afraid."

"I meant what I said, Highness."

"I'm sure you did. If only every Sword of the Realm were so sincere in their oaths, this would be a much easier land to govern." He sat in his throne, crouching forward, elbows resting on his knees, meeting Vaelin's gaze with tired eyes. "Got old, didn't I?"

"We all did, Highness."

"Not you, you barely look a day older. I was expecting some wizened creature from the depths of the Emperor's dungeon. But here you are, looking like you could take on every knight at the fair with barely a laboured breath."

"The Emperor's hospitality was generous, but lonely."

"I'm sure." Malcius reclined in his throne. "You know why I took your father's estate, I presume?"

"You needed to ensure my loyalty."

"I did. I see now it wasn't necessary. But I had to be sure. You have no notion of the plots that surround my family. Every day word comes of a new group of conspirators, hatching murderous schemes in darkened rooms."

"The Realm was always rich in wild rumour, Highness."

"Rumour? If only it was just that. Two months ago they found a fellow in the palace grounds with a poisoned blade and the Catechism of the Faith tattooed on his back and chest, every word of it. I gave him a quick death, which is more than my father would have done, eh?"

Janus would have tortured him for a month, if he was feeling generous, two if he wasn't. "Indeed, Highness. But one madman doesn't make a plot."

"There are others, be assured of that. And I must face them on my own, Aspect Arlyn wants no part of it. Since the war, your former Order has regained much of its independence."

"Even in your father's day Aspect Arlyn was keen to draw a distinction between the Crown and the Faith."

"The Faith." The King's voice was soft and faintly bitter. "When trouble brews in this Realm like as not you'll find the Faith stirring the pot. Ardents and Tolerants at each other's throats, Aspect Tendris and his ridiculous attempts to turn his bureaucrats into warriors. It's supposed to unite us, instead it threatens to tear itself apart and this Realm with it." His eyes fixed on Vaelin again. "And each side will wish to enlist your support."

"Then each side will be disappointed."

The King blinked, straightening in surprise. "I know you have left the Order behind, but the Faith too? What forced you to this? Did the Emperor make you worship the Alpiran gods?"

Vaelin suppressed a laugh. "Merely the hearing of a truth, Highness. The Faith was not tortured from me, nor do I look to any god for comfort."

"It seems you are more of a danger to the harmony of the Realm than I realised."

"I am a danger to no-one, provided they offer no harm to me or mine."

Malcius sighed again then smiled. "Lyrna did always like you for your . . . complexity."

Lyrna . . . It was strange, but it only occurred to him now that the princess had been absent from the court today. "She is at the fair, Highness?"

"No, gone north to conclude a treaty with the Lonak. If you can believe such a thing."

Lyrna treating with the Lonak. The thought of it was absurd and appalling in equal measure. "You offered them peace?"

"Actually the offer came from their High Priestess. But she would only talk to Lyrna. A Lonak tradition apparently. Only the word of a woman can be trusted by the High Priestess, men are too easily corrupted." He grimaced at the doubt on Vaelin's face. "I had to take the chance. We've lost enough blood and treasure fighting the wolfmen, don't you think?"

"Fighting us is what they live for."

"Well, perhaps they want to start living for something else. As do I. This land needs to be reborn, Vaelin. Remade into something better. United once more, truly united, not forever riven by our borders and our faiths. The Edict of Toleration was but the first step. Reshaping our towns and cities is the next. Improving the fabric of the Realm will improve the souls of its subjects. I can do what my father never did despite all his wars and his scheming. I can bring peace, a lasting peace that will make this land great again. But I need your help."

And so to the price. "You have my loyalty, Highness. However, I would be more secure in my service if I knew my sister was given her due."

The King waved a hand. "Done, I'll have the papers signed today. You can have all that your father owned. But you cannot remain here, not in Asrael."

"In truth I had intended to ask your leave to depart the Realm, once my father's estate is restored."

The King frowned. "Depart? To where?"

"You recall Brother Frentis, I'm sure. I believe he still lives. I intend to find him."

"Brother Frentis." The King shook his head, voice heavy with sorrow. "He died at Untesh, Vaelin. They all did. Every man under my command."

He was on a ship, bound somehow, his scars were burning . . . "Did you see it, Highness? Did you see him fall?"

The King's gaze became distant, brow creased with reluctant

memory. "Again and again we fought them off, Frentis at my side for much of it. And he was a sight to see, throwing himself into the thickest fight, saving us time and again. The men called him the Faith's Fury. Without him the city would have fallen on the first day, not the third. I sent him to bolster the southern section that morning. The Alpirans were like a wave boiling over a harbour wall in a storm."

He ran a hand through his hair, once rich red-gold, now thinner and shot through with streaks of grey. Vaelin noted how his hand shook. "They wouldn't kill me. No matter how many I cut down, how hard I hacked and cursed at them. When they finally bore me down they roamed the city killing every Realm Guard they could find, the deserters, the wounded, it didn't matter. But me they kept alive. Only me."

He was on a ship . . . "In any case, Highness. I believe my brother to be alive, and request your leave to search for him."

The King gave a grim smile and shook his head. "No, my lord. I'm sorry, but no. I require a different service from you."

Vaelin gritted his teeth. *I could just leave,* he thought. *Leave this sad, tired man to his dreams and his phantom plots. An oath compelled before an audience of pampered sycophants is just another lie, like the Faith.*

Malcius rose from his throne to point to a large embroidered map of the Realm on the wall, his finger tracking from Asrael to a large blank expanse above the Great Northern Forest. "There, my lord, is where I require your service."

"The Northern Reaches?"

"Quite so. Tower Lord Al Myrna passed away last winter. His adopted daughter's been running things since then, but since she's a Lonak foundling of no breeding whatsoever, I can hardly allow such a state of affairs to continue." The King straightened, speaking in formal tones. "Vaelin Al Sorna, I hereby name you Tower Lord of the Northern Reaches."

He could refuse, state his unwillingness and walk from the palace without a hand raised against him. Malcius was effectively barred from acting against him for fear of raising rebellion the length of the Realm. But the notion evaporated when the blood-song gave a sudden and unexpected crescendo of assent. The music faded quickly but the meaning was clear enough: *The path to Frentis lies in the Northern Reaches.*

He bowed low to the King, replying in formal tones. "An honour I gladly accept, Highness."

CHAPTER SEVEN
Lyrna

Why hasn't she killed me?

Davoka's eyes flared in warning, her hand firm on Lyrna's mouth, it smelt of woodsmoke. Lyrna swallowed, did her best to stem the harsh torrent of her breathing and raised a questioning eyebrow. Davoka's eyes flicked to her right. Lyrna strained to see but could only discern the dim greyness of the tent wall, still thumping in the mountain wind. She looked back at Davoka, both eyebrows raised now. The Lonak woman's eyes were elsewhere, gaze tracking along the tent wall, the bare muscle of her arms tensed in readiness.

It was only the smallest sound, a faint whisper of parting cloth. Lyrna's eyes picked out a pinprick of gleaming metal in the tent wall, growing into a knife point then a blade at least ten inches long. The whisper grew into a shout of ripping canvas as the knife slashed downward, the tent wall parting to reveal the face of a man, a Lonak warrior if Lyrna was any judge, shaven-headed and tattooed across the forehead, teeth bared in a killing snarl.

Davoka lunged, her knife taking the Lonak under the chin, his head jerking up and back as she forced it deeper, finding the brain. She pulled the knife free and threw her head back, her scream vast and savage. From outside came an instant clamour of alarm, shouted orders and the cacophony of men in combat.

Davoka hefted her spear, pushing her gore-covered knife into Lyrna's hand. "Stay here, Queen." Then she was gone, diving through the gash in the canvas into the blackness beyond.

Lyrna lay on her back, the bloody knife sitting in her open hand, wondering if a person's heart could truly burst with overuse.

"HIGHNESS!" A rasping shout from outside. Brother Sollis.

"Here," she croaked through a sand-dry throat, coughed and tried again. "I'm here! What is happening?"

"We are betrayed! Stay insi—" He broke off and there came a harsh clang of colliding steel followed by a grunt of pain. More shouts, voices raised in cries of challenge or shock. She could hear many Lonak voices amongst the riot of sound.

A sharp thwack jerked her gaze to the roof of the tent where a steel-tipped arrow dangled from the canvas, caught by its fletching.

GET UP! her mind screamed.

Another thwack, another arrow, lower this time, coming straight through the fabric to thump into the fur an inch from her leg, the shaft quivering.

Get up! If you stay here, you will die!

The knife sat ungripped in her open palm, a bead of blood dripping from the hilt and onto her skin. The heat of it was enough to shock her into motion. She gripped the knife, gore seeping between her fingers, and forced herself to her feet and out into the night.

The campfire surged as Sollis threw another log on the flames, bloodied sword in his other hand, ducking as an arrow buzzed overhead. The two other brothers, Hervil and Ivern, were positioned in front and rear of her tent, strongbows ready with notched arrows. Out in the darkness, beyond the fire, battle raged unseen, the tumult of combat revealing no sign of victory or defeat.

"Stay down, Highness!" Sollis commanded and Brother Hervil reached up to grasp her forearm, pulling her to her knees.

"My apologies, Highness," Hervil said with a grin. He was a veteran brother, his craggy features painted red in the fire.

"How many are there?" she asked him.

"Hard to say. We've killed at least ten already. That Lonak bitch has fucked us." He grinned again. "Pardon my low-born tongue, Highness."

"The Lonak bitch just saved my life," she told him. "She's not to be harmed, do you hear?"

A harsh yell drew her gaze to the south of the camp where three Lonak warriors came screaming into the light, war clubs and hatchets raised. Brother Hervil loosed two arrows, so fast his hands blurred, two Lonak falling. Sollis dispatched the third with a single sword-stroke, combining a parry with a riposte in the same fluid arc of steel. The Lonak staggered back, throat agape, and Hervil put a shaft in his chest for good measure.

"Thirteen," he chuckled. "Haven't had such a fruitful night for years."

Something thrummed in the darkness off to the left and Hervil threw himself onto Lyrna, bearing her to the ground with a suffocating weight, jerking as something made a hard smacking sound. She squirmed beneath him, fighting to draw enough breath to voice a protest, then felt a warm torrent staining her shift. Hervil's face was inches from hers, features slack, half-lidded eyes dim. She touched a hand to his craggy face, feeling the warmth drain away. *Thank you, brother.*

"Highness!" Sollis hauled the body off, pulling her upright, eyes widening at the blood making the shift cling to her breasts and belly. "Are you hurt?"

She shook her head. "Where is the Lord Marshal?"

"Fighting I assume." He turned back to the darkness, eyes searching, sword point held low. The song of battle was fading, the shouts and thuds of combat lessening until the only sound was the ceaseless northern wind.

"Have they gone?" Lyrna asked in a whisper. "Did we win?"

Something leapt out of the black void beyond the fire, something pale and quick and lithe, dodging under Sollis's sword, side-stepping Brother Ivern's arrow, launching itself at Lyrna, hatchet raised. Lyrna's shock was such that time slowed as the figure descended towards her, her eyes drinking in every detail of the assailant. It was a girl, no more than sixteen years in age, chest encased in a wolf skin, finely muscled arms bringing her hatchet down, and her face . . . There was no snarl here, no screaming fury, this was a face of serene joy and doll-like beauty.

Lyrna lurched backwards, the knife in her hand coming up in a slash born of pure instinct. It jarred on something, coming loose and tumbling off into the dark. The Lonak girl reeled away, spinning to the ground. Her gaze flashed at Lyrna, a red line running from her chin to her brow. *Her eyes are very blue,* Lyrna noted.

Sollis charged the Lonak girl, sword arcing down with enough force to cleave her to the ribs, meeting only hard ground as she leapt clear, pivoting to face him, hatchet ready.

"Kiral!" Davoka came running out of the blackness, leaping the fire, bloodied spear levelled.

The Lonak girl's gaze flashed at Lyrna, blue eyes bright and joyous, blood streaming from her new scar, teeth bared in a fierce smile. Then she simply wasn't there, vanished into the night like a snuffed candle.

"Kiral!" Davoka screamed after her, halting at the edge of the firelight. *"Ubeh vehla, akora!" Please, sister, come back.*

Nersa was dead, pierced by half a dozen arrows a few yards from her tent. Lyrna assumed the Lonak had mistaken them in the darkness. If so, the lady may well have saved her life by drawing so many arrows. She watched a guard sergeant wrap the body in a cloak to be taken to the base of the hill where a large pyre was under construction.

"A moment please," she said as he lifted the body. *There should be no guilt,* she thought, knowing it to be a lie, her hand tracing through the lady's hair, finding something amongst the tresses, a tortoiseshell comb of scant value. *I didn't kill her.*

"Thank you," she told the sergeant, taking the comb and stepping back.

They counted over a hundred Lonak bodies, mostly boys and men but also a dozen or so women and girls. Lord Marshal Al Smolen, sporting a bandaged hand and a spectacular multicoloured bruise on his jawline, reported the loss of twenty-three guardsmen plus six more wounded. Over half the horses had been lost, scattered or slaughtered, Sable amongst the dead. Lyrna had only a small affection for the animal but still felt the loss. The remaining mounts were all bred for war and unlikely to offer so comfortable a ride.

Davoka sat by the smouldering remains of the fire, spear resting on her shoulder. She had said nothing since the battle, offering neither argument nor contrition despite several calls for her immediate execution, all of which Lyrna had refused.

"She led us into this, Highness," Smolen insisted. "Half my men are dead thanks to this wolf bitch."

"My word is given, Lord Marshal," Lyrna told him. "Do not make me give it again."

She went to sit opposite Davoka, seeing the sadness that shrouded her face. *"It's time for truth between us,"* she said in Lonak.

The Lonak woman's head rose, a faint glimmer of amused surprise in her eyes. *"So I see."*

"The Mahlessa's rule is not complete, is it?"

"She commands peace with the Merim Her, the greatest and most vile enemy in our history. There was . . . disagreement amongst the clans. Voices were raised in dissent. We killed those who questioned her, of course, but there were always more, too many to kill. The Mahlessa named them as varnish, to be driven from their clans, and so they formed a clan of their own. The Lonakhim Sentar."

"Sentar? I do not know this word."

"It's rarely spoken now, a tale from the days before your people came across the sea to steal our lands. The Sentar were a war-band composed of the greatest Lonakhim warriors, chosen for outstanding

skill and courage, the Mahlessa's own shining spear. The Sentar won our greatest victory over the Seordah, and would have led us to dominion over all this land but for the arrival of the Merim Her. They were all killed in the Great Travail, when our people fled to the mountains, holding the pass long enough to allow the remnants of the Lonakhim to secure a new home here. Now they are reborn, a twisted perversion of past glory."

"The girl who tried to kill me, she is your sister?"

Davoka closed her eyes and nodded. *"Kiral. We were born to the same mother. The gods were kind to take her before she could see what she has become."*

"And what is that?"

"Something vile, something that kills without reason and speaks poison. She is their leader, called the true Mahlessa by those varnish who follow her." She opened her eyes, meeting Lyrna's gaze. *"It was not always this way with her, something . . . changed her."*

"What something?"

Davoka fidgeted in discomfort. *"That which is known only to the Mahlessa."*

Lyrna nodded, knowing she would reveal nothing more on this subject. "Will she come for us again?"

"When she sent me to the pass, the Mahlessa dispatched three war-bands to hunt down the Sentar. It was hoped this would force them to fight instead of coming for you. It seems my sister managed to evade them." She glanced over her shoulder at the base of the hill where Smolen's guardsmen were piling up the Lonak bodies. *"The Sentar are strong in number, and they will not stop."*

"Then we shouldn't linger." It was Brother Sollis, speaking in Realm Tongue. Behind him a pyre was burning, Brother Hervil's body wreathed in flame. The Order was never slow in seeing to its dead. "If we push hard, we can be back at the pass before nightfall. I'll find you a suitable horse, Highness." He turned to go.

"Brother Sollis," Lyrna said, making him pause. "This expedition is under my command and I have given no instruction to end it."

Sollis's gaze flicked to Davoka then back to Lyrna. "You heard what she said, Highness. There can be no chance of success now. We cannot survive another attack on this scale."

"He's right," Davoka said, switching back to Realm Tongue. "Too many men, too many wounded. We leave a trail my sister can follow eyes closed."

"Is there another way?" Lyrna asked. "A path for a smaller party, harder to track?"

"Highness . . ." Sollis began.

"Brother," Lyrna cut in. "The Order does not answer to the Crown, it is true. Therefore, you have my leave to depart without risk of disfavour and my thanks for your service." She turned back to Davoka. "Is there another way?"

The Lonak woman gave a slow nod. "Yes. But great risk, and there can only be . . ." She grimaced, then held out a hand, fingers splayed. "This many. No more."

Five, including me. Meaning only four swords against the Departed know how many more of these Sentar. She knew Sollis spoke wisdom, the correct course was a speedy return to the pass and on to the much-missed comforts of the palace. But Davoka's words had added fuel to her burning need for evidence. *That which is known only to the Mahlessa . . .* There was evidence here, she knew it, and more to be had at the Mountain of the High Priestess.

She got to her feet and beckoned Smolen over. "Choose your three best men," she told him. "They will accompany me north. Brother Sollis will guide you back to the pass."

"I prefer to stay, Highness," Sollis said. She could tell he was fighting to keep the anger from his voice. "With your permission, Brother Ivern and I will go with you."

"And I am my best man, Highness," Smolen informed her. "And even if I wasn't, you must know I would never leave your side."

"My thanks to you both." She pulled her fur about her shoulders, glancing up at the forbidding peaks ahead, the tops shrouded in cloud, hearing a distant note of thunder. *Let's see what you can tell me.*

Her new horse was named Verka, a Lonak word which meant North Star in honour of the single blaze of white on his chest. He had been Brother Hervil's mount and was, Sollis assured her, the most placid horse in the Order's stables. From the way Verka reared and tossed his head as she hauled herself into the saddle she suspected the dutiful brother was merely attempting to salve her trepidation. However, despite her initial misgivings, the warhorse proved an obedient mount, responding to her touch willingly enough as they followed Davoka's swift-trotting pony.

She led them south for several hours, setting a punishing pace, the journey unbroken by any rest stops. Sollis rode in front of Lyrna with Ivern behind and Smolen bringing up the rear, their eyes constantly scanning horizon and hilltop. Lyrna had been similarly vigilant when the journey began but lost her enthusiasm as the strain took its toll. *Why couldn't I have been more interested in physical pursuits?* she grumbled, feeling every step of Verka's hooves on the rough ground. *One hour away from my books wouldn't have killed me. But this bloody horse might.*

They turned north again before twilight, spending an uncomfortable and fireless night in the lee of a great boulder, the others taking turns on watch whilst Lyrna huddled in her furs, exhaustion for once ensuring sleep, albeit fitful. Her dreams were different this night, instead of the dying King, Nersa came to stand before her, back in Lyrna's private garden at the palace. The lady smiled and laughed, as she often had, bent to smell the flowers and run a hand through the cherry blossoms, and all the time blood flowed from the arrows jutting from her chest and neck, leaving a red trail wherever she walked . . .

Despite the many aches and pains that greeted Lyrna's waking, she was thankful when morning came.

◆ ◆ ◆

Lyrna met the ape that afternoon. For hours they had pressed on through a succession of gully and canyon, laboured up a score of hills, always climbing, the air growing ever more chill and the trail ever more narrow.

Davoka called a welcome halt when they had climbed an especially rock-strewn path to a summit of sun-bathed boulders. Their onward course was obvious; an ever-more-narrow and winding trail atop a ridge snaking away towards two great mountains, the largest they had seen so far. The ridge seemed to disappear into a gap between the peaks. Eyeing the constricted and winding path, Lyrna could appreciate why Davoka had insisted on keeping their party small. Guiding a full company of guards along this path would have taken days if not weeks.

She slid from Verka's back with the now-customary groan and found a large boulder behind which to evacuate the royal bladder. She was rising from the crouch when she saw it, no more than a dozen paces away. An ape. A very large ape.

It sat, regarding her with black eyes above a doglike snout, a sprig of half-chewed gorse in its leathery paw. Seated, it was at least five feet tall and covered from brow to rump in thick grey fur, ruffling in the wind.

"Don't look at its eyes, Queen." Davoka stood atop the boulder behind her. "Pack leader. He'll take it as a challenge."

Lyrna duly averted her eyes from the ape's face, keeping it in sight with furtive glances as it rose to stand on all fours, a wide yawn revealing a set of vicious fangs. It raised its head to utter a short coughing hoot and five more apes appeared out of the surrounding rocks. They were marginally smaller but no less threatening in appearance.

"No moving, Queen," Davoka said softly. Lyrna noted she grasped her spear with a reverse grip, ready for throwing.

The pack leader gave another hoot and bounded away, leaping from one rock to another with soundless precision, the five others following with similar expertise. Within seconds they had vanished.

"Don't like our smell," Davoka said.

Lyrna walked back to their temporary camp on weak legs, her heart hammering, slumping down next to Smolen with an explosive sigh.

He frowned at her. "Is something wrong, Highness?"

"You are mad, woman!" Sollis barked at Davoka. "This is your safe path?"

The mountain loomed ahead of them, slopes of black ash broken by huge boulders ascending to a summit wreathed in roiling smoke, lit by the occasional burst of orange fire accompanied by a vast rumbling that made the earth tremble beneath their feet.

"No other way," Davoka insisted. She was busy divesting her pony of tack, throwing the saddle down the slope and freeing its head of the bridle. She gave the animal an affectionate scratch on the nose then slapped a hand against its rump, sending it trotting back along the ridge-top trail they had followed for the five days it had taken to get here. "Can't take horses," the Lonak woman said. "Slope too steep and they don't like fire."

"*I* don't like fire," Lyrna told her.

"No other way, Queen." Davoka hefted her spear, shouldered her leather satchel and began to ascend without another word or a backward glance.

"Highness," Sollis said, "Forgive me but I must advise . . ."

"I know, brother. I know." She waved him to silence, watching Davoka ascending the ash slope with her long-legged strides. "Does it have a name? This mountain."

It was Brother Ivern who answered. A much younger man than Sollis or the fallen Hervil, he had nevertheless acquired an impressive knowledge of the Lonak and their lands. "They call it the Mouth of Nishak, Highness," he said. "Nishak being their god of fire."

Lyrna took hold of her skirt, lifting it clear of the ash and starting forward. "Well, let's hope he's sleeping. Loose the horses, good sirs."

But Nishak, it seemed, wasn't sleeping today. Several times Lyrna found herself stumbling to her knees as the mountain shook, feeling a rush of heat as the summit belched fire into the sky. The air stank of sulphur and the ash made her cough to the point of retching, but she kept on, endeavouring to keep Davoka's striding form in sight. Finally, the Lonak woman paused to rest, sheltering on the cooler side of a boulder, taking a sip from her water flask as Lyrna collapsed beside her.

"This." Davoka slapped a hand on Lyrna's riding gown. "Too heavy, take it off."

"I don't have anything else," Lyrna gasped and gulped water from her own flask.

Davoka opened her satchel and extracted a jerkin and trews of soft leather. "I have. Long for you, but I make them fit." She laid out the trews for tailoring and drew her knife. "You strip."

Lyrna glanced at the three men standing nearby, all studiously looking elsewhere. "If any of you turn, I'll see you in the Black Hold," she warned them.

Sollis said nothing, Smolen coughed and Ivern suppressed a chuckle.

Standing naked on the slopes of a volcano whilst a Lonak woman dressed her was one of the more bizarre experiences Lyrna could recall, made somewhat more awkward by Davoka's frank words of appraisal. "Firm thighs, hips not too narrow. Good. Strong children you'll bear, Queen."

Brother Ivern snickered, earning a harsh rebuke from Sollis.

It was done within the hour. Princess Lyrna Al Nieren stood in Lonak clothing, ash staining her face and her unwashed hair hanging in a long greasy mass. Davoka had offered to shear it for her but she refused, tying it back with a leather thong which at least kept it out of her eyes. "How do I look, Lord Marshal?" she asked Smolen, knowing he was the most likely to lie.

"Glorious as ever, Highness," he assured her with impressive sincerity.

"Brother!" Ivern called to Sollis, pointing down the slope.

Sollis shielded his eyes to take in the view. "I see them. About fifty, I'd say."

"Closer to sixty," Ivern said. "We have perhaps five miles on them."

Lyrna followed their gaze, seeing a line of ponies making their way along the ridge. *Sentar.*

"Good," Davoka commented, resuming her climb.

"Good?" Lyrna said. "How can this be good? We were supposed to lose them by coming here."

Davoka didn't turn. "No, Queen. We weren't."

Lyrna sighed, gathered her things and started after her.

The sun was beginning to dip behind the mountains by the time they reached the summit, a caldera fully half a mile across. Smoke rose in unending billowing columns and the stench of sulphur was so thick Lyrna had to fight her rising gorge. She risked a glance over the rim of the caldera, beholding a vision of roiling lava pools spouting gobbets of molten rock into the air, before the heat forced her back. Davoka sat a few yards below the rim, gazing intently at the sun as it descended below the jagged peaks to the west. Her gaze occasionally flicked to the dim shapes of their pursuers, a rising cloud of dust betraying their progress.

"Ready your bows," she told Sollis and Ivern. "Might need to slow them down."

"We're just going to sit here?" Lyrna demanded. She had tried to keep her temper in check so far but the circumstances were fast eroding her self-control. "Shouldn't we, perhaps, be moving on with all possible haste?"

Davoka shook her head, speaking in Lonak. *"Nishak will kill us if we take another step. We must await his blessing."* She shifted her gaze to the sun again, waiting until it was fully concealed by the mountains, then closed her eyes and began to chant.

"Are you . . ." Lyrna sputtered and spat ash from her mouth. "Are you praying to your god? Have I followed you here and doomed myself and these men so you can seek aid from an imaginary magic man who lives in a mountain?"

Davoka ignored her, eyes closed and chanting.

Lyrna was tempted to shake the Lonak woman but realised it would most likely earn an angry blow which in turn would force Smolen to kill her, or at least try to. She could only stand and watch, fuming like the mountain they stood on, as darkness descended.

"She's not praying, Highness," Ivern told her, watching the Lonak woman with an intense curiosity. "She's counting."

"That's three hundred yards by my reckoning," Sollis said, eyes fixed on the Sentar below, bow in hand. The slopes were bathed in an orange glow, the mountain's fiery breath reflecting from the smoke clouds. He took an arrow from his quiver and notched it, drawing and loosing with only the barest hesitation to fix his aim. Lyrna watched the arrow arc towards the cluster of pursuing Sentar, falling amongst them with little sign of having caused any injury or delay.

Ivern moved off to the left and both brothers began loosing arrows in a slow, deliberate repetition of notch, aim and release. Lyrna fancied she saw a brighter plume of dust rise from the onrushing Sentar which might indicate one or more had fallen. In any case, they showed no sign of slowing.

"I'm not to be taken alive, Lord Marshal," she told Smolen.

Davoka stopped counting and rose to her feet. "Sentar don't want you alive," she said, then called to Sollis and Ivern. "Save your arrows. No need now."

"So where is he?" Lyrna said, too tired and defeated to even feel angry. "Where is the great Lonak fire go—"

The mountain shook with a violence they hadn't felt before, tipping them off their feet, a fresh blossoming of black smoke rose from the caldera and barely fifty yards below the summit molten lava erupted from a dozen different places. It gushed forth in glowing streams, flowing down the slope and coalescing into a great river of fire, the Sentar disappearing amidst the fiery current, the roar of the mountain drowning out the screams they must have voiced.

Davoka got to her feet, arms raised to bathe in the heat, reciting in Lonak, *"At the count of two hundred and twenty past the fall of the sun on the third day of the sixth month, Nishak speaks and blesses the south face of the mountain. Know this and mark it well, for Nishak is the most generous of gods."*

The descent of the north side of the Mouth of Nishak took most of the night. There was less ash on these slopes and Lyrna found the going easier, though the growing chill as they left the fiery warmth of the mountain behind made her pine for her heavy riding gown.

They made shelter on a narrow ledge snaking alongside the base of the mountain, a rocky overhang providing shelter from a fresh downpour. Davoka allowed their first fire in days, fashioned from the stunted gorse bushes that sprouted between the rocks. Lyrna kept as close to it as she could, too chilled to sleep. Davoka took the first watch as the men slept, the brothers in eerie silence, Smolen tossing fitfully. She sat on the lip of the ledge, long legs dangling over the sheer drop of more than a hundred feet, spear within easy reach.

"I regret my anger," Lyrna told her through chattering teeth. "My words were foolish. I didn't mean to insult your god."

Davoka shrugged, replying in Lonak. *"Your insult means nothing to Nishak. He has always been here. He will always be here. Whenever the Lonakhim have need of fire."*

"I-I'm sorry, also, for your . . ." Lyrna spasmed with cold and forced the last words out. ". . . sister. A death like that, is n-not to be wished on . . . anyone."

Davoka turned to her, eyes narrowed in concern. She rose and knelt by Lyrna, taking hold of her hands then touching knuckles to her forehead. "Too cold, Queen."

She shrugged off her fur vest, placing it around Lyrna's shoulders then pulling her close, arms and legs wrapped tight around her. Lyrna was too weak to protest.

"My sister lives, Lerhnah," Davoka whispered to her. *"My sister who is not my sister. I feel it. She rages out there in the dark. She's*

lost us for now, but she'll find us soon. Whatever took her chose well, her skills are great indeed."

"Wh-whatever took her?"

"It was not always this way with her. She was . . . never a warrior. A skilled huntress yes, Kiral means wildcat in the ancient tongue. She could track prey with such skill many thought she carried the gods' blessing. But she never sought battle, not even against your kind.

"Then came the day she happened upon one of the great apes of the western hills. It was birthing season and they are fierce in protecting their young. Kiral was badly mauled. She lingered for days, seemingly beyond the shaman's skills. The Mahlessa had given me leave to be at her side for the end. I sat and watched her until all breath was gone. She died Lerhnah, I saw it. It shames me but I wept for my sister, the only tears I have ever shed, for she was precious to me. Then she spoke, she was dead but she spoke, 'Tears are not fitting for a Mahlessa's guard.' I looked into her eyes, her living eyes, and I did not see my sister there, nor have I since."

"Will you . . . fight her . . . when she comes again?"

"I will have to."

"Will you . . . kill her?" Lyrna's head began to loll and her vision swam as exhaustion began to overtake her.

"No!" Davoka shook her, drawing a groan of complaint. "Can't sleep now. Sleep now, won't wake up come the light."

Won't wake up come the light . . . Would it really be so bad? What was she now in any case? Useless, childless, unwed sister to a foolish king, seeking proof of the impossible through this mad endeavour. *Nersa died, Brother Hervil died. Why shouldn't I?*

"Lerhnah!" Davoka took hold of her face, shaking it, hard. "No sleep."

Her head came up with a snap and she blinked, chill-born tears streaming from her eyes. "Do you love your husbands?"

Davoka's face showed a momentary relief then she laughed. "That is your word."

"What is the Lonak word?"

"*Ulmessa.*" *Great and deep affection. Affection for one not of your blood.*

"*You feel this for them?*" Lyrna asked.

"*Sometimes, when they're not doing the foolish things men do.*"

"*Years ago I felt it, all the time. For a man who looked at me and saw something vile.*"

"*Then he was a fool and you are well rid of him.*"

"*He was no fool, he was a hero, not that he knew it. We could have ruled the Realm together, he and I, as my father had ordained. It would all have been so very easy.*"

"*Your father was leader of all the Merim Her, was he not?*"

"*He was. Janus Al Nieren, Lord of Asrael and ruler by conquest of the Unified Realm.*"

"*Then why did you not honour his wishes? Take this man you wanted, be king and queen together?*"

"*Because I couldn't kill my brother, as you can't kill your sister.*"

Brother Sollis stirred and rose, barely making a sound, pausing at the sight of a half-naked Davoka embracing the Princess of the Unified Realm.

"Queen is too cold," Davoka told him. "Fetch more wood."

She had recovered enough by morning to stumble in Davoka's wake as they reached a valley floor and continued north. She was aware the Lonak woman had slowed her pace and found her constant scrutiny disconcerting, as if she feared her charge would drop dead at any moment. Smolen and Ivern took turns helping, lifting her clear of streams and half carrying her when it seemed she was about to collapse. They rested more often today, brief but welcome pauses during which Davoka or Sollis would force her to eat the dried beef and dates the brothers carried, though her appetite seemed to have all but disappeared.

"She needs rest and shelter," Smolen said late in the afternoon. "We cannot make her go any further." There was an edge of panic to his voice and his gaze had taken on a certain wild-eyed cast.

"Do not speak for me . . ." Lyrna began then choked off as a coughing fit took her.

Davoka directed a questioning glance at Sollis. The Brother Commander gave a reluctant nod.

"Two or three miles that way," Davoka said, pointing east with her spear. "A village. We shelter there."

"Is it safe?" Lyrna croaked.

The guarded look in Davoka's eyes as she turned away was answer enough.

The village consisted of a few dozen stone-built dwellings contained within a solid wall. It sat atop a pear-shaped hill rising from the floor of a broad valley through which a fast-flowing river wound its way south. Davoka led them to a marker stone at the base of the hill where a rough gravel track ascended to a gate in the wall. She reversed her spear, resting it on the ground, point first, and waited.

"Which clan lives here?" Sollis asked her.

"Grey Hawks," she responded. "Big hate for the Merim Her. Many Sentar come from Grey Hawk villages."

"*But you expect them to help us?*" Lyrna asked.

"*I expect them not to question the word from the Mountain.*"

It was the best part of an hour before the gate swung open, thirty or more men on ponies emerging, descending the hill at the gallop. "Do not touch your weapons," Davoka told the men as the Lonak party neared.

The rider at the head of the group reined to a stop a short distance away, holding up a hand to halt the other riders. He was a large man wearing a vest of brown bear's fur and the most extensive tattoos Lyrna had seen yet, covering his forehead, neck and arms in a whirling confusion of unreadable symbols. He sat, regarding them in silence, face impassive, then trotted forward until he loomed over Davoka. A war club and hatchet hung from his belt.

"*Servant of the Mountain,*" he greeted Davoka.

"*Alturk,*" she responded. "*I require the shelter of your home.*"

The big man guided his pony past Davoka and towards where Lyrna was slumped against the packs. She could sense the tension of Smolen and the brothers as they fought the impulse to reach for their swords.

"You are the Queen of the Merim Her," the big man said to Lyrna in passable Realm Tongue. "I had heard you scarred the false Mahlessa. Now I see that to be a lie." He leaned forward in his saddle, dark eyes glowering. "You are weak."

Lyrna forced herself to stand and fought down a cough. *"I did scar her,"* she replied in Lonak. *"Give me a knife and I'll scar you too."*

Something twitched in the big man's face and he reclined in his saddle, grunted then turned his mount back towards the village. *"My door is always open to the Servants of the Mountain,"* he told Davoka before spurring to a gallop.

"You spoke well, Queen," Davoka told her with grave respect.

"Next to history," Lyrna replied, "diplomacy is my favourite subject." With that she vomited before falling into a dead faint.

CHAPTER EIGHT
Reva

*W*orld Father, I beg you, do not deny your love to this
miserable sinner.

Reva had chosen the topmost room in the house.
In truth it was more an attic, the roof featuring a good-sized hole
she had inexpertly repaired with some nailed-on boards. She sat
on a small cot, the room's sole furnishing, sliding her knife along
a whetstone. The Darkblade was arguing with his sister downstairs,
or rather she was arguing with him, voice loud and angry, his soft
and soothing. Reva hadn't known Alornis could get angry. Kind,
generous, given to laughter despite her many troubles, but not angry.

The drunken poet was singing in the courtyard outside, as he
often did when the hour grew late. She didn't recognise the song,
some sentimental doggerel about a maiden waiting for her lover
by a lake. She had thought his fondness for song might have been
stilled by the presence of so many onlookers, but if anything the
crowd of wide-eyed idiots gathered beyond the cordon of Palace
Guard only seemed to encourage him.

"Thank you, thank you," she heard him say, no doubt offering
a bow for their non-existent applause. "Every artist appreciates
an audience."

"Easy for you to say, brother!" Alornis's shout came through
the floorboards. "This is not your home!" A door slammed and

Reva heard the drumming of feet on the stairs, making her eye the attic door in trepidation. *Why did I choose one without a lock?*

She fixed her gaze on the knife blade as it scraped along the whetstone. It was a fine knife, the finest possession she had ever owned in fact. The priest told her the blade was fashioned by Asraelin hands but that shouldn't prevent her from using it. The Father did not hate the Asraelins, but their heresy made them hate him. She must care for this knife, hone it well, for with it she would do the Father's work . . .

The door flew open and Alornis stormed in. "Did you know about this?" she demanded.

Reva kept working the blade on the stone. "No, but I do now."

Alornis took a deep breath, mastering her anger, wandering in a small circle, fists clenching and releasing. "The Northern Reaches. What in the name of the Faith am I supposed to do in the Northern Reaches?"

"You'll need furs," Reva said. "I hear it's cold there."

"I don't want any bloody furs!" She paused at the small, cracked window set into the slanting roof, sighing heavily. "I'm sorry. This isn't your fault." She came and sat on the bed, patting Reva's leg. "Sorry."

World Father, I beg you . . .

"He just doesn't understand," Alornis went on. "Spent his life wandering from one war to another. No house, no home. No idea that leaving here would be like leaving my soul behind." She turned to Reva, eyes bright and moist. "Do you understand?"

My home was a barn where the priest would beat me if I didn't hold a knife the right way. "No," Reva said. "This place is just bricks and mortar, tumble-down bricks and mortar at that."

"It's my bricks and mortar, half-ruined though it may be. Thanks to my darling brother it now actually belongs to me, after all these years. And as soon as it belongs to me, he makes me give it up."

"What would you do with it? It's a big place and you are . . . small."

Alornis smiled, eyes downcast. "I had notions, dreams really.

There are many like me, many who want to learn to do what Master Benril can do, or acquire the knowledge his Order holds, but barred from it because of sex or differing faith. I thought this could be a place to teach them, once I'd learned enough."

Reva watched Alornis's hand on the fabric covering her thigh, feeling the warmth of it, how it made her burn . . . She sheathed her knife and got up from the cot. *World Father, do not deny your love to this miserable sinner.*

She went to the window, looking through the dirt-encrusted glass at the fires of the crowd beyond the cordon. *A fine frothing of Faithful fools,* the poet had called them, speaking uncharacteristic wisdom.

"More come every day," she said. "Just half a dozen two days ago, now more than fifty. All seeking your brother's support, or just a word of acknowledgment. In time his silence will make them angry, an anger they'll turn on you when he's gone on his King's mission."

Alornis raised her eyebrows, giving a short laugh. "Sometimes you sound so old, Reva. Older than him in fact. You've spent far too much time together."

I know. Too long waiting for him to fulfil their bargain. Too long stilling her tongue, fooling herself it was because she wanted more lessons with the sword, more knowledge to use against him when the time came. Too long living this lie, too long with *her.* Every day she felt the love of the Father move further away, the priest's cries coming to her in her dreams, the cries he uttered through raging spittle the day he gave her the worst beating of her life. *Sinner! I know what vileness lurks in your heart. I have seen it. Filthy, Fatherless sinner!*

"Your brother's right," she told Alornis. "You have to go. I'm sure you'll find others to teach, and they say there are many wonders in the north. You won't be short of things to draw."

Alornis gave her a long look, the smallest crease appearing in her smooth brow. "You're not coming, are you?"

"I can't."

"Why not? Many wonders, you said. Let's see them together."

"I can't. There is something . . . else I must do."

"Something else? Something to do with your god? Vaelin says you are fierce in your devotion, but I've not heard you say a word about him."

Reva was about to protest then realised it was true. She had never told Alornis about the Father's love, or the warmth it gave her, how it fuelled her mission. *Why?* The answer came before she could suppress it. *Because you don't need the Father's love when you're with her.*

Filthy, Fatherless sinner!

"Across the valley, deep and wide," came the poet's voice from outside as he started up a new tune. "With my brothers by my side . . ."

Reva went to the window, pushing it open with difficulty, yelling into the dark. "Oh, shut up, you drunken sot!"

Alucius fell silent and for once there was a murmur of appreciation from the crowd.

"We leave tomorrow," Alornis said in a soft voice.

"I'll travel with you a ways," Reva said, forcing a smile. "Your brother has a bargain to keep."

The King had supplied horses and money, a large bag of money in fact, some of which Al Sorna had given to her. "A holy quest requires funding," he said with a grin.

Reva had taken the money with a glower, slipping away as they packed. It was easy to avoid the crowd, simply wade into the river a short way then follow the bank for a hundred yards. She made her way to the market, bought new clothes, a fine cloak waxed against the rain, and a sturdier pair of boots, shaped for her feet by an expert cobbler who told her she had dancer's toes. From his grimace she divined this wasn't a compliment. He gave her directions to her next port of call, not without a note of suspicion in his voice. "What would a dancer be wanting there?"

"Gift for my brother," she told him, paying a little extra to forestall any more curiosity.

The swordsmith's shop fronted a yard which rang with the constant fall of hammer on steel. The man in the shop was old and surprisingly thin, though the burn scars discolouring the knotted muscle of his forearms told of a life in the smithy. "Your brother knows the sword, lady?"

Not a lady, she wanted to snap back, disliking the pretence of respect. Her accent and lack of finery marked her clearly enough and any respect he felt owed more to the bulging purse on her belt. "Well enough," she told him. "He'd like a Renfaelin blade, the kind a man-at-arms might use."

The smith gave an affable nod and disappeared into the recess of his shop, returning with a sword of very basic appearance. The handle was of unadorned wood and the hilt a thick bar of iron. The blade was a yard of sharpened steel ending in a shallow point, free of any etching or decoration.

"Renfaelins are better at armour," the smith told her. "Their swords have no art, more a club than a blade, in truth. Why don't you let me show you something a little finer."

And more expensive, she thought, eyes drinking in the sight of the sword. *He carried one just like this, and made art aplenty with it.*

She nodded at the smith. "Perhaps you're right. My brother's a slighter fellow than most, about my size, truth be told."

"Ah. A blade of the standard weight would not suffice, then?"

"Something lighter would be better. But no less strong, if possible."

He considered a moment then raised a hand indicating she should wait, disappearing again to emerge shortly after with a wooden case a yard or so long. "Perhaps, this may suit."

He opened the case, revealing a weapon with a curved blade, single-edged, less than an inch across and a handspan shorter than the Asraelin standard. The guard was a circle of bronze moulded into an unfamiliar design, the hilt wrapped in tight-bound leather for a strong grip and long enough to be grasped by two hands.

"You made this?" she asked.

The old smith smiled in regret. "Sadly no. This comes from the Far West where they have strange ways of working steel. See the pattern on the blade?"

Reva looked closer, discerning dark regular swirls the length of the steel. "Is it writing?"

"An artifact of its fashioning only. They fold the blade, you see, over and over, then coat it in clay as it cools. Makes for great strength, but without the weight."

Reva touched a hand to the hilt. "May I?"

The old man inclined his head.

She hefted the sword, stepping back from the counter and going through one of Al Sorna's sword scales, the most recent one he'd taught her, designed to foil an attack by multiple opponents in an enclosed space. The sword was only a little heavier than the stick she practised with and well balanced, giving a faint musical note as it sliced the air. The scale was brief but strenuous, requiring several fully extended thrusts and a double pirouette to finish.

"Beautiful," she said, holding the blade up to the light. "How much?"

The smith was looking at her with a strange expression, reminiscent of the looks men had given Ellora when she danced. "How much?" Reva repeated, putting an edge on her voice.

The smith blinked and smiled, replying in a somewhat thick voice. "Do that once more and I'll throw in the scabbard for free."

She made it back to the house in good time, sloshing up to the courtyard to find Al Sorna saying his good-byes to the drunken poet. "You could come with us," he said.

Alucius demurred with a florid bow. "The prospect of isolation, cold and constant threat from savages, all at a far remove from a decent vineyard, is a delightful one, my lord. But I think I'll pass. Besides, without me, my father will have no-one left to hate."

They clasped hands and Al Sorna went to his horse, glancing at Reva and taking in the sword strapped across her back. "Was it expensive?"

"I bargained it down."

He pointed at a grey mare, saddled and tethered to the post beside the well. The priest had tutored her in riding and she slipped onto the mare's back with practised ease, undoing the tether and falling in alongside Al Sorna. Reva watched Alornis embrace Alucius, fighting down the lurch in her chest at the tears shining in the girl's eyes, the way the poet thumbed them away, speaking soft words of comfort.

"You know he loves her, don't you?" she asked Al Sorna, keeping her voice low. "That's why he comes here every night."

"Not to begin with. I expect the King was keen to ensure my sister's interests didn't stray beyond matters artistic."

"He's a spy?"

"He was. With his father out of favour, I doubt he had much choice. It seems Malcius has more of Janus in him than I thought."

"And you allowed him to keep coming here?"

"He's a good man, like his brother before him."

"He's a drunkard and a liar."

"Also a poet and, on occasion, a warrior. A person can be many things."

There was a commotion amongst the watching throng, the guardsmen raising their pole-axes in warning as a man in a black cloak rode through the crowd. She heard Al Sorna groan in consternation. The man halted before the guards, speaking in a loud voice heavy with authority. The guard captain gave an emphatic shake of his head and a terse gesture of dismissal. Reva noticed the other guards stiffen as several more black-cloaked men appeared out of the crowd, all armed.

"Come on," Al Sorna said, nudging his horse into motion. "Time for you to meet a kindred spirit."

The man on the horse was thin to the point of gauntness, hollow cheekbones shaded beneath deep-seated eyes, his close-cropped hair steel-grey and thinning. He wore an expression of deep scrutiny as he offered Al Sorna a respectful nod, his gaze dark and piercing as if he were trying to cut away the Darkblade's skin and glimpse the soul beneath. Reva noted how the guards and the black-cloaked men eyed each other with wary eyes whilst the crowd looked on in rapt silence.

"Brother," the gaunt man said. "It gladdens my heart, and the hearts of all the truly Faithful, to see you safely returned to us."

Al Sorna replied in clipped tones, devoid of any warmth or regard. "Aspect Tendris."

"I told him he wasn't welcome, my lord," the guard captain said.

"And why would he say that, brother?" the gaunt man asked. "Why should you ever bar your door to your brother in the Faith?"

"Aspect," Al Sorna said. "Whatever it is you want, I can't give it to you."

"Not true, brother." The Aspect's voice became fierce, his eyes wide with conviction. Reva noticed his voice was pitched loud enough to be caught by all ears in the crowd. "You can join with us. My Order welcomes you, as your own does not."

Reva shifted in her saddle, settling the sword more comfortably on her back. *This man is mad,* she decided. *Some lunatic luminary of their heretic faith, so lost in its lies his reason has fled.*

"I no longer have an Order," Al Sorna informed the Aspect, his own voice at an even level. "Nor do I wish another. I am commanded by our King to undertake Lordship of the North Tower."

"The King," Tendris rasped. "A man in thrall to a Denier witch."

"Watch your tongue, Aspect!" the guard captain warned, causing his men to take a two-handed grip on their pole-axes. The black-cloaked men began reaching for their weapons.

"Enough of this!" Al Sorna barked, the implacable note of command in his voice sufficient to forestall further movement, even the crowd seemed to have frozen. However, there was one, Reva saw, who seemed immune to the command, one of the black-cloaks, a large, blocky man with broad, brutish features and a strikingly misshapen nose. He was careful, keeping his movements small as he shifted something beneath his cloak.

"You've stated your case and had your answer," Al Sorna told the Aspect. "Now take yourself off."

"So this is what you've become?" Tendris grated, his horse fidgeting as it read his mood, his wide-eyed gaze shifting from Al Sorna to Reva. "A Faithless slave of the Crown, shamelessly parading his god-worshipping whore about—"

Reva's knife came free of its sheath in a blur. She rose in the saddle, leaning forward as the knife left her hand, barely five feet from the Aspect. It was one of her more clumsy efforts, as she had to account for the shifting of her horse, and the knife tumbled untidily as it flew past the Aspect's ear to bury itself in the shoulder of the man with the misshapen nose. He screamed, high and shrill, collapsing to his knees, the loaded and drawn crossbow he had been raising clattering to the cobbles.

The guard captain barked an order and his men moved forward, pole-axes levelled. The other black-cloaks began to draw their swords but stopped at a shout from the Aspect. The crowd drew back at the violence, some scattering, others retreating a ways before turning to stare at the spectacle.

Al Sorna guided his horse forward a few paces, looking down at the large brother as he rolled on the ground, groaning then gasping as he drew Reva's knife from his shoulder, staring at the bloody blade in horror. "Don't I know you?" Al Sorna asked.

"You have shamed the Order, Iltis," the Aspect scolded the fallen brother before addressing Al Sorna. "This man acted without my sanction."

"I'm sure, Aspect." Al Sorna smiled at the unfortunate Brother Iltis. "He had a debt to repay, I know."

"Brother, I beg you." Tendris reached out to grasp the Darkblade's forearm. "The Faith needs you. Come back to us."

Al Sorna turned his horse, breaking the Aspect's grip. "There is nothing to come back to. And you and are I done here."

The guards took charge of Brother Iltis, dragging him away as Reva dismounted to retrieve her knife. "And I'm not his whore!"

she called to Tendris as he rode away, his brothers trotting in his wake. "I'm his sister! Haven't you heard?"

"Kindred spirit?"

Al Sorna shrugged and smiled. "I thought you'd get on better. He's as wedded to the Faith as you are to the Father's love."

"That man is a mad heretic wallowing in delusion," Reva stated. "I am not."

Al Sorna just smiled again and spurred on ahead. They were on the north road, having exited Varinshold a mile or so back, Alornis riding in morose silence amidst their escort, a full company of the Mounted Guard. Evidently, the Darkblade's King was keen for him to reach his destination.

Another mile brought them within sight of a grim castle of dark granite. It was not as tall as the Cumbraelin castles she had seen, the inner wall only some thirty feet high, but it was larger, enclosing several acres within its walls. There were no pennants flying from the towers and Reva wondered what Asraelin noble could afford the upkeep of such a mighty stronghold. Al Sorna had reined in a short distance ahead and she spurred her mare to a trot, pulling up at his side. "What is this place?"

Al Sorna's gaze stayed on the castle, his face betraying a sadness she hadn't seen before. "You need to wait here," he said. "Tell the captain I'll be an hour or so."

He kicked his stallion into motion, riding towards the gate in the castle's outer wall at a steady trot. Upon reaching it he dismounted and rang a bell hanging from a nearby post. After only a few moments a tall, blue-robed figure appeared at the gate. He was too far away to make out his features, but Reva had the sense he was smiling in welcome. The tall man pulled the gate open and Al Sorna went inside, both of them quickly vanishing from view.

"The first time he went through that gate was the last time my father ever saw him." Alornis sat on her horse a few yards away, regarding the castle with deep suspicion.

"This is the home of the Sixth Order?" Reva asked.

Alornis nodded and dismounted. She moved with a smooth precision, clearly no stranger to the saddle, holding something up to her horse's mouth, the white-nosed mare chomping on it with evident appreciation. "You can always win a horse's heart with a sugar lump," she said, patting the animal's flank then reaching for her saddlebag. "You and I have something very important to do."

That's not me.

The girl depicted on the parchment was very pretty, despite a slightly off-centre nose, with a tumble of lustrous hair and bright eyes that seemed to gleam with a life of their own. Despite Alornis's obvious flattery, Reva was compelled, even a little chilled, by the talent on display. *Just charcoal and parchment,* she wondered. *Yet she makes them live.*

"Hopefully they'll have canvas and pigment in the Northern Reaches," Alornis said, adding a few strokes to the shadows under the too-perfect curve of Reva's jawline. "This one's definitely worth painting."

They sat together under a willow tree some distance from the castle walls. Al Sorna had been inside for close to two hours. "Do you know why the Darkblade came here?" she asked Alornis.

"I'm starting to realise that understanding my brother's actions may be a task beyond me." She looked up from her sketch. "Why do you call him Darkblade?"

"It's the name my people gave him. The Fourth Book foretold a fearsome heretic warrior who wields his sword with the aid of the Dark."

"Do you believe such silliness?"

Reva flushed and looked away. "The love of the Father is not silliness. Do you consider your Faith silly? Bowing down to the imaginary shades of your ancestors."

"I don't bow down to anything. My parents now, they were devoted in their adherence to the Ascendant Creed, the path to perfection and wisdom, attainable through the right combination of words, a poem or a song that could unlock all the secrets of the soul and with it, the world. They used to drag me along to their meetings, held in secret in those days. We'd gather in basements and recite our creeds. Mumma would get cross when I giggled through mine. I thought it all such nonsense."

"So she beat you for your heresy?"

Alornis blinked at her. "Beat me? Of course not."

Reva looked away again, realising she had made a mistake.

"Reva?" Alornis put her sketch aside and came to sit beside her, touching a hand to her shoulder. "Were you . . . ? Did someone . . . ?"

Filthy, Fatherless sinner! "Don't!" She jerked away, rising, walking to the other side of the willow, the priest's words hounding her. *"I know what lies festering in your heart, girl. I saw your eyes on her . . ."* The hickory cane he used fell with every word as she stood there, arms at her sides, forbidden to move, or cry out. *"You befoul the Book of Reason! You befoul the Book of Laws! You befoul the Book of Judgement!"* His last blow caught her on the temple, sending her to the barn floor, dazed and bleeding onto the straw. *"By rights I should kill you, but you are saved by your blood. This mission given to us by the Father Himself saves you. But if we are to succeed, I must beat the sin from you."* And he did, until the pain was such she felt nothing more and blackness engulfed her.

She was on her knees in the grass, hugging herself. *Filthy, Fatherless sinner.*

Al Sorna returned from the Sixth Order's castle as the afternoon sun began to wane. He said nothing, motioning the guard company into their ranks and riding on without pause. His silence stayed in place until nightfall when they made camp and ate a supper of bland but hearty soldier's fare. Reva sat across from Alornis, eating mechanically and avoiding her gaze. *Too long,* she thought continually. *Too long with him. Too long with her.*

There was a scrape of boot leather and she looked up to find

Al Sorna standing over her. "It's time I fulfilled our bargain."

They left Alornis at the fire and found a spot amongst the field of long grass fringing the road, far enough away to be out of earshot. Reva sat on the grass cross-legged as Al Sorna crouched nearby, meeting her gaze intently. "What do you know about your father's death?" he asked. "Not what you've imagined. What do you truly know?"

"The Eleventh Book relates how he was mustering his forces at the High Keep to meet your invasion. You led an attack, using the Dark to find your way into the keep. He died bravely, but the Trueblade of the World Father was cast down by superior numbers and Dark skill."

"In other words, nothing. Since there were no survivors amongst his followers, whoever wrote this Eleventh Book of yours wasn't there. He wasn't mustering an army. He was waiting, with a hostage, someone I cared about. He used her to compel me to disarm so he could kill me. And he didn't die bravely, he died confused and maddened by something that made him kill his father."

Reva shook her head. The priest had warned her many times it would be this way when she moved amongst heretics. *They won so they get to write the story.* But still the words needled her. Reluctant as she was to admit it, there was a truth to the Darkblade. He hid things, left many things unsaid, but still there was a basic honesty to him. And, unlike her unknowable father, she could actually hear his words. "You lie," she said, forcing conviction into her tone.

"Do I?" His gaze was unwavering, holding her fast. "I think you know the truth in my words. I think you've always known it's your father's tale that's the lie."

She tore her gaze away, closing her eyes. *This is his power,* she realised. *This is where his Darkness resides. Not in his sword, in his words. A clever trick, to speak a lie through a mask of truth and trust.* "The sword," she said, voice hoarse and thick.

"We were in the Lord's chamber at the High Keep. My brother threw an axe that took him in the chest. He died instantly. I recall his sword tumbled off into the shadows. I didn't take it, nor did I ever see any of my brothers or my men with it."

"You said you knew where to find it."

She knew the answer before he voiced it, but still the words cut her, worse than any stroke of the priest's cane. "I lied, Reva."

She closed her eyes. A fiery tremble covering her from head to toe. "Why?" was all she could say, the word spoken in the faintest whisper.

"Your people say I have the Dark. But that, as a much wiser soul once told me, is a word for the ignorant. It's like a song, a song that guides me. And it guided me to you. It would have been so easy to lose you in the forest that first night, but the song told me to wait for you. Told me to keep you close, teach you what you hadn't been taught by whoever sent you for me.

"Didn't you ever wonder why you were only taught the knife? Not the bow or the sword, or anything that might have given you a chance against me? Given just enough skill to make you a threat, just dangerous enough to make me kill you. The blood of the Trueblade fallen to the Darkblade. A fresh martyr. There was someone else there that night when you came for me. My song found them when it found you. Someone followed you, waiting, watching. A witness, hungry for another chapter to the Eleventh Book."

She rose to her feet and he rose with her. The sword shifted on her back, like a snake uncoiling for a strike. "Why?" she said.

"Your father's followers need me. They need their great heretic enemy. Without me they're just a group of madmen worshipping the ghost of another madman. You were sent in search of a thing that can't be found, in the hope that I would kill you, birthing more hate to fuel their holy cause. Your only value to them is in your blood and your death. They care nothing for you, but I do."

The sword came free of the scabbard, straight and true as an arrow as she flew towards him. He didn't move, didn't twist, didn't dodge, just stood still, expression unchanging as the sword point pierced his shirt and flesh. Reva realised she was crying, a dimly remembered sensation from childhood, when the priest had first taken her and his beatings had seemed cruel. "Why?" she grated through tears.

The sword point had penetrated the shirt and inch of flesh. Only a small thrust and the Darkblade would be gone to his well-deserved eternity of torment.

"For the same reason I now deny my song though it screams at me to let you go," he said, face and voice lacking any trace of fear. "For the same reason you can't kill me." His hand came up, slowly reaching out to caress her cheek. "I came back to this land to find a sister. Instead I found two."

"I am not your sister. I am not your friend. I seek the sword of the Trueblade to unite all in the love of the Father."

He gave a small sigh of frustration, shaking his head. "Your World Father is nothing more than a thousand-year-old collection of myth and legend. And if he did exist, his bishops say he hates you for what you are."

The trembling grew to a shudder, making the sword vibrate in her grip. *One small thrust* . . . She reeled away, stumbling to the ground.

"Come with us, Reva," he said, imploring.

She scrambled to her feet and began to run, through the shifting dark of the long grass, tears streaming back from her eyes, the sword blade flickering as her arms pumped, stifling a sob as his plaintive call echoed after her. "REVA!"

CHAPTER NINE
Frentis

The seed will grow . . .

The itch began the morning after they killed the old man in the temple. Frentis woke with the woman's naked flesh pressed against him, features serene and content in slumber, locks of dark hair tumbling over her face, stirring a little in her soft, untroubled breath. He wanted very much to strangle her. She had been exultant as she used him, nails digging into his back, her thighs firm around his waist, panting riddles in Volarian as she moved. "We have . . . the whole world now . . . my love . . . Let the Ally play his games . . . Soon I'll play mine . . . And you . . ." She paused, smiling as she pressed a kiss to his forehead, sweat dripping from her breasts onto his scarred chest. "You will be the piece that wins the whole board."

Lying there, his body lined with sunlight from the slatted windows, he willed his arms to move, his hands to reach for her throat, forcing every ounce of desire into the command. But his arms stayed at his side, relaxed and unmoving. Even now, lost in sleep and whatever nightmares she thought dreams, still she bound him.

He noticed the itch as he let his eyes wander the ornate ceiling of her inn room. It was a small, faint tickle in his side, just below the rib cage. He assumed it must be one of the numberless bugs that seemed to be everywhere in this corner of the empire, but there was a rhythm to it, a slight but constant scratch too regular to be the nibbling of a bug.

The woman stirred, rolling onto her back, eyes opening, a lazy smile on her lips. "Good morning, beloved."

Frentis said nothing.

She rolled her eyes. "Oh don't sulk. That man was singularly undeserving of your noble concern, believe me." She got out of bed, walking naked to the window, peering through the slats at the street. "Seems we've caused a little commotion. Only to be expected. These irrational wretches are bound to react badly when one of their gods fails to stop her own temple burning down."

She turned away, yawning and ruffling her tangled hair. "Go get dressed. Our list is long and so is the road."

He went to his own room, drawing a wide-eyed gasp from the serving girl in the hallway. He closed the door on her blushing embarrassment and started to dress. The itch was still there and he was now allowed sufficient freedom to look, fingers probing the flesh under his rib cage. There was nothing, just the thick scar line that ran from his side to his sternum . . . wait. It was only the smallest change, a slight shift in the texture of his damaged flesh, from rough to smooth. He could see no difference but his fingers told another story. *Is it . . . ? Can it be healing?*

He recalled the woman's alarm when she saw the old man's blood on his face, the way she had bound him, eyes alive for any change in his state, and the old man's last sputtering words. *The seed will grow . . .*

The binding flared with an impatient jab and he finished dressing. Healing or not, she bound him as tight as ever.

They went to the docks and booked passage to the Twelve Sisters aboard a compact merchant vessel. The captain was an aged veteran of the seas and eyed Frentis with no small amount of suspicion, saying something to the woman which made her laugh. "He says you look like a Northman," she said in Volarian then gave the captain an answer in Alpiran which seemed to satisfy him. He pointed them to a spot on the mid-deck amongst a collection of caged chickens and spice barrels. They were gone from the harbour within the hour, sails unfurled to catch the north-westerly winds.

"How I hate seas, ships and sailors," the woman said, gazing out at the waves with a grimace. "I once sailed the ocean to the Far West, endless weeks sharing a ship with slaves and fools. It was all I could do not to kill them all mid-voyage."

There was a shout from one of the crew and they turned to see a young sailor pointing off the starboard bow, yelling in excitement. Frentis and the woman joined him at the rail along with a cluster of crewmen, all jabbering in Alpiran. At first he could see nothing to arouse such interest then noticed a thrashing in the waves some two hundred yards distant, a great sail-like tail rising out of the water. *Whale*, Frentis decided. He had seen them before, off the Renfaelin shore, impressive beasts to be sure but hardly an uncommon sight for a sailor.

The thrashing abruptly increased and a flash of red appeared amidst the foam, a great pointed head rising from the spume, jaws widened to reveal rows of bright teeth. It disappeared back into the water, a huge tail rising shortly after, more than forty feet in length, the skin shining in the sun, stripes of pale red on the dark grey topside, the underside milky white. The tail whipped from side to side and was gone. The water soon calmed, the red-slicked surface broken only by the bubbles rising from the depths.

"Red shark," the woman said. "Unusual for them to come so close to shore."

The crew dispersed after some happy chatter. It seemed this was a good omen.

"They say Olbiss the sea god gave the shark a whale to sate his hunger so we could sail safely on," the woman observed, turning her face to the sea to conceal her contemptuous grin. "It'll take more than a whale to sate mine."

Land hove into view four days later, a great mountain appearing out of the morning mist. It seemed unnaturally dark to Frentis as the wind pushed them closer, but soon he realised it was covered in forest from top to bottom. She had brought him to another jungle.

Their vessel moored up on a narrow jetty reaching out into a natural harbour on the south shore of this island. The woman named it as Ulpenna, easternmost of the Twelve Sisters, the islands that formed the broken bridge between the continents. He followed her along the jetty to a sizeable town of wooden buildings. In contrast to the ramshackle slave market at the Volarian riverbank, this jungle town displayed an elegance and age indicating many years of settled occupation. The houses were mostly two-storey affairs with ornate wooden statues on every veranda, each one different.

"Each house has its own god," the woman explained, once again reading his thoughts. "Each family its own guardian."

They stopped at a tavern and ate a meal of heavily spiced chicken stew, the woman striking up a conversation with the man who served them. Frentis's Alpiran remained poor but he picked out the words "law" and "house" amongst the babble.

"No guards," the woman commented when they were alone. "A trusting fellow this magistrate. Popular too, by all accounts. Not what you'd expect for a lawmaker."

They lingered at the tavern until late afternoon then took the only road, a track of dry red clay trailing out of town and upwards into the jungled slopes of the mountain. They followed the road for another hour before the woman led him onto a side track, through the dense jungle until they came to a large house. It was an impressive three-floored structure built on a ledge in the mountainside, shuttered windows open to the evening breeze coming in off the sea.

"Just the magistrate," the woman told Frentis as he stripped down to his trews, taking off his boots and smearing earth over his exposed flesh. "Apparently there's a wife and three children, but you don't have to concern yourself with them." She tweaked his nose a little. "Isn't that kind of me? Now off with you, my love."

The information from the tavern had been correct, there were no guards. A servant tended the small garden at the rear of the house and another lit lamps on the porch. Frentis approached through the thick undergrowth at a crawl, lying still when he got to within twenty feet of the south-facing wall. He lay against the carpet of vegetation until nightfall then crept forward to the wall. It was an easy climb, the ornamentation favoured by house-builders here provided plentiful handholds.

He hauled himself onto the top-floor veranda, finding an open door. Inside a child was sleeping in a large bed, a small dim shape in the bedcovers. He moved through the room on silent feet and into the hallway beyond, finding two other rooms on this floor, each occupied by sleeping children, before making his way downstairs. There were two more rooms here, one a book-filled space he took as a study, empty of any readers, the other a bedroom, the covers on the bed neatly pulled back in readiness. He returned to the landing, hearing the sound of voices from the ground floor.

The staircase creaked as he descended to the hallway, but his step was too light to draw any attention. The voices came from a room at the front of the house, a man and a woman talking on the other side of a closed door. Frentis found a shadowed corner, crouched and waited.

He fancied the itch had grown worse today, building steadily to a true irritation. The binding was loose enough to let him scratch at it, although this seemed to have no effect at all, and once again his fingers revealed a change in the texture of the scar, more smooth flesh amongst the damaged tissue . . .

His head snapped up as the door opened, a woman emerging, glancing back to say something, face lit by the glow of the room. She was somewhere past her fortieth year, a handsome woman dressed in pale blue silks with bound-up hair and an easy smile. A male voice came from the open door and she gave a small laugh then turned away, walking to the staircase and ascending, oblivious to Frentis's presence.

He waited until he heard her enter the bedroom above then went to the door. The woman had left it slightly ajar and he could see the man inside. He was seated at a desk, facing a window affording a fine view of the sea, humming to himself as he read a scroll. He was of middling height, portly and balding, more grey in his hair than black. Frentis wondered what his name was as he pulled the dagger from the sheath at the small of his back.

"A single thrust," the woman said as they made their way up the mountain. They had sat in the jungle until morning, watching the house and waiting for the screams. They began to climb accompanied by the grief-filled cries of the magistrate's wife, moving away from the road and the town where people were like to start asking questions about new arrivals when news of the murder became known. "Neat and quick," the woman continued, climbing without any obvious strain. "Aren't you going to thank me for letting you give him an easy death?"

Frentis kept climbing, saying nothing.

They came to the summit as the sun climbed to its apex, the woman turned towards the west, arms wide. "The Twelve Sisters in all their glory."

They stretched away into the mist-shrouded distance, a line of eleven jungle-clad islands rising from the sea. "For centuries not even the bravest soul would dare to live here," the woman went on. "It's said there was a great cataclysm, great enough to shatter the land-bridge joining our continent with what is now the mainland of the Alpiran Empire. What caused it none can say, though legend offers a thousand explanations. The Alpirans say the gods battled the nameless and their wrath was such the earth shook with enough fury to drown the bridge. The tribes to the south have it that a fiery globe fell from the sky bringing destruction in its wake. There's even an old story in Volarian about a mighty but foolish sorcerer who summoned something he couldn't control, something that ravaged the land before dragging him screaming back to the void. Whatever it was, when it was done the land-bridge had become what you see now, twelve islands. Wild stories abounded of the great evils and magics still lurking here in the aftermath of the shattering, beasts that could talk like men, men that were more like beasts. It must have been a shock to the first Alpiran explorers who dared to come ashore, finding nothing but stinking jungle."

She started down the western slope. "No time to enjoy the view, beloved. We'd best be off this rock by nightfall. You *can* swim, can't you?"

The channel between Ulpenna and its nearest neighbour was at least five miles wide at it narrowest point. The woman had him fashion a small raft for their pack from the light wood that littered the beach, lashed together with vines hacked from the jungle. He pushed it ahead of him with both arms, legs pumping. He had always been a strong swimmer, but that had been in the stretch of the Brinewash curving around the walls of the Order House. This was very different, the ceaseless swell of the sea and the darkness of the water as the sun began to descend conjured fresh images of the great red-striped shark as it devoured the whale.

The woman laughed, turning onto her back, leg kicking lazily in the water, completely at ease. "Don't worry. We're far too meagre a meal for a red shark to bother with. He does have smaller cousins though." She laughed again and swam ahead as his fear lurched to an even higher pitch.

They made it to the far shore without undue incident, though Frentis could swear something rough and scaly had brushed his leg beneath the waves. He gathered driftwood and stacked it in a crude cone. The woman held her hand to it, grunting in pain and delight as the flame lashed out to ignite the timber, a line of blood appearing beneath her nose almost immediately. She wiped it away with a casual flick of her thumb, but he took note of the way she flexed her hand as the flames subsided, and the shudder of suppressed agony in her shoulders. *There's always a price to pay, my love.*

They sat by the fire to dry off as the darkness deepened and a half-moon rose high above.

"Can you sing?" the woman asked. "I've always had a yen to hear my lover sing to me beneath a moonlit sky."

For once Frentis was happy to reply without any encouragement. "No."

She frowned at him. "I can make you, you know that."

Frentis stared into the fire, saying nothing.

"You're wondering who he was," she said. "Why his name was on our list."

The itch flared anew, almost burning now. He fought down the impulse to wince and kept his hands resting on his knees. If she knew of his discomfort, the woman gave no sign, tossing dry twigs into the fire as she spoke on, "I'm sorry to tell you he wasn't a bad man, quite the opposite from what I could gather. A fair and learned judge, immune to influence or bribery. The kind of man who is trusted by all, rich and poor. The kind of man people look to in a crisis." She tossed a final twig into the fire, offering Frentis a sad smile. "That's why he was on the list. His worthiness killed him, not you. You are merely the instrument of a long-planned enterprise."

She rose, moving to sit at his side, wrapping her hands around his arm, her head resting on his shoulder. He knew they must have made a pretty picture, young lovers huddled together on a moonlit beach, but her voice held no vestige of prettiness when she began to speak again. It was a harsh, sibilant whisper, barely controlled, the voice of a madwoman.

"I know this pains you," she said. "I remember that pain, my love. Though it was many lifetimes ago. You think me cruel, but what do you know of true cruelty? Is the tiger cruel when it takes the antelope? Or the red shark when it claims the whale? Was your mad king cruel when he sent you off to fight your hopeless war? You mistake purpose for cruelty, and I have always had a purpose. I am not mindless. When we are done with this list I promise you we'll write one of our own, and then there will be no pain when you strike off a name, only joy."

She snuggled closer, sighing in contentment . . . and the itch burned like fire.

They killed twice more in the Twelve Sisters. A merchant's clerk on Alpenna, throttled by the woman in an alley as he searched for a place to piss away the night's wine. Next was a tavern girl in Astenna, lured to Frentis's room by the silver he spun before her eyes, making it dance along his knuckles. She giggled as she followed him up the stairs, giggled as he stood aside with a bow at the door, giggled in the room as he lit a lamp and closed his arms around her. Once again the woman let him make it quick.

They found a ship before the sun was up and sailed away with the morning tide. The ship docked at Dinellis four days later, a huge bustling port even larger than Mirtesk. The guise of lady and bodyguard had been abandoned by now, replaced by husband and wife, though this time she played the role of cowed mouse and had him act the domineering braggart, spoiled son of a Meldenean merchant come to oversee his father's trade. Dinellis yielded another victim from her list, a rotund innkeeper persuaded to join them for a cup of wine on their veranda by a boisterous Frentis. They left him there, staring sightlessly at the harbour, his empty wine cup still resting on his extensive belly.

The days took on a nightmarish monotony as they journeyed north, finding listed names along the way. There was no pattern to this list, at least none he could decipher. A village washerwoman ten miles north of Dinellis, a strapping farmhand two days later, a half-blind and deaf old man the day after that. If not for the fact he had seen the man with the too-familiar voice hand her the list, he might have thought it just a delusion of her fractured mind, an illusion giving her permission to kill at random. But there was a control to her killing now that told him this mission was not recreational, the savagery that had so disgusted him when she killed the old man in Hervellis replaced by a terrible efficiency. Whether she did the killing or forced him to it, little was left to chance. Their victims were observed and killed when opportunity arose, quickly if not cleanly, and they were gone well before any alarm could be raised.

A carpenter in Varesh. Another magistrate in Raval. A bandit leader in the hills to the west.

"Well, he was a tough one." The woman angled her head at the body of the bandit, shaking blood from her short sword.

Frentis dodged a spear thrust from the last of the bandit's men, the five others all lay about their camp, bloodied and lifeless. The camp had been hard to find, taking several days tracking through rocky hills. When they finally came upon it the woman eschewed waiting for darkness in favour of walking in and killing them all. "We've scant time for artistry, my love."

The bandit leader had fought hard, if briefly. His men hadn't run when he fell, bespeaking a genuine friendship and respect amongst these rogues.

The final bandit wore his hair in long, tightly bound braids, an intricate array of decorative scars etched around his eyes and mouth. He cursed Frentis in an unfathomable torrent of Alpiran and redoubled his efforts, fury putting too much strength into his final spear slash, the barbed blade arcing wide, leaving him exposed. Frentis's boot took him square on the jaw, felling him unconscious to the dusty rock.

"He's seen us," the woman said, the binding forcing Frentis to bring his sword to bear on the fallen bandit's neck . . .

. . . *the itch burned, bright and fierce, so bright he wondered it didn't burn through his shirt and blind her* . . .

. . . the blade stabbed down, severing the spine. The bandit spasmed once and died.

They took the bandits' horses, squat, wide-legged animals little bigger than ponies, and rode hard towards the north. The horses withered as night drew on but the woman wouldn't stop and they rode them to death before the next morning. Two days' walk brought them in sight of Alpira, the empire's capital.

"Magnificent isn't it?" the woman said. "They can't build a road worth a turd but they can build a city."

Alpira was a vast square grid of countless houses and towers, bordered all around by huge sloping walls fifty feet thick. Frentis would have been awe-struck by the sight of it but for the images of murder that now crowded his head. *The farmhand had approached them with a wide smile, stepping away from his plough with raised arms, thinking them travellers in search of direction. Frentis's dagger had opened his neck with a single slash and they watched him thrash on the ground until he bled his life away.*

"See?" the woman was saying, finger pointing. "The dome of the Emperor's Palace." The dome seemed to shimmer with a white fire as it reflected the afternoon sun. "Clad in silver, every inch of it. I wonder what it'll look like when it burns."

They made camp atop a nearby hill, watching the city as night fell, a spectacle of lights appearing as the shadows grew long, the city resembling an unnaturally well-ordered spider's web.

The woman took a piece of waxed parchment from the pack, unfolding it to briefly scan the names it held, then tossed it onto the fire where it blackened and curled in the flames. "You still haven't reckoned it out, have you?" she asked. "What this has all been for?"

Frentis watched the last fragments of parchment burn and said nothing.

"Do you know what scrying is?" she persisted.

He wanted to ignore her, but found he needed to know why she had made him spill so much blood. If he could make some kind of sense of it, then perhaps the images wouldn't plague him with such ferocity.

"I heard one of my brothers talk of it once," he said. "Brother Caenis, he knew many things."

"I see. And what did knowledgeable Brother Caenis have to say about scrying?"

"It's a thing of the Dark. A way of seeing the future."

"Quite so. But it's a far-from-exact art, and a rare gift. The Council have been scouring the empire and beyond for centuries to find those with this gift, all with but one object, to divine what will happen when we finally come to take this land. Decades of scrying, most of it under torture, produced our list. Each name recurring again and again in the visions forced from the seers. The magistrate on Ulpenna would have rallied a fleet of armed merchant ships to harry our supply lines. The clerk was destined to be a master strategist in naval warfare, architect of a great victory. The whore in the tavern would discover a talent for archery, becoming a legend when she killed our admiral on the deck of his flagship. I assume you can guess the rest. Our list was a list of heroes, my love. By removing them we ensure success and eternal glory for the Volarian Empire."

The sound that rose from his chest was so unfamiliar it hurt his throat. A laugh, in truth more a grating mirthful cough, making the woman narrow her eyes. "Do I amuse you, my love?"

Her anger just made him laugh harder, choking off as she flared the binding, leaning forward, hands flexing. "I will not be mocked. You saw me drink the blood of the last man who mocked me. Do not forget what I can do."

He was surprised to find she had left him freedom to speak. "You won't," he rasped. "Mad bitch that you are, you're actually in love with me."

She became very still, fists clenched now, face twitching. "It seems you know more about cruelty than I gave you credit for." She reclined slowly and unclenched her fists. "I asked what amused you."

This time the binding left no room for silence. "There are millions of people in this empire," he said. "Not slaves, free people, more than can be counted. Janus sent the largest and finest army ever mustered by the Realm and we couldn't hold three cities for more than a few months. You think because we killed the people on your list this empire is ripe for the taking? You think amongst all the millions there won't be any to take their place? I hope your vile race does try to take it, and I hope I live long enough to see their ruin."

She gave a laugh of her own, short, almost wistful. "Oh my love, if only you knew how childish you are, how small your mind is. You talk of taking an empire, and in truth those idiots on the Council dream of little else, selling themselves like the cheapest whores to the Ally. They can have this empire. *I* want more, and I'll have it, with you at my side."

The itch, dormant for much of the day, began again. Not so painful now, but an insistent throbbing ache.

"But first," the woman said, getting to her feet and brushing dust from her clothes, "we have the last name on our list to strike through. And this time, since you find me so amusing, I think I'd like you to play with them a while first. It's a child you see, and children do so love to play."

The villa stood on a plateau to the west of the city. It was a large horseshoe-shaped structure, two storeys tall, comprising a stable and workshop as well as a lavishly decorated main house, all set within well-ordered groves of acacia and olive trees. White-cloaked guards patrolled the grounds in pairs. From the number visible, Frentis guessed there was at least a company garrisoned here.

They had approached via a narrow fissure in the southern slope of the plateau. It would have been a perilous climb in daylight but at night their success in scaling it seemed miraculous. He knew he had the woman to thank for the smooth precision with which he had made his way up the rock, hands and feet finding purchase with faultless accuracy. Somehow the binding enabled her to convey her skills to him, along with her bile. The itch hadn't stopped and he worried continually it would prove such a distraction he would slip, but the binding and the woman's Dark skill left no room for error and they reached the plateau's edge without incident.

He hung at her side as two guards passed by above, fingers clamped to the ledge, sweat bathing him as the strain told. But his hold never wavered and he suspected, if she so wished, she could have him hang there until he starved. She waited until the voices of the guards had faded then hauled herself up, sprinting into the gardens, Frentis trailing ten feet behind. They moved fast but with barely any sound, halting in tree-cast shadows to allow patrols to pass. They were both dressed head to foot in black cotton, the metal hilts of their swords and daggers blackened with ash to conceal any telltale gleams. The guards were a vigilant lot, speaking to each other in infrequent murmurs, their eyes constantly scanning for intruders. Whoever lived here was clearly worthy of the best protection the Emperor could offer.

It took over an hour before they made it to the rear of the main house. The windows on the ground floor were all securely shuttered and this side of the building was bare of any decorative fixtures that would have afforded useful handholds. The woman took something from the silk sheath on the underside of her wrist, a small garrotte he had seen her use on the merchant's clerk in the Twelve Sisters, ten inches of shining steel wire stretched between two wooden grips. She moved to one of the windows, briefly inspected the iron padlock on the shutters, then looped the garrotte wire around the U-shaped piece of iron to which it was secured. Her hands moved in a blur, the scrape of the wire on the metal seemed like a scream after so much time spent in silence. Frentis kept watch as the woman worked. In the distance he could see two white-cloaks moving through the gardens, left to right, then right to left, following a pattern that took them ever closer to the house. He and the woman were concealed in the shadow cast by the stables but that would offer scant protection when the white-cloaks came within thirty paces or so.

There was a *ping* then a clatter as the lock came free of the shutter, the woman catching it before it could hit the ground. She pulled the shutters apart and climbed through, Frentis following, closing the shutters behind them. They were in a kitchen, the cook fire still glowed from the day's work and rows of hanging copper pots gleamed in the half-light. The woman drew her sword and moved to the door.

Most of the servants would be abed in one of the side buildings at this hour, but there were still a few tending to nightly chores in the main house. They found an old man lighting lamps in the hallway, the woman's sword piercing his neck from behind before he even sensed their presence. A pretty young maid swept a broom over the marble steps ascending from the main lobby, she had time to gape at them before Frentis's thrown dagger took her square in the chest. He pulled it free as they climbed the stairs. By now the itch had grown to a tiny pinprick of purest agony in his side, the kind of agony that would have sent him screaming to his knees but for the binding.

The next floor yielded three more servants, all dispatched with quiet efficiency. The woman opened successive doors until she found her quarry. The boy half rose in his bed as the light from the hallway bathed him, yawning and rubbing at his eyes. He was nine or ten years old and stared at them with a strangely fearless wonder, saying something in a sleepy murmur.

"You've never had a dream like us, boy," the woman said, then nodded at Frentis. "Bring him." She turned and walked along the hallway to another door, pushing it open and provoking a startled shout from an unseen female occupant.

Frentis entered the boy's room, standing over him, hand outstretched. The boy looked at his hand then at him, his eyes suddenly absent of sleep and full of terrible understanding. *I'm sorry*, Frentis wanted to say, standing there, tormented to the edge of reason by the binding and the agony in his side. *I'm so sorry*.

The boy's head slumped and he took Frentis's hand, allowing himself to be led from the room, padding alongside in his silk pyjamas as they went through the door the woman had opened.

He found her tying another woman to a chair, her head slumped forward, dark hair dangling as the woman bound her with ropes torn from the drapes over the windows. When she was done she took hold of the woman's hair, jerking her head back, revealing a face of arresting beauty, the kind of face that belonged on one of the Alpirans' god-worshipping statues. The bound woman was dressed in a white silk robe, the ropes leaving red weals where they bit hard into her tanned flesh. The woman slapped the beautiful face, once, then twice. The bound woman's eyes flew open at the second slap, bright green and darting about in alarm.

"Beloved," the woman said in Realm Tongue, "allow me to present the Lady Emeren Nasur Ailers, former ward of the Emperor Aluran Maxtor Selsus, and widowed bride to Seliesen Maxtor Aluran, the fallen Hope of this empire."

The Lady Emeren drew a great breath, tilting her head back.

"Scream and the boy dies," the woman said.

Emeren closed her eyes, the breath hissing from her through gritted teeth. "Whoever you are . . ." she began in accented but well-spoken Realm Tongue.

"Forgive me," the woman said. "My etiquette is not what it was. You must, of course, be fully informed of who we are. This handsome fellow is my lover and soon to be husband, Brother Frentis, formerly of the Sixth Order of the Faith and the Unified Realm. As for myself, I haven't had need of a name for many years, so let's just call me a servant of Volarian Imperial interests, for the time being anyway."

Frentis watched the calculation on the Lady Emeren's face, the way her eyes shifted from the woman to Frentis and the bloody dagger in his hand, then to the silent boy holding his other hand. It was only when she looked at the boy that he saw true fear in her eyes.

The throbbing in his side was like a spike, plunging into his flesh, over and over . . .

"If you know so much," Emeren said, her voice even and well controlled, "you know I hold no power in this empire. I have no sway with the Emperor. My death will cause him no hurt."

"Hurting the Emperor is not our object," the woman replied. She went to the large bed, sitting down and bouncing on the soft mattress, her legs dangling over the side, a little girl at play. "I thought you might like to know something," she said. "Regarding your recent visit to the Meldenean Islands. Did you know, if you had succeeded in your artful scheme, you would have given immeasurable aid to our enterprise? We've given up trying to take Al Sorna, now it's just his death we seek. He's there in every scrying, every vision we wring out of the seers. The endless impediment, saving those we want dead, killing those we want alive. Your much-mourned husband for instance."

Emeren's eyes flashed at her, fury burning amidst the fear.

"Oh yes," the woman went on. "The visions were quite clear. Had he survived his encounter with Al Sorna, Seliesen Maxtor Aluran would have orchestrated the assassination of your Emperor, blaming it on agents of the Unified Realm, sparking another war, a war that raged for years, sapping the strength of the empire and making him a monster, the greatest tyrant in Alpiran history, and the doom of his people. For when our forces landed, there would have been scant strength to oppose them."

"My husband," the Lady Emeren grated, "was a good man."

"Your husband lusted for the flesh of other men and found you repellent." The woman's gaze shifted to the boy at Frentis's side. "Surprised he managed to get a child on you though. Still, duty makes us perform the most vile acts. Take my darling betrothed here. I know what I'm about to make him do will cause him great and terrible pain, but I will do it. For it is my duty to educate him in the nature of our bond. He doesn't love me, you see. To love a man and not have that love returned is . . ." She sighed, offering a sad smile to Emeren. "Well, I think you know. The blood of your son, spilled in front of his mother's eyes, will turn his soul a darker shade, bind us closer. For every time we kill together our bond grows. I know he feels it, my song tells me so."

The sickening fear gripping Frentis deepened into terror as he saw a tear trace down the woman's cheek, her eyes wide in adoration as she gazed at him. "Take his fingers first, my love. Nice and slow . . ."

. . . the throbbing was almost continuous now, barely pausing between each stab of agony . . .

He tugged the boy to his knees, tightening his grip, forcing the fingers apart, placing the blade of his dagger against the knuckle of his smallest digit . . .

Something made a loud crashing sound downstairs, followed by a fierce shout in Alpiran.

"HEVREN!" the Lady Emeren screamed, putting every ounce of her strength into the cry, straining against her bonds, neck muscles bulging.

The instant thunder of boots on marble could be heard through the open door.

"Oh bother!" the woman sighed, springing from the bed and moving to the door, drawing her sword. "No time for play, after all, beloved. I'll be downstairs. Make sure of them both and don't linger."

Alone with them, Frentis took hold of the boy's hair, drawing his head back, placing the dagger against his exposed throat . . .

The throb exploded in his side, a nova of all-consuming pain, burning every thought from his head and swamping the binding. He staggered, letting go of the boy, reeling in a welter of pain.

The boy ran to his mother, tugging at the bonds that bound her to the chair. *"Unteh!"* she shouted at him, shaking her head frantically. *"Emmah forgalla. Unteh! UNTEH!"*

He won't run, Frentis thought, seeing the boy continue to tug at the ropes.

He was surprised to find he could move, despite the pain raging in him from head to toe. *He could move.* He took a step, he actually took a step of his own volition, though the binding still compelled him to slit the throats of this boy and his mother. It was still there, flaring away, but compared to the pain that exploded from his side, it was little more than an irritant.

From downstairs came the sound of combat, multiple voices raised in challenge and fury, steel clashing, then a loud *whoosh*, like a first spark touched to oil-soaked kindling on a pyre. Screams followed and a pall of smoke started to fog the hallway beyond the door.

Frentis stumbled towards Emeren and the boy, limbs twitching as he fought for control through the pain. He collapsed against her, a shout of agony erupting from him to wash over her face. She twisted away in disgust and terror, screaming again as his dagger came up, wavering as he strove to control it. The boy launched himself at Frentis, kicking, punching, biting. He hardly felt it, focusing all his will on the dagger, bringing its trembling tip onto the rope across Emeren's chest. One final spasm of muscle and it was done, the rope parting and falling away. He released the dagger, letting it fall into her lap, rolling onto his back, convulsing in pain.

The binding was flaring with a new ferocity, the pain in his side slowly diminishing. *Not enough,* he thought, teeth gritted as he writhed on the floor. *The seed didn't grow enough.*

He was aware Emeren was standing over him, dagger in hand. The look on her face was one of mingled rage and confusion. "S-sorry . . ." he sputtered, spittle flying from his lips, "So . . . s-sorry . . ."

Her eyes bore into him as her son tugged at her hand. "Entahla!"

Frentis wanted to scream at her to run, but the resurgence of the binding left no room for further forbidden action. She gave Frentis a final glare of frustration and fled, lifting the boy into her arms and running from the room. She turned to the left, wisely opting not to take the stairs to the lobby.

The binding closed on him like the fist of a giant, forcing him to his feet with an implacable command: HELP HER!

He ran for the stairs, sword drawn, descending to the lobby to find the woman locked in combat with a white-cloaked guardsman. The walls of the lobby were covered in fire, thick black smoke blanketing the ceiling. The woman attacked the guardsman with every vestige of skill she could muster, her blood-streaked mouth snarling, but he was no easy opponent, fending off her blows with rapid counterstrokes of his sabre. There was something familiar about him, a tall black-skinned man with pepper-grey hair and the lean weathered features of a veteran. Catching sight of Frentis he grimaced, side-stepped a lunge from the woman and launched himself towards the stairs.

Frentis parried the sabre thrust and countered with a slash to the guardsman's eyes, but he was quick, dodging past the blade with inches to spare, leaping up several stairs to turn and face them. He met Frentis's gaze, eyes bright with desperation and fury, torn between continuing the fight or running to check on the fate of the lady and her son.

They're safe, Frentis wanted to say, but of course, the binding wouldn't let him.

A shout caused him to turn back to the woman, finding her battling two more guards who had braved the flames now licking around the open door. The grey-haired guardsman saw his chance and thrust at Frentis. He managed to twist away before the sabre point found its target but the edge left a shallow cut on his back as it sliced through his black cotton shirt.

He launched a kick at the guardsman's chest, the boot impacting on his breastplate and sending him sprawling. There was no time to press his advantage as the woman called him to her side. She retreated back from her two opponents, Frentis stepping in to fend them off as she sheathed her sword and pointed both clenched fists at the nearest wall. She screamed as the flames burst forth, two columns of raging fire striking the wall and blasting through in a haze of cinders. She collapsed as the flames faded from her hands, blood streaming in red rivers from her nose, ears, eyes and mouth.

Frentis caught her before she could fall, lifting her onto his shoulder, parrying a final thrust from one of the guardsmen then sprinting through the hole she had blasted in the wall.

The villa grounds were a confusion of running guards and swirling smoke. Frentis ran to the rear of the house, seeking the stables, hoping he didn't catch sight of Emeren and the boy, knowing what the binding would force him to do. The stables were full of guards and servants trying to save the horses from the inferno now engulfing the main house. Frentis picked out a large stallion, rearing in alarm as a stable boy attempted to lead him away. He felled the boy with a blow to the back of the head and caught hold of the reins, hoisting the woman onto the stallion's back then vaulting up behind her. The horse ran without need of encouragement, desperate to be away from this place of fire and terror.

They were free of the smoke in a few heartbeats, galloping hard to the west as the villa burned and tumbled to ruin in their wake.

PART II

The exact origins of the people comprising the mass migration into the Northern Reaches, now known as the onslaught of the Ice Horde, remain a mystery. Their language and customs were uniquely unfamiliar to both Realm subjects and the Eorhil and Seordah warriors who confronted their invasion. The vast majority of the Horde died in the carnage following their rout on the plains, only a pitiful remnant fleeing back to the ice. Consequently, opportunities for the scholar to gain a full picture of their society are limited to the experience of Realm-born witnesses, an inevitably skewed interpretation full of prejudice and fanciful tales of Dark skills and unfeasibly monstrous war-beasts. What is clear from the available evidence is the merciless ferocity of the Horde towards any man, woman or child not of their tribe and the unusual level of control they exerted over their animals, large numbers of which were employed in the line of battle.

—MASTER OLINAR NUREN, THIRD ORDER,
THE NORTHERN REACHES: A HISTORICAL SKETCH,
THIRD ORDER ARCHIVES

Verniers' Account

I cowered against the ship's rail, shrinking from the fierce inquisition of the foul-smelling man.

"I do not know," I said.

The man drew a knife from somewhere. It must have been hidden in his clothing for I had seen no weapon on him when he boarded the ship. The blade was at my throat quicker than I would have thought possible, his free hand coming up to grab my hair, pulling my head back, his reeking breath washing over me. "Where is he, scribe?"

"Th-the Northern Reaches," I babbled. "King Malcius sent him there when he returned to the Realm."

"I know that." The knife blade burned as he pushed it deeper into my skin. "Where is he now? What did the Battle Lord tell you of him? What messages were sent to him?"

"N-none! I swear. He was hardly mentioned. The Battle Lord seemed to have a hatred for him."

The foul-smelling man leaned closer, eyes searching my face, no doubt looking for signs of deceit.

"I trust you'll compensate me for any loss," the general said. "I had intended making considerable use of this one."

The foul-smelling man grunted and released me, stepping away. I sagged against the rail, fighting to keep upright. Collapsing to the deck would have been deemed an insult to my master. The general's wife came closer and handed me a silk kerchief. I held it to the shallow cut on my neck, blood staining the finely embroidered material.

"You have been interrogating the captives, as ordered?" the man demanded of the general. He stood by the table, helping himself to wine, downing a cup in a few short gulps, red liquid spilling down his chin and staining his already besmirched clothing.

"Yes." The general's eyes were narrow as he regarded the dirty man before him, his tone hard with reluctant compliance. "Plenty of tall tales about this Darkblade they seem to hate so much. No actual information. They find the idea that he would come to their aid ridiculous."

"Really?" The man turned his gaze on me once more. "Come here, scribe."

I walked to the table on unsteady legs, avoiding his gaze.

"You travelled with him to the Isles," the man said. "Do you think it ridiculous that he'd come to save those who hate him?"

I recalled the tale Al Sorna had told me during the voyage, all the trials and battles that had coloured his life. But the clearest memory was the day of the challenge, the Shield lying senseless, Al Sorna walking away and sheathing his sword. I had reasons of my own to hate him, I still thought of Seliesen every day, but it was a hatred that had dimmed that day, never quite dying, but no longer burning with the same passion. "Forgive me, Master," I said to the general. "But he will come to fight you, if he can. Here or anywhere else."

"Of course he will." The man drained another cup of wine and tossed it away, the dregs spilling on the exquisite map. He stalked from the table, walking back to his boat.

"You have no intelligence to offer?" the general called after him.

The man glanced over his shoulder. "Yes, don't expect it to be easy." He vaulted the rail with considerably more athleticism than a man of his years should have been capable, landing in the boat and barking an order at the slaves on the oars. The boat pulled away and made its way back to the shore, the man standing immobile in the prow. I felt I could still smell him even at this distance.

Fornella said something in a soft voice, a quotation, one of my own, from the *Third Canto* of Gold and Dust: Meditations on the Nature of Politics. "'Judge a nation best by its allies.'"

The assault began at midday, hundreds of boats carrying thousands of Varitai and Free Swords across the river to land under the walls of Alltor, greeted by swarms of arrows from the defenders. Some boats never made it to land, so saturated with arrows their oars went limp and they drifted away on the current. More fell as they leapt from the boats and tried to form ranks. The general opined he had been wise in issuing shields to his men, something he was keen for me to record.

"A few planks of wood nailed together and held aloft by two or three men," he said. "A simple antidote to these supposedly fearsome longbows of theirs."

Despite his antidote, however, I still counted over two hundred dead under the walls by the time the first battalion made it to the nearest breach. The ballista ships had been moved closer, their projectiles now consisting of great bundles of oil-soaked rags, lit with a torch just before being launched over the walls. From the rising smoke it seemed several fires were already raging in the city. "Fire is the bold commander's greatest ally," the general quipped, making me wonder how many of these he had prepared in advance. From his wife's rolling eyes, I suspected quite a few.

The battle raged in the breaches for near an hour, Volarian soldiery thrashing in an arrow-lashed knot that seemed to be making little forward progress. Having judged the time right, the general had his flag-men signal the Kuritai to begin their assault. The single battalion advanced across the causeway at the run, scaling ladders held aloft. Although the general had been correct in deducing most of the Cumbraelin defenders would be concentrated at the breaches, the Kuritai were still subjected to a fierce arrow storm, over two dozen falling before they reached the walls, the ladders swinging up to rest on the battlements. It seemed to me they lost at least half their number as they attempted to climb the ladders, one tumbling to the ground every second or so. Eventually though, a solid knot of them managed to claw their way onto the battlements, a small cluster of black amidst the grey-green throng of Cumbraelins seeking to throw them back. The general watched the scene through a spyglass for a moment then barked a command to his flag-men. "Send the reserve!"

Two battalions of ladder-bearing Free Swords advanced across the causeway. They lost fewer men to the Cumbraelin archers as the Kuritai kept the defenders on the wall occupied. The Free Swords scaled the wall in two places, drawing more defenders away from the Kuritai, who were now hacking their way inwards. There was a sudden convulsion in the Cumbraelin ranks and they drew back, disappearing from the walls in the space of a few moments. At one of the breaches there came a great shout of triumph as the throng of Volarian attackers finally broke through.

"And so it ends," the general mused with a studied lack of outward triumph. He handed the spyglass to a nearby slave then went to sit down, stroking his chin in a display of careful reflection. "The greatest siege in Volarian history, concluded thanks to nothing more than sound planning and a few hours' work." He glanced at me to be sure my pen was still busy. "Perhaps the Council will let you name the city," Fornella said. "Tokrevia?"

The general flushed and made a show of ignoring her.

"Though Burning Ruin would appear to be more appropriate," she went on, gazing at the numerous columns of smoke rising from the city.

"We'll rebuild," the general snapped.

There was no triumph on her face as she gazed at the city, just a faint melancholic repulsion. "If your soldiers leave us any slaves to do the work."

Another two hours passed as the general waited for confirmation that the city had fallen, growing more impatient by the minute, pacing the deck and ordering the overseers to hand out beatings for minor offences committed by the slave-sailors. Finally, a boat approached from the shore, bearing a man in the all-black armour of a Division Commander. The man climbed onto the deck with fatigue etched into his face, features blackened with smoke and a bandaged cut on his upper arm. He saluted the general and bowed to his wife.

"Well?" Tokrev demanded.

"The walls are ours, Honoured General," the officer reported. "However it seems the Cumbraelins never intended to hold them. They have constructed barricades within the city, houses demolished to bar the roads and create a killing ground, archers thick on the rooftops. We've lost more men in the streets than we did in the breaches."

"Barricades!" Tokrev spat. "You come before me and whine about barricades. Tear them down, man!"

"We broke through the first an hour ago, Honoured General. But found another a hundred yards beyond. And all hands in the city are raised against us, men and women, old and young. We have to fight for every house, and their witch seems to be everywhere."

The general's voice became very quiet. "Say one more word about the witch and I'll have you flayed as an example to your men."

He walked to the prow of the ship, staring at the city.

"Perhaps an order to rest and reorganise might be appropriate," Fornella said. There was an edge to her voice that told me she wasn't making a suggestion. "Consolidate our gains."

Tokrev stiffened and I saw his fists clench behind his back. He turned to the Division Commander. "Halt the advance and reorder your ranks, and gather all the lamp oil you can. We attack again when it gets dark, and when we do we won't fight for every house, we'll burn them. Understood?"

That night the city of Alltor had gained a great orange crown, the glow reaching up to obscure the stars. The general had ordered me to remain on deck and record the spectacle, retreating to his own cabin with a pleasure slave he had brought from the shore, a girl of no more than fifteen years. Fornella lingered on deck, her shawl wrapped tight about her shoulders. If the sounds emanating from below caused her any concern, she gave no sign, joining me at the prow to regard the city with the same sombre expression.

"How old is this place?" she asked me.

"Almost as old as the Fief of Cumbrael, Mistress," I replied. "At least four centuries."

"Those twin spires are a temple to their god, are they not?"

"The Cathedral of the World Father, Mistress. Their holiest site, I believe."

"Do you think that's what inspires them to such feats of resistance? A holy mission to defend the home of their god?"

"I couldn't say, Mistress." Or perhaps they realise that all you can offer is slavery and torment, so they prefer to die fighting.

"That man today," she said. "The stinking fellow. Don't you want to know who he was?"

"It is not my place to ask, Mistress."

She turned to me with a smile. "So convincing in your role, and yet a slave for just a few weeks. You must want to live very badly." She turned her back on the city, resting against the prow with her arms crossed. "Would it surprise you to know that he wasn't a man at all? Merely a shell filled with the ghost of something fouler than his stench."

"I . . . know nothing of such things, Mistress."

"No, you wouldn't. It's a well-kept secret, known only to the Council and a few, like me, too important not to be told. Our filthy, shameful secret." There was a distance in her eyes as she spoke, a spectre of unwelcome memory.

She blinked, shaking her head slightly. "Tell me about this Al Sorna," she said. "Who exactly is he?"

CHAPTER ONE
Vaelin

"I miss her too."

Alornis glanced up from her wood carving, dark eyes hard, as they had been for the past four weeks. Compelling her on this journey had done little to endear him to her, and Reva's disappearance had only made things worse. "You didn't even look for her," she said.

Despite the accusation in her tone he was encouraged by the fact that this was the most she had said to him since the morning she woke to find Reva gone. The long journey through Nilsael, and their time on this ship as they voyaged to the Northern Reaches, had been marked by a refusal to engage him in anything more than the most basic conversation.

"What choice did I have?" Vaelin asked her. "Tie her up and bind her to a horse?"

"She's alone," Alornis said, returning to her carving, the short curved knife whittling away at the figure. She had started it when they first boarded the ship, a distraction from the sea-sickness that had her heaving over the rail for the first few days out from Frostport. Her stomach had settled in the week since, but her anger hadn't, the knife chiselling at the wood in quick, tense flicks of her wrist. "She had no-one," she added softly. "No-one but us."

Vaelin sighed and turned his eyes to the sea. These northern waters were much more fractious than the Erinean, the waves rising steep and the unceasing wind possessed of a cutting chill. The ship was named the *Lyrna* in honour of the King's sister, a narrow-hulled, two-masted warship of some eighty hands, augmented by Vaelin's company of Mounted Guard who had been ordered to stay with him for the next year. The guard captain, a well-built young noble named Orven Al Melna, was punctilious in affording Vaelin every measure of respect his lordly status required, acting as if he were in fact under his command rather than the more truthful role of gaoler; the King's insurance against any changes of heart.

"What did you tell her?" Alornis had moved to his side, her expression still guarded but not quite so fierce. "You must have told her something to make her leave us."

This had been a worry for some time now; what to tell her. *What lies to tell her,* he corrected himself. *I lie to everyone, why not her?* He would tell his sister, his trusting sister who didn't know he was a liar, that Reva had fled due to her god-worshipping shame, born of her acceptance of his tutelage and her feelings for Alornis, feelings the bishops held as a sin. It was perfect, mixing in enough embarrassment to forestall further questions on the matter.

He opened his mouth but found the words died in his throat. Alornis still regarded him with angry eyes, but there was trust there too. *She looks at me and sees him. Did he ever lie to her?* "What did Reva tell you about her father?" he asked.

And so he told her, all of it. From the day he was taken to the House of the Sixth Order to the night he returned to his father's house. Unlike the tale he had told the Alpiran scholar on the voyage to the Isles, this was his unvarnished and complete account, every secret, every death, every tune from the blood-song. It took a long time, for she had many questions, and another week had passed before it was done, the shore of the Northern Reaches appearing on the horizon the morning he finished.

"And the song lets you see her?" she asked. They were in the cabin the first mate had given up for the Tower Lord and his sister. She sat cross-legged on her bunk, the near-completed carving resting in her lap. She had continued to whittle away as he told his tale, the figure becoming more refined with every passing day, in time revealed as a statue of a tall, lean man with a bearded face. She had borrowed some varnish from the ship's carpenter and was carefully applying it to the wood with a small sable brush, making it shine like bronze. "Sherin, wherever she is?"

"At first, when I had learned how to sing," he replied. "But the visions faded over time. It's been more than three years since I had any sense of her at all."

"But still you try?" His sister's gaze was intent, entirely lacking in disbelief. There had been some initial scepticism when he first told her of the blood-song but he borrowed a trick from Ahm Lin's tale of his apprenticeship and had her hide his belt-knife somewhere on the ship whilst he stayed in the cabin. He found it within a few minutes, slotted into a gap between two ale barrels in the hold. She tried again, this time enlisting the help of a sailor to hide it in the crow's nest. Vaelin had opted not to climb up after it, simply calling on the look-out to toss it down. She hadn't required any further demonstrations to trust his word.

"Not for some time now," he said. "Hearing the song is one thing, singing is another. It's very taxing, possibly deadly if I put too much effort into it."

"That thing that had taken Brother Barkus, you searched for it?"

"I catch glimpses now and then. It's still free in the world somewhere, deceiving, killing at the command of whatever it serves. But the images are vague. I suspect it can mask itself somehow. How else could it hide in Barkus for so long? It's only when it thinks of me that the glimpses come, its hatred enough to burn through the mask."

"Will it come for you again?"

"I expect so. I doubt it has much choice in the matter."

"What happened when you called at the Order House?"

Again he was tempted to lie to her, the information garnered during his visit left a bitter taste and he had no desire to voice it. But instead of a lie he chose concealment. "I met the Aspect."

"I know that. What did he tell you?"

"Not just Aspect Arlyn. I met the Aspect of the Seventh Order. And no, I won't tell you who it is. For your own protection." He leaned forward, holding her gaze. "Alornis, you must always be careful. As my sister you are a target. That's why I brought you with me, that's why I'm telling you this tale. The Northern Reaches are safer than the Realm, but I've little doubt that thing and its cohorts can reach for us here if they choose to."

"Then who can I trust?"

His gaze dropped. *I've told her nothing but truth so far, why stop now?* "Honestly, no-one," he said. "I'm sorry, sister."

She looked at the statue in her hand. "When father died, did you . . . ?"

"Just the echo of it. He'd already passed the day I sang for you. You were watching the pyre with your mother. It was snowing. There was no-one else there."

"No," she said, with a small smile. "You were there."

The North Tower came into view two days later. It was an impressive structure, wider at the base than the top, some seventy feet tall, surrounded by a stout wall half as high. It had the look of the older castles Vaelin had seen in Cumbrael, no hard angles and a general lack of statuary or ornamentation, a fortification from another time, after all it had stood here for near a century and a half.

The port was busy with fishing smacks and merchant vessels, their crews hauling ropes and oars to make way for the *Lyrna* as she made a stately progression to the quayside. Captain Orven ordered his men down the gangplank first, lining them up in two ranks, polished armour gleaming. They made something of a contrast to the line of twenty men in dark green cloaks standing at the opposite end of the wharf. Their line was somewhat uneven and their armour, mostly of hardened leather rather than steel, had a non-uniformity to it that wasn't exactly ragged but neither was it particularly tidy. Most of the green-cloaked men were dark-skinned, the descendants of exiles from the southern Alpiran Empire, and none seemed to be less than six feet tall. Standing in front of the line was an even taller man, also in a green cloak, and a diminutive dark-haired woman in a plain black dress.

"How do I look?" Vaelin asked Alornis at the head of the gangplank. He was dressed in a fine set of clothes supplied by the King's own tailor, a white silk shirt embroidered with a hawk motif on the collar, trews of good cotton and a long dark blue cloak trimmed with sable.

"Very lordly," Alornis assured him. "You'd be even more so if you actually wore that thing rather than just carry it around." She pointed at the canvas bundle in his hand.

He placed a smile on his face and turned to walk down the gangplank, approaching the dark-haired woman and the tall man, both giving a formal bow.

"Lord Vaelin," the woman said. "I bid you welcome to the Northern Reaches."

"Lady Dahrena Al Myrna," Vaelin returned the bow. "We've met before, although I daresay you don't remember."

"I remember that day very well, my lord." Her tone was carefully neutral, her handsome Lonak features lacking expression.

"His Highness sends his warmest regards," Vaelin went on. "And sincere gratitude for your dutiful labours in continuing to administer this land for the Crown."

"His Highness is most kind," Lady Dahrena replied. She turned to the tall man at her side. "May I present Captain Adal Zenu, Commander of the North Guard."

The captain's tone was less than neutral, and absent of any note of welcome. "My lord."

Vaelin glanced at the line of mismatched men. "I assume this is not the entirety of your command."

"There are three thousand men in the North Guard," the captain replied. "Most gainfully employed elsewhere. I didn't think it appropriate to gather more than was strictly necessary." He met Vaelin's gaze, waiting a while before adding, "My lord."

"Quite right, Captain." Vaelin beckoned to Alornis. "My sister, the Lady Alornis Al Sorna. She will require suitable quarters."

"I'll see to it," the Lady Dahrena said. Vaelin was heartened to find she managed to summon a smile for his sister as she bowed. "Welcome, my lady."

Alornis returned the bow a little awkwardly; noble manners were new to her. "Thank you." She offered another sketchy bow to the captain. "And you, sir."

The captain's bow was considerably more accomplished and his tone markedly warmer than when he had addressed his new Tower Lord. "My lady is very welcome."

Vaelin looked up at the tower looming above, a dark mass against the sky, birds flocking around the upper levels. The blood-song rose with an unexpected tune, a warm hum mingling recognition with an impression of safety. He had a sense it was welcoming him home.

The base of the tower was surrounded by a cluster of adjoining stone-built buildings comprising the stables and workshops required for the smooth functioning of a castle. Vaelin guided the horse they had given him through the main gate and into the courtyard where the servants of the tower had been arrayed in welcome. He dismounted and made an effort to speak to a few, finding only clipped responses and a few obvious glares of hostility.

"Friendly bunch, these Reach dwellers," Alornis muttered as they made their way inside. Vaelin patted her on the arm and kept smiling to all they met, though it was starting to make his face ache.

The Lord's chamber was situated on the ground floor of the tower, a simple unadorned oak chair sitting on a dais looking out on the large circular space. Against the wall stone steps ascended in a spiral to the next level. "Remarkable," Alornis said, drinking in the sight of the chamber with evident fascination. "I didn't think a ceiling of such size could be supported without pillars."

"There are great iron beams in the wall, my lady," Captain Adal told her. "They reach from the foundations all the way up to the top of the tower. Each floor is suspended from the beams, counterweights stop them from falling in on themselves."

"I didn't know our forebears were such skilled builders," Vaelin commented.

"They weren't," the captain replied. "This is actually the second North Tower, built by my people when we were granted refuge here. The original was only half as tall and had a tendency to list."

Vaelin's gaze was drawn to a large tapestry hanging behind the Lord's Chair. It was about twelve feet long and five feet high, embroidered with a battle scene. An army comprising warriors clad in a variety of armour, and bearing varying forms of weaponry, advanced against a host of men and women clad in furs, all with a savage aspect, standing alongside great cats with teeth like daggers. Overhead, birds of prey crowded the sky, an unfamiliar species larger than any eagle, their talons outstretched as they flew towards the polyglot army.

"The great battle against the Ice Horde?" he asked Dahrena.

"Yes, my lord."

He pointed at the birds. "What are these?"

"We called them spear-hawks, though in truth they're a descendant of the eagle, bred for war. The ice people used them the way we use arrows."

He peered closer, picking out the figure of the former Tower Lord, Vanos Al Myrna, a great bear of a man pointing a war hammer towards the Horde. Next to him stood a smaller figure with long dark hair and a bow in hand. "This is you?" he asked in surprise.

"I was there," she replied. "As was Captain Adal. We all were, every Realm subject in the Reaches old enough to bear arms, fighting alongside the Eorhil and the Seordah. The Horde made no distinction between combatant and civilian, all hands were needed to fight them off."

"Especially since no aid was forthcoming from the Realm," the captain added.

Vaelin's gaze lingered on the war-cats amongst the ranks of the Ice Horde and the blood-song swelled, turning his thoughts to the north-west. *So, they found refuge here after all.*

Dahrena gave a sudden gasp and he looked up to find her regarding him with a wide-eyed stare.

He raised an eyebrow. "My lady?"

She flushed and tore her eyes away. "I'll show you to your rooms, my lord."

"Please do."

The room was situated three floors up, high enough to afford a clear view of the town and surrounding country. A large fur-covered bed was set against the wall and a sturdy desk stood in front of the south-facing window. A stack of papers sat on the corner of the desk next to a quill and a full inkpot.

"I've readied the petitions and reports for your perusal, my lord," Dahrena said, gesturing at the papers. They were alone, the captain having offered to show Alornis her own rooms on the floor above. "Anything urgent is tied with a red ribbon. You may want to read the letter from the shipbuilders guild first."

He glanced at the documents, finding a red-ribboned letter on the top of the pile. "My thanks for your thoroughness, my lady."

"Very well. If you'll excuse me." She bowed and turned to the door.

"What is it?" he asked before she could leave.

She hesitated, turning back with obvious reluctance. "My lord?"

"Your gift." He sat in the chair in front of the desk, reclining with his hands behind his head. "I know you have one, otherwise you couldn't have felt mine just now."

Her previously expressionless face became shadowed by fear, quickly replaced by anger. "Gift, my lord? I do not understand your meaning."

"Oh, I think you do."

They stared at each other in silence, she with resentment shining in her eyes, he realising the depth of distrust he would find here. "Where do I find my brother?" he asked when it became plain she was determined not to answer his question. "The blond fellow with the pretty wife and the war-cat."

The Lady Dahrena gave a faint snort of amused annoyance. "She said you would know. That there was no point in lying to you."

"She was right. Did she also tell you that you have nothing to fear from me?"

"She did. But she knows you, I do not. And neither do the people your King has sent you to rule."

"I think you mean our King."

She closed her eyes for a second, sighing in suppressed anger. "Quite so, my lord. I misspoke. Sella and her husband can be found at Nehrin's Point, a settlement twelve miles to the northwest. I know *they* will be pleased to see you."

He nodded, picking up the letter on the top of the stack. "What do they want? These shipbuilders."

"The merchants guild have reduced the stipend they pay for the upkeep of their ships. They say the drop in trade thanks to the Alpiran war has reduced their profits too much. The shipbuilders request that you reinstate the original price under the King's Word."

"Do these merchants speak the truth?"

She shook her head. "Trade in certain goods has reduced, but the price of bluestone has doubled since the war. More than enough to make up the losses in other commodities."

"The bluestone price has increased due to its rarity, I assume?

King Janus once told me the seams were thinning every year."

Dahrena frowned. "I cannot account for what our late king told you, my lord. But the mines have continued to produce a steady flow of stone for years. In fact my father was obliged to slow production to prevent the price from falling. It's doubled in price due to the fact that Realm ships can no longer carry it directly to Alpiran ports."

Vaelin swallowed a bitter laugh. *Another strand to the old schemer's web revealed as a lie.* He opened the letter and signed his name to it, feeling her gaze on his hand as he laboured over the letters. "The shipbuilders' request is granted," he said. "What else do you have for me?"

Her gaze moved from his clumsy signature to the stack of letters. "Well," she said, moving to the desk and opening the next petition, "it seems Captain Adal needs to buy the North Guard some new boots . . ."

They held a banquet for him in the Lord's chamber that evening, a lavish but tense affair attended by the leaders of the town guilds, the senior brothers and sisters from those Orders maintaining mission houses in the Reaches, and a large number of merchants. They were the least taciturn, engaging the new Tower Lord in conversation whenever the opportunity arose, each working in a request for a private audience when time allowed. Dahrena had already warned him her father conducted all meetings in the presence of witnesses, a surety against accusations of graft, and he replied to every request with a statement that he saw no reason why such a wise practice should not continue.

He found himself seated alongside the representatives of the Faith at the top table. Only the Second, Fourth and Fifth Orders had Houses in the Reaches. The Sixth had never established itself here, local security resting in the hands of the North Guard by royal command. Dahrena said the official reason was that the security of the greater Realm was deemed of higher importance in the Sixth's already long list of responsibilities, but her father always suspected it had more to do with Janus's keenness to keep them well away from his supply of bluestone.

Vaelin was surprised to find Brother Hollun of the Fourth Order the most talkative of the Faithful. A rotund and jovial fellow with the permanent squint of the near-sighted, he talked at length about the history of the Reaches and his Order's work in keeping accurate records of local trade, especially where bluestone was concerned. "Did you know, my lord," he said, leaning closer to Vaelin than was strictly necessary, probably to get a clear look at his face, "more money passes through the three banks in this town in a month than in the whole of Varinshold in a year?"

"I did not, brother," Vaelin replied. "Tell me, how regular is your correspondence with Aspect Tendris?"

"Oh"—the black-robed brother gave a shrug—"perhaps once a year a letter comes, usually with advice on how to ensure the Faith of my junior brothers doesn't waver in these difficult times. At so far a remove from the Order House, we can hardly expect to occupy the Aspect's attention when other matters are more pressing, I'm sure."

Sister Virula of the Second Order was less talkative. She was a thin woman of middling years with a somewhat morose air, her conversation limited to softly spoken complaints about Captain Adal's refusal to provide an escort for her intended mission to the horse-tribes of the Eorhil Sil. "An entire nation barred from the Faith through simple lack of will, brother," she told Vaelin, seemingly incapable of addressing him by his correct honorific. "I can assure you my Aspect is very displeased."

"Sister," Dahrena said in a weary tone. "The last group of missionaries sent to the Eorhil Sil were found bound and gagged outside the tower gate. My father raised the matter at the autumn horse trade and the answer was quite clear; they don't like to hear your bad talk about the dead."

Sister Virula closed her eyes, briefly recited the Catechism of the Faith under her breath and returned to her soup.

The Fifth Order was represented by Brother Kehlan, a man of some fifty or so years with a serious look who regarded Vaelin with the same wary suspicion he saw on most faces around him.

"Would I be right, brother," he asked the healer, "in judging you the longest-serving member of the Orders in the Reaches?"

"I am, my lord," Kehlan replied, pouring himself some more wine. "Some thirty years now."

"Brother Kehlan came north with my father," Dahrena explained, touching an affectionate hand to the brother's sleeve. "He has been my tutor for as long as I can remember."

"Lady Dahrena has an excellent knowledge of the healing arts," Kehlan said. "In truth she's more my tutor these days than I am hers, what with all the curatives she brings back from the Seordah. They're often remarkably effective."

"You visit with the Seordah, my lady?" Vaelin asked her. "I was given to believe they forbid entry to their forest."

"Not to her," Kehlan said. "In fact I doubt there's a path in the Northern Reaches she couldn't walk in complete safety." He leaned forward to meet Vaelin's gaze, some wine sloshing from his over-filled cup. "Such is the respect and affection she commands here."

Vaelin gave an affable nod in reply. "Of that I have little doubt."

"Are the Seordah very fierce, Lady Dahrena?" Alornis asked. She was seated on Vaelin's left and had said little all evening, clearly disconcerted by the unfamiliarity of the circumstance. "All I know of them are rather fanciful tales from the histories."

"No fiercer than I," Dahrena replied. "For I am Seordah."

"I thought my lady was of Lonak descent," Vaelin said.

"I am. But my husband was Seordah, and so, by their custom, am I."

"You have a Seordah husband?" Alornis asked.

"I did." Dahrena looked down at her wine cup, smiling sadly. "We met when the Horde came out of the north and my father called for aid from the Seordah, he was amongst the thousands who answered. I would have married him the very day I met him but for father's insistence I wait for my majority. After we were wed I lived amongst them for three years until . . ." She sighed and took a sip of wine. "The war between Lonak and Seordah has never ended. It raged long before your people came here and will no doubt rage for centuries to come, claiming many more husbands."

"I'm sorry," Alornis said.

Dahrena smiled and patted her hand. "Love once and live forever, so the Seordah say."

The sadness in her eyes stirred memories of Sherin, her face the day he had placed her in Ahm Lin's arms, the hours he spent watching the ship take her away . . .

"Might I enquire what plans my lord has for the morrow?" Brother Hollun said, calling his attention back to the table. "I have several months' worth of records requiring the Tower Lord's signature."

"I have business at Nehrin's Point," Vaelin replied. "I would like to introduce my sister to some friends I'm told reside there. We'll see to the records when I return, brother."

Sister Virula stiffened at mention of the settlement. "Do I understand, brother, that you intend to visit the Dark Clave?"

Vaelin frowned at her. "Dark Clave, sister?"

"Just silly rumours, my lord," Dahrena said. "The kind that always beset those with unfamiliar ways. The Reaches have ever been a refuge for exiles, people of differing faiths and customs, outlawed in their homelands. A long-standing tradition of the Tower Lord's dominion."

"One not to be overthrown without very careful consideration," Brother Kehlan said, downing what was probably his sixth cup of wine. "New blood enriches us, Vanos always said. Something you'd do well to remember."

Vaelin found he didn't like the threat in the man's voice, drunk or not. "Brother, if serving me is such an irksome task, you have my leave to return to the Realm at your earliest convenience."

"Return to the Realm?" Kehlan grew red in the face, getting to his feet, shaking off Dahrena's restraining hand. "This *is* my realm, my home. And who are you? Some vaunted killer from the mad king's failed war?"

"Brother!" Captain Adal came forward, grasping the healer's arm and pulling him away. "You forget yourself. Too much wine, my lord," he said to Vaelin.

"Do you have any notion of the greatness of the man you pretend to replace?" Kehlan raged on, tearing free of Adal's grip. "How much these people loved him? How much they love her?" His finger stabbed at Dahrena who sat with eyes closed in despair. "You are not needed here, Al Sorna! You are not wanted!" He continued to rant as Adal and another North Guard hustled him from the chamber, leaving a taut silence in his wake.

"And I thought this evening was destined to end without any entertainment," Vaelin said.

The words provoked only a small ripple of laughter, but it was enough to herald a return of conversation, albeit muted.

"My lord." Dahrena leaned close to Vaelin, speaking in hushed but earnest tones. "My father's death was very hard on Brother Kehlan. The illness that took him was beyond his skill to heal. He has not been himself since."

"He spoke treason," Sister Virula said, her voice a touch smug. "He said King Janus was mad. I heard him."

Dahrena gritted her teeth and pressed on, ignoring her. "His service to this land has been unmatched. The lives he has saved . . ."

Vaelin rubbed at his temples, suddenly weary. "I'm sure I can forgive the drunken outburst of a grieving man." He met her gaze. "But it can't happen again."

She nodded, forcing a weak smile. "My lord is kind. And there will be no repetition of this, you have my word."

"I'm glad." He pushed his chair back and got to his feet. "My thanks for all your attention today, my lady. Now, if you'll excuse me, I find myself sorely in need of rest."

"The Eorhil named him He Who Trails Fire When He Runs. On account of his mane." The stable master smoothed a hand over the horse's flank. It was a handsome beast, thickly muscled though not so toned as a well-bred Realm mount, but tall at the shoulder, his coat a dark russet brown save for his mane which had a tinge of red to it. "Not ones for short names the Eorhil. I just call him Flame."

"He's young," Vaelin observed, checking the horse's teeth and noting the absence of grey in the hairs on his snout.

"But smart as a whip and well trained, my lord," the stable master assured him. He was a broad man in his thirties, Nilsaelin judging by his accent, sporting a patch over his left eye and naming himself only as Borun. He had greeted Vaelin's early-morning appearance at the stables with brisk affability, absent any of the resentment the Tower Lord was becoming accustomed to.

"He was traded from the Eorhil when still a colt," Borun said. "Was to be Lord Al Myrna's next mount. Lady Dahrena thought it fitting he should come to you."

Vaelin scratched Flame's nose, receiving a contented snort in response. *At least this one won't bite.* "I'll need a saddle. And a mount for my sister."

"I'll see to it, my lord."

Alornis appeared as the horses were being led into the courtyard, yawning and swaddled in furs. Even in summer the Reaches retained a chill for much of the small hours. "How far is it?" she asked. There was a redness to her eyes that made Vaelin suspect she had partaken of more wine than she should the night before.

"A few hours' ride, usually," Dahrena advised, climbing onto her own horse. "But we have a call to make first. I should like to show you one of the mines. If you are agreeable, my lord?"

"Certainly." He inclined his head at Alornis, then at her horse. She yawned again, muttered something and hauled herself into the saddle with an audible groan.

As well as Orven's guardsmen, they rode in company with Captain Adal and two of his men, taking the north road into heather-covered hills. The road had a well-maintained surface of hard-packed gravel and proved a busy route; they had to make way for several heavily laden carts along the way.

"When my father first took on the Lordship it was just a narrow dirt track," Dahrena said when Vaelin commented on the quality of the road. "The stone had to be carried to the dock on packhorses. He used the King's coin to build the road and the King's Word to make the merchants pay towards its upkeep."

They rode together at the head of the column. The mix of rigid neutrality and anger from the previous day seemed to have abated, but he could still sense a guardedness in her demeanour. *Probably still worrying over the drunken healer,* he thought.

"You don't intend to stay, do you?" he asked.

She gave him a sidelong glance and he knew she was wondering what his song had told him, although his words came from nothing more than careful observation. "I had thought I might return to the forest," she said. "For a time."

"A pity, I should have liked to bestow a title on you."

She arched an amused eyebrow at him. "Aren't titles within the gift of the King?"

"And in this land I exercise his Word. How does First Counsel to the North Tower sound?"

She laughed then sobered when she saw his serious intent. "You want me to stay?"

"I'm sure the people of these Reaches would greatly appreciate it. As indeed, would I."

She rode on in silence for a time, brows drawn in thought. "Ask me again when you've seen the mine," she said, then spurred on ahead.

The mine was a gaping wood-braced maw torn into the side of a squat mountain, around which a number of wooden buildings were clustered. The miners were mostly stocky, pale-skinned men with candles pressed into leather straps worn about their heads. They offered cursory bows to Vaelin and deeper ones to Dahrena, ignoring a barked command from the mine foreman to gather in ranks to properly greet the Tower Lord.

"Insolent hill-born dogs!" he shouted at them, although Vaelin had a sense his anger was a little forced. The foreman was somewhat taller than his charges, with a cleaner face and a thick Renfaelin brogue. "Ye'll have to forgive them, m'lord," he said. "Don't know no better." He raised his voice. "Been shagging goats and smoking five-leaf their whole lives, the scum!"

"Oh, fuck a rock ape, Ultin," called a tired voice of unseen origin.

Ultin flushed and bit down on his anger. "My own fault, m'lord. I'm too soft on 'em. Anyhow, welcome to Reaver's Gulch."

"Lord Vaelin would like to see the workings," Dahrena told him.

"Of course, my lady, of course."

He lit a lamp and led them to the mine entrance. Alornis gave the inky blackness of the shaft a brief glance and promptly announced she would prefer to remain above ground, taking her ever-present parchment and charcoal off to find something interesting to draw. Dahrena and Vaelin followed Ultin along the shaft, the damp walls shining in the lamplight. They passed a pair of miners pushing a wheeled barrow laden with rock to the surface. The descent couldn't have covered more than two hundred yards but the rising heat and musty air stirred a sense that they were descending to the very bowels of the earth. Vaelin was starting to wish he had followed Alornis's example by the time they came to a halt.

"Here we are, m'lord." Ultin lifted his lamp, illuminating a cavernous space where a dozen or so miners were chipping at the walls with picks, others roaming the cavern floor to heave the hewn rock into barrows. "The richest seam in the Reaches. Finest quality stone too. Despite what that liar at Myrna's Mount might tell you."

Vaelin moved closer to the wall. He was surprised how clearly the bluestone stood out in the rock, small azure beads shining in the grey stone. "I once owned one as big as my fist," he murmured. "I used it to hire a ship."

"And the other matter, Ultin," Dahrena said. "Lord Vaelin needs to see that too."

Vaelin turned to find him giving her a questioning glance. She responded with a nod and he led them towards a small side tunnel leading off from the cavern. They followed him along the increasingly narrow passage for a good quarter hour, eventually coming to the end where Ultin's lamp revealed a sloping length of rock about twenty yards long. At the foreman's expectant look Vaelin moved closer to the slope, seeing something there besides bare stone, a thick yellowish vein running through it from end to end. He turned to Dahrena with a questioning glance. "Is it . . . ?"

"Gold," she confirmed. "And Master Ultin assures me, for well he knows such things, it's of the purest quality."

"That it is, m'lord." Ultin ran a hand along the yellow vein. "Grew up working the gold seams in west Renfael, and I've never seen so much of it in one place, nor so pure."

Vaelin squinted at the seam. "Doesn't look like so much."

"You misunderstand me, m'lord. When I say one place, I mean the Reaches, not just this mine."

"There's more?"

Dahrena touched the foreman on the arm. "Master Ultin, if you could give me a moment with the Tower Lord."

He nodded, lighting the candle in his head-strap and handing her the lamp before making his way back along the passage.

"We've found many such seams," she told him when Ultin's footsteps had faded. "These past four years, the deeper we dig the more we find."

"Then I must confess my surprise King Malcius failed to mention such good fortune."

Dahrena pursed her lips. "Good fortune for him could mean ruin for this land," she said.

"Did your father know of this?"

"It was at his order that no word of it was sent to the Realm.

To this day it's known only to the Miners Guild, Brother Kehlan and myself."

"An entire guild knows of this but says nothing?"

"The hill people are very serious in the oaths they give. They were here long before the first Asraelin ship appeared on the horizon. They know what will happen if word of this spreads to the wider Realm."

"The wider Realm is greatly troubled at present. Such riches could alleviate considerable suffering, not to mention fund our King's many ambitions."

"That may be, my lord. But it will also bring the Realm down on us like a plague. Bluestone is one thing, gold is another. Nothing so inflames men to lust and folly like the yellow metal we find with every shaft we sink. Everything will change, and believe me, this land and its people are worth preserving."

"Oath or no. A secret like this holds too much value to be kept forever. By accident or betrayal it will become known."

"I am not suggesting we strive to keep it concealed for all the ages. Just the scale of it. The King can have his gold, build all the bridges and schools he likes with it, just not all at once."

She was suggesting treason, and, judging by the intensity of her gaze, she knew it.

"You show great trust in me," he said.

She shrugged. "You . . . were not what I expected. Besides, as you say, it was a secret you would have learned soon enough."

He turned back to the seam, looking at the dull gleam of the yellow metal in the lamp's glow. Greed had never been a preoccupation for him and he had always found its power difficult to understand, but it was an undeniable power nonetheless. He searched for the blood-song but found no music, no notes of either warning or acceptance. *This decision, seemingly of such import, may in fact be irrelevant.*

"Lady Dahrena Al Myrna," he said, turning back to her. "I ask you formerly to accept the title of First Counsel to the North Tower."

She gave a slow nod. "I gladly accept, my lord."

"Good." He began to work his way back along the narrow passage. "When we return to the tower, I shall require your assistance in composing a suitably restrained letter to the King advising him of our good fortune in finding a new supply of gold, albeit of relatively small quantity."

They emerged blinking in the sunlight, finding Captain Adal waiting with a scroll in hand. Nearby a newly arrived North Guard was removing the saddle from an exhausted horse. The captain's face was grave as he handed Vaelin the scroll. "From our northernmost outpost, my lord. The news is three days old."

Vaelin looked down at the scroll and the meaningless scrawl it contained. "Perhaps you could just . . ."

"I agree, my lord, this lettering is appalling," Dahrena said, reading the scroll over his shoulder, her eyes widening at the contents. "This is confirmed?"

Adal gestured at the new arrival. "Sergeant Lemu witnessed their transit himself. He's not a man prone to excessive flights of imagination."

"Transit?" Vaelin asked.

Dahrena took the scroll and read it through again. He was disturbed to note her hands shook as she held it. "The Horde," she said in a soft murmur. "They came back."

CHAPTER TWO
Lyrna

S he awoke to find a little girl sitting on her bed, staring at
her with wide blue eyes. Her head felt as if it were being
pummelled from within by a tiny man with a large mallet
and her mouth was so dry she could only croak a hello in Lonak
at the girl. She angled her head and kept staring.

"It's your hair, Queen." Davoka was sitting on a neighbouring
bed, naked save for a loincloth. "No Lonak with gold hair."

Lyrna pulled back the furs that covered her and swung her legs
off the bed, sitting up with a groan provoked by the multiple aches
rippling from her back to her toes. Davoka rose and poured water
into a wooden cup, holding it to Lyrna's lips. Shorn of clothing,
Davoka was an even more impressive sight, her body an epic of
muscle, scars and tattooed flesh. She put the cup aside when Lyrna
had drained it, holding a hand to her forehead. "Fever gone. Good."

"How long have we been here?"

"Three days."

Lyrna cast her gaze about the room, seeing walls of stone
covered in decorated goatskins and complex hangings fashioned
from strips of leather and wood carvings, some depictions of
animals and men, others so unfamiliar as to be abstract.

"*This is the woman's hall,*" Davoka told her, slipping into her
own tongue. "*Used for birthing. Men are not allowed here.*"

Lyrna felt something teasing her hair and looked up to see the little girl tracing her fingers through the gold tresses, eyes still wide with fascination. *"What's your name?"* she asked her in Lonak, smiling.

The little girl cocked her head. *"Anehla ser Alturk,"* she said. *Alturk's daughter.*

"She doesn't have a name yet," Davoka explained. She shooed the girl away with a flick of her hand. She scampered to a corner and sat on the floor, still staring at Lyrna.

Davoka took a flask from her pack and handed it to Lyrna. "Redflower," she recognised, sniffing it.

"Take your pain away."

Lyrna shook her head and handed it back. "Redflower makes a slave of those who drink it."

Davoka frowned at her then laughed, taking a small sip from the flask. *"Queen makes things hard for herself. I see this."*

Lyrna rose from the bed, taking a few experimental steps. The slight chill to the air made for a not-unpleasant tingle over her naked flesh. "Brother Sollis and the others?" she asked.

"Unhurt but kept apart from the village. Only Alturk speaks to them, and no more than he has to."

"He's the leader of these people?"

"Clan Chief of the Grey Hawks. He holds dominion over twenty villages and their war-bands. No other save the Mahlessa can command so many."

"You trust his loyalty?"

"He has never questioned the word from the Mountain."

Lyrna detected a slight hesitancy to Davoka's tone. *"But will he continue to do so?"*

"He has led many raids against your people, lost blood and kin to your gods-hating brothers. My people are taught to hate you from the day they are born." She nodded at the little girl in the corner. *"You think she doesn't hate you? She's probably only here so she can tell her father what words we speak."*

"And yet the Mahlessa wants peace. Even though it threatens to break your nation apart."

"*Words from the Mountain are not to be questioned.*" Davoka threw a clay pot at the little girl, making her flee the hall. "*Tell your father that!*" she called after her.

She turned back to Lyrna, eyes surveying her nakedness. "Too thin, Queen. Need to eat."

The next three days were spent in isolation at the woman's hall, eating the food Davoka prepared and slowly rebuilding her strength. She was allowed to wander a few steps from the entrance where two Lonak warriors stood, regarding her in scowling silence and ignoring whatever greetings she offered. Davoka was never more than six feet from her side, and always armed. She caught a glimpse of Sollis at the far end of the village, practising a sword scale with Brother Ivern outside a small stone hut ringed with ten more warriors. She waved and the Brother Commander stopped, pausing for a moment then raising his sword in a brief salute. Brother Ivern followed suit, albeit with more of a flourish to the flash of his blade. She laughed and bowed in return.

Despite being repeatedly chased away by Davoka, Alturk's daughter continued to return, her wide blue-eyed stare unwavering. Lyrna showed her how to work poor Nersa's tortoise-shell comb through her hair, an activity she seemed to find tirelessly engaging.

"*You have brothers and sisters?*" Lyrna asked her, sitting on her bed with her back to the girl, whose small hands were guiding the comb through the long mane, still damp from washing.

"*Kermana,*" the girl replied. *Any large number not easily counted.* "*And ten mothers.*"

"That's a lot of mothers," Lyrna observed.

"*Used to be eleven, but one joined the Sentar so Alturk killed her.*"

"That's . . . very sad."

"*No it's not. She beat me more than the others.*"

"Must've been her blood mother," Davoka commented. "They always beat you more."

"*How many mothers for you, Queen?*" the girl asked Lyrna. Like Davoka she was unable to comprehend the difference between a queen and a princess.

"*Just one.*"

"*Did she beat you?*"

"*No. She died when I was very young. I have little memory of her.*"

"*Was it on the hunt or in battle?*"

"*Neither. She just got sick.*" Like my father, although she died too soon whilst he died too late.

A woman appeared at the entrance, young in years but no less fierce in aspect than the warriors outside. Davoka had marked her as Alturk's eldest daughter, charged with bringing them food and fuel, a task she usually performed in stern-faced silence. "*You are to bring the Merim Her to the Tahlessa's fire tonight,*" she told Davoka. Her gaze tracked to Lyrna, taking in the sight of her younger sister tending hair. She barked a harsh command, beckoning to the girl who grimaced in annoyance but obediently slid off the bed to trot to her side.

"*Leave that,*" the young woman commanded, seeing the comb she still held in her hand.

"*She can have it,*" Lyrna said. "*A . . . queen's gift.*"

"*The blood of Alturk need no gifts from you,*" the woman snarled back, twisting the comb from the girl's grasp, drawing a pained sob.

"*I said let her keep it!*" Lyrna got to her feet, meeting the woman's gaze.

The Lonak woman was almost shaking in rage, her hands inching towards the antler-handled knife in her belt.

"*Mind the word of the Mountain,*" Davoka told her in a quiet voice.

The woman seethed for a moment more then tossed the comb back to her sister, her furious gaze never leaving Lyrna. The little girl looked at the comb in her hand then threw it on the floor and stamped on it. "*Merim Her are weak!*" she hissed at Lyrna then ran from the hall.

The young woman gave Lyrna a final sneer of disdain before following.

"You are not queen here," Davoka said. "Never forget they hate you."

Lyrna looked down at the fragments of tortoise-shell. "They do," she agreed, then turned to Davoka, smiling faintly. *"But you don't, sister."*

Predictably, Alturk's dwelling proved the largest in the village, a stone-walled circle some twenty paces in diameter with a slanted roof of slate. Night had fallen by the time Davoka led Lyrna inside, finding the clan chief seated before a raging fire, the flames rising from coals heaped into a pit in the centre of the floor. He was alone save for a young man who stood at his shoulder, arms crossed and favouring Lyrna with the customary glower, and a large hound which sat at his feet gnawing on an elk bone.

"I understand," Alturk began in Realm Tongue, apparently finding the offer of a greeting a pointless affectation. "My first daughter gave offence to the queen."

"It was nothing," Lyrna told him.

"Nothing or not, she showed weakness in failing to properly mind the Mahlessa's command. I whipped her myself."

"We are grateful for your consideration," Davoka told him in Lonak before Lyrna could say anything.

He accepted the words with a nod, looking Lyrna up and down. "You are strong enough to travel." There was no question in his tone.

"We will depart on the north-eastern trail come the dawn," Davoka said. *"I require ponies and an escort. A full war-band should be enough."*

The young man standing at Alturk's shoulder gave a scornful laugh, falling to silence at a glare from the clan chief. *"You can have the ponies, but there is no war-band to send with you,"* Alturk said. *"The hunt for the Sentar has taken all my warriors save the few I can spare to guard the villages."*

Davoka's jaws bunched and her response was edged with suppressed anger. *"I have counted over two hundred warriors in this village."*

Alturk shrugged. *"The Sentar are many, and your sister's blood-thirst insatiable. The Grey Hawks look to their Tahlessa for protection, I will not deny them."*

"But you would deny the word from the Mountain."

Alturk got to his feet. He wore no weapons but the power evident in him was threat enough. *"The Mahlessa sends no command for me to muster arms for your onward journey. I have honoured the word of the Mountain by providing succour to this gold-haired quim you fuss over like a nesting she-ape."*

Davoka gave a shout of fury, hefting her spear, a war club appearing in the hand of the young Lonak as she did so.

"NO!" Lyrna said, raising a hand and stepping in front of Davoka. *"No, sister. This will do no good."*

The Lonak woman looked away, nostrils flared as she fought the desire for battle, then slowly lowered her spear. Lyrna turned to Alturk. "Tahlessa, I thank you for your hospitality. I, Princess Lyrna Al Nieren of the Unified Realm, am in your debt. We shall be on our way come morning."

The pony they gave her made Lyrna pine for poor slaughtered Sable. It was an ill-tempered beast, prone to unbidden trotting and likely to rear in protest at the slightest provocation. It also had the boniest back she had ever encountered, the thin goatskin saddles the Lonak used offering little protection for her behind which now perched on what felt like a jumble of rocks covered with a thin blanket. Smolen seemed similarly discomfited by his mount, squirming somewhat as they trekked away from the Grey Hawk village, whilst Sollis and Ivern were fairly at ease on their ponies and Davoka, of course, rode hers as if she had known it for years. She led them on at a brisk trot, keen to cover as much distance as possible before nightfall. Lyrna glanced back at the village before they crested a rise at the north end of the valley, wondering if Alturk's daughter would find the lock of golden hair she had hidden in the women's hall, deep in a gap in the stone walls, only reachable by small hands.

"I trust you were not mistreated, good sirs," Lyrna said to the three men as they traversed a shallow stream.

"Only if silence is a form of torture, Highness," Ivern replied.

"For you it usually is," Sollis muttered.

"No time for talk," Davoka told them. "Need to be at the rapids by sun fall." She kicked her pony to a canter, obliging them to follow suit.

As always, Lyrna found the relentless hours in the saddle irksome, but not quite so miserable an experience as before. Her back and legs didn't ache so much and her thighs seemed to have become more resistant to chafing. She was also aware her ability as a rider had improved, where before she had struggled constantly to stay in the saddle at the gallop, now she moved in concert with the horse, even experiencing a small thrill in the exhilaration of speed as her hair trailed in the wind and the pony's hooves drummed on the earth. *Perhaps I'm becoming Lonak,* she thought with a grin.

They came to the rapids by late evening, a raging torrent some fifty paces wide, stretching away on either side as far as they could see. Davoka led them eastward, following the course of the river until they found a deeper stretch where the current was not so fierce.

"This is not a ford," Sollis observed.

"Ponies can swim," Davoka said. "So can we."

"Erm," said Lyrna in a small voice.

"The current's too swift," Sollis insisted. "We should press on, find a better spot."

"No time," Davoka said, dismounting and leading her pony to the riverbank. "Sentar will already have our trail. We swim."

"I can't," Lyrna said, eyeing the swirling eddies churning the river's surface.

"No choice, Queen," Davoka said, making ready to leap into the water.

"I said I can't!" Lyrna shouted.

The Lonak woman turned with a quizzical expression.

"I can't swim," Lyrna went on, unable to keep the sullen defensiveness from her voice.

"Not even a little, Highness?" Ivern enquired.

"Forgive me for not spending my childhood in your order, brother!" she rounded on him. "My tutors were clearly remiss to the point of treason in not teaching me to swim, for it's well-known such a skill is of great value to a princess."

He winced a little under the tirade, but was unable to fully suppress a smirk. "Well, it is now."

"Mind your tongue, brother!" Sollis snapped.

"We must cross," Davoka stated.

"Well, I agree with Brother Sollis," Lyrna replied, crossing her arms and forcing all the regal authority into her voice she could muster. "We should find a better spot, somewhere not so deep . . ."

She trailed off as Davoka approached her with a purposeful stride. "Don't!" Lyrna cautioned her.

Davoka ducked down and lifted Lyrna over her shoulder, turning back to the river. "Rock apes can swim, no-one teaches them. So can you."

"Brother Sollis, I command you . . ." Lyrna had time to sputter before finding herself in the air. The chill of the water was shocking, numbing her from head to toe in an instant. There was a moment of deafness, her vision crowded with bubbles, before she bobbed to the surface, dragging air into her lungs with a shout. As Sollis had predicted, the current was swift, carrying her downriver a good twenty paces before she managed to scramble to the bank, flailing and kicking until her feet found purchase on the rocky shallows. She crawled from the water, shivering and retching. Smolen appeared at her side, helping her up with careful hands. "You insult the person of our princess!" he raged at Davoka as she strode to join them.

"See," she said to Lyrna, ignoring Smolen's outburst. "You swim well eno—"

Lyrna punched her in the face. She put all her strength into the blow but it rebounded from the Lonak woman's jaw without any obvious effect, whilst provoking an instant flare of agony in her fist.

There was a moment's silence as Smolen put a hand on his sword hilt, Lyrna shook the pain from her hand and Davoka rubbed the small bruise on her jaw. She grunted and a smile ghosted across her lips. "Hold on to the pony's neck," she told Lyrna, turning away. "You be fine."

In the event, the crossing was less hazardous than Sollis feared, although Smolen came adrift from his pony halfway across and had to be rescued by Ivern before the current took him away, the young brother managing to snare the Lord Marshal's tunic as he swept past. Lyrna clamped her arms around her pony's neck and hung on as the animal kicked through the torrent. It seemed unafraid of the water, though its snorts indicated it found her an unwelcome burden. It was done in the space of an hour, all five of them safely making the opposite bank in varying stages of bedraggled exhaustion.

"Can't rest," Davoka said, climbing onto her pony's back and spurring towards the north.

They trailed after her until they made it to the cover of a thick pine forest some ten miles from the river. Davoka discovered a shallow cave in a ravine where they took turns to sleep until morning. Lyrna found herself chilled to the point of shaking once more but there was no return of the sickness that laid her low beneath the Mouth of Nishak and she woke with the dawn, aching but refreshed enough to continue.

She moved to Davoka's side as she crouched at the mouth of the cave, eyes scanning the walls of the ravine. "Any sign?" Lyrna asked her.

Davoka shook her head. "No sign, no scent. They hunt for us, but not in this forest." Her tone indicated this wasn't necessarily good news.

"I'm sorry I hit you," Lyrna said.

Davoka turned to her with a puzzled frown. "Sorree?"

Lyrna searched for the Lonak equivalent, finding there wasn't one. "*Illeha*," she said. *Regret or guilt, depending on the inflection.*

"*Lonakhim hit each other all the time*," Davoka replied with a shrug. "*If you'd tried to knife me, things would be different.*" She rose and moved back into the cave, kicking at the feet of the sleeping men. "*Rouse yourselves, limp-pricks. Time to go.*"

They cleared the forest by midmorning, riding hard to the north-east. The country here was less mountainous than they had experienced so far, distinguished by numerous broad grassy plains between the peaks. Lyrna's new-found skill in the saddle allowed her to match Davoka's speed and they rode side by side for a time until Davoka reined to an abrupt halt, her eyes alighting on something to the west. Lyrna followed her gaze, picking out a dust-cloud rising above the horizon. "Sentar?" she asked.

"Who else?" Ivern said.

"Highness!" Smolen stood in his stirrups, pointing to the south where another dust cloud was rising.

Lyrna turned to Davoka, finding her looking ahead at the mountain range to the north, no doubt calculating the distance.

"It's too far," Sollis said, unhitching his bow. There was no particular alarm to his voice, just a faint note of resignation.

"Queen can go," Davoka said. "We hold them back."

Lyrna looked at the cloud to the west, picking out the dark smudges appearing out of the haze. She stopped counting at fifty. "There are too many, sister," she said. "But thank you."

Davoka met her eyes, and for the first time there was a sense of confusion there, a reluctance to comprehend the finality of the moment. Lyrna supposed she had never tasted defeat before. "I'm . . . sorree, Lerhnah," Davoka said.

Lyrna surprised herself by responding with an unforced and genuine smile. "It was my choice," she said, then surveyed the three men now arranged in a circle around her, Ivern and Sollis with their bows ready, Smolen with his sword drawn. "Good sirs,

I thank you for your service and express my sincere regret for leading you on this mad enterprise."

Sollis just grunted, Smolen offered a grave bow of respect and Ivern said, "Highness, I believe a kiss from you would see me into the Beyond with no regrets at all."

She stared at him and was gratified when he actually blushed. "My apologies, Highness . . ." he stammered.

She moved her pony alongside his and leaned over to plant a kiss on his lips, letting it linger a while before drawing back. "Good enough?" she asked.

For once it seemed words were beyond him.

"*Sekhara ke Lessa Ilvar!*" Davoka shouted, drawing Lyrna's attention away from the dumbfounded brother. *We live in the sight of the gods. An expression of thanks for godly blessings, usually unexpected.*

The Lonak woman was staring at the dust-cloud to the south, the riders now clearly visible. Riding in front was a large man in a bearskin vest, a massive war club in his hand. *Alturk!*

For a moment Lyrna thought the clan chief had come to join in their imminent slaughter, which seemed strange considering he had already enjoyed ample opportunity to do them all the harm he wished. But instead Alturk led his band towards the west, at least five hundred warriors riding at full gallop, placing themselves between Lyrna's party and the onrushing Sentar.

The two war-bands met in a headlong clash some two hundred paces distant. The wind was brisk, dispelling the dust to afford a clear view of the battle, Lonak warriors assailing each other with club, hatchet and spear in a ferocious melee, accompanied by a continuous chorus of war cries and the screams of their ponies. She saw Alturk in the thickest part of the fight, laying about with his club and hatchet, foe after foe falling before him.

Davoka gave a shout and kicked her pony into motion, soon becoming lost in the swirl of combat, Lyrna catching brief glimpses of her spear whirling and stabbing amongst the confusion.

Three Sentar emerged from the melee to charge at them, war

cries high and shrill. The brothers' arrows plucked two from their saddles in quick succession and Smolen rode out to confront the third, ducking under the warrior's spear and hacking his pony from under him with a slash to the flank. Ivern finished the rider with an arrow as he rolled on the ground.

The battle seemed to end as quickly as it had begun, the surviving riders coming to a halt, Grey Hawk warriors dismounting to finish the wounded. Alturk trotted towards them, a bloody hatchet in his belt and a gore-encrusted war club in his hand. The young man who had stood at his shoulder at their last meeting rode at his side.

"Queen," Alturk greeted her with a nod. "You are hurt?"

She shook her head. "It seems I am in your debt once more, Tahlessa. Though it might have been polite if you had shared your plan before we set off."

Alturk's only expression was a slight curl of his lip. She couldn't tell if he was amused or disdainful. "A trap is not a trap without bait."

There was a shout of fury from behind him and Lyrna looked to see Davoka leading a captive from the corpse-strewn aftermath of the battle. She had bound the girl's hands and dragged her along with a rope lashed around her neck.

"*You take her to the Mountain?*" Alturk asked as Davoka sent her sister sprawling with a jerk of the rope. Lyrna was surprised by the note she detected in the Tahlessa's voice: concern, albeit reluctant.

"*She will be judged by the Mahlessa,*" Davoka replied.

"*I saw her kill five of my men.*" Alturk's gaze remained fixed on the scarred girl. "*I claim her by right of blood—*"

"*A claim made far too late,*" Davoka cut in, glancing towards the young man at Alturk's side, then back at the clan chief. "*And you have judgement of your own to make.*"

Alturk's face clouded and he gave a sombre nod. "*True enough.*"

The young man frowned. "*Father . . . ?*"

Alturk's war club caught him on the side of the head, sending him senseless to the ground. The clan chief beckoned two of his warriors closer. *"Bind this varnish. We judge him tonight."*

Davoka had earned a deep cut on her shoulder which Sollis cleaned and stitched with practised hands, the Lonak woman sipping redflower and gritting her teeth against the pain as he worked. They were encamped on the plain amongst the Grey Hawk war-band. They seemed subdued in the shadow of victory, their fires untouched by song or noises of celebration. The reason was no mystery; he knelt, arms bound and head bowed before Alturk's fire, a son awaiting his father's judgement. He had raged for hours, as the sun waxed and the shadows grew, screaming scorn and insults at his former clansmen. *"You betray the Lonakhim . . . you will make us slaves to the Merim Her . . . throw our borders wide so they can take all we have fought to defend . . . they will defile us . . . make us weak . . . make us like them . . . The Mahlessa is false, her word is not the word of the gods . . ."*

There was no attempt to silence him, no punishment meted out for his blasphemy. They let him rant himself to exhaustion, refusing to acknowledge any sound he made. *Varnish,* Lyrna thought.

"How did you know he had betrayed us?" she asked Davoka when Sollis had finished tending to her wound.

"Same way his father did. No other ears to hear of our route." She glanced at their own captive, secured with strong rope to an iron stake thrust deep into the ground, the chin-to-brow scar Lyrna had given her red and angry in the fire's glow. She had said nothing since her capture, slumping onto whatever patch of ground she was led to, her expression one of vague annoyance, untroubled by fear.

When the moon rose high Alturk stood up, war club in hand, and walked to his son's side. The Grey Hawks gathered round as he raised his arms. *"I call you, my brothers in war, to witness judgement,"* the clan chief said. *"This wretched thing that was once my son kneels in disgrace. He has shunned the word of the Mountain, he has spoken false words. These are not the actions of the Lonakhim. And so he will be judged."*

There was a murmur of assent from the gathered warriors, a tense expectation stealing over them as Alturk moved closer to his son. But instead of striking the man down he tossed his war club aside and knelt beside him. *"But as he is judged, so must you judge me, for it is my weakness that has led us to this. My weakness that made me beg for this wretch's life years ago when he lay defeated by the worst of the Merim Her. My weakness that made me return to our clan with no word of his transgression or the shame that shrouded my heart. I begged like the weakest of men for his life and this is my reward, the only reward such weakness deserves. I, Alturk, Tahlessa of the Grey Hawks, ask for your judgement."*

For a moment Lyrna suspected this was merely pantomime, a show of contrite humility by a noble leader, but the rising murmur of confusion and anger from the band told her there was no theatre here; Alturk's words were sincere. He wanted judgement.

A man emerged from the ranks of the war-band, a veteran warrior judging by his age, whip thin and short of stature but commanding enough respect to still the rising babble with a raised war club. He regarded the kneeling clan chief with an expression of sombre regret. *"Our Tahlessa asks for judgement,"* he said. *"And by the truth of his own words, judgement is warranted. I, Mastek, have been this man's brother in war since he was old enough to climb onto his pony. Never have I seen him flinch from battle. Never have I seen him turn his sight from a hard choice or a hard road. Never have I seen him weak . . . until now."* The old warrior closed his eyes for a second, swallowing, forcing his next words out: *"I judge him weak. I judge him no longer fit to be our Tahlessa. I judge that he should share the same fate as the varnish that kneels at his side."* He surveyed the band. *"Are there any who would speak against this?"*

There was no response. Lyrna could see no anger on their faces, just grim acceptance. She understood what was happening now, these men were as bound by their customs as any Realm subject was bound by law. This was no vengeful mob, it was a court, and judgement had been passed.

A harsh peal of laughter cut through the silence, loud enough to echo across the plains. Kiral's gaze was bright with glee as she regarded the doomed clan chief, teeth bared as she laughed, shaking with amusement. Davoka rose, rushing over to slap the girl to silence. It did no good, the laughter raging on and on, seeming to increase with every slap. Finally Davoka jammed a gag in her sister's mouth, tying it off tight at the base of the skull. It muted the laughter but failed to stop it completely, Kiral rolling on the ground, tears of mirth streaming from her eyes. She caught sight of Lyrna, eyes gleaming in the firelight, and winked.

Lyrna turned back to the war-band, seeing Mastek step towards his former Tahlessa, war club ready in a two-handed grip. *"I offer you the knife, Alturk,"* he said. *"In remembrance of the battles we have fought together."*

Alturk shook his head. *"Kill me but don't insult me, Mastek."*

The warrior gave a nod, raising the club.

"WAIT!" Lyrna was on her feet, striding through the knot of warriors, stepping between Alturk and the advancing Mastek.

The old warrior stared at her, eyes wide in astonished fury. *"You have no voice here,"* he breathed.

"I am Queen of the Merim Her," she told him, voice raised so they could all hear. *"Called to parley by the Mahlessa herself, granted safe passage and all respect due my rank."*

Davoka appeared at her side, eyes scanning the crowd with considerable anxiety. *"This is unwise, Queen,"* she murmured to Lyrna in Realm Tongue. *"This is not your realm."*

Lyrna ignored her, fixing Mastek with a harsh glare. *"The Grey Hawks have spilled blood and lost warriors in my defence, they have honoured the word from the Mountain."* She pointed at the kneeling Alturk. *"All at this man's order. This places me in his debt. Amongst my people an unbalanced debt is the greatest dishonour. If you kill him without a reckoning, you dishonour me, and you dishonour the Mahlessa's word."*

"I need no words from you, woman," Alturk grated, head bowed, his large hands gouging into the earth. "Is the well of my shame not deep enough?"

"He is varnish," Lyrna told Mastek. *"Judged as such by his own war-band. His words no longer have meaning for the Lonakhim."*

Mastek slowly lowered his war club, fury still shining in his eyes but the slump of his shoulders told of something more—relief. *"What would you have us do?"*

"Give him to me," she said. *"I will present him to the Mahlessa. Only she can balance the debt I owe him."*

"And this one?" Mastek pointed his club at Alturk's son.

Lyrna looked down at the young man, at the hatred in his face. He spat at her, wrestling against his bonds and trying to rise before swiftly being forced back to his knees by the surrounding warriors. *"Weak!"* he snarled at them. *"This Merim Her bitch makes you her dogs!"*

Lyrna turned back to Mastek. *"I am not in his debt."*

He sang his death song as they looped a rope about his already bound hands and lashed it to the saddle of Mastek's pony. Turning to face the rising sun, Alturk's doomed son sang a dirge in lilting Lonak, most of the words archaic and unknown to Lyrna but she noted the phrase "vengeance of the gods" repeated several times. He was jerked from his feet in mid-song as Mastek spurred his mount into motion, dragging him away at the gallop, the rest of the band closing in around as they rode hard for the south. Davoka commented she had once seen a man last a whole day being dragged behind a pony. Alturk watched his former clansmen disappear from view and said nothing.

Lyrna felt Sollis's eyes on her as she went to her pony, checking his hooves for signs of injury and working the worst of the knots from his mane. "Do you have something to say, brother?" she asked.

Sollis's expression was as unreadable as ever but there was a new tone in his voice, the suppressed anger she usually detected replaced by what might have been respect. "I was just thinking, Highness, that the Lonak may have it right," he said. "We are riding with a queen after all." He gave a small bow before going to see to his own mount.

The mountains closed in again as they journeyed north, the peaks broader and higher even than those found around the Skellan Pass, the summits shrouded in perpetual cloud. The tracks they followed became ever more narrow, winding around hill-side and mountain in increasingly treacherous spirals. The first night out from the scene of the Sentar's defeat they camped on a precipice above a drop Ivern judged at near five hundred feet, a damp blanket of mist descending as night came.

Alturk sat apart from them, still and silent at the edge of the precipice, not troubling to eat or make a fire. Lyrna had begun to approach him but stopped at an emphatic shake of the head from Davoka. Instead she went to sit opposite Kiral. Davoka had positioned the girl beside a smaller fire, as far from their own as was practicable, both legs bound together since there was no soft ground to stake her to. She regarded Lyrna with an incurious glance, reclining against a rock, every inch a bored adolescent.

"Does it hurt?" Lyrna asked her, gesturing at her scar.

Kiral frowned. "*I don't speak your dog tongue, Merim Her bitch.*"

Not all gambits work, Lyrna thought with a rueful grimace. "*The scar I left you with,*" she said. "*Does it pain you?*"

The girl shrugged. "*Pain is a warrior's lot.*"

Lyrna glanced at Davoka, seeing the wariness in her eyes as she watched their conversation. "*My friend thinks you are no longer her sister,*" she said. "*She thinks her sister has been claimed by you, that what lives behind your eyes is no longer the girl she cared for.*"

"*My sister is blind in her devotion to the false Mahlessa. She sees lies where she should see truth."* Lyrna could see no particular emotion in the girl's face, finding her tone flat, like a child reciting one of the catechisms of the Faith.

"And what is this truth?" she asked.

"The false Mahlessa seeks to slay the spirit of the Lonakhim, to turn the sight of the gods from us, to leave us with no stories for our fires or our death songs. Peace with you, then peace even with the Seordah. What will that make us? Will we grub in the earth as you do? Make slaves of our women as you do? Labour in service to the dead, as you do?" Again the same flat tone, fanatical invective delivered without a hint of passion.

Lyrna nodded at the hulking form of Alturk, dim and forlorn in the mist. *"Do you know why I saved him?"*

"Merim Her are weak. Your heart is soft, you imagine a debt where there is none. He followed the false Mahlessa's word, you owe him nothing."

Lyrna shook her head, eyes searching the girl's face. *"No, I saved him because I saw that you wanted him dead. Why is that?"*

Nothing, not even a flicker of concern or a sign of deceit when she replied, *"He has ever been the Sentar's persecutor. Why would I not wish him dead?"*

There's no evidence here, Lyrna decided. The girl was strange indeed, quite possibly insane, but that was hardly proof of Davoka's conviction. She got up to return to her place by the main fire.

"I heard a strange thing about Merim Her women," Kiral said as she rose.

"And what is that?"

For the first time there was some animation in the girl's face, a malicious curl to her lips. *"Custom forbids them a man until they are joined. And after that they are only allowed their one husband. Is that true?"*

Lyrna gave a small nod.

"But you, Queen, are not joined." Her gaze ranged over Lyrna, it was not the gaze of any adolescent girl, Lonak or no. *"You've never known a man."*

Lyrna said nothing, watching the girl's features as she laughed, soft mocking rasps. *"I'll make you a bargain, Queen,"* she said. *"I'll answer any question you have with an honest tongue, and all I ask is a taste of that unsullied peach between your legs."*

Is this it? Lyrna wondered. *Is this finally my evidence?* "What are you?" she asked.

The girl's laughter subsided after a moment and she lay back against the rock with the same bored expression as before. *"I am Kiral of the Black River Clan and true Mahlessa to the Lonakhim."* She looked away, staring into the fire, still and indifferent, her face blank of all expression.

Lyrna returned to the larger fire, sitting down at Davoka's side. The Lonak woman seemed reluctant to meet her gaze. "I can't kill her, Lerhnah," she said after a moment, a note of apology in her tone.

Lyrna patted her hand and settled down to sleep. "I know."

Two more days brought them within sight of the Mountain, the home of the Mahlessa. It rose from the floor of a small valley nestling between two of the tallest mountains, a circular spike of stone, curving up from a wide base to a needle-sharp point at least three hundred feet in the air. It seemed to shimmer in the sunlight, but as they drew nearer Lyrna saw it was honeycombed from base to top with balconies and windows, all hewn out of the rock. From the weathering of the surface she judged this a truly ancient structure, the architecture so unfamiliar as to appear alien, like something from a distant land never visited by modern eyes.

"The Lonakhim built this?" she asked Davoka.

She shook her head. *"It was waiting for us at the end of the great travail. Proof that the gods had not turned their sight from the Lonakhim. For who else could craft such a gift?"*

They entered via a tunnel, the walls ascending to meet overhead in an elegant arch of stone. There were no guards at the mouth of the tunnel and they proceeded unchallenged into the Mountain's interior. After a hundred paces the tunnel opened out into a broad courtyard, ringed by balconied walkways bathed in sunlight shafting through the many circular windows. A number of women were waiting there, some armed and wearing similar garb to Davoka, others dressed more simply in robes of black or grey. Their age ranged from young to old and none seemed perturbed by their appearance, although the sight of Kiral provoked some hard stares from the women bearing arms.

"*I see you had an interesting journey,*" a short, blunt-faced warrior said, coming forward to take the reins of Davoka's pony. "*I trust you have a story for the fire.*"

"*More than one.*" Davoka dismounted, favouring the blunt-faced woman with a warm grin. "*We need rooms, Nestal.*"

"*Ready and waiting.*" Nestal's gaze roamed their company, settling on Lyrna. "Queen," she said, with an incline of her head. "The Mahlessa asked that you be brought to her as soon as you arrived." She turned to Kiral, her expression hardening. "Together with this one."

Lyrna had expected the Mahlessa to make her home on one of the Mountain's upper floors but Davoka led her to a stairwell in the centre of the chamber, the spiral course descending into shadow.

"No!" she barked when Smolen and the two brothers attempted to follow. "Stay here. Men do not look upon her."

Smolen seemed about to protest but Lyrna held up a hand. "I doubt your sword would aid me here, Lord Marshal. Wait for me."

He bowed and stepped back, standing stiffly at attention, every inch the loyal guards officer, albeit one without armour or any vestige of his former finery save his sword and the boots he had contrived to retain, and even they had lost their previous mirror-like sheen. For the first time in days it occurred to her that her own appearance was hardly more edifying. No more ermine robes or finely tailored riding gowns, just sturdy leather garb and hardy boots, scuffed and dusted from the trail. But for her hair she might well have been taken for Lonak.

"Please, sister!"

She looked round to see Kiral resisting Davoka's tug on her leash. Her once-passive features now so riven with fear it almost seemed she wore a mask. *"Please,"* she begged in a terrorised rasp. *"Please if you ever thought me your sister, kill me! Do not take me to her!"*

She continued to beg and struggle as Davoka took hold of her and forced her to walk down the stairwell, her pleas becoming plaintive shrieks as they descended into the shadows. *No fear of death,* Lyrna thought. *What awaits her below is worse.*

She smoothed her hands over her dusty, trail-marked clothing and followed them down.

Chapter Three
Reva

S he ran, until her lungs burned and her legs ached, she ran. Away from the road, away from him, away from the *lies*, through the long grass and into the trees. She ran until exhaustion sent her sprawling in a painful tangle of sword and cloak. Scrambling to her feet, she cast about for landmarks, chest heaving from exertion and panic. *He'll come after me, hunt me down, make me listen to more lies . . .*

She began to run again, tripping almost immediately as her fatigued foot found a tree root. She fell to her arms and knees, sobbing in hard, aching jerks, her mind racing. *If he did exist, his bishops say he hates you for what you are . . . You were sent in search of a thing that can't be found in the hope that I would kill you . . . A fresh martyr . . .*

"LIES!" Her voice resounded through the trees, wild and feral. The trees, however, had no answer save for the creak of wind-stirred branches.

She sat back on her haunches, face raised to the sky, mouth wide as she drank the air. She knew now Al Sorna wasn't coming in pursuit, his skills were such that finding her would have been a simple matter, but here she sat, alone. She remembered the edge of despair in his voice as he called after her, a note of defeat . . . *I now deny my song though it screams at me to let you go.*

Follow your song, Darkblade, she thought. *I'll make my own.*

She ran a shaking hand through her too-long hair, her sluttish, Asraelin hair. *Filthy, Fatherless sinner . . .*

The priest! The priest will have answers to these lies. She would return to him and he would speak the truth and the World Father would once again bless her with his love, prove she was not hated, prove the sin had been beaten from her, prove she was worthy of His holy mission . . . Worthy to carry her father's sword.

The sword. The prospect of returning to the priest without it, demanding he answer the Darkblade's lies no less, was absurd. But if she had the sword, his face would reveal all the truth she needed. The sword was the truth.

She opened her eyes to the stars, picking out the Stag. The fore-hoof, she knew, pointed almost directly due south, towards Cumbrael, the Greypeaks . . . and the High Keep. Perhaps it was still there, lying unclaimed in a shadowed corner of the Lord's chamber, waiting for her. If not, then she had little chance of finding it elsewhere.

The thought came to her as she started to rise, a swift treacherous whisper in her mind. *Go back. They will welcome you.*

"With lies!" she hissed back.

With love. When did the priest ever show you that?

"I care nothing for his love, or theirs. The love of the Father is the only love I need."

She got to her feet, brushing loose soil from her clothes, and began to walk towards the south.

The bow was fashioned from wych elm and pale cream in colour, the centre of the stave smooth and shiny with use, the wood on either side ornately carved, one side showing a stag the other a wolf. It was different to the ash bow Al Sorna had made for her, abandoned the day she ran from him, longer and somewhat thicker, no doubt making for greater power and range.

The bow's owner lay on a blanket of grass in the lee of an aged tree stump, several miles from the nearest road. His eyes were closed in an apparently blissful slumber, his mostly white beard stained red and an empty earthenware wine jug in his lap. At his side a bored-looking sheep-hound, all shaggy fur and dolorous eyes, gazed up at Reva with a complete absence of alarm, only angling its head in a curious manner as she crept closer to gently lift the bow from the drunkard's arms. The quiver of arrows was too firmly wedged beneath his back so she left it. Arrows were more easily made than bows.

She had gone about twenty paces when she stopped, eyeing the carving on the stave and finding it even more fine than she first thought. On the upper side the stag stood with its antlers lowered in readiness for combat whilst below it the wolf crouched, teeth bared in a snarl. The craftsmanship was remarkable, the carvings finished to a level that told her this was an item of considerable worth.

The sword is all, the priest had said. *The Father will forgive all sins committed in pursuit of the sword.*

Reva sighed, retraced her steps, placed the bow back in the drunkard's arms and sat down to wait for him to wake. After a while the sheep-hound came over, sniffing and whining for scraps of the rabbit she had snared the day before. The old man woke with a start at the dog's appreciative bark as she fed him a morsel.

"What!" He clutched at his bow, fumbling for an arrow. "Whaddya want, ya whore ya!"

Reva watched him fail to pull an arrow from the quiver, abandon the attempt and reach instead for the small knife in his boot, wild eyes becoming still and rapt at the sight of the single gold piece she held up.

"That's a nice bow," she said.

The arrow smacked into the tree trunk with a sharp thwack, buried in the wood up to at least a handspan of its length. It was a practice arrow, just a sharpened yard of wind-fallen ash with no head or fletching, and yet she had found her mark from a distance of twenty paces.

The old man had named himself a shepherd although there was no sign of a flock for miles around. He claimed the bow was a souvenir from a forgotten campaign against the Cumbraelins, when he was but a lad and the lord's men came to take him for a soldier, though his poor mother wept. Reva thought the tale unlikely. The bow was a fine weapon but it was not Cumbraelin in design. She assumed the shepherd had either stolen it or won it at gaming. In any case he had been too eager to be off with his new-found wealth to provide a fuller explanation of the bow's origins, striding his unsteady way across the sheepless meadow, wine jug in hand and his sad-eyed dog trailing after.

She had been travelling for two weeks now, keeping off the roads and sheltering in woodland at night, hunting where opportunity rose, suppressing her hunger and always following the Stag's hoof south. There were few people about, the drunken shepherd the first she had seen for several days. This far from the roads there was little chance of encountering either traveller or outlaw, although she kept a wary eye out for the latter.

That evening the bow reaped a moor hen, plucked, spitted, cooked and eaten before the sun fell. She knew her time with Al Sorna had weakened her, the weeks of sleeping on a full belly leaving her too much in thrall to her hunger. Every night she offered thanks to the Father for delivering her from the Darkblade's lies and begged His forgiveness for her sinful indulgence.

After eating, she drew her knife, taking hold of a length of her ever-growing hair and making ready to cut. It had become a nightly ritual, her determined purpose waning as she touched the blade to the sluttish curls, never actually cutting. She told herself she needed to maintain the disguise. *Asraelin women don't wear their hair so short* . . . And she had yet to cross into Cumbrael. It had nothing to do with vanity, or the many times Alornis had said how she liked the way it caught the sun.

Liar. The priest's voice followed her into sleep as she sheathed her knife and huddled in her cloak. *Fatherless, sinning liar* . . .

◆　◆　◆

Another week brought her within sight of the Greypeaks, a jagged blue-misted outline on the horizon. Woodland grew thicker here, covering the foothills rising in height the further south she walked. Game was sparse, her kills amounting to a solitary partridge and a somewhat aged hare too slow to scamper out of the arrow's path. Two nights more and she judged herself within a half-day's march to the mountains proper. The exact location of the High Keep was unknown to her but the days when it had been forbidden for any Cumbraelin to even speak of it were long over, her father's martyrdom had seen to that. She knew of a village situated just over the river forming the border with Asrael. The priest had indicated that pilgrims could find assistance there, for all Sons of the Trueblade must journey to the High Keep to honour the Father's most blessed servant.

She found a pool of clean water beneath a small cascading waterfall, stripped and bathed, washed her clothes as best she could and lay them out to dry as she reclined on a rock in the sunlight, gazing up at the drifting majesty of the clouds. As ever, when her thoughts strayed, she thought of Al Sorna and his lessons, of Alornis and her drawings, even of the drunken poet and his awful songs. It was wrong, she knew, indulgent, sinful, and she always begged the Father for forgiveness afterwards, but for a short time every day, she let her thoughts wander over the memories, waiting for the moment when the treacherous voice would whisper its enticements: *It's not too late. Turn around, go north. Take ship to the Reaches. They will welcome you . . .*

She punished herself with sword practice, flashing through the scales faster and faster until her vision swam and she nearly dropped from exhaustion. As the light faded, she piled up some ferns for a bed and settled down to sleep, for once not bothering to hold the knife to her hair, though in truth it was now long enough to warrant a trim, just enough to keep it out of her eyes.

She awoke to screams, the sword coming free of the scabbard in a blur as she rolled to a crouch, eyes searching the blackness of the forest for enemies. Nothing . . . *Wait.*

Her nose picked up the scent before she saw it, smoke on the breeze, the yellow flicker of a tall fire through the trees. The scream came again, shrill, agonised . . . female.

Outlaws, she decided, rising from the crouch. *Not my concern.*

More screams, a babble of incoherent pleading, choked off into sudden terrible silence.

Reva thought of the outlaws she had killed at Rhansmill, of corpse-fucking Kella and the others who had not troubled her sleep one whit since.

She sheathed the sword to conceal its gleam, shouldered the quiver, hefted the bow and started forward, moving as Al Sorna had taught her when they hunted, foot raised only enough to clear the ground, strides short, crouched low. The flickering cone of the fire grew as she neared it, flames rising high from logs stacked in the centre of a clearing, dark forms moving in silhouette, a voice raised in fierce conviction.

She dropped to the ground when she got within thirty paces of the fire, crawling forward, the bow in her left hand, the string resting on the upper side of her forearm. A few moments of crawling brought something into focus, something that made her stop. A heavyset man standing with his back to the fire, eyes scanning the forest with diligent attention. He wore a sword on his back and cradled a crossbow in the crook of his arm, drawn and loaded. A sentry. No outlaw was ever so conscientious or well armed.

Reva crept a little closer, slow and careful, fingers sweeping the ground for twigs or dry leaves which might betray her, unseen by the sentry who, she now saw, wore a black cloak. *The Fourth Order.*

The voice became clearer as she closed, the speaker moving into view, a lean, sallow-faced man, also cloaked in black, gesticulating towards something off to the right as he spouted an unhesitating tirade: ". . . as Deniers you live, as Deniers you will die, your souls cast forth into oblivion, finding no refuge amongst the Departed, the falsehood that makes you wretched in this life will earn you an eternity of solitude in the Beyond . . ."

Reva waited until the sentry's eyes shifted to the left then rose as high as she dared, following the direction of the speaker's frantic gestures. There were four of them, all bound and gagged, a man and a woman, plus a little girl no more than ten years old and a beefy boy maybe five or six years older. Two black-cloaked brothers stood behind them with swords drawn. The boy was the most animated of the group, straining against his bonds which consisted of a stave thrust between his elbows and his back, lashed tight enough to gouge the bare flesh of his arms. A six-inch length of wood had been jammed into his mouth and tied in place with twine. Spittle flowed over his chin as he raged, his eyes alive with fury, not directed at the ranting black-cloak but beyond him at the fire.

Reva looked closer and saw there was a darker form visible through the flames, something blackened and vaguely human in shape, something that gave off a stench of burning meat.

"You!" the sallow-faced speaker pointed an accusing finger at the bound man who, unlike the boy, knelt in his bonds with his head bowed in dumb submission. "You who have ensnared your children in this falsehood, corrupted them with your Denial, you will witness the fate you have reaped for them."

One of the black-cloaks took hold of the man's hair and jerked his head back, revealing a face curiously absent of fear or rage, the eyes tearful but showing no sign of terror as the ranting brother loomed closer.

"See this, Denier," he hissed, face twisted and red in the fire's glow as he took hold of the little girl, dragging her to her feet. "See what you have wrought."

The girl squealed and twisted in his grip but he lifted her easily, advancing towards the fire. The beefy boy's scream was choked by his gag as he surged to his feet only to be clubbed to the ground by one of the brothers, a sword hilt coming down hard between his shoulder blades.

Reva's eyes took in the scene in the space of a heartbeat, the ranter, the two by the captives, the sentry. Four that she could see, no doubt more she couldn't, all well armed, none of them drunken outlaws. It was a hopeless prospect, and this was not her mission. The choice was clear.

The sentry died first, taken by her knife as she stepped out of the blackness, clutching at the gaping wound in his throat and falling face-first to the ground with barely a groan. Reva sheathed the knife, notched an arrow to the bow and sent it into the back of the ranter as he raised the girl above his head. He collapsed instantly, dropping the girl who thrashed at him with frantic kicks of her small legs, scrabbling free.

Reva had time for one more arrow as the two remaining brothers recovered from their shock and turned to face her, swords ready. She chose the one closest to her, the one who had been forcing the man to witness the girl's end. He was quick, dodging to the left as she drew a bead on his chest, but not quick enough. The shaft took him in the shoulder, sending him sprawling. She drew her sword and advanced on the other, killing the wounded brother with a slash to the neck as she passed.

His companion moved from behind the captives, raising a crossbow. With a howl the beefy boy launched himself at the brother, his shoulder connecting with an audible crunch of breaking ribs, pitching the black-cloak into the fire. He screamed and flailed in the flames, tumbling free to roll on the ground, voicing his pain in a continuous torrent of high-pitched yelps.

A shout drew Reva's attention to the left where three more brothers came charging out of the blackness, crossbows raised. Reva glanced at the boy, crouched on his knees, eyes wide and pleading above the gag.

She turned and sprinted for the trees, ducking to scoop up the fallen bow, a crossbow bolt fluttering her hair before the darkness claimed her.

She stopped after twenty paces, turned and crouched, taking two great breaths then forcing stillness into her body as she waited. The three black-cloaks were all anger and confusion, aiming kicks at the boy to vent their fury before heaping earth on their smouldering brother, babbling at each other about their next course of action, standing in a row, outlined against the fire.

Not so hopeless a prospect after all, Reva thought, raising the bow and taking aim.

The boy was named Arken, his sister Ruala, the mother Eliss and the father Modahl. The body on the fire belonged to Modahl's mother, her name had been Yelna although Ruala and Arken called her Gramma. Reva had no inclination to ask the only surviving brother his name so kept on calling him Ranter.

"God-worshipping witch!" he cried at her from his place slumped against a tree trunk, his legs splayed out on the earth before him, slack and useless. Reva's arrow had punched clean through his spine, leaving him dead below the waist. Sadly, his voice was unaffected. "Only with the aid of the Dark could you slaughter my brothers so," he accused, waving an unsteady finger at her. His skin was pale and clammy, his eyes increasingly dull. Killing him would have been a mercy, but Modahl had stopped her wielding the knife the night before.

"He was going to burn your daughter alive," she pointed out.

"What is mercy?" he said, his long face tense with fresh grief but still devoid of any anger, his eyebrows raised as if he were asking a sincere question.

"What?" she replied, frowning.

"Mercy is the sweetest wine and the bitterest wormwood," Eliss, the mother, said. "For it rewards the merciful and shames the guilty."

"The Catechism of Knowledge," Arken informed Reva, heaving a black-cloaked body onto the fire. His voice had a bitter edge to it. "She's obviously Cumbraelin, Father," he said to Modahl. "I doubt she wants to hear your lessons."

Catechism? "You are of the Faith?" she asked in surprise. She had expected to find them adherents of one of the myriad nonsensical sects appearing out of the shadows since the Edict of Toleration.

"The true Faith," Modahl said. "Not the perversion followed by these deluded souls."

Ranter said something, scattering earth with his breath. It sounded like "Denier lies!"

"Tell me if this hurts," Reva said, reaching down to pluck her arrow from his back. It didn't, he couldn't feel it.

The burnt brother had also survived her attack but succumbed to his wounds before the sun came up. He had screamed for quite some time and once again Modahl had stood in her way when she went to silence him. Nonplussed, she busied herself with aiding Arken in consigning the bodies to the fire.

"This one was skilled," she commented, hefting the legs of the tallest brother, the last one to fall. "Expect he was Realm Guard before the Fourth Order took him."

"Not skilled enough for you," Arken said, lifting the corpse by the shoulders. "I'm glad you made him suffer."

Was that what she had done? She had certainly played with him a little. After the others had fallen to her arrows, he had managed to duck the final shaft, running for the safety of the forest. She met him at the edge of the clearing, sword in hand. He was fast, experienced and knew many tricks. She knew more, and was faster. She made it last longer than it should, feeling her skill grow with every parry and thrust, every scar she left on his face or arms, like a lesson with Al Sorna only played for real. She finished it with a thrust to the chest when she caught sight of the little girl weeping on the ground, still bound and gagged.

Forgive me my indulgences, World Father.

Modahl said the words as the flames grew high, calling on his family to thank Yelna for the gift of her life, to remember her kindness and wisdom and to reflect on the flawed choices that had brought these unfortunate men to their end. Reva stood apart, cleaning the blood from her sword, seeing how Arken's face darkened as his father spoke on, glaring at him with a fury that seemed to border on hatred.

Morning brought a light rain and the sound of Ranter's voice, rousing her from a fitful sleep. The fire had burned down to a pile of black-grey ash, the rain washing it away to reveal a jumble of human bone and grinning skulls.

"Oh my fallen brothers!" Ranter cried. "To be taken by the Dark. May the Departed cleanse your souls."

"Not the Dark," Reva told him, yawning. "Just a knife, a bow, a sword and the knowledge to use them."

Ranter started to voice a reply but choked instead, coughing and rasping. "I . . . thirst," he croaked.

"Drink the rain."

The brothers had left a clutch of good horses, food for several days, plus a decent harvest of coin. Reva chose the tallest of the horses, a somewhat feisty grey stallion with the rangy look of a mount bred for the hunt, and scattered the rest. At Modahl's insistence the brothers' weapons had all been heaped onto the fire the night before, Arken making a disgusted noise when his father gently but firmly tugged the sword he had claimed from his grasp.

The family's wagon was still intact along with the oxen that pulled it, although the contents had been badly ravaged, evidenced by the sight of Ruala crying over the ripped and tattered remains of her doll.

"We were heading for South Tower," Arken said. "We have family there. It's said Tolerants have less to fear under the gaze of the Tower Lord of the Southern Shore."

"They hunted you," Reva said.

Arken nodded. "Father is keen to speak the words of Toleration to all who will listen. He hopes to find more willing ears in the south. It seems Aspect Tendris didn't relish the prospect."

Reva's gaze was drawn to the sight of Modahl laying out a blanket in the back of the wagon, casting aside sundry items as he endeavoured to clear a space. "What are you doing?" she asked.

"For the injured brother," he explained. "We must find him a healer."

Reva moved close to the man and spoke very quietly into his

ear. "If you attempt to make your daughter share a wagon with that piece of dung, I'll hack his head off and throw it in the river."

She lingered for a moment, eyes meeting his to ensure he understood. Modahl's shoulders slumped in weary defeat and he began ushering his family onto the wagon.

"There's a village some miles east of here," Reva said. "I'll ride there with you if you wish."

Modahl seemed about to protest but his wife spoke up first, "That would be greatly welcome, my dear."

Reva mounted the grey hunter and trotted over to where Ranter was slumped against the tree.

"Will you . . . kill me now . . . witch?" he enquired between rasps, his eyes two black coals in the pale wax of his face.

Reva took a full canteen from the hunter's saddle and tossed it into his lap. "Why would I do that?" She leaned forward, casting a meaningful glance at his useless legs. "I'm hoping you live a very long time, brother. If the wolves or the bears don't get you, of course."

She turned the hunter and cantered after the wagon as it trundled on its way.

The village proved a strange place, Cumbraelin and Asraelin living side by side and speaking a strange accent that seemed to accommodate only the most jarring vowels from both fiefs. It was clearly an important way-station from the numerous travellers and wagoners milling about. Wine going north, steel and coals going south. A company of Realm Guard was in evidence, the soldiers policing the crossroads about which the village clustered, ordering diversions and clearing blockages to ensure the trade kept moving. A temple to the World Father stood on the south side of the crossroads, facing a mission house of the Fifth Order on the other side.

"The Order will have salve for your cuts and such," Reva told Modahl. "Best if you tell them it was outlaws. They stole but were on their way quickly. No need to trouble the guards."

Modahl gave a slow nod, his eyes betraying a severe wariness. *No room for killers in his heart,* Reva surmised. *Even though he'd tend to them if they lay dying. What comedy their faith is.*

"Our thanks go with you," Eliss said as Reva tugged on the grey's reins. There was genuine warmth in her eyes, and gratitude. "We would welcome your company on the road come the morrow."

"I'm bound for the Greypeaks," she replied. "But I thank you."

She guided the horse further into the village, glancing back to see Arken gazing after her from the rear of the wagon, raising a hand in hesitant farewell. Reva waved back and rode on.

The inn was the smallest of the three found in the village, a sign above the door proclaiming it as the Wagoner's Rest. The interior was crowded with travellers and drovers, mostly men with wandering hands, quickly withdrawn at the sight of a half-bared knife. She found a stool in a corner and waited for the serving girl to come round. "Shindall owns this place?" she asked.

The girl gave a wary nod.

Reva handed her a copper. "I need to see him."

Shindall was a wiry man with a fierce growl to his voice. "What's this you bring me?" he demanded of the serving girl as she led Reva into a back room where he sat counting coin. "Makin' me lose count with some boney wh . . ." He trailed off as his eyes found Reva's face.

She placed her thumb on her chest, above her heart, and drew it down, once.

Shindall gave a barely perceptible nod. "Ale!" he barked at the serving girl. "And a meal, the pie not the slop."

He pulled a chair over for Reva to sit at the table, his eyes fixed on her face as she unbuckled her sword and removed her cloak. He waited until the serving girl had come and gone before speaking, a hushed reverent whisper. "You are *her*, aren't you?"

Reva washed down a mouthful of pie with a gulp of ale and raised an eyebrow.

Shindall's voice dropped even further and he leaned closer. "The blood of the Trueblade."

Reva smothered a surprised laugh, the man's earnestness was both funny and disconcerting. The light in his eyes calling to mind the dozens of idiot heretics who had gathered at Al Sorna's house. "The Trueblade was my father," she said.

Shindall stifled a gasp, clasping his hands together in excitement. "Word came from the priest that we should expect news of you soon. News that would shake the foundations of the Heretic Dominion. But I never thought, never dreamed I would see you myself, certainly not here in this hovel where I play innkeeper."

Word came from the priest . . . "What did he tell you?" she enquired, keeping her tone light, only mildly curious. *That I'd be dead soon? That you had a new martyr to worship?*

"The priest's messages are brief, and vague, for good reason. If the Fief Lord or the heretic King were to intercept them, too much clarity could undo us all."

She nodded and returned to her meal. The pie was surprisingly good, steak marinated in ale and baked with mushrooms in a soft pastry.

"If I may," Shindall went on. "Your mission, though I would never dare ask its object, is it complete? Do we finally draw near our deliverance?"

Reva gave a bland smile. "I need to find the High Keep. The priest told me you had charge of seeing pilgrims safely there."

"Of course," he breathed. "Of course you would want to undertake the pilgrimage, whilst time remains." He rose and went to a corner of the room, the one least favoured by the lamplight, bending down to lift a brick from the base and extract something from the space behind.

"Drawn on silk," he said, placing a rectangle of material in front of her, no more than six inches across. "Easy to hide, or swallow should you need to."

It was a map, simply drawn but clear enough to follow, a line stretching from a cluster of icons she took to be the village, winding its way past mountain and river until it ended at a black symbol shaped like a spear-point.

"Six days' travel from here," Shindall told her. "Not so many pilgrims these days so the way should be clear. There are friends of ours there, playing the role of beggars in need of shelter."

"It's not garrisoned?" she asked in surprise. She had been considering various notions of how best to sneak into the keep under the nose of the Fief Lord's guards.

"Not since the Trueblade fell. The drunken whore-chaser in Alltor seems happy to let it fall to ruin."

Reva finished her meal, draining the rest of the ale. "I'll need a room for tonight," she said. "And a stable for my horse." She offered him payment which he refused, leading her to a room on the upper floor. It was small and not especially clean but the sight of the narrow bed, the first she had seen since leaving the Darkblade's house, dispelled any misgivings.

"I met him once," Shindall said, lingering at the door, eyes still fixed on her face. "The Trueblade. It was not long after the Father had saved him from the outlaw's arrow, the scar was still fresh, red like a ruby, bright in the morning air when he stood up to speak. And his words . . . so much truth to hear in the space of a few moments. I knew then I had heard the Father's call in those words." His gaze was intense and the thickness in his voice reminded her of the swordsmith in Varinshold when he said, "You have his eyes."

Reva placed her cloak and sword on the bed. "Do the Realm Guard patrol the peaks?"

Shindall blinked, then shook his head. "The lowland roads only, most likely places for outlaws. Don't get 'em in the mountains, too cold I expect." He placed a lit candle on the room's only table and went to the door. "Earliest bell's at the fifth hour."

"I'll be gone by then. My thanks for your diligence."

He gave her a final glance before leaving the room, swallowing before he said, "Seeing your face is the only thanks I'll ever need."

She had never been to the Greypeaks before and found the sheerness of the mountains disconcerting, unassailable cliffs rising on all sides to ever-greater heights the deeper she went. The air held a perennial chill made worse by frequent drizzle or descending mist. The road ended at a broad, swift-running river tracking away towards the east. She began to follow it, the silk map having told her it provided the most direct route to the keep, the grey hunter snorting in protest as she guided him over the rock-strewn bank.

"Snorter," she said, smoothing a hand along his neck. "That's what I'll call you."

A clacking scatter of stone made her turn in the saddle, seeing another rider arriving at the road's end. Reva sat and waited for him to catch up, a large boy on a small horse.

"Did you steal that?" she asked as Arken drew level.

"The brothers' coin," he said, coughing then fidgeting in his too-small saddle.

Reva sat in silence, watching him blush and cough some more.

"I stay with them one more day and I'll kill him," he said eventually. "And I owe you a debt."

A faint rumble of thunder sounded overhead and Reva looked up to find a dark bank of cloud approaching from the west. "We'd best move back a ways from the river," she said, kicking Snorter forward. "It's like to flood when it rains."

"He was just a wheelwright," Arken said. "Skilled and a little more learned and Faithful than most men in the town, but still just a wheelwright. Then one day the Aspect of the Second Order came to visit the mission house and father went to her for catechism. After that, everything changed."

They had found shelter from the rain in a narrow crack in a cliff face. It kept the worst of the deluge off but was still too damp for a fire, obliging them to huddle in their cloaks, warmed only by the breath of the horses.

"Every spare hour spent speaking to any who would listen," Arken went on. "Every spare coin gone to pay the blocker to print his tracts, handed out for free to any who'd take them, me and my sister standing in the street hour after hour whilst he droned on. The worst thing was some people actually stopped to listen. I hated them for that. If no-one had listened, he might have given it up, and the Fourth Order might have left us alone. Your god has no Orders, does he?"

"This world was made by the will of one Father," she said. "So we might know his love. One world, one Father, one church." *Venal and corrupt though it is.*

Arken nodded then sneezed, a bead of water lingering on the tip of his nose.

"Will they look for you?" Reva asked.

His face became downcast. "I doubt it. Words were said."

"Words are not arrows, they can be taken back."

"He ordered us to do *nothing*!" Arken's jaw clenched, his fists balled beneath his cloak. "Just sat there when they came riding out of the woods, whispering his catechisms. What kind of man does that?"

A faithful man, she thought. "What did he have to say that angered them so much?"

"That the Faith had lost its way. That we were guilty of a great error, that the Red Hand had twisted our souls, made us hate when we should have loved. Made us kill where we should have saved. That the persecution of the unfaithful had raised a wall between our souls and the Departed. One day a brother from the Fourth came to the house with a letter from his Aspect. It was polite but firm: stop speaking. Father ripped it up in his face. Two days later the shop burned down."

Snorter began stomping the rock with his fore-hoof, head jerking in impatience. She was starting to understand his moods, and inactivity was not something he appreciated. She got up, taking a carrot from the saddlebag and holding it to his mouth as he chomped. "You don't owe me any debt," she told Arken. "And travelling with me could prove . . . dangerous."

"You're wrong," he said. "About the debt. And I don't care about any danger."

His gaze was full of earnest intent, and something more, which was a shame. *Still just a boy,* she thought. *Despite all his troubles.* "I'm looking for something," she told him. "Help me find it and the debt between us is settled. After that, you go your way."

He nodded, smiling a little. "As you wish."

She took something from the saddlebag and tossed it to him. "Your father forgot to check the Ranter for weapons."

He turned the knife over in his hands, pulling the blade free of the scabbard. It was a long-bladed weapon of good steel, well balanced, the ebony hilt cross-etched for a strong grip. "I don't know how to use it. Father wouldn't even let me have a wooden sword when I was younger."

She peered out at the rain, seeing it was starting to dwindle into a light drizzle, and took hold of Snorter's reins to lead him from the crack. "I'll teach you."

It was like playing with a child, a child half a foot taller and twice the bulk of her, but a child nonetheless. *He's so slow,* she wondered as Arken stumbled past, his sheathed knife missing by an arm's length as she dodged away. She leapt onto his back and put her own knife to his throat. "Try again," she said, jumping clear.

She saw a slight flush on his face as he turned towards her, a flustered hesitancy in the way he hefted his knife. *It's not shame,* she realised. *I'll have to stop jumping on him.*

For the next four days she spent an hour at night and another in the morning attempting to teach him the basics of the knife, finding it a mostly hopeless task. He was big and strong but had none of the speed or agility required to match even her weakest efforts. In the end she told him to put the knife away and concentrated on unarmed combat. He did better at this, mastering the simpler combinations of kick and punch with relative ease, even landing a stinging blow on her arm as they engaged in some light sparring.

"I'm sorry," he gasped as she rubbed at the bruise.

"For what? My fault for being too"—she ducked under his

guard, delivered a hard open-handed smack to his cheek and twisted away before he could react—"slow. That's enough for tonight. Let's eat."

She was aware allowing him to stay was another indulgence, meeting a need for human company unfulfilled since her escape from Al Sorna. Also, he had taken on the role of menial without complaint, making the fire, seeing to the horses and cooking the meals every night with an almost martial efficiency. *This is unfair,* she thought, watching him cut strips of bacon onto the skillet. *I don't need his help. And the way he looks at me . . .* It wasn't lustful exactly, or leering in any way. More a kind of longing. *Still just a boy.*

The High Keep came into view the next day, a jagged spike in the distance. From the tales she had heard of the place she had expected something grander, taller, a fabled castle fit for her father's martyrdom, but its lack of glamour became more obvious the closer they came. There were large holes in the walls and jagged gaps in the battlements, as if some giant had come along and taken a few bites out of the stonework. The road on the earthen ramp leading up to the gates was marked by patches of broken stone and home to a herd of long-horned mountain goats, feeding on the weeds sprouting from the paving and paying them scant heed as they passed.

"It's amazing!" Arken enthused as they stood before the gate, looking up at the walls rising above. "Never knew a tower could rise so high."

A squeal of metal called their attention to a door set into the gate, seeing an aged face peering out from the shadowed interior. "Got nothing here worth stealing," it said.

Reva made the sign of the Trueblade and the hostility faded from the face. "Best come in," it said then disappeared back into the gloom.

The old man stood back as she entered. Reva found it impossible to guess his age, anywhere past his seventieth year was her best estimate from the sagging wrinkles dominating his features. He wore mean clothing which she doubted had seen a wash-stone for some months, his torso wrapped in a threadbare blanket. He carried a head-high staff, more, she suspected, for support than armament from the way he leaned on it. "Vantil," he introduced himself. "And I think I know who you are." He nodded at Arken, left standing outside with the horses. "Him I don't."

"He has my trust," Reva said.

That seemed to be enough for Vantil as he began hobbling towards a steep flight of stone steps. "'Spect you want to see the chamber first."

"Yes." Reva found her heart was beating harder than it had when she faced Ranter and his brothers. "Yes I would like that."

It was just a room. Larger than the others they passed on the way, and in a similar state of disrepair, but still just a room, chill stone and shadow, empty save for a high-backed chair facing the door. At her request Vantil provided a torch and she began to scour the shadows, playing the flame over the walls, behind the pillars, beneath the chair.

"Don't you want to pray before the chair?" Vantil asked, clearly puzzled by her behaviour.

Reva ignored the question, completing her first search of the room and immediately starting another, then another. Every corner of the chamber examined, every possible hiding place prodded, every shadow banished with the torch. *Nothing.*

"How long have you been here?" she asked Vantil.

"Came not long after the Trueblade fell."

"You must know what I seek here."

The old man shrugged. "To offer prayers for the Trueblade. To speak to the Father in the place of his holy martyrd—"

"He had a sword. Here in this room when he died. Where is it?"

Vantil could only shake his head in bafflement. "No sword here, and I know this keep better than any living soul. Everything got taken, if not by the Darkblade's cutthroats then by the Fief Lord's House Guards."

"The Darkblade didn't take it," she muttered. "When did the Fief Lord's men come?"

"They come every year, make sure the place is empty of pilgrims. We hide in the mountains until they're gone. The last visit was two months ago."

So many miles for nothing. It wasn't here, Al Sorna's men didn't take it which left the Fief Lord, in Alltor.

"Do you have somewhere I can rest for tonight?" she asked Vantil.

"The blood of the Trueblade is welcome here for as long as she likes." He fidgeted for a moment, his staff beating on the stones a few times. "The, ah, prayers?" he asked.

Reva gave the chamber a final glance. *An empty chair in an empty room.* No sign of the Trueblade, not even a bloodstained stone to mark his passing. *Did he ever think of me?* she wondered. *Did he even know I lived?*

"The Father knows well the depth of my love for the Trueblade," she told Vantil, moving to the door. "I'll need a bed for the boy as well."

CHAPTER FOUR
Frentis

He found a hiding place in the hills several miles from the villa, a cluster of rocks atop a rise affording a clear view of the surrounding scrub desert, with sufficient brushwood for fuel and a rudimentary shelter. He set the stallion loose, whipping it towards the south in the hope it would lead any pursuers away. She continued to bleed that first night, thick streams of red flowing from her nose, ears and eyes, the dampness on her trews indicating she bled from everywhere she could. He stripped her and continued to wipe the blood away until, slowly, the flow began to ebb. She lay pale, naked and senseless, her breathing shallow, no fluttered eyes or groans to signal she might be dreaming. It occurred to Frentis that she might never wake, and if so, he could well be sitting here watching over her corpse for the rest of his life. The binding was as strong as ever, the itch vanished. He was hers again, even though she was defenceless, even though he wanted to sink his knife into her chest over and over. Instead he nursed her, kept her warm and sheltered against the night's chill, until her eyes snapped open on the morning of the third day.

She smiled when she saw him, gratitude shining in her eyes. "I knew you couldn't abandon me, my love."

Frentis stared back, hoping she saw the hatred in his gaze, and said nothing.

She pushed aside the cloak he had used to cover her, stretching and flexing her limbs. She was thinner, but still lithe and strong . . . and beautiful. It made him hate her even more.

"Oh don't sulk," she said with a groan. "They were a necessity. For us as well as the Ally. You'll understand in time."

She grimaced at the sight of her blood-soiled clothing but pulled on the black cotton shirt and trews without hesitation. "Do we have food?"

He pointed to the only game he had been able to catch, a rock snake, caught, skinned and filleted the day before. He hung the strips of meat over a low-burning fire to smoke, finding it surprisingly tasty fare.

The woman fed on the remaining snake with evident gusto, grunting in pleasure as she chewed and swallowed. "A man of unending talents indeed," she said when finished, grease shining on her lips. "What a fine husband you'll make."

They struck out in a north-easterly direction before the sun grew too hot to permit travel. A shallow rain pool nestling in a shaded crevice amidst the rocks provided a decent supply of water, though the going was hard due to the meagre sustenance of the last few days. A day and a half of slogging through the scrub brought them in sight of the coast, the woman judging them a good twenty miles north of Alpira.

"The port of Janellis lies another half-day north," she said. "We'll need to do some stealing, now that we're just beggars in rags."

Frentis hadn't stolen anything of true value since his days as a pickpocket on the streets of Varinshold, the thievery he had been encouraged to indulge in during his time at the Order House had been much less lucrative in monetary terms. It transpired his childhood skills hadn't deserted him, a few hours wandering the streets of Janellis netted two full purses and a decent collection of jewellery, sufficient for new clothes and a room at a suitably unremarkable inn. They were husband and wife again, newly wed and in the flush of marital bliss, seeking a ship to the northern ports to visit relatives. The innkeeper recommended a merchantman due to depart for Marbellis the next morning.

"I was expecting more of a reaction," the woman mused that night, lying next to him. Her using had been gentler tonight, she had kissed him for the first time, trying to make their intimacy a reality he supposed. The binding forced him to reciprocate, to kiss and caress, hold her close as she shuddered against him. Afterwards she entwined her legs with his, fingers smoothing over the hard muscle of his belly.

"The wife and son of their fallen Hope die in a fiery calamity," she said. "And not a voice speaks of it."

Frentis willed the itch to return, to bring back the wonderful liberating agony that had allowed him to *move*, to be a man who saved rather than killed. He was careful to keep the truth from his thoughts, calling up images likely to provoke guilt and despair in an effort to mask the true outcome of their mission. *The farm-hand, the innkeeper, the boy staring up from the bed . . .*

"Perhaps the Emperor has stifled the news," she wondered. "Sparing his people the shock of it. First the Hope, now this, just as he's about to announce a new Choosing. Not that there's anyone to choose now that bitch is dead." She giggled a little, sensing his surprise. "I'm afraid I wasn't entirely honest, darling. It wasn't the boy's name on the list, it was his mother. He was just my little lesson for you. No, she was the prize, the one name that had to be struck through, Emeren Nasur Ailers, the Emperor's choice as the new Hope, future Empress of the Alpiran Empire." She lay her head on his shoulder, voice fading as sleep took her. "Doesn't matter who he chooses now, all hope is gone . . ."

The voyage to Marbellis took another eight days, all the time playing the loving young couple for the merchantman's crew. They were a cheerful lot, given to ribald jokes and unsolicited advice concerning Frentis's husbandly duties, although his meagre Alpiran forced him to limit his responses to embarrassed laughter. In their cabin at night, when she was done, he would use the limited freedom allowed him to explore the scar where the itch had burned. There was a definite change in the texture now, the smoothness more discernible, and he had a sense it might have grown in size. But still no itch, no freeing surge of pain. *Grow,* he implored continually, trying to keep his frustration in check lest she sense it.

They docked at Marbellis with the morning tide, exchanging farewells and a final bout of raucous banter with the sailors as they descended the gangplank. "Right." The woman turned to survey the city beyond the quay. "Time to find some scum."

Like all ports, Marbellis had districts where wise feet didn't tread. In Varinshold it had been the entire western quarter, here it was smaller, a cramped slum of listing terraces clustered around the warehouse district. As they walked the streets, evidence of the Realm Guard's occupation was still plain in the gaps in the terraces and patches of ash-blackened wall. The bustle of the docks and the liveliness of the people told of a city that had healed a great deal in the years since the war, but the poorer recesses still showed the scars of battle.

"They say a thousand women or more were raped when the walls fell," the woman commented as they passed a hollowed-out shell that had once been a home. "Many of them had their throats cut afterwards. Is that how your people celebrate victory?"

I wasn't here, he wanted to say but stilled his tongue. *Here or not, doesn't matter. Every soul in the army was stained by Janus's war.*

"Ah, guilt for the crimes of others." She wagged a finger at him. "Won't do, my love. Won't do at all."

She chose a wineshop in the darkest alley they could find, ordering a bottle of red with a conspicuous display of coin then settling down to wait at a table facing the door. Several patrons, mostly men in various states of dishevelment, got up and left in the few minutes following their arrival, leaving them alone save for a man sitting in an alcove, the smoke from his pipe pluming in the shadow.

"Always go for the one who lingers in a place like this," the woman advised, lifting her wine cup to the man in the alcove and offering a bright smile. "He'll have the keenest eye for opportunity."

The man took another puff on his pipe then rose and sauntered over to their table. He was short, wiry but with a fighter's face, displaying several gaps in the teeth he bared in a mirthless smile. Although Frentis judged him to be from northern climes he spoke to the woman in Alpiran.

"I speak the Realm's tongue," she replied. "And no, I have no need of five-leaf, thank you."

The man inclined his head. "Ah, so it's the redflower you're after." His accent was thick and familiar, Nilsaelin. He pulled a chair over to sit down at the table, helping himself to wine. "Available, but expensive. Not like the Realm here. The Emperor thinks redflower a great evil."

"We're not looking to buy any . . . amusements." She gave a furtive glance around the shop, dropping her voice. "We need passage to the Realm."

The wiry man sat back in his chair, grunting in amusement. "Good luck to you. Alpiran ships don't dock there any more. You may have heard. There was this small matter of a war, y'see."

The woman leaned closer, voice soft and intent. "I have heard there are . . . other ships for hire. Ships not so bound by the Emperor's strictures."

His face lost any vestige of humour, the eyes narrowing. "Dangerous talk, from a stranger."

"I know." Her voice dropped to a whisper. "We need to be gone from here. My husband . . ." She nodded at Frentis. "He is from the Realm, we met before the war. Things were so much easier then, our union was blessed by my parents, but now." She put a sorrowful expression on her face. "The years since the war have been hard for us, shunned by family and neighbours alike. In the Realm though, perhaps we'll find a welcome."

The wiry man raised his eyebrows, giving Frentis a long look of appraisal. "From the Realm, eh? Whereabouts?"

"Varinshold."

"Yeh, I can hear that in your voice. What brought you to the empire? You look more a soldier than a merchant."

"A sailor," he said. "Started as a cabin boy when things got difficult in the quarter. Needed to leave."

"Difficult how?"

"One Eye."

"Ah." The wiry man drained his wine cup. "A name I know. Y'heard he died years ago now?"

"Yes. I didn't weep."

A faint smile twisted his lips. "I might have a name or two for you. But it'll cost."

"We can pay," the woman assured him, displaying the fullness of her purse.

He stroked his chin, giving every impression of careful consideration before nodding. "Wait here. I'll be back by the ninth bell."

The woman watched him leave before turning to Frentis with a raised eyebrow. "One Eye?"

He drank some wine, saying nothing until she flared the binding. "My scars," he hissed through the pain. "He was the one who gave me my scars. My brothers killed him for it."

"So," she murmured, letting the binding fade, "you were one of the Messenger's." There was a gravity to her voice as she said this, an unwelcome realisation. The look she turned on him was intense in its scrutiny, like the time in the temple, only this time she refrained from torture. After a moment she blinked, shaking her head and patting his hand. "Forgive my doubts, beloved. But the centuries have made me cautious."

She rose from the table, adjusting the short sword beneath her cloak. "We'd best adjourn to await our benefactor."

They climbed onto the roof of a shed overlooking the alley and waited. The wiry man returned a good deal before the ninth bell, with four rather larger companions. They entered the shop in a rush, re-emerging almost as quickly. The largest of the wiry man's companions rounded on him, hushed threats accompanied by hard jabs to the chest.

"Don't kill any," the woman whispered. "And keep the lingerer conscious."

It was Frentis's experience that the larger and more aggressive a man was, the poorer his fighting ability. Large men, especially those employed in criminal pursuits, were more accustomed to intimidation than combat. So it was scant surprise to find the man he dropped behind failed to duck the blow that crunched into the base of his skull, or that his even larger companion simply gaped and failed to react to the spinning kick that caught the side of his head. The third one, the least physically impressive, managed to pull his knife free before the woman's punch found the nerve centre behind his ear. The fourth was swift enough to swing at her with a cudgel. She ducked under it, delivered a knee-cap-smashing backward kick and finished him with a blow to the temple.

She drew her sword and advanced on the wiry man, now cowering against the alley wall, hands raised and eyes averted. She placed the point of the sword under his chin and forced his face up. "We'll take those names now."

"This is supposed to impress me?" The smuggler looked down at the wiry man's beaten and bloody form with a mix of disdain and amusement. He had led them, after some persuasion, to a warehouse seemingly full of nothing but tea chests. The smuggler, plus several crew-mates were playing dice behind a wall that wasn't a wall. He was a powerfully built man, speaking in a Meldenean accent, with a sabre propped within easy reach. His comrades were all similarly well armed.

"This is a demonstration," the woman said, tossing the smuggler a bulging purse. "Of the consequences of failing to keep a bargain."

The smuggler considered the purse a moment then aimed a kick at the wiry man's huddled back. "This one goes about with four others. Where're they?"

"They felt sleepy." The woman held up their remaining purse plus a clutch of the jewelled bracelets Frentis had stolen. "Yours when we reach the Realm. This one says you're due to make another run past the King's excisemen. Consider us just a little extra cargo."

The smuggler pocketed his new earnings then waved a hand at two of his men, nodding at the wiry man. They hauled him upright, dragging him off to the dark recesses of the warehouse. "I'm grateful for the business, but he shouldn't have told you my name."

"I've already forgotten it," the woman assured him.

The smuggler's vessel was little larger than the river barges Frentis remembered from childhood, but with a deeper hull and a taller sail. The crew numbered only ten men besides the captain, moving about their tasks with quiet efficiency and none of the ribald chatter of the merchantman's sailors. They were pointed to a small section of deck near the prow and told not to move from it, meals were brought to them and none of the smugglers attempted to engage them in conversation. It made for a dismal voyage, unleavened by the woman's unending voice and a thick bank of fog greeting them halfway across the Erinean on the fourth day out.

"I've only been to your Realm once," the woman said. "This must have been, oh, a century and a half ago. The scryers had picked out a minor noble who was likely to scheme his way to Kingship in a few years. It was a fairly easy kill as I recall, the man was a pig, ruled by his appetites, all I had to do was play the harlot. I killed him before he could touch me, of course. A single punch to the centre of the chest, a difficult technique I'd been trying to master for years. It was odd, but when Janus started his rise several decades later, the Ally gave no instruction for his death. Seems your mad king fit his plans perfectly."

The fog began to lift in the early evening of the seventh day, revealing the dark mass of the Realm's southern coastline a few miles off the port bow. The captain ordered a change of course, the small ship tacking towards the west. Frentis kept a close watch on the misted shore until a familiar landmark came into view, a free-standing column of rock nestled in a narrow cove.

"Something of interest?" the woman enquired, sensing his recognition.

"The Old Man of Uhlla's Fall," he said.

"Meaning?"

"We're about thirty miles east of South Tower."

"Can we land here?"

The Wolfrunners had spent the months prior to the mustering at South Tower chasing smugglers along this coast, and he knew the channel surrounding the Old Man was far too narrow for a ship, but an easy prospect for the smuggler's rowboat. He nodded.

"The captain first," she said, moving towards the steps leading down into the hold. "I'll see to the lower deck."

For all his ruthlessness and impressive physique the captain proved a feeble opponent, barely managing a parry with his sabre before the short sword took him in the chest. The first mate was a tougher prospect, fending him off with a boat hook for several seconds, calling for help in between voicing curses in a language Frentis didn't know. But curses and courage availed him nothing. He died hard but, like the rest of the crew, he died.

"Why is it called Uhlla's Fall?" the woman asked. They were on the bluffs overlooking the cove, the rowboat abandoned on the shingle beach below. Beyond the Old Man the smugglers' ship ploughed a steady course towards the rocks beneath the cliffs, the tiller having been lashed in place by the tightest of the woman's knots.

"Never thought to ask," Frentis said, not caring that she would sense the lie. Caenis had told him the story, the cove had been named for a woman, lovelorn when her man was called to sea in service to some forgotten king's war. Every day she would climb the Old Man's treacherous flanks to stand on the summit and watch for his return. For weeks then months she climbed, through sun and rain, snow and gale. Then one day his ship hove into view, and when she could see him waving from the prow, she cast herself from the Old Man, finding death on the rocks below. For he had been untrue to her before he sailed, and she wished that he witness her end.

They watched the ship carry its lifeless crew onto the rocks, the hull splintering with a booming crack, the flailing sail dragged into the waves by the swaying mast. It was already half-sunk when they turned away. Night was coming in fast and a stiff breeze brought the sea's chill to sting at their faces.

"Is your face known in South Tower?" the woman asked.

This time his reply was truthful, "I doubt there are any who would recall it." With Vaelin Al Sorna in attendance when the King's grand army gathered for invasion, who was likely to remember any other brother of the Sixth Order? He cherished all his memories of Vaelin but to stand beside him in a crowd was to know what it was to be invisible.

The journey to South Tower took the rest of the night, the woman having no desire to linger near the site of a shipwreck sure to attract salvage hunters before long. The sun was rising over the rooftops of the town by they time they paused to rest. South Tower was walled all around, the structure that gave it its name rising above the other buildings, a slender crenellated lance reaching into the morning sky. They entered via the western gate, still man and wife. He noticed she seemed to have forsaken all other guises and wondered if she had come to believe it was true.

The guards on the gate were thorough in searching them, finding them weaponless, their swords having been concealed in a grassy mound a mile away, and possessed of just enough coin to permit entry. One of them questioned the woman's curious accent but Frentis told him she was from the Northern Reaches which seemed to satisfy him. They were allowed entry with a stern warning that vagrancy was not tolerated within the walls and they had to be gone by the tenth bell if they failed to find a lodging.

The South Tower from which Frentis set sail six years before had possessed all the bustle and noise of a thriving port, the quay crowded with ships waiting to carry the army across the Erinean. This was a quieter place, the streets free of the laden carts and hawkers he remembered, sloping down to a harbour where at most a dozen ships were berthed. *No more silk, no more spices,* he thought, recalling the colours and scents of the market. *Janus cost us more than just blood.*

They found an inn near the tower precincts and ate a meal served by a plump woman who fussed around them with an energy born of having little else to occupy her time. "The Northern Reaches you say?" she gushed at the woman. "Long way from home, deary."

The woman clasped Frentis's hand, caressing the back of it with her thumb. "I'd have travelled the whole world if he'd asked me."

"Aww, aren't you the loveliest. It was all I could do to walk across the room for the bugger I was shackled to." Their heart-warming story earned a free helping of apple pie and a discount on the room.

There was no using that night, she sat on the bed, silent and immobile whilst he stood by the window watching the street. There was a tenseness to her he hadn't seen before, a wariness to her gaze. *She doesn't know what's coming,* he decided.

The realisation earned him a stern look of rebuke, but she held off on flaring the binding. She rarely hurt him now, and there had been no repeat of the intense scrutiny from the wineshop in Marbellis. *She thinks me hers completely,* he thought. *Like a dog whipped to the perfect pitch of obedience.* His hands burned to explore the scar again, feel the smooth, healed flesh that broke the pattern. He kept the imprecation in his mind as quiet as he could, but never let it falter: *Grow!*

The moon had risen by the time a shadow played across the

cobbles on the street outside, its owner unseen and moving with an unhurried fluency. Frentis turned to the door and the woman rose to her feet. For the first time he could remember they were unarmed and wondered if it was by accident or design.

There was a soft knock on the door and the woman nodded at Frentis to open it. The man standing outside was equal in stature to Frentis though at least a decade older, with sharp but handsome features, his black hair swept back from a smooth forehead. He was dressed in plain clothes and sturdy boots, scuffed from many miles of travel. Like them, he was unarmed but Frentis knew a warrior when he saw one. It was plain in the set of his shoulders, the way his green eyes took in every detail of the room in a single glance, lingering first on Frentis then fixing on the woman, instinct finding the greatest threat.

"Please come in," the woman said.

The man entered slowly, keeping a good two arms' lengths from the woman and standing close to the window.

"He fears us, beloved," the woman observed as Frentis closed the door.

A flicker of anger passed across the man's well-made face. "I fear nothing but the loss of the Father's love," he said, the accent cultured but clearly Cumbraelin.

The woman gave a soft sigh of disgust, but kept any ridicule from her tone. "You have a name?"

"My name is for the Father to know."

Frentis had heard this before, when they had been chasing after those child-stealing fanatics in Nilsael. They had been led by a priest, excommunicated by the Church of the World Father for heresy but still a priest in his own mind, crying out his prayers in defiance before Dentos put an arrow through his eye.

The woman turned to him with a raised eyebrow as she sensed his remembrance. "He's a priest," he told her. "They give up their birth names when they take their orders. The church gives them a new one, known only to them and their god."

A fresh curl of disdain twisted the woman's lips before she

forced a smile at the priest. "I assume great promises were made in return for your assistance."

"Not promises, assurances." The man became agitated, a red flush creeping into his cheeks. "Proof was given. You do the World Father's work. Is this not so?"

Frentis could tell the woman was suppressing a laugh. "Of course. Forgive my testing words. But we have to be careful. The, ah, servants of the World Father have many enemies."

"And different faces, it seems," the priest said in a soft murmur.

"I was told you would have word," the woman went on. "Of Al Sorna."

"He was in Varinshold a month ago. The heretic King sent him to the Northern Reaches as Tower Lord."

"I was given to understand there was a stratagem. Something either fatal or damaging."

"There was. The results were . . . unexpected."

"They usually are where he's concerned."

"Steps have been taken. The Reaches are not so far." He produced a small leather wallet, placing it on the bed and stepping back.

The woman reached for the wallet and briefly leafed through the contents. "My list is complete," she said. "We have an appointment in Varinshold."

"Another name has been added. Although this is a task well within my skills, the Messenger insisted it be left to you. The Tower Lord of the Southern Shore keeps an efficient household, but there are occasions when he makes himself vulnerable."

The woman extracted a sheet from the wallet, a block-printed image of a white flame on a black background. Frentis knew it well, the fanatics the Wolfrunners hunted would deface the homes of the Faithful with it after killing the parents and stealing the children: the Pure Flame of the World Father's Love.

"I was told to tell you that the Fief Lord alone is not enough," the woman said. "The whore has to die too."

His gaze tracked from her feet to her face, eyes bright with enmity and voice heavy with righteous conviction. "All whores have to die."

She moved in a blur, appearing in front of him, her face inches from his, hands open in clawlike readiness.

The priest took an involuntary step back before mastering himself.

"When I see you again," she said. "Perhaps I'll arrange for you to meet this god you're so fond of."

The priest's gaze shifted between them and Frentis had a sense of how threatening they must appear; her fury and his stillness. *He has no notion of what we are,* he realised. *No clue as to the true nature of his bargain.*

The priest moved to the door in silence and left without a word.

"Go and kill that sow downstairs," the woman instructed. "We made too great an impression on her."

"Your realm is an insane place," she commented the next morning, watching the Tower Lord of the Southern Shore and his lady hand out alms to the poor. There were only two South Guard in attendance despite the large number of beggars lined up outside the tower gate.

"In Volaria," she went on, "no-one goes hungry, slaves are no use when they starve. Those freeborn too lazy or lacking in intelligence to turn sufficient profit to feed themselves are made slaves so they can generate wealth for those deserving of freedom, and be fed in return. Here, your people are chained by their freedom, free to starve and beg from the rich. It's disgusting."

There weren't always so many, he thought but didn't say. *But I was one of the few, even though I never begged.*

They took some rags from a pair of drunken vagrants found passed out in a dockside alley, draping the stinking garments over their own clothes and veiling their faces with scrapings of dirt and threadbare cloth. The plump innkeeper's kitchen had supplied two knives of good steel, freshly sharpened and well hidden beneath their rags.

The Tower Lord stood next to a table piled high with clean clothing, greeting each stooped unfortunate with a smile and a kind word, waving their thanks away. His lady looked to the children, handing out sweets or guiding them and their mothers, if they had one, to a secondary line headed by a pair of grey-robed brothers from the Fifth Order.

Grow, he implored the itch as they joined the line, shuffling ever closer to the Tower Lord. But there was no answer from the itch, not now and not last night when he held a pillow over the plump woman's sleeping face.

"See to the guards," the woman whispered. "The generous fellow is mine. Oh, how I despise hypocrisy."

Grow!

The Tower Lord's face was vaguely familiar, though Frentis couldn't conjure his name. Had they met during the war? A Sword of the Realm somehow spared the slaughter to return home to Lordship and charitable pursuits? He greeted every unfortunate differently, free of stock phrases or forced conviviality, some even by name. "Arkel! How's the leg? . . . Dimela, still off the grog I trust?"

Grow!

He reached under his rags, gripping the sandalwood handle of the knife.

"Ah, new faces." The Tower Lord smiled as they reached the head of the line. "Welcome, friends. And what can I call you?"

GROW!

"Hentes Mustor," the woman said, loud enough for all the crowd to hear.

The Tower Lord frowned. "I don't . . ."

Her first blow was deliberately non-fatal, designed to produce as much shock amongst the onlooking poor folk as possible, this was as much theatre as murder. The Tower Lord gasped in pained astonishment as the knife blade sank into his shoulder, the woman ripping it free, crying, "In the name of the Trueblade!" before bringing it down again, this time straight at his heart. The Tower

Lord, surely once a soldier, managed to raise his arm in time to block the knife, the blade sinking deep into his forearm.

The two guards were quick to recover from the shock, charging forward with pole-axes lowered, the one in front pitching to the ground as Frentis's knife throw found the gap in his armour between chest and neck. Frentis darted forward, snatching up the fallen pole-axe and delivering an overhead swing at the second guard. His parry was swift, however, and his riposte the precise jab of a veteran, nearly skewering Frentis through the thigh. He managed to side-step the thrust and replied with a whirling sweep to the guard's legs, sending him sprawling.

There was a shout behind him and he turned to see the woman advancing on the Tower Lord, now on his back, bleeding freely from both wounds, legs working to push himself away.

"Die, heretic!" the woman screamed, raising the knife. "Such is the fate of the Father's ene—"

A pair of skinny arms wrapped themselves around her, pulling her back. It was one of the ragged beggars, the grog-addicted woman the Tower Lord knew by name, Dimela.

The woman jerked her head back into Dimela's face, breaking teeth in a plume of red. The beggar-woman howled but held on. More arms reached out to grab the Tower Lord's assailant, an old man clutching at her legs, a cripple swinging his crutch at her midriff, more and more closing in until she was lost from view in a press of rags and unwashed flesh.

Please! Frentis begged. *Please die!*

But the binding surged, fiercer and stronger than ever. *HELP HER!*

He delivered a hard kick to the helmeted head of the fallen guard then charged into the throng of flailing poor folk, the pole-axe laying about with deadly effect, four of them felled in as many seconds as he tried to hack his way through, all the time hoping the binding would suddenly fade as the beggars tore the woman's life from her.

He was halfway through the crowd when it happened, a blast

of heat and a surge of flame burning a hole in the centre of the throng, people reeling back in shock and pain, screams and panic amidst the sudden smoke.

Frentis fought his way through the dazed remnants of the crowd, finding her on her knees, bloodied as he knew she would be, both from use of the stolen gift and the attentions of the mob. Her face was a red mask of malice and fury. Behind her Dimela's body lay in a twisted tangle of scorched rags and flesh. Frentis dragged the woman to her feet and they ran.

"One hundred and seventy-two years," she said, voice soft, reflective, but the anger still shining in her eyes. "That's how long it's been since I last failed, beloved."

Frentis had known many sewers in his time, they made for fine hideaways or speedy thoroughfares beneath the streets of Varinshold and later he had helped Vaelin seize Linesh via its shit-choked underground channels. This one was the cleanest so far, wider too with well-pointed brickwork and a ledge or two to rest on. The stench, however, was everything he remembered.

Making for open country would have been suicide with the South Guard sure to be ranging in strength, so he followed his street-born instincts and dragged her to the sewers. They followed the flow to the outlets in the harbour, waiting for night when the evening tide would allow them to swim away.

"One hundred and seventy-two years." She turned her gaze on him, beseeching a response and freeing his mouth of the binding.

She wants comfort, he thought. *Commiseration for her failed murder.* Not for the first time, he wondered at the depth of her madness.

"There's a difference," he said.

She was baffled, shaking her head and gesturing for him to continue.

For the first time in weeks he smiled. "Between a hungry beggar and a sated slave."

Chapter Five
Vaelin

"Our patrol put their numbers at about four thousand. Crossing from the ice here." Captain Adal's finger picked out a point on the map unfurled on the table before them. "They were following a south-westerly course."

"Last time they made straight for North Tower," Dahrena said. "Killing everything in their path."

"Four thousand," Vaelin said. "A large force but hardly a horde."

"Just a vanguard, no doubt," Adal replied. "Seems they learned a lesson from their last attempt."

"As I understood it, the Horde was destroyed in their last attempt."

"There were some survivors," Dahrena said. "A few hundred. Just women and children. Father let them go, though there were many who argued for their death. We always wondered if there were more, waiting beyond the ice to plague us again."

Adal straightened, turning to Vaelin and speaking formally. "My lord, I request permission to sound the muster."

"Muster?"

"Every man of fighting age in the Reaches will be called to arms. Within five days we will have six thousand men under arms plus the North Guard."

"We'll also send word to the Eorhil and the Seordah," Dahrena added. "If they respond as they did before, the full army will number more than twenty thousand. But it will take weeks to marshal them. Enough time for the Horde to cross in strength whilst their vanguard wreaks havoc on the settlements to the north."

Vaelin reclined in his chair, regarding the lines Adal had drawn on the map. They had ridden hard to be back at the tower before nightfall where Adal selected one of the more detailed maps of the Reaches from the collection in the Lord's chamber. From outside came the tumult of men readying for war as North Guard and Captain Orven's men sharpened their steel and saddled their horses. He had hoped the days of maps and battle plans were behind him, that here in the Reaches there would be no more need to orchestrate slaughter, but as ever, war contrived to find him. He took some solace from the fact that the blood-song was strangely muted, not entirely devoid of warning, but free of the strident urgency he recalled from when he had planned the attack at the Lehlun Oasis, the plan that cost Dentos his life.

"How strong was the Horde when it came before?" he asked.

"We can only guess, my lord," Adal said. "They moved in a great mass and formed no ranks or regiments. Brother Hollun's official history puts the figure at over one hundred thousand, including children and old folk. The Horde was not so much an army as a nation."

"The northern settlements have been warned?"

Dahrena nodded. "Gallopers were sent as soon as the news reached us. They will be readying their own defences, but their numbers are small and without help they won't last long."

"Very well." Vaelin rose. "Captain, sound your muster. Choose good men to take charge of the levies and secure the tower and the town against siege. We will lead the North Guard and the King's men north to provide what aid we can to the settlers."

"Over half my guardsmen are posted throughout the Reaches," Adal pointed out, his gaze flicking to Dahrena. "That gives us barely fifteen hundred men."

"All the better." Vaelin lifted his canvas-wrapped bundle from the table and went to the stairwell. "We'll ride so much faster. Lady Dahrena, I realise you may wish to remain here, but I must request that you accompany us."

She frowned in surprise and he knew she had been preparing an argument against being left behind. "I . . . shall be glad to, my lord."

They rode hard until the night grew dark, making camp in the foothills about twenty miles north of the tower. Alornis had been furious as he said good-bye at the tower steps, but he remained adamant. "Battle is no place for an artist, sister."

"And what am I supposed to do?" she said. "Just sit around for days worrying over your fate?"

He took hold of her hands. "I doubt these are capable of remaining idle." He pressed a kiss against her forehead and went to where a guardsman stood holding Flame's reins. "Besides," he said, climbing into the saddle, "I need you to be seen about the place. The presence of the Tower Lord's sister will reassure the townsfolk. No doubt many will be asking for news. Tell them everything is well in hand."

"And is it?"

He trotted closer, leaning down and speaking softly. "I have no idea."

The North Guard demonstrated an effortless ability to form a camp within what seemed like moments, fires readied, horses tethered, saddles stacked and pickets posted with no shouted orders or instruction from Captain Adal. The King's Guard made something of a contrast with their neatly aligned fires and tents, plus an end-of-day inspection from Captain Orven who fined two men for poorly polished breastplates.

"Makes a change from the desert, eh, my lord?" he said, joining Vaelin at the fire he shared with Dahrena and Adal. He had found a wolf fur from somewhere and tugged it about his shoulders before blowing into his hands.

"You were at the Bloody Hill?" Vaelin asked.

"I was. My first battle in fact. Took an Alpiran lance in the leg during the last charge, lucky for me. The healers took me to Untesh and put me on a ship back to the Realm. Otherwise, I'd've been at the King's side when the city fell."

"They killed everyone but him, didn't they?" Dahrena asked.

"Indeed, my lady. I'm the only survivor from my entire regiment."

"Seems Alpirans are just as savage as the Horde, then," Adal commented. "My people have many stories of the oppression they suffered at the hands of the Emperors."

"They weren't savages," Vaelin said. "Just angry. And not without good reason." He turned to Dahrena. "I need to know more about the Horde. Who are they? What do they want?"

"Blood," Adal said. "The blood of any not born into their Horde."

"That's their creed? Death to all outsiders?"

"It's what they do. We never had any notion of their creed. The language they speak is an unfathomable babble of clicks and snarls, and any prisoners we took were too savage to keep alive long enough to get any sense from them."

"I heard they fight with beasts," Orven said. "Giant cats and hawks."

"That they do," Adal said. "We were fortunate they never had more than a few hundred of the cats. Not an easy thing to stand in ranks facing a charge from those monsters, I can tell you. The spear-hawks, though, they had those by the thousand, screaming out of the sky to tear at your eyes. Even today, you'll see many a man in the Reaches sporting an eyepatch."

"How did you beat them?" Vaelin asked.

"How is any battle won, my lord? Guts, steel and"—Adal glanced at Dahrena with a small grin—"good intelligence of the enemy's dispositions."

Vaelin raised his eyebrows at her. "Good intelligence?"

She gave a somewhat forced yawn and got to her feet. "If you gentlemen will excuse me. I should rest for the morrow's journey."

◆   ◆   ◆

Two more days' riding brought them to the first settlement, a stockaded clutch of dwellings in the shadow of a ridge-back mountain, the southern slopes marked by numerous mine-works. They were greeted at the gate by a North Guard sergeant and a greatly worried town factor.

"Any news, my lady?" the factor asked Dahrena, sweat-damp hands clasping and releasing. "How long before they fall upon us?"

"We've seen no sign of them yet, Idiss," Dahrena assured him. There was a tightness to her voice that spoke of a palpable dislike. She gestured at Vaelin. "Do you have no greeting for your Tower Lord?"

"Oh, of course." The man gave Vaelin a hurried bow. "My apologies, my lord. Welcome to Myrna's Mount. We are *very* pleased to see you."

"Any word from the other settlements?" Vaelin asked him.

"None, my lord. I fear for them."

"Then we'd best not linger." Vaelin turned Flame away from the gate, pausing as the factor reached out to clutch at his reins.

"But surely, my lord, you can't leave us. We have just two hundred miners with swords, and only a dozen North Guard."

Vaelin looked at the man's hand on his reins until he removed it. "A good point, sir." He raised his gaze to the North Guard sergeant. "Gather your men. You ride on with us."

The sergeant glanced at Adal, receiving a nod in response, then marched off to collect his men.

"You leave us defenceless!" Idiss cried. "Naked before the Horde."

"Then you have my leave to make for North Tower," Vaelin told him. "The road behind us is clear. But if you care for this place and its people, perhaps you would prefer to stay and fight for them."

Idiss, it transpired, had a fast horse, raising a sizeable cloud of dust in its wake as he galloped south.

"The head of the Miners Guild has agreed to take on the factorship," Dahrena advised, emerging from the gate an hour later. "At my urging they've armed the womenfolk too, which gives them over three hundred and fifty swords to hold the wall." She mounted her mare and met Vaelin's gaze. "Idiss is a cowardly, greed-shrivelled soul, but he was right. If the Horde come, this place will fall in an hour, at most."

"Then it rests with us to ensure they never get here." He waved a command at the ranks of horsemen behind him and spurred towards the north.

They called at the three settlements north of Myrna's Mount over the next two days, finding only fearful miners and no word of the Horde. Thankfully, these were led by hardier souls than Idiss and their defences were well prepared. Vaelin offered each the option of making for Myrna's Mount where greater numbers might offer more protection, but they all refused.

"Been hewing stone from these hills near twenty years, m'lord," the factor at Slade Hill told him, a burly Nilsaelin with a large axe strapped across his back. "Didn't run from those frost-arses last time, not runnin' now."

They pressed on into the plains where the wind swept down with a chill that seemed to cut through clothing like a steel-tipped arrow cuts through armour.

"By the Faith!" Orven cursed through clenched teeth, blinking away tears as the wind lashed at his face. "Is it always like this?"

Adal laughed. "This is just a balmy summer day, Captain. You should try it in winter."

"There are no more mountains between us and the ice," Dahrena explained. "The Eorhil call it the black wind."

They halted after ten miles and Vaelin ordered scouts sent east, west and north. They all returned by late evening, having found no trace of the Horde.

"This makes no sense," Adal said. "They should be well into the mountains by now."

Dahrena suddenly straightened, her gaze switching to the west, eyes bright with expectation.

"My lady?" Vaelin asked.

"It seems we have company, my lord."

It came to him then, a faint rumble of thunder, but constant, and growing.

"Saddle up!" he barked striding to where Flame was tethered, sending men scrambling for their horses.

"There's no need," Dahrena called after him. "The Horde don't ride. We have other visitors."

The dust-cloud grew in the west, coming ever closer, the thunder rising as it neared. The first riders came into view, mounted on tall horses of varying colour, each carrying a lance with a horn bow strapped to every saddle, more and more resolving out of the dust until Vaelin lost count. They reined in a short distance away, the dust settling to reveal what must have been over two thousand riders, men and women. Their pale-skinned faces were an echo of the hawk-faced Seordah Vaelin had met years ago, their hair uniformly black and tied into braids. Their clothing was mostly of dark brown leather decorated with necklaces of bone or elk antler. They sat waiting in silence, not even a snort rising from their horses.

A lone rider trotted forward, making unbidden for Vaelin. He halted a few paces away, looking down on him in stern appraisal. He was not a tall man, but there was an evident strength to him, his face lined but possessed of the kind of leanness that made guessing his age difficult.

"What is your name?" the rider asked in harshly accented Realm Tongue.

"I have a few to choose from," Vaelin replied. "But the Seordah call me Beral Shak Ur."

"I know what the forest people call you, and why." The man reclined in his saddle a little, his features taking on a frown. "Ravens are rarely seen on these plains. If you want a name from us, you must earn it."

"I will, and gladly."

The rider grunted, reversing the hold on his lance and throwing it into the ground at Vaelin's feet. Despite the hardness of the earth the steel point was buried up to the hilt, the lance shuddering with the force of the throw. "I, Sanesh Poltar of the Eorhil Sil, bring my lance to answer Tower Lord's call."

"You are very welcome."

Dahrena came forward to welcome the Eorhil chieftain with a broad smile. "I never doubted you would find us, plains-brother," she said, reaching up to clasp his hand, their fingers entwining.

"We hoped to find the beast-people first," he replied. "Make you a gift of their skulls. But they leave us no tracks to follow."

"They elude us also."

This seemed to puzzle the horseman. "Even you, forest-sister?"

She shot a guarded look at Vaelin. "Even me."

That night they ate dried elk meat with the Eorhil. It was tough but tasty fare, improved by a few seconds over the fire, washed down with a thick white beverage possessed of a pungent aroma and a palpable kick of spirits.

"Faith!" Orven exclaimed, wincing after his first taste. "What is this?"

"Fermented elk milk," Dahrena said.

Orven suppressed a disgusted shudder and handed the fur-covered skin back to the young Eorhil woman who had appeared at his side as they gathered round the fire. "Thank you, lady. But no." She frowned then shrugged, saying something in her own language.

"She wants to know how many elk you've hunted," Dahrena translated.

"Elk? None," he replied, nodding and smiling at the young woman. "But many boar and deer. My family has a large estate."

Dahrena relayed his reply, provoking a puzzled exchange.

"She doesn't know what an estate is," Dahrena explained. "The Eorhil have no understanding of how one can own land."

"Or even that the plains they live on are owned by the crown," Adal put in. "One of the reasons they saw no need to fight the first Realm settlers. You can't claim something that can't be owned, so why fight over it?"

"Insha ka Forna," the young woman said to Orven, patting her chest.

"Steel in Moonlight," Dahrena said with a small smile. "Her name."

"Ah, Orven," the captain said, patting his own chest. "Orrvennn."

This provoked another exchange with Dahrena. "She wanted to know what it means. I told her it's the name of a great hero from legend."

"But it isn't," Orven said.

"Captain . . ." Dahrena paused to smother a chuckle. "When an Eorhil woman chooses to tell a man her given name, it's a *considerable* compliment."

"Oh." The captain gave Insha ka Forna a broad smile, finding it returned. "Is there a suitable response?"

"I think you just gave it."

A short while later Dahrena bade them good night and rose from the fire, making her way to the ingenious contrivance she had carried with her since leaving the tower. Seemingly little more than a bundle of elk-hide and wood, a few minutes' work formed it into a small but serviceable shelter, equal to any of the tents used by the King's Guard. Some of the North Guard carried similar items, though most were content to sleep in the open clad only in a wrapping of furs.

Vaelin waited for a time before going to speak to her. His questions had been mounting over the course of their journey and he had delayed long enough in seeking answers.

"My lady," he greeted her as she sat outside her shelter.

She didn't reply and he noticed her eyes were closed, her hair fluttering across her face in the chill wind with no sign she felt it.

"You can't talk to her now, my lord." Captain Adal appeared next to the shelter. His ebony features were outlined in red from the fires and tense in warning.

Vaelin looked again at Dahrena, seeing the absolute stillness of her face, the way her hands sat in her lap, absent of any twitch. The blood-song rose with a familiar note: recognition.

He gave the captain an affable nod and returned to the fire.

"Steel Water Creek," Dahrena said the next morning. "It's about forty miles north-east of here. It's the only supply of freshwater large enough to service so many this far south of the ice. It seems reasonable to assume the Horde will be camped there since they don't appear to be moving."

"Just a reasonable assumption?" Vaelin asked. "Is there no other source for this intelligence, my lady?"

She avoided his gaze and bit back an angry retort. "None, my lord. You are of course free to discount my advice."

"Oh, I think it would be churlish to ignore the words of my new First Counsel. Steel Water Creek it is."

They rode in a three-group formation, Vaelin with the North Guard and Orven's men in the centre and the Eorhil on both flanks. He had heard many tales of the horsemanship of the Eorhil and saw now they were well-founded, each rider moving in concert with their mount in an unconscious reflex, like a single animal forged to range across these plains. He was aware they were limiting their speed to keep pace with the Tower Lord's men, and one had opted to join their company for the ride. Insha ka Forna rode at Orven's side on a piebald stallion a hand taller than the captain's own warhorse, her braids streaming back from a face wearing a faintly smug expression.

It was late in the afternoon by the time they came upon them, a large camp on the eastern bank of the creek, numerous fires seeping smoke into the ice-chilled wind. Vaelin called a halt two hundred paces from the camp, signalling for both flanks to spread out and ordering his own men into battle formation. He took the canvas bundle from where it was lashed to his saddle, placing a hand on the largest knot. *One tug and it's free.* He knew it would shine very bright today, the sound it made as it cut the air would be another song of blood, one he sang so well. It had remained sheathed and bound since the day he faced the Shield of the Isles. He hadn't liked the way it felt when he drew it that day, the way it fit in his hand . . . so *comfortable*.

"My lord!" Captain Adal's shout brought his gaze back to the camp, seeing a solitary figure walking towards them. A cluster of people had gathered at the fringes of the camp, it may have been an illusion of the light and the distance but they all appeared thin to the point of emaciation: gaunt, flesh-denuded faces poking out from their furs, staring at their enemies with numb expectation free of any anger or hate.

"I see no weapons, my lord," Orven said.

"A trick, no doubt," Adal replied. "The Horde always had a thousand tricks."

Vaelin watched the lone figure continue towards them. He was squat but thin, like the rest of his people, and considerably older, walking with a slow but purposeful gait, aided by what seemed to be a large gnarled stick but soon revealed itself as a long thighbone from some unknown beast, covered all over with intricate carvings and script.

"*Shaman!*" Adal hissed, unlimbering his bow. "My lord, I request the honour of first blood."

"Shaman?" Vaelin asked.

"They command the war-beasts," Dahrena explained. "Train them, lead them in war. We never learned how they did it."

"He doesn't appear to have any beasts," Vaelin observed as the squat man came to a halt twenty yards away.

"More fool him," Adal said, raising his bow.

"Stop that!" Vaelin commanded, his voice snapping through the ranks, absolute in its authority.

Adal gaped at him, his bow still drawn. "My lord?"

Vaelin didn't look at him. "You are under my command. Obey my order or I'll have you flogged and dismissed."

He angled his head as he studied the squat man, ignoring Adal's choking fury as Dahrena sought to restrain him. The shaman took hold of the bone in both hands and held it out before him, trembling and swaying in the black wind.

Vaelin felt it then, the blood-song's note of greeting to a gifted soul. Dahrena stiffened in her saddle, her calming hand falling from Adal's shoulder. Vaelin inclined his head at the shaman. "It seems we are called to parley, my lady."

Fear made her eyes wide and her face white, but she nodded and they trotted forward, halting to dismount before the shaman. Up close his emaciation was a painful thing to see, the bones of his face white under skin that seemed no more than wet paper wrapping a butcher's leavings. A black-and-grey tangle of hair grew from his head to his shoulders, a few talismans hanging unpolished in the unkempt tresses. The tremble was not just fear, Vaelin saw, but hunger, bringing a harsh realisation: *They don't come for war, they come to die.*

"You have a name?" Vaelin asked him.

The shaman gave no response, planting the bone on the earth before him, both hands resting atop it, his gaze taking on owl-like focus as he stared into Vaelin's eyes. The gaze fixed him, drew him closer. There was a moment of concern as something stirred in his mind. *A trick, like Adal said.* But the blood-song was unwavering in its welcome and he let the stirring continue. It was like a memory, a forgotten vision of another time, but it was not his.

People, clad in furs, and beasts. Bears, huge white-furred terrors, all labouring through a blizzard. Many are wounded, many are children. Riders appear out of the blizzard, dressed all in black, swords and lances stabbing and slashing . . . blood on the snow . . . so much blood . . . The riders wheel and turn, laughing as they kill, more and more charging out of the snow as the fur-clad people scatter. A man raises a great bone-staff and his bears turn on the riders, mauling and rending, killing many . . . but there are more . . . there are always more . . .

The vision faded, the shaman's face still and unspeaking above the tip of his bone-staff.

Vaelin looked at Dahrena, noting the horror on her face. "You saw it?"

She nodded, hiding her trembling hands within her furs and drawing back a little. He could tell she wanted to flee, that this squat old man with no weapon save a length of bone, terrified her. But she stayed, drawing breath in gulps, refusing to look away.

Vaelin turned back to the shaman. "You flee these men, these riders?" It was clear from the man's frown he didn't understand a word. Vaelin sighed, glanced back at the ranks of guards and Eorhil, then *sang*. It was just a small note, unlikely to call forth any blood, conveying the sense of his query, coloured by his memory of the shaman's vision.

The old man straightened, eyes widening, then nodded. He met Vaelin's eyes again and soon another vision filled his mind.

A dark mass of people trekking across an ice field, the backs of their great white bears rising and falling amongst the throng as they flee, always westward, always away from the riders . . . no time to rest . . . no time to hunt . . . only time to flee . . . or fall out and die. The old people are first, then the younger children, the tribe bleeding its life away as it moves across the white expanse. The bears grow maddened by hunger, rending them from the shamans' control. Hardy warriors weep as they cut them down and share out their meat, for without their bears, what are they? By the time the plains are in sight, they know their nation has died . . . They ask for nothing save a peaceful death.

Dahrena wept as the vision faded, gasping as tears streamed down her face. "What callous fools we are," she whispered. Vaelin sang again, filling his song with the image of the battle tapestry from the tower; the Horde and its terrible beasts.

The shaman gave a disgusted grunt, replying with a vision of his own. *The battle is fierce, no quarter is given, cats and bears tear at each other with mindless fury, the spear-hawks blacken the sky as they meet in a roiling cloud above, birthing a rain of blood and feathers, the warriors fight with spear and bone-club. When the red day is done the Bear People have shown the Cat People the folly of war on the ice. They see them no more, for they take themselves off to the southern plains, soft and cowardly in their desire for easier prey.*

Bear People. Vaelin raised his gaze to the camp, seeing only starving men and women, a few children, no old folk, and no beasts at all. *They lost their bears, they lost their name.*

He looked again at the shaman, singing for the final time, recalling the image of the riders in black and ending the song with a questioning note, feeling the familiar wave of fatigue that told him he had sung enough for now.

For the first time the shaman spoke, his mouth twisting as it formed perhaps the only foreign word he knew. *"Volarriahnsss."*

He ordered the North Guard to give up half their rations and sent all but a dozen back to their postings. Captain Adal, whose sullen fury was becoming more irksome by the second, was dispatched south to call an end to the muster and send riders informing the Seordah their warriors were not needed.

"Cat People, Bear People," he hissed at Dahrena before leaving, just within Vaelin's earshot. "*They* are still Horde. They cannot be trusted."

"You didn't see, Adal," she whispered back, shaking her head. "The only thing we have to fear from them is the guilt of letting them die."

"This won't be popular," he warned. "Many will still call for vengeance."

"My father always took the right course, popular or not." She fell silent and Vaelin sensed she was looking in his direction. "Things have not changed so much."

The Eorhil took their leave in the evening, Sanesh Poltar raising a hand to Vaelin as his people took to their mounts. "Avensurha," he said.

"My name?" Vaelin asked.

The Eorhil chieftain pointed to the north where a single bright star was rising above the horizon. "Only one month in a lifetime does it shine so bright. It's said no wars can be fought under the light it brings."

He raised his hand again and turned his horse towards the east, galloping away with his people, all save one.

"She won't leave, my lord." Captain Orven stood at rigid attention, avoiding his gaze. Nearby Insha ka Forna was handing out strips of dried elk meat to a clutch of children, using hand gestures to warn them against bolting it down too quickly. "I asked the Lady Dahrena why. She said I, ahem, already knew."

"Do you want her to leave?"

The captain coughed, brows furrowing as he sought to formulate a reply.

"Congratulations, Captain." Vaelin clapped him on the shoulder and went to find Dahrena.

She was with the shaman, crouched next to an old woman propped on a litter. She was even thinner than the other tribesfolk, her chest rising and falling in shallow heaves, mouth agape and eyes unfocused. The shaman stared down at her with such a depth of desolate sorrow Vaelin had no need of any visions to tell him this was a man watching his wife's final moments.

Dahrena took a vial from her satchel and held it over the old woman's mouth, a few clear drops falling onto her parched tongue. She stirred, frowning a little, mouth closing over the fresh moisture. Some light returned to her eyes and the shaman bent down to take her hand, speaking softly in his own language. The words sounded harsh to Vaelin's ear, a guttural rush of noise, but even so, there was tenderness in it. *He tells her they're safe,* he surmised. *He tells her they have found refuge.*

The old woman's gaze tracked across her husband's face, the corners of her mouth curling as she tried to smile, then freezing as the light faded from her eyes and her chest halted its labour. The shaman gave no reaction, remaining crouched at her side, holding her hand, near as still as she.

Dahrena rose from the old woman's side and walked over to Vaelin. "I have something to tell you," she said.

"My people call it spirit walking." They sat together beside a fire on the periphery of the Bear People's camp. It was quiet, the tribe consuming their new supplies in silence and tending to their sick with not a voice raised in celebration. *They still think of themselves as dead,* Vaelin thought. *They lost their name.*

"It's difficult to describe," Dahrena continued. "Not really walking, more like flying, high above everything, seeing great swathes of the earth all at once. But I have to leave my body to do it."

"That's how you found these people," he said. "That's how you found the Horde."

She nodded. "Easier to plan a battle when you know the enemy's line of march."

"Does it hurt?" he asked, thinking of the blood that flowed whenever he sang for too long.

"No, not when I'm flying, but when I return . . . At first it was exhilarating, joyous. For who hasn't dreamt of flying? I'd heard tales of the Dark, and knew it to be a thing to fear. But the flying was so wonderful, so intoxicating. I had just said farewell to my twelfth year when it happened. I was in my bed, awake but content, my thoughts calm, or as calm as the thoughts of a thirteen-year-old girl can be. Then I was floating, looking down at a small girl in a large bed. I was fearful, thinking I had drifted into a nightmare. In my panic my thoughts turned to my father, and so I flew to him in his room, poring over papers late into the evening as he always did. He reached for his wineglass and knocked over an inkpot, staining his sleeve and cursing. I thought of Blueleaf, my horse, and flew to her in the stables. I thought of Kehlan and flew to him, where he was pounding herbs in his chamber with a mortar and pestle. What a wonderful dream this was, just think of something and I would fly to it, see them without their seeing me. And more, more than just them, the *colour* of them, the shine of their souls. My father was shrouded in a bright, pale blue, Blueleaf a soft brown and Kehlan seemed to flicker, red one minute, white the next. I flew high, as high as I dared, looking down at the entirety of the Reaches, all the shining souls, like the stars above reflected on a great mirror.

"But strangely, in this dream, I began to grow tired, and so I returned to my body. The bed felt a little chilly but not enough to prevent sleep. The next morning at breakfast father wore a shirt with an ink stain on the sleeve and I knew it had been no dream. It scared me, but not enough to stop me; the joy had been too great. And so I continued to fly, every spare moment, soaring out over the mountains and the plains, watching the Eorhil hunt the great elk, dancing in the storms that swept out of the ice. Then one day I flew out over the western ocean for miles and miles, hoping to glimpse the shore of the Far West. But the time grew long and I knew my father expected me at dinner, so I flew back to my body. It was like pulling on a skin made of ice, the shock of it made me scream and scream. My father found me, shaking on the floor of my room as if I'd just been pulled from an icy lake.

"That was when I told him. He wasn't afraid, wasn't shocked. He put me to bed, called for warm milk and stayed at my side until the chill had faded. Then he took my hand and told me, in great detail, what your people do to those with gifts such as mine. No-one was ever to know."

"Then came the Horde?"

"Two summers later. I'd been careful, never flying for more than an hour at a time, and always at night, leaving my body seated before a well-stoked fire. I saw their first slaughter, a blue-stone caravan making its way south from Silvervale. Two score drovers slain in a rush of war-cats and spear-hawks. The warriors wandered amongst the dead with knives, cutting off trophies, and their shine was a dark, dark red. I had never seen a soul snuffed out before. Mostly it was like wind blowing through a clutch of candles, but there was one, shining brighter than the others. It rose and the world seemed to bend around it, like a whirlpool, drawing it in, taking it somewhere . . ."

Vaelin leaned closer as she trailed off. "Where?"

"I know not. But for an instant I had a glimpse of what lay beyond the whirling. It was so very dark." She fell silent and hugged herself for a moment, shivering. "I'm grateful it's something I've only witnessed once."

"Your gift brought enough warning for Lord Al Myrna to prepare a defence?"

She nodded. "I ran to him with the news, blurting it out in front of Adal and Kehlan. He swore them to secrecy, an oath they've kept these many years, although I'm sure there are those who suspect, and those like Sanesh who just seem to *know*."

"The Eorhil have no fear of the Dark?"

"Like the Seordah they respect it, for they know it can be misused, but they do not fear those who possess it unless given reason." She raised an eyebrow at him in expectation.

Like for like, he thought. *Secret for secret.*

"The Seordah call it the blood-song," he said.

Her face took on a slight echo of the fear he had seen when the shaman shared his vision. "A Seordah told you this?"

"A blind woman. She called herself Nersus Sil Nin. I met her in the Martishe."

The fear on her face deepened and her next words were marred by a tremor. "Met her?"

"On a clear summer's day in the dead of winter. She said it was a memory, trapped in stone. She told me my name in the Seordah tongue."

"Beral Shak Ur," she said, fear turning to mystification. "She named you?" She blinked, shaking her head. "Of course she did."

"You know of her?"

"All Seordah drawing breath know of her, but none have seen her . . . save me."

"When?"

"After my husband died." She was deeply troubled, he could tell, like someone receiving unwelcome tidings they knew would always come. "The words she spoke . . . But, I was so sure . . . when he died . . ." She trailed off, lost in thought.

"Your husband?" Vaelin prompted.

The look she gave him was guarded to the point of anger, slowly fading to sombre distress. "I must think on this. My thanks

for your honesty, my lord. I am glad my trust was not misplaced."
With that she rose and went to her shelter.

Vaelin turned his gaze to the north, picking out the bright star
Sanesh had named him for, higher over the horizon now, brighter
even than the moon. *Avensurha . . . No wars can be fought under
the light it brings.*

It's a good name, he thought with a smile. *For once, a good
name.*

CHAPTER SIX
Lyrna

S he started down into darkness, so black and absolute only the touch of her hands and feet on the stone could guide her, that and the terror-filled sobs of Davoka's sister. She had ceased begging, voicing only whimpers and the occasional anguished howl as they descended, ever deeper. At first Lyrna thought the light an illusion born from her vision-starved mind, it was so faint, little more than a thin pinkish haze around Davoka's tall form, but growing with every step. By the time they reached the bottom they were bathed in a deep red glow.

The chamber was huge, the circular floor, walls and ceiling paved in precisely measured slabs of marble. There were numerous openings in the walls, tall enough to walk through, black holes inviting oblivion. The red glow emanated from a large circular well in the centre of the chamber from which a column of thick steam ascended to an identical opening above.

Davoka dragged the weeping Kiral towards the well and Lyrna followed. The heat from the steam was too intense to allow them to approach closer than a dozen feet. Lyrna squinted, peering through the steam at the circle in the ceiling, seeing only the wet walls of a marble-tiled shaft ascending into the centre of the refashioned mountain above.

"There were great copper blades set into the lower shaft when we first came here."

She stood in the entrance to one of the tunnels. A dark-haired woman, dressed in a plain robe of black cotton that left her arms bare, her skin painted a pale crimson in the glow from the well. "The shaft below was choked with rubble," she went on, coming closer.

Kiral clutched at Davoka's legs, whispering, *"Please, sister! Pleeeaase!"*

The young woman paid her no mind, stopping a short distance from Lyrna and offering a smile of welcome. "Three hundred feet below us an underground river meets a channel of Nishak's blood, producing a constant rush of steam, ascending through the well to meet four blades arranged in a cross, suspended from a great iron rod that reached up to the third level of the tower above. A curious mystery, wouldn't you say?"

Watching her face as she spoke, Lyrna was struck by the surety in it, the confidence exuded by a woman of such youth, speaking Realm Tongue with no trace of an accent, her gaze level and only mildly curious.

"The steam would make the blades turn," Lyrna said. "Like a windmill."

The young woman's smile broadened. "Yes. Sadly, such novelties were lost on the Lonakhim who first set eyes on this place and the blades were destined to become much-needed pots and pans, the great iron rod melted down for hatchet blades. It was only when I ordered the stone cleared from the well that the purpose of the blades became clear. After every renewal I promise myself I will order the fashioning of new blades, for I would dearly love to see them turn once more, but I never do." Her gaze shifted to the cowering girl at Davoka's feet. "There is always a fresh distraction, after all."

"What was it for?" Lyrna asked. "The power harnessed by the blades?"

"That is an unanswerable question. The rod ended in a great

cog, whatever it turned gone to dust centuries ago. Though, I suspect it had something to do with heating the carved mountain that stands above us."

She stood regarding Kiral's trembling form in silence for a moment, then raised her gaze to Davoka, speaking in Lonak, *"This is your sister's body?"*

"It is, Mahlessa."

"If I return her, she will be . . . changed. And not just with scars. You understand this?"

"I do, Mahlessa. I know my sister's heart. She would wish to return to us, whatever the cost."

The Mahlessa gave a small nod. *"As you wish. Bring her."*

"No!" Kiral shrieked, trying to crawl away. Davoka hauled her upright, forcing her towards the well.

"You think this thing fears me," the Mahlessa said to Lyrna. "You are mistaken. What it fears is the punishment that will greet its failure when I return it to the void."

Kiral screamed and begged in a constant babble of fear, she thrashed, she spat, she cursed. It did no good. Davoka forced her to the edge of the well, sweat bathing them both. The Mahlessa moved to stand next to Kiral and Lyrna saw not a bead of sweat on her skin. She reached out to pick up a bottle sitting on the edge of the well. It was small, the glass cloudy, a dark liquid just visible inside.

"Her hand," the Mahlessa told Davoka, pulling the stopper from the bottle. Lyrna saw a wisp of vapour rise from it and a foul stench assailed her nostrils. Davoka drew her knife and severed the binding on Kiral's wrists, forcing one arm behind her back and extending the other to the Mahlessa.

"For all the misery and sorrow sown by these things," she said to Lyrna, reaching out to caress Kiral's hand, fingers tracing over the skin of the spasming fist, the girl's screams now hoarse grunts from a ravaged throat. "You would think their number legion, but there have never been more than three. This one is the youngest, female when she was first snared and twisted, only capable of taking female shells and then no more than one at a time until death releases her. Also not so skilled in her deceit. Her brother is more accomplished, able to control several shells at once regardless of gender, living for years behind the masks without arousing the suspicion of even those who loved them from birth. Her sister, well, let's just say it would be best if you never met her. Century upon century of murder and deceit, weaving their skein of discord throughout the world, now seeking to bring their master's great scheme to fruition. Only three, snared by the depth of their own malice. But from where does malice spring? If not from fear . . . and pain."

She lifted the bottle and poured a single drop of liquid onto Kiral's hand.

The vastness of the pain and fury erupting from the girl's throat was enough for Lyrna to close her eyes and fight down a wave of nausea. Weeks of threat and repeated exposure to the sight of violent death may have hardened her, but the sheer inhuman ugliness of this sound cut through her new-grown callus like a healer's scalpel. When she looked again the girl was on her knees, her face clasped between the Mahlessa's hands, eyes wide and unblinking.

"Pain is just the door," the Mahlessa said. "Fear is the lever, the tool that scrapes away the filth infecting this girl's mind, latched onto her gift like a leech." Kiral shuddered, gibberish issuing from her lips amidst a cloud of spittle. "For even this thing fears true oblivion, and if it stays to face me, I will rend it to nothing."

Kiral sagged, eyes closing, falling free of the Mahlessa's grip, cradled by Davoka, a steaming red-black sore covering the back of her right hand.

Lyrna swallowed bile and went to press her fingers against the girl's neck, finding the pulse strong.

"*How . . . how long?*" the voice behind her was thin, choked with confusion and sorrow.

Lyrna looked up and saw that the Mahlessa had vanished, the confident young woman replaced by a fearful girl, staring at her in confusion, slender arms hugging herself tight. The same face, the same slender form, but a different soul.

"*Mahlessa?*" Lyrna asked, rising and moving to her.

The girl uttered a sound that was part sigh and part laugh, just a pitch below hysteria, her eyes finding the bottle in her hand. "*Yes, oh yes. I am the Mahlessa. Great and terrible is my power . . .*" She faltered to silence with a mirthless giggle.

"*Five summers,*" Davoka said. "*Since the renewal.*"

"*Five summers.*" The girl's gaze roamed over Lyrna, taking in her hair before looking directly into her eyes. "*The Merim Her queen. She's been waiting for you, such a long time. So many visions . . .*" Her hand came up to caress Lyrna's cheek. "*Such beauty . . . Such a shame . . . What does it feel like?*"

"*Mahlessa?*"

"*To have killed so many. You see, I only killed my mother . . .*"

Then she was gone, the face of a scared girl abruptly replaced by ageless surety, her hand falling from Lyrna's face as she retreated.

"What did she tell you?" the Mahlessa asked.

Lyrna forced herself not to retreat further, though the spiral stairs now appeared very inviting. *You wanted evidence,* she reminded herself. *Here it is.*

"She said she killed her mother," she replied, striving to keep the tremor from her voice.

"Ah yes, a sad story. A beautiful young girl, kindly and possessed of the healing touch, but also quite mad, murderously so. It's always the way with the healing touch, some facet of its power works to unhinge the mind. Every gift has its price. In this case the persistent delusion that her mother was possessed by Jeshak, the hating god. Having killed her mother, of course there was no place for her in her clan. They wouldn't kill her because of her gift, for all Lonakhim know that the gifted can only be judged by the Mahlessa. She wandered the mountains until Davoka found her and brought her to me. The perfect vessel, one of my finest in fact. Though she does have a tendency to get loose more often than her predecessors."

She returned to Kiral's side, reaching down to clasp her ravaged hand. The girl spasmed, coming awake with a jerk, trying to pull away as Davoka held her. "*I . . . sister?*" Her eyes found Davoka's face. "*I . . . was cold.*"

The Mahlessa released her hand and Lyrna was unable to contain the gasp that rose from her chest. It was healed, the red-black sore gone, the skin still showing some faint scars, but whole once again. *Evidence.*

"It does drain one so," the Mahlessa said, flexing her own hand, a crease appearing in her smooth brow. "More than any other gift. Perhaps that's where the madness comes from, the loss of self with every healing." She rose once more and stepped back, addressing Davoka, "*Alturk is here?*"

"*He is, Mahlessa.*"

"*A lost and broken man, no doubt. A Tahlessa without a clan. It may be kinder to allow him to throw himself into the Mouth of Nishak.*"

"*I owe Alturk a great debt . . .*" Lyrna began but the Mahlessa just waved a dismissive hand.

"Have no fear, my Queen. He's far too valuable to waste indulging his self-pity." Her gaze lingered on Kiral's still-confused face as she addressed Davoka once again. "*Ten centuries of life teaches me the folly of discarding insight gained from a hard lesson. The thing that took your sister was wise enough to play on the history of the Lonakhim; the legend of the Sentar is enduring, and appealing. You will tell Alturk he is now the Tahlessa Sentar, the true Sentar, blessed by the true Mahlessa. He will go forth from here, scouring every clan for their finest warriors. They will number one thousand, no more, no less. They will not hunt, they will not feud, they will only train for war and fight at my command.*"

Davoka gave a solemn nod. "*Mahlessa, I beg a place in the Sentar. I will be your eyes, your voice to the thousand . . .*"

The Mahlessa shook her head with a smile. "*No, my bright spear, I have a greater mission for you.*" She turned to Lyrna once again. *"Though you may consider it more a curse. Take your sister above, she will need to rest. The queen and I must talk further."*

Davoka gently pulled Kiral to her feet, the girl staring about her in a blend of wonder and fear, which only deepened when her gaze found Lyrna. *"She saw it,"* she whispered, drawing back. *"She heard it . . . She knew . . ."*

"Calm now, little cat," Davoka soothed her. *"This is Lerhnah, Queen of the Merim Her. She is a friend to us."*

Kiral swallowed, looking down at the tiled floor, guilt replacing fear. *"It wanted her . . . Wanted to hurt her, worse than all the others . . . I felt the want . . ."*

Lyrna went to her, placing a hand under her chin and lifting it. *"I know it was not your want,"* she said. *"Your sister is my sister too, and so I will be yours."*

Kiral stared at her with an expression close to awe. *"It feared you . . . That's why it wanted to hurt you so much . . . You were new . . . Unexpected . . . No ilvarek had revealed your nature . . ."*

Ilvarek . . . The word had an archaic inflection, and was similar to the Lonak word for sight, or vision, but spoken with a gravitas that gave Lyrna pause. *"Ilvarek, I do not know this word."*

"Take your sister above, Davoka," the Mahlessa said again, her voice soft but carrying an unmistakable note of command.

Davoka nodded and led Kiral to the spiral steps, the girl whispering as she ascended. *"When it slept I saw its nightmares . . . It strangled its own baby . . ."*

"Allow me to show you something," the Mahlessa said as Kiral's voice faded. "Something only Lonakhim eyes have ever seen."

The darkness in the tunnel proved less absolute than Lyrna had expected, the walls possessed of a faint green luminescence providing enough light for them to make their way without the aid of a torch. "It's a kind of powder found in the western hills," the Mahlessa explained. "Possessed of an inner light that never fades. Carried here in great quantities and painted onto the walls by whoever carved the Mountain. Ingenious, don't you think?"

"Quite," Lyrna agreed. "Almost as ingenious as you, Mahlessa?"

There was a pause and she knew the woman was smiling. "How so?"

"A trap is not a trap without bait. My mission here, at your invitation, was an irresistible target for that thing you just banished, as I'm sure you knew it would be."

"Indeed I did."

"Good men and women died to get me here. Your people and mine."

"Good men and women die all the time. So do the bad ones. Surely it's better to die with a purpose."

"But far better to live with one."

"A choice we do not always get to make. Take my people for example, they did not choose for the Merim Her to descend upon our shores like a plague. They did not choose to be hunted like animals for three decades. They did not choose to carve out a home amidst the frozen mountains with the pitiful remnants of what strength was left them." Lyrna was struck by the absence of anger in the Mahlessa's words, her tone light and conversational, as if they were two ladies at court discussing the finer points of one of Alucius's poems.

"I cannot account for the crimes of my ancestors," she said, her own tone less than conversational. "But I will have to account for the lives lost in pursuit of the peace you offered. My lady Nersa's parents will find scant comfort in the knowledge that their daughter died in service to your purpose."

A laugh, very soft, very slight. "I suspect they have little time left for grief or comfort. None of us do."

She stopped as the tunnel ended, opening out in a huge circular chamber, as least three times the size of the one they had left. There was no well here, the only illumination coming from the green-glowing powder painted onto the floor and ceiling, much brighter than in the tunnel, bright enough to read by in fact.

Curiously, whilst the floor and ceiling were bright the walls were dark. Also the air was dry, carrying a faint musty tinge.

"Princess Lyrna Al Nieren," the Mahlessa said, stepping into the chamber and raising her arms. "I bid you welcome to the memory of the Lonakhim."

Books, Lyrna realised following her into the chamber, her eyes roaming over the walls, stacked floor to ceiling with countless books and scrolls. She found herself drawn to them immediately. Some were massive, giant tomes requiring many arms to lift, others tiny enough to fit into the palm of her hand. She lifted the nearest volume, only dimly aware that it may have been diplomatic to ask permission first. It was leather-bound, with an intricate design etched into the cover, and, despite its age, the pages were intact and pliant enough to turn easily instead of cracking to dust. The script they held was beautifully rendered, illuminated with gold leaf and coloured inks, but completely indecipherable.

"*The Wisdoms of Reltak,*" the Mahlessa said. "His only philosophical work. He's usually more concerned with astronomy. The first Lonakhim scholar to calculate the circumference of the moon. Though Arkiol argues he was out by about twenty feet."

Lyrna raised her gaze from the book, frowning at the word "scholar" being used in conjunction with "Lonakhim."

"Oh yes," the Mahlessa said. "We were not all warriors once. Before your people came, whilst the Seordah wandered their forests, losing themselves in communion with the earth, my people studied, we observed, we crafted great works, we wrote great verse. What you see here is only a fragment, the salvaged remains of our achievement. If we had been left alone, another century perhaps, even the mysteries of this mountain would have been within our grasp. Sadly, for all our wisdom, we never discovered how to smelt iron. A small thing, you might think, but wars are often decided by small things."

"Did you know him?" Lyrna asked, holding up the book.

The Mahlessa laughed and shook her head. "Even I am not that old. Though I did make the acquaintance of one of his descendants, a many-times-great-grandson. I watched him starve to death during the travail."

Lyrna returned the book to the stacks. "Who were you, before?"

"Just a girl who had too many nightmares. I still do. I'm looking at one of them right now." There was no humour now, just serious scrutiny and keen intellect. It had been many years since Lyrna had met an equal, a soul as attuned to nuance and deceit as she was. She was shamed by it, the deaths of so many still weighed on her, but this moment made her grateful for the journey that had brought her here. To look into a face that saw all of her, no need or opportunity for concealment, no charm or tears to deflect unwelcome insight, no prospect of manipulation, just cold reason and the weight of history packed into these books. The novelty of it was a guilty delight.

"Ilvarek," she said. "A vision. That's what it means."

"The closest translation in your language is 'scrying.' You know this word?"

"A Dark ability to peer into the future."

"I do not peer. The future stares at me and I stare back, and when I do I see you."

"And what am I doing?"

The Mahlessa's expression clouded. "One of two things." She moved to a scroll perched atop a stack of books, lifting it and holding it out to Lyrna. "This is for you."

"A gift?"

"A treaty. The war between our peoples is over. Please accept my congratulations on successfully negotiating this peace."

Lyrna went to her and took the scroll, unfurling it to find two blocks of finely scribed text, the one above in Realm Tongue, the other in the same alien script as the book. "There are no terms," she said. "Just a statement that the conflict between us is ended."

"What more would you want?"

"It's customary for us to squabble over borders, tributes and such."

"Borders are always changing, and I'll take your role in bringing down the false Mahlessa as more than sufficient tribute, one I'll reward with a gift. You wear a knife do you not?"

Lyrna's hand went to the chain about her neck. "A trinket only. It poses no threat. I can't even throw it properly."

"Not yet." The Mahlessa held out her hand, Lyrna noticed she still held the small bottle in her other hand. "Give it to me."

Kiral's scream and the stench of the bottle's contents were still vivid, so Lyrna hesitated before lifting the chain over her head and placing the knife in the Mahlessa's open palm.

"You wonder what this is," she said, taking hold of the knife by the handle and lifting the bottle until it was poised over the blade. "The Lonak scholars were not just poets and mathematicians, they were also chemists. Centuries ago they concocted a substance that would produce the most pure and absolute pain a human can endure and still live, though only if a tiny amount is used." She tipped the bottle and a single drop of dark viscous liquid fell onto the blade, the foul vapour rising again, making Lyrna step back and cover her nose. The liquid spread across the steel, the vapour fading, then seemed to disappear, like water seeping into cloth.

"Here." The Mahlessa held the knife out to Lyrna. "It won't hurt you. When mixed with steel it only comes to life if it touches blood."

"Why would I need such a thing?" Lyrna asked, making no move to take the knife.

"To do one of the two things I see you do."

It was clear she would say no more on the subject. Tentatively, Lyrna reached out and touched a finger to the knife, feeling only cool metal.

"Never be without it," the Mahlessa said as Lyrna took the knife and pulled the chain over her head.

"I will always keep it, in any case," Lyrna replied. "It's the only gift I've ever cherished."

The Mahlessa's gaze remained serious but there was surprise

there too. "You are not what I was expecting. The *ilvarek* painted a very different picture."

"Was I taller?" Lyrna asked with a small laugh.

"No, you were ambitious. You cared nothing for the lives lost reaching this place, just more pieces on your Keschet board. This meeting was to have made you furious, the truth of the ilvarek provoking hatred, making you swear vile retribution and tear up the treaty you hold in your hands. Something has changed in you, Lyrna Al Nieren. Was it guilt I wonder, some crime committed out of the ilvarek's sight? So terrible the guilt forged a new facet to your soul."

Father I beg you . . . "I'd hazard," Lyrna said, "there are more crimes in your ledger than mine."

"Ensuring the survival of my people compelled me to terrible acts, it is true. I have lied, I have corrupted, I have tortured and I have killed. And every crime I would commit again a thousand times to secure the same end. Remember this, Queen, when you watch the flames rise high, remember this and ask yourself: would I do this again?"

She moved closer, lifting the book Lyrna had examined and holding it out to her. "Removing even the smallest scrap from this place is punishable by death, but for you I think I can make an allowance. The meditations on divinity are particularly interesting. Reltak has much to say on the folly of dogma."

"I can't read it."

"I think we both know a translation is well within your abilities. The Lonakhim text in the treaty will provide sufficient clues, I'm sure. And my bright spear will be there to help. She reads very well."

"Davoka?"

"It is customary for nations at peace to exchange ambassadors, is it not? She will be mine."

"Her . . . diplomacy will be very welcome. I shall of course arrange for a suitably qualified Realm official to present himself here as soon as possible."

"As you wish, there's no hurry. Just make sure you send a woman, unless you want your ambassador to gift me your Realm in its entirety."

"Men are so easily captured by your beauty?"

"No, by the gift of a woman who died three centuries ago. Oddly, it only works on men."

Lyrna took the book. "I regret I have nothing to offer in return."

The Mahlessa's scrutiny faded to an aspect of sombre reflection. "You are the gift," she said. "Confirmation that it has all been for something." She held out her hand and Lyrna took it. "They come, Queen, they come to tear it all down. Your world and mine. Look to the beast charmer when chains bind you."

"Mahlessa?"

But she was gone again, replaced once more by the fearful girl, her hand trembling in Lyrna's grasp, head cocked, eyes looking into hers with desperate fear. *"How does it feel?"* she asked and Lyrna realised she was repeating her question from before, unaware of time having passed since.

"I have killed no-one," Lyrna told her.

"Oh . . ." Her eyes roamed Lyrna's face. *"No . . . Not there yet . . . But they will be."*

"What will?"

The girl smiled, teeth bright in the green glow. *"The marks of your greatness."*

She made her way back to the steam chamber then up the spiral steps to the surface. She had lingered for more than an hour, asking question after question. *"Who is the master the Mahlessa spoke of? What is his scheme? Who is coming to bring it all down?"*

The fearful girl's answers were no more than a jumble of confusion and riddle. *"He waits in the void . . . He hungers . . . Oh how he hungers . . . My mother said I was the kindliest soul ever to grace the Lonakhim, I cut her throat with my father's knife . . ."*

After a while her rambling faded to silence and she slumped to the floor, listless, eyes vacant. Lyrna waited a while longer for the Mahlessa to return, but knew instinctively it wouldn't happen. *We will never meet again.*

She sighed and touched the girl on the shoulder. *"Did you earn a name?"*

"Helsa," the girl replied in a whisper. *Healer, or saviour in the archaic form, depending on the inflection.*

"I'm glad to have met you, Helsa."

"Will you come to see me again?"

"I hope so, one day."

This brought a smile, slipping from her lips as the vacant stare returned to her eyes. Lyrna squeezed her shoulder and returned to the tunnel. She didn't turn for a final look, the sadness was too great.

She found the brothers and Smolen waiting for her when she returned to the surface. They were alone, the women who had greeted them gone to whatever duties the Mahlessa ordained.

"Alturk?" she asked Sollis.

"He left, Highness. Davoka spoke to him and he left."

"Didn't even say good-bye," Ivern commented. "I was hurt."

"Davoka?" Lyrna asked.

"Off caring for her sister somewhere," the young brother said. "They've given us rooms the next level up."

Lyrna nodded, looking down at the scroll in her hand.

"Your mission was a success, Highness?" Smolen ventured.

"Yes." She forced a smile. "A great success. Rest well tonight, good sirs. We leave for the Realm come the dawn."

The journey back to the Skellan Pass took the better part of two weeks, Davoka choosing an easier but longer route than the varied paths that brought them to the Mountain. Lyrna had offered to take Kiral with them but the Lonak woman refused. "Better cared for at the Mountain."

"But you only just got her back," Lyrna objected. "Don't you want to stay a while? You can join me at court at any time."

Davoka shook her head. "The Mahlessa commands," was all she said.

In the evenings they would collaborate in translating *The Wisdoms of Reltak*, although Davoka found his verses somewhat troubling. "'Divinity retains the appearance of insight,'" she read one evening, brows creased with a deep frown. "'When in reality it celebrates ignorance. Its tenets are so much clay, and when the clay sets, it becomes dogma.'"

She looked at Lyrna over the top of the volume. "I don't like this book."

"Really? I find it rather charming."

In the mornings Davoka would tutor her with the throwing knife, something they had neglected on the journey north. Brother Ivern soon joined in, finding a thin but broad piece of wood to use as a target. Sometimes he would toss it into the air, sending his own knives into the centre with a disconcerting speed and accuracy.

"I was always the best at toss-board," he said. "Won more knives than any novice brother my age. Only Frentis could hope to match me."

Frentis. A name Lyrna knew, her brother had spoken it many times. "You knew Brother Frentis?"

"We were in the same group at the Order House, Highness."

"The King praises his courage highly. He said Untesh would have fallen on the first day if not for Brother Frentis."

Ivern gave a sad smile. "That sounds like him. After the Test of the Sword he was sent to the Wolfrunners and I was sent here. I'm ashamed to say I was jealous, thinking him the lucky one."

As the days passed she began to improve with the knife, finding the target with greater frequency, seeing the truth in Davoka's words: *Throw again . . . Again and again until you hit. Then you know how.*

On the last morning, with the pass only one day's ride away, as Ivern's board fell to earth with her knife embedded in the centre, she could finally say she knew how.

◆ ◆ ◆

Their return to the pass was greeted with some celebration and no small amount of surprise. The garrison had grown with the addition of a full regiment of Realm Guard cavalry, ordered by the King to venture into the Lonak Dominion in search of her. Fortunately, they had arrived the day before and preparations for their unwise expedition were far from complete.

"But you were attacked, Highness," the regiment's Lord Marshal objected when she told him to be ready to escort her south the next day. "Surely, the savages require some punishment. I would consider it an honour . . ."

She held up the scroll. "We are now at peace with the Lonak, my lord. Besides, the only punishment you'll find north of the pass will be your own."

Her gaze was drawn to Brother Sollis, noting the way he straightened as he received news from one of his brothers. He caught her eye and came over. "Tidings from the Realm, Highness. It seems there was an attempt on the life of Tower Lord Al Bera. He lives but is grievously wounded. Witnesses lay the blame on Cumbraelin fanatics."

Lyrna stifled a groan. *End one war and there's another brewing at home.* "What has the King commanded?"

"The Battle Lord musters the Realm Guard with orders to root out the fanatics. Fief Lord Mustor has been ordered to render assistance but whether his people will do so is another matter."

"I see. Then I had best not linger. Lord Marshal, we leave within the hour."

The Lord Marshal bowed and strode away, shouting orders. Lyrna turned back to Sollis. "It seems our farewell must be brief, brother. I know there is no gift or favour I can offer that you will accept, so I can only offer my thanks, for my life and the success of this mission."

"It was . . . an interesting journey." He hesitated. "There were other tidings, Highness. Lord Al Sorna has returned to the Realm."

Vaelin . . . "Returned?" She heard the shrillness in her voice and coughed. "How?"

"The Emperor released him, apparently in gratitude for some heroic service. The details are a little vague. He arrived at Varinshold some weeks ago. It seems he has left our Order. King Malcius sent him to the Northern Reaches, as Tower Lord." *The Northern Reaches . . .* For once her foolish brother had made the right move, although she found herself wishing he had waited a little before making it. "Please thank Brother Ivern for me," she told Sollis. "Convey my regrets I have no more kisses to offer."

"I think one was more than enough, Highness."

"Where will you go?" she asked. "Now there is no-one here for you to fight."

"I go where my Aspect commands, Highness. And there's always someone else to fight." He gave a bow lower than any he had offered before, straightened and turned to walk towards the squat tower at the south end of the pass.

A Realm Guard sergeant hurried up to her, leading a fine grey mare. "The Lord Marshal offers you this gift, Highness," the man said, holding out the reins. "From his own stables."

Lyrna turned to scratch the nose of her pony. She had taken to calling him Surefoot in recent days, something Davoka seemed to find amusing and baffling in equal measure; the Lonak did not name animals they might have to slaughter for meat in the winter months. "I have a mount, sergeant," she said, climbing onto the saddle, feeling the now-familiar bones of Surefoot's back. "Shall we be off?"

In Cardurin, cheering people thronged the streets, bunting decorated the myriad bridges between the tall buildings and townsfolk cast flowers along her path through the city. When she reached the main square the city factor made a florid and somewhat long speech praising her as a peacemaker and deliverer. "Anything Your Highness commands, this city will provide," he finished, with an elaborate bow.

Lyrna shifted a little on Surefoot's back as the crowd fell to expectant silence. "A bath, sir," she said. "I should very much like a bath."

So she bathed in a suite of rooms at the factor's mansion, twice, and chose clothes provided by the city's finest dressmakers whilst Davoka looked on with a wary scowl. "Can't ride in those," she said. "Or fight."

"I'm hoping my riding and fighting days are over," Lyrna replied. "This one," she said to the serving girl, pointing at a long gown of dark blue chiffon and discarding her bathrobe. The girl gasped and looked away, blushing furiously. *"Never seen a queen's tits before,"* Lyrna explained to a puzzled Davoka.

She put on the dress and stood before a long mirror, taking satisfaction from the way it complimented her figure, though it was looser around the waist than she would have liked, the consequence of so many days in the saddle she supposed. She paused at the sight of her face, half expecting the journey to have left some mark on her, some hardening or weathering to her features, but saw only the same face she had always seen, except . . . Was there something new in the set of her eyes? An openness that hadn't been there before?

"You are . . . v-very beautiful, Highness," the serving girl stammered, having recovered enough wit for flattery.

"Thank you," Lyrna said with one of her best smiles. "Please lay out the riding gown for the morning and pack these others for me."

She spent a few hours at the banquet the factor had convened in her honour, sitting through more speeches from various town notables and suffering the inane chatter of their wives. The only oratory she offered was a reading of the Mahlessa's scroll, which she ordered be copied and sent to every corner of the Realm. From the speeches and conversation it was clear these people saw her as more a victor than a peacemaker, as if she had won a great battle rather than merely survived a perilous journey to return with a piece of parchment. Watching the laughing, and increasingly drunken faces around her, she found herself pondering the Mahlessa's words. *They come, Queen, to tear it all down . . . Your world and mine.*

She sighed into her wine cup. *Now I have the evidence, what to do with it?*

They moved on the next morning, though the town factor had been vociferous in his entreaties that she stay a little longer. "Your greatness enriches our city, Highness." Judging by the gifts they had attempted to bestow on her and the scale of the ongoing celebrations, Lyrna thought it more likely they would bankrupt themselves if she lingered another day. She did accept one thing, a copy of the Mahlessa's scroll, inscribed on velum and illuminated with an image of her astride Surefoot as she arrived at the gates of the city, scroll in hand. Apparently the Scribes Guild had worked on it through the night and the ink was barely dry.

They were two days south of Cardurin when one of the Lord Marshal's scouts galloped up with news she had been dreading with every southward step. "Fief Lord Darnel comes to greet her Highness, my lord."

"An enemy, Queen?" Davoka asked, seeing Lyrna's sudden tension.

"You remember the man I told you about?"

Davoka nodded as a line of horsemen appeared on the horizon. *"He comes?"*

"No, his opposite."

Fief Lord Darnel had lost none of his good looks in the years since their last meeting, a blessedly brief exchange of greetings at her brother's coronation. He wore no helm but was otherwise fully clad in armour inlaid with intricate blue enamel, riding an all-black stallion, long dark hair streaming back from his finely sculpted face, every inch the lordly knight. *Nobility is a lie,* her father had once told her. *A pretence that high standing comes from anything more than money or martial prowess. Any dolt can play the noble, and as you'll discover in time, daughter, it's mostly dolts who do.*

"Princess!" Lord Darnel exclaimed, reining to a halt and dismounting to fall to one knee. Behind him his retinue of more than fifty knights did the same. "I bid you welcome to Renfael.

Forgive my failure to offer you a suitable welcome, but word of your coming only reached me yesterday."

"Fief Lord," Lyrna replied. She gestured at Davoka. "May I present, the . . . Lady Davoka, Ambassadress of the Lonak Dominion."

Darnel rose from his bow, squinting up at the Lonak woman with a poorly concealed grimace of distaste. "So it's true then? The savages have finally yielded."

Lyrna saw Davoka's hand tighten on the haft of her spear and was sorely tempted to let her act on her anger. The stories about Darnel's actions during the fall of Marbellis were well-known, and none of them flattering.

"Nothing has been yielded," Lyrna told him. "We have agreed a peace. That is all."

"A pity. They always made such good sport. The first man I killed was a Lonak, if you could call such as him a man."

"I can't let you kill him," Lyrna told Davoka as her spear began to lower.

"You learned their tongue?" Darnel said with a laugh. "Such accomplishment in one so lovely . . ."

"Did you have other business, my lord?" Lyrna cut in. "We have many miles to cover, and the King awaits my safe return."

"There was a matter of some import, if we could talk alone for a moment."

She was tempted to refuse but the lack of civility already on display was making a poor show in front of so many Realm Guard and knights. "Very well." She dismounted, murmuring to Davoka in Lonak, *"Don't stray too far."*

They walked a short distance from the ranks of horsemen, Lyrna all too aware of so many eyes taking in the scene. "There is one in this fief," Darnel began, "who plots against my Lordship, speaking falsehoods, impugning my honour at every turn. I think you would agree, Highness, that treason against me is tantamount to treason against the crown."

Lyrna avoided providing an affirmation, answering with a question, "And who is this malcontent?"

Darnel's mouth twisted around the word. "Banders!"

"Baron Hughlin Banders? The most beloved knight in Renfael, and one of the few captains to return from the Alpiran war with any vestige of honour. This is the man you would name a traitor?"

"I would rule my fief in the King's name, as ordained by the tenets that bind this Realm in unity."

How could a man see so much and change so little? she wondered. It was still there, everything that had made her discount her father's wishes in a heartbeat, in his face, his stance; the ingrained assumption of right, the knowledge of his own brilliance. *What a dreadful child he must have been . . . and still is.* "This is a free Realm," she pointed out. "And all may voice their thoughts without fear of persecution."

"Not when such thoughts amount to sedition. The man *holds court,* Highness. Lords and commons go to him for counsel, though he holds no position in this fief. A beggar knight in fact."

"A beggar you would kill, my lord? Hardly a knightly ambition."

"Despite the lies you may have heard about me, I am not without mercy. Exile seems the most just sentence."

Also, the least likely to raise the commons against you. Darnel's display of cunning annoyed her; she preferred him as a dolt.

"Exile and forfeiture of property," the Fief Lord added. "I will of course, make provision for any dependents."

There was a weight to these last words that gave her pause. *Not just revenge on an old adversary,* she decided. *He wants more.* "I will bring your concerns to the King," she said, turning away. "Now, if there's nothing else . . ."

"Only my undying love."

The sincerity in his voice was disturbing, as was the intensity in his eyes. She hadn't noticed before how darkly blue they were. Another place, another man, she might have found reason to linger in the sight of such eyes, but here she just wanted to mount her pony and ride away as fast as possible.

"That matter was settled . . ." she began, keeping her voice low.

300 · ANTHONY RYAN

"Not for me." He stepped closer and she could tell he was resisting the impulse to reach for her. "Not for one day since. Have you never wondered why I remain unmarried? Why I strive every day to keep the King's peace though justice cries out for me to gather my retainers and burn Banders's holdfast down around him? Him and every other ungrateful wretch in this fief. For you, Lyrna. So that you might see me . . ."

"I've seen you," she said, voice hard and flat. "And I've seen enough."

His jaws clenched as he looked down, his voice thin but deep in regret. "That is your final word?"

"My final word regarding you was spoken to my father eight years ago, and I see no reason to speak another."

When he raised his face the sincerity of his affection remained, albeit dimmed by anger. "If your brother had died at Untesh, you would be queen now. It must have been very *affecting* to see him return safely home."

"I assure you, if my brother had perished, you would have been on the first ship back to the empire, presented in chains to account for your crimes."

"Crimes?" He laughed, harsh and short. "You talk of crimes, as if war is a game, as if rules mean anything in a slaughter, as if they have ever mattered for us, Lyrna. I *see* you." He came closer still, dark eyes intent and questing. "I see you, the face you hide from the court and the commons. But I see it, because I see it in me, and I see everything we could be. A union between us would see the whole world at our feet in a decade."

"When did it happen?"

He frowned. "Highness?"

"When madness supplanted mere cruelty."

His face froze as if she had struck him, a rigid fury seizing him from head to toe. Davoka's pony gave a loud snort as she walked him within a spear throw of the Fief Lord.

"I believe," Darnel grated, "Al Sorna has returned to the Realm, and no longer enjoys the protection of the Sixth Order.

A challenge can be made and accepted. Tell me, would you prefer his head or his heart as a tribute?"

"It is my fervent hope, my lord, that you make such a challenge. Then I'll be able to choose my tribute from whatever remains of you. Perhaps I'll send it to Marbellis as a small token of recompense."

He stood still for a moment, frozen in his anger, face quivering before he mastered himself. "I should like, Highness," he said, his voice a soft rasp, "for you to remember the words you have said to me today. I should like you to remember them for a very long time."

"Then I regret to tell you, my lord, that I intend to forget them just as soon as you are out of my sight. A circumstance I expect you to bring about forthwith."

He could refuse, she had no power to command him. She could only expect. It was usually enough, but would it suffice for this handsome madman?

He closed his eyes, breathing softly, a faint whisper coming from his lips, "Faith save me, but I had to try." When he opened his eyes there was no more anger, not even any cruelty, just numb acceptance. He gave a bow, formal and correct in every way, turned to march back to his horse, mounting and riding away without another word.

"*Send me after him,*" Davoka said, watching Darnel and his knights crest a rise and disappear from view. "*It'll be done tonight. His heart stops when he sleeps. No blame will arise.*"

"*No,*" Lyrna said, walking back to Surefoot.

"*I know men like him, Lerhnah. I've killed enough to know them very well. That one won't stop until he's made you bleed.*"

Lyrna mounted the pony, meeting Davoka's eyes and giving a firm shake of her head. The Lonak woman gritted her teeth but said no more.

"Lord Marshal Al Smolen," Lyrna called, the Guard commander quickly riding to her side with a smart salute. "A change of course, my lord. We make for the holdfast of House Banders."

CHAPTER SEVEN
Reva

They saw the cathedral spires first, jutting over the crest as they led their horses up the hill. "Faith!" Arken breathed, gazing at the cathedral as they reached the top. The two spires rose from the centre of the city like twin arrows. "How tall are they?"

Reva replied with a quote from the priest, "Tall enough to match the Father's glory."

Alltor was another place she had never been, but the priest had told her many stories of the city named for the World Father's first and greatest prophet. *A whole city built in the Father's honour, a wonder of marble and beauty when it first rose, shaming the wooden hovels of the Asraelins.* Looking at the city stretched out before her, Reva couldn't quell a suspicion that the priest's description may have been coloured by the assumption she would never set eyes on the place. It was smaller than Varinshold, confined within its walled island in the middle of the Coldiron River, and not quite so smelly, at least from this distance. But she saw no wonder in it, just a jumble of stone buildings under a thick haze of smoke from a thousand chimneys. Only the cathedral came close to matching the visions the priest had conjured in her girlish mind, and even that was a soot-blackened shadow of her imaginings, the marble of the spires darkened from centuries of windblown grime.

"Do you have family, here?" Arken asked. Recent days had seen his questions become more frequent, and irksome. But she found herself unable to lie to him, her answers brief but always truthful.

"Yes." She climbed onto Snorter's saddle and started down the slope. "An uncle."

"Will we be staying with him?" She could hear the hope in his voice. Sleeping in the open every night had dispelled any boyish notions of grand adventure, and the prospect of room and board was no doubt very welcome.

"I hope not," she replied. "I don't think he'd be pleased to see me."

It was market day and the guards on the gate were too busy collecting dues from the hawkers to bother with them much. Reva had hidden her weapons under a blanket strapped across Snorter's back and Arken kept his knife concealed within his shirt. They rode through without incident but were soon snared by the throng of the market. Reva had to dismount to calm Snorter as he began to rear, nostrils flaring with the stench of so many people. "Don't like it, do you?" she said, holding a carrot to his mouth. "Not bred for cities, eh? Me neither."

An hour of shoving and squeezing bought freedom from the crowd, delivering them to a maze of narrow streets bordering the market square. They found an inn with a stable after what seemed like an age of aimless wandering. Snorter and Arken's squat horse, named Bumper for his less-than-comfortable back, were ensconced in the stable boy's care whilst Reva paid five coppers for a room she could share with her brother.

"Brother, eh?" the innkeeper said with a knowing leer. "Doesn't look like you."

"You won't look like you if I let him have his way for five minutes," Reva replied. "How do we get to the Fief Lord's manor from here?"

The man seemed unruffled by the threat, merely chuckling a little as he said, "Just keep headin' for the spires, you'll find it.

Stands opposite the cathedral. Petitioning day's not till Feldrian though."

"We'll wait."

His grin broadened. "Then I'll need another two days in advance."

She left the weapons in the room with Arken, cautioning him not to open the door too wide if the innkeeper came sniffing, then went to find the manor. As instructed, she kept the spires ahead of her, marvelling ever more at their height, until the streets fell away to reveal the great central square. It was paved from end to end in granite, clouds of pigeons flocking and breaking continually on the stones, the cathedral rising on her left, the largest structure she had ever seen, so tall she wondered it could remain upright. On the opposite side of the square stood a large three-storey building of many windows, surrounded by a ten-foot wall topped with steel spikes. Pairs of guards patrolled the walls and a squad of five manned the main gate. She counted four archers on the roof. Clearly her uncle was very conscious of his security.

She circled the manor several times, keeping to the shadows as much as possible, counting another four archers on the back roof and four guards on the rear gate. The walls were in an excellent state of repair and there was a good twenty yards between them and the nearest cover. The guards were alert and changed at intervals of two hours. There would be a drain within the grounds allowing access from the sewers, but she had a strong suspicion whoever had care of her uncle's person would ensure that too was guarded.

No way in, she concluded, perching herself on the cathedral steps with an apple she had purchased from a nearby vendor.

"Here for the petitions?" he asked her as she took a bite. "Don't have the look of a city girl, way you're staring at everything."

"My stepmother claimed the farm when Dadda died," she replied, munching. "The sow won't give me and my brother our share."

"Father save us from greedy women," he said. "A tip for you, don't appeal to the lord, appeal to the whore."

"The whore?"

"Aye, he's only got the one these days. An Asraelin no less. She does much of his thinking for him, and they say she's a fair judge, whore and heretic though she is."

She favoured him with a smile. "My thanks, old fellow."

"I'm not so old," he replied in mock outrage. "Not so long ago you'd've been glad to earn the eye from me." His humour faded as his eyes lit on something behind her. "That time already," he said, moving back from his cart and falling to one knee.

Reva turned to see a procession entering the square from the north, people kneeling as they passed. In the lead a young man in a priest's robe walked with a measured gate, holding aloft a silken banner emblazoned with the flame of the World Father. Behind him walked five men side by side, robed in the dark green worn only by bishops, all holding a book in each hand. At the rear walked an old man in a plain white robe, his gaze fixed firmly ahead, giving off an aura of calm dignity, only slightly spoiled by the bulge of belly beneath his robe.

"Kneel girl!" the fruit vendor hissed. "Do you want a flogging?"

The Reader, Reva realised as she knelt, watching the procession mount the steps a few yards away. The priest had always been very clear on the first target for her father's sword. *Corrupt leader of the corrupted church. Near as vile a traitor to the Father as the drunkard in the manor.*

She watched the white-robed man as he lifted his skirts to ascend the steps. His face was unremarkable save for a somewhat hooked nose, lines of age, and no particular shine to his eyes bespeaking either evil or goodness. The church held that the Reader heard the Father's voice every time he read from the Ten Books. An absurd notion, since the Father had clearly ordained there should now be eleven books. This old man, with his belly and his sycophants, was the worst kind of heretic, deafening himself to the Father's voice for fear he may lose power over the church.

One thing at a time, she thought as the procession disappeared into the cathedral, turning back to the manor. *No way in . . . except on petitioning day.*

The next two days were spent familiarising herself with the city streets and gleaning as much information as she could about the interior of the Fief Lord's manor.

"Sits in his chair on a platform in the main hall," the innkeeper said. "People come, plead their cases, it all gets written down then a week later he gives his judgement, or rather what judgement the whore tells him to give."

"Doesn't it make people angry?" she asked, careful to keep her tone merely curious. "The fief being governed by some Asraelin strumpet."

He cackled; she noticed he did that a lot. "Would do if she wasn't so good at it. Streets are clean, trade is good, outlaws under control, more so here than in the other fiefs so I hear. Wasn't like this in his father's day, I can tell you."

From what she could gather, petitioners would line up at the front gate in the morning, the proceedings commencing at the tenth hour, though the Fief Lord's punctuality was often lacking. Petitions were heard until the sixth hour past noon, the order they were heard in determined by lot. It was tradition for the Fief Lord to provide a meal for the petitioners at midday. "It's no banquet," the fruit vendor told her. "But it's a decent spread, takes all the servants in the manor to dish it out."

Servants . . . Lots of them moving about, pages and maids.

She sat with Arken on the cathedral steps that evening, waiting for a cart to trundle up to the gate.

"The thing you're after is in there?" he asked, sounding dubious.

"I believe so."

"And you're going to steal it?"

"You can't steal what's yours by right . . . But yes. Is that a problem?"

"Stealing from a Fief Lord." He grimaced and shook his head. "They'll kill us if we're caught."

"No, they'll kill me. You're not coming." She held up a hand as he started to protest. "I need you to secure our escape. You'll wait with the horses at the city gate."

"And if you don't come?"

"Then ride away, fast."

"I can't . . ."

"This isn't a story and it isn't a song, and you're not some noble warrior who can rescue me. You're right, if I'm caught, I'm dead, and your waiting around will make no difference. You will take the horses, and the money, and go."

Her gaze was drawn back to the manor as a cart arrived, laden with wine and sundry foodstuffs. The guards opened the gate and a troop of servants emerged to unload the cart, mostly men, but also a few women. She watched them closely, drinking in the details of their garb. *A pale blue scarf tying back their hair, skirts black, blouses white.*

"Where would I go?" Arken was asking, sounding very young.

She watched the servants disappear back into the manor. "North," she said. "The Reaches. If you present yourself to the Tower Lord and mention my name, I'm sure he'll find a place for you."

His voice was hushed when he spoke again, reverent almost. "You know Lord Al Sorna?"

She got to her feet, brushing dust from her trews. "Certainly, I was his sister."

She bought a plain white blouse, a blue scarf and two skirts, one black, one green. She spent the evening before petitioning day sewing them together, green outside, black inside. She had seen how punctilious the guards were in searching visitors to the manor so discounted the notion of concealing a weapon beneath the skirts. If need be, she could always find the kitchens where there would be knives aplenty. Come the morning she presented herself at the manor gate, clutching a scroll bearing a fictitious claim against an imaginary stepmother. She was a little flustered, the farewell with Arken had been awkward, the boy leaning close to press a kiss to her cheek then retreating with a hurt look as she pulled back in alarm.

"Remember, don't wait," she said. "If I'm not there an hour after the gate opens in the morning . . ."

"I know," he said, scowling a little.

She hoped he would be content with a squeeze to his hand and took herself off to the manor. She got there early but a line of over a dozen people had already formed, the number soon growing to well over two hundred by the time the gate opened. A House Guard emerged to walk down the line, a sack held open in his hands, each petitioner reaching in to extract a wooden peg as he did so. Reva duly plucked one when her turn came, doing her best to look anxious.

"Six!" exclaimed the old woman behind her, reading the symbol carved into the peg Reva had drawn. The woman's own read fifty-nine. "I'll be here all bloody day, with my old legs about to buckle any second as well."

Reva thought the woman had a fairly sturdy look to her, but made a sympathetic face. "Don't worry, grandmother. We'll swap, here." She held out the peg.

The woman squinted in suspicion. "How much?"

"The Father loves a generous deed," Reva told her, smiling broadly.

"Oh." The woman glanced at the cathedral then held out her own peg. "Righto."

From behind came shouts of discord as the last peg was chosen. "Not my problem," the guard with the sack called over his shoulder as he made his way back down the line. "Come back next month."

They were soon ushered through the gate, each searched for weapons before being allowed to proceed into the grounds beyond, a bizarre mix of ornate topiary and fruit trees, then into the manor itself. The petitioners were required to gather in the main hall, situated at the end of a short hallway featuring few doors, all having the varnished look of many years' disuse. In the hall a cordon of guards stood before a raised platform where an empty chair waited. When all one hundred petitioners had been led in, a guard held up a hand to silence the murmur.

"Bow for Fief Lord Sentes Mustor, most loyal servant of the Unified Realm and ruler by the King's Word of the Fief of Cumbrael."

Reva had positioned herself at the rear of the hall so only had a partial view of the man who emerged from a side door. He was of average height, somewhere past his fiftieth year, well dressed but with a long tangle of unkempt hair, walking with a slight stoop. When he sat down she had a clear view of his face, finding it far from edifying: sunken cheekbones, sallow unshaven skin and eyes that were unnaturally red, even for a drunkard. She had expected to find some vestige of her own features there, some echo of shared blood, but there was nothing, making her wonder if she favoured her mother more than her father.

The guard tapped the butt of his pole-axe on the floor and spoke again. "Keep silence for the Lady Veliss, Honorary Counsel to the Lordship of Cumbrael."

The woman who stepped onto the platform was dressed simply in a skirt and blouse, not dissimilar to the garb of the maids Reva had so keenly observed the day before, distinguished only by the bluestone amulet hanging on a golden chain that did much to draw the eye to her ample bosom. Her hair, tied back in a simple ponytail with a blue ribbon, was a dark but natural shade of brown and her comely features, full-lipped and apple-cheeked, were free of paint.

"Filthy whore," an anonymous male voice muttered close to Reva, though not loud enough to reach the ears of the guards.

The Lady Veliss smiled and opened her arms in a gesture of welcome, speaking in precise tones but the coarseness of her Asraelin accent giving the lie to her noble title. "On behalf of Lord Mustor, I bid you welcome. Please be assured that all petitions will be heard today, and will receive careful deliberation before judgement is made. Patience, as the Father tells us, is amongst the finest virtues." She smiled again, showing bright and perfect teeth.

"Like the Father would soil his sight on you," the unseen voice muttered.

"We shall proceed," Veliss went on. "Number one. Please come forward and state your name, home and case."

The first petitioner was an old man complaining on behalf of his village about a recent increase in rents, blaming it on his landlord's taste for spoiling his son. "Buys him a new horse every month, milord. Ain't right, people goin' hungry and there's a lad no more than twelve riding about on a brand-new stallion."

"Your landlord's name?" Veliss enquired.

"Lord Javen, milady."

"Ah. I believe Lord Javen lost his eldest boy at Greenwater Ford, did he not?"

The man gave a stiff nod. "Along with half the lads in the village, milady. And they weren't lost in the ford, they were slaughtered afterwards, having surrendered on promise of honourable treatment."

Veliss gave a tight grimace, Greenwater Ford had been an Asraelin massacre after all. "Quite so." She looked towards the pair of scribes sitting at a desk to the side of the platform, one of them looking up and nodding. "Your case has been noted," Veliss told the old man. "And will receive urgent consideration."

And on it went, one complainant after another, each with a similar tale of woe; unfair rents, unjust disinheritance, theft of land, one young girl asking for sufficient alms to buy her grandfather a new wooden leg, lost in service to the Fief Lord's mighty forebear. "I think this one can be decided now," Veliss said, gesturing for a servant to come forward with a purse from which she handed the girl twice the amount she had asked for, drawing an appreciative murmur from the crowd. *This one's no fool,* Reva judged. *Uncle is wise in his choice of whore.*

The last petitioner of the morning proved the most interesting, a man of middling years and somewhat shorter than most, but impressively muscular, his belly free of any paunch despite his age, the hard muscle of his arms discernible under his shirt.

Archer, Reva decided as the man bowed and stated his particulars. "Bren Antesh, Tear Head Sound, seeking permission to convene a company of archers."

For the first time the Fief Lord stirred in his chair, eyes narrowing at the man's name. "There was a Captain Antesh at Linesh," he said in a voice of gravel. "Was there not?"

The archer nodded. "Indeed, my lord."

"They say he saved the Darkblade's life," her uncle continued, raising a murmur from the crowd. "Can that possibly be true?"

A faint smile came to Antesh's lips as he said, "That's not a name I use, my lord. There is no Darkblade, it's a story for children."

Some of the murmurs became angry mutters. "Heresy! It's in the books . . ." The voices fell silent as a guard slammed his pole-axe stave on the stone floor.

The Fief Lord seemed unaware of the commotion, wiping a hand over his bleary eyes as he went on, "A company of archers, eh? What on earth for?"

"The young men at the Sound grow lazy, my lord. Given to drunkenness and brawling. The bow brings focus to a man's gaze, trains the body and the mind, gives him the skill to feed his family, and pride in having done so. Deer are plentiful in our woods but few possess the skill to hunt them, save with a *crossbow*," he added with a disdainful curl to his lip. "I will tutor the lads in the bow, so that they may know the skills of their fathers."

"Along with a monthly stipend from me into the bargain?" the Fief Lord asked.

Antesh shook his head. "We ask for no payment, my lord. We will craft our own bows and shafts. We merely seek leave to form a company and practise freely. "

"And should I require the service of this company in time of war?"

Antesh hesitated and Reva saw he had anticipated, but dreaded, this question. The tone of his answer had a certain heaviness to it. "We will be yours to command, my lord."

The Fief Lord's gaze became distant with remembrance. "As a boy I was good with bow, better than my brother in fact. Hard to believe I could best him at anything, I know. Had I not been . . . distracted by life, perhaps I'd have muscles like you, eh, Captain?"

The archer replied quickly, neatly side-stepping the opportunity for transgression. "If my lord would care to pick up the bow again, I'd happily teach him."

Mustor laughed a little. "A man who hits the mark with words as well as arrows." He turned to the scribes, raising his voice. "The Fief Lord of Cumbrael hereby grants the men of Tear Head Sound leave to convene a company of archers under the captaincy of"—he fumbled, waving a hand at the archer—"Master Antesh here, for a term of one year." He turned his gaze back to Antesh. "After that we'll see."

The archer bowed. "My thanks, my lord."

The Fief Lord nodded and rose to his feet, looking expectantly at Lady Veliss. "Lunch?"

Servants brought trestle tables and benches into the hall, soon laden with bread, chicken, cheese and bowls of steaming soup. As the vendor had said, the fare was simple but hearty, the petitioners falling to the meal with enthusiasm. The Fief Lord and Lady Veliss retired to enjoy a private meal and Reva found herself seated next to the sturdy old woman from the line. Her case had been heard, a claim against her former employer for unpaid wages, but she stayed for the food.

"Sewed dresses for that ungrateful bitch for near ten years I did," she said around a mouthful of chicken. "Wore my fingers to nubs. One day she says she's had enough of my waspish tongue and sends me packing. Well, the lord's strumpet'll see to her, all right."

Reva nodded politely as the woman ranted on, eating a small portion of food and watching the servants come and go, mostly via a large door in the east wall. They were an efficient lot, moving with brisk purpose and little talk, causing Reva to suspect the

Lady Veliss had small tolerance for lazy servants, which meant she was likely to know them all, if not by name, certainly by sight.

She waited a short while before asking a passing servant girl the way to the privy, being pointed to a smaller door in the western wall. She found the stalls empty and quickly went about her change of garb, removing the skirt and turning it inside out, pulling her hair into a tight tail before tying the blue scarf in place. *Deception is a matter of expectation,* the priest had told her once. *People do not question what they expect to see. Only the unusual draws the eye.* People expected a serving girl in this house to move quickly and speak little, and so she did, emerging from the privy with an unhesitant stride, going to the table to lift some empty plates and taking them to the eastern door. She was gratified by the fact that the old woman didn't even glance up from her plate as she passed by.

She stood aside as other servants exited the door, thankfully too intent on their own tasks to afford her any attention. The door led to a long corridor ending in a flight of steps which she judged led down to the kitchens. The numerous voices echoing up the stairwell made her discount any notion of trying to secure herself a knife just yet. She placed the plates on a nearby windowsill and went looking for a hiding place. Only one door in the corridor walls was unlocked, opening into a cupboard holding nothing more exciting than a collection of mops and brooms. However, fortune had also provided a large wicker basket piled high with laundry. A few moments squirming and she was safely concealed beneath the mound of mingled bedclothes and garments. Discovery seemed a faint possibility, since with so much clearing up to do after the petitioners had left, any laundry duties would probably be left for the morrow. With little else to occupy her, she went to sleep.

She awoke to the soft impact of more laundry being piled on top of the concealing mound, hearing a muffled exchange of tired voices, cutting off as the door closed. She balled her fists and started counting, stopped at a hundred and started again, extending a finger every time she began a new count. When all ten digits were extended she balled her fists once more and forced herself to repeat the process three more times, only then did she push her way out of the laundry basket, groping for the door in the pitch-darkness. She opened it a crack and peered out onto the dimly lit corridor. Nothing, no footsteps, no voices. The house was at rest.

She divested herself of the heavy double-skirt, having worn her trews underneath the whole time, then crept out into the corridor, ears straining, still hearing nothing. Satisfied, she rose and made for the stairway. The kitchens were large and empty, the only sound coming from a few steaming stock-pots left on the long iron range. Her eyes soon picked out the gleam of metal next to the chopping block. The knives were neatly laid out on the table, offering a wide choice, from large broad-bladed cleavers to needlelike skewers. She chose a plain butcher's knife with a six-inch blade and good balance to the handle, pushing it into the leather strap she had tied to her ankle before donning the skirts.

As she expected, the kitchens led to another stairway which she hoped would provide access to the Fief Lord's private chambers, where he was sure to keep any items of value. She climbed the stairs with slow, softly placed steps, careful not to raise the slightest noise. The first room she came to held a long dining table, polished surface dark and gleaming in the light from the oil lamps, the walls covered with tapestries and paintings, mostly portraits. She annoyed herself by allowing her eyes to linger on the faces gazing out from the canvases, searching once more for echoes of her own features, but finding only the distinctive jawline and broad nose that characterised her uncle's visage.

The dining room adjoined a library, three high walls of book-laden shelves. In the centre of the room sat a writing desk where a book lay open, the silk ribbon trailing across the centre of the page, a few handwritten sheets of parchment next to it. Reva paused as she passed, turning the book to read the title on the cover; *Of Nations and Wealth* by Dendrish Hendrahl. The writing on the sheets was precise, scribed by a tutored hand. *The price of wine defines this fief,* she read. *Its wealth therefore derives from the vine. The most important man in the fief? Is it the man who owns the vine or the man who picks the grapes?*

Reva returned the book to its previous state and moved on, finding another stairwell at the far end of the library. The sight of the room on the next floor up provoked a sudden leap in her heart. *Swords!*

The room was windowless, lit by a candelabrum hanging from the ceiling, the light from the numerous tiered rows of lamps playing on the swords that covered all four walls. The floor was wooden and springy underfoot as she ventured further, drawn to the nearest sword, a plain but well-made blade of the Asraelin pattern, as were most of its brothers. They were each held in place by iron brackets and easily lifted. Reva's gaze was drawn to the white plaster above the sword racks, finding it decorated with faded but readable paintings, men frozen in the lunge or the parry. This, she realised, was a room for sword practice. Her father must have learned his skills in this room. What better place for his brother to keep it?

Her eyes roved the walls, seeing more and more Asraelin blades, here and there an archaic long sword or a poniard, but none that matched Al Sorna's description or the example the smith had shown her . . . *Wait!*

It hung in the centre of the far wall, a twin to the sword in the smith's shop, except . . . the handle was finely made and bore an engraved silver emblem; a drawn bow ringed in oak leaves, the crest of the House of Mustor. *Can it be?* Her fingers played over the handle, her eyes noting the uneven edge of the blade and the scratches on its surface. This sword had seen use, this sword had been carried to war. Perhaps her uncle had the handle made when he brought it back from the High Keep, finding some vestige of decency to honour his fallen brother.

This is it! she decided, grasping the handle and lifting the sword from its bracket. *It has to be.*

She closed her eyes, held it close, the blade cold against the skin of her forearms, fighting the hammer of her heart. *At last . . .*

She exhaled slowly, calming herself. Success would only come when she and Arken were free of this city. She would return to her cupboard and wait for the morning, conceal the sword in a basket of laundry and leave via the front gate under the gaze of the guards.

She returned to the stairwell, casting a brief glance upwards . . . and saw a hand. It jutted from behind the corner, lying on the stone ten steps up. It was small, skin smooth and youthful though speckled with blood, the fingers slender but unmoving.

The sword was heavy and clumsy in her grasp, making her pine for her own Far Western blade, but still she reversed her grip on it, holding the point low as she ascended the steps. The girl lay on her back, eyes wide and staring, blue scarf askew on her head, the white of her blouse dyed red from the gaping wound in her neck. The blood still flowed, this was recent.

Reva's eyes tracked to the steps above, seeing bloody footprints on the stone, overlapping each other in a red collage. *More than one. Probably more than two.* The realisation was cold and implacable. The Sons, it had to be. *The Sons are here, and they have not come for me.*

Her immediate instinct was to flee. The manor would soon be in an uproar, bringing danger but also the chance to slip away in the confusion, carrying her prize . . .

They're going to kill my uncle.

That this undeniable fact was unwelcome surprised her. Her only living blood relative, a man she had never met but been raised to despise, was about to die alongside his Asraelin whore. *A just end for the Father's betrayer, and for his heretic slut.* She tried to force some passion into the thought but it remained a listless inward recitation of long-held dogma, empty and insincere in the face of the atrocity confronting her gaze.

What about her? she wondered, continuing to stare at the face of the murdered girl. *What end did she deserve?*

She found herself climbing the stairs, stepping over the corpse on silent feet, sword held in front of her in a two-handed grip. The bloody footprints faded as she climbed higher, but still left enough gore for her to follow, all the way to the top. She crouched before turning the final corner, using the blade of the butcher's knife as a mirror, edging it out to afford a view of the last flight of steps, seeing dark shapes moving in a gloomy hallway. No-one had been left to guard their line of retreat, a curious error . . . unless there was no expectation of danger.

She turned the corner and ascended to the hallway. There were three of them, dressed all in black, including the silk scarves covering their faces. Each held a sword, light Asraelin blades, not the like the clumsy bar of sharpened steel she held. They were crouched before a door, outlined in yellow light from the room beyond where voices could be heard, a man and a woman. The woman sounded tense, angry even, the man weary, and drunk. The words "archers" and "foolish" were audible amidst the muffled babble. The man closest to the door reached up to grasp the handle.

"Why did you kill the girl?" Reva asked.

They whirled as one, the man close to the door rising to his full height, green eyes staring at her in appalled recognition, eyes she knew well.

She took an involuntary step back, the sword sagging in her grasp, air escaping her lungs in a rush. "I"—she choked, coughed, forced the words out, holding up the sword—"I found it. See?"

The green eyes narrowed and a voice came from behind the scarf, hard, flat and certain, as it had been every time he beat her. "Kill her!" the priest said.

The man closest to her lunged, sword extended, the point seeking her neck. Her counter was automatic and largely the fruit of Al Sorna's teaching, the heavy sword coming up to sweep the stabbing point aside as she stepped back, ducking under a following slash. Behind her attacker the priest kicked the door open and charged in, sword raised for a killing thrust, a shout of astonishment sounding from a female throat.

Reva side-stepped another thrust, jabbed fingers into her attacker's eyes then brought the heavy sword up and round to hack into his leg below the knee, biting deep into the flesh. She left him writhing and screaming, leaping clear and charging into the bedroom.

The priest's companion had his back to her, slashing repeatedly at something on the bed, something that wriggled in a thick welter of bedclothes, feathers billowing as the blade tore through the quilts. Reva slammed the sword into his back, putting all her weight behind the blade as it speared him between the shoulder blades to jut an inch from his chest, blood erupting from his mouth as he arched his back, collapsing lifeless to the floor.

Reva had expected to find the Fief Lord dead but instead he gaped up at her from his protective swaddle of quilts, his only injury a small cut to the cheek. Shouts of fury dragged Reva's gaze to the other side of the bed where the priest was battling the Lady Veliss. She lunged at him with a short rapier, teeth bared in a snarl, a torrent of foul abuse issuing from her lips with every thrust. "You cock-munching fucker! I'll make you eat your own balls!"

For all her fury, Reva was impressed with her control, the thrusts were quick, precise and not over-extended, forcing the priest back, away from the bed. He parried without difficulty, the blade moving in a fluid series of arcs, the way it had when he blocked Reva's attempts to find a way past with her knife. Despite her skills, Veliss proved to be outmatched, the priest finding an opening as he feinted a jab at her eyes then swung a punch to her face, sending her sprawling.

Reva scooped up the fallen sword of the man she had killed, placing herself between the priest and the bed.

He stared at her in outraged frustration. "You forsake the Father's love with this betrayal!" he screamed, skin reddening about his eyes. "Al Sorna's Darkness has twisted you!"

"No," she whispered, hating the tears that streamed from her eyes. "No, you did that."

"Filthy, Fatherless sinn—"

She lunged, fast and low, the blade straight and true, finding his thigh, coming free bloody as he twisted away with a howl.

A shout and the thunder of many feet drew her gaze back to the door before she could press the advantage. The priest hefted a stool and threw it at the nearest window, glass shattering amidst the billowing curtain. He glanced back at her once, eyes bright with hate, then turned and ran, leaping through the remains of the window.

Reva dropped her sword and stared at the curtain as it coiled in the night breeze, the sky beyond black and empty. Metal scraped from scabbards and shouts of challenge filled her ears as rough hands closed on her.

"STOP!" The command filled the room, stilling the tumult.

The Fief Lord cursed as he disentangled himself from the bedclothes, stumbling into her gaze though she barely saw him, her eyes still fixed on the curtain and the window.

"Look at me," he said, voice gentle, fingers soft on her chin. She looked into the red-rimmed eyes of her uncle and saw tears there as he smiled, his lips forming a fond murmur. "Reva."

CHAPTER EIGHT
Frentis

They lived in the wild for ten days, deep in the forested hills north of South Tower, far away from any roads or likely patrol routes. Still they were hunted, the South Guard venturing far and wide with dogs and trackers, forcing them to move camp every day, sometimes laying false trails towards the Cumbraelin border. The need to keep moving made hunting a rare luxury so they grew hungry, sustained by what mushrooms and roots they could scavenge on the move, huddling together for warmth at night for they dared not risk a fire.

The woman was mostly silent now, still brooding over her failure, a new uncertainty having crept into her gaze. Frentis wanted to find comfort in the change, to be heartened by this signal of frailty, but instead saw a greater threat brewing behind her eyes. He knew her now, though he hated the knowledge, knew that whatever reflection she indulged in could only lead to a fiercer devotion to killing. She might hate others for their gods but she worshipped murder with all the fervour of the worst Cumbraelin fanatic.

"I do not blame you, beloved," she said one night, the first words she had spoken in days. "Do not think that. I can only blame myself, I see that now. My love for you has made me exultant, Revek's gift complacent, and so I allowed myself the illusion of invulnerability. A hard lesson, as are all true lessons."

On the tenth day they found an old forester's cottage, overgrown and tumbled down, but retaining enough shelter to conceal a fire come nightfall. Frentis went foraging and returned with the usual roots and mushrooms but also a hand-caught trout, heaved from a nearby stream when it ventured too close to the bank. He gutted it, wrapped it in dock leaves and baked it in the fire, the woman wolfing down her share with feral enthusiasm. "Hunger is always the best seasoning," she said when it was all gone, the first smile in days appearing on her lips.

Frentis finished his own meal and said nothing.

"You're worried," she went on, shuffling closer, pressing herself against his side. "Wondering who's next when we get to Varinshold. Although, I think you already know."

Frentis found he much preferred her introspective mood, and was allowed enough freedom to say so. She rarely bound his tongue now, seeming to find some comfort in the rare words he spoke, however lacking in affection they might be. *Why couldn't you just die in South Tower?* he wanted to say, but paused. He knew they were approaching something, a moment of fulfilment for whatever insane purpose she served, and he had divined sufficient insight by now to know what that would mean. "Are you open to a bargain?" he asked instead.

This drew a frown of genuine puzzlement. "A bargain, my love?"

"My love," he repeated. "You call me that all the time, and you mean it, don't you? You've lived so long, but you've never loved, not until me."

Her face lost all expression, save a faint wariness to the eyes, and she nodded, probably in expectation of another barb or hate-filled declaration.

"You want me, all of me," he continued. "You can have me. We can be together, for as long as you want, you'll never have to force me again. I'll never fight you again. We go, we leave, we find some forgotten place, far away from people. And we stay there, just you and me."

Her face remained immobile but for a faint twitch to her lips, an occasional blink to her eyes.

"You can read my feelings," he said. "So you know I am sincere in this."

When she spoke her voice was thick, whether with anger or sorrow he couldn't tell. "You think that's what I want?"

"No, it's what I'm offering."

"In return for what?"

"Turn away from this path, no more killing. Abandon whatever task waits in Varinshold."

She closed her eyes and turned away, profile red and perfect in the firelight. "When I was as young as you are now, I knew only hate. A hate as bright and glorious as any love, the kind of hate that calls across the void when married to a gifted song, finding the ear of something that also had a bargain to offer. And I made it, beloved. I made that bargain, sealed it in an ocean of blood, so I can't make yours."

She opened her eyes, turning to him, her expression betraying such a depth of sadness and confusion he found it hard to look at her. "You talk of finding a forgotten place. There are no forgotten places, not for the Ally. Our only chance is to fulfil his scheme, don't you see? Give him his moment of triumph, the last stroke of the brush to his grand design, only then can we make our own. Then, my love, then I promise you, there will be no need for forgotten places, no need to hide. We'll give him his victory, then burn it all down and him with it."

He looked away and she moved closer, her arms slipping around his waist as her head rested on his shoulder. "I'm going to kill you," he said. "You must know that."

She kissed his neck and for once he didn't flinch, though he had the freedom to do so. "Then, beloved," she said in a whisper, breath hot on his neck, "you would doom yourself and every soul in this world."

They hid for another three days until all sign of pursuit had faded, the forest free of the distant barking of dogs or the scent of soldiers' fires. They journeyed north, remaining cautious, avoiding roads and well-trammelled tracks, too wary even to risk stealing from the few farmhouses they saw. The woman's purpose consumed her now, allowing no chance of failure. She spoke rarely, made no more use of him at night. They travelled, they slept, they foraged, nothing more.

It was another two weeks before they reached the flatlands and the road to the Brinewash Bridge, both notably thinner and besmirched from so long in the wilds, something the woman seemed to find comfort in. "Escaped slaves are rarely well-fed," she said the night before they were to enter the city. They camped on the riverbank a few miles upstream from the bridge, lacking any coin for the toll and wary of drawing the eye of any guards who might be in attendance.

"We met in the pits," she told him. "Two slaves thrown into the same cell in expectation we would breed. I was stolen from my people as a girl, one of the fierce northern tribes will do, the name doesn't matter. They're renowned warriors, many of the Kuritai are bred from stock stolen from the northern wastes. I expected you to be bestial, inflicting your lust upon my innocent flesh, instead you were kind, in time love bloomed between us and we contrived an escape. Our journey across the empire was an epic of trial and bloody adventure, until we made it to Volar and concealed ourselves upon a ship to the west, sailing all the way to Varinshold, where you will be recognised by a kindly lord at the docks."

She smiled thinly, reading his surprise at the mention of the kindly lord. "This has been long planned, my love. The Ally has many tools."

They swam across in the morning, the rising sun raising mist from the river as they fought the current to make the opposite bank. At the western gate, guards waved approaching wagons to the side and pushed back travellers seeking entry. The reason became clear shortly afterwards as the first regiment trooped through the gate. Frentis recognised the standard, a boar with red tusks, the Thirtieth Regiment of Foot, wiped out at Untesh and now evidently reborn. Behind them came the Sixteenth, the Black Bears, followed by one regiment after another until it seemed the whole Realm Guard was on the march. They edged closer to a group of onlookers, hearing the words "Cumbrael" and "Tower Lord" most amongst the general chatter.

"Not such a failure after all," the woman murmured as the Realm Guard continued to troop past.

Frentis counted ten full regiments of foot and five of cavalry before the final contingent emerged, a contrast to the others with their dark blue cloaks, mail and leather helms, marching under a banner emblazoned with a running wolf above a tower. Their Lord Marshal was younger than most men of such rank, possessed of an aura of competence and toughness undiminished by his comparatively slight stature. He was also dressed in the garb of a brother of the Sixth Order.

The binding surged as Frentis tried to call out, the words trapped in his chest the instant he thought them. The woman gave a regretful smile as she forced him to turn his face away. "Not a time for reunions, my love."

So he was prevented from watching Caenis lead his Wolfrunners from Varinshold, and none of the veterans had cause to let their gaze linger on the bedraggled but sturdy beggar in the crowd.

The western quarter was much as he remembered, a little cleaner perhaps, but all the streets, alleys and doorways of his youth were intact, although it seemed to have shrunk in the interval. As a child it had been a vast maze, one minute a playground for an impetuous thief, the other a deadly battleground when the gangs went to war. He was permitted to linger outside a boarded-up hovel on Jape Street. The woman who once lived there had long, straggly hair and eyes dulled with too much redflower, and a man who stank of piss and gin, knifed and bled dry behind a tavern over some forgotten grievance before Frentis was old enough to form a clear memory of his face. The straggle-haired woman disappeared soon after, to a brothel he heard, though some said she'd given herself to the river. If she had a name, he never knew it.

"Don't worry," the woman said, squeezing his hand. "It'll all be gone soon enough. No more grim reminders for my husband."

She led him to the warehouse district, halting before one with a chalked symbol on the door, a circle within a circle. She hammered on the door and waited. The man who answered the door was dressed in the mean garb of a sailor but Frentis knew him immediately as Kuritai, his stature and bearing made it obvious. He gave the woman a nod of respect rather than the full bow that would have been required in Volaria, then stepped aside. The warehouse was stacked high with barrels save for a bare section of floor in the centre where ten more Kuritai waited, scabbarded short swords within easy reach. They bowed to the woman as she entered. "Who is One here?" she asked.

The Kuritai from the door stepped forward. "I am, Mistress."

"Everything is in readiness?"

"It is, Mistress."

"What is your allotted target?"

"The palace. We attack one hour after your arrival there. After that we rendezvous at the north gate for the assault on the House of the Sixth Order."

"How many?"

"All of the hidden companies, Mistress, plus a contingent of Free Cavalry. There should be five hundred in the assault force."

The woman glanced at Frentis. "It won't be enough. When the general comes ashore tell him the force is to be tripled, on my authority."

"Yes, Mistress."

She looked around, nose wrinkling at the musty air in the warehouse. "Is there any food in this shit-hole?"

The were given oatmeal porridge flavoured with berries, the standard fare of the Kuritai Frentis knew so well from the pits. Despite the growing dread that gripped him, his hunger made him wolf down two bowls in quick succession. He was scraping the bowl clean with his spoon when someone began pounding on the warehouse door.

The woman nodded to the One who gestured to two of his men. They drew swords and faded into the shadows on either side of the door before he opened it. The man who entered was tall and finely dressed, with smooth, somewhat delicate features marred by a fearful but determined expression. The woman rose as he came forward, offering him a respectful bow. "My lord."

The man nodded, his eyes fixing on Frentis. "This is really him? The King will be quick to spot an impostor."

"I assure you, my lord, this is Brother Frentis, brave comrade of King Malcius risen from the dead, as promised."

The man's gaze didn't lift from Frentis. "Which hand does the King favour?"

Frentis replied without hesitation. "He writes with his left but wields a sword with his right. As a boy, his father forced him to suppress his natural inclination to use his left in sword practice, fearing it would be a disadvantage in battle."

The man grunted in apparent satisfaction and the woman said, "Why would we seek to deceive you, my lord? Have we not kept every promise made so far?"

He ignored her question, eyes tracking around the warehouse. "Where is your usual agent? His face I know."

"You'll see it again, soon. When the city is ours and our arrangement complete."

"I have another stipulation."

It was just a slight curve to her lips, the smallest crease to her brow, but Frentis saw that this finely dressed lord had just earned himself a swift death. "Stipulation, my lord?"

The man nodded, licking his lips. He kept his hands within the folds of his sable-trimmed cloak, but Frentis knew they were shaking. "Princess Lyrna will soon return to Varinshold. The King will want her at his side when he welcomes his old comrade. She is not to be harmed, not in any way. She will be secured and placed in my care. My continued cooperation depends on this. I hope that's clear."

The woman inclined her head. "The princess is famed for her beauty, it would be churlish of us to deny you an additional reward."

A flash of anger lit his eyes. "She must never know of my part in this . . . enterprise. My survival, and elevation, will be portrayed as merely the wise actions of a pragmatic man."

The woman smiled and Frentis thought, *Slow death.* "Yet more stipulations, my lord. But fear not, it will all be as you say." She guided him back to the door, her face a perfect representation of servile respect, the face a servant shows to a kindly master. "The ship should arrive in the next day or two. Word will be sent when it's time for you to discover Brother Frentis."

She held the door open for him with a deferential nod. The lord seemed about to speak again, no doubt earning himself an even slower demise, but thought better of it and made a hasty departure.

"What do you think, my love?" the woman asked Frentis, returning to his side. "Burning or flaying?"

"The traditional death for traitors to the Realm is hanging," he replied. "But I think burning would suit that one better."

That night he watched her sleep and implored the Departed to return the itch to his side with every ounce of will he could summon. When they failed to respond he asked their forgiveness and prayed to all the Alpiran gods he could recall, the Nameless Seer the old man had served, Olbiss, the sea god, Martual, the god of courage Vaelin's mason friend had carved in Linesh. They gave no answer and so he abandoned all hope of ever being accepted into the Beyond and turned to the Cumbraelin World Father. *If you're there, release me, bring back the pain. I will forsake the Faith, I will leave the Order and serve you all my days. JUST SET ME FREE!*

But the World Father, it seemed, was as deaf as every other god or departed soul.

For the next two mornings they climbed to the roof of the warehouse as the tide swelled the harbour waters. Ships put out to sea whilst others arrived and all the while the woman's eyes scanned the horizon.

"My bargain is still offered," Frentis told her on the second day, hating the desperation in his voice, knowing he was finally a beggar. "Please."

She kept her gaze fixed out to sea and said nothing.

The sail appeared shortly after the tenth bell, the ship resolving through the mist into a medium-sized trading vessel, Volarian colours flying from the mainmast. It had a somewhat drab appearance, sails and wood darkened with age and use, sitting low in the water, carrying a heavy load.

"Plea—" Frentis began but stopped as she flared the binding.

"No more words, my love." She turned away from the sea and went to the ladder propped against the warehouse roof. "It's time."

They dressed as stevedores, faces shadowed beneath broad-brimmed hats, going to the harbour and waiting for the ship to berth. The gangplank was duly lowered and they went aboard without preamble, attracting no attention from the sailors on deck as they went below. A well-built man of middle years awaited them in the hold, his black jerkin marking him as the owner and captain of this vessel. He gave the woman a deep bow. "Most honoured citizen."

The woman's gaze went past him to the contents of the hold, ranks of seated men, silent, waiting. Perhaps three hundred, all Kuritai. "The fleet?" she asked.

"Waiting beyond the horizon," the captain said. "They attack at nightfall. All other vessels we met on the sea were taken and burned, the crews with them. These ghost-worshippers have no knowledge of our approach."

She began to undress. "We need clothes, the kind worn by the lowliest of the crew."

They exchanged their ragged garb for thin cotton trews and

shirts which made them look only slightly less beggared than before. "No need for restraint," the woman told the captain.

"Off my ship, you worthless bitch!" he railed at them, hounding them across the deck, brandishing a whip. "Go and take your Realm dog with you!"

The woman cowered away from him, sheltering beneath Frentis's protective arm. They hurried to the gangplank and fled to the wharf. "Count y'selves lucky you're not feeding the sharks!" the captain called after them. "That's the proper reward for stowaways."

They stood on the wharf, clutching each other, a few onlookers having paused to watch the spectacle announced by the captain's tirade. Frentis stared about in amazement. "Varinshold!" he breathed.

The woman embraced him, tears of joy shining her eyes. "We're truly here, Frentis! After so long."

A tall man in a sable-trimmed cloak stepped from the small crowd, a frown of recognition on his smooth brow. "Are you . . ." His eyes widened in amazement as he drew closer and he bowed low in grave respect. "Brother Frentis!" He straightened, turning to the crowd. "Brother Frentis is returned to the Realm!" He beckoned a man to him, one of his servants from the way the man scurried to his side. "Run to the palace. Give word to the guard that I will bring Brother Frentis before the King with all dispatch."

The man bobbed his head. "I shall, Lord Al Telnar."

The crowd chattered as Al Telnar led them away, their faces joyous, a few even awed. *They think me a hero,* Frentis realised, offering a tight smile in return as some called out to him, deaf to his silent plea: *Kill me!*

CHAPTER NINE
Vaelin

They stayed with the Bear People for another three weeks, the first days spent dispelling their hunger with the steady stream of supplies coming from the south, and also the occasional delivery of elk meat from Eorhil hunting parties. Despite their deliverance, the mood of the Bear People remained largely joyless, though some of the children were more given to laughter as the days passed. Others continued to perish from the depredations of their trek across the ice, mostly the old, and a few dozen fur-wrapped bundles were left out on the plain in that first week. The Bear People did not burn or bury their dead, knowing the wild would reclaim any flesh left to it soon enough.

The shaman's name was far beyond the ability of Vaelin's tongue to pronounce, but from the visions he divined it as some concordance of bearlike ferocity and great knowledge, so took to calling him Wise Bear. They communicated mainly through visions but Vaelin found it too taxing to share his own with any regularity, so began to teach the old man Realm Tongue, with Dahrena's help.

"Bear!" he said, thumping a hand to his bone-staff when she had managed to communicate a desire to know what animal it derived from.

"And these?" she asked, her fingers playing over the many symbols carved into the bone. "Words?"

The old shaman frowned, seemingly surprised by her ignorance. Vaelin was beginning to understand that the knowledge of the Dark possessed by this man far exceeded their own. He never seemed to tire from the use of his gift, despite his age, and his facility with Realm Tongue grew rapidly thanks to his ability to share visions of the words they conveyed. This time, however, Dahrena's question seemed to have stumped him.

"Writing," Vaelin said, singing a little, a small sensation of words captured in text.

"Ahhh." Wise Bear nodded in understanding then shook his head. "No . . . words." His hand smoothed over the myriad markings on the bone-staff. "Power."

They were ready to move on by the second week, Dahrena leading them on a south-westerly course. "There's an inlet some fifty miles along the coast," she explained. "The forest has game and the waters offer good fishing. There was a settlement there many years ago but it was abandoned when the bluestone mine proved too poor to sustain the effort of surviving the winter. I doubt these people will have that problem though."

During the journey Vaelin was able to piece together a clearer picture of the events which had driven these people from their home. Wise Bear told of countless years on the ice, warring with the Cat People to the west or trading with the Wolf People to the north. Life remained unchanged until the Cat People grew ambitious. It seemed a new shaman had arisen amongst them, great and powerful in his command of beasts. Under his hand the Cat People became ever more discontented, looking with envious eyes on the vast hunting grounds enjoyed by their neighbours. They couldn't hope to defeat them alone, of course, for all the war-cats and spearhawks they bred, and so sought alliance with the iron-shapers south of the ice. Traditionally, they had been looked on with a mixture of bafflement and contempt, living in the same dwelling all year round, shutting themselves away when the snows fell, valued only for the iron tools they fashioned and traded for furs. But recent centuries had seen them change, seen them range further and further north, and not always with the intent of trade. Children were taken, later seen dragged away south in chains. The Bear People exacted vengeance of course, for a feud cannot be turned from on the ice, many iron-shapers were killed, but there were always more, and the Cat People's shaman saw an opportunity for alliance.

"But you defeated them," Vaelin said, recalling the vision of the great clash between cat and bear. "Drove them into these lands where they perished."

"Lost . . . many men," Wise Bear said. "Many bears. Too many."

Their victory had been no more than a respite, and a costly one. When the Volarians came north in force they were too weak in number to stand against them. The Wolf People fled east, the Bear People west, and the ice was lost to them forever.

The inlet was known as the Mirror Sound for the placidity of its waters which offered a clear reflection of the tall-forested slopes rising on either side. Dahrena guided them to the site of the former settlement, now a ramshackle stockade on the eastern shore, the wooden dwellings overgrown with creepers and moss. Wise Bear gave it only the most cursory of glances before turning his attention to the water. "Boats," he said.

"I can have some brought here," Vaelin offered but the shaman shook his head.

"Make boats."

He disappeared into the forest with a group of the younger men and women and soon the sound of chopping wood was echoing through the trees. They returned some hours later with a number of midsize tree trunks and set about stripping the bark. When the trunks were bared they were split with some well-placed axe blows and the ice folk began hollowing them out and shaping the rounded sides into hulls. Within two days the Bear People had a fleet of ten boats with ever more being fashioned on the shoreline. They had also begun to pull a regular supply of fish from the inlet, mostly cod and a few salmon.

They made no effort to repair the settlement, even pulling

some of the huts down for firewood. Their own shelters were easily collapsible rounded structures of twisted branches covered with skins or foliage. "We move," the shaman said in response to Vaelin's query about where they intended to make their home. "People are home . . . not place."

The first child was born that night, a girl, brought to term by a combination of her mother's will and the sacrifice of her family, who starved so she would eat. The shaman emerged from the shelter holding the child aloft as she squirmed and cried towards the heavens, calling out his unfathomable blessing, raising the ice folk to their feet in hushed reverence. Vaelin felt it lift then, the pall of despair that had covered these people since he met them, seeing smiles on some faces, tears on others. They may have lost their name but they were alive again.

He took his leave the next morning, having agreed to return in two months with fresh supplies, although, given the Bear People's proficiency as hunters he doubted they would need any. Wise Bear's mood was warm with gratitude as Vaelin clasped his hand in farewell, but also held a note of foreboding. "Volariaanns," he said. "Won't stop."

"They can't reach you here," Vaelin said. "If they come, we'll fight them together."

The shaman's expression was sorrowful, a deep sense of apology colouring the vision he sent: *an army, dark ranks of infantry and cavalry, stretched out across a frozen plain, more than could be easily counted, heading south towards a distant port.* "Not coming . . . for us," he said. "For you."

He rode in silence for much of the day, the old man's vision stuck in his mind, unwelcome but compelling.

"They called the baby Dark Eyes," Dahrena told him, riding alongside. "In honour of you."

He nodded, still distracted. *He tells of an army marching on the Realm, but the blood-song has no note of warning. And Volaria is an ocean away.*

"I shall be glad to get home," Dahrena said. "It's been a few years since I spent so long in the saddle. I'm afraid I've grown too fond of comfort."

"I should like to call on my friends before we return to the tower," he said. "If you would care to accompany me."

"I would, my lord." She lapsed into silence for a moment, then gave a small laugh.

"My lady?"

"Just a thought, something Brother Kehlan said, 'They're sending us a warmonger.' In fact they sent a peacemaker."

That night he sat apart from the fire where Dahrena kept company with Captain Orven and the Eorhil woman, far enough away to escape the distraction of voices, and began to sing. He found his sister first, dabbing paint onto a canvas in her room at the tower, a rendering of the harbour, the ships and sailors depicted with her usual unnerving precision. She seemed rapt by her work, content, but it pained him to see her alone.

Reva was next, the first time he had sought her out. The relief at seeing her safe was palpable as he watched her offering a much-missed scowl to a buxom woman holding a scroll. They appeared to be in a library of some kind and he could see the twin spires of the Alltor cathedral through the window. It was strange to see Reva in a dress, squirming in discomfort and boredom as she listened to the woman, who seemed vaguely familiar. He saw Reva's scowl deepen before she voiced a no-doubt-biting insult. However, the woman just laughed and reached for another scroll.

He found Caenis encamped with the Realm Guard, sitting in council with the other Wolfrunner officers. Their expressions had a uniform tension he knew well; the faces of men sent to war. *More discord in the Realm?* he wondered as his unease deepened. *Or something worse?*

Caenis himself seemed as unconcerned as ever in the face of impending battle, issuing orders with the unhesitant surety Vaelin remembered. But the song carried a sorrowful note as he watched his brother and he knew their last words weighed on him.

He moved on, feeling the creeping chill that would soon force a halt to his song, spending his remaining strength on a final effort to find Frentis, but as ever it proved hopeless. The song became discordant, the images fragmented, a cluster of rocks in a scrub desert, a burning house, a ship approaching a harbour . . . This last proved the most compelling, even though it lasted barely a few seconds, the tune becoming more ominous as the ship ploughed through the waves, hull and sails dark from age . . .

The chill lurched, dragging heat from his body, and he knew it was time to stop. He started to open his eyes, seeking to quiet the song but it kept on unbidden, the vision shifting, fixing on a road tracking through the Urlish Forest, a young woman with golden hair riding a pony at the head of a cavalry regiment, a tall Lonak woman at her side. *Lyrna* . . . The princess had grown yet more beautiful in the intervening years, but whatever recent trials she had endured seemed to have brought a change in her that went beyond beauty. There was an ease to her manner that hadn't been there before, the way she laughed with the Lonak woman spoke of genuine friendship. Also the fierce intellect she had hidden so well now shone in her eyes, unbound and unsettling. The song's tone deepened as the vision lingered, Lyrna's face filling his mind as the ominous note heralded by the sight of the aged ship stretched then built until it was almost like a scream . . .

He coughed, feeling blood spatter onto his chin. He was on his back, retching, the chill so intense he trembled from head to foot. "Lie still, my lord." Dahrena's voice was a whisper, her hands warm on his face, brow furrowed in concern. "I fear you have been somewhat foolish."

"When I lived with the Seordah, I met a woman. Very small, very old, but every soul in her tribe afforded her the greatest respect." Dahrena added more fuel to the fire as she spoke, Vaelin huddling in his cloak, as close to the flames as he dared. The chill had lessened somewhat but still he trembled.

"I sensed her gift," Dahrena continued. "And she sensed mine.

The Seordah are not like us, they speak openly of the Dark, discuss it, try to understand it, even though true understanding still eludes even the wisest amongst them. She told me something about the nature of gifts, she told me that the greater the gift the greater the price it exacts. For this reason she rarely used her own, for it was great indeed, but every instant of its use brought death one step closer, and she wished to see her grandchildren grow. I only saw her use it once, when the summer came. Fires are common in the great forest during the summer months, the tinder grows dry and it only takes a single bolt of lightning to set whole swathes alight. The Seordah do not fear the fires of summer, in fact they welcome them, for they thin the forest where it grows too thick to hunt, and bring forth stronger trees from the cindered ground. But sometimes the fires grow large, and when two or more fires meet they birth an inferno that destroys more than it renews. And that summer was very hot.

"When it came it moved so fast there was no outrunning it, the way it leapt from tree to tree, as if it were some great hungry beast, and we were its next meal. It surrounded the camp on all sides, we huddled in the centre and my brothers and sisters sang their death songs. Then this small, old woman stepped forward. She spoke no incantations, made no gestures, just stood and stared at the fire. And the sky . . . the sky became black. The wind came down, chill and cold, bearing rain, a rain so heavy it bore us to the ground with the weight of its waters, so much I feared I had been saved from burning only to drown. Steam billowed as it met the fire, covering us all in a dense mist, and when it faded the fire had gone, leaving damp, blackened stumps, and an old woman lying on the ground, bleeding as you bled just now."

Vaelin rubbed his hands together, trying to keep the chatter from his teeth. "D-did she live?"

Dahrena gave a small smile and nodded. "Just one more season. To the best of my knowledge she never used her gift again. It was strange but the summer ended that day, rain and wind replacing sun and heat until autumn brought golden relief. She told me she had tipped the balance too far and it would take time for the scales to right themselves."

Dahrena extended a hand towards the fire, fingers wide in the warmth. "Our gifts are us, my lord. They do not come from elsewhere, they are as much a part of your being as your thoughts or your senses, and like any other action they require fuel, fuel that burns with the use, as this fire will burn until it's nothing but ash." She withdrew her hand, her face serious. "As First Counsel, I ask that you exercise greater care in future."

"S-something comes," he stammered, clenching his teeth in frustration. "My song brings warning."

"Warning of what?"

Lyrna's face . . . The song like a scream . . .

He closed his eyes against the vision, fearing the song would return, knowing he wouldn't survive another verse. "I don't kn-know. B-but there is one amongst the gifted who may, one who lives at the p-place they call the Dark Clave . . . A man named Harlick."

She wanted him to spend the next day resting but he refused, clamping himself to Flame's saddle and staying there by sheer effort of will, though Captain Orven had to reach out and steady him a few times. The guardsman was clearly disconcerted by his Tower Lord's sudden and unexplained illness but wise enough not to voice any unwelcome questions. Insha ka Forna however, felt no such restraint, offering several caustic observations to Dahrena throughout the day. He thought it best not to ask for a translation, though from the discomfort on Orven's face, it seemed his knowledge of the Eorhil language had grown considerably.

The chill had begun to abate by midday, and by the time they made camp all trace of the tremble had disappeared. But the vision lingered, the princess's face capturing his thoughts with maddening compulsion. Throughout his captivity he had never sought her out when he sang, more through indifference than spite. His anger towards her had faded that day on the Linesh docks, but he never grew any more regard for her than his already healthy respect for the sharpness of her mind. Her ambition had been too great, the crime they shared too terrible to allow for affection or friendship. There were times though, when he felt the song tug at him, singing the tune he recalled from his last vision of her, when she had wept, alone with no-one to see. But he had always resisted the song's call, concentrating instead on Frentis and, occasionally, Sherin. Finding no more than the vaguest glimpses of the former and increasingly dim visions of the latter.

Is it because she feels our love gone? he often wondered. He understood now the blood-song was not limitless, that he could seek out only those he knew, those who had touched his soul somehow, and even then the clarity of the vision varied. His first visions of Sherin had been bright and clear, like looking through well-polished glass, gradually becoming more opaque as time passed. His last glimpse had seen her alongside Ahm Lin, standing in a courtyard set within a house of completely unfamiliar design, exchanging words with a man in plain clothing, unarmed but exuding a warrior's nature. Vaelin saw how the man tried to hide his regard for Sherin, but it was clearly considerable from the way his eyes tracked her. Vaelin knew his own face had once held a near-exact expression. The vision faded, leaving hurt and regret in its wake. He didn't search for her again for almost a year, and when he did all he could find was a sensation of clear air and great height, as if she stood atop a mountain . . . That and something more; she had been happy.

The journey to the place Sister Virula called the Dark Clave, and Dahrena called Nehrin's Point, took the best part of another week, tracking through mountain and forest. They took hospitality from a few settlements along the way, Vaelin gaining an appreciation of the hardships and rewards on offer to those who chose to make a life in the Reaches.

"Came north four years ago, m'lord," a gap-toothed Asraelin bargeman told him at Lowen's Cove, a small port serving the mines some forty miles south of Mirror Sound. "Worked barges on the Brinewash from a boy, till the Fleet Lord scooped me up for my three years under the King's flag. Half the fleet's gone now, sold off to settle the war debts. Got left on the quay with no more than the shirt on my back, worked passage on a freighter to the Reaches. Came ashore penniless, now I got a wife, son, house and third share in my own barge."

"You don't miss the Realm?" Vaelin asked.

"What's there to miss? There a man is born to his station, here he makes his own. And the air." The bargeman put his head back and breathed in deeply. "It's clearer, sweeter. In the Realm I was always choking."

Nehrin's Point sat on a promontory overlooking a sickle-shaped bay where waves pounded a beach of white sand. There were perhaps forty houses, well-built with thick stone walls against the sea-borne wind. They arrived in late afternoon when a stream of children were emerging from one of the larger buildings. There was no sign of any Faith presence or guard house.

Vaelin made for the large building where a blond, bearded man played with an equally blond boy of no more than six years age. The boy was throwing stones at the blond man, his small hands plucking them from a pile at his feet, the man batting them away with a stick. Despite his age the boy had a good arm, his throws fast and precise, but the blond man smacked every stone from the air with unerring precision as the stick moved in a blur, stopping as he caught sight of Vaelin, giving a pained grunt as one of the boy's stones thumped into his chest.

"Got you, Father!" the boy yelped, jumping with excitement. "Got you! Got you!"

Vaelin dismounted a short distance away, walking towards the blond man who dropped his stick and ran to embrace him.

"Brother," Vaelin said.

"Brother." Nortah laughed. "I could hardly believe it was true, but here you are."

Vaelin drew back, seeing the curious stare of the boy, and the settlers beyond who had all paused to take in the sight of the

Tower Lord. The blood-song's note of recognition grew loud in proximity to so many gifted.

"Artis," Nortah told the boy. "Give greeting to your uncle Vaelin."

The boy stared for a few seconds more then gave an awkward bow. "Uncle."

Vaelin returned the bow, feeling the song's volume dip a little. *The boy has no gift.* "Nephew. I see you have your father's arm."

"You should see him with a sling," Nortah said. He turned to bow as Dahrena joined them. "My lady. Your visit is welcome, as always."

"Teacher," she replied, returning the bow.

"There was talk of the Horde," Nortah said. "My fellow townsfolk were concerned."

"It wasn't the Horde," she replied. "Just starving people in search of refuge. Which the Tower Lord provided."

"Cheated of battle, brother?" Nortah enquired, a small glint in his eye. "That must have been a bitter pill."

"One I swallowed happily."

Nortah's gaze went to the canvas bundle hanging from Vaelin's saddle. His eyes narrowed but he didn't press the matter. "Come, come." He turned, beckoning them to follow, taking Artis's hand. "Sella will be anxious to see you."

They found Sella hanging freshly washed sheets on a rope fixed to the side of a single-storey house. Nearby, a girl of about four sat astride a huge cat which padded back and forth, the girl giggling as she bounced on its back. The horses began to fidget in alarm as the cat bared its daggerlike fangs. Vaelin and Dahrena dismounted and he ordered Orven to make camp a good distance away.

Sella came to him with a bright smile, gloved hands touching his in welcome. She was as lovely as he remembered, though considerably more pregnant, her dress billowing in the wind around the bulge of her belly. *Twins,* her hands said as she tracked his gaze. *Boy and girl. The boy will be named Vaelin.*

"Oh, don't curse him with that," he said, squeezing her hand.

Never a curse. Always a blessing. She extended a hand to Dahrena who came forward to take it. "It's been far too long."

Snowdance came padding up, grown to full size since the fallen city, pressing her great head against Vaelin's side, purring like distant thunder as he played a hand through her fur. The little girl on her back stared up at Vaelin in wide-eyed curiosity. The blood-song stirred in recognition and he felt a sudden tumble of images in his head, *toys and sweets and laughter and tears . . .* He grunted, blinking in discomfort.

Sella clapped her hands and the images faded. The little girl pouting a little as her mother wagged a finger at her. *Apologies,* her hands said to Vaelin. *Her way of saying hello. Doesn't realise not everyone can do what she can.*

Vaelin crouched down, coming level with the girl's gaze. "I'm your uncle Vaelin," he said. "Who are you?"

A murmur in his mind, soft and shy. *Lohren.*

Sella clapped her hands again and the girl frowned and spoke in a sullen voice, "Lohren."

"I'm very pleased to meet you, Lohren."

"I had a dream once," she said, smiling broadly. "I saw you on a beach, it was nighttime and you were killing a man with an axe."

Sella took her hand and tugged her from Snowdance's back, her free hand making the sign for food as she pulled her daughter towards the house.

"Don't worry," Nortah said. "You should hear the dreams she has about me."

Sella gave them fish pie and potatoes cooked in an onion broth whilst Nortah related the tale of their journey from the fallen city to the Reaches. "Took us the best part of four months, and not all made it."

"The Lonak?" Vaelin asked.

"No, curiously they never troubled us. It was the cold, the winter came early, caught us on the plains. If not for the Eorhil we'd surely have starved. Gifted folk can do many things, but they can't conjure food from thin air. The Eorhil fed us and guided us to the tower where Fief Lord Al Myrna, thanks to the Lady

Dahrena's kind influence, saw fit to grant us tenancy of the long-unused settlement at Nehrin's Point."

"Your mother and your sisters?" Vaelin asked.

Nortah's face clouded. "Mother had passed the year before we arrived, my sisters . . ." He trailed off and Sella clasped his hand. "Well, not everyone is able to master their fear of the Dark. Hearing your niece's voice in your head before she's old enough to talk can be a little disconcerting. Hulla is married to a North Guard sergeant, Kerran a merchant. They live in North Tower and don't feel obliged to visit."

Vaelin finished his meal before broaching another subject. "Is Harlick still with you?"

"In a manner of speaking," Nortah replied. "Lives by himself in a hut on the beach, scribbling away from dawn to dusk. Never lets anyone read whatever it is he writes though. Most are content to leave him be, except for Weaver. Trades the baskets he makes for food to keep them both fed."

Vaelin pushed back from the table. "I and the lady must speak with him, if you'll excuse us."

You'll stay with us tonight, Sella signed. *We have room.*

The house was certainly large enough to accommodate several visitors. Nortah had described how it had been built by an exile from the Alpiran Empire who saw fit to continue his tribal tradition of keeping multiple wives.

"He hit one of them," Lohren chipped in. "Hit her hard, and made the other ladies angry. They all stabbed him." She took a firm grip of her fork and began to thrust it into a bread roll. "Stab! Stab! Stab!" She stopped with an annoyed grimace when Sella clapped her hands again.

"I should be glad to stay," Vaelin told Sella, turning to Dahrena. "If my lady would care for a walk on the beach?"

"I've seen war, inferno and the souls of murderous men," Dahrena commented as they strolled along the sand to Harlick's hut. Night was coming on and the surf was high, her hair an inky tumble in the wind. "But that little girl scares me more than all of it combined."

"Such power is bound to breed fear," Vaelin assented. "Her gift will be hard to bear as she grows older."

"At least now she has a gifted uncle to help protect her."

"That she does."

"How many years since you last saw the teacher?"

"Why do you call him that?"

"It's the only name he gives himself, and it's what he does. Every day save one, the children gather in his school. Some of the adults too, those that have trouble with numbers or letters. He teaches them all, and well. In his own way he's gifted too."

He recalled Nortah's patience with Dentos before the Test of Knowledge, his ability to get Frentis to sit still for instruction and the rapidity with which he had trained the Wolfrunners' company of archers. *All those years a teacher at heart. Had he stayed with the Order no doubt he would have been Master of the Bow in time.* "It must be over eight years," he said. "Since the fallen city. It's good to see them settled here."

"There were those who counselled my father to send them on their way," she said. "The Eorhil had been free in describing their abilities, arousing the fears of the Realm folk."

"But he listened to you."

"In truth I think he would have granted them sanctuary in any case. He had the kind of heart that couldn't pass up a generous deed."

Her words brought unwelcome memories of Sherin and he was pleased to find them nearing the hut. It was a ramshackle structure of driftwood with a slate roof and a stove-pipe chimney. There were no windows but a glow of candlelight emanated from the half-open door. A broad-shouldered man in a sleeveless jerkin sat on the sand outside, his curly blond hair ruffled by the wind as he worked, muscular arms flexing as his deft hands intertwined broad-bladed sea grass. A pile of completed baskets lay in the lee of the hut.

"Weaver," Vaelin greeted him. "Good to see you again, sir."

The broad, handsome face looked up, a faint smile curling the lips. The blue eyes tracked from Vaelin to Dahrena, blinked and returned to the work in hand. "Not hurt," he said.

The door creaked, opening to reveal a slightly built man with long ash-grey hair, and a less-than-welcoming expression. "What do you want?" he asked Vaelin. His voice was hard with resentment, possibly at their intrusion or perhaps the fear Vaelin had induced at their last meeting.

"Same as before, brother," Vaelin told him. "Answers to difficult questions."

Harlick shook his head, turning back inside. "I have no answers for you. Just let me be . . ."

"Your Aspect would disagree, I think." Harlick paused and Vaelin continued, "I met him recently. Your name came up. Would you like to know the context?"

The librarian sighed through gritted teeth and went back inside, leaving the door open. Vaelin bowed to Dahrena, "My lady, shall we?"

Harlick's hut was furnished with a simple table, chair and narrow cot. An iron stove stood in the corner, a recently boiled kettle steaming atop the hob. The table was piled high with parchment, several quills scattered about the pages amongst inkpots, most empty. By far the most salient feature of the hut, however, was the scrolls, stacked against the far wall, twenty high from floor to ceiling.

"Do you forget them?" Vaelin asked. "Once you've written them down?"

Harlick made a harsh grating noise that might have been a laugh as he moved towards the stove.

"I am remiss, my lady," Vaelin said. "Allow me to present Brother Harlick of the Seventh Order, former scholar to the Great Library in Varinshold. Brother, this is the Lady Dahrena Al Myrna, First Counsel to the North Tower."

Harlick offered Dahrena a shallow bow. "My lady. Please forgive the meanness of my home. I have freshly brewed tea if you would care for some."

Dahrena returned the bow with a polite smile. "Another time, sir."

"Just as well." Harlick lifted the kettle from the hob. "I only have enough for one more cup." He spooned some leaves from a clay pot into a small porcelain cup and poured in the water.

"Your Aspect had a story to tell," Vaelin said. "About a forest and a dead boy."

He was impressed by the absence of a tremble in Harlick's hand as he stirred the tea leaves. He did, however, cast a guarded look at Dahrena.

"I hold no secrets from this lady," Vaelin told him.

Harlick sighed and shook his head. "You are a liar, my lord. We all hold secrets. I expect the lady has a whole bushel of her own, and I'm certain you do."

He's different, Vaelin decided. *Lost his fear somehow.* His gaze wandered to the scrolls covering the far wall. *Something he read perhaps?*

"Tell me," Harlick said, sitting on the only chair and sipping his tea. "Did my Aspect give you a message for me? A command to answer your questions?"

"No," Vaelin replied. "But he did tell me your mission here was not some sacred trust. You do not enjoy his favour. You are lucky, in fact, to be alive, and this"—he cast his gaze around the hut—"is your punishment. You are in exile."

"As are you." Harlick sounded weary, putting his cup aside and reclining in his seat. "If you're here for vengeance, just get it done. My actions may have been misguided but they were driven by honest and unselfish intent."

For the first time in years Vaelin felt a true anger building in his breast. "Misguided? You set assassins to kill me in the Urlish. Instead they killed my brother. A boy of just twelve years. They cut his head from his shoulders. Were you there for that? Did you linger to see the results of your *unselfish intent*?"

"My lord," Dahrena said in a quiet voice and Vaelin realised he was advancing on the scholar, fists clenched.

Harlick merely stared up at him, face impassive save for a mild curiosity.

Vaelin took a deep breath and stepped back, forcing his hands open. "You know of my gift?" he asked when his breathing had calmed enough to speak in an even voice.

"Manifestations Volume One," Harlick recited in a flat tone. "Index Four, Column One. All known instances recorded amongst the Seordah, none concurrent. Seordah name translates as 'Song of Blood' or 'Blood Song' depending on inflection. Known manifestations in the Realm at the time of writing: none. All detected manifestations to be reported to the Aspect with extreme urgency." He met Vaelin's eyes then spoke on. "Addendum: known manifestations in the Realm: One."

"When?" Vaelin asked. "When did you know?"

"Before you did, I expect. The prophecy was unusually unambiguous. 'Born of the healer and the Lord of Battle.' Who else could it be?"

"And what else did this prophecy tell you?"

"'He will fall to the One Who Waits under a desert moon and his song be claimed by reborn malice.'" Harlick took another sip of tea. "I was not prepared to see that happen."

"The Aspect told me there was another prophecy, one not quite so pessimistic. One you chose not to believe."

"We all make choices. Some are harder than others."

"So you hired assassins to prevent the prophecy ever coming true."

"How would I go about hiring assassins? A scholar of the Grand Library is not so resourceful, especially since I knew my Aspect would be unsympathetic to my intent. But as it transpired, research revealed an interested party who had ample knowledge of such matters. A king's First Minister is required to dirty his hands on numerous occasions, I expect."

A king's First Minister . . . "Artis Al Sendahl. Nortah's father hired the men?"

"And required little persuasion, I assure you. He made a show of reluctance at first but a few whispers of my Dark knowledge and he was all enthusiasm, his duty to the Realm demanded it no less. Plus with the Battle Lord's boy tragically taken from the Order, there would be no reason to keep his own son shackled to them."

"But when your scheme failed . . ."

"We had made great efforts to conceal our involvement, but your Order is persistent. It took them two years or more to ferret out the truth, and when they did . . . my Aspect was not pleased. I expect the matter was communicated to the King in due course, hence Lord Al Sendahl's execution, supposedly on charges of corruption."

Janus's words, from years ago: *He wasn't a thief of coin, he was a thief of power.* Nortah's father was executed for exercising the power to kill, a power reserved to the King.

"There was someone else there that night," he said to Harlick. "The assassins spoke of another one. One they feared. Who was it?"

The scholar sipped some more tea. "I know of no other." For the first time there was some fear there, just a small flare to the nostrils, a slight twitch to the mouth . . . and a discordant note from the blood-song.

"You know my gift," Vaelin reminded him.

Harlick put down his tea cup and said nothing. Vaelin felt his fists begin to curl again, knowing he could beat it out of Harlick if he chose to, for all his apparent unconcern the man remained a coward at heart. "There are others," he said. "Others in the Seventh Order who shared your belief. You did not act alone." The blood-song's murmur confirmed it as Harlick maintained his silence. "Even now," Vaelin went on. "All these years later, you cling to your delusion. That what you did was right."

"No," Harlick replied. "All prophecies are false. I see that now.

Those with the gift for scrying are usually mad, driven so by the swirl of visions clouding their thoughts and dreams. It is not the future they see, just possibility. And possibility is infinite. Wouldn't you agree? But for chance it could well have been some malign soul from the Beyond standing before me now, possessing your gift and made Tower Lord no less. Fortune may have proved me wrong, but only by the most slender margin."

"Not fortune," Vaelin said. "Blood, most of it innocent, much of it spilled by my hand."

Harlick gave only a slight nod by way of acknowledgment, regarding Vaelin in resigned expectation. "Thank you for allowing me my tea, my lord."

Vaelin gave a mirthless laugh. "Oh, I'm not going to kill you, brother. Arrogant wretch though you may be, I have too much use for you. And there is a great deal for you to balance. You are hereby appointed Archivist of the North Tower." He waved a hand at the hut's contents, moving to the door. "Gather your things and be ready to leave by morning. We will have much to discuss at the tower. My lady?"

She paused to offer a stunned Harlick a bow of congratulation then followed him from the hut.

"I do not like that man," she said as they walked back along the beach.

Vaelin glanced back at the hut, seeing the scholar's wiry figure outlined in the doorway. "I doubt he likes himse—"

It hit him like a hammerblow, the screaming note of the song surging once more to an instant crescendo. He staggered, feeling blood flow from his nose, collapsing to the sand as the scream brought a vision . . . *Flame, all is flame, all is pain and fury . . . A man dies, a woman dies, children die . . . And the scream never ends . . . The flames swirl, coalesce, two dark patches appear, forming into eye sockets as the flames shape themselves into a skull, then a face, perfect and beautiful . . . And familiar . . . Lyrna, formed of fire . . . Screaming.*

CHAPTER TEN
Lyrna

The holdfast of Baron Hughlin Banders lay thirty some miles from the Asraelin border, a sprawling structure of varying architecture and mismatched brickwork, some new, some clearly ancient. It sat in the centre of a large estate of forest and rolling hills, well-stocked with deer. They arrived as evening was coming on, greeted a good distance from the main house by a company of knights, over fifty fully armoured men approaching in battle order. The company's leader revealed a nose marked by a single horizontal scar as he raised his visor, his evident suspicion dissipating at sight of Lyrna. Despite his ruffian-like appearance he possessed the cultured vowels and manners of a blood-born knight.

"My most abject apologies, Highness," he said, having dismounted to sink to one knee, head lowered. "Such a large party, we mistook your intent."

"Do not concern yourself, my lord," Lyrna replied. She had always found the elaborate manners of the Renfaelin knightly class somewhat tedious and was in scant mood to indulge them now. "I come in search of Baron Banders. Is he at home?"

"He is, Highness." The knight rose and quickly remounted. "Allow me the honour of escorting you to his presence."

Baron Banders was waiting at the door to his home, unarmoured but holding a scabbarded long sword. Behind him a young woman stared up at Lyrna, clutching the hand of a lanky youth, who, despite his height, couldn't have been more than fourteen.

"Highness." Banders's tone and expression were both carefully neutral as he sank to one knee before her. "I bid you welcome. My home is yours."

"And I'll gladly stay the night, my lord," she replied, slipping from Surefoot's back to stride forward, extending a hand. "But I do require a promise from you first."

His eyes widened a little at the hand she placed before his lips, famously a sign of great favour she rarely bestowed, before pressing a kiss to her fingers. "Promise, Highness?" he asked, rising as she stepped back.

"Yes, no banquets." She smiled. "I should like only a quiet meal tonight, and the pleasure of your company of course."

He introduced the young woman as Ulice, his ward, and the boy as Arendil, her son. No family names were offered but Lyrna's eyes picked out the similarities between Banders's and Ulice's features with ease, the colour and set of their eyes were almost identical. The lack of a family name marked her as an unacknowledged bastard, though one enjoying her father's care if not his name judging by the clothes she wore. Strangely, the boy's face showed only a slight similarity to his mother and none at all to his grandfather. His eyes were blue whilst theirs were brown and his hair, an untidy cascade of dark curls reaching to his shoulders, made a stark contrast to the sandy mane of his mother and the thinning grey crop adorning Banders's pate.

They ate a well-cooked but not lavish meal in the main hall, Davoka clumsily dismembering her food with the alien cutlery the servants placed beside her plate with every course. She eyed Lyrna's actions closely, attempting to copy her grip on the various utensils, mostly without success.

"*Eat however you wish,*" Lyrna told her. "*There will be no offence.*"

"You learned my ways," Davoka replied, frowning in concentration. "I learn yours."

"You speak Lonak!" Arendil exclaimed, staring at Lyrna in open astonishment. Banders thumped a hand onto the table and the boy quickly added, "Highness."

"Speaks it better than me, sometimes," Davoka said, chewing a mouthful of quail. "Knows words I don't."

"The princess's accomplishments are a great example," Ulice said. She had a shy demeanour, almost fearful, but the gaze she offered Lyrna was rich in honest admiration. "And now she brings a peace that has eluded men for centuries. Would that all ladies could be so accomplished."

"I hear it's a hard country north of the pass," Banders said. "Never been there meself. Fought plenty of Lonak though." His gaze shifted to Davoka, who grinned back as she chewed.

"Thankfully, those days are now behind us," Lyrna said. She lifted her goblet, raising it in a formal toast. "Will you drink with me, my lord? To peace?"

Banders's smile was faint but he lifted his goblet readily enough, drinking as she did. "Peace is always welcome, Highness."

"Indeed. It also seems to be a concern for your Fief Lord. I had occasion to meet him on the road."

Ulice's fork made a loud clatter as she dropped it onto her plate. She blanched as Lyrna's gaze swung to her, looking down, now visibly pale.

"Are you well, my lady?" Lyrna asked her.

"Forgive me, Highness," she replied in a whisper. Next to her, Arendil reached out to clasp her hand, face drawn in worry.

"Perhaps, Highness," Banders said in a somewhat hard tone, "talk of the Fief Lord can wait until after dinner. Such a subject has a tendency to turn the stomach."

The rest of the meal was eaten in silence, save for Davoka's queries about the food placed in front of her. "Jellee?" she said, prodding the quivering castle-shaped dessert with a spoon. "*Looks like snot.*"

"I'm sure, my lord," Lyrna said, "you require no lecture on the Realm's recent troubles."

They were in the main hall, alone save for a pair of wolfhounds, both of whom seemed to have taken a liking to her, laying their heads on her knees as she sat beside the great marble fireplace. Banders stood by the mantel, his expression still guarded but she could see the anger in him. "No, Highness," he replied. "I surely do not."

One of the wolfhounds gave a loud huff and she ruffled the fur behind his ears. "With the attempt on Tower Lord Al Bera's life there may be more discord ahead," she said. "Renfael has been largely free of the riot and lawlessness seen in the wider Realm. I assume you agree it would be best if it remain so."

"I seek no discord. Only to preserve what is mine."

"By traducing the reputation of your Fief Lord?"

"His reputation was sullied beyond redemption years ago, even before the war. I speak the honest truth, and only when asked."

"And how often are you asked?"

Banders picked up a poker and prodded at the coals in the fire with quick, hard jabs. "There are many who find the thought of being ruled by that man a stain on their honour. If a knight comes to me for honest counsel, should I turn him away?"

"You should seek to preserve the King's peace. Your standing in this fief, and the Realm, is very high. No other knight enjoys such regard. But high standing brings responsibility, asked for or no."

He looked down, reminding her once again of Ulice and her obvious parentage, but not her son with his long dark curls. *Only to preserve what is mine . . .*

"Why have you not acknowledged your daughter?" she asked. "Or your grandson?"

Banders straightened, keeping his gaze averted. "I . . . do not grasp your meaning, Highness."

"You have no wife, no other children. Your daughter, born outside the bounds of marriage or no, is still your blood. And clearly you cherish her greatly. Yet you withhold your name."

He rose from the fire and turned away, hands clasped behind his back. "These are private matters . . ."

"My lord, I have travelled too many miles and seen too much to suffer the burden of petty courtesies. Please answer my question."

He gave a heavy sigh and turned back, meeting her gaze, his face more sorrowful than angry. "Ulice's mother was . . . of mean station, a miller's daughter. I knew her from childhood, my father was always too wrapped up in his gaming and his whores to offer more than the laxest discipline. So I was free to associate with whomever I wished, and do as I pleased. And as I grew to manhood it pleased me greatly to make Karla my wife. But, for all his loose ways and disregard for propriety, my father would have none of it. That the daughter of the mill should bear the next heir to his lands and titles, those he hadn't pissed away on cards or women that is. Unthinkable. When he died I hoped for a more sympathetic reply from Theros, but the old Fief Lord believed in the sanctity of knightly blood with all the vehemence others afford to the Faith. So, I gave up my entreaties and Karla and I lived together in this house as man and wife, though never formally joined. She was taken from me when Ulice was born, I have never sought another."

"Your grandson?" Lyrna asked. "Ulice seems young to be a widow."

Banders's expression hardened once again. "Is it Your Highness's habit to ask questions to which you already know the answer?"

Dark hair, dark blue eyes . . . I will of course, make provision for any dependents. "Lord Darnel."

"Ulice was young," Banders went on. "Barely fifteen, brought to join me at the Fief Lord's holdfast. Darnel and I were never friends, he saw his father's regard for me and hated it, for Theros had never shown him more than disappointed scorn. His pursuit of my daughter was revenge, though she didn't see it as such, head full of the girlish notion that all knights are heroes. So when the handsome son of the Fief Lord professed love to her, why would she not believe him? He cast her aside of course, when she told him she was with child, laughed at her, and at me when I brought the matter to Theros.

He beat the boy bloody, as was his wont, right there in the Lord's chamber in front of all the ladies and retainers. Beat him until it seemed he'd killed him. Sadly, he hadn't. I left the lord's service the next day, took my daughter home and raised my grandson. I sought some recompense at the Summertide Fair a few years later, I believe you were there that day. I'd have had it too if one of his retainers hadn't thumped me from behind with a mace."

"Darnel has never married," Lyrna recalled.

"And fathered no other children. None that are known in any case."

"So if you were to acknowledge his mother, Arendil becomes of noble birth. A noble son with the Fief Lord's blood. A claimant to the Lord's Chair."

"Darnel came here, shortly after I returned from the war, demanding his son by right. I told him he had no son. His retinue was only twenty strong, all callow youth. His old retainers had died to a man at Marbellis. I had over fifty knights at hand, all veterans of the desert. It pains me greatly that I didn't decide to settle the matter then and there."

"He hasn't abandoned his claim then?"

Banders shook his head. "He wants his heir within his own grasp, either to be moulded into another monster or discarded as he sees fit. But if I give Arendil my name, it's as good as an open claim to the Lord's Chair. Renfael will go to war."

"Then I thank you for your restraint."

"It will not be I who sunders this fief, Highness. But, should it happen, with the King's help, I can at least heal it. Our Fief Lord can only inflict wounds, not heal them."

She was tempted to caution his tongue, but she had drawn the truth from him with impolite insistence after all. "There can be no war in this fief," she said. "Not at any cost. You understand?"

He looked back at the fire and gave a tense nod.

"I ask for patience, my lord, and forbearance of difficult duty. Tomorrow Arendil will accompany me to Varinshold where I will counsel the King to offer him royal patronage. He will receive education and undertake service to the Crown, far beyond the reach of his father. His mother is free to accompany him if she wishes, I shall certainly be glad of pleasant company at the palace."

"This estate is their whole world," Banders said, voice soft. "Having seen more of the world beyond it than I would ever have wished, I dreamt that I might spare them the sight of it."

Lyrna patted the wolfhounds a final time and rose from the chair, drawing a whine of protest from the larger of the two. "The price of noble blood is that we do not choose our paths in life, just the manner of walking them. I shall retire, my lord. You will wish to speak to your family."

She had expected tears from Ulice but her gratitude was a surprise. "Wisdom *and* compassion," she said the next morning, fighting a fresh bout of sobs as they said farewell on the gravel pathway before House Banders. "May the Departed preserve you always, Highness."

Lyrna reached out to grasp her arm as Ulice began to bow. "Enough of that, my lady. I do wish you would come with us."

"Fath—the baron needs me." Ulice wiped her eyes with both hands, forcing a smile. "I can't leave him here all alone. And a mother should know when to send her son forth, don't you think?"

Lyrna squeezed her arm. "I do indeed."

"May I crave a promise, Highness?" Ulice went on before Lyrna could move to mount Surefoot. "You have already done more than I could ever . . ."

"Just ask," Lyrna said, then smiled as the woman blanched at her tone. "Please."

Ulice came closer, speaking in a whisper. "Never let the Fief Lord take him. Hide him, send him far across the sea, but do not ever let him fall into his father's hands." The woman's apparent timidity was gone now, her face a mask of maternal fury.

Lyrna clasped her hands and pressed a kiss to her cheek, whispering close to her ear. "I'll see the raping bastard dead before he gets within a mile of your son. You have my word."

Ulice stifled a gasp of relief and stepped back, extending a hand to Arendil who stood scowling next to his grandfather. "Come, bid your mother farewell."

His mother may have been overflowing with gratitude, but Arendil was a picture of sullen, adolescent resentment. "Does it have to be now?" he said in a dull voice. "Why not in the winter, or next year?"

"Arendil!" his mother snapped, extending her hand again.

The boy's scowl deepened and he seemed about to speak again when his grandfather's knee prodded him forward. "Don't insult Her Highness with tardiness, boy."

Davoka trotted her pony closer, leading a horse by the reins, the fine grey mare the regiment's Lord Marshal had offered Lyrna at the pass. "Here," she said, tossing the reins to Arendil. The boy looked down at them, his lips curling. "Got my own horse," he said.

"Perhaps it is a little too big for him," Lyrna said to Davoka. "Do we have something more suited to a child?"

"I can ride it!" Arendil retorted, putting a foot into the stirrup and hauling himself into the saddle with practised ease. "Just not mine, is all."

Ulice went to his side, clasping his hand and pressing a kiss to it. After a moment Banders came forward and gently pulled her away. Lyrna saw the flush of Arendil's cheeks and turned away. "Baron! My lady!" she said, raising her voice to ensure the surrounding cavalry could hear. "My thanks for your hospitality. Rest assured your orphaned ward will receive the finest education at the King's court."

Banders put his arm around his daughter's shoulders and pulled her close as Lyrna turned Surefoot and led the regiment from the estate.

They made good time and were encamped on the northern fringes of the Urlish three days later, Lyrna and Davoka engaging in the now-nightly ritual of knife throwing. The Lonak woman had obtained an additional brace of knives, presumably from some unsuspecting brother at the pass, which enabled Arendil to join in, though his lack of skill was obvious.

"Boy hasn't been taught to fight," Davoka observed as Arendil's latest throw went wide of the cleaved log they were using as a target.

"I have!" Arendil replied. "I can ride and use a lance and a sword. Grandfather taught me. Every day since I was eight. I even have my own armour, though I wasn't allowed to take it."

"Armour," Davoka scoffed, sending a knife close to the centre of the log. "The steel-bellies were always easy to kill, just had to wait for them to camp. Only dangerous when they had something to charge at."

"You can choose some armour when we get to the palace," Lyrna assured Arendil, her own throw smacking into the upper edge of the log. "We have endless corridors full of it, rack upon rack of swords too. It always struck me as odd that the Realm Guard cost so much to arm when we had so many swords going to waste as ornaments."

"Grandfather has lots of swords too, spears as well. He brought them back from the desert war."

"Does he talk of it?" Lyrna asked him. "His time in the war."

"Oh yes, though it makes him sad sometimes. The betrayal of Lord Al Sorna weighs on him. He says if the army had known of it, every man would have stayed and died to stop the Alpirans taking him, even the Cumbraelins."

Lyrna decided she liked him then, the openness and disregard for titles were a quiet delight, though they would make him easy meat at court. And as for Davoka . . .

"It is not a good place," she told the Lonak woman that night.

They sat by the campfire, Arendil sleeping soundly in his tent. Davoka sat on her wolf fur, long legs stretched out, cutting strips of dried beef into her mouth with a hunting knife. "Dangerous?" she asked in Realm Tongue. Lyrna had noted it was almost all she spoke now.

"In many ways, most unknown to you. The people there lie as

if it were a virtue. Your closeness to me will arouse suspicion and envy in some. Others will seek to turn it to advantage. You must keep a guard on your tongue, and do not look for trust."

Davoka grinned as she chewed. "If I have your trust, I need no other."

"You may call me queen, sister. But I do not rule here; at the palace my counsel is tolerated, discarded or accepted as my brother sees fit. I fear my trust will not be enough to spare you the cruelties that await us there."

"It's your home, yet you speak as if you hate it."

Hate it? Was it possible to hate a place she knew so completely? A place drained of mystery in childhood. But there had been so many faces over the years, so many lost to the noose or the wars. Lord Artis, power-greedy fool though he had been, she had always appreciated his pragmatism. Fat Lord Al Unsa and his clumsy dancing, as corrupt as a man could be yet he always made her laugh. And Linden, poor loving, idiot Linden . . . And Vaelin.

"Perhaps I do," she admitted. "But there is nowhere else for me."

"Cannot your brother rule without your counsel?"

"He certainly tries to, though I'm loath to abandon him even so. Perhaps one day, when the Realm is calmer, then I'll find another home."

Davoka grinned. "Plenty of space at the Mountain."

Lyrna laughed. "I doubt the Mahlessa would welcome my presence." *But there is always the Northern Reaches . . .*

"This forest is very old," Davoka said, eyeing the dense woodland fringing the road with evident unease. Lyrna had noted her dislike of forest before, the constricting trees were a stark contrast to the tundra and mountains she knew so well. "I can smell the age of it."

"The Urlish is the largest expanse of forest in the Realm," Lyrna replied. "Preserved by the King's Word and dwarfed only by the Great Northern Forest, at least on this continent."

Davoka frowned at her. "Continent?"

"The landmass across which we travel."

"There are others?"

Lyrna was about to laugh then saw the honest curiosity in Davoka's eyes. *She knows so much, and yet so little.* "Four that are known to our maps," she said. "All much larger than this one. Probably more besides, but no Realm subject has yet journeyed so far and returned."

"Not so," Arendil put in. "Kerlis the Faithless. It's said he travelled around the world twice, and currently makes his third such journey."

"Just a story," Lyrna said. "A myth."

"It can't be," the boy insisted. "Uncle Vanden swears he met him once, near thirty years ago."

"And who is Uncle Vanden?"

"Grandfather's cousin, a great and mighty knight in his time. I call him Uncle because he acts as such. He's very old."

"Old enough to meet the man who never dies, eh?"

Arendil's scowl returned. "It's true. Uncle wouldn't lie. It happened when he was in service to the Warden of the North Shore. He was wounded in a battle with some smugglers and became separated from his men in the craggy rocks that cover the coast near the mountains. He says he stumbled about for hours, fearing he would bleed his life away, then he found Kerlis sheltering amidst the rocks with some strange people. Uncle was near death by then but there was a little boy amongst them with the Dark, a touch that could heal."

Lyrna's interest began to pique. "A healing touch?"

"I know it sounds fanciful, and Grandfather told me it was just the dreamy ramblings of an old man. But Uncle showed me the scar, a patch of mottled skin on his shoulder, all puckered and rough to the touch, but the centre of it smooth and unscarred in the shape of a hand, a child's hand."

Davoka gave a sullen grunt and spurred her pony to a canter, moving ahead until she was out of earshot. "Such talk upsets her," Lyrna explained. "Finish the story."

Arendil's gaze was guarded, as if he feared she had some mockery in store, but he continued after a moment's hesitation. "Although the boy had closed his wound, Uncle sickened with fever. Kerlis and the others saved him from the rising tide, taking him to shore and making a fire. Kerlis sat with him that night as he shivered and waited for death, and it was from his own lips that Uncle heard the tale. How he had been cursed by the Departed, though not, as the legend says, for simple Faithlessness, but for refusing a place in the Beyond, refusing to join with them. So they had closed him off from all doors to death, even the great emptiness that awaits the unfaithful. Twice he had circled the world, Uncle said. Twice he had returned to this land, come to help those he could, all the while searching."

Lyrna was familiar with the story of Kerlis the Faithless but this was a new wrinkle to the tale. Kerlis was a cautionary figure, a lost soul endlessly wandering the earth, friendless and desperate for release. A passive victim, not a searcher. "Searching for what?" she asked.

"Uncle asked him the same thing. He said he thought Kerlis expected him to die, hence the freedom with which he spoke. He leaned close to my uncle and spoke in a whisper, 'For what I was promised. One day there will be one amongst the gifted folk of this land who can kill me. I'll know him when I see him. Until then I'll strive to save as many as I can, for in years to come he may well be born to those I save. In a few years most birthed by this generation will be scattered or slaughtered, and I'll take myself off again. My third circling of the world, my lord. I wonder what I'll see.' Uncle fell into a feverish slumber then, and when he awoke, somehow still living, Kerlis and the strange folk were gone."

An old man's dreamy ramblings indeed, Lyrna thought, more in hope than conviction. What she had witnessed in the Mahlessa's chamber plagued her waking hours and her dreams. *I searched so far for evidence, now I have it why does it seem such a burden?*

The forest began to thin after two more days, eventually opening out into the grassy plain surrounding the walls of Varinshold.

The eighth bell was tolling as they approached the north gate and the City Guard were lighting the great oil lanterns on either side of the entrance. Unlike Cardurin there was no bunting or cheering crowds to greet her entry to the city. It seemed her brother felt no need to mark her success and safe return with a public celebration. *Probably saving the coin for another bridge,* she thought. The usual gawkers and well-wishers lined the streets as the cavalrymen cleared a path for her, and there were a few calls of welcome or congratulation, but none of the adulation she had found in the north. In fact most onlookers seemed more interested in Davoka, some gaping and pointing at the sight of a Lonak riding through the streets of the capital, and a woman at that. Davoka bore the scrutiny with stoic calm, but Lyrna saw her hand tighten on her spear as some ribald comments arose from the spectators.

The crowd was a little thicker at the palace, the guards obliged to become more aggressive in ensuring her passage to the main gate where she was met by a balding, portly man with a wide smile. "Highness," he greeted her, bowing low.

"Lord Al Densa," she replied. Al Densa was master of the royal household and normally gave off an aura of perpetual calm, though today he seemed a little more lively.

"The King sends his apologies for failing to greet you in person, Highness," the portly lord told her. "But today's joyous event has commanded his attention."

"Event?" Lyrna enquired, dismounting from Surefoot's back and handing the reins to a groom.

"More a miracle in truth, Highness. Brother Frentis is returned to the Realm, safe and well, all the way across the ocean. The Departed be thanked for their care of him."

Frentis? Of all the souls lost at Untesh, Frentis was the one that haunted her brother the most. "Joyous news indeed," she said.

"I hate to trouble you with correspondence so soon," Al Densa went on, producing a small scroll and handing it to her. "But the King seems keen to afford the fellow all cooperation."

"Fellow?" Lyrna unrolled the scroll, revealing neat and well-scribed lines of Realm Tongue, although the letters were formed with some unusual flourishes.

"An Alpiran scholar, Highness. Come to write a history of some kind. The King thinks indulging him will offer a chance at healing the rift between our nations."

Lyrna's eyebrows rose at the sight of the signature on the scroll. "Verniers Alishe Someren. The Emperor's personal historian. He's here?"

"He was, Highness. The King acceded to his request to accompany the Realm Guard on their excursion to Cumbrael. However, as you see from his letter, he is very keen to secure an audience with you."

She was familiar with Verniers' work of course, though it suffered in translation from Alpiran. She had intended to work on her own version of his Cantos, if she ever got the time. *A historian seeks the truth, at least a good one does. He comes to ask about my father and his mad war.* "Of course I'll see him," she told Al Densa. "Please arrange the meeting as soon as he returns."

Al Densa bowed. "I shall, Highness. For now, however, the King requests your attendance in the throne room. Brother Frentis and his companion are being conveyed there as we speak."

"Companion?"

"A Volarian woman. It seems they were slaves together. The details are vague as yet, but clearly we can look forward to a tale of great adventure."

"Clearly." Lyrna beckoned Davoka and Arendil closer. "The Lady Davoka, Ambassadress of the Lonak Dominion, and Squire Arendil of House Banders, soon to be made ward of the King. They require suitable lodgings."

"Of course, Highness."

"For now I'll take them to my rooms. Tell the King to expect me shortly."

"Brother Frentis!" Arendil enthused as Lyrna led them along the many corridors to her suite in the east wing. "He's almost as great a hero as Lord Al Sorna. Will I get to meet him?"

"I expect so," Lyrna replied. "And when you meet the King do try to remember to call him 'Highness.' Such niceties are expected of palace guests."

Her rooms were as she remembered, every furnishing and ornament just as they had been left. Her many books sat on their long shelves in the order she had decreed, the leather bindings dusted and shining but otherwise untouched. The desk where she spent so many hours held the full ink bottle and freshly cut quills she required be placed there every morning. And her bed, her wonderful bed. So soft, so warm . . . so very big. It was strange, everything else in the room seemed to have shrunk, but the bed had somehow contrived to grow.

Who lives here? she wondered, going to the desk and placing *The Wisdoms of Reltak* next to the stack of parchment. *Which lonely old woman lives here and spends her days in endless scribbling?*

She permitted her maids some fussing before ordering a suitable gown laid out and food brought for her guests. "I don't know how long this will take," she told Davoka when she had exchanged her riding gown for a blue silk dress with a gold-embroidered bodice. She stood in front of the mirror as one of the maids pushed her coronet into the remolded mass of her hair. "Best if you wait here with the boy. I'll arrange a time for you to meet the King on the morrow." She turned as Davoka failed to answer, finding the Lonak woman staring at her, a faint frown on her brow. "What is it?"

"You are . . . different," Davoka said softly, eyes tracking over Lyrna's form.

"Just trappings, sister," she replied in Lonak. *"A disguise in fact."* *Save for this,* she thought, fingering the throwing knife hanging from the chain about her neck. She had taken to wearing it openly since leaving the pass but decided it was probably best to keep

it hidden once again, so took it off to hide behind the laces in her bodice. *Never be without it.*

"Princess Lyrna Al Nieren!" The page at the door announced her entry with a booming voice, thumping a staff onto the marble floor of the throne room three times. Lords only got one thump of the staff, Aspects two, she and the queen three. It was one of the rituals her father had instigated on assuming the throne. She had once asked him the significance of the thumping staff and received only a wry smile in response. *All ritual is empty,* Reltak had written. The more of the long-dead Lonakhim scholar she read, the more she appreciated his insight.

"Sister!" Malcius came to greet her, his embrace warm and close. "Your adventures had me greatly worried," he whispered into her ear.

"Not so much as I. We have much to discuss, brother."

"All in good time." He stepped back and extended his hand to the two figures standing in the centre of the room, a young man and woman, dressed in mean clothing, but also both handsome of face and athletic of build. The man was well muscled with a stern visage, his features possessed of a hungry leanness. The woman was no less striking, lithe like a dancer and darkly beautiful. She seemed somewhat overawed by her surroundings, keeping close to the man's side and casting wary glances at the assembled lords and guards.

"You are in time to join me in a joyous occasion," Malcius said, moving towards the young man. "Brother Frentis." He shook his head in wonder. "How you gladden my heart!"

Lyrna moved to her usual seat on the left of the throne, pausing to press a kiss to the queen's cheek on the way and exchange hushed greetings with her niece and nephew. "Did you bring me a gift, auntie?" little Dirna asked.

"I did." She tweaked her niece's nose, drawing a giggle. "A Lonak pony for you and a new playmate for your brother. We'll all go riding tomorrow."

"I come . . ." Brother Frentis was saying in a halting voice as she took her seat. "I come, Highness. To beg . . . forgiveness."

"Forgiveness?" the King replied with a laugh. "Whatever for?"

"Untesh, Highness. I couldn't hold the wall . . . My men . . . My failure saw the city fall."

"The city was always going to fall, brother. Do not seek forgiveness for an imagined failing."

Lyrna noticed Lord Al Telnar, one-time Minister of Royal Works, standing at the far side of the room. His expression, normally one of smug self-satisfaction or obsequious solicitation, was oddly tense as he offered her a bow. She had heard from a maid that he had been the one to recognise Frentis at the docks that very day, a perfect opportunity to curry lost royal favour. *So where is his triumph?* she wondered. *Or his customary leer?* The man had been another unwelcome suitor over the years, one she dismissed with almost as much alacrity as she had dismissed Darnel, but like the Fief Lord it hadn't dimmed his ardour.

"For all the long years of slavery and torment," Brother Frentis was saying, "it has been my one ambition to stand before you and crave your pardon."

"Then it grieves me to disappoint you," Malcius replied, moving forward with his arms wide, enfolding Frentis in a warm embrace. "For no pardon is required." Malcius drew back a little, his hands on the brother's shoulders. "Now, tell me of how you came to be here, and in company with such a lovely associate."

Frentis smiled a little, head downcast, nodded, and reached up to clasp the King's head between both hands, jerking it up and to the side, breaking his neck with a loud crack.

The knife was in Lyrna's hand as she rose to her feet. She had no memory of having drawn it from her bodice. The screams began as the shocked stillness turned to confusion and rage, as the queen shrieked and the lithe woman dodged a guard's pole-axe and drove a punch into his throat. Lyrna's knife flew from her hand and buried itself in Frentis's side. He convulsed instantly, back arching, a scream every bit as terrible as Kiral's erupting from his throat, collapsing onto the marble floor, jerking as the agony wracked him.

The Volarian woman turned from the dead guard at her feet, gaping in shock at the sight of Frentis's writhing form, his jerks ending abruptly, limbs suddenly slack. A single Volarian word issued from her lips in a whisper: *"Beloved?"*

"Kill her!" cried the queen in terror and grief. "Kill them both!"

Guards charged from all sides of the room, pole-axes levelled. The woman paid them no heed, her gaze fixing on Lyrna, face rendered ugly with malice and revenge. She extended both arms as the guards closed, and flame erupted from her hands.

Lyrna staggered back in shock, reeling from the heat as the woman whirled, her flames engulfing guards and lords as they swept the room. Lyrna saw little Dirna bathed in fire, her mother next, then little Janus, their bodies charred and blackened in seconds. Lyrna would have screamed but for the choking stench of smoke and burning flesh, making her crawl and rasp on the floor.

"You took him from me!" the woman screamed at Lyrna, advancing towards her on unsteady legs, blood flowing from her eyes in thick red tears. *"You took my beloved! You festering cunt!"*

A figure came staggering out of the swirling smoke as the woman raised her hands towards Lyrna, reaching out to restrain her. *Al Telnar!* Lyrna realised in shock.

The lord shouted at the woman as he grappled with her, his words lost amidst the roaring flame. The woman bared her teeth in a feral snarl and drove her hand open-palmed into the centre of his face. Al Telnar staggered back, sinking to his knees, his nose driven back into his skull, then collapsed lifeless to the floor.

Lyrna scrabbled back as the woman lurched closer, arm raised, flames erupting . . . and she burned.

CHAPTER ELEVEN
Frentis

Agony erupted as the knife sank into his flesh, instantly spreading to seize his entire body. He heard screams he knew were his own as his legs gave way. It was like being squeezed by a fist made of a million jagged steel points, the pain so intense he felt his reason slipping away, memory fading amidst the torment. Vaelin, the Order, the woman . . . the King's eyes just before he killed him, the brightness of them—a man finding relief from guilt. Far away there were more screams, a great heat filling the air, but it was so dull, beyond the wall of pain that surrounded him. He retained sufficient reason for one more thought: *At least I won't live to suffer the guilt.*

Then it changed, the agony born of the knife blade shifted as it met something, an echo of a previous pain, a seed, stunted, prevented from growing, now given new life. *The seed will grow . . .* The steel-point grip faded, replaced by something worse, a burning, a searing fire ripping through him, covering his skin, finding his scars. It reached a crescendo then, the pattern of scars covering his torso flaring with a force greater than any he had known before . . . Then it was gone. All the pain, gone in an instant . . . along with the binding.

Air escaped him in a rush as he rolled on the floor, the sensation of freedom overwhelming. His hands found his chest, searching for the scars, finding only smooth flesh. They were gone, healed and disappeared. *No scars, no binding. I can move. I CAN MOVE!*

He began to rise then grunted as a fresh pain gripped his side where the princess's knife was still embedded. *An Order knife*, he thought in wonder, tugging it free. The cut was bad, bleeding freely, but not fatal. He surged to his feet, finding himself standing amidst an inferno. Blackened and burning bodies lay everywhere, flame and smoke covered the walls, the King's corpse lying before him, dead eyes open, meeting his own.

A shout to his left dragged his gaze away, finding the woman, flame streaming from her hands towards the prone form of Princess Lyrna. For an instant it caught her hair, her face, raising a scream of terror and agony. "No," the woman said, stilling her flames, stumbling towards Lyrna, blood dripping from her face. "Too quick. You I'll have raped every day for a year. You I'll have cut, one piece at a time. You I'll ha—"

The pole-axe blade slammed into her back and erupted from her chest. Her back arched as blood fountained from her mouth. She hung there for a moment, head lolling to the side, her eyes finding his face. "Beloved," she said, showing red teeth in a smile of complete devotion. Frentis twisted the blade and watched the light fade from her eyes.

More screams from the princess as she found the strength to rise, her hands scrabbling at her face and hair as they beat down the flames.

"Princess . . ." He went to her but she reeled away, still screaming, running through the smoke, her blue gown lost in the haze. He ran after her, rebounding from flaming walls, stumbling over corpses. The smoke faded as he found the corridor. Screams echoed in the distance as the princess continued her unreasoned flight. He ran on, pausing at the sight of a guardsman's body a short way along the corridor. This one wasn't burned, his throat gaping open. Slit from behind, a single stroke. *Kuritai. They're here. It's started.*

He took the guardsman's sword and ran on, following the princess's screams, finding more bodies with every turned corner, bloody streaks staining clean palace marble. The screams were soon lost amongst the rising cacophony of terror and combat as the Kuritai abandoned stealth and began their work in earnest. He found a maid standing amidst four bodies in a courtyard, staring about in shock, for some reason still holding a basket of laundry. Before he could approach her a Kuritai appeared from the shadowed arches behind to cut her down with a single thrust through the back.

Frentis held up a hand as the man came for him, short sword raised, speaking in Volarian. "The King has been dealt with. I have orders to secure his sister."

The Kuritai hesitated, his sword dropping only a fraction, but it was enough. Frentis's sword point scraped past the opposing blade, taking the man in the eye, punching through to the brain. Frentis tugged the sword free and ran on.

More bodies, more Kuritai killing servants and soldiery alike with typical efficiency, too many to fight. Any who tried to block his path were killed, otherwise he ran on. There was a joy in the familiar feel of the Asraelin sword in his hand as it parried and cut, years of Order training returning in an instant. *I am no slave,* he remembered, side-stepping a thrust and severing his assailant's arm. *I am a brother of the Sixth Order.* Freedom was exhilarating, adding speed to his flight through the palace. There should have been guilt; he had just killed the King of the Unified Realm, he had left a trail of death the length of the Alpiran Empire, but the absence of the binding was too wonderful to allow the onset of despair. That, he knew, would come later.

They should have killed me in the pits, he thought as he ran. *I'll turn this invasion into their ruin. I'll wring blood from their army until their empire's bled white.*

He drew up short at the sight of a guard officer fighting two Kuritai in a hallway lined with huge paintings. He was a Lord Marshal of horse judging by his uniform, and a skilled swordsman, managing to keep two such able opponents at bay, though they were slowly backing him into a corner, his parries becoming more desperate as they closed for the killing blow.

Frentis took the princess's throwing knife from his boot, still red with his blood, and threw it at the nearest Kuritai, the blade sinking into the base of his skull. His companion stepped back from the Lord Marshal, his gaze finding Frentis, then dropping into a defensive stance he recognised from the pits. The Lord Marshal saw his chance and aimed a thrust at his chest.

"No!" Frentis shouted but it was too late, the Lord Marshal had taken the bait. The Kuritai ducked under the blade, rolling and jabbing upwards with his short sword, the blade sinking deep into the guardsman's chest.

Frentis charged the Kuritai as he vaulted to his feet, spinning to parry the first thrust, replying with one of his own, only blocked with instinctive speed. Frentis took in the man's features, finding recognition there. *The One who answered the door to the warehouse,* he realised. *A Kuritai captain.* The man's face was devoid of expression, betraying no surprise at finding himself fighting a man who had been at the mistress's side the night before. It was the way with these automata. Bred and trained for war, conditioned with drugs and Faith knew what other Dark devices. Made perfect killers, immune to fear or distracting insult. Even so, he had killed many, and now would kill one more.

It was a scale from his days under Master Sollis, drilled into him with merciless precision, for use against a skilled enemy. A series of slashes and thrusts, delivered with dizzying speed, all aimed at the face, forcing the opponent to raise his blade, leaving the midriff open, not for a sword but a kick. Frentis's boot took the One full in the sternum, bone breaking with an audible crunch. The Kuritai slumped against the wall, blood coming from his mouth, but finding the strength for a final thrust. Frentis swept it aside and cut his throat with the backswing.

"K-King . . ." the fallen Lord Marshall stuttered, staring up at Frentis, his face white from loss of blood.

Frentis went to his side, looking at the wound and seeing it was hopeless. "The King is fallen," he said. "But Princess Lyrna lives. I need to find her."

"Brother . . . F-Frentis, is it not?" the guardsman asked in a croak. "I saw . . . with the Wolfrunners, years ago . . ."

"Yes. Brother Frentis." *I am a brother of the Sixth Order.* "And you, my lord?"

"S-Smolen . . ." He coughed, staining his chin with blood.

"My lord, your wound . . . I cannot . . ."

"Care not for me, brother. L-look for her in the east wing . . . Her rooms are there . . ." He smiled as his eyes began to dim. "Tell her . . . It was a great thing to travel so far . . . with the woman I loved . . ."

"My lord?"

The smile faded from the Lord Marshal's lips and his features slumped into a lifeless mask. Frentis gripped his shoulder and turned away, turning a corner and running in what he hoped was an eastward direction. The palace was empty here, no more bodies, although the sounds of slaughter still echoed through the halls. He passed a broad window and saw flames rising in the city. He paused, taking in the sight of the Volarian fleet crowding the harbour, well over a thousand ships, disgorging a great mass of soldiery onto the wharfs, a constant stream of boats carrying more from the ships outside the harbour wall. He could see no Realm Guard, just Varitai and Free Swords, forming ranks and moving off at the trot, spreading throughout the city in accordance with a well-rehearsed design. *This has been long planned my love . . .*

Varinshold will fall this night, he realised, tearing his gaze away and running on. He would find the princess and spirit her from the city. Then to the Order House with warning of the impending attack.

He came upon more bodies as he entered the east wing; it was separated from the main palace by a narrow courtyard, several corpses lying amongst the rosebushes and cherry blossoms. A tumult of combat came from the doorway ahead, shouted challenges in an unfamiliar language. A woman's voice.

He charged in, finding four Kuritai battling a tall tattooed woman wielding a spear, the blade trailing blood as she whirled it. One was already down and she speared another through the leg as he stepped forward to make an unwise thrust, twisting away before the others could close. *Lonak,* Frentis realised, noting her tattoos and the indecipherable abuse she yelled at her attackers. Crouched to her rear was a lanky youth clutching a long sword, staring at the melee with wide-eyed indecision. Frentis was impressed he hadn't run.

He killed the wounded Kuritai with a slash to the neck, took another down with a thrust to the back, parried the third's slash and stepped back as the Lonak woman speared him in the guts. She finished him with a bone-crushing stamp to the neck and whirled to face Frentis, spear levelled. "Who are you?" she demanded in Realm Tongue.

"I am a brother of the Sixth Order," he replied. "Come in search of Princess Lyrna."

"You wear no cloak," she said, eyes narrowed in suspicion.

"Brother Frentis?" the lanky youth came forward, staring at him. "Could you be Brother Frentis?"

"I am," he said. "Is the princess here?"

The Lonak woman lowered her spear, though her suspicion still lingered. "This place falls to deceit," she told the boy. "Don't give your trust so easy."

"This is Brother Frentis," he replied. "And you saw what he just did. If we cannot trust him, there is no-one to trust."

"The princess," Frentis repeated.

"She's not here," the boy said. "We haven't seen her since she went to meet with the King. I'm Arendil, this is Davoka."

"You are far from the mountains," Frentis observed to the Lonak woman.

"I am ambassador," she replied. "What has happened here?"

"The King has been assassinated, also his queen and the

children. Princess Lyrna has fled, badly wounded. We must find her."

The Lonak woman's eyes lit with rage and concern. "Wounded! How?"

"She burned. The assassin . . . had a Dark ability with fire."

Davoka hefted her spear. "Where is this *assassin*?"

"Dead by my hand. We have no time for this. A Volarian army comes ashore as we speak and this city will be in their hands within hours." He cast around at the empty palace halls. *She will not be found here.* "We have to leave," he said. "Get to the Order House."

"Not without my queen," Davoka stated.

"If you linger here, you'll die and she'll still be unfound." He gestured at the long sword in the boy's hands. "Can you use that?"

The boy took a firmer grip on the hilt and nodded.

"Then next time do so, don't just stand there." He started for the courtyard, Arendil trotting after.

"Davoka," he paused to hiss at the Lonak woman. "Please!"

Frentis ran on, making for the western wall. The gates would be in Volarian hands by now, they would have to find another way. He glanced back on reaching the wall, seeing Davoka's tall form following. He moved right for another forty feet or so until he found it, a shallow drain leaking foul-smelling water into the city sewers through a channel in the base of the wall.

"We won't fit," Arendil said, nose wrinkling at the smell.

The channel was barely one foot high, though fortunately without bars. "Strip," Frentis told him, pulling off his shirt. "Smear yourself with shit. It'll ease your passage."

He went first, scooping up muck from the drain water to cover his chest and arms. He cast the sword ahead of him then lay down and crawled through, straining to squirm into the sewer beyond, skin scraped and chafed by the rock, his knife wound stinging from the foulness that would surely infect it. With a final grunt he hauled himself free of the channel, bending down and extending a hand to the boy. He pushed his long sword through then followed, coughing and retching from the stench. Davoka was next, her spear clattering past them before her head appeared, teeth bared as she tried to pull herself free. Frentis and Arendil took hold of her arms and hauled her out, Arendil gaping at her bare though shit-covered breasts. She cuffed him on the side of the head and retrieved her spear.

"How do we find our way down here?" Arendil asked, rubbing his stinging head.

Frentis found he had a laugh in him. "How does anyone find their way around their home?"

He tried for the northern river outlet first, it was closest and offered the prospect of the north road, the quickest route to the Order House. He had Davoka and Arendil wait whilst he crawled through the pipe to the river, peering out at the half-obscured north gate on the far bank. Varitai were already manning the gatehouse with more on the walls, including several archers. He had hoped to crawl along the bank and through the channel under the city wall but they would be seen almost instantly and swimming upriver against the current was impossible.

"No good," he reported after crawling back. "The walls are lost."

"No other way?" Davoka asked.

"Just one." He didn't like it, the route was tortuous and would add miles to their journey to the Order House, but all other avenues would be well guarded by now. For all his detestation of the Volarians, their efficiency demanded considerable respect.

"You were there," Davoka said as he led them on an easterly course through the maze of tunnels, splashing through the foul waters that still made Arendil retch with every other step. "You saw this assassin?"

The King's eyes . . . the sound his neck made as it broke, like a dry piece of driftwood . . . "I was."

"There was no warning? No chance to stop it?"

"If there had been, I would have taken it."

A pause as she fumbled for the right words. "The *gorin* . . . character of the assassin? Their name?"

"A Volarian woman. I never knew her name." He held up a hand as a sound echoed through the tunnels, a brief shout, quickly cut off. He crouched, waiting, listening. Faint whispers came to him, rough voices in argument, the words indistinct.

Frentis crept forward, sliding his feet along under the water, pausing at a corner as the voices became clearer. Two of them, both male. "I ain't staying down 'ere all fuckin' night," a guttural whisper, the words pitched high in desperation.

"Then go for a nice walk outside," a calmer response, but still edged with fear. "Make some new friends."

A pause, then a sullen mutter, "Must be somewhere better'n this shit pipe."

"There isn't," Frentis said, stepping round the corner.

The two men crouched in the tunnel ahead gaped at him then surged to their feet. The smaller of the two, shaven-headed with a gold earring, carried a long-bladed dagger. His companion, a large man with a mass of shaggy black hair, brandished a cudgel as Frentis came closer.

"Who the fuck are you?" the large man demanded.

"I am a brother of the Sixth Order."

"Balls, where's your cloak?" He advanced raising the cudgel with a snarl, stopping short as Frentis's sword point appeared under his chin.

"Proof enough?" Frentis asked.

The smaller man seemed about to intervene then caught sight of Davoka advancing along the tunnel, spear levelled. "No offence, brother," he said, pushing the dagger into his belt and raising his hands. "I'm Ulven and this fine fellow is known as Bear, account of his hair, see? Just two honest folk seeking refuge."

"Really?" Frentis angled his gaze, studying the large man's fearful visage. "When this one used to collect for One Eye he was called Draker and you were called Ratter, on account of your trustworthy nature."

The smaller man drew back, eyes narrowed. "I know you, brother?"

"You used to call me shit-bag when you gave me a kicking. The night I gave One Eye his name you were right behind him as I recall."

"Frentis," the man breathed, partly in amazement, but more in fear.

"Brother Frentis," he corrected.

Ratter swallowed, glancing behind him in preparation for flight. "That . . . was a lotta years gone, brother."

He had often dreamed of a chance for vengeance, recompense for all those beatings, all his stolen loot. Killing them would be so easy, he was so well practised after all.

"One Eye blamed us, y'see," Ratter went on, backing away. "For not spotting you that night. We had to leave the city for years, lived like beggars we did."

"How terrible for you." Frentis looked into Draker's eyes, seeing only fear, like the bandit in the desert, or the smuggler's first mate . . .

"We're making for the harbour-pipe," he said, withdrawing the sword point and moving on, Ratter shrinking away as he passed. "You can come, but I hear one ounce of shit from either of you, you're done. Understand?"

It took a good hour's worth of sloshing through the sewers before they came to the pipe jutting out from the harbour wall. As they moved, the sounds of Varinshold's fall echoed down through the drains, screams of torment and terror, roaring fires and the thunder of collapsing walls. Here and there they heard the unmistakable song of combat, clashing steel and rage . . . followed by the screams of the defeated.

"Faith!" Ratter breathed, gazing up at blood dripping from a drain in the tunnel ceiling. "Never thought I'd feel sorry for the City Guard."

Frentis peered through the pipe at the harbour, seeing Volarian ships clustered around the quays, more offshore still disgorging troops into their boats. He judged the distance to the nearest ship at little over a hundred paces, well within bowshot and there was a fair chance of being seen, but he was hoping most of the archers were employed elsewhere. In any case there was no other option.

"Mind if I go first, brother?" Ratter volunteered. "Clear the way like?"

"Fuck that," Draker replied. "Why should you be first?"

"Because whoever's last is most likely to get an arrow in the back," Frentis said. He beckoned Arendil closer. "There's a ten-foot drop onto the rocks below the pipe," he told the boy. "The tide's on the turn so we won't have to swim. Keep to the rocks and head north. That'll bring you round the headland. When the ships are out of sight, wait for us." He nodded to Davoka. "You next. Then you two," he added as Ratter started to speak again.

Arendil took a deep breath then climbed into the pipe, shuffling along then dropping from sight. Davoka paused before following. "If you die?"

"The Order House is twelve miles west. Find the north road and follow it."

She nodded then followed Arendil through the pipe. Frentis turned to find Ratter and Draker tossing a coin. Ratter lost, much to Draker's delight. "Enjoy your arrow, y'little bastard," he said, squirming into the pipe with difficulty.

"Fat sod's going to block the bloody thing," Ratter grumbled as Draker seemed to take an age to haul his bulk along. Finally, after much squirming, his great shadow disappeared from the pipe, heralded by a shout as he landed on the rocks below.

Ratter needed no urging to follow, scrambling into the pipe and dropping from view in a scant few seconds. Frentis crawled after, drinking in the sudden rush of fresh sea air as his head emerged from the pipe. He levered himself free and dropped to the rocks, his feet sliding on the wet stone but managing to remain upright. He saw Draker shambling his way towards the headland, already overtaken by Ratter. Frentis glanced back at the ships in the harbour, seeing plenty of activity but no sign they had been seen.

He moved off, leaping from rock to rock. As a child he often came here at low tide, sometimes there would be something worth finding amongst the flotsam washing up onto the rocks, but mostly he just liked to jump from one to the other. It was good practice for the rooftops he hoped to graduate to one day, when he was old enough to do some proper stealing.

"Don't leave me, brother," Draker huffed as he overtook him.

"Then hurry up." Frentis paused at a harsh clanking sound behind them, turned and leapt, catching Draker by the legs and bearing him to the rocks. Something made a loud ding as it rebounded from the stone, spinning away into the gloom.

"What was that?" Draker gasped.

"Ballista bolt," Frentis said. "Seems we've been seen."

"Oh Faith!" Draker was on the verge of weeping. "Oh Faith what now?"

"You were a lot more impressive when I was a boy." Frentis raised his head, finding a lantern glowing on the prow of the nearest ship, dim shapes moving about the spiderlike silhouette of the ballista, working the windlass with leisurely ease. *Bored and practising on some strays*, Frentis decided. *Free Swords, not slaves.* "We're in luck," he told Draker, standing up and raising his arms.

The large man gaped at him. "What are you doing?"

"Keep going," Frentis ordered, waving his arms.

"What?"

"Run!" The ballista clattered as one of the crew hit the release. Frentis stood stock still, counted off two heartbeats, then dropped to his knees. The bolt sailed overhead and skittered away amongst the rocks. He heard Draker babbling a constant stream of curses as he fled.

From the ship came the sound of voices raised in consternation, a few laughs of appreciation at the welcome distraction. Frentis turned and walked slowly towards the headland, not glancing back. A ballista was a fearsome weapon, but it wasn't a bow, and these men could never be as skilled as a well-drilled team of slaves.

He was obliged to duck three more bolts before reaching the headland, by which time Draker had disappeared from view. He paused to wave at the ship before rounding the final outcrop, provoking a chorus of disappointment. Most of the crew now seemed to have gathered on the prow to watch the entertainment. Frentis cupped his hands around his mouth and shouted back in Volarian, as loud as his lungs would allow: "LAUGH ON! YOU'RE ALL GOING TO DIE HERE!"

PART III

Students may be forgiven for believing the figure of the Holy Reader to be ancient and original to the Cumbraelin form of god worship, a sacred trust embodying the will and authority of the World Father in a human vessel at the prophets' behest. However, mention of such a figure can be found nowhere in the Ten Books and the organisational template for the church as it currently stands is hard to discern amongst their varied and often contradictory contents.

The earliest recorded investiture of a Holy Reader dates back only some three centuries, and even then this role seems to have been conceived as little more than an honorary title bestowed on particularly devout clerics. The ascendancy of a man holding absolute and unquestioned leadership of the church did not become an established institution until two hundred years after its arrival in the land now known as Cumbrael, and not without considerable opposition.

—ASPECT DENDRISH HENDRAHL,
FALLACY AND BELIEF: THE NATURE OF GOD WORSHIP,
THIRD ORDER ARCHIVES

Verniers' Account

The general's wife released me as dawn was starting to break over the smoking city. The sounds of battle had abated a little earlier, but so far no messenger had appeared with word of victory, and the steady stream of Volarian wounded stumbling through the breach told of a battle far from won. The wounded were all Free Swords. The slave soldiers, naturally, were left to expire where they fell.

The general had remained below with his pleasure slave as I related what I knew of Al Sorna to his wife, leaving nothing out and taking hours over the telling, Alltor continuing to smoke before us. Her curiosity was keen, and she asked many questions, though it seemed to me she had contrived to form a fanciful picture of the Hope Killer's abilities.

"So you never saw him exhibit these great powers your people speak of?" she asked when I had related a few of the myriad tales told about Al Sorna in the empire.

"He is just a man, Mistress," I replied. "Greatly skilled and cunning, it is true. With the kind of keen insight that many might mistake for some form of magic. But I saw no real evidence he could read minds or commune with beasts, or the souls of the dead for that matter."

"When he comes to face my beloved husband, will he display

this cunning, do you think? Some clever design to save this city from destruction."

There was a sardonic lilt to her voice confirming my sense of a deep fatalism to this woman, an impression that there was no novelty to what she witnessed here, the outcome preordained, inevitable and not entirely relished. "I expect so, Mistress," I replied.

"A great strategist then." She laughed a little. "I've met a few of those. One of them was so convinced of his own genius he sent fifty thousand men to burn in an oil-soaked swamp. Tell me, if Al Sorna had commanded the Realm Guard against my husband, would the outcome have been the same?"

The question was dangerous, as she must have known, and any answer I gave potentially fatal. "Such a thing cannot be judged, Mistress."

"Oh, I think it can, especially by a man so well versed in history and all its battles, as you."

Her tone was insistent, I had to answer, knowing any flattery of her husband would be recognised, and unappreciated. "The Battle Lord was overconfident," I said. "And saw no reason to suspect treachery from an ally. Al Sorna would not have been gulled so easily."

"And what of the weight of numbers against him. You said yourself it was a decisive factor."

"At the Lehlun Oasis, Al Sorna was able to turn the course of the entire Imperial elite with only a few hundred men. If there is a path to victory here, he will find it." She raised an eyebrow and I realised my mistake, adding "Mistress," with my heart thumping and fresh sweat chilling my brow.

"I was starting to wonder if you would ever forget yourself," she said.

"Forgive me, Mistress . . ." I babbled but she waved me to silence, returning her gaze to the smoking city. "Is there a wife somewhere, my lord Verniers?" she asked after a moment. "A family waiting for you back in Alpira?"

This reply required little thought, I had voiced it many times. "I have always been too preoccupied with my work to allow for such distractions, Mistress."

"Distractions?" She turned to regard me with a smile. "Love is a distraction?"

"I . . . wouldn't know, Mistress."

"You're lying. You've loved someone, and lost them. Who was she, I wonder? Some studious girl awed by the great scholar? Did she write poetry?" She pouted in mock sorrow. But for my all-consuming dread, the hatred I felt in that moment would have caused me to pitch her over the side and laugh as she drowned.

I chose the safest course, I lied. "She died, Mistress. In the war."

"Oh." She winced a little, turning away. "That's very sad. You should get some rest. My beloved husband will have more slaughter for you to record on the morrow, no doubt."

"Thank you, Mistress." I bowed and strode to the steps leading to my cabin, trying not to run. Her husband's innate cruelty was frightening, but now I knew by far the greatest danger on this ship came from his wife.

I slept for perhaps two hours, dreaming my dreams of chaos and blood as the nightly epic of the Realm Guard's defeat returned yet again. The Battle Lord's face when he saw them turn to charge his own flank . . . Brother Caenis trying to rally those who fled . . .

On waking I forced down the gruel that had been left at my door and spent some hours converting my notes from the previous day into a suitably misleading account of the Volarian assault, being sure to note the careful preparations the general had made for a prolonged struggle within the city walls.

I was called to the deck a short while later, finding he had convened a council of war, his senior officers standing around the map table as he listened to a report from the division commander. "We had some success with burning them out, Honoured General," the man said, fatigue and grime etched into his face. "But they were quick to adapt, creating breaks between the streets, preventing the fires from spreading. Also, much of the city is constructed from stone, it doesn't burn so easily. And the men . . . fire knows no friend, it claimed almost as many of ours as of theirs. Morale is . . . poor."

"If your soldiers are so keen on shitting themselves," the general replied, "we have overseers aplenty skilled in the art of flogging obedience into reluctant men." His gaze swivelled to the nearest unfortunate, a Free Sword commander with smoke-blackened features and a recently stitched cut on his cheek. "How about you? Hand out any floggings yesterday?"

"Four, Honoured General," the man replied in a hoarse voice.

"Then make it six today." His gaze roamed the table in search of more prey. "You!" He jabbed a finger at a man clad in the garb of the engineers who serviced the ballista and mangonels. "My little trick with the prisoners. Did you try it?"

"We did, Honoured General," the man confirmed. "Fifty heads cast over the walls, as you instructed."

"And?"

The man faltered and the division commander spoke up. "The enemy have prisoners of their own, Honoured General. They threw fifty heads back at us over the barricades."

"The witch's doing," the commander of a Varitai battalion muttered softly.

The general's eyes blazed at him, his finger shooting out like a spear. "This man is demoted to the ranks. Get him out of my sight and make sure he's in the first charge today."

He fixed his gaze on the map as the miscreant was led away. "Against all sense and history," he murmured. "When the walls fall the city falls, and the victors reap the reward of plunder and flesh. It has always been thus." His head came up, eyes finding me. "Is that not so, my scholarly slave?"

It could be a trap or just a sign of his ignorance. In either case I had no time to ponder a careful lie. "Forgive me, master, but no. There is a historical parallel for this current . . . difficulty."

"Parallel," he repeated softly, straightening to bark a laugh, heartily echoed by the relieved officers. The general spread his arms, eyebrows raised. "Then educate us ignorant Volarian fools, oh great Verniers. When and where for this parallel?"

"The Forging Age, Master. Near eight hundred years ago, the wars that forged the Volarian Empire."

"I know what the Forging Age was, you Alpiran wretch." He glared at me in suppressed rage and I experienced a certainty that my continued existence owed much to his wife's influence. "Go on," he rasped when his anger subsided.

"The city of Kethia," I said. "For which the modern province of Eskethia is named. It was last to fall to the Imperial host, holding out for the better part of a year before the walls fell, but the battle didn't end. The city's king, a renowned warrior and, legends say, great user of magics, inspired his people to feats of endurance beyond imagining. Every house became a fortress, every street a battlefield. It's said despair and terror gripped the Imperial soldiery, for surely this city would never fall."

"But it did," the general said. "I've walked the ruins of old Kethia myself."

"Yes, Master," I said. "The tide of battle turned when the Council appointed a new commander, Vartek, known to history as the Spearpoint, for he always led his men into battle, always the first to meet the enemy line. His fearless example dispelled his men's fears. It took weeks of fighting, but Kethia fell, all the menfolk killed and the women and children taken as slaves."

Silenced reigned, the general staring at me in frozen fury. I kept as still as I could, my face impassive. Readers should understand that my words were not courageous, I had intended no insult in the obvious implication they held. I had merely obeyed the command of my master by voicing historical fact, at least as far as the sources relate it.

"Honoured Husband." Fornella had appeared on deck, dressed in a simple gown of white muslin, a red satin shawl over her shoulders. She went to her husband's side and placed a wine cup next to his hand. "Have another drink, true-heart. Perhaps it'll distract you from the ancient doggerel my expensive slave offers."

Slowly the general lifted the wine cup and drank, his gaze remaining fixed on me for long enough to ensure knowledge of impending and severe punishment. "How many slaves have we taken in this province?" he asked, turning to the divisional commander.

"Not so many as from the others, Honoured General. Perhaps three thousand."

"Five hundred heads tomorrow then," the general told the engineer. "Have them blinded first. Exact some pain before the beheading, within earshot of the barricades, make them call to their families. Any of ours they behead in answer are no loss. Only a coward becomes a prisoner. If they're still fighting the day after, make it a thousand more." He drained the wine cup and tossed it aside, grinning at me. "See, slave? I too know how to provide a fine example."

CHAPTER ONE
Reva

"I will not wear that."

The Lady Veliss smiled, holding the pale blue dress up as Reva backed away. "But it complements your hair so," she said. "At least try it on."

"Where are my own clothes?" Reva demanded.

"Burned, I hope. Such rags are hardly fit for the niece of the Fief Lord."

"Then leave me as I am." She wore a plain cotton shift left by the maid who had brought breakfast. Her uncle's guards had brought her to this room the night before, the manor in an uproar as Veliss commanded every room and closet searched for more intruders. Reva had little awareness of the commotion, dazed by a welter of despair and grief that left her drained, capable only of stumbling along as she was bade, deaf to any question. *Kill her,* the priest had said. *Kill her . . .*

The room held a large bed onto which she had collapsed almost immediately, curling up to hug her knees, hating the tears flowing down her face. *Kill her . . .* The sleep that claimed her had been dreamless and absolute. When she awoke she was naked beneath the bedclothes and a maid was placing a breakfast tray on the dressing table as a guard stood by the door. She had never imagined she would be so senseless as to allow herself to be undressed without waking.

Veliss's eyes tracked over her with unabashed admiration. "I should love to. But I think your uncle would appreciate a tad more modesty." She tossed the dress onto the bed and continued to stare at Reva, a faint smile curling her full lips.

"You are unseemly," Reva muttered, reaching for the dress.

Veliss laughed a little, turning to the door. "A guard will escort you down when you're ready."

Her uncle was in his garden, seated at a small table amidst the topiary in company with a bottle of wine, already three-quarters empty although Reva judged the hour as somewhere past the ninth bell. Lying next to the bottle was the sword she had stolen the night before. The Lady Veliss stood nearby, reading from a scroll.

"My brave niece!" The Fief Lord's smile was broad and warm as he rose to greet her. She allowed herself to be embraced, grimacing a little at the stain of wine on his breath as he pressed a kiss to her cheek.

"How did you know my name?" she asked as he drew back.

"Ah, so your grandparents named you for her." He returned to the table, gesturing at the empty chair. "I'm glad."

"Grandparents?" she asked, staying on her feet, casting her gaze around the gardens. *So many guards.*

"Yes." He seemed puzzled. "They raised you, did they not?"

At that moment Reva abandoned all thought of escape. She went to the empty chair and sat down. "My grandparents are dead," she said. "My mother is dead. My father . . ." She fell to silence for a moment. He needed little education on her father. "Why didn't you let them kill me?"

He laughed and poured more wine into his glass. "What kind of uncle would that make me?"

"You knew my mother?"

"Indeed I did. Not so well as your father, obviously. But I

remember her very well." His reddened eyes roamed her face. "Such a very pretty thing. So lively too. Little wonder Hentes fell for her so. When I saw you I thought her ghost had come to save me. You are her very image, but for your eyes. They are all Hentes."

Fell for her? The priest had left her no illusions about her parents' relationship. *Your mother was a whore,* he had told her simply. *One of many to tempt the Trueblade before the Father graced him with His word. Now you have the chance to redeem her sin, give meaning to your misbegotten life.*

"If only she hadn't been a maid, they might have married," her uncle continued. "Your grandfather's rage was a thing to see when it transpired you were on the way. There had been other girls over the years, of course, a smattering of bastards, but none he wanted to keep. Reva was packed off back to her parents' farm with a suitably large purse, and Hentes sent to the Nilsaelin border to deal with a particularly nasty band of outlaws. When word reached him of your mother's death in childbirth, I wondered if it wasn't his sorrow that made him so reckless. The old Hentes would never have charged a bowman standing thirty feet away."

"'Though a sinner, the man who would become the Trueblade never shirked his duty,'" she quoted. "'He was wounded in service to the people, taken by the arrow of a lawless man. For days he lay in pain, senseless to the world, until the Father's word woke him to a new purpose.'"

"You know the Eleventh Book then?"

"Every word." *Beaten into me, until I knew it better than he did.*

"That man last night," the Fief Lord said. "You knew him, didn't you?"

She nodded, finding herself unable to speak of the priest.

"Then you know his name," Veliss said, looking up from her scroll. "His companion, the one you maimed, seems reluctant to tell us."

"It's unlikely he knows it. The Sons rarely use their true names, even to each other."

"The Sons." Her uncle sighed, sipping more wine. "Of course. Who else? Always the bloody Sons."

"Except," Veliss observed, regarding Reva with the same brazen interest she had shown in the bedroom. "Now we have a daughter in our hands."

"A niece," the Fief Lord said in a flat tone. "*My* niece, counsellor."

"Do not mistake me, my lord. After all, like you, I owe this *interesting* young woman my life. I wish nothing more than to please her . . ."

"The maimed prisoner," he interrupted. "Did he have anything else of interest to impart?"

"It's all here." She tossed the scroll onto the table. "Usual fanatical nonsense. Reclaiming the fief for the World Father, ending the Heretic Dominion. It took some time before he became cooperative."

Lord Mustor picked up the scroll, squinting as he read. "The maid?" he asked. "That's how they got in."

"It seems she was sympathetic, didn't expect her reward to be a slit throat. I must be more rigorous in selecting future employees. I'm having her room searched now, though I doubt we'll find anything." She turned again to Reva, her expression harder now. "The name," she said.

"I never knew it," she replied. "Priests do not share the names given them by the Father."

Veliss exchanged a glance with Mustor, a faint look of triumph on her face. "It doesn't mean anything," he said in a warning tone.

"Perhaps not yet." Veliss moved back from the table with a brisk flex of her wrists. "Though it does give me another avenue to explore with our prisoner. If you'll excuse me, my lord." She bowed to Reva. "My lady." She began to walk away then paused at Reva's side, resting a hand on her shoulder. "Oh, I've arranged for a gift for you. A token of my esteem you might say. It'll be here presently." A final wink and she was off, striding along the gravel path back to the manse, full of purpose.

"Is she torturing him?" Reva asked.

"Nothing so vulgar," he replied. "At least not until it becomes necessary. Lady Veliss is skilled in the concoction of certain herbal mixtures that can have a loosening effect on the tongue, and also the mind, which makes the questioning fairly tricky. My counsellor's manner can be somewhat . . . unsubtle, at times. But she is loyal to this fief, and to me. Have no doubt."

"I don't like the way she looks at me."

Lord Mustor laughed as he poured the remaining wine into his glass. "Take it as a compliment. She's very choosy."

Reva found this was a topic she didn't wish to explore further and reached out to touch her fingers to the sword's hilt. "You saved it," she said. "Kept it. I should thank you for that."

He frowned in puzzlement. "Your great-grandfather's sword has been hanging on the practice-room wall for as long as I can remember. I was curious as to why you should go to such lengths to steal it."

"Great-grandfather?" She groaned, withdrawing her hand. "I thought . . ." *I have come so far, for nothing.*

"You thought this belonged to Hentes?" His eyebrows rose in understanding. "The sword of the Trueblade. A great and holy relic indeed. I wish I had it."

"You do not?"

"Lost in the High Keep when he died. Vanished by the time it occurred to me to retrieve it. I would have asked Al Sorna to force those dungeon rats in his regiment to give it up, but my stock wasn't particularly high at the time."

"All a waste then," she said, voice soft. "I have travelled so many miles, lying, hurting and killing along the way. All in search of something that can't be found."

"The priest. He set you on this path?"

"He sent me to die. I see it now. Al Sorna was right. I was to be the new martyr, the rallying cry for the reborn Sons of the Trueblade. That's what the priest made me, ever since I was old enough to walk, he raised me to be a corpse."

"Do you remember nothing before, nothing of your grandparents?"

"There are . . . images of other people, faces I knew before his. I think they were kind. But they always seemed a dream. And he was so very real, his every word the Father's truth. Except he was a liar. What does that mean, Uncle? What of the Father's love now?" Tears were coming again and she was obliged to use the lace cuffs of her ridiculous dress to wipe them away.

Her uncle drained his glass and waved it at a servant who trotted off to fetch another bottle. "Allow me to impart a secret, my wonderful niece." He leaned closer, voice dropping to a whisper. "I may cultivate the image of a godless sinner, but I have never doubted that the Father's gaze rests upon me. I feel it, every day, a great and terrible weight . . . of disappointment."

She found she couldn't contain the laugh, mirth and tears mixing on her face.

"But there's more," he went on. "Who but the Father could bring me such a great gift? A saviour and a niece on the very night assassins come to kill me. Tell me you do not see His hand in this, and I'll not believe you."

He turned at the sound of the main gate opening. "Ah, it seems my counsellor's gift has arrived."

Reva rose in alarm at the sight of the approaching group, four guards, pushing a broad-shouldered youth ahead of them. She ran forward as they came to a halt, Arken sporting a blue-black bruise under his eye. "What have you done to him?"

"Apologies, my lord," the guard sergeant said as Mustor sauntered over. "The boy saw us coming and jumped from the inn window. Wouldn't listen to reason."

Reva touched a hand to Arken's bruise, wincing. "I told you not to wait."

He gave a sheepish grimace. "Didn't want to go to the Reaches on my own."

The Fief Lord coughed in expectation. "It seems," Reva said, "we'll be staying with my uncle after all."

◆ ◆ ◆

They gave her a maid, a quiet woman with mercifully few questions, but a keenness to her gaze making Reva suspect her principal duty consisted of providing reports to Lady Veliss. She was given more dresses and a suite of rooms on the floor below those her uncle shared with his counsellor. She wondered if there was any significance to the fact that Arken was housed in a separate wing.

"He's just my friend," she had insisted in answer to the Fief Lord's query over breakfast the next day.

"An Asraelin friend," he pointed out.

"Just like Lady Veliss," she returned.

"Which gives me a wealth of experience in fending off the jibes of those in this fief who still hunger for independence. If you are to be my acknowledged niece, a certain . . . discretion will be required."

She chose to ignore the obvious irony of being lectured on discretion by so famous a whore chaser. "Acknowledged niece?"

"Yes. Wouldn't you like that?"

"I . . . don't know." In fact she had little notion of what course to follow next. The priest was a lie, the sword a myth, and the Father's love . . . "I thought I might journey to the Northern Reaches. I have friends there."

"Al Sorna, you mean." There was a sourness to his voice that told her she had finally found someone not in awe of her former tutor. "I don't think I like the notion of my niece in proximity to that man. Trouble finds him with far too much regularity."

"So I am your prisoner, now? Kept here to do your bidding."

"You are free to go where you wish. But don't you want to stay a while with your lonely old uncle?"

Reva was puzzling over an answer when the Lady Veliss arrived to join them. Breakfast was usually eaten in the large dining hall with the portraits on the walls. Veliss and the Fief Lord had a curious habit of sitting at opposite ends of the long table, obliging them to converse in shouts.

"Any more intelligence to impart, counsellor?" Mustor called to her as she sat down to a plate of bacon, eggs and mushrooms.

"Sadly our prisoner contrived to expire under questioning," she shouted back, shaking out her napkin. "Too much drum-weed in the mix. All I managed to extract were a few ramblings about some great and powerful ally, able to match the Darkness that perpetuates the Heretic Dominion." She shook her head. "These fanatics grow ever more deluded." She cast a critical gaze over Reva. "You'll need to change, love. Something more formal, and pleasing. It's the Father's Day, and we have a service to attend."

"Service?"

"The date of Alltor's first prophecy approaches," her uncle said. "Three weeks hence. The Reader himself will conduct a service in the cathedral on each Father's Day until then."

"Services are a perversion of the Ten Books," Reva said, in remembrance rather than conviction. "No rituals are stipulated in the books. The truly loved need no empty ceremony from the venal church."

"Did the priest teach you that?" he asked.

She nodded. "And much more."

"Then perhaps there may be some wisdom to the Sons' delusions. In any case, perversion or not, I would greatly appreciate your attendance. I think the Reader will find you most interesting."

She tried on four dresses before finding one Veliss approved of, a black tight-bodiced contrivance with lace sleeves and a high collar. "It itches," Reva grumbled as they formed a procession before the main gate. A squad of guards lined up on either side and they started forward at a sedate walk, making their way through the gate and into the square beyond.

"Power comes at a price, love," Veliss replied through bared teeth, maintaining the smile she offered to the townsfolk lining the square.

"What power?"

"All power. The power to rule, to kill or, in your case this fine morning, the power to incite the lust of the old goat you're about to meet."

"Lust? I have no desire to incite lust in anyone."

Veliss turned to her with a quizzical expression, her smile suddenly genuine. "Then I'm afraid you're in for a lifetime of disappointment."

Inside, the cathedral seemed a vast wonder of ascending arches and tall windows, the stained glass casting multi-coloured rays across the pillars. The air was thick with incense as they made their way to the balcony on the western wall, the raised seats offering a fine view of the interior. In the centre of the space below stood a podium surrounded by ten lecterns.

It took an age for the whole congregation to assemble, finely attired nobles and merchants in the foremost rows, poorer folk behind, the poorest lining the walls. Reva had never seen such a multitude in one place, and found herself squirming under the weight of so many curious eyes. "Is the whole city here?" she whispered to her uncle.

"Hardly. Perhaps a tenth. There are other chapels in the city. Only the most devout come here, or the richest."

The sound of a bell pealed forth, stilling the murmur of conversation. After a moment the white-robed figure of the Reader appeared, preceded once again by his five book-bearing bishops. They went to each of the lecterns, placing the books with careful reverence before stepping back, hands clasped together and eyes downcast as the Reader ascended the podium. He surveyed the congregation with a faint smile then raised his gaze to the balcony, smiling at the Fief Lord, at Lady Veliss, and paling somewhat at the sight of Reva, the smile slipping from his lips, making them sag on his aged face like two wet slugs.

That, Reva decided, *is not the expression of a lustful man.*

The Reader seemed to recover his composure quickly, turning and opening one of the books, his voice strong and clear as he read, "'There are two types of hate. The hatred of the man who knows you and the hatred of the man who fears you. Show love to both and they will hate you no longer.'"

The Tenth Book, Reva recognised. *The Book of Wisdom.*

"Hatred," the Reader repeated, raising his gaze to the congregation. "The World Father's love, you would think, would be enough to banish all hatred from the hearts of men. But, of course, it is not. For not all men open their hearts to such love. Not all men allow themselves to listen to the words in these ten books, and many who do make only a pretence of hearing their truth. Not all men have the courage to cast off their old ways, to banish sin from their hearts and make a new life under the Father's gaze. In return for what He offers, the Father asks so very little, he offers you love. His love. A love that will preserve your soul for eternity . . ."

Reva's boredom grew as he droned on, her collar itching worse than before as she tried not to fidget. *What am I doing here?* she wondered. *Showing respectful obedience to an uncle I don't even know. Alongside his whore no less.*

She was seized by a desire to leave, just get up and walk out. Uncle had said she was free to go where she wished, and she wished to be somewhere far away from this old man's twaddle. *But his expression when he saw me,* she remembered. *Not lust, fear.* She had scared him, badly, and she found she wanted to know why.

Although it seemed a century, the Reader spoke for perhaps an hour, pausing now and then to read another passage from one of the books, then launching into another rambling diatribe on the Father's love and the nature of sin. As a child, one of her few pleasures had been those periods of respite when the priest would educate her in the Ten Books, reading every passage with such passionate conviction she couldn't help but be swept along in the torrent of words. The respite was always brief though, for he would test her after every reading, hickory cane poised to punish any fumbled recitation.

She found no echo of the priest's passion here in this vaulted cavern of glass and marble, just an old man's empty dogma. *It can't all be a lie,* she thought, fighting a rising sense of desperation. *Even Uncle Sentes feels the Father's love. There must be truth here somewhere.*

The Reader's last words were lost to Reva as she indulged in memories of time spent with Alornis, finding she badly wanted to see her draw again. Finally, he fell silent and walked from the podium as the congregation rose from their seats, heads bowed. The bishops, who had remained standing throughout, though some were almost as old as the Reader, retrieved their books from the lecterns and followed in solemn silence. The bell pealed once more and the cathedral began to empty. A few of the nobles and merchants attempted to linger at the balcony steps to beg a word with the Fief Lord but were shooed away by the guards.

"Right," Uncle Sentes said when the last of the congregants had filed out, standing and offering Reva his hand. "Let's see what the old bastard has to say for himself."

"Your niece, my lord?" The Reader's voice was carefully modulated, just enough surprise mixed in with the serenity. They had been conveyed to his private chambers by a coldly servile priest who couldn't disguise his disdain for Veliss, or a suspicious sneer at Reva. She resolved to punch him on the way out.

"Indeed, Holy Reader," Uncle Sentes replied. "My niece, soon to be acknowledged as such. It would be an honour if you would witness the warrant, as well as serving to still any silly doubts amongst the people. I've had the document prepared."

Lady Veliss placed the scroll she held on the Reader's desk, unfurling it and securing the edge with an inkpot. "Where I've marked, if you please, Holy Reader."

The Reader barely glanced at the document, apparently finding it difficult not to look at Reva, his expression not so fearful now. *Some lust in him after all,* she thought. "How old are you child?" he asked.

She couldn't say where the certainty came from, but she had no doubt he already knew her age, probably to the day. "Eighteen years this summer, Holy Reader," she replied.

"Eighteen years." The old man shook his head. "At my age the years speed by so. It seems no more than a week since your father came to me, seeking guidance. He wanted so badly to marry your mother, and, though it grieves me to say so in your uncle's hearing, I counselled him to do so, in defiance of his father. 'The joining of hearts is to be rejoiced at.'"

"'And only a sinful man will sunder those joined in love,'" Reva concluded. *The Second Book, The Book of Blessings.*

The Reader smiled and sighed in pleasure. "I see the Father's love burns bright in you, child." He picked up a quill, dipping it in the inkpot to add his signature to the document formalising her acknowledgment as Lady Reva Mustor, Niece to Fief Lord Sentes Mustor of Cumbrael. Veliss reclaimed the scroll and moved back to the Fief Lord's side, blowing gently on the wet ink.

"I do so hate to trouble you further, Holy Reader," the Fief Lord said. "But I have grave news to impart."

The old man gave a placid nod. "The Realm Guard marches towards our borders once more. Grim tidings indeed. We can only trust the Father's benevolence will save us from further ravishment."

"The Realm Guard will spend a month or so wandering around woods and hills seeking the fanatics who attacked the Lord of the South Tower. Having found nothing, they will go home. A necessary demonstration for the Asraelin populace. I have the King's Word on it." Her uncle's red eyes for once were clear and bright with scrutiny as he read the Reader's expression. "No, the news I must impart is far graver. You see my niece is not only accomplished in her knowledge of the Ten Books, she also wields a sword with great skill, even more skill than my late brother in fact."

"Really?" The Reader gazed at Reva in wonder. "The Father is generous with his blessings, it seems."

"Doubly generous," Uncle Sentes said. "For he contrived to place her in my manor the very night three assassins came to kill me. But for her I wouldn't be standing here."

The Reader's shock was genuine, she could see it, the start that made his aged jowls wobble, the slight frown of consternation;

the face of a man suffering an unpleasant surprise. "The Father be thanked you are not hurt, my lord," he gasped. "The assassins, do they live?"

"Sadly, no. One was slain by my wonderful niece, a second by my guards." He paused, his gaze still fixed on the Reader's face. "But one escaped. A man my niece insists is a priest in your church."

The Reader's alarm was also genuine, but not so surprised as before. *He knows,* Reva thought. *He knows who the priest is.* She found her fists clenching as the old man made a show of sorrowful reflection.

"Sadly the priestly calling does not make us immune from misguided notions," he said. "Your brother's words, heretical though they were, found many willing adherents, including some amongst the priesthood. I shall, of course, exhaust every resource available to the church to bring this rogue to justice. If you could furnish a description . . ."

Veliss produced a second smaller scroll and placed it on his desk. "Ah, efficient as ever, my lady," the Reader said. "It shall be copied and distributed to every chapel within days. The fugitive will find no refuge in the church, I assure you."

Reva took a step towards him, fists aching now, finding her uncle's hand on her arm, gentle but firm.

"Your consideration is appreciated, Holy Reader," he said. "I believe we have troubled you enough for one day."

"Feel free to trouble me on all days, my lord." He smiled at Reva. "Especially if the company you bring is so delightful as today."

Her uncle tugged her arm and started for the door, but Reva didn't move just yet. "'Deceit,'" she said to the Reader, "'is the hardest sin to divine, for many a lie is spoken in kindness, and many a truth in cruelty.'"

He kept it from his face, but his eyes gleamed with it, just for a second: anger. "Quite so, my dear. Quite so."

"Reva," Uncle Sentes said from the door.

Reva bowed to the Reader and followed her uncle from the room. The sneering priest stood in the hallway, regarding her with unmistakable contempt.

"Pardon me," Reva said, pausing. He was a tall man and she was obliged to look up at him, though not tall enough to be out of reach. "Your nose appears to be bleeding."

He frowned, fingers coming up to touch his nose, coming away clean. "I don't . . ."

His head snapped back from the force of the blow, nose breaking, though not with enough force to kill him. He stumbled backwards to collide with the wall, sinking to the floor, blood streaming down his face.

"My mistake," Reva said, moving on. "Now it's bleeding."

"That was unbecoming," Uncle Sentes reproached when they had returned to the manse, going to the library where a fresh bottle of wine was already waiting. Lady Veliss, however, seemed to be smothering a laugh.

Reva slumped into a chair, unbuttoning her hateful collar and scratching furiously. "That old man is a liar," she stated.

"Evidently," he replied, removing the cork and sniffing the bottle's contents. "Umblin Valley, five years old. Very nice."

"So that's it?" Reva asked. "He lies to your face and you do nothing?"

The Fief Lord merely smiled and poured the wine.

"We imparted a warning," Veliss said, glancing up from her desk, the one Reva had paused at during her mission to retrieve the sword. Veliss was still engaged in study of the same book, the one about money and wine-making, her desk stacked high with copious notes. "The great hypocrite will be on the defensive now."

"Where I would like to keep him for good," Uncle Sentes added. "Something your vaunted grandfather never quite managed."

"He knows," Reva said. "The priest, where he is. I can tell."

"Hungry for vengeance, love?" Veliss asked. "Did he treat you so badly?"

Filthy, Fatherless sinner . . . Reva got up from the chair, moving to the door. "I'm going to change."

"It would help if we knew more about him," Veliss said, making her pause. "About how you were raised. Where exactly was it? A castle, a cave in the mountains?"

"A barn," she replied in a mutter before leaving the room.

She went to her room, undressing with an urgency that left several rips in the dress, tossing it into a corner. She changed into her preferred garb of riding trews and loose-fitting blouse, provided at her insistence despite Veliss's objections. *I'll find him myself*, she decided as she laced up her boots. *Sneak into the cathedral tonight and make the old man spill his secrets* . . .

There was a knock on the door, soft but insistent. She opened it to find her uncle there, his expression kind but insistent. "A barn?" he said.

She sighed, moving back and sitting on the bed. He came in, closing the door and sitting next to her. She was surprised to see he had no bottle with him. They sat in silence for a moment, Reva trying to form words that might make some sense to him. "It was big," she said eventually. "The barn. No animals, no ploughs, just me and him, and a lot of straw. My first clear memory is of climbing up and down the beams. If I fell, he'd beat me."

"He did that many times?"

"More than I could count. He was skilled with the cane, leaving no scars, save this one." She pulled back her hair to reveal the mark above her right ear from the time he had beaten her unconscious.

"Do you know where it was, this barn?"

"It sat amidst broad fields, the grass was long and visitors were rare, stern men who looked at me with odd expressions. He called them his brothers, they called him the Truepriest. There was one man though, different from the others. He came only once or twice a year, and the priest would make me stay in the shadows when he did. I couldn't hear what they spoke of, but I'm fairly certain the priest called him 'my lord.'"

"Can you describe him?"

"Broad across the shoulders, not particularly tall. He had a bald head and a black beard."

She saw recognition dawn in his eyes. She waited for him to name the man but instead he said, "Go on. What else can you remember?"

"As I grew older he began to take me to the village where he went for supplies. I had little experience of other people and hardly any notion of how to act around them, shouting and pointing in excitement the first time. That earned me a beating. 'You must not be noticed,' he said. 'You must pass through the lives of others leaving no mark.' Later he would send me on my own at night, either to steal or to contrive a means of overhearing a conversation. Practice for my holy mission, I suppose. I began to know the villagers quite well, their gossip giving me a fine insight into their lives. The baker's wife was carrying on with a tinker who came by every two weeks. The wheelwright had lost a son at Greenwater Ford. The village priest was far too fond of the ale. Then one night, I happened upon an open window . . ." *I knew her only as the carpenter's daughter. She stood before a basin, guiding a washcloth over her skin. The light from the lantern seemed to make her skin glow, her hair like gold . . .*

"Reva?" Uncle Sentes prompted.

She shook her head. "The priest had been following me, every night, without my knowledge. I lingered by that window too long. The next day he gave me this." She touched a hand to her scar.

"The name of the village?"

"Kernmill."

This seemed to confirm a suspicion in his mind and he nodded. "I'm sorry, Reva," he said, putting an arm around her shoulders, pulling her close. "I may not be the best Fief Lord, but I'm resolved to be the best uncle. And as a present to my niece I intend to find this priest and watch when you gut him. Would you like that?"

She blinked away tears and returned his embrace, whispering. "Yes, Uncle. I should like that very much."

The days that followed saw her settling into a routine at the manor. Practice in the sword room with Arken in the mornings, lunch with Veliss and the Fief Lord in the afternoon followed by an interminable hour or more of sitting in the corner whilst one or both of them met with some merchant or lord asking for something. Evenings saw her free to go riding with Arken, her uncle having secured a place in the stables for Snorter and Bumper. They would range beyond the walls until night came, hunting when opportunity arose. Arken had acquired a longbow from somewhere, proving capable of drawing it which was still more than Reva could do, although his ability to find his mark was meagre compared to her skill with the wych elm. Every Feldrian she was also required to sit through the petitions, Veliss quizzing her on their relative merits when the whole boring palaver was done.

"I don't know," she groaned as Veliss asked her opinion on a disputed land grant. The land had been gifted to a former House Guard by her grandfather and now his two eldest sons were fighting over it. "Divide it in half or something."

"The quality of the land is variable," Veliss explained. She had a seemingly infinite well of patience despite Reva's continued air of tired indifference. "Rich pasture sits alongside rock-strewn bog, like a patchwork of good and bad cloth. Such land is not easily divided."

"Then tell them to sell it and split the money between them."

"The elder brother would like that I'm sure, but the younger lives on the land with his wife and children and wants to stay."

"'All land is the Father's gift,'" Reva quoted, stifling a yawn. "'But only the man who works the land can lay claim to it.' The Seventh Book, Alltor's judgement on the greed of landlords."

"So just give the land to the younger brother and risk angering the elder?"

"Is he an important man?"

"Not especially, but he does enjoy the patronage of some minor nobles."

"Then his anger shouldn't matter. Are we done yet?"

That afternoon she went to badger her uncle for news of the priest, something that had become a near-daily ritual. She found him in his rooms, buttoning his shirt whilst a large man in a grey robe stood at the window, holding a small bottle up to the light as he shook it.

"Reva," the Fief Lord greeted her. "Do you know Brother Harin?"

The large grey-robed man turned to offer her a bow. "The niece I've heard so much about? Can't say I see a resemblance, Sentes. Too pretty by half."

"Yes. Fortunately for her, she favours her mother."

Reva found herself unable to suppress a pang of suspicion at the presence of the large man. "You are a healer?"

"Indeed, my lady. Once Master of Bones at the House of the Fifth Order, sent by my Aspect to care for your uncle . . ."

"And all the heretic Faithful I allow to remain in this city," Uncle Sentes interrupted. "Don't forget them." There was a hardness to his tone making Brother Harin raise his eyebrows and hand the Fief Lord the small bottle in silence.

"Same dose as before?" her uncle asked.

"Probably best to increase it. Four times a day . . ."

"Mixed with clean water, yes I know."

Brother Harin pulled a leather satchel over his shoulder. "I'll be back next week." He went to the door and gave Reva another bow before leaving.

"He doesn't address you properly," she said.

"Because I told him not to. Seems a little silly to stand on ceremony with a man who's had his finger up your arse."

She nodded at the bottle. "What is that?"

"Just a little tonic." He placed it on a table. "Helps me sleep. You've come to ask about the priest."

"Let me hunt for him," she said. "Send me and I'll bring him back bound and ready for judgement in a month. I swear it."

"This is hardly the best time, with the Realm Guard roaming our borders people are uncertain enough. Uncovering whatever schemes the Reader may have indulged in will only add to the alarm."

"You know who that man is, the one the priest called a lord. I could tell."

"I don't know, I suspect. And I'll not upset a long-worked-for peace by proceeding on suspicion alone. We'll act, Reva, you have my promise. But we'll act soft and slow so the old bastard doesn't see us coming."

"I can be stealthy," she insisted. *You've no idea how stealthy . . .*

He shook his head. "I don't doubt your abilities but I need you here. The people must become accustomed to seeing you at my side."

She bit down her disappointment. "Why? You've acknowledged me. Why do they need to see me?"

This gave him pause, his brows creasing in realisation. "You don't know, do you? You honestly have no notion at all."

"No notion of what?"

"Reva, you may have noticed but there are no children in this house. Nor are there likely to be. I had no heirs, no-one to follow me to the Chair. But now, I have you."

She felt a cold hand creeping across her chest. "What?" she said in a thin sigh.

"A few of your father's . . . indiscretions have come calling over the years. Some seeking acknowledgment, only to be disappointed. Most just asking a favour or a full purse. I was happy to send them all on their way. Until you, Reva. How old were you when the priest took you away from your grandparents, do you think?"

"I know how old, he told me. I was six."

"Your father died nigh on nine years ago. That means he took you three years before Hentes assassinated our father and plunged this fief into war. Of all Hentes's children, he came for you. He saw what I can see."

She shook her head in confusion. "What can you see?"

"The next Mustor to sit in the Lord's Chair." He moved closer, taking her hand and pressing a kiss to her cheek. "Sent to me by the Father Himself, for surely He heard my prayer."

"A girl can't be a Fief Lord," Arken said as they rode out that evening, cantering along the causeway and off towards the forested hills to the north.

"Fief Lady," Reva said, the cold hand still gripping her chest. Her tone was flat, the enormity of her uncle's words leaving no room for emotion.

"That doesn't sound right," Arken said. "You'll have to think of something better. Countess maybe."

"You only get countesses in Nilsael." She pulled on the reins, Snorter coming to a halt. She sat in the saddle for a long time, the coldness gradually giving way to a heart-thumping bout of terror. "I can't stay here," she decided in a tremulous voice. "I should never have lingered."

"Your uncle has been good to you, to us."

"Because he wants an heir."

"Not just that. He loves you, I can tell."

Or the memory of his brother, the man he couldn't be. Reva ran a shaking hand over her forehead. "The Northern Reaches," she said. "We can go there. You said you'd like that."

"When there wasn't anywhere else . . ."

"We can go now. We have horses, weapons, money . . ."

"Reva . . ."

"I can't do this! *I'm just a filthy, Fatherless sinner! Don't you understand?*"

She spurred Snorter to a gallop, making for the trees. She was halfway there when something made her pull up, another horse cresting the hilltop ahead. It moved with the ragged trot of an exhausted animal, foam covering its flanks and mouth, the rider slumped forward, barely able to keep himself in the saddle. Well-honed instincts brought one word to mind. *Trouble.*

She watched them straggle closer, Snorter stirring beneath her, nostrils flaring at the unwelcome stench of a fellow horse near death, keen to keep running. *The Northern Reaches,* Reva thought. *Al Sorna will welcome you.*

She kicked Snorter into motion, closing the distance to the horse. The rider was so exhausted he barely noticed when she reached out to grab the reins, tugging his mount to a halt. *Realm Guard,* she noted from his garb, taking in the red-brown smears on his breastplate and the empty scabbard on his saddle. "Where's your sabre?" she asked.

His head snapped up in alarm, a face of encrusted sweat and dried blood, regarding her in naked terror before he blinked and took in his surroundings. "Alltor?" he croaked.

"Yes," Reva replied. "Alltor. What has happened to you?"

"To me?" The man bared his teeth, a strange light in his eyes as he giggled. "They killed me, girl. They killed us all." His giggle turned into a full laugh, the laugh into a choking cough before he slumped forward, falling from the saddle. Reva dismounted, taking the waterskin from Snorter's saddlebag and holding it to the guardsman's lips. He coughed again, but was soon gulping down water in great heaves.

"I . . . need to see the Fief Lord," he gasped when he had drunk his fill.

Reva looked back at the city, shrouded in the pall rising from many chimneys, the dim outline of the manor where the servants would be preparing the evening meal, and the great twin spires, home to a great old liar. "I'll take you to him," she said. "He's my uncle."

CHAPTER TWO
Vaelin

"The Volarian Imperial Army is formed of three principal contingents," Brother Harlick said, voice rising and falling as he bounced along on the back of a pony. "The citizen conscripts known as Free Swords, the great mass of slave-soldiery known as Varitai, and the Kuritai, highly trained slave-elite of fearsome reputation. A basic structure that has been in place for nearly four hundred years."

At Vaelin's command he had been talking constantly for hours, relating all he knew about the Volarian Empire as they journeyed back to the tower. "Individual units are grouped into battalions, which are in turn grouped into a division comprising eight thousand men when at full strength. A typical division will include both Free Swords and Varitai with smaller specialist contingents of engineers and Kuritai. An army grouping consists of three or more divisions under the command of a general . . ."

Vaelin had insisted on setting off the night before, having recovered from the vision which laid him low on the beach. Despite its intensity, the vision had been brief, the chill lingered but without the same depth as before, although the images it left brought all the discomfort he could want, the conclusion inescapable. *Something very bad has happened.*

He could offer only a brief farewell to Nortah and Sella, sensing their alarm and feeling a liar for the comforting words he spoke as he left. "It's likely nothing," he had said. "I grow overly cautious with age."

"Burning!" little Lohren was saying in a sing-song voice as he made for the door, jumping in excitement. "Burning houses! Burning people! Bad men burning everything! Uncle's going to kill them!"

He roused Captain Orven, finding scant surprise at the sight of the Eorhil woman's head poking out from his tent as he stumbled into his boots. "Battle order," Vaelin told him. "Scouts on both flanks. Torches for every man. Send a squad to the beach, they'll find a man in a hut. He's coming with us. If he objects, tie him to a horse."

"Officers of general rank are typically drawn from the small but immensely wealthy ruling class," Harlick was saying. "The only class of Volarian society entitled to wear red. Although such privileged status affords the chance of high command, appointments are given only to those of proven leadership experience . . ."

"What do they come for?" Vaelin broke in. "What do they want?"

Harlick thought for a moment, perhaps considering a complex response, but seeing Vaelin's expression replied simply, "Everything, I imagine."

He began a description of the working practices of the Volarian Governing Council but Vaelin waved his hand. "That's enough for now."

The Lady Dahrena had ridden in silence, her expression one of controlled concern as she listened to Harlick's knowledge. "I know this reaction may seem excessive . . ." Vaelin began but she shook her head.

"I trust my lord's . . . judgement."

"I regret the necessity of making my next request . . ."

"Tonight," she said. "When we return to the tower."

"It's not too far?"

"It's a fair distance, but I have managed it before, during the riots after the Aspect Massacre. Father was concerned the Realm might be undone."

"My thanks, my lady."

"Thank me when I bring news all is peace and harmony."

"I fervently hope to." *Hope all you want,* his doubts mocked him. *You know what she'll tell you.*

Dawn was breaking as they clattered through the cobbled streets of North Tower, the courtyard gates swinging open as they approached. Vaelin climbed down from Flame's back, fighting weariness and calling for Captain Adal.

"My lord." The captain's greeting was clipped, his hard gaze evidence he still smarted from Vaelin's threat of dismissal.

"Sound the muster," Vaelin told him, ascending the steps to the tower. "Every North Guard is to report here forthwith. Send emissaries to the Eorhil and the Seordah. The Tower Lord calls for all the warriors they can send."

"My lord . . . ?"

"Just do it, please, Adal," Dahrena said, moving past him and making for the stairs. "I'll need a few hours," she called to Vaelin before disappearing from view.

For want of another resting place, Vaelin slumped into the Lord's Chair, wincing against the din of shouted orders as Adal went about his business. *Can I do this again?* he wondered. The canvas bundle rested on his knees, feeling heavier now.

"Vaelin?" Alornis stood before him, a shawl over her shoulders, feet slippered against the chill of the stone floor. Her eyes were wide with uncertainty and her gaze continually drawn to the commotion outside. He noticed her fingers were stained with dried paint.

He held out a hand and she came to him, sinking down to rest against his knees. "What's happening?" she asked in a small voice.

"It seems, as ever, my mother is shown to be a very wise

woman." He smiled as she frowned up at him, teasing the hair back from her eyes. "There's always another war."

"The palace is a ruin," Dahrena said, her features pale and eyes red with recent tears. However, her voice was clear and free of any tremble as she made her report. "Bodies lie thick in the streets. Volarian ships fill the harbour. People line the docks, hundreds of them, in chains."

Vaelin had convened a council in his rooms on the upper floor. Captain Adal stood by the window, arms crossed. Brother Kehlan, invited at Dahrena's insistence, sat at her side, face drawn in concern. Also present, at Vaelin's invitation, was Brother Hollun of the Fourth Order, clutching a bundle of scrolls, eyes wide with unabashed fear as he regarded Dahrena. She had waved aside Vaelin's suggestion she contrive to conceal her gift from those not already party to the knowledge. "After what I saw, I fear secrets are of small use now. Besides, I've long suspected most already know."

Seated in the corner was Brother Harlick. Although appointed archivist to the tower he made no notes of the meeting, Vaelin knowing he would remember every word spoken here for transcription later. Alornis sat at Vaelin's side, hands clasped tight to conceal the tremble that had begun the night before. *She worries for Alucius,* he thought. *And Master Benril.*

"The Realm Guard?" he asked Dahrena.

"I saw no sign of them, my lord. Clearly the City Guard made a stand in several places, to no avail."

"The King? Princess Lyrna?"

"I lingered over the palace as long I could, seeing only corpses and blackened ruin."

Vaelin nodded and she sat down, Brother Kehlan grasping her hand as her head slumped in sorrow and fatigue. "Captain," Vaelin said. "What is our strength?"

"Over two thousand have answered the muster so far, my lord. The remainder should arrive within seven days. The North Guard on hand numbers three thousand and will be at full complement when the outlying companies report in. That may take over two weeks, given the distances involved."

"It's not enough," Dahrena said. "The army I saw must number five or six times our strength, even if the Seordah and the Eorhil answer our call."

"Expand the muster," Vaelin told Adal. "All men of fighting age, including the miners and fishing folk."

Adal gave a slow nod. "I shall, my lord." He gritted his teeth in hesitation.

"Problem, Captain?" Vaelin asked him.

"There's been some grumbling already, my lord. Amongst the men."

"Grumbling?"

"They don't want to go," Brother Kehlan said when Adal hesitated further. "Half of them were born here and have never seen the Realm. The other half will be well pleased if they never see it again. They ask, not without justification, why they should fight for a land that sent no aid when we faced the Horde. It's not their war."

"It will be when the Volarians get here," Dahrena said before Vaelin could give vent to his anger. "I saw their souls, they burn with greed and lust. They won't stop at Varinshold, or Cumbrael or Nilsael. They will come here and take all we have, and any they don't kill will be made slaves."

Vaelin took a breath to calm his temper. "Perhaps if you spoke to the men, my lady," he said. "I feel your word will carry great weight."

She nodded. "Of course, my lord."

Vaelin turned to the captain. "And any further *grumbling* must be stamped on, hard. I rule here by the King's Word, not by their consent. Their war is what I say it is."

"The question of numbers is still pertinent, my lord," Brother Hollun said. He had scribbled some figures on a piece of parchment and placed them under Vaelin's gaze.

"Just tell me," Vaelin ordered the rotund brother.

"With an expanded muster, I calculate we will have perhaps twenty thousand men under arms, a figure at least doubled by the Eorhil and Seordah. We have one warship in harbour and the merchant fleet numbers a little over sixty ships, half of which are currently at sea. To transport so many men and horses to the Realm, with weapons and supplies, will take at least four round-trips."

"Assuming we are spared storms," Captain Adal added.

"A moot point," Vaelin said. "We won't sail, we'll march."

Dahrena's head came up slowly. "There is only one land route to the Realm from the Reaches."

It had happened as he surveyed the map earlier, a clear note of confirmation from the blood-song when his eye tracked over the dense mass of symbols comprising the Great Northern Forest. The note had summoned a memory, a blind woman in a clearing on a distant summer day. "I know."

They established a camp outside the town for the growing army, the mustered men falling into their assigned companies with well-practised ease. Tower Lord Al Myrna had insisted on four musters a year to ensure their discipline didn't slacken. The new recruits were a mixed bunch of artisans, miners and labourers, many openly resentful at the interruption to their lives, although Captain Adal had been quick to crush any signs of mutiny and Dahrena's repeated speeches to each batch of new arrivals did much to assuage any doubts over the need to muster. "Many of you ask, 'What would Tower Lord Al Myrna have done?'" she would say. "I tell you as his daughter his course would have been the same. We must fight!"

Adal set the North Guard to work training the recruits and picked out those he knew had distinguished themselves in the battle against the Horde, making them sergeants or captains. The lack of equipment was a worry, although every smith, tailor and cobbler in North Tower was working to exhaustion to produce the weapons, armour and boots needed by an army. Vaelin knew every day spent in building their strength was precious, but the need to begin the march was a constant nag. *Varinshold fallen in a day. Where do they strike next?* Dahrena had offered to revisit the Realm every day if need be, but the depth of fatigue that had gripped her after her first foray convinced him it would be best if she saved her strength. "When we get through the forest," he said. "Then you'll fly again."

"You're so sure they'll grant us passage?" she asked as they toured the camp, Vaelin keen to be seen by as many of the men as possible. "My father was the only Realm subject allowed to walk there, and even then he was permitted no weapon or escort."

He just nodded and moved on, his gaze drawn to the sight of two men sparring with wooden swords amidst a circle of onlookers. The taller of the two batted his opponent's stave aside and swept his legs from under him in a smoothly executed combination of strokes. The tall man helped the defeated recruit to his feet, spreading his arms wide with a broad grin. He was a well-built fellow with long hair, tied back and reaching down to the middle of his bare back, his skin slick with sweat, toned muscle shining. "Number four! Who's next?"

Despite his evident skill he was young, barely twenty by Vaelin's reckoning, with the confident swagger of youth. "Cowards!" he berated the audience with a laugh when none stepped forward. "Come on! Three silvers for the man who can best me!" He laughed again then sobered as he caught sight of Vaelin in the crowd. His grin flickered for just an instant, his gaze narrowing as the bloodsong told Vaelin an unwelcome truth.

"How about you, my lord?" the young man called, holding up his wooden stave in a salute. "Care to honour a simple shipwright with some gentle sparring?"

"Another time," Vaelin said, turning away.

"Come come, my lord," the young man called again, a slight edge to his voice. "You wouldn't want these good men to think you afraid. Many already wonder why you wear no sword."

One of the North Guard in the crowd stepped forward to

rebuke the man but Vaelin waved him back. "What's your name, sir?" he asked the young man, stepping into the circle and taking off his cloak.

"Davern, my lord," the man replied with a bow.

"Shipwright eh?" Vaelin handed his cloak to Dahrena and stooped to retrieve the wooden sword from the earth. "Skills like yours don't come from swinging an adze."

"All men should have interests beyond their work, don't you think?"

"Indeed." Vaelin stood before him, meeting his eyes. Davern hid it well, but Vaelin saw it—deep, festering hatred.

Davern blinked and Vaelin's stave came up, feinted towards his head, avoided the parry, sweeping under his guard to place a single hard jab in the centre of his chest. Davern back-pedalled, arms windmilling as he sought to retain his balance before collapsing heavily onto his rump, much to the amusement of the crowd. There was a jingle of coin amongst the laughter as men settled bets.

"Don't look at a man's eyes," Vaelin told Davern, offering his hand. "The first lesson my master taught me."

Davern ignored the hand, scrambling to his feet, all sign of joviality vanished from his face. "Let's go again. Perhaps I'll teach you one."

"I don't think so." Vaelin tossed the stave to the North Guard. "Make this man a sergeant. Have him teach the sword to his brothers."

"The offer is always open, my lord!" Davern called after him as he retrieved his cloak from Dahrena and walked on.

"Have a care around that one," she cautioned. "I think he means you harm."

"Not without cause," Vaelin replied in a murmur.

He found Alornis outside his tent on returning from his daily tour. He had chosen to live amongst the men, setting up a tent on the fringes of the encampment. His sister's brush was busy on the canvas propped on her easel. She had made it herself with tools borrowed from the tower's carpenter, an ingenious contrivance of three hinged legs, easily folded into a single block less than a yard in length. She had become a common sight about the camp, bag of brushes over her shoulder and easel under her arm as she moved about, stopping to paint when something caught her eye. Her latest was a rendering of the whole camp, each tent and paddock depicted with the precision Vaelin still found unnerving. "How do you do it?" he wondered, looking over her shoulder.

"The same way you do what you do." As he sank onto a nearby stool, she turned, dipping a cloth into some spirit and cleaning her brush. "When do we march?"

We? He raised his eyebrows at her but chose to ignore the word. They had argued enough over this already. "Another week. Maybe longer."

"Through the forest and into the Realm. I assume you have a plan for when we get there."

"Yes. I intend to defeat the Volarians then come home."

"Home? That's how you think of this place?"

"Don't you?" He looked beyond the camp at the town and the tower rising beyond, framed by the dark northern sea. "I've felt it since we got here."

"I do like this place," Alornis replied. "I wasn't expecting to find it so interesting, so many colours. But it's not my home, my home is a house in Varinshold. And if Lady Dahrena has it right, it's now most likely a burnt-out shell." She looked away for a moment, eyes tight against fear-born tears. When she spoke again her gaze was hard, the words repeated several times over the preceding days. "I will not be left behind. Tie me up, lock me in a dungeon. I'll find a way to follow."

"Why?" he asked. "What do you think you'll find there, besides danger, death and suffering? It will be war, Alornis. Your eyes may find beauty in everything you see but there's none to be found in war, and I would spare you the sight of it."

"Alucius," she said. "Master Benril . . . Reva. I need to know."

Reva . . . His thoughts had turned to her many times, his song surging at every instance, the note one he knew well, the same note from the night assassins came for Aspect Elera, the note that had impelled him through the Martishe in pursuit of Black Arrow, and through the High Keep in search of Hentes Mustor, implacable in its meaning. *Find her.* He had resisted the impulse to sing, seek her out, fearing becoming trapped in the vision once again, this time for good.

"As do I," he said. "Present yourself to Brother Kehlan in the morning, I'm sure he'll be glad of another pair of hands."

She smiled, coming closer to press a kiss to his forehead. "Thank you, brother."

He held a council of captains every evening, reviewing progress in training and recruitment. Seven days on and their numbers had swollen to well over twelve thousand men, though only half could be counted as soldiers.

"We'll have to train on the march," Vaelin said as Adal pleaded for a month's delay. "Every day spent here costs lives in the Realm. Brother Hollun reports the full complement of weapons and clothing will be ready in just five more days. It seems an enterprising merchant kept a warehouse full of halberds and mail as a speculative investment. When every man is armed and armoured, we march."

He dismissed them shortly afterwards, Dahrena waiting with a bundle of papers in her arms.

"Petitions?" he asked.

She gave an apologetic smile. "More every day."

"I'll happily defer to your judgement if you'll set aside those requiring my signature."

"These *are* those requiring your signature."

He groaned as she placed the bundle on the map table. "Did your father really do all this himself?"

"He would read every petition personally. When his eyes started to fail him he'd have me read them aloud." Her fingers played on the papers. "I . . . could do the same for you."

He sighed and met her gaze. "I can't read, my lady. As I assume you deduced at our first meeting."

"I do not seek to criticise. Only to help."

He reached out and took the topmost scroll, unfurling it to reveal the jumble of symbols on the page. "Mother tried to teach me, but I was always such a restless child, unable to sit in a chair for more than a few moments, even then only if there was food on offer. When she did force me to try I just couldn't make sense of the letters. What she saw as poetry or history was a meaning-less scrawl to me, the letters seeming to jump about on the page. She kept at it for a while, until eventually I could write my name, then the sickness took her, and the Order took me. Little need for letters in the Order."

"I have read of others with similar difficulty," Dahrena said. "I believe it can be overcome, with sufficient effort. I should be glad to help."

He was tempted to refuse, he had little time for lessons after all, but the sincerity in her voice gave him pause. *I have won her regard,* he realised. *What does she see? An echo of her father? Her fallen Seordah husband? But she doesn't see it all.* His gaze was drawn to the canvas bundle in the corner of the tent, still unwrapped despite all the woeful tidings. Every time his fingers touched the string he found his reluctance surging anew. *She has yet to see me kill.*

"Perhaps for an hour a night," he said. "You could tutor me. A welcome diversion after the day's march."

She smiled and nodded, taking the scroll from him. "'The Honourable Guild of Weavers,'" she read. "'Begs to inform the Tower Lord of the scandalous prices being charged by crofters on the western shore to maintain the supply of wool . . .'"

An encampment at night was always the same, regardless of the army or the war. Be it desert, forest or mountainside, the sights, smells and sounds never altered. Music rose from amongst the canvas city, for every army had its quota of musicians, and voices lifted in laughter or anger as men came together to gamble. Here and there the quieter knots of close friends clustered to talk of home and missed loved ones. Vaelin felt a certain comfort in the familiarity of it all, a reassurance. *They become an army,* he decided, walking alone along the fringes of the camp, beyond the glow of the many fires. *Will they fight as one?*

He halted after a few moments, turning to regard the saw-toothed outline of the tree-line a short distance away. *Skilled with a blade, but not so light on his feet,* he thought as the blood-song's note of warning began to rise. "Do you have something to discuss with me, Master Davern?" he called into the shadows.

There was a pause then a muffled curse, Davern the ship-wright appearing out of the gloom a moment later. He wore his sword at his side, hand tight on the handle. Vaelin could see a faint sheen of sweat on his upper lip, however his voice was even as he spoke. "I see you continue to go about unarmed, my lord."

Vaelin ignored the comment. "Have you rehearsed this moment?"

Davern's composure suffered a visible jolt. "I do not understand . . ."

"You intend to tell me your father was a good man. That when I killed him I shattered your mother's life. How is she, by the way?"

Davern's mouth twitched as he fought down a snarl. The moment stretched, Vaelin sensing the man's desire to abandon pretence. "She burned with hatred for you until the day she died," the shipwright said finally. "Gave herself to the sea when I was twelve years old."

The memory returned in a rush of unwelcome sensation. *The rain, beating down in chilled sheets, the sand streaked with blood, a dying man's whisper, "My wife . . ."*

"I didn't know that," he told Davern. "I'm sorry . . ."

"I do not come for your apology!" The young man took a step forward, his snarl unleashed.

"Then what do you come for?" Vaelin asked. "My blood to wash away all the grief? Remake those shattered lives? Do you really imagine that's what you'll earn here, rather than just the noose?"

"I come for justice . . ." Davern advanced further, placing his free hand on the scabbard, ready to draw, halting as Vaelin voiced a laugh.

"Justice?" he said as the mirth faded. "I looked for justice once, from a scheming old man. He gave it to me, and all I had to give him was my soul. All that I did for you and your mother. Didn't Erlin tell you?"

"Mother said he lied." There was a faint note of uncertainty in Davern's tone, but his snarl remained in place, the note of warning taking on a deeper pitch. *A lifetime's hatred can't be dispelled with a few words.*

"Erlin sought to soften her anger, with lies," Davern went on. "To deflect me from my cause, and my cause is just."

"Then you should kill me now and have done." Vaelin spread his hands. "Your cause being just."

"Where is your sword?" Davern demanded. "Fetch your sword and we'll settle this."

"My sword isn't for the likes of you."

"Curse you! Fetch your sw—"

There came a faint snapping sound from the tree-line, no louder than a breaking twig.

Vaelin charged Davern, catching him about the waist, his sword half-free of the scabbard as they tumbled to the earth. The air made a groaning sigh a foot above their heads.

Davern thrashed, kicking out as Vaelin rolled away. More snaps from the tree-line. "Roll to the right!" he barked at the shipwright, jerking himself to the left as at least ten arrows thudded into the earth about them.

"What?" Davern shouted in confusion, stumbling to his feet.

"Down!" Vaelin commanded in a fierce hiss. "We are attacked."

Another snap and Davern threw himself flat, the arrow a black streak against the dim sky.

Not him, Vaelin realised, eyes fixed on the infinite void of the trees. *The song's warning wasn't for him.*

"Run for the camp," Vaelin told Davern, removing his cloak. "Raise the alarm."

"I . . ." Davern looked about wildly, still hugging the ground. "Who?"

"Longbowmen, if I'm any judge." Vaelin tossed his cloak into the air, seeing it dance as the shafts tore through it. "Run for the camp!"

He surged to his feet and ran towards the trees, counting to three then dropping as another volley whistled overhead, rising and charging again, weaving from side to side until the first of them came in sight, a hooded figure rising from the long grass no more than ten feet away, bow half-drawn. Vaelin darted towards him, dropping and rolling, the arrow missing by inches. He surged to his feet, delivering an open-handed blow to the archer's chin, felling him instantly. Another charged from the left, bow abandoned for a long-bladed knife. Vaelin snatched up the fallen man's bow and brought it round in a wide arc, the stave connecting with the attacker's head as he closed. The man stumbled back, slashing wildly. Vaelin stood, remaining still for a heartbeat then diving to the side as an arrow flew past to bury itself in the stumbling man's chest.

Another archer rose before him as he ran to the right, bow fully drawn. *Fifteen feet,* Vaelin judged. *Too far and too close.* A shadow appeared behind the archer, a silver flash of metal cutting him down with a single stroke. Davern turned from the corpse as a hooded figure came for him, raising a crescent-bladed axe. Davern ducked the blow and slashed at the man's side but he was clearly no amateur and blocked the stroke with the haft of his axe, catching the shipwright with a backhanded blow that sent him sprawling.

Too far, Vaelin thought again, sprinting towards the hooded figure as he raised his axe for the killing blow.

Something inhuman growled in the darkness, a great shadow flicking across Vaelin's path and the man with the hatchet was gone. Hooves drummed the earth and a rider came from the shadows, the long staff in his hand whirling as he sent another hooded figure senseless to the earth. More growls, yells of terror and running feet . . . then screams, mercifully short, five of them, one after the other.

"Brother," Nortah said, reining in beside him, eyes wide with concern and blond hair trailing in the wind. "Lohren had a dream."

Davern was emerging from the healing tent when Vaelin arrived the next morning, a large bandage covering his nose and a spectacular bruise colouring the surrounding flesh.

"Broken then?" Vaelin asked.

Davern glowered at him and gave no response.

"I owe you thanks," Vaelin went on. "Or did you save me so you could kill me later?"

"Dis changesh noddin," Davern stated.

"Pardon?"

Davern flushed, licked his lips and tried again with slow deliberation. "Thish changes nothing."

"Ah." Vaelin nodded and moved past him. "Good to know. You have men to train, Sergeant."

Inside, he found his sister applying a poultice to the face of a well-built man with a shock of black hair and a bruise on his jaw that made Davern's seem positively dull. He sat on a stool, flanked by Captain Adal and one of his North Guard, wrists and ankles constrained by shackles, the chains jangling as he twisted towards Vaelin, face full of hate, spittle coming from his mouth as he tried to voice his threats. Alornis took a backward step, wincing from the fury on display.

"His jaw's broken," Brother Kehlan said from the other side of the tent where he was grinding herbs in a pestle. "Who knew the teacher had such a strong arm?"

"I did." Vaelin moved to Alornis's side, touching her arm in reassurance. "You frighten my sister, sir," he told the shackled man.

The man grunted something at him, spouting more spittle, a bead of it finding Vaelin's face. "Quiet!" Adal barked, cuffing the man on the back of the head.

"Enough of that!" Kehlan said. "I'll have no torture in this tent."

"Torture, brother?" Adal scoffed, then leaned down to whisper in the shackled man's ear. "I think I'll wait for him to heal first. Wouldn't want it over too soon."

"Secure him to the main post and leave us," Vaelin said. Adal gave a reluctant nod and did as he was bade, roping the man to the post and leaving with his comrade. "And you, brother," Vaelin told Kehlan.

"I said no torture," the old brother insisted.

"Come along, brother." Alornis went to his side and tugged him towards the tent flap. "His Lordship is above such things." She raised a questioning eyebrow at Vaelin. He nodded back and she gave a grim smile before leaving.

"You're the only one to survive," Vaelin told the shackled man, placing the stool before him and sitting down. "The fellow I hit would probably have lived also, but my brother's war-cat is not always easily restrained."

The man just maintained his baleful glare. *Some fear, mostly hate,* Vaelin surmised from the song.

"Ten Cumbraelins arrive on a ship three weeks ago," he said. "Hunters by trade, hence their bows. Come to the Reaches in search of bear, the furs and the claws fetch a high price and they're increasingly scarce in the Realm. It was a good story."

Same fear, same hate, a little grim amusement.

"So," Vaelin went on. "Gold or god?"

More fear mingling with uncertainty. The man's brows furrowed, his emotions a jumble for a second then settling on a sense of contempt.

"God then," Vaelin concluded. "Servants of the World Father come north for the glory of killing the Darkblade."

The confusion deepening, fear building . . . and something more, an echo . . . no, a scent, faint but acrid, foul and familiar, buried deep in this man's memory, so deep he doesn't even know it's there.

"Where is he?" Vaelin demanded, moving closer, staring into the archer's eyes. "Where is the witch's bastard?"

Bafflement, more contempt. He thinks me mad, but also . . . suspicion, an unwelcome memory.

"A man who is not a man," Vaelin went on, voice soft. "Something that wears other men like masks. I can smell him on you."

A surge of fear mixed with recognition.

"You know him. You've seen him. What is he now? An archer like you?"

Fear only.

"A soldier?"

Fear only.

"A priest?"

Terror, swelling like oil poured on flame . . . A priest then . . . No, no note of recognition. Not a priest. But he knows a priest, he answers to a priest.

"Your priest sent you here. You must have known he was sending you to your death. You and your brothers."

Anger, coloured by acceptance. They knew.

Vaelin sighed, getting to his feet. "I'm not overly familiar with the Ten Books, as you might imagine. But I do have a friend who could recite them at length. Let's see if I have it right." He closed his eyes, trying to remember one of Reva's many quotations. "'Of the Dark there can be no toleration amongst the loved. A man cannot know the Father and know the Dark. In knowing the Dark he forsakes his soul.'"

He stared down at the bound man, sensing what he had hoped to sense. *Shame.*

"You looked into his eyes and saw a stranger," he said. "What was he before?"

The man looked away, eyes dulling, his emotions quieter now. *Shame and acceptance.* He grunted, head bobbing as he forced sound through his crippled mouth, spittle flying as he repeated the same garbled word, unknowable at first but gaining meaning with repetition. "Lord."

"Put him on a barge to the settlements on the northern coast," Vaelin told Adal outside. "He's to be taken far into the forest and released with his bow and a quiver of arrows."

"What for?" Adal said in bafflement.

Vaelin moved off towards his tent. "He's a hunter. Perhaps he'll find a bear."

Nortah was waiting with Snowdance and Alornis when he got to the tent, the great cat's purr a contented rumble as she ran a hand over the thick fur on her belly. "She's so beautiful."

"Yes," Nortah agreed. "Pity there are no boy cats for her to make beautiful babies with."

"There must be, somewhere," Alornis said. "Her kind would have been bred from a wild ancestor."

"In which case they'll be far beyond the ice," Vaelin said, accepting the cup of water Nortah passed him.

"Did he tell you anything?" his brother asked.

"More than he wanted to, less than I would have liked." He glanced at the pack Nortah had brought, noting the sword propped against it.

"Lady Dahrena's gift," Nortah explained. "One I asked for. A man should have a weapon if he's to ride to war."

"War is no longer your province, brother. I sent no recruiters to Nehrin's Point for a reason. You belong with your family."

"My wife believes my family will only be safe if we lend our aid to your cause."

"We?"

"Come." Nortah clapped him on the shoulder. "There are some people you should meet."

He led Vaelin to where four people waited on the outskirts of the camp, one of whom Vaelin already knew. Weaver stood staring at the ground, his usually bland but affable expression replaced by one of deep discontent, his hands constantly twitching at his sides. "Why did you bring him?" Vaelin asked Nortah. "He's not made for this."

"I didn't bring him. He just came, deaf to all entreaties to go home. He'd like some flax, or twine. Anything he can weave really."

"I'll see to it."

"This is Cara," Nortah introduced the slight girl at Weaver's side. She was perhaps sixteen with wide dark eyes, stirring a memory of a little girl peering out from behind her father's cloak at the fallen city.

"My lord," the girl said in a small voice, eyes continually darting about the camp. Despite her timidity, the blood-song's greeting was strong. *Whatever her gift,* Vaelin decided, *it has power.*

"And Lorkan." Nortah's voice held a note of reluctance as he gestured at the young man standing nearby. He was a few years older than the girl and also slim of stature, but had none of her reticence.

"A considerable honour, my lord!" He greeted Vaelin with a deep bow and a bright smile. "Never would I have thought such a lowly soul as I could count himself a comrade to the great Vaelin Al Sorna. Why, my dearest mother would weep with pride . . ."

"All right," Nortah said, cutting him off. "Talks too much but he has his uses."

He moved on to the final member of the group, and the most imposing, a large, bearlike man with an extensive beard and a mass of grey-black hair.

"Marken, my lord," the big man introduced himself in a Nilsaelin accent.

"He may be able to help," Nortah said. "With your want of intelligence."

The bodies had been placed in a tent on the edge of camp, the few valuables they possessed handed out as payment to the soldiers who would do the grim work of burying them in accordance with Cumbraelin custom. Marken moved to the closest one, a stocky man, as archers often were, his final grimace of terror frozen and incomplete, half his face having been torn away by the war-cat's claws. Marken seemed untroubled by the gory sight, kneeling and touching his palm to the corpse's forehead, eyes closed for a second, then shaking his head. "All a jumble. This one was half-mad long before Snowdance got to him."

He moved on, touching a hand to each corpse in turn, pausing at the fourth, judging by the lines on his face the eldest of the group. "Better," he said. "All a bit red and cloudy, but sane, after a fashion." He looked up at Vaelin. "Does my lord have a particular point of interest? It'll make things easier."

"A priest," Vaelin said. "And a lord."

Marken nodded, placing both hands on the dead man's head, eyes closed. He remained in the same position for several moments, unmoving, breathing soft, face placid beneath the beard. After a while Vaelin wondered if he was still present in his own body or, like Dahrena, able to fly beyond himself, except he burrowed into the mind of a corpse rather than soaring above the earth.

Eventually the big man opened his eyes with a pained grunt, moving back from the corpse, a sense of accusation in the gaze he turned on Vaelin. "My lord could've warned me of the nature of the thing I sought."

"My apologies," Vaelin replied. "Does that mean you found it?"

"The hair's a little thicker on the sides of his head," Marken told Alornis, pointing at her sketch. "And his mouth is not so wide."

Alornis's charcoal stub added a few fluid strokes to the image, wetting her finger to smudge some lines. "Like this?"

"Yes." Marken's beard split to reveal a brace of white teeth. "My lady is the gifted one here."

"That's him?" Vaelin asked as Alornis handed him the sketch. It showed a broad-faced man, balding, bearded, eyes narrow. He wondered if Alornis had indulged in Master Benril's liking for artistic licence in adding a cruel twist to the mouth.

"As close a resemblance as memory allows, my lord," Marken said. "That's the face of the thing's mask all right."

"You felt it? When you saw it in the dead man's memory?"

"I saw it, behind the mask. We always see more than we know, but it lingers." He tapped a stubby finger to the side of his head. "Especially when we see something we don't really understand."

"You have a name for this face?"

Marken's beard ruffled in an apologetic grimace. "My gift is limited to what they see, my lord. What they hear is beyond my reach."

Vaelin placed the sketch next to the one Alornis had already completed, showing a younger man of handsome aspect, though his sister had opined his nose and chin were a little too sharp. "And this is the priest?"

"Can't say for sure, but he's the one the dead man and the others deferred to. His most vivid memory, besides Snowdance bearing down on him, was of this man talking. They were on a dock somewhere, about to board ship."

Vaelin stared at both sketches for a long time, hoping for a note from the song, hearing nothing.

"Shall I show master Marken to the meal tent?" Alornis said, breaking his concentration.

"Yes, of course." Vaelin offered a smile of gratitude to Marken. "My thanks sir."

"We are here to help, my lord." The big man got to his feet with a groan, rubbing his back. "Though I wish this war had come a few years earlier."

◆ ◆ ◆

He found Nortah at the butts they had arrayed along the river-bank. He had brought his own bow, an Eorhil weapon similar to their old Order strongbows. It seemed his skill had actually increased since their service, the shafts flying towards the target with unerring speed and precision, the other archers pausing to watch the spectacle.

"You've drawn an audience," Vaelin observed.

Nortah glanced at the onlookers and sent his last arrow into the centre of the butt. "A small one. You don't have many archers in this little army."

"Mostly hunters and a few veteran Realm Guard from the settlements," Vaelin acceded. "How would you like to be their captain? Perhaps pick out some likely extra hands from the recruits."

"As my lord commands."

"I don't command anything from you, brother. In fact I'm sorely tempted to send you home."

Nortah's expression became sombre, upending his bow and resting his hands on the tip. "It wasn't only Lohren who had a dream, brother. She just dreamt of you fighting many men with bows. She thought it so exciting. Sella . . . Sella dreamt she watched us die. Me, Lohren and Artis, and the twins yet to be born. All of us, taken, tortured and slaughtered before her eyes, as Nehrin's Point burned. If you had heard her screams, you would know why she sent me and why I came, though I relish no part of what we are about to do."

"Can you . . ." Vaelin hesitated then made himself say it. "Do you think you'll still be able to kill?"

Nortah raised an eyebrow and for an instant the bearded teacher disappeared, replaced by the caustic youth with the bitter tongue. "Do you? *I* have a shiny new sword. Yours seems to be wrapped up and hidden from the world."

Maybe I'm worried unsheathing it will loose something worse than an invading army. He left the thought unsaid and changed the subject. "These companions of yours. I know Weaver's power, and I've seen what Marken can do. What of the other two?"

"Cara can call the rains, though you'll want to think long and hard before asking her to do so. The effect is . . . dramatic, but the consequences unpredictable."

"And the boy?"

"Lorkan can't be seen."

Vaelin frowned. "I can see him."

Nortah just smiled. "It's . . . difficult to explain. No doubt, before this is over there'll be plenty of opportunity for a demonstration."

"No doubt." Vaelin reached out to clasp his brother's hand, finding the grip strong, and warm. "I'm glad you're here, brother. Be quick about picking your men. Tomorrow we march for the Realm."

CHAPTER THREE
Lyrna

Water . . . Falling . . . A slow, regular liquid beat, birthing an echo.

Am I in a cave? Later, she would remember this as her first coherent thought as Queen of the Unified Realm. Her second being the fact that she was now queen. Her third would be a silent wail of despair at the agony searing its way into her mind, summoning horror and making her thrash and scream . . . *The flames spouting from the Volarian woman's hands, Malcius, Ordella, Janus, little Dirna, the stench of her skin and hair as it burned . . .* She choked as the scream spluttered to silence. There was something in her mouth, something hard and unyielding clamped between her teeth. She tried to pull it free but found her hands unwilling to respond, restrained somehow. It occurred to her that she should open her eyes.

Darkness, broken by a dim shaft of light, hazy shapes huddled in catacombs. A cave after all. *But why is it swaying so? And why do chains dangle from the ceiling?*

A jerking movement from one of the huddled shapes commanded her eye, a loud retching reaching her ears along with the spatter of vomit. Silence returned, save for a faint whimpering, the occasional jangle of linked metal, and the creak of protesting wood.

Not a cave. A ship.

"So," a soft, gravelled voice muttered in the shadows to her left. "The screamer's awake again."

Her eyes peered into the shadows, seeking a face, seeing only the dim outline of a shaven head, blocky and gleaming from the light above. A grunt as the blocky head tilted. "Don't look so mad now. Pity, you'll soon wish you were."

Lyrna tried to speak, but found the words caged by whatever was clamped into her mouth, secured in place by leather straps about her head. She looked down at her hands, seeing a faint glint of old metal on her wrists. She gave a tug, chains snapping taught, the shackles chafing her skin.

"Overseer thought you were a nuisance," the voice said. "Wanted to toss you overboard. The master wouldn't have it. My Volarian isn't good, but I think he said something about breeding stock."

Lyrna heard no malice in the voice, just indifferent observation. She grimaced as the pain returned, closing her eyes as tears seeped forth, the agony sweeping across her scalp and face in waves. *Her skin, her hair, burning . . .*

She abandoned herself to the sobs that wracked her, collapsed to the damp wooden planking, shuddering in sorrow, drool flowing around the gag. It could have been hours, or days even, before exhaustion took her. She was always grateful there were no dreams lurking in the void that claimed her.

She jerked awake as something hauled on the gag, straining her neck as she was dragged to her knees, staring up at a very large man in a black leather jerkin. He leaned close, eyes staring into hers in appraisal, grunting in satisfaction then reaching behind her, undoing the straps and removing the gag. Lyrna coughed, retching and gasping, then choking off as the large man enclosed her face with his hand, pulling her eyes back to his. "No . . . screaming," he said in broken Realm Tongue. "You. No more screaming. Or." He raised something in his other hand, something long and coiled with an iron handle. "Understanding?"

Lyrna managed to move her head in a fractional nod.

The large man grunted again and released her, moving away, boots splashing in the bilge water. He paused to nudge a huddled shape with the handle of his whip, voicing a tired curse, leaning down to unlock the shackles with the key hanging around his neck then barking something over his shoulder. Two men, not quite so large, appeared from the shadows to lift the shape between them, carrying it towards the steps above Lyrna's head, the only feature of the hold to be fully bathed in the light from above. Lyrna glimpsed a face through the gaps in the steps as they took the body aloft, a woman, her features slack and pale in death, but Lyrna had a sense she had been pretty.

The overseer, as Lyrna had intuited him to be, found two more bodies amongst the host of huddled shapes, both also dragged aloft, presumably to be cast overboard. She couldn't tell how many others were shackled here, the furthest reaches of the hold were too shrouded in shadow, but counted over twenty within view. *A space of ten yards square, holding twenty. The average Volarian slave ship is eighty yards long. There are perhaps one hundred and fifty people in this hold.*

Off in the gloom the key rattled anew followed by a fearful sob. The overseer appeared again, pulling a stumbling figure behind him, a girl, slender, young, dark hair veiling her face, tears audible as she was led aloft.

"Third time for that one," the shaven-headed shadow said. "Not a good place to be pretty, this ship. Lucky for us eh?"

Lyrna tried to speak, finding the words stuck in her sand-dry throat. She coughed, summoning as much moisture to her mouth as she could, and tried again. "How long?" she asked in a rasp. "Since Varinshold."

"Four days, by my reckoning," the voice replied. "Puts us maybe two hundred miles across the Boraelin."

"You have a name?"

"I did, once. Names don't matter here, my lady. You are a lady, are you not? That dress and that voice don't come from the streets."

Streets. She had been running through streets, screaming, the pain taking all reason as she ran from the palace where all was flame and death, ran and ran . . . "My father was a m-merchant," she said, a tremor colouring every word she spoke. "My husband also. Though they hoped to ascend one day, by the King's good graces."

"I doubt anyone will ascend again. The Realm has fallen."

"The whole Realm? In just four days?"

"The King and the Orders are the Realm. And they're gone now. I saw the House of the Fifth Order burning as I was led to the docks. It's all gone."

All gone. Malcius, the children . . . Davoka.

Her gaze was drawn upwards as more feet sounded on the steps. One of the overseer's not-so-large servants led a slim young man down into the hold, securing him to a free set of manacles a few feet from Lyrna.

"Another popular pretty face," the shaven-headed man muttered.

"Necessity breeds forbearance, brother," the young man replied in a light tone that jarred on Lyrna's ear. She had to agree he was pretty, his features delicate, reminding her of Alucius, before the war and the drink.

"Filthy degenerate," shaven-head said.

"Hypocrite." The young man grinned at Lyrna. "Our screaming lady has regained her senses, I see."

"Not a lady after all," the gravelly voice replied. "Just a merchant's wife."

"Oh. Pity, I should have liked some noble company. No matter." The young man bowed to Lyrna. "Fermin Al Oren, Mistress. At your service."

Al Oren. Not a name she knew. "Your f-family has property in Varinshold, my lord?"

"Alas no. Grandfather gambled away every bean before I was born, leaving my poor widowed mother destitute and me obliged to restore our fortunes through guile and charm."

Lyrna nodded. *A thief then.* She turned to shaven-head. "He called you brother."

The shadowed face gave no response but Fermin was quick to reply in his stead. "My friend is fallen from the sight of the Departed, Mistress. Cast down amongst the wretched for his grievous attempt on the . . ."

The shaven head lunged forward, chains straining, the slatted light revealing brutish features and a misshapen nose. "Shut it, Fermin!" he ordered with a snarl.

"Or what, exactly?" the noble thief returned with a laugh. "What can you threaten now, Iltis? We're not fighting over scraps in the vaults any more."

"You were in the dungeons together," Lyrna realised.

"That we were, Mistress," Fermin confirmed, grinning at Iltis who had slumped back into the gloom. "Our hosts came for us the morning after the city fell, killed the guards that had been foolish enough to linger, killed most of the prisoners too. But preserving the strong and"—he winked at her—"the pretty."

Slave, Lyrna thought, crouching to peer at the bracket to which her chains were fashioned. *I am a slave-queen.* The thought provoked a shrill giggle, threatening to build to more screams. She forced it down and concentrated on the bracket, her fingers describing a half loop and plate of iron, secured into the oak beam with two sturdy bolts. She couldn't hope to work it loose. The only way these shackles were coming off was via the overseer's key.

"You have a name, Mistress?" Fermin asked as she reclined against one of the beams supporting the steps.

Queen Lyrna Al Nieren, Daughter to King Janus, Sister to King Malcius, Ruler of the Unified Realm and Guardian of the Faith. "Names don't matter here," she said in a whisper.

The following day the overseer found no further corpses which seemed a signal to begin giving them better food, thick porridge with berries replacing thin gruel. *Weeded out the weaklings,* Lyrna surmised. *And starved slaves are no use.*

She watched the overseer closely during his visits, her eyes constantly on the key about his neck as he stooped to examine his stock, the key dangling, but never low enough to grab. *Even if I could, he would beat me down before I could use it.* She glanced over at Iltis slurping his porridge, meaty fingers scooping out the dregs from the bowl, licking them with gusto. *Fourth Order,* she decided. *One of Tendris's Ardent brutes. Not so easy to beat down.*

She dropped her gaze as the overseer stopped beside her, leaning down to unlock the chains from the bracket. "Up!" he commanded, nudging her with his whip handle.

She rose, swaying on unsteady legs, muscles shuddering with cramp. The overseer pulled her into the light, taking hold of her face and turning her head from side to side, eyes narrowed in scrutiny, lip curled in disgust. "Too much damage," he muttered in Volarian. "Even the crew won't fuck you with a face like that." Without a pause he reached down to lift her skirt, rough hands mauling, exploring. Lyrna choked back vomit and kept as still as possible. "Or maybe they would," the overseer mused, rising and unlacing her bodice, hands and eyes exploring her breasts.

No screaming, Lyrna thought, closing her eyes and clenching her teeth as his thumb traced over her nipple. *No more screaming.*

"Not stupid either," the overseer said, turning her face to him again. "What were you I wonder? Rich man's whore? Prize daughter of a wealthy house?" He searched her face for understanding as he spoke. Lyrna stared back with eyes wide, her fear only half pretence.

The overseer grunted, stepping back and gesturing with his whip. "Sit!"

Lyrna slumped back to the boards and he relocked her manacles, leaving her fumbling at her bodice as he stomped up the steps. *Davoka would have slit his belly and laughed as his guts spilled out. Smolen would have hacked his head from his shoulders in a trice. Brother Sollis would have . . .*

THEY ARE NOT HERE!

She breathed deeply, forcing the tremble from her hands,

leaning down to lace up her bodice with deliberate care. *You have no protectors here. No servants. You must serve yourself.*

Night-times were the worst, the other captives often given to terrors, calling out in their sleep for lost loved ones or begging for release. Lyrna slept only fitfully, waking often thanks to the pain and the memories. This night it had been the Volarian woman again, but instead of flame it was water that gushed from her arms, great torrents of it, filling the throne room . . .

She rose to her customary crouch, waiting for her heart to calm itself. The dreams were vivid, no doubt because she had repeatedly forced herself to examine every facet of what she witnessed in the throne room, realising for the first time that her fearsome memory could be a curse as well as a gift. She spared herself nothing, every word spoken by Brother Frentis, every nuance of expression, every lick of flame.

He had been flawless, she thought. *Perfect in every way. Not like an act at all. A damaged man, noble in his humility, returning home after an epic of tribulation. The woman too, every inch the timid escaped slave. All gone the moment my brother died. And her rage when I killed Frentis, no acting there.* Her thoughts lingered on the woman's face, the grief and rage as the blood began to stream from her eyes. *Unexpected,* Lyrna decided. *Frentis wasn't supposed to die. Not part of the plan.* Which begged another question. *What else did she need him for? Or was it just the rage of a woman who loses her lover?* The Mahlessa's words came to her, as they often did as she pondered the mystery of it all. *Three of these things . . . His sister . . . you wouldn't want to meet her.* Could it be? Had she survived an encounter with the third malicious agent the Mahlessa spoke of?

A fresh spasm of pain clutched at her scalp, making her stifle a gasp. Perhaps survive was not the right word. *A mountain of questions but no answers. No evidence. But I'll have it, however many years it takes . . . However much blood I have to spill to get it.*

Her eyes were drawn to a movement off to her left. It was Fermin, leaning forward with a hand extended towards the deck, his finger moving from side to side as he smiled down at something between his feet. Lyrna followed his gaze, seeing a small black rat on the planking, staring up at the moving finger, its head matching the movement with exact precision, as if it were being pulled along by an invisible string.

Lyrna's chains made a small clanking sound as she leaned forward for a better view. Fermin's head came up in a start, expression void of any humour now. His fingers spasmed and the rat scampered off into the shadows. He looked away as Lyrna continued to stare, the Mahlessa's words now singing in her head like a triumphal bugle: *Look to the beast charmer when chains bind you.*

"So, my lord," she asked Fermin the next morning, "what manner of thief were you?"

For once he seemed reticent, reluctant to meet her gaze. "A poor one, given my capture."

"When you are . . . taken aloft," she persisted. "You must have seen how many hands crew this ship."

His gaze met hers. "Why would that interest you, Mistress?"

There was a rattle of chains as Iltis shifted behind her, as she hoped he would. "Do you wish to be a slave?" she asked him. "Used like this for all your days? What fate do you think awaits you in their empire?"

"A better fate than being cast into the ocean. I'll suck every cock they thrust at me and bare my arse to a thousand more. Shame is not my vice. But fear is. I intend to live, mistress of no name." He turned away. "Scheme all you want, I'll have none of it."

"Forget him," Iltis said in a dismissive rumble. "A coward will be of no use to us in any case."

Lyrna turned to him. "Us, brother?"

"Don't play with me, woman. I see your eyes covering every corner of this hold. What have you seen?"

She turned towards him, shuffling as close as she could, speaking softly, but still loud enough for Fermin to hear. "My family were merchants, as you know. We traded with Volarian ships. A ship this size will have a crew of perhaps forty men, fifty at most."

Iltis frowned. "So?"

"There must be at least one hundred and fifty people in this hold. Odds of three to one, if we can loose them."

"Many will be too weak to fight, and half are women."

"Give a woman a good reason and she'll fight a hundred men. And a weak man becomes strong when fired with fear and hatred."

The man beside Iltis stirred, raising his head. Iltis turned a hard stare on him. "Breathe a word of this and you'll wake up with a broken neck."

The man shook his head, sitting up and shuffling closer. He was sturdy, though not so large as Iltis, with a prominent jaw and a scars on both cheeks marking him as either outlaw or soldier. "Get these chains off," he said. "And I'll rip the throats from a dozen of the fuckers with my bare hands."

Outlaw, Lyrna decided.

Iltis regarded the earnest face of the outlaw in silence for a moment then turned back to Lyrna. "The overseer's key. You have a way to get it?"

No. "Yes. But we need to be patient. Wait for the right time. Speak to those around you, keep your words soft, but warn them to be ready."

"How do we know we can trust them all?" Iltis enquired. "Some may sell us for favoured treatment or a promise of freedom."

"We have no choice," Lyrna said, glancing over her shoulder at Fermin, now huddled with his back to them, though she saw his fists were clenched. "Trust must be risked."

The word was passed from captive to captive, questions whispered back and forth throughout the day. They were afraid, but none save for Fermin said no, and none sold them to the overseer. *Still free at heart,* Lyrna thought. *Not yet moulded into slaves.*

She had questions relayed to the slender girl who was taken aloft most often. *How many in the crew? How many are armed?* The next time she was led to the steps her hair was pulled back from her face, her eyes still leaking tears, but lit with a determined light. Upon being returned to the hold her answers came back. *Thirty crewmen. Fifteen guards, positioned about the hold entrance, working in shifts of five at a time.*

She waited until Iltis was asleep before speaking to Fermin again. He sat, half-turned towards the hull, eyes closed, a slight frown on his brow, as if straining for some faint sound. Lyrna listened and picked up a distant, lilting drone.

"Whale-song," she said.

Fermin's eyebrows rose and a grim smile came to his lips. "Not for long."

Abruptly the whale-song ended and a moment later the hull reverberated with the echo of a crushing impact. "Red sharks," said Fermin. "They're always hungry."

"You can hear their hunger?"

He turned back to her, expression closed once more.

"I know what you are," Lyrna said. "Beast charmer."

"And I know you're not some merchant's daughter. Did the overseer have it right? A rich man's whore? I know you understood every word he said."

"Whores get paid. Slaves don't."

"What do you want from me?"

"To do what you do. Steal. Or rather have your little friend steal for you."

"The overseer's key."

"Quite so."

"We unshackle everyone and storm the ship. That's your great plan?"

"If you have another, I should very much like to hear it."

"I have a plan, of my own. You see it's the master of this fine vessel who calls for me. He's a man of considerable property, a large estate near Volar, a wing of his house given over to his collection of young men from all the corners of the world. I'll be his first from the Realm, pampered and cared for whilst you'll be squirting out babies every year until your womb dries."

"That's your ambition? To be kept like a pet until you grow too old to interest him."

"I'll be on my way long before then, don't worry. A whole empire to explore, so many treasures to steal."

"Leaving everything behind? Your city, your mother?"

She saw that one hit home, the twitch of his mouth speaking of a suppressed pain.

"What of her?" Lyrna prodded. "Do you know what became of her when the city fell?"

He rocked back and forth, hugging his knees and suddenly appearing very young. "No," he said in a whisper.

"You said you provided for her. That's why you took to thieving, isn't it? For her. Don't you want to know if she still lives?"

"How do we know anyone still lives back there? How do we know anyone remains free?"

"I know it. And I think you do too."

"When the City Guard caught me she bribed the lord of the dungeon to make sure I was fed. The King allows a few comforts in the dungeons now, if you can pay for them. At least, he did." He closed his eyes, hugging his knees tighter. "She's dead. I know it."

"With all your heart? Because with all my heart I know there are still free people in our Realm, and they are fighting whilst we languish here."

He opened his eyes and she saw tears shining. "You're not a whore," he said hoarsely. "No whore ever spoke like that."

"Help us. We'll take this ship and sail back to the Realm. I will help you find her, you have my word."

He gritted his teeth, breath exhaling in a hiss. "I always used weasels," he said after a moment. "Rats aren't suited to thieving. I'll need time before the bond is strong enough for such a complex task."

"How long?"

"At least three days."

Three days. An unwelcome delay, but Volaria was still a long way off, and three more days of improved diet could only aid them when the time came. She nodded. "Thank you."

He gave a faint grin. "I hope there are some sailors amongst this lot, otherwise we'll be running a great risk just to set ourselves adrift in a broad ocean."

The rat dropped the berry in front of Fermin, sitting back and staring up with bright eyes, whiskers twitching. Fermin smiled fondly at the rodent and blinked, the rat scurrying off in a blur. It reappeared after only a few moments bearing another berry, adding it to the growing pile at Fermin's feet.

"Don't like this," Iltis whispered. His face was shadowed but Lyrna knew it was tense with suspicion. "Use of the Dark is a denial of the Faith."

Lyrna was tempted to point out that none of the original catechisms made any mention of the Dark and the strictures against it only appeared in Realm Law following the time of the Red Hand. But she doubted Iltis was the kind of man for whom reasoned discussion held much meaning. "We have no choice," she whispered instead. "No other way to get the key."

"She's right," the scar-faced outlaw said. "I'd even give my soul to the Cumbraelin god to get out of this pit."

Iltis made a grunting noise, his bulky form hunching over in anger. "Heresy comes easy to the weak of Faith. Mine has never wavered."

"We don't get that key, you'll have years of slaving to test your precious Faith," the outlaw replied provoking a lurching snarl from Iltis.

"This isn't helping," Lyrna said.

Iltis ground his teeth and relaxed back against the hull, lost to the shadows once more.

"You understand your part in this?" Lyrna asked the outlaw.

He nodded. "Get to the tiller, kill the helmsman. Three of the strongest men will be with me."

"Good." She turned to Iltis. "Brother?"

"Once the shackles are off, wait for the guards to come for the nightly inspection. Strangle them with our chains and take their weapons. Take five men and kill the others on deck. The overseer's cabin is at the stern next to the master's. Kill the overseer first, then the master."

"I'll lead the others against the crew," Lyrna said. "Try to herd them towards the port rail, keep them bottled up. We'll need you to help finish them off, so be quick."

"We'll be lucky if half of us are still breathing by the end," the outlaw said.

I'll consider us fortunate if it's a quarter, she thought. "I know. Do the others?"

"They know." He swallowed and forced a smile. "Better a free corpse than a living slave, eh?"

Fermin pronounced his rat ready the following night, the animal now so completely within his control it would sit in his upturned hands, staring ahead with an unnerving stillness. "He's a clever one," Fermin said. "Not weasel clever, but still smart enough for tonight's escapade."

Lyrna felt a fresh wave of pain sweep over her head, making her grimace. The pain had changed over the last two days, becoming more concentrated in certain places, no doubt where the flames had seared the deepest into her flesh. Added to the pain was a hard ball of nausea in her gut. The Lonak had a word for it, *Arakhin*: the weakness before battle. "Then let's be about it," she said.

Fermin lowered the rat to the deck where it promptly scampered towards the steps, hopping from one to the other until it was lost from view. Fermin reclined, eyes closed. Lyrna breathed slow and even as the moments stretched, trying to calm the sickness building in her belly, feeling the silence thicken around her as the others waited. She studied Fermin's face as he continued to sit with his eyes closed, seeing the occasional twitch or frown and wondering what it meant. *Does he see through its eyes?* she wondered as a faint smile came to the thief's lips.

"He's got it," he whispered, making Lyrna's heart leap. "That's it, jump down, then back under the d—" His eyes flew open as a spasm of pain shook him from head to toe. He convulsed then doubled over, retching.

"Fermin!" Lyrna called to him. "What is it? What happened?"

The heavy fall of boots on the deck echoed throughout the hold, all eyes raised to track their progress. The footsteps halted, a pause, then something small splashed into the square of moonlit bilge water below the steps, something with black fur and a broken back.

Fermin stopped vomiting, righting himself and staring at the planking on the hull, his brows deeply furrowed in concentration.

The overseer descended the steps at a leisurely pace, the tip of his whip sliding over the wood as he made an unhurried entrance, standing in the moonlight and nudging the dead rat with his boot. "How very interesting," he murmured in Volarian.

Fermin gave a pained grunt, his breathing heavy, sweat shining on his skin as he continued to stare at the hull.

"Magic," the overseer said in Realm Tongue, raising his gaze. "One here, with magic. Who?" His whip uncoiled with a flick of his wrist, sliding across the planking like a snake. "All here, trade for one with magic." He moved to the outlaw, staring into his eyes. "Understanding?"

The outlaw was shaking with fear, a fear so absolute it seemed certain he was about to spill every secret. Instead he closed his eyes and shook his head. *Better a free corpse than a living slave.*

The overseer shrugged and moved back, turning away, then twisting with cobralike speed, his whip moving too fast for the eye, the skin on the outlaw's already scarred cheek splitting open as the crack reverberated throughout the hold.

"Who?" the overseer said again, his eyes roving, the outlaw sobbing in pain.

Fermin gave an audible gasp, sagging as yet more sweat streamed down his back, drawing the overseer's eye. As he started towards him Lyrna jangled her chains, rising the bare few inches they permitted, speaking in Volarian. "It's me! I have the magic!"

The overseer's gaze narrowed, a very small grin on his lips as he moved towards her. "Should have guessed," he said in Volarian. "Rare to find one, but when I do it's usually the smartest." He held up the key on the chain about his neck. "Sent your little friend for this. Clever, it nearly worked. But now I'll have to kill ten of these as an example. Not you though, you're worth a thousand of them. But you do get to choose."

He moved back to the moonlit square, spreading his arms with a laugh. "So choose, you burnt bitch! Which of these do you want to watch d—"

The ship lurched, throwing him from his feet, the planking on the hull behind splintering, water streaming through in miniature fountains. The overseer staggered forward, falling onto Iltis and the outlaw. For a moment he gaped up at the big brother, face blank with shock. Iltis brought his blocky head forward to connect with the overseer's nose, bone breaking and blood streaming. The overseer sagged as the outlaw twisted, wrapping his legs around the Volarian's midriff, holding him in place as Iltis continued to bring his head down. More breaking bone, more blood.

"The key!" Lyrna shouted.

Iltis stared at her, blood streaming down his face, he blinked as the fury abated and understanding returned. With the outlaw's help he rolled the overseer onto his back, fumbling for the key.

"I can't . . ." Fermin said in a faint drone of exhaustion. Lyrna turned to see him slumped, blood streaming from his nose and eyes. "I can't stop him . . . now. You have to be quick."

"Got it!" Iltis said, pulling the key towards his manacles, stubby fingers attempting to manoeuvre it into the lock.

Something impacted on the hull once more, the planking splintering further, more water gushing forth, the level rising about their feet. Iltis cursed as the key was jerked from his fingers, spinning in the air and landing at Lyrna's feet. She crouched down, hands plunging into the water, searching, panic threatening to strip her reason away . . . There, smooth metal under her fingertips. She grasped it tight, holding it up to her manacles, forcing the tremble from her hands as she twisted the lock to meet it. *Slow, don't rush . . .* The key slotted into the lock, turned and the manacles fell away.

She stood, uncaring of the ache that burned in every muscle, surveying the few faces not hidden in shadow, seeing the terror and desperation, the pleading in every gaze. *The steps are near, and this ship will sink before long . . .*

She freed Iltis first, then the outlaw. "Guard the steps!"

"What about taking the ship?" the outlaw asked.

Lyrna glanced at the splintered hull and moved on to the next captive, a woman about her own age, sobbing in gratitude. "Soon there won't be any ship to take," she said, helping the woman to her feet.

She freed the next man in line and handed him the key. "Free the others. Hurry."

She went to Fermin, finding him near senseless with exhaustion, although the blood had stopped flowing. "Wake up!" She slapped him across the face. "Wake up, my lord!"

Focus returned to his gaze and he groaned in protest as she hauled him upright. "What is it?" she said. "What did you do?"

"They're always hungry," he said in a whisper.

The ship tilted, the captives shouting in alarm as something scraped along the hull, the ever-rising water sloshing about. A guard came trotting down the stairs, probably sent to check on the overseer, drawing up in shock at the sight of Iltis and the outlaw. He turned to shout something at his comrades above but the outlaw whipped his chains around the man's legs before he could speak, pulling him onto his face and dragging him down the remaining steps. Iltis forced him under the rising waters, keeping him submerged until his thrashing subsided.

"See if he has another key," Lyrna said.

Iltis searched the corpse but raised his hands in a helpless gesture.

Lyrna surveyed the captives, maybe twenty were free now, and the water kept rising.

"Can you keep it at bay?" she asked Fermin in desperation. "Until everyone is freed?"

He smiled, revealing bloodstained teeth. "Given all I have to give . . ."

The deck exploded, a huge fountain of water gushing forth and in the centre a great triangular head, impossibly wide jaws opening, revealing row upon row of spear-point teeth. The jaws closed on two of the captives, cutting through both like a scythe through straw, the gushing water turned red. The head thrashed from side to side, more wood splintering, the whole ship shuddering with the force, then it was gone.

"Convinced him we were a whale," Fermin said to Lyrna, the water nearly at his shoulders. He met her gaze. "My mother's name is Trella. Remember your promise, my Queen."

Iltis's large hands grabbed her, pulling her towards the steps as the water rose to cover Fermin's head. Iltis pushed her ahead of him, up the steps and onto the upper deck. All was confusion, a few freed captives milling about, the crew either frozen in shock or desperately trying to launch their boats, deaf to the orders shouted by a tall man in a black robe.

"We need a boat," Lyrna said.

Iltis nodded, striding towards the nearest boat, laying about with his chains, the outlaw fighting at his side as they forced a path, the remaining captives following in a dense knot. Some crewmen fought, others fled, most just stood and stared.

Lyrna found one of the guards on his knees, twitching fingers exploring the bleeding gash Iltis had left on his forehead. She pulled the short sword from his scabbard and strode to where the tall black-robed man stood shouting his pointless orders from a hoarse throat. He had his back to her so could offer no defence as she thrust the blade into it. He shouted in shock and pain as he sank to his knees.

"I would like you to know," she said in Volarian, placing her mouth close to his ear, "that from this day every moment of my life will be spent rending your empire to dust and flame. I'll give your regards to your collection when I burn your estate to the ground, Master."

She left the sword embedded in his back and ran to the boat. The crew were now solely concerned with preserving themselves and the prisoners had a free hand in heaving it over the side, a task made easier by the fact that the sea was now almost level with the rail. The outlaw vaulted into the boat, reaching back to help a captive aboard, the slender girl who had been so popular with the crew. Lyrna noticed her nails were bloody and broken.

The ship shuddered once more and the sea swamped the deck. Lyrna found herself lifted by Iltis and thrust at the boat, catching hold of a cleat, the outlaw hauling her aboard with the aid of the others. Iltis pulled himself over the side and lay panting on the deck amidst the survivors. Lyrna counted five in all, ragged, exhausted, and all looking at her.

Not much of a kingdom, she thought, surveying the boat as they rose and fell at the ocean's whim. She glanced over her shoulder, seeing the ship's mainmast slipping beneath the waves amidst a swirling cluster of flotsam. "Do we have any oars?"

CHAPTER FOUR
Frentis

They ambushed a Free Sword cavalry patrol on the north road, four men having the misfortune to dismount for a piss close to where they lay in the long grass. Davoka's spear took one, Frentis's sword two more whilst Ratter and Draker wrestled the fourth to the ground as he struggled to remount his horse, cudgel and knife rising and falling in a frenzy after which they squabbled over who got his boots. Davoka covered herself with a bloodstained jerkin taken from the man she killed and Frentis took the sword belt and scabbard from another, throwing away the long-bladed weapon favoured by Volarian cavalry and replacing it with his own Asraelin blade. He also found some bandages in the saddlebags to bind his knife wound which had begun to burn with increasing persistence, drawing sweat from his brow and adding an unwelcome cloudiness to his vision.

Daylight was coming on fast as they mounted up and rode west, Arendil riding double with Davoka. Ratter and Draker clearly demonstrated their lack of experience on horseback as they bounced along behind. Frentis had expected them to take to their heels as soon as they reached the beach on the other side of the bluffs, but for some reason they stayed, perhaps fearing his retribution, though he suspected their loyalty had more to do with the Volarians who now seemed to be everywhere. They passed two more patrols in the space of an hour, too distant to offer a threat, but then spied a full regiment of cavalry cresting a hill half a mile ahead.

"This is hopeless, brother," Ratter said. "The road is choked with the bastards."

He was right, the most direct route to the Order House was denied them, leaving only one option. "The Urlish," he said, turning his horse towards the great mass of trees to the north. "Six miles in and we'll be at the river. We can follow it to the house."

"Don't like the forest," Draker grumbled. "Got bears in there."

"Rather them than that lot," Ratter said, kicking at his horse's flanks. "Come on you bloody thing!"

Frentis spurred to a gallop, hearing a shrill pealing from the Volarian cavalry, similar to a noble's hunting horn. They had been seen. The trees soon closed in, forcing them to slow to a canter, the ground becoming so rough they had to dismount. Frentis strained for signs of pursuit but heard only the song of the forest. *Probably decided we weren't worth the effort.*

He removed the saddlebags from the horse and slapped a palm against its rump, sending it trotting off into the trees. "We walk from here," he told the others.

"Thank the Faith!" Draker groaned, climbing down from the saddle and rubbing his backside.

"The house we go to," Davoka said. "It's the home of the blue cloaks?"

"That's right." *My home.*

"These new *Merim Her* seem to know much," Davoka went on. "They will know of your House, your Order."

"Yes." Frentis hoisted the saddlebag over his shoulder and began to walk north.

"Then they will attack it," she persisted, striding alongside. "Or already have."

"Then we had best not linger." The wound in his side flared again, making him hiss in discomfort, but he kept walking.

They came to the river around midday and paused for a brief rest, Draker and Ratter collapsing on the bank with a flurry of curses. Frentis took off his shirt and began to change the bandage on his wound. Davoka came over to peer at it, nose wrinkling as she sniffed, saying something in her own language.

"What?" Frentis asked.

"Wound is . . ." She fumbled for the right word. "Sick, more sick."

"Festering," he said, fingers gently probing the cut, still leaking some blood but also now swollen and angry, lines of deeper red tracing through the surrounding flesh. "I know."

"I heal it," she said, glancing around at the undergrowth. "Need to find the right plants."

"No time," Frentis told her, tossing aside the used bandage and extracting another from the saddlebag.

"I do it." Davoka took the bandage and wrapped it around his midriff, binding it tight. "Shouldn't leave it like this. Kill you before long."

Killed by a princess, he thought. *A fitting end.* "We need to move on," he said, getting to his feet.

They followed the river west, keeping back from the bank, shrouded by the trees. After a while they saw a barge, drifting with the current, ropes and blocks swaying, the sail tumbled from the rigging and covering the deck. There was no sign of any crew.

"What does it mean?" Arendil wondered.

"We're close to the house," Frentis said. "Barges rarely travel this far upriver except to bring us supplies."

It was another mile before they saw it, a column of black smoke rising above the trees, Frentis breaking into an immediate run. Davoka called to him but he ran on, the wound now a burning cinder in his side and his vision starting to swim. He stumbled to a halt at the sight of the first body, a man in a blue cloak, propped against a tree, face white as marble. Frentis went to him, searching the face but seeing a stranger. *Young, probably newly confirmed.* The brother had a sword within reach of his right hand, the blade dark with dried blood. His chest was encrusted with his own, the earth beneath him damp from it.

"What is death?" Frentis whispered. "Death is but a gateway to the Beyond and union with the Departed. It is both ending and beginning. Fear it and welcome it."

He got to his feet, swaying a little, wiping sweat from his eyes, stumbling on. He found more bodies, all Kuritai, at least a dozen littering the forest, a few still moving despite their wounds, quickly dispatched with the point of his sword. A hundred yards on he found another brother, a tall man with two arrows in his chest. Master Smentil, the tongueless gardener. *You always let me get away,* Frentis thought, recalling his apple-stealing missions to the orchard. *And they always tasted so sweet.*

His gaze was drawn to a strange sight, another dead Kuritai, but instead of lying on the forest floor he was impaled on the broken stump of a tree branch, hanging at least ten feet in the air, blood dripping into a growing puddle below.

Frentis staggered as a fresh bout of pain and fever tore through him. Tearing his eyes from the bloody spectacle of the impaled man, he stumbled on but managed only a few more steps before the pain forced him to his knees. *No!* He tried to crawl forward, seeing more blue-cloaked corpses ahead. *I need to go home.*

"Brother?" The voice was soft, cautious and familiar.

Frentis rolled onto his back, chest heaving, dazzled by the sun blazing through the swaying leaves above, the light dimming as a very large shadow came into view. "Were I a suspicious man," Master Grealin said, "I might see some significance in your returning to us on this particular day."

The shadow disappeared and Frentis felt himself being lifted, head lolling as he was carried away.

It was dark when he awoke, starting from the feel of fingers on his wound. "Lie still," Davoka said. "You'll work them loose."

He relaxed, feeling a bed of soft ferns under his back, looking up at a roof of cloth. "Fat man's cloak makes a good shelter," Davoka said, wiping her hands and settling back on her haunches. Frentis looked down at the wound, grunting in disgust at the mass of wriggling white maggots covering it.

"Forests are full of dead things, rotting away," Davoka said. "The white worms only eat dead flesh. Another day and they clean the wound." She pressed a hand against his forehead, nodding in satisfaction. "Not so hot, good."

"Where," Frentis coughed and swallowed. "Where are we?"

"Deeper in the forest," she said. "Trees are thick here."

"The fat man? Is he the only one?"

She gave an expressionless nod. "I tell him you're awake."

The years had done little to diminish Master Grealin's girth, though there was a hollowed-out look to his face as he settled his bulk next to Frentis, flesh hanging from prominent cheekbones below sunken eyes.

"The Aspect?" Frentis asked without preamble.

"Dead or captured, I expect. The storm broke far too quickly, brother, and with the regiment off chasing shadows in Cumbrael . . ." He spread his hands.

"Who did you see fall?"

"Master Haunlin and Master Hutril were both cut down on the walls, though they certainly made them pay for it. I saw Master Makril and his hound charge into the battalion that broke through the gate, but by then the Aspect had ordered us to flee and I was running for the vaults. There's a passage, built centuries ago for just such an emergency, it leads from the vaults all the way into the Urlish. Myself, Master Smentil and a few brothers made it through but they caught us on the other side."

Frentis was struck by the absence of emotion in Grealin's tone, his voice clear but distant, almost as if he were telling one of his innumerable stories of the Order's history. "They killed the boys too," he said, sounding more puzzled than outraged. "All the little men, fighting like wildcats to the last." A faint, fond smile came to his plump lips and he lapsed into silence.

"Does this mean you are now Aspect?" Frentis asked after a moment.

"You know Aspects do not ascend by virtue of seniority. And I hardly think I stand as the best example of the Order's ethos, do you? But it does mean that, until we can join with our brothers in the north, we are all that remains of the Order in this fief."

"You were right." Frentis paused to cough, accepting the canteen Grealin passed to him and gulping some water.

"Right?" he enquired. "About what?"

"To be suspicious of my return. My presence here is no co-incidence."

A glimmer of the old twinkle shone in Grealin's eye. "I have a feeling you are about to tell me a very interesting story, brother."

"The Lonak woman and the others," Grealin said some hours later, the forest now pitch-dark save for the glow of the campfire outside the shelter. "I trust you've told them nothing of your enforced role in our King's sad demise?"

"I told them it was an assassin, an assassin I killed. Master, I seek no pardon for my crime . . ."

"It was not your crime, brother. And I can see no good arising from any misguided honesty. Indulge your guilt when this war is won."

"Yes, Master."

"This woman with whom you journeyed. You're certain she's dead?"

Her red smile, the love shining in her eyes before he twisted the blade . . . Beloved . . . "Very."

Grealin fell to silence, lost in thought for several long minutes. When he spoke again it was a reflective murmur. "She stole a gift . . ."

"Master?"

Grealin blinked then turned to him with a smile. "Rest, brother. Sooner you're mended the sooner we can plan our war, eh?"

"You intend to fight?"

"That is our Order's charge, is it not?"

Frentis nodded. "I am glad we are of like mind in this."

"Hungry for revenge, brother?"

Frentis felt a smile come to his lips. "Starving, Master."

He knew it was a dream from the slow even beat of his heart, free of hatred or guilt; the heart of a contented man. He stood on a beach, watching the surf crash on the shore. Gulls soared low over the waves and the air had a bitter chill, harsh on his skin but welcome all the same. There was a child playing near the water's edge, a boy of perhaps seven years. Nearby a slender woman stood, close enough to catch the boy should he venture too close to the waves. Her face was turned from him, long dark hair twisted and tangled in the wind, a plain woollen shawl about her shoulders.

He walked to her, feet soft on the sand, keeping low. She kept her gaze on the boy, seemingly deaf to his approach, then spinning as he closed, catching the arm he sought to wrap around her neck, a kick sending him sprawling to the sand.

"One day," he said, scowling up at her.

"But not today, beloved," she replied with a laugh, helping him up.

She pressed herself against him, planting a soft kiss on his lips, then turned back to the boy as his arms enfolded her. "I did say he would be beautiful."

"You did, and you were right."

She shuddered against the wind, pulling his arms tighter about her. "Why did you kill me?"

Tears were falling down his face, his contented heart vanished now, replaced by something fierce and hungry. "Because of all the people we killed. Because of the madness I saw in your eyes. Because you refused this."

She gasped as his arms tightened, ribs breaking. The boy was caught by a wave and began to jump in the water, laughing and waving at his parents. The woman laughed and coughed blood.

"Did you ever have a name?" Frentis asked her.

She convulsed in his arms and he knew she was smiling her red smile once more. "I still do, beloved . . ."

He was woken by shouting, rolling from his bed of ferns and feeling every muscle groan in protest. He looked at the wound, finding it bandaged with no sign of maggots. He was light-headed and possessed of a monstrous thirst, but the fever was gone, his skin cold to the touch and free of sweat. He pulled on his dead man's jerkin and emerged from the shelter.

"The brother I know," Ratter was shouting at Master Grealin. "You I don't, fat man. Don't give me no fuckin' orders."

Frentis looked on in wide-eyed wonder as the master failed to beat the wiry thief to the ground. Instead he gave a patient nod and clasped his hands together. "Not orders, good fellow. Merely an observation . . ."

"Oh, bugger off with the big words—"

Frentis's cuff caught Ratter on the side of the head and sent him sprawling. "Don't talk to him like that," he stated, turning to Grealin. "Problem, Master?"

"I thought a little reconnaissance might be in order," Grealin replied. "A brief ranging to ascertain if we are truly alone here."

Frentis nodded. "I'll go." He gave a brief but formal bow to Davoka, presently engaged in skinning a freshly caught rabbit by the fire. "My lady ambassador, would you care for a stroll?"

She shrugged, handing the half-skinned catch to Arendil and reaching for her spear. "Like I showed you. Keep the fur."

"Master Grealin's words are to be respected at all times," Frentis told a sullen Ratter, now rubbing his head. "And his commands obeyed. If you can't do that, feel free to leave. It's a big forest."

"Your sleep is troubled," Davoka observed as they struck out in an easterly direction. In addition to his sword Frentis carried an

Order-fashioned bow Arendil had had the presence of mind to retrieve from one of the fallen brothers, although his foresight hadn't extended to securing more than three arrows.

"The fever," Frentis replied.

"In sleep you speak a tongue I don't know. Sounds like the barking of the new *Merim Her*. And your fever is gone."

Volarian. I have been dreaming in Volarian. "I've travelled far," he said. "Since the war."

Davoka halted and turned to face him. "Enough shadow talk. You know of these people. Your coming brought celebration, followed by death and fire. Now you speak their tongue in your dreams. You are part of this."

"I am a brother of the Sixth Order and a loyal servant of the Faith and the Realm."

"My people have a word, *Garvish*. You know this?"

He shook his head, increasingly aware of how she held her spear, a measured distance between each hand, grip tensed and ready.

"One who kills without purpose," she said. "Not warrior, not hunter. Killer. I look at you, I see *Garvish*."

"I always had a purpose," he replied. *Just not my own.*

"What happened to my queen?" she demanded, her grip tightening.

"She was your friend?"

The Lonak woman's mouth twisted as she suppressed something deep felt, and painful. *Carrying some guilt of her own,* Frentis surmised.

"My sister," Davoka said.

"Then I grieve for you, and for her. I told you what happened. The assassin burned her and she fled."

"The assassin only you saw."

Beloved . . . "The assassin I killed."

"Seen and killed only by you."

"What do you think I am? A spy? What purpose would I serve in leading you and the boy here to skulk in a forest?"

She relaxed a little, the grip on her spear loosening. "I know you are *Garvish*. Beyond that, we'll see."

They kept on towards the east for five hundred paces then turned north, circling around in a wide arc until the trees began to thin. "You know this forest?" Davoka asked.

"We would train here often, but never this deep. I doubt even the King's wardens come this far in more than they have to. There any many stories of those who ventured into the deep woods and vanished, swallowed by the trees and wandering until hunger claimed them."

Davoka gave an irritated grunt. "In the mountains you can see. Here only green and more green."

They stopped in unison as a sound reached their ears, distant but clear. A man screaming in pain.

They exchanged a glance. "We risk the camp," Davoka said.

Frentis notched an arrow and set off at a run. "War is ever a risk."

The screams trailed off to a piteous wailing as they neared, replaced by something else, a thick, savage cacophony of growls stirring a rush of memory for Frentis. He slowed to a walk, moving forward in a crouch, keeping to the thickest brush. He held up a hand to signal a halt and raised his head, nostrils flared, a pungent scent coming to him on the breeze stirring yet more memories. *Upwind*, he thought. *Good.*

He lowered himself to the forest floor and moved forward at a crawl, Davoka moving beside him with equal stealth until the expected sight came into view through the foliage. The dog was huge, standing over three feet at the shoulder, thick with muscle from haunch to neck, the snout broad and blunt, ears small and flat. It growled as it fed, occasionally pausing to snap at the three other dogs clustered around, its jaws red and dripping gore.

Scratch, Frentis thought in automatic recognition, knowing the foolishness of the thought with instant chagrin. This animal was not quite Scratch's size and its snout was mostly free of the scars for which his old friend was named. He often wondered what became of him, assuming he had been lost or killed when Vaelin sacrificed himself at Linesh. Wherever he was, this wasn't him. This was a slave-hound pack leader, and it had made a kill.

"Please!" Frentis's head came up in a jerk at the call from above, finding himself staring at a girl's face, a pale oval of wide-eyed terror framed by dark oak leaves.

The pack leader left off feeding to issue a curious grunt at the new sound, raising its nose, nostrils flaring. Something pink and red dangled from its jaw, Frentis taking a moment to recognise it as a human ear.

"Oh please!" the face in the branches called again and the pack leader gave a loud rasping yelp, its brothers closing in around as they charged towards the oak barely fifteen paces from where they lay. The oak was old, and tall, the trunk thick and gnarled. Scant obstacle for a slave-hound. Frentis had seen Scratch clamber halfway up a birch without breaking stride.

He raised his head from the brush, casting his gaze about. *No Volarians, yet. But they'll soon come to see what the dogs brought down.*

"Don't let them get close," he told Davoka and stood up.

He waited for the first dog to leap up the trunk then sent an arrow through its back, the beast slumping back to earth with a faint whine. The others turned, snarling, the pack leader charging straight for them, the other two circling round. *Scratch was always so clever,* Frentis remembered.

He made sure of the kill, waiting for the pack leader to close then putting the arrow in his eye. The animal's momentum kept it coming as the arrowhead found its brain and its legs gave way, tumbling towards him. He leapt the corpse, dropping the bow and drawing his sword, slashing at the dog closing from the side, the blade slicing through its nose. It reared back, head shaking furiously from side to side, still snarling in fury . . . then pitching over dead as Davoka's spear punched through its rib cage.

She pulled the weapon free then whirled on the remaining

dog, now standing still, blinking in confusion, beginning to cower as Davoka charged.

"Wait!" Frentis called, too late as the Lonak woman skewered the animal through the neck.

"Strange," she commented, wiping the spear-blade on the dog's pelt. "Come at you like an enraged rock ape then cower like a sick pup."

"It's . . . in their nature." His gaze was drawn to the sight of the girl dropping from the branches of the oak. She landed heavily on bare feet and ran to them, terror still lighting her gaze. She was perhaps fourteen, dressed in a fine but somewhat besmirched dress, her hair showing the semblance of a noble fashion.

"Thank you, thank you, thank you!" She flung herself against Frentis, hugging him tight. "The Departed must have sent you."

"Erm," Frentis said. The war, the pits and a long journey of murder hadn't prepared him for a circumstance like this. He touched the girl lightly on the shoulders. "There, there."

She continued to sob into his chest until Davoka came over to tug her off. The girl started at the sight of the Lonak woman, pulling away and sheltering behind Frentis. "She's a foreigner!" she hissed. "One of them!"

"No," Frentis told her. "She's from somewhere else. She's a friend."

The girl gave a dubious whimper and continued clutching at Frentis's sleeve.

"Are there more of you?" he asked.

"Just Gaffil. We ran from the wagon. He hit one of the whippers and we ran."

"Gaffil?"

"Lady Allin's steward. He must be here somewhere." She stepped away, raising her voice. "Gaffil!" She fell silent as Davoka pointed her spear at something in the brush, something that might once have been a man.

"Oh," the girl said in a small voice and fainted.

"You're carrying her," Davoka stated.

Her name was Illian Al Jervin, third daughter to Karlin Al Jervin, recently favoured by the King for the quality of his granite.

"Granite?" Davoka asked with a frown.

"Stone," Frentis explained. "You build things with it."

"The King loves to build!" Illian said. "And Father's quarries make the best stone."

"Quarries don't make stone," Arendil scoffed, stirring the stewpot suspended over the fire. "You take stone from them."

"What do you know?" Illian rounded on him. "You're a Renfaelin, and a peasant if I'm any judge."

"Then you're not," he replied evenly. "My grandfather is Baron Hughlin Banders . . ."

"Enough!" Frentis said. "Lady Illian. You spoke of a wagon."

She made a face at Arendil and continued her tale. "I was visiting with Lady Allin, she often invites me when father's away. We saw smoke rising from the city, then those men came. Those horrid men, with whips and dogs . . ." She trailed off, sniffling.

"You were captured?" Frentis prompted.

"All of us, apart from the older servants and Lady Allin . . . They k-killed them all, right there in front of us. We were chained up together and put in wagons. They already had other people in the wagons. Mostly commoners but people of quality too."

"How many?" Frentis asked, choosing to ignore her unconscious snobbery.

"Forty, maybe fifty. They were taking us back to the city, anyone who cried out or even gave them a bad look was whipped. There was a woman in the wagon next to ours, captured before they came for us. One of the whippers t-touched her, she spat at them and they cut her throat, her husband was chained beside her. He screamed until they beat him senseless."

"How did you get away, my lady?" Master Grealin asked.

"Gaffil had a small pin in his boot, he used it to do something to the locks on the chains and they came off."

"*He* would have been useful," Ratter muttered.

"He freed everyone in the wagon and told us to wait until the trees were closer. When they were he hit one of the whippers with his chains and we ran. There were ten or twelve of us when we started running, soon it was just Gaffil and I. Then we heard those dogs." She fell silent, face tensed against more tears.

"Other than the men with whips," Frentis said. "Were there guards? Soldiers?"

"There were some men on horses with swords and spears. Perhaps six or seven."

Frentis smiled and gestured at the stewpot. "Eat, my lady. You must be hungry."

He inclined his head at Master Grealin and Davoka and they went a short distance into the trees, beyond earshot of the others.

"Two thieves and a couple of children," Grealin said. "Plus a fat old man. Not an impressive army, brother."

"Armies need recruits," Frentis pointed out. "And thanks to her ladyship we know where to find some."

"Be miles gone by now," Davoka said.

"I doubt it. No slaver's likely to leave his dogs behind."

They had dragged the bodies of the dogs a good two miles north before doubling back to the camp. Finding the trail of those who came in search of them wasn't especially difficult, though keeping Ratter and Draker quiet enough to follow without being detected was another matter.

"See?" Davoka said in a fierce whisper, picking up a broken twig from the forest floor. "Wood is dry. Step on it and it cracks." She tossed it at Draker. "Look where you step."

It was early evening before they found them, encamped in the more open fringes of the forest. Master Grealin waited with Illian and Arendil as Frentis led the others forward. "Wait until you see me," he whispered to Ratter and Draker then beckoned Davoka to follow as he circled around to the right. The four wagons were arranged in a square, rows of cowed people chained within. There were six guards on the perimeter and five slavers sitting around a fire, one of them weeping openly.

Overconfident, Frentis decided, noting the casual saunter of the guards between the wagons. *Shouldn't have ventured so far in.*

He crept up behind the nearest guard, waited until his closest compatriot disappeared behind a wagon and slit his throat with a hunting knife. *Free Sword mercenary,* he judged from the man's non-uniform gear.

He caught Davoka's eye and pointed to the next guard, sitting on a wagon wheel with his back to the trees and guiding a whetstone over the blade of his short sword. Frentis didn't wait for the spectacle and moved to the wagons, close enough to hear the slavers' conversation.

"Raised 'em from pups," the crying man was saying. "Trained 'em myself."

"Cheer up," one of the his companions said with a sympathetic smile. "Fuck one of the boys we found. Always perks me up."

"When I find who did my pups," the weeper went on. "I'll do plenty of fuckin' all right." He brandished a long-bladed dagger. "With this."

A shout came from the other side of the camp quickly followed by the din of an untidy scuffle; Ratter and Draker failing to remain hidden. Frentis drew his sword, keeping the hunting knife in his left hand, and stepped from behind the wagon. "In compensation for your loss," he told the man with the long dagger, "I'll kill you last."

"No moving!" Davoka told Draker as she stitched the cut on his arm. The big man gritted his teeth with a whimper, arm trembling as the needle did its work.

"Serves you right, you clumsy bugger," Ratter said. He sported a livid bruise on his cheek and badly scraped knuckles from beating one of the slavers half to death. The freed captives had gathered round to finish the job.

Altogether they had rescued some thirty-five people, none appearing to have passed their fortieth year, an even mix of men and women, plus a few barely in adolescence. There was also a decent haul of weapons and loot gathered by the slavers, some of which the captives had immediately begun to squabble over.

"This belonged to me old mum!" a young woman insisted as she hugged an antique vase in a tight grip.

"That belongs in the house of Lady Allin, as you well know," Illian scolded. "Brother"—she tugged at Frentis's sleeve as he passed—"this servant seeks to thieve from her employer."

Frentis paused, staring hard at the young woman with the vase. After a moment she swallowed and handed it over. He turned it over in his hand, noting the artistry of the decoration, an exotic bird of some kind flying above a jungle, reminding him of the country south of Mirtesk. "Beautiful," he said, and threw it against the nearest tree.

"Weapons, tools, clothing and food only," he said, raising his voice, the squabblers falling silent. "That's if you're going to stay with us. This Realm is at war and any who stay are soldiers in that war. Or grab whatever loot you can carry and run, though I'd be surprised if you didn't find yourself back in a slaver's wagon within days. This is a free Realm, so I leave the choice to you."

He moved on then paused at the sight of a man sifting through the pile of assembled weapons. He was thin with long hair veiling his face, but there was a familiarity to his movements, a noticeable limp as he sifted through the pile. He stopped, recognising something, his hair parting as he knelt down to retrieve it.

"Janril!" Frentis rushed over, extending a hand to the one-time bugler of the Wolfrunners. "Faith, it's good to see you, Sergeant!"

Janril Norin didn't look up from the assorted weaponry, lifting a sword from the pile. It was a Renfaelin blade, plain but serviceable. Janril sat back on his haunches, grasping the hilt, his fingers playing over the blade. Frentis took in the many bruises on his narrow face. *They slit her throat . . . Her husband screamed until they beat him senseless . . .*

"Janril," he murmured, crouching at the minstrel's side. "I . . ."

"We were sleeping when they came for us," Janril said in a dull tone. "I hadn't posted a guard, didn't think we needed one so close to the capital. This"—he tapped the sword—"was under our bed, all cosy and tucked up in a blanket. I'd barely got a hand to it when they dragged us out. Sergeant Krelnik gave it to me the day I left the Wolfrunners. Said all men needed a sword, be they minstrel or soldier. Apparently he picked it up the night we stormed the High Keep. Don't know why he kept it so long, not much to look at, is it?"

Janril's gaze swivelled to Frentis, who knew he was looking into the eyes of a madman. "You kill them all?" the minstrel asked.

Frentis nodded.

"I want more."

Frentis touched a hand to the sword blade. "You'll have it."

CHAPTER FIVE
Reva

"The entire Realm Guard?" Uncle Sentes asked.

The cavalryman nodded, the brandy glass in his hand trembling. It was his third measure but seemed to have done little to calm his nerves. "Save those regiments not quartered on the coast or borders, my lord. Forty thousand men or more."

Reva watched her uncle slump in his chair. Apart from Lady Veliss and the cavalryman, they were alone in the Lord's chamber.

"How is this possible?" Veliss asked the man.

"They were so many, my lady. And the knights . . ." He shook his head, trailing off and choking down more brandy before continuing. "Smashed into our flank and cut down two full regiments before we knew what was happening. By then the Volarians were coming on in full strength."

Uncle Sentes continued to sit silently in his chair and Lady Veliss seemed unable to formulate another question, tracing a less-than-steady hand over her forehead.

"Let me see if I have this right," Reva said as the silence stretched. "The Realm Guard was two days out from Varinshold when word came of invasion. Correct?"

The cavalryman nodded.

"The Battle Lord turns you all around, a day later you're drawn up against the Volarians then Fief Lord Darnel appears on the horizon with his knights."

"We thought he'd come to aid us. Though the Departed know how he could've gotten there so quickly."

"You are saying," Veliss put in, "that Fief Lord Darnel is a traitor? That he led his men against the King's host?"

"I am, my lady. And as for the King, I met some refugees from Varinshold on the road. Word is the King's dead."

Silence reigned and Reva wondered at her lack of exultation. *The King of the Heretic Dominion lies slain and all I feel is dread.*

"There were no survivors?" Veliss pressed. "The Battle Lord?"

"Last seen charging the Volarian line, alone," the cavalryman replied. "As for survivors, Lord Marshal Caenis had rallied the Wolfrunners and a few other regiments for a rear guard, but they were sorely pressed last I saw. My own Lord Marshal sent me and four others to bring news to you here, I was the only one to make it."

"Thank you," Uncle Sentes said in a faint tone. "Please leave us to consider your tidings. Quarters will be provided."

The cavalryman nodded, rising to his feet, then hesitating. "You should know, my lord. The tales I heard on the road leave little doubt as to the nature of our enemy. These Volarians do not come just for conquest, but for slaves and blood. They cannot be treated with."

Lady Veliss gestured at the door with a polite smile, leading the man from the chamber. "Lord Darnel seems to have found grounds for treaty," she commented when the door closed.

"Darnel is a self-glorying fool," the Fief Lord replied with little emotion. "Though I never thought his vain ambition would lead him to this. One wonders what they promised him."

"I told the guard captain on the gate to send scouts north," Reva said. "If they come, we should have warning."

"I seriously doubt it's a question of 'if.'" He turned to Veliss who stood with a hand covering her mouth, eyes distant. "No counsel for me, my most trusted advisor?"

Veliss swallowed and glanced at Reva.

"My heir should hear your wise and honest guidance, don't you think?" he told her.

"Five pounds of gold lie waiting in the basement of this manse," Veliss said. "Swift horses in the stables and a well-attended port an hour's ride south."

Reva found herself on her feet, advancing towards the woman with fists clenched.

"He desires honest counsel," Veliss protested, backing away.

"Reva!" Uncle Sentes barked as she reached for the Asraelin woman. "Leave her be!"

"Just a whore after all," Reva said, glowering at Veliss but stepping back.

"In recognition for your good and faithful service to this fief," Sentes told Veliss, "you may take one of those pounds of gold, and a swift horse of your choosing, and depart with no recrimination."

A flush of anger marred Veliss's face. "You know I won't do that."

"But you would have me do it?"

"I would have you live. You heard what the soldier said. If the Realm Guard can't oppose them, what chance have we?"

Uncle Sentes rose from his chair and went to the long window at the rear of the chamber, looking out at the grounds and the rooftops jutting above the manor wall. "Did you know this city has never been taken? My grandfather held it against Janus's father for a whole summer. Eventually, the besiegers grew more starved and diseased than the besieged and they went back to Asrael, leaving half their army behind. Janus, always wiser than his father, never even tried to take this city, he knew all he had to do was keep ravaging the fief."

"What's to stop the Volarians doing the same?" Veliss asked.

"Nothing. Nothing at all." Uncle Sentes turned back from the window, smiling at Reva. "You, my wonderful niece, are also free to take . . ."

"What do you intend, Uncle?" she broke in before he could finish.

An unfamiliar expression came to his face as he looked at her, an odd smile of contentment on his wine-red lips. *Pride,* Reva realised after a second. *He finds pride in me.*

"When I first went to enjoy the hospitality of King Janus's court," the Fief Lord said after a moment, "before I developed my appreciation for wine, and other pleasures, I had a liking for games. Especially cards. They have a complex game in Asrael called Warrior's Bluff, where victory depends largely on how you bet. Stake too much and your opponents know you have the better hand, too little and they see your bluff. I must have played a thousand games, becoming rather rich in the process I must say. Eventually it was difficult to find others willing to play against me and I found other distractions."

"So," Veliss said. "How much do you intend to stake now?"

"Warrior's Bluff gets its name from one particular hand, the Lord of Blades and the five other cards in the martial suit. Even if every other player holds cards with grater value, if you hold the Warrior's Bluff, the game is yours." He moved to Veliss and embraced her, Reva seeing how her fists bunched in his tunic, the knuckles white. Uncle Sentes drew back and kissed her softly on the cheek. "I intend to stake it all, my lady, for I suspect the Lord of Blades sits high in our deck."

The commander of Alltor's City Guard stood tall and straight, breastplate gleaming, his grey whiskers neatly groomed. Behind him the six hundred men of the guard stood in ranks, all similarly polished and straight-backed. Beside them stood the four hundred some men who made up the Fief Lord's House Guard, all at least six feet tall as tradition dictated. *A thousand men to hold a city,* Reva thought as her uncle stepped onto the back of a cart. *It won't be enough.* As many times as she had fought, she had never seen battle so had no experience to support the gloomy conclusion, but the cavalryman's tale had left little room for optimism.

The muster had been called less than an hour before, convened on the gravelled parade ground next to the barracks. Rumours were already flying: the cavalryman's appearance at the gate had been well marked, so many of these men would no doubt suspect trouble was brewing, yet every face betrayed only the stoic discipline of the long-serving soldier. The wind was stiff, stirring dust and setting cloaks and banners aflutter, her uncle obliged to shout to make himself heard.

"War comes to us," he called. "Unsought and unjust, brought to our shores by the foulest race this world has yet to birth. I do not beg your loyalty, I do not seek to persuade. I tell you simply you must stand here and fight what comes or face death if you are fortunate and slavery if you are not. Our enemy brings no other gifts. I give you all this day as your own. Go home, be with your families, look into the face of your wife and imagine her raped, look on your children and see them as corpses. Look at this city and see it as a burnt and wasted shell. Then, come the morning, decide if you will stand with me and my valiant niece, as we defend this city."

He turned to step down from the cart, pausing in surprise as voices were raised in the ranks, a few at first but soon building until a great cheer ascended from every soldier present, fists and swords raised to punch the air. Reva scanned the chanting faces in the ranks, seeing mostly fear and sweat, but also something more. *Not courage. Desperation, or is it hope? They find hope in a drunkard's words.*

The commander of the City Guard strode forward as the Fief Lord stepped down from the cart, saluting smartly.

"Lord Arentes?" her uncle asked.

"I know I speak for my men, my lord," the man said in formal tones, his back just as straight as before. "We need no day for reflection. The defence of this city requires every hour at hand."

"As you wish. No doubt you will have requests to make in due course." He extended a hand to Reva. "The Lady Reva will stay at your side throughout the preparations, any requests will be made through her."

The old guardsman gave Reva the briefest glance of examination, too quick to judge his reaction, but she heard a certain tightness to his tone when he replied to her uncle. "As my lord wishes."

Uncle Sentes leaned close to kiss her cheek, whispering, "Keep an eye on the old buzzard for me."

"I'd like Arken to assist me," she said as he drew back.

"I'll send him along." He went to his carriage, leaving her with the Lord Commander.

"I thought I might tour the walls, my lady," he said. "If you would care to join me."

The walls were fashioned from great blocks of granite, each taller than she was, held in place by virtue of their sheer weight. "Stood unbroken for four hundred years, my lady," Lord Commander Arentes said in answer to her query. "Some cracks showing in the lower stones, but I'll still stake the city on their strength."

Reva recalled one of the stories about Al Sorna's exploits during the desert war. The details were vague, and Al Sorna himself had simply ignored or waved away any question she voiced about those days, but it had something to do with the Alpirans sending great engines against the city he had seized.

"Aren't there engines?" she asked. "Devices capable of bringing down walls like these."

Arentes gave an indulgent chuckle as they strode along the battlements where his men were busy stacking weapons. "Not like these, I assure you. A castle may fall to siege engines, given enough time, but the walls of Alltor have stood against the greatest such devices Asraelin cunning could devise. No, the battle will be won here." He slapped a hand on one of the crenellations forming the battlements. "To take this city they'll have to climb these walls, and when they do . . ." He sniffed, narrowing his gaze. "Well, they'll find they're not facing Asraelins now."

"I'm Asraelin," Arken said. "And I believe there are about two hundred others who make their home here."

"Then, young man, I fervently hope they fight for it better than the Realm Guard fought for their fief."

Arken drew breath for a retort but Reva motioned him to silence. "The Volarian army is said to be huge," she said. "But we have barely a thousand men."

"Yes," Arentes admitted with a sigh. "I would ask that your Lord uncle call every man of fighting age to assist in the defence. Plus all those we can gather from the wider fief whilst time allows."

"What of their families? Do we bring them here too?"

"Hardly. Sieges are not just won with battle, but also hunger. The fewer mouths to feed within these walls the better."

"So we just leave them out there to face slavery and death, whilst their men fight for us?"

"This is war, Lady Reva. And Cumbraelins know well how to bear the cost of war."

"You won't be bearing it," Arken pointed out. "You'll be safe behind these unbreachable walls of yours."

Arentes stiffened. "My lady, I doubt His Lordship permits you to keep this Asraelin commoner at your side so he can offer insults to his betters."

This man is a pompous fool, Reva decided. She inclined her head, smiling. "My apologies, my lord. Shall we complete the tour?"

By nightfall Lady Veliss had added over three thousand men to the rolls, about half possessing longbows or sundry weaponry. Messengers were sent to all corners of the fief commanding men of fighting age to report to Alltor within three weeks. At Reva's urging a paragraph had been added to the message offering sanctuary within the city walls for any who sought it. Veliss had protested, echoing the objections of Lord Arentes, but the Fief Lord overruled her. "If we can't offer protection to our own people, what worth will they see in us?" he enquired, although Reva detected a certain calculation in his gaze as he spoke, making her wonder if her influence served a deeper purpose.

Every day, parties of woodsmen brought freshly cut ash and willow back from the surrounding forests to be fashioned into arrows, the smiths working hard to churn out the thousands of arrowheads needed. Food was stockpiled and the warehouses in the merchants' quarter were soon so full of grain the grounds of the manor were given over as extra storage space. A note from the Fief Lord to the Reader requesting use of the cathedral vaults for the same purpose received a terse response: "The Father's House is not a shed."

In fact the impending siege seemed to have had little effect on the Reader's schedule. He and his bishops still made the daily procession through the square, though not so many were inclined to kneel, busied as they were by the myriad tasks allotted by Lady Veliss. The Reader's services also continued uninterrupted, often to mostly empty pews, though some reported his sermons were more impassioned and compelling than usual.

"Doesn't mention the war at all," a House Guard told Reva as she and Arken helped him carry bushels of arrows up to the battlements. "Seems most fond of the Sixth Book these days."

The Book of Sacrifice. "Any particular passage?" she asked.

"Oh, what was it last time?" The guard hefted a bushel onto the growing pile above the main gate. "The one about how Alltor's children refused to leave him when the mob came for him."

"'The blades of the unloved shone bright beneath the moon,'" Reva quoted. "'The blood of the martyred brighter still.'"

"That's the one. Can't claim to be that fussed about it all, but the wife insists we go. The last Reader though, now there was a man you could listen to all day. He really made the books sing."

New recruits began arriving in large numbers towards the end of the first week. About a hundred a day at first, swelling to over four hundred within ten days, many with families in tow. Most of the older men carried longbows whilst the younger often bore swords or pole-axes handed down by their fathers, though many had no more than bill-hooks or any farm implement with an edged blade. A few brought no weapon at all and Uncle Sentes was obliged to empty the manse's sword room to meet the need.

"This one I'll keep, I think" he said, holding up his grandfather's sword as the others were carried through the gates to be handed out. "Bag me a few Volarians with it, eh?" He made a few clumsy swings with the sword as Reva looked on.

"I'm sure I'll bag enough for both of us, Uncle," she said.

"Oh no." His tone was emphatic. "You will stay by me and Lady Veliss for the duration of this siege."

Reva gaped at him. "I will not . . ."

"You will, Reva!" It was the first time he had raised his voice to her and she found herself taking a backward step from the anger in his face. Seeing her alarm his expression softened. "I'm sorry."

"I fight," she said. "It's what I do. It's all I can do. All I can offer you and these people."

"No. You offer more than that. You offer hope, hope that this fief will survive what comes to tear it down. And that hope cannot die. I have seen battle, Reva. It knows no favourites, it claims the strong and the weak, the skilful and the clumsy." He extended a hand and she took it. "The old and the young. I need your word. You will stay by me and Lady Veliss."

His grip was gentle, but insistent. "As you wish, Uncle."

He squeezed her hand and turned back to the manor.

"The Lord of Blades," she said. "You're so sure he'll come?"

"Aren't you? You know him better than I."

"The Reaches are many miles away, and who knows what lies between him and us. And all the people of this fief have ever offered him is fear and hatred. Why would he come?"

He put a hand around her shoulders as they walked through the gardens, rows of grain sacks ascending on both sides, the topiary animals all cut down days ago. "When the High Keep fell, I found Al Sorna crouched over your father's body, reciting one of their catechisms. For some reason he seemed genuinely upset. He also ordered the bodies of your father's men given a proper burial under the Father's gaze. Whatever hatred our people may level at him, I don't think he returns it. He'll come, I have no doubt of it. We'll just have to ensure there's something here for him to save when he does."

She took to sparring with the House Guards most afternoons, two or three at a time assailing her with practice swords as she danced her dance, deflecting every blow and landing her own. None seemed to be affronted by defeat at the hands of a teenage girl, if anything they seemed heartened by her skill, a few even seeing something of the divine in it.

"The Father guides your sword, my lady," the senior sergeant said after she had sent two more of his men stumbling into each other. His name was Laklin, a stocky veteran of battles against various outlaws and rebels, and a survivor of Greenwater Ford. He was also the first Cumbraelin she had met, besides the Reader, who came close to matching her knowledge of the ten books. "'The Loved need not fear the tides of war or the swords of evil men, for the Father will allow them no defeat.'"

Nor suffer them to bring war to the Unloved, Reva completed the quotation, thinking it best left unsaid.

Her gaze was drawn to the edge of the parade ground where a new company of recruits were giving their names to a harassed-looking Lady Veliss. She was an oft-seen presence throughout the city, two assistants in tow burdened with numerous scrolls and ledgers as she signed permissions on behalf of the Fief Lord and kept records of men and supplies, all meticulously transcribed into a single leather-bound volume come the evening. More than once Reva had found her slumped across it in the library, snoring faintly. Reva noted the suspicion on her face as she took down the name of the man before her, an archer heading a company of some thirty men. *Bren Antesh,* Reva recalled. *True to his word.*

She bowed to the sergeant and excused herself, walking over to Veliss, finding her giving Antesh a hard stare. "No other names to give?" she asked with pointed deliberation.

Antesh seemed puzzled as he shook his head. "What other name would I have, my lady?"

"A few come to mind," Veliss replied.

"Captain Antesh, is it not?" Reva said. "My uncle will be glad to see you kept your promise."

The archer gave her a brief look of appraisal before offering a deep bow. "You must be Lady Reva."

"I am. If Lady Veliss is done with you, I'll show you to your place on the walls."

Veliss took her arm and led her a short distance away. "Do not trust this man," she stated in a low voice. "He is not who he claims to be."

Reva frowned. "He comes in answer to his Fief Lord's call, in accordance with a solemn promise. Those do not seem the actions of an untrustworthy man."

"Just have a care around him, love." Veliss's voice lost much of its smoothed vowels as she reached out to clasp Reva's hand. "You know much, but not enough. Not by half."

The intensity in her gaze and voice provoked an unwelcome doubling of Reva's heartbeat. "I know this man comes to fight for the people of this fief," she said, disentangling her hand from the lady's grip. "Him and thousands more. No sacks of gold or swift horses for them."

"You know why I said that."

"I know we have little time to indulge your suspicions. What place do you have for them?"

Veliss sighed and produced a letter from the bundle she carried, folded and sealed. "It seems your uncle anticipated the captain's dutiful return. He's to be made Lord Commander of Archers. He'll choose his own place."

"Lord Antesh," the archer mused as Reva walked the walls with him. "My wife will be pleased, at least. Perhaps I'll buy that pasture she's been on about."

"Your wife is not with you?" Reva asked.

"I sent her and the children to Nilsael. They'll make their way to Frostport and, if this city should fall, on to the Northern Reaches where I have reason to believe they will be made welcome."

"The Tower Lord owes you a debt, I know."

"The Tower Lord will make them welcome because they are in need of shelter, for such is his nature. Any debt between us ended with the war."

"My uncle is certain he'll come to our aid."

The archer gave a soft laugh. "Then I pity any Volarians left to face him." He moved to the chest-high wall between the crenellations, eyes dark with calculation as he looked out at the causeway leading away from the main gate. "Easy to see why this place has never fallen. Only one very narrow line of march and all year round the surrounding waters remain too deep to ford."

"Lord Commander Arentes is sure the issue will be decided at the walls."

"You don't sound convinced, my lady."

"By all accounts, Varinshold fell in a single night. The greatest city in the Realm taken, the King slain and his host defeated in a few days. I know little of armies and wars, but such feats must require preparation, plans months or years in the making."

There was some surprise in the look he gave her, but also a measure of relief. "Glad to see the Fief Lord has exercised sound judgement in choosing his heir, my lady. You reason the Volarians must have similarly-long-laid plans for us?"

"It's not widely known, but an attempt was made on my uncle's life the very night you came to petition him. Had the assassins succeeded, the fief would now be in turmoil and there would be no-one to organise the defence."

"Must've been a clumsy bunch, these assassins, to have failed so."

"Indeed they were."

"If my lady is correct, then the Volarians' plan has failed and they have little option but to lay siege."

"Perhaps. Or perhaps we've yet to see the whole of their design.

Tell me, what do you know of the Sons of the Trueblade?"

His gaze clouded and he turned to the river. "Fanatical followers of your late father, or so I hear. They found little purchase in the southern counties, people are more pragmatic in their devotions there. You think they have a hand in this?"

"I know it." She paused, watching him as he scanned the river from bank to bank, his archer's eyes no doubt calculating ranges. "Why does Lady Veliss greet you with such suspicion?" she asked him.

"Not for any allegiance to the Sons, I assure you." He glanced back at her, his eyebrows raising as he noticed the wych-elm bow she carried. "Father's sight, my lady. Where did you find that?"

She hefted the bow and shrugged. "I bought it from a drunken shepherd."

Antesh reached out a tentative hand. "May I?"

She handed the bow to him, frowning as his eyes roamed the stave, fingers playing over the carvings, a smile coming to his lips as he thrummed the string. "I thought them all lost."

"You know this bow?" she asked.

"Only by reputation. I had occasion to draw one of its sisters as a child. Straightest shaft I ever loosed." He shook his head and handed it back to her. "You really don't know what this is?"

She could only shake her head. "The shepherd had some tall tale about an old war. I wasn't really listening."

"Well, there may have been some truth to the tale, for the five bows of Arren were all lost in war, the war that brought this fief into the Realm in fact. My lady, what you hold is a veritable legend of Cumbrael."

Reva looked at the bow. She had often marvelled at the artistry of the carvings, and knew it as a weapon of considerable power, but a legend? She began to suspect she was the foil for some archer's joke, a veteran's prank on an impressionable recruit. "Really?" she said with a raised eyebrow.

Antesh, however, betrayed no sign of humour in his reply, "Really." A frown creased his brow and he straightened from the wall, his gaze more intense now, tracking her from head to toe. "Blood of the Mustors carrying a bow of Arren," he said in a soft tone.

After a moment he blinked, abruptly turning away and hefting his own bow. "I should be about my lordly duties, my lady."

"I should like to hear more," she called after him as he strode away. "Who is this Arren?"

He just held up a hand in a polite wave and strode on.

The scouts returned the following day, two exhausted riders relating their tale to the Fief Lord and assembled captains in the Lord's chamber. "The border lands are burning, my lord," the older of the two said. "Everywhere people flock southwards, tales of slaughter and cruelty told by every soul we questioned. Rumours were wild and many, but it seems clear that the King is truly dead and Varinshold fallen along with most if not all Asrael."

"Any news of Princess Lyrna?" the Fief Lord asked. "I had heard she was on some mad peace mission to the Lonak."

The soldier shook his head. "It seems she returned the very day the Volarian fleet descended, my lord. They say the palace burned taking every Al Nieren with it."

"Did you see any Realm Guard at all?" Lady Veliss asked.

"A few stragglers only, my lady. Wasted wild-eyed men, shorn of armour and weapons, fleeing south as fast as they could. We did find a motley company yesterday seemed to have some fight left in them, only a hundred men or so. We told them to make their way here."

"The Volarians?" the Fief Lord asked. "You saw them?"

The man nodded. "The vanguard only, my lord. I reckon maybe ten miles south of the border as of six days ago. I estimate over three thousand horse and twice as many light infantry, moving south at a fair lick."

"We now number some thirteen thousand, my lord," Lord Arentes pointed out. "Giving us a temporary advantage."

"Our trained men number no more than half that," Antesh

said. "And we've only a few hundred horse. We couldn't hope to match them in open field."

"And we shan't," Uncle Sentes stated firmly as Lord Arentes drew breath to speak again. "Thank you, good soldiers," he said to the two scouts. "Get y'selves something to eat in the kitchens. Tell the cook I said to give you the red from the Malten Vale."

"The vanguard," Lady Veliss said after the soldiers had gone. "Perhaps a fifth of their army?"

"More like a tenth," Antesh said. "Even if only half the tales from Asrael are true, the force needed to subdue the entire fief must be massive."

"And they've no need to secure their northern flank thanks to Lord Darnel's treachery," Uncle Sentes said. "They'll have to garrison the towns they've taken, allocate troops to mop up the countryside. But we shouldn't delude ourselves. The force that comes will outnumber us greatly." He turned to Antesh. "Which begs the question, do we have arrows for all of them?"

The archer gave a regretful grimace. "I estimate we need at least four times the number already stockpiled, my lord."

"The fletchers are working to exhaustion as it is," Lady Veliss said. "I've also drafted in every carpenter and woodworker in the city."

"Draft more," the Fief Lord said. "Every pair of idle hands not crafting arrows from now on will receive no rations until they do. Lord Arentes, send half your men to the forest and bring back every tree and sapling they can cut in the time that remains to us."

"Not just wood, my lord," Antesh said. "We need iron for the heads."

"This city is awash in iron," Uncle Sentes said. "I see it in every window, every railing and weather vane. Scour this manor and take all the pots, pans and ornaments you need, then scour the city." He paused to draw breath, his cheeks suddenly pale.

"Uncle?" Reva said, moving to his side.

He grinned at her, patting the hands she laid on his arm. "Your uncle is old and tired, my wonderful niece." He took her hands and climbed to his feet, Reva feeling the tremble in his grip. "And hasn't had a drink in hours," he added to the assembled captains, drawing strained laughter. "You have your orders, good sirs and lords. Be about them if you will."

Reva and Lady Veliss helped him up the stairs to his rooms. "The blue bottle, if you would my lady," he said to Veliss. She fetched it and he held it to his mouth, draining the liquid inside, smiling faintly then doubling over, face contorted in pain, the empty bottle tumbling to the carpet.

"I'll fetch Brother Harin!" Veliss said, hurrying from the room.

Reva knelt before him, clasping his trembling hands once again. "What is this?" she asked. "What ails you?"

Air rushed from him as he reclined, gasping but smiling. "My life, Reva. My life ails me."

Brother Harin's face was grave as he closed the door behind him, Veliss and Reva awaiting his word in the hallway. "I've doubled his dose," the healer said. "Given him a flask of redflower which should ease his pain."

"You said the curative would buy him years yet," Lady Veliss said.

"Restful years, my lady. Not war years. Exhaustion does not help his condition."

"What condition?" Reva said.

Harin glanced at Veliss who gave a tense nod. "Your uncle has drunk a lot of wine in his time, my lady," the brother told her. "More in fact than I would have thought it possible for a man to drink and still be living at his age."

"He's not yet sixty," she said in a whisper.

"Liquor does unfortunate things to a man's insides," Harin explained. "The liver in particular."

"What if he stopped?" Veliss asked. "Just stopped completely. No more wine. Not ever."

"It would kill him," Harin replied simply. "His body requires it, even though it's killing him."

"How long?" Reva asked.

"With rest, perhaps six months, at most."

Six months . . . I've known him for barely three. "Thank you, brother," she said, feeling a slow tear trace down her cheek. "Leave us now, if you would."

He bowed. "I'll call again tomorrow."

Veliss moved beside her, fingers touching her hand. "He didn't want you to know . . ."

Reva took her hand away, wiping the tear from her face. *No more of this,* she decided. *No more weeping.*

"The grain stocks," she said in a voice void of emotion. "How long will they last?"

Veliss hesitated then spoke in a clear voice, her tone coloured by just the slightest quiver. "Given the expanded population, perhaps four months. And only then if carefully rationed."

"Send the House Guard forth. Every scrap of food, every cow, pig and chicken within fifty miles of this city is to be brought here. All unharvested crops will be burned, all wells spoiled, anything that might give succour to our enemy destroyed."

"There are people working those farms . . ."

"Then they'll find shelter here, as the Fief Lord promised. Or they can take their chance with the Volarians."

She moved to the door to the Fief Lord's rooms. "I wish to talk to my uncle, alone."

He was seated at his desk, a glass of wine at his side, his grandfather's sword propped nearby, the quill in his hand moving over a sheet of parchment. "My will," he said as she closed the door. "Thought it was about time."

"Veliss can have the books," she said.

"Actually, there's a parcel of land to the north she always liked. Nice big house, well-kept gardens."

"Why didn't you tell me?"

He sighed, tossing the quill aside and turning to her. "I was afraid you'd run," he said. "And I wouldn't have blamed you if you had."

"And yet you curse me with all this anyway."

He reached for his wineglass, taking a sip. "Did you know, according to Veliss's figures, I am the most successful lord ever to sit in the Chair? In the history of this fief no other lord has produced so much wine, generated so much wealth or overseen such a period of peace and harmony. And will I be celebrated for it when I'm gone? Of course not, I'll always be the drunken whore chaser with the mad brother. But you, Reva, you will be the saviour of Cumbrael. The great warrior, blessed by the World Father Himself, who threw wide the city gates and sheltered all within these walls against the vile, godless storm. I had expected it to take years, welding the people's hearts to you. Thanks to the Volarians, it'll barely take months."

She shook her head in grim amusement. "I had thought Veliss the schemer. Turns out it was you."

He gave an injured groan. "Try not to hate your old uncle. I shouldn't wish to carry such a thought to the Fields."

She went to him, putting her arms around his shoulders and planting a kiss on his head. "I don't hate you, you drunken old sot."

The first Volarians arrived three days later, a troop of cavalry appearing on the horizon about midday, lingering for no more than a few minutes before disappearing from view. Reva ordered scouts in pursuit and had riders sent out with orders to hasten any refugees to the city and call in the foraging parties. The scouts reported back within the day; the Volarian vanguard was no more than fifteen miles distant. She waited until darkness and the last trickle of beggared people had filtered through the gates before ordering them closed.

"Do we fetch the Fief Lord?" Antesh asked her as they stood atop the bastion over the main gate, looking out at the causeway and the pregnant darkness beyond.

"Let him sleep," she said. "I suspect there'll be plenty to do in the morning."

They came as the sun rose over the eastern hills, cavalry first, moving at a sedate pace, their ranks tidy and well-ordered as they made their way to the plain beyond the causeway. The infantry followed soon after, tightly arrayed battalions in front, marching with an unnerving uniformity of step, the formations that followed more open, their pace less regular. The Volarian host arranged itself with the kind of precision and speed that could only arise from years of drill, cavalry on the flanks, the disciplined infantry in the centre, looser formations behind.

"Slave soldiers in the front rank," Veliss said. "They call them Varitai. Those behind are conscripts, Free Swords. I read it in a book," she added in response to Reva's quizzical frown.

"They have slaves in their army?" she asked.

"Volaria is built on slaves," her uncle said. "It's what they came for." He wore a heavy cloak, hand resting on Reva's shoulder, his breath laboured, although his red-rimmed eyes still shone as bright as ever.

"No engines," Antesh observed. "No ladders either."

"All in good time, I'm sure," Uncle Sentes said. "Though I suspect they're about to try and scare us to death."

Reva followed his gaze, seeing a lone rider emerge from the Volarian ranks to gallop along the causeway. He reined in over a hundred paces from the gate, staring up at them, his long cloak billowing in the wind. He was a tall man, wearing a black enamel breastplate, a scroll clutched in his fist. His gaze found the Fief Lord and he gave a shallow bow, a grin of contempt on his lips as he unfurled the scroll.

"Fief Lord Sentes Mustor," he read in accented but clear Realm Tongue. "You are hereby ordered to surrender your lands, cities and possessions to the Volarian Empire. Peaceful compliance with this order will ensure just and generous treatment for yourself and your people. In return for your cooperation in overseeing the transfer of power to Volarian authority you will receive . . ."

"Lord Antesh," Uncle Sentes said. "I see no recognisable flag of truce, do you?"

Antesh pursed his lips and shook his head. "Can't say as I do, my lord."

"Well then."

". . . swift transportation to any land of your choice," the Volarian was saying, the scroll held in front of his eyes. "Plus one hundred pounds in gol—" He choked off as Antesh's arrow punched through the scroll and the breastplate beyond. He tumbled from the saddle and lay still, the scroll pinned to his chest.

"Right," the Fief Lord said, turning away. "Let me know when the rest get here."

CHAPTER SIX
Vaelin

He found it impossible to gauge the Eorhil woman's age. Somewhere between fifty and seventy was his best guess. Her face possessed many lines, her lips cracked with age and her long braids iron-grey. But there was a leanness and evident strength to her that bespoke an ageless vitality, her back straight as she sat cross-legged on the other side of the fire, her bare arms strung with knotted muscle. Behind her the great gathering of Eorhil warriors waited, some dismounted, most not, over ten thousand riders come in answer to the Tower Lord's call. The Eorhil woman's name, translated by Insha ka Forna, was unusual amongst her people as it consisted of but one word: Wisdom.

"You ask much, man of tower," the young Eorhil had cautioned. "Not since war with beast people do so many come. Then they knew old tower man, you they don't. Wisdom will decide."

They had been sitting like this for much of the afternoon, the woman staring at him through the smoke rising from the fire. He heard no note from the blood-song, she possessed no gift, at least none it could recognise. Ten days' march had brought them here to the lake the Eorhil called the Silver Tear, a small placid body of water shining amidst the great expanse of the plains where the Eorhil were already waiting with their full number.

"Al Myrna wanted a quiet life," Wisdom said finally in flawless Realm Tongue, Vaelin starting at the sudden break in the silence. "A man with many battles in his past, tired of war. Our trust in him was built on that weariness. It's the man of energy who hungers for war, and you, Vaelin Al Sorna, are a man of considerable energy."

"Perhaps," he replied. "But I've seen enough battle also. It pains me to lead so many to war once more."

"Then why do it?"

"Why does any man of reason go to war? To preserve what is good and destroy what is not."

"The Volarians seek to destroy your homeland. But that is far from here."

"Your forest sister has seen the hearts of these people. They will not stop at my homeland. And I have seen what they did to the ice people. They will take all they can, from the Seordah, the Lonak and you."

"And if we give you our warriors, the bright promise of our youth, how many will return?"

"I do not know. Many will fall, I do not deny it. I do know that the Eorhil will have to fight the Volarians, either on these plains or in my realm."

"To reach your realm we must travel through the forest. You expect the Seordah to allow this?"

"I expect them to heed the words of the blind woman."

Wisdom gave a start of her own, stiffening as her gaze narrowed. "You've seen her?"

"And spoken with her."

The Eorhil woman's mouth twitched and he discerned she was fighting fear. She got to her feet, muttering, "We named you wrong." She stalked back to her people, casting her final words over her shoulder. "We will ride with you."

"Wisdom," Vaelin read slowly, pronouncing each syllable with care.

"Good," Dahrena said. "And this?" Her finger moved on to the next word.

"Aah-greeed?"

She smiled. "Very good, my lord. A few more weeks and you won't need me at all."

"I very much doubt that will be the case, my lady." He reclined in his chair, yawning. The evening drill had been hard, far too many men still stumbling about with faint notion of the difference between right and left, clumsiness made worse by fatigue from the day's march, but there was no other choice if they were to have a hope of facing a disciplined enemy.

They were four days from the lake, the Eorhil scouting ahead and covering the flanks as they moved south towards the forest, now no more than a week away. Dahrena fretted over the fact they were yet to meet any Seordah but he told her to stow her worries, forcing more certainty into his tone than he actually felt. *Just tell them you met a blind woman from several centuries hence, and they'll throw their arms wide in welcome?* he asked himself. *Do you really suppose it'll be that easy?*

But the blood-song was unchanged; the route to the Realm lay through the forest. So he marched his army, trained them for two hours in the morning and two hours at night, suffered the grumbling and doubts of his captains and spent a blessed hour before slumber learning letters with the Lady Dahrena.

He was finding a joy in the words the more he learned, the poetry his mother had tried to impart now laid bare, the emptiness of the catechisms glaring and obvious when captured in ink. It gave him a deeper appreciation of the gift enjoyed by Brother Harlick, the power and the beauty of it, to have an entire library in one's head.

Dahrena sat at the table they shared, adding the final words to the treaty formalising the Eorhil's alliance to their cause, including an unasked-for grant of ownership over the northern plains in perpetuity. The treaty would require ratification by the monarch of the Unified Realm, assuming they could find one.

Vaelin had ordered Brother Harlick to draw up a list of those with a legitimate claim to the throne should the Al Nieren line prove extinct. It consisted of just four names.

"King Janus lost much of his family to the Red Hand," Harlick explained. "Many of the survivors perished in the wars of unification. These"—he held up the list—"are the only blood relatives still living in the Realm, to the best of my knowledge, since it's several years since I lived there."

"Anyone of note?" Vaelin asked.

Harlick considered the list. "Lord Al Pernil is a famed horse-breeder, assuming he still lives. My lord, you may have to consider the possibility that there is no surviving heir to the throne of the Unified Realm. If that's the case, other options will have to be considered."

"Options?"

"The Realm is not the Realm without a monarch. And in a time of chaos people will look to the strongest man for leadership, regardless of blood or station."

Vaelin studied the man's face, wondering if some fresh design lurked behind his eyes. "More honest and unselfish intent, brother?"

"Merely the observations of a well-read man, my lord."

"Well, confine your observations to those subjects I ask you to consider." He moved to the map table, his eyes picking out Alltor, the blood-song flaring as it always did whenever his thoughts turned to Reva. Recently there had been a change in the tone, an ominous counterpoint to the usual compulsion. *They come for her,* he decided. *And she won't run.*

"The population of Alltor?" he asked Harlick.

"The King's census ten years ago put the total at some forty-eight thousand souls," the brother replied without hesitation. "Though, in times of siege it could be expected to double." He paused. "That's where we're going?"

"As fast as the men can stand it."

"The distance . . ."

Vaelin shook his head. "Is immaterial. We march to Alltor, even if it's only to survey a ruin. That's all for now, brother."

Four days' march saw a dark uneven line appear on the horizon. It thickened as they marched, growing into a great wall of trees, stretching away on either side as far as eyes could see. Vaelin ordered the army to camp a half mile short of the forest and bowed to Dahrena. "Allow me to escort you home, my lady."

Nortah guided his horse closer, Snowdance padding alongside. "We should go too," he said. "The sight of a war-cat may ward against anger at your intrusion."

"It's more likely to provoke it," Dahrena told him. "In any case, my people will not harm us. I'm sure of it." Vaelin detected a wariness to her gaze as she eyed the forest, indicating a lack of conviction in her own words.

"If you don't return?" Nortah asked.

Vaelin was tempted to offer a flippant response but seeing Dahrena's unease decided on a reasoned reply. "Then I name you as my successor, brother. You will lead the army back to the tower and prepare against siege."

"You imagine these people will follow a simple teacher?"

"A teacher with a war-cat." Vaelin grinned and spurred Flame into motion.

The blood-song swelled as they neared the forest edge, not in warning, but welcome. It subsided to a soft contented note as the trees closed in around them, the air cool and musty with the myriad scents offered by all forests. Dahrena reined to a halt and dismounted, her face raised to the canopy of branches, eyes closed and a faint smile on her lips. "I missed you," she said softly.

Vaelin dismounted and left Flame grazing on a patch of long grass, his eyes scanning the trees and finding a man standing between two elms, watching him with a deeply furrowed brow.

"Hera!" Dahrena gave a joyous yelp and ran to the Seordah, jumping to embrace him.

The man seemed less joyful as she drew back, his smile of

welcome strained. His hair was long and streaked with grey, swept back from a hawk-nosed face, stirring Vaelin's memory.

"Hera Drakil," he said, moving towards the man. "Friend to Tower Lord Al Myrna. I . . ."

"I know who you are," Hera Drakil said, his accent thick but clear. "Beral Shak Ur, though I had hoped to be hunting in the dream age when your shadow fell on this forest."

"I come with friendship . . ."

"You come with war, ever the way with the Marelim Sil." The Seordah laid an affectionate hand on Dahrena's cheek and turned away. "Come, the stone waits."

There were a dozen Seordah chiefs waiting, five women and seven men, all of an age with Hera Drakil who sat in their centre of their line. He had led them to a small clearing some miles into the forest, in the centre of which stood a stone plinth. The shape and height of the stone reminded Vaelin of one he had seen before, although whilst the stone in the Martishe had been overgrown with weeds and creepers, this was free of any vegetation, the carved granite seemingly unmarked by age or weather. In the trees beyond he could see many other Seordah, faces concealed in shadow, but he made out bows and war clubs amongst the shifting silhouettes. *Warriors*, he thought. *Waiting for something.*

Vaelin and Dahrena sat before the dozen chiefs, finding no welcome in any gaze. One of them said something, a woman with a crow feather in her hair.

"We give you no leave to enter," Dahrena translated. "Yet here you are. She asks for a reason why they shouldn't kill you."

"I come to seek your help," Vaelin replied as she related his words to the chiefs. "A great and terrible enemy has attacked my people. Soon they will come to the forest, bringing fire and torment . . ."

Hera Drakil held up a hand and Vaelin fell silent as the Seordah spoke in his own language. "Your people could not take this forest from us," Dahrena related. "Though they tried. Why should we fear these newcomers when we do not fear you?"

"My people saw wisdom in making peace. Our enemy has no such wisdom. Ask your sister, she has seen their hearts."

The chiefs' gaze turned to Dahrena who nodded and spoke at length in the Seordah tongue, no doubt relating what her gift had revealed of Varinshold's fate and the Volarians' nature.

"You face a cruel foe indeed," she translated when one of the other chiefs responded to her tale, a wiry man with a foxtail hanging about his neck. "But it is your foe, not ours. The wars of the Marelim Sil are their own."

Vaelin paused, pondering how best to phrase what he hoped would silence their doubts. "I am named Beral Shak Ur by Nersus Sil Nin. I tell you true that I have seen and spoken with the blind woman. She has blessed the course of my life. Can any here claim the same?"

He saw some flickers of uncertainty on the faces of the chiefs, but no shock or fear, and certainly no change of heart.

"If the blind woman blesses you," Dahrena related the words of Hera Drakil as he pointed over Vaelin's shoulder, "she will hear you now."

Vaelin turned, regarding the stone for a moment then getting to his feet. "You don't have to." Dahrena moved to his side as he approached the stone, looking down at the smooth flat surface with the single perfectly round indentation in the centre. "Let me talk to them. With enough time, they'll listen."

"Who am I to deny them a show?" he asked. "One I suspect they've been expecting for a long time."

"You don't understand. Seordah have been coming here for generations, usually the old and the sick, some the mad. All come to touch the stone and seek the blind woman's counsel. Most just touch it, wait for a time then leave disappointed, but some, only a very few . . . Some it takes, leaving their bodies empty."

"Except you," he said. "You said you had seen her."

"After my husband died . . ." Her eyes went to the stone, clouded with sorrowful remembrance. "My grief was such I didn't care if I lived. I came here in search of some kind of answer, some reason. If that was denied me then I would happily accept death. The blind woman . . . She showed me something to live for." Her hand reached out, hovering over the surface of the stone. "It put me back in my body, because she willed it."

"Then," he said, stepping closer. "Let's hope she finds me similarly worthy."

The granite was cool under his palm, but he felt no other sensation, no change in his song, but when he looked up Dahrena and the Seordah were gone. It was night and a woman sat at a fire, face turned away from him but he knew her instantly. "Nersus Sil Nin," he greeted her, walking to the fire. She was older than he remembered, lines deeply etched into the flesh around her red marble eyes, her hair entirely white. She blinked and glanced up at him.

"You're older," she said. "And your song is stronger."

"You said I should learn its music well."

"Did I? It was so long ago. There have been so many visions since." Her hand reached down to the stack of firewood at her feet, tossing some branches into the flames. "Still serving your Faith?" she asked.

"My Faith was a lie. Though I think you knew that."

"Is à lie really a lie if it is honestly believed? Your people sought to make sense of the world's many mysteries with their Faith. Misguided perhaps, but based on a truth not fully revealed."

The thing that lived in Barkus, the cruelty of its laugh. "A soul can be trapped in the Beyond."

"Not all souls, only those with a gift. This power, this fire that burns in you and I, doesn't cease burning when our life fades."

"And when it slips into the void. What then?"

Her aged lips formed a smile. "I suspect I'll discover that myself before long."

"Something lives there, in the void. Something that takes these souls and twists them, making them serve its purpose, sending them back to take the bodies of other gifted."

Her eyebrows rose in faint surprise. "So, it grew after all."

"What grew? What is it that lives there?"

She turned her blank eyes to him, face heavy with regret. "I do not know. All I know is that it *needs*. It hungers."

"What for?"

She voiced her answer with a flat certainty making doubts redundant, "Death."

"Can you tell me how to defeat it?"

She closed her eyes and shook her head. "But I can tell you it has to be fought, if you care about this world and its people."

He looked up at the small patch of night sky visible through the branches above, seeing the seven stars of the sword. This high in the sky meant it was early autumn here, though how many years before his time was an unfathomable mystery. "Has it happened yet?" he asked. "Have my people come to take this land?"

"I'll be many years dead before that happens. Though I've had enough visions from that time to make me thankful for it."

"And the future? The future of this land?"

She stared into the fire for some time and he suspected she wouldn't answer, but eventually she said, "You are as far into the future as I've seen, Beral Shak Ur. After you, there is no future. None that I can see."

"And yet you would have me fight?"

"My gift is not absolute. Many things remain hidden. And in any case, what else would you do? Give up your hope and sit waiting for the end?"

"Your people require persuasion to grant passage through the forest. What do I tell them?"

Her brow creased into an amused frown. "Tell them I said they should. That might help."

"And that will be enough?"

Her frown turned into a laugh, bitter and short. "I haven't the faintest notion. The people you find in this forest may speak my language and share my blood, but they are not my people. Those who come to touch the stone are shadows of former greatness and beauty. They gather in tribes and pursue their endless feuds with the Lonak, myth and legend has replaced knowledge and wisdom. They have forgotten who they were, allowed themselves to be diminished."

"If they don't join with me, then even that shadow of your greatness will be gone, along with any chance that it might one day be rebuilt."

"What is broken remains so. It is the way of things." She turned to the stone. "We did not craft these vessels of memory and time, they were here long before us. We merely divined their use, and even then they prove fickle, taking the minds of those they deem unworthy. Once a people far greater than the Seordah crafted wonders and built cities the length and breadth of this land. Now, even their name is lost forever."

She turned back to the fire and fell silent, features sagging with fatigue. "I had hoped our final meeting might be joyous, that when you came it would be with tales of a wife and family, a long life lived in peace."

He reached for her hand, knowing it would feel nothing, but let it hover there for a moment. "It grieves me to disappoint you so."

She said nothing and he sensed that her vision was fading. He returned to the stone, extending his hand then hesitating. "Good-bye, Nersus Sil Nin."

She didn't turn around. "Good-bye, Beral Shak Ur. If you win your war, return to the stone. Perhaps you'll find someone new to talk to."

"Perhaps." He pressed his palm to the stone, daylight returning in an instant, banishing the night's chill. He drew a breath, forcing authority into his voice as he turned to address the Seordah. "The blind woman has spoken . . ."

He trailed off when he saw their gaze was elsewhere, all twelve Seordah chiefs now on their feet staring at something to the side of him. Dahrena stood nearby, eyes wide in wonder. He turned and the song surged.

The wolf sat on its haunches, green eyes regarding him with the scrutiny he remembered so well. He couldn't recall its being so large before, standing at least as tall as he. After a moment it licked its lips and raised its snout, a great howl rising to the sky, loud enough to banish all other sound, filling the ears of all present to the point of pain.

The wolf lowered its snout, the howl fading and for a heartbeat silence ruled the forest, then it came, rising from the trees for miles around, the answering howl of every wolf in the Great Northern Forest. On and on it went as the wolf rose to trot forward, its great head level with his chest, nostrils twitching as it sniffed him. He could hear its song, the alien tune he remembered from the day Dentos died, the music so strange as to be baffling, but one note was clear and unmistakable. *Trust. It has trust in me.*

The wolf nuzzled his hand, its tongue lapping once, then turned and bounded away, a blur of silver in the trees, soon vanished from sight. The great howling faded with it.

Hera Drakil and the other Seordah came forward, forming a circle around him, the shadowy warriors emerging from the trees to surround him, men and women of fighting age all holding their war clubs out before them as one. Hera Drakil raised his own club, holding it flat and level. "Tomorrow," the Seordah chief said, "I will sing my war song to the rising sun, and guide you through this forest."

"No fires are to be lit, no wood cut, no game taken. All men will remain in their companies and not wander away from the line of march. We walk only where the Seordah tell us."

He saw some of his captains exchange wary glances, Adal's face betraying the most unease. "And punishment for transgression, my lord?" he asked.

"Punishment won't be needed," Vaelin said. "The Seordah will enforce these rules, of that they have left me in little doubt."

"I would be remiss, my lord, if I did not report the temper of the men," Adal went on. "Open dissent is quickly quelled, as per your order, but we cannot still every tongue."

"What is it now?" Vaelin ran a weary hand through his hair. The meeting with Nersus Sil Nin had left him troubled, the scarcity of knowledge she could impart leaving an irksome uncertainty. Also, he was coming to realise why he had never relished command. *They're always so endlessly malcontent.* "Boots too hard? Training too tough?"

"They're scared of the forest," Nortah said. "Not that I blame them. Scares the life out of me and I've yet to set foot in it."

"I see," Vaelin said. "Well, any man too craven to walk through some trees has my permission to leave. Once they've surrendered their arms, boots, supplies and any pay they've received to date, they can make their way home and wait for a Volarian fleet to appear and enjoy the ensuing spectacle of slaughter. Perhaps then they'll consider the true price of cowardice." He rested balled fists on the map table, sighing through gritted teeth. "Or you could just give me a list of the most vocal grumblers and I'll have them flogged."

"I'll speak to them," Dahrena said as the captains fidgeted in uncomfortable silence. "Allay some fears."

Vaelin gave a wordless nod and gestured for Brother Hollun to give his daily report on the state of the supplies.

"What did she tell you?" Dahrena asked when the captains had been dismissed. From outside the tent came the noise of the camp breaking up as the army prepared to march into the forest. "To have befouled your mood so."

"It's more what she didn't tell me," he replied. "She had no answers, my lady. No great wisdom to guide our path. Just a tired old woman suffering her final vision of a future she hates."

Dahrena said nothing for a moment, but her gaze lingered on his face. He noticed it had done so since they returned from the forest. "The wolf," she said. "You've seen it before."

He nodded.

"So have I. When I was very little, the night father found me, it blessed me with its tongue . . ." Her gaze was distant, almost trance like. She blinked, shaking her head and rising. "I should go and make some speeches."

In the end there were none who refused to enter the forest, Dahrena's words once again carrying sufficient weight to ensure loyalty. *They love her,* Vaelin decided, seeing the ease with which she moved amongst the men, the laughter she exchanged, seemingly able to recall every face and name without effort. He knew it was not a gift he held, most men who had followed him had done so out of duty or fear. He could only hope their love for her and fear of him would be enough when they finally met the Volarians.

The North Guard were first to enter the forest, dismounted and leading their horses through the trees, dozens of Seordah warriors on all sides looking on in stern silence. Vaelin led the First Regiment of Foot next. He had divided the army into ten regiments of about a thousand men each, numbered accordingly, though he had allowed them to decide on their own banners. The First were mostly miners and had adopted a banner showing crossed pickaxes on a blue background. They were led, albeit with much assistance from a North Guard sergeant, by Foreman Ultin from Reaver's Gulch.

"Me, walking the great forest," he said in wonder, eyes wide as he stared about. "Commanding a regiment at y'lordship's side, too. And my old dad said I'd never climb no higher than emptying the foreman's piss-bucket."

"How long since you left Renfael, Captain?" Vaelin asked him.

"Just Ultin, if you please, m'lord. Even the lads can't keep a straight face when they call me captain." He glanced back at his men. "Ain't that right, you disrespectful dogs?"

"Kiss my hole, Ultin," one of the men in the front rank said. He blanched a little at Vaelin's stare and quickly looked down. Vaelin stilled the rebuke on his tongue, seeing the sweat on the man's forehead and the fear on his comrades' faces, their eyes constantly roaming the trees.

"More'n fifteen years, m'lord," Ultin said. "Since I left the old stinkhole I called home. Can't say as I miss it much. Just another mean mining village, full of mean people paid mean wages by a mean lord. One day I heard about the Reaches from a tinker, said a miner could earn four times as much there, if he didn't mind the cold and the savages. Got meself on a ship soon as I had enough for a berth. Never gave no thought to goin' back, till now."

If there's anything to go back to, Vaelin thought.

Each regiment was given a Seordah guide, Hera Drakil leading the First, his communication confined mostly to pointing or holding up a hand to signal a halt. He seemed even more reluctant to engage with Vaelin than he had at their first meeting, avoiding his gaze and keeping to his own language, forcing Dahrena to continue as translator. *The wolf,* Vaelin surmised. *They don't appreciate being made to feel fear in their own forest.*

The Seordah chief led them to a clearing around a shallow creek where they would camp for the night. In accordance with Vaelin's orders no fires were started and the men were obliged to huddle in their cloaks, eating cold hard-tack with some cured meat. There was little talk and no singing, men often starting at the sounds of the forest.

"What's that?" Ultin asked in a whisper as a faint wailing came to them from the surrounding blackness.

"Wild cat," Dahrena said. "Looking for some female company."

Vaelin found Hera Drakil perched on a large boulder in the middle of the creek. The water was shallow but the splashes gave ample signal of any visitors, the Seordah's eyes narrowing at Vaelin's approach. He offered no greeting and went back to unstringing his bow, a flat-staved weapon with a thick leather-wrapped centre. Vaelin noticed his arrows were headed with some kind of dark shiny material rather than iron. "Can you pierce armour with those?" he asked.

Hera Drakil took one of the arrows and held it up, the edge

of the head catching the moonlight and Vaelin saw it was glass rather than flint. "From the hill country," the Seordah said. "Have to fight the Lonak to get it. Cuts through anything if you get close enough."

"And that?" Vaelin nodded at the war club placed within reach. It was about a yard long, double curved like an axe handle with a notched grip and a blunt head resembling the misshapen head of a shovel. A wicked ten-inch spike protruded from the wood an inch short of the head. "Will it hold against a blow from a sword?"

"Why not try?" The Seordah looked him up and down. "Except you have no sword." He laid his bow aside and picked up the club, holding it out to Vaelin. He took it and tried a few swings, finding it light, the grip comfortable. The wood it was fashioned from was unfamiliar, dark and smooth, the grain hardly perceptible under his fingers.

"Black-heart tree," Hera Drakil explained. "Wood is soft when it's cut and shaped, grows hard like rock when placed in fire. It won't break, Beral Shak Ur."

Vaelin inclined his head and handed the club back. "You haven't asked what the blind woman told me."

"She said we should join with you. Her visions are well-known to the Seordah."

"But you were going to deny her words."

"Your people have no gods, neither do mine. The blind woman lived many years ago and had visions of the future. Most came true, some did not. We are guided by her, we do not worship her."

"What do you worship?"

For the first time the Seordah's face showed some sign of amusement, a grin coming to his lips. "You are standing in what we worship, Beral Shak Ur. You call this place the great forest, we call it Seordah, for it is us and we are it."

"To fight our enemy you'll have to leave it."

"I've done so before, when I went to see your land with the

last Tower Lord. I saw many things there, all of them ugly."

"What you'll see this time will be uglier still."

"Yes." The Seordah put his club aside and rested back against the rock, closing his eyes. "It will."

CHAPTER SEVEN
Lyrna

"I t's there again!" Murel said, pointing in alarm and making
the boat pitch as she rushed to the bow. "Do you see?"

Lyrna looked at the sea, catching sight of the great fin
before it slipped under the water once more. *They're always hungry.*

"Maybe it likes us," the outlaw with scarred cheeks suggested.
His name was Harvin and he claimed to have once commanded
a band thirty men strong, his capture and imprisonment the
result of betrayed love for a beautiful woman of noble birth, a
story Iltis had greeted with open contempt.

"Sold out by some tavern doxy you forgot to pay, more like,"
he had laughed.

They bickered constantly, often to the verge of violence and
Lyrna had given up trying to placate their temper. If one killed
the other, then at least the rations would last longer.

"Fell in love with the brother's beautiful face when it rammed
the hold," Harvin continued. "Just couldn't stay away."

"You criminal scum!" Iltis bridled.

Lyrna turned away as the argument began its inevitable esca-
lation, eyes scanning the waves for sign of the shark. Four days
adrift on the ocean and their only companion a red shark. She
wondered why it didn't simply tip the boat over and eat them at
its leisure. If it could sink a ship, what challenge did their boat

represent? Her thoughts kept returning to Fermin's last smile, his bloody teeth. *Given all I have to give . . .*

Next to her, Murel stiffened as the fin reappeared, her scabbed fingertips going to her mouth. It was closer this time, tracking an arcing course towards them through the swell. Murel closed her eyes and began reciting the Catechism of Faith. Lyrna put an arm around her shoulders as the fin grew ever larger, Iltis and Harvin abruptly forgetting their argument. The fin veered away some twenty yards short of the boat, the red-striped body of the shark rising from the water, a huge black eye gleaming above the waves for a moment. Murel opened her eyes, whimpered and closed them again. The shark gave a brief thrash of its tail and disappeared under the surface.

"It's gone," Lyrna told a sobbing Murel. "See?"

The girl could only shake her head and slump down in exhausted fear, her head resting in Lyrna's lap.

Lyrna surveyed her small wooden kingdom of five hungry souls and wondered again if it might have been kinder to abandon them to the hold. They had managed to scavenge some supplies from barrels found bobbing in the water the morning after the ship went down, mostly pickled fish that made her gag the first time she tried it: however, hunger had soon overcome such qualms. Her biggest fear had been the lack of fresh water but this soon disappeared under the weight of rain that threatened to swamp the boat on a daily basis, forcing them to bail continually, albeit untroubled by thirst. Their oars consisted of two short splintered planks from the ship's deck, the outlaw and Iltis spending much of the first day paddling a westward course until a quiet youth named Benten, a fisherman from Varinshold and the only sailor amongst them, pointed to the early evening stars and judged them fifty miles east of where they had started the night before.

"Means we're a good ways south of Varinshold," he said. "The Boraelin currents flow east at these climes. Paddle all you want, won't make any difference."

East. Which meant Volaria, in the unlikely event their food held out that long. Lyrna had read enough sea stories to know the extremes to which hunger could force desperate people, the tale of the *Sea Wraith* looming largest in her mind. She had been one of her father's first warships, built at considerable expense and some said the finest ever to sail from a Realm port. She had disappeared in a storm off the northern coast sometime in the second decade of Janus's reign, presumed lost for months but eventually found drifting south by Renfaelin fishermen. They had discovered only one crewman on board, a gibbering loon gnawing on the thigh-bone of one of his crew-mates, a pile of skulls stacked neatly on the deck. On her father's orders the *Sea Wraith* had been burned and sunk so that no sailor would set foot on her again.

Murel's head shifted on her lap and Lyrna saw that she was sleeping, faint groans of pain coming from her half-open lips as the dreams made her relive the torments she had suffered on the ship. Lyrna resisted the impulse to caress her hair, knowing any touch was like to provoke a flurry of screams. *I'm sorry,* she thought as Murel's eyelids fluttered and she jerked in her sleep. *Seems I won't be bringing down their empire after all.*

The boat pitched again and Lyrna looked up to see Benten standing in the stern, hand shielding his eyes against the sun as he gazed east.

"The shark?" Lyrna asked him.

The young fisherman maintained his vigil for a moment more then stiffened, turning to her with a grave face. "A sail."

The others all turned, the boat threatening to tip over with the movement. "Volarian?" Iltis asked.

"Worse," Benten said. "Meldenean."

The Meldenean captain rested his arms on the rail and stared down at them with faint curiosity and no small amount of contempt. "I think I prefer you land-bound enslaved, it seems fitting somehow."

Iltis brandished the chains he had kept at his side, probably, Lyrna suspected, for killing Harvin should it become necessary. "Slaves no longer, freed by our own hand."

"And the ship?" the captain enquired.

"Sunk, along with our captors."

"And anything of value they may have carried." His gaze roamed the boat, lingering first on Murel then finding Lyrna's scars. "And what use did they have for you, my beauty?" he asked with a grin.

Lyrna forced her anger away, knowing if they sailed on it meant death for everyone in this boat. "I am well learned," she replied, knowing the true reason would only provoke more laughter. "And speak many languages. The master wanted a tutor for his daughters."

"Really?" the captain asked, continuing in Alpiran, "Have you read *The Cantos of Gold and Dust*?"

"I have." *And very nearly once met the author.*

"Where does the heart of reason lie?"

"In knowledge, but only when married to compassion." *A word I hope holds some meaning for you,* she added silently.

The captain's gaze narrowed a little. "And Volarian?" he asked slipping back into Realm Tongue.

"Yes."

"Read it as well as speak it?"

"I do."

He waved at his crew. "Bring her aboard. Leave the others."

"No!" Lyrna shouted. "All of us. Whatever you need my skills for, I'll only help if you take all of us."

"You're in no position to bargain, my burnt beauty," he replied with a laugh. "But, just to demonstrate my generosity, we'll take the pretty one too."

One of the crewmen at the rail suddenly straightened, finger shooting out with a shout of alarm. Lyrna turned, seeing the shark's head break the surface no more than fifty yards away. It rolled onto its side, jaws wide, teeth gleaming. The Meldeneans immediately began to work their rigging as the captain barked orders, glaring down at Lyrna in consternation. She placed a foot on the edge of the boat. "All of us," she called to him. "Or I jump."

They took the others to the hold, Iltis and Harvin reluctantly surrendering their chains at the sight of so many bared sabres. The captain pushed Lyrna into his cabin, a cramped space of rolled maps and locked chests, one of which he hefted onto a squat nailed-down desk, turning a key in the heavy lock and lifting the lid. He extracted a scroll with a broken seal and handed it to her. "Read."

She unfurled the scroll and scanned it, absorbing the contents in barely a few seconds, but deciding it would be best to delay her translation. This man had far too keen an eye for her liking. "From Council-man Arklev Entril to General Reklar Tokrev," she began in a slow laboured voice. "Officer commanding the Twentieth Corps of the Volarian Imperial Host. Greetings, honoured brother-in-law. I assume congratulations are in order though of course a full account of your inevitable victory has yet to reach us. Please extend my warmest affection to my honoured sister . . ."

"Enough," the captain said. He took a small leather-bound book from the chest, exchanging it for the scroll. "This one."

Lyrna turned the first few pages and suppressed a wry smile as she placed a puzzled frown on her brow. "This . . . makes no sense."

His gaze narrowed further. "Why?"

"The letters are all jumbled, mixed up with numbers. Perhaps some kind of code."

"You know of such things?"

"My father used codes in his business. He was a merchant, always worried his competitors would discover his prices . . ."

"Can you solve it?" he interrupted.

She shrugged. "Given time, it may be possible . . ."

The captain took a step closer, assailing her with his breath.

"Believe me, land-bound, you do not have the luxury of time."

"I would need to discover the key."

"Key?"

"All codes require a key, the basis for the cypher. Likely to be known only to a few . . ."

He took her by the arm and pushed her from the cabin, across the deck towards the hold, still clutching the book. She was led past the others, crouched in the shadows and surrounded by crewmen, Murel looking up at her with fearful eyes. The captain stopped at a locked door near the stern, a crewman standing guard. "Open it," the captain ordered.

The door swung open, releasing a powerful stench, her senses assailed by a blend of excrement, urine and stale sweat. She fought down her gorge as the captain pushed her inside. A man was huddled in the dark corner of the cabin, hair long and greasy, his clothes the ragged remnants of a uniform, stained with his own filth. Heavy manacles were fastened to his wrists and ankles. From the stench Lyrna surmised he had been here for several days.

"If he moves, beat him down," the captain growled at the crewman who drew a cudgel and stepped closer. "Moves like a snake this one. Stuck a hidden stiletto through the eye of the only man in my crew who spoke his pig tongue." The captain jabbed the toe of his boot into the stinking man's ribs, drawing a pained gasp. He stepped back, jerking his head at her. "If there's anyone alive knows this key, it's him."

Lyrna crouched down and edged closer to the captive, all too aware of the guard's proximity, the brass handle of the dagger jutting from his boot gleaming in the half-light. The man squinted at her as she drew closer and she had the impression of a handsome face under the filth and dried blood. "Sending monsters to plague me now," he muttered.

"How do you come to this?" Lyrna asked him in his own language.

"So they've found a clever monster," he replied. "Tell this pirate dog he'd best kill me soon for when our fleet finds him . . ."

"If you want to live, shut your mouth and do what I tell you," Lyrna said in as placid a tone as she could manage. "Believe me when I say your life is of no worth to me and I'll laugh when they throw you to the sharks. However, if I can't convince the pirate you're being cooperative, they're likely to throw me in after you. Now, how do you come to be here?"

He angled his head at her in calculation and Lyrna detected a keen mind behind the arrogant sneer. *Like Darnel but with brains,* she thought. *Not a pleasant prospect.*

"Betrayal," he said. "Deceit. The lies of a slave, for only a fool ever trusts a slave. An island of riches, he promised me. Stolen by the greatest Meldenean pirate ever to live, long thought a legend but he had a map and was willing to trade it for freedom. It was only a few days' diversion from our route, I didn't see the harm."

"But when you get to the island you find this lot waiting instead of the fabled treasure."

He gave a weary nod.

"You're right," she said. "You are a fool."

He thrashed at her, chains jangling, becoming still when the guard stepped closer and placed his cudgel under his chin.

"I'll tell them nothing," the Volarian stated, glaring at her above the cudgel.

"He says he wants passage to an Alpiran port," she told the captain in Realm Tongue. "In return for the key."

The captain nudged the guard who removed the cudgel and stepped back. "Well I'm feeling generous," he said stroking his beard. "So I'll start with his left hand, one knuckle at a time. Tell him that's the only payment he'll get."

"You don't have to tell them anything," she told the Volarian. "Just make them think you have." She shuffled closer, holding up the leather-bound book. "They want the key to this code. If they think you've shared it, I can pretend I'm able to decipher it. But it'll take time, maybe long enough for your fleet to find us."

"Keen to be a slave are we?"

"Did it once, wasn't so bad compared to this lot. The Volarians wouldn't come near me because of my face, these dogs aren't so discerning."

"What's to stop them killing me when I've played this little farce?"

"I'll tell them they need to keep you alive, that the code is complex and I'll need more help with it."

"Why should I trust you?"

"Because I'm not going to tell them they have the son of a Council-man in their clutches." She gave a pointed glance at the tattered red shirt he wore, the gold-embroidered emblem on the breast a match for the seal on the scroll the captain had shown her. "Quite a prize to carry back to the Isles. Do you think your father's career will stand the shame of it? Or yours?"

He raised his head, eyes intent and searching. "Who are you, monster woman?"

"Just an escaped slave trying to stay alive."

He stared at her in silence for several moments, face drawn in anger but otherwise impassive. "Show me the book," he said finally.

She opened the book and leaned closer, finger tracking along the text. "I've heard it said," she murmured, "that only Volarians who own over one hundred thousand slaves are permitted to wear red."

"You heard correctly," he muttered, nodding as if in agreement as she peered closer at the text.

"You are young to have amassed such a fortune." She raised her eyebrows in apparent understanding.

"My father's gift on achieving my majority." His tone was one of reluctant assent. "A third of his assets. He gave me the pick of the pleasure slaves." He gave her a sidelong glance, eyes tracking over her burns. "Sorry if I disappoint, my dear. But I don't think I have a place for you."

Lyrna gave a final nod, sitting back on her haunches and closing the book. "Thank you for that," she said.

"I keep my bargains," he replied evenly.

"No, I meant for making it easier."

He frowned. "Wh—"

Lyrna twisted, snatched the dagger from the guard's boot and plunged it into the Volarian's chest. *The centre,* Davoka had said. *Always aim for the centre of the chest and you'll find the heart.*

The air whooshed from her as the captain threw her to the floor, advancing with a drawn dagger. "You treacherous bitch!" Lyrna gasped for air as he dragged her upright, forcing her against the wall of his cabin, dagger poised at her throat. "And they say my people are untrustworthy."

"You . . ." She coughed and dragged air into her lungs. "You can trust me."

"I can trust you'll knife me or my men when our backs are turned."

"You can trust me to translate the book."

"What proof do I have of that? All I saw was you exchange some pig talk with that filth before you stuck him."

She met his eyes. "You were sent for his ship."

He loomed closer, the tip of his dagger pricking her skin. "What was that?"

"For that book. The Ship Lords sent you to take his ship and that book."

His face twitched and she saw him bite down his next words. He moved back a step, dagger poised. "You see far too much, burnt beauty."

She spoke in a rapid tumble, gasping the words out without pause. "Twenty-eight gold bars stamped with the crest of House Entril twelve barrels of wine from Eskethia a ceremonial short sword engraved with a poem of thanks from the Ruling Council to General Tokrev in recognition of his victory . . ." She ran out of breath and stared at him, seeing the hesitation in his knife hand. "That's what you found in their hold, wasn't it?"

"How do you . . . ?"

"It's listed in the book, on the first page."

"You only saw it for a second."

"That was enough."

"It was in code."

"A substitution matrix based on a descending numerical order. Not especially difficult if you know how. And now I'm the only soul on this ship, and I suspect in this half of the world, who can read it."

He took the book from where he had stuffed it into his belt and held it out. "Then do it."

She straightened, waiting for her breath to calm. "No."

"I already told you, you are in no position . . ."

"To bargain?" She grinned. "Oh I think I am."

The men from the boat were given their own corner of the hold, plus fresh clothing and food. Lyrna and the two other women, Murel and Orena, were given the first mate's cabin to share.

"You're sure?" Murel asked in her soft whisper.

Lyrna held out her hand for the small mirror she had seen the girl trying to hide. "Yes."

The mirror was backed with silver, ornately engraved in the manner favoured by Alpiran smiths from the northern ports, the motif of a man engaged in combat with a lion typical of the style. She traced her fingers over the image for a moment then turned the mirror over.

She always wondered why there were no screams, no tears, no despair sending her into thrashing hysterics. She felt it all, inside, a raging, burning storm of anguish and pain, but all she actually did was sit and stare at the burnt stranger in the mirror. Most of her hair was gone, the scalp a mottled relief of red and pink flesh. The flames had caught the upper side of her face, the scars ascending from the bridge of her nose, the line of seared skin slanting diagonally from left cheekbone to right jaw, like an ill-fitting mask worn to scare children on the warding's night.

I am no queen, she thought, staring into the eyes of the burnt stranger. *What artist will ever paint this portrait? And what do I tell the mint to stamp on the coins?* The thought drew a laugh, making Murel start, no doubt wondering if she had slipped into madness.

Lyrna handed the mirror back to her. "Thank you."

"What happened in the hold?" Orena asked, a slim woman with dark brown hair and eyes, the abuse she had suffered evident in the bruises on her neck, but less traumatised by her ordeal than Murel. However, she was smart enough to be afraid.

"I killed a Volarian," Lyrna said, seeing little point in deceit.

"Why?"

"To secure our place on this ship."

"And where is this ship headed exactly?"

"The Meldenean Isles. From there we can make our way back to the Realm."

"In return for what?"

Lyrna lifted the book from the bed where she had placed it, thumbing through the middle pages. "A small service. Don't worry, the captain has agreed none of us will be touched provided I perform adequately."

"Not so sure about that," the woman muttered, pacing the cabin, arms crossed. "These pirates . . . I don't like how they look at us. The slavers were bad enough. Never thought I'd miss my husband, the fat fool."

Murel slumped onto the bed. "If he was fat and foolish, why did you marry him?" she asked.

Orena gave her a quizzical look. "He was rich."

Lyrna concentrated on the book as they chattered. For the most part it was the dull minutiae of military correspondence, lists of supplies, expected lines of advance. She took note of the fact that the Volarians had extensive plans for the occupation of all the fiefs save Renfael, recalling Darnel's final words at their last meeting. *Faith help me, I had to try.*

Has the steel-clad fool finally given me reason to hang him? she wondered, deciding it was a question for another time. *The Ship Lords sent their best men for this. There has to be a reason.*

Whoever had written the text was clever enough not to rely exclusively on the code. Certain place names had been substituted. She was able to identify The Eerie as Varinshold due to the description of the street plan, and Crow's Nest was obviously Alltor; what other city sat on an island? Others were less obvious. Gull's Perch was barely described as was Raven's Loft, though mention of mines led her to suspect it as the Northern Reaches. *I pity whoever they send to take them,* she thought. However, the longest description was afforded to Serpent's Den, a complicated place of numerous ports and sea channels. The description was also followed by an extensive plan of attack.

It is imperative, she read, *that as many ships as possible be gathered for the assault on the Serpent's Den following the successful investment and pacification of The Eerie. The assault must take place before the onset of the winter storms. Admiral Karlev will take command of the strike squadrons, primary importance being afforded to denying the enemy use of their ports . . .*

She rose from the bed and went to the door, hauling it open, the guard outside stepping forward with his hand on his sabre hilt. He had been the one guarding the dead Volarian and seemed keen not to get too close. "I need to see him," she said.

"I'm trusting you to keep our agreement," she told the captain in his cabin. "But I think you'll agree it's best if I share this now."

He had needed little persuasion; if anything, she seemed to be confirming a long-held suspicion. He ordered all excess weight cast overboard, even the gold bars captured from the Volarians, and every sail raised. Due to the prevailing currents they had to tack south before striking east, the captain hounding every inch of efficiency from his crew.

"What's happening?" Iltis asked as the escapees clustered around Lyrna in the hold.

"The Volarians move against the Meldenean Isles," she said. "We hasten there with warning."

"And our fate when we arrive?" Harvin enquired.

"The captain has given his word we'll be released. I have reason to trust it."

"Why?" the outlaw pressed.

"He'll need me to convince the Ship Lords."

Foul weather descended two days later, the captain trimming as little sail as possible as the sea rose in great angry swells and the wind threatened to rip the crew from the rigging. The cease-less pitching of the ship sent most of her compatriots heaving, only she and Benten remaining immune.

"Sailed before, my lady?" the young fisherman asked during a slight lull in the storm as the others bent over the rail, Harvin raising his head between retches to voice the most colourful curses she was yet to hear.

"Pig-fucking sons of whores!" he ranted, much to the amuse-ment of the crew.

"I'm not a lady," she told Benten. "And before this my sailing experience consisted of a few barge trips up the Brinewash." *The last with my niece and nephew, before I travelled north. Janus spotted an otter climbing onto the riverbank with a freshly caught trout flapping in its mouth, clapping his hands and jumping in delight . . .*

"My lady?" Benten said, a note of concern in his voice.

Lyrna touched a hand to her eyes and found them wet. "Mistress," she corrected. "Just a simple merchant's daughter."

"No." He gave a slow but emphatic shake of his head. "You certainly are not."

The storm abated after six full days of fury, all sails hauled into place to catch the westerly winds as the sun dried the deck. Lyrna took to wearing a scarf over her mottled scalp, finding the sun's heat painful on her scars. It was to lead to a near-disastrous incident when one of the crew offered her a mocking bow, presenting her with a larger scarf. "For your face, Mistress," he explained.

Iltis had laughed, issuing great hearty peals of mirth as he strode across the deck, proffering an appreciative hand to the Meldenean, who proved fool enough to take it.

"How's he supposed to work the rigging with both arms broken?" the captain demanded a short while later. The fight had been brief but brutal, the crewman Iltis had crippled resembling a recently landed fish as he flopped about on the deck whilst the brother, Harvin and Benten exchanged punches with his mates. The captain barked out a restraining order when one of the crew drew his sabre.

"One of our number is a sailor," Lyrna replied. "He can take his place."

She sensed there was something forced about the captain's ire, his curt treatment of the injured crewmen evidence of an already scant regard. "He'd better," he growled but said no more, stomping off to berate the helmsman for letting the bow wander too far from the compass.

She found Iltis being nursed by Murel in the hold, the girl's slender hands dabbing a reddened cloth to his bruises. Lyrna said nothing but pressed a kiss onto his stubbled head. It was gone in an instant, but she fancied she saw a smile twitch on his lips before he growled and turned away.

It became her habit to linger above as night fell. Orena and Murel had a tendency to jabber away for hours until sleep claimed them, usually about matters of the meanest consequence. Lyrna suspected there was a deliberate shallowness to their conversation, an avoidance of recent trauma in talk of past loves and girlhood escapades, a trauma she hadn't fully shared thanks to her burns. She didn't begrudge them their distractions but found she needed the comparative quiet of the foredeck to continue the ceaseless examination of evidence.

At first all contemplation had been coloured by the events in the throne room, a central horror that commanded her every thought, birthing uncomfortable conclusions. *A plan years in the making,* she decided. *To prepare such a perfect assassin. And who would have thought Al Telnar would die a hero?* She experienced a momentary shame at her many clipped dismissals of the lord's approaches over the years. Clearly he had been a better man than she judged him, braving Dark fire to save her without care for his own life. But, hero or not, she couldn't help but conclude he would still have made a terrible husband.

She began to realise concentration on a single event was obstructing the consideration of other evidence. She recalled a phrase from *The Wisdoms of Reltak*: "Beware the seduction of the quick conclusion. Do not indulge in the answer you desire until you know all you need to know."

Subduing a city the size of Varinshold would require an army of thousands, she reasoned. *Even with Realm Guard absent . . . The Realm Guard, marching forth with the invasion only days away. A case of remarkable ill fortune brought about by the attack on the Tower Lord of the Southern Shore . . .* She strove to recover every scrap of detail she had learned about the attempt on the Tower Lord's life. *Two assassins, Cumbraelin fanatics . . . Two assassins.*

She should call it merely a suspicion in the absence of other evidence, but allowed herself a certainty. *Brother Frentis and the Volarian woman. They've been busy.* Incredibly, she felt a sense of regret at Frentis's death. *How much more evidence could I have wrung from him if he'd lived? But* she *lives, no doubt killing ever more as her countrymen rape my lands.*

She looked down at her hands, finding her fists clenched, as they had been when she stabbed the Volarian. She recalled the twitch of the dagger in her hand as his heart had given a final convulsive beat after the blade pierced it. *She can kill,* she mused. *But now so can I.*

CHAPTER EIGHT
Frentis

The Free Sword held the blade up to the moonlight, running an admiring eye over the edge, smiling a little as he picked out the grey flames trapped in the metal. Truly a valuable prize to take home.

"That doesn't belong to you," Frentis told him as he vaulted over the battlement.

A Kuritai might have had a chance to parry the thrust, but this man had none of the unnatural reflex required. The hunting knife took him in the throat, stilling any shout he may have been trying to voice, Frentis holding him down until his twitching ceased. He crouched, looking down at the courtyard, seeing only a few Volarians pacing back and forth from one familiar doorway to another, all Free Swords. *Kuritai too valuable to waste on guard duty,* he thought.

His gaze roamed the Order House, drinking in the sight, every corner, rooftop and brick as he remembered, with an important difference. No blue-cloaked figures walking the walls this night, just an infestation of Volarians.

He took the dead Free Sword's cloak, exchanging the Order sword for his own, and walked at a sedate pace towards the nearest guard, killing him with a knife throw when he got close enough for the man to make out his face. He completed a full circuit of the walls in an hour, killing every guard he encountered, only one managing to put up a fight, a veteran sergeant in the gatehouse with a swarthy, sun-bronzed look, probably from the southern empire. He managed a parry or two, shouting for assistance from his dead comrades before the star-silver blade slipped past his short sword to punch through the breastplate and into his belly. Frentis finished him with the hunting knife and found a shadow, waiting for someone to come in answer to the sergeant's shouts. None did.

He slipped from the shadow and lifted a torch from its mounting, standing atop the battlements and waving it back and forth three times. Within seconds they emerged from the tree-line, over a hundred shadows running full pelt for the gate, Davoka's tall form in the lead. Frentis made his way to the courtyard, lifting free the great oak plank that held the gates closed. He didn't wait for the others, finding the doorway which led to the vaults and descending the steps at a run. The heavy door securing the Order's supply store was guarded by two Kuritai, indicating the Volarians put some value on what they kept here. Frentis saw little point in further stealth and shrugged off his stolen cloak, advancing with sword in one hand and hunting knife in the other. As expected the guards betrayed no sign of alarm and drew their weapons, arranging themselves into a dual fighting formation he recognised from the pits, one behind the other, the one in front crouched, the one behind standing.

It was over in six moves, one less than his best performance in the pits. Feint towards the one in front, leap and slash at the one behind forcing the parry, extend a kick into his chest sending him reeling, block the thrust of the crouching man, open his neck with the backswing and send the hunting knife spinning into the eye of the other as he rebounded from the wall.

He retrieved his knife, took the keys from the hook in the wall and unlocked the doors. The vaults were as dark as he remembered, a faint glow of torchlight glimmering in the depths. He advanced with caution, keeping low, ears alive for any sound, hearing only the laboured breathing of a man in pain.

They were chained to the wall, arms raised and wrists shackled.

The first was dead, hanging slack and lifeless, signs of recent torment covering his broad chest. *Master Jestin, never to forge another sword.* Frentis steeled himself against grief and moved on, finding more tortured corpses, brothers mostly but he recognised Master Chekril amongst them, making him wonder over the fate of the Order's dogs.

He judged the next one dead also, a thin man of middle years, head slumped and dried blood covering his bare torso, then stifled a shout as the man jerked, chains rattling and wild eyes finding Frentis's face. "Died," Master Rensial said. "The stables burned. All my horses died."

Frentis crouched at his side, the mad eyes fixed on his face. "Master, it's Brother Frentis . . ."

"The boy." Rensial's head bobbed in affirmation. "I knew he would be waiting."

"Master?"

Rensial's head swivelled about, manic gaze scanning the surrounding blackness. "Who would have thought the Beyond so dark?"

Frentis rose and tried each key until he found the one that unlocked the master's manacles, putting an arm around his midriff to help him up. "This is not the Beyond, and I am truly here to take you away. Do you know where they put the Aspect?"

"Gone," Rensial groaned. "Gone to the shadows."

Frentis paused at the sight of another dim glow, a narrow rectangle of light in the black void. *Master Grealin's chambers.* Racks of weapons, probably all looted but it was worth a look. He helped the stumbling master to the wall and let him slump to the floor. "A moment, Master."

He drew his sword and advanced towards the door, nudging it fully open with his boot. A man of slight build knelt on the floor beside a table bearing a corpse, rivulets of blood streaming over the table's edge and onto the floor. "Please," the kneeling man whispered in Volarian, Frentis taking in the fresh blood that covered his arms.

He ignored the man as he continued to beg, moving to the corpse. He had been a sturdy man, the part-shredded skin of his chest covered in hair and those patches of his head not marred by triangular burns evidence he had possessed a thick mane. His features, mostly a mass of livid bruises, had been broad and, Frentis recalled, somewhat brutish in life, except when he tracked, then they came alive. His eyes, now vanished from their sockets, would dart about with the kind of sharpness only a wolf could match.

"So he didn't die when the gate fell," Frentis murmured. He looked around the chamber where Master Grealin had once lived and kept his meticulous records of every weapon, bean and scrap of clothing the Order possessed. All the ledgers were gone, replaced by neatly arrayed metal implements, gleaming and very sharp.

"Please," the man with the bloody hands sobbed, a pool of liquid spreading out across the stone floor from where he knelt. "I only do as I am commanded."

"Why was this done to him?" Frentis asked.

"The battalion lost many Free Swords to this man, the commander's nephew amongst them."

"You are a slave," Frentis observed.

"I am. I only do as I . . ."

"Yes. You said." The tumult of battle came to them through the vaults, the Free Sword garrison finally waking to their danger.

Frentis moved to the door. "This battalion commander, where is he quartered?"

It transpired the commander had taken over Master Haunlin's old chamber, fortuitously positioned so as to overlook the courtyard. Frentis left the shutters on the windows open so the prisoners could hear the slave do his work. They knelt in the courtyard, twelve survivors from a garrison of over two hundred, most of them wounded. He had let them stew a while as he visited the kennels, returning to find all displaying a gratifying level of terror.

"Your commander wasn't very forthcoming," Frentis told them, some starting at the sound of their own language. "The man who led our order was called Aspect Arlyn. We know he was here when the gate fell. The first man who tells me where he is gets to live."

From above came a sound Frentis had heard in the pits; castration always produced a uniquely high-pitched scream.

One of the men convulsed and vomited, drawing breath to speak but the man next to him was quicker. "You mean the tall man?"

"Yes," Frentis said as the other prisoners all began to jabber at once, falling silent as the surrounding fighters stepped closer with swords raised. He stood before the man who had spoken first. "The tall man."

"A-an officer from the general's staff took him, b-back to the city. Just after we took the fortress."

"It's a house." Frentis dragged the man to his feet, pulling him towards the gate, passing Janril Norin on the way, the one-time minstrel waiting with his Renfaelin blade resting on his shoulder. "Don't be too long about it," Frentis ordered.

He dragged the man through the gate as the screams began in the courtyard, drawing his knife and severing his bonds. "Go back to the city, tell your people what happened here."

The man stood staring at him in shock for a moment then turned and stumbled into a run, falling down several times before he disappeared from view. Frentis wondered if he should have told him he was running in the wrong direction.

Davoka was mostly silent during the journey back to the camp, avoiding his gaze. *Garvish,* he thought with a sigh.

"I know what the Lonak do to their prisoners," he said when the silence grew irksome.

"Some Lonakhim," she returned. "Not I." Her gaze shifted to the slight form of the slave, stumbling along with eyes wide in constant expectation of death. "What play will you make with him?"

Frentis uttered a shallow laugh. "Not play, work."

"You're not *Garvish*," he heard her say as he walked on ahead. "You're worse."

Master Grealin greeted them with wide arms and a broad smile, enfolding a confused Rensial in a warm embrace.

"My horses burned," the mad master told Grealin with earnest sincerity.

The big man gave a sad smile as he stepped back from his brother. "We'll get you some more."

"Over two hundred killed," Frentis reported to Grealin a short while later. "A large number of weapons captured, plus sundry armour, food and a few bows. And our special new recruits of course. We lost four."

"The value of surprise should never be underestimated," the master observed.

They sat together on the riverbank a short walk from the camp where over three hundred souls now made their home. They had been accumulating refugees and freed slaves for the past few weeks, some electing to move on when it became clear they were expected to fight, most deciding to stay. Even so their fighting strength numbered barely a hundred, the remainder too young, old, sick or ill trained to carry a weapon against the Volarians. Before last night their victories had been small, confined to raiding slavers' caravans and Volarian supply trains.

"They'll be coming," the master said. "Now we've proved ourselves more than a nuisance."

"As we knew they would. Master, about the Aspect . . ."

Grealin shook his bald head. "No."

"I know many ways in . . ."

"To search an entire city for one man, who for all we know languishes in the hold of a slave ship halfway across the ocean by now. I'm sorry, brother, but no. These people need their champion, now more than ever."

The slave was sitting where he left him, silent and unmoving beside the shelter Davoka shared with Illian. The girl stared at him in open curiosity as she stirred the pot of soup hanging over the fire, the rising aroma convincing Frentis her talents, whatever they were, didn't reside in cookery.

"Brother!" She brightened as he moved to his own tent, unbuckling the sword from his back. "Another victory. The whole camp is afire with it. Did you really kill ten of the beasts?"

"I don't know," he replied honestly.

"Take me next time," Arendil said in a sullen voice, prodding the cook fire with a stick. "I'll kill more than ten."

"You couldn't kill a mouse," Illian said with a laugh.

"I am a trained squire of House Banders," the boy retorted. "Dishonoured by being left here with you whilst my comrades win glorious victory."

"The camp must be guarded," Frentis told him in a tone that indicated he had heard enough on this subject.

He took a bowl and scooped some soup from the pot, moving to squat down at the slave's side. "Eat," he said, holding it in front of his face.

The slave took the bowl and began to eat with mechanical obedience, holding it to his lips and drinking the less-than-flavoursome contents without sign of reluctance.

"You have a name?" Frentis asked when he had finished.

"I do, Master. Number Thirty-Four."

Numbered slave. A specialist, trained from childhood for a particular task. *This man can't be more than twenty-five, but I'll wager he's taken far more lives than I, none of them quickly.*

"I'm not a master," he told Thirty-Four. "And you are not a slave. You're free."

The slave's face betrayed no joy at this news, just bafflement as he voiced a quotation with an oddly stilted intonation. "Freedom, once lost, cannot be regained. Those not born free are enslaved by the weakness of their blood. Those enslaved in life forsake freedom by virtue of their own weakness."

"That sounds like something you read," Frentis observed.

"Codicils of the Ruling Council, Volume Six."

"Well, forget the Council and the empire. You're a long way from both, and this Realm has no slaves."

Thirty-Four gave him a cautious glance. "You do not bring me here to exact revenge?"

"You only do as you are commanded, since you were old enough to remember. Am I correct?"

Thirty-Four nodded, reaching into his tunic and extracting a small glass vial on a chain about his neck. "I need this, it numbs the pain . . . my pain. It's how I do what I do."

Frentis eyed the pale yellow liquid in the vial and felt an echo of the binding flicker across his chest. "And if you stop taking it?"

"I . . . hurt."

"You're a free man now, you can take it or not, as you wish. You can stay with us or go, as you wish."

"What do you want of me?"

"You have skills, they will be useful to us."

Davoka arrived, dumping the sack of grain she had carried from the Order House next to the fire and scowling at the sight of the slave. She accepted a bowl of soup from Illian, spooning some into her mouth and promptly spitting it out. "No more of this for you," she told Illian, taking the soup pot and tipping the contents into a patch of ferns. She went to her tent and returned with a captured Volarian knife, tossing it to the girl. "You learn to hunt. Arendil, make more soup."

Illian looked at the knife in her hand with obvious delight, waving it at Arendil with a taunting snicker.

"Come, we check the snares," Davoka said, hefting her spear. She paused beside Frentis, scowling again at Thirty-Four. "Find another place for him," she said quietly. "Don't want him near the children."

She strode off with Illian scampering after. "I'm not a child," the girl said. "I'll be old enough to marry in a year and a half."

Arendil aimed a kick at the soup pot, grumbling, "I'm the blood heir to the Lordship of Renfael, you know."

Frentis rose, gesturing for Thirty-Four to follow. "Allow me to show you something."

Janril sat opposite the captive, honing the edge of his sword with a whetstone. The Volarian was large, impressive muscles bulging on the arms pulled back and secured to the trunk of an elm with strong rope. His face was a patchwork of cuts and bruises, one of his eyes swollen shut and his lips split with recent damage.

"Anything?" Frentis asked Janril.

The sergeant gave a silent shake of his head, narrowing his gaze at the sight of Thirty-Four. "He may be able to help," Frentis told him.

Janril shrugged and rose to kick the feet of the bound man, his head snapping up, the one good eye casting about in alarm before understanding returned and it narrowed into stern defiance.

"He was wearing that when we took him." Frentis pointed to the medallion hanging from Janril's neck, an embossed silver disc showing a chain and a whip. "We believe he may be a man of some importance."

"Guild-master's sigil," Thirty-Four said. "He'll have command of fifty overseers. I've seen this man before, when the fleet was mustering. I believe he answers to General Tokrev himself."

"Really?" Frentis said, stepping aside so the captive had an unobstructed view of Thirty-Four. "That is interesting."

The single eye widened considerably at the sight of the slave. "Our new recruit has some questions," Frentis told the guild-master.

They left them alone for a time, Thirty-Four crouched next to the guild-master as he spoke, the words tumbling from his damaged lips with scarcely any hesitation. The torturer hadn't touched him at all.

"A large caravan returns from the province to the north in three days," Thirty-Four reported a short while later. "The lord of that land provided a list of subjects he thought would make good slaves."

Master Grealin straightened as Frentis related the torturer's words. "Lord Darnel cooperates with his people?"

Thirty-Four gave a slight shrug when Frentis related the question. "I do not know who that is."

This has been long planned, Frentis thought with a grimace. "What else? Any word of our Aspect?"

Thirty-Four shook his head. "He knows nothing of that, his sole concern is slaves and profit."

"Is he going to be any more use?"

"He has numbers, figures on the slaves shipped back to the empire, likely returns on his master's investment."

"Get what you can out of him. Especially about this general he answers to. When you're sure you've got it all, turn him over to Sergeant Norin."

"I promised him a quick death. He begged for it."

"A promise made to an animal is no promise at all," Janril said when Frentis explained. It was the most he had spoken in days.

"You will stay?" Frentis asked Thirty-Four.

The slight man took the vial from about his neck and pulled off the stopper, his hands shaking as he hesitated, then tipped the contents away. "I will, but I have a condition."

"I leave the manner of the slaver's death to you."

Thirty-Four shook his head. "No. I want a name."

"Your role," Frentis said to Illian and Arendil, lying alongside him in the long grass. "Repeat it to me."

Arendil rolled his eyes in annoyance but Illian spoke up with prim eagerness. "We walk the road, stumbling about as if wounded. When the caravan comes we sit down and wait."

Frentis surveyed their appearance one last time, satisfying himself the dried rabbit's blood and ragged clothing would suffice. "And when it starts?"

Arendil spoke first, drawing a glare from Illian. "Get to the wagons and free the captives." He brandished one of the keys they had been given. Experience had revealed the slavers were lazy about changing their locks and the keys they had captured would undo most manacles.

"Davoka will run to you as soon as the attack begins. Do not stray from her side."

He glimpsed the Lonak woman's stern look of disapproval from her position a few yards away and avoided her gaze, bringing the young ones had not been her idea.

"I thought Lonak children learned war at an early age," he had said when she voiced her objections back at the camp.

"They are not Lonakhim," she replied. "Both have known nothing but comfort."

He knew she had a deeper reason, her eyes seeing another overly comforted soul when she looked at them, especially Illian. "War comes to this forest soon," he said. "The games we've been playing up until now are over. They need to be prepared."

A short shrill whistle sounded to the north, making the fighters sink deeper into the grass. Frentis turned to the two youths he intended to put in harm's way. "It's time."

They played their part well, although Illian's stumbles were somewhat elaborate and Arendil's a little stiff. The caravan crested the low hill a few hundred paces to the north, a full company of Free Cavalry riding in escort. The officer at the head of the column raised a hand at the sight of the two youngsters sitting in the road and the caravan came to a halt. Frentis watched the Volarian captain scan the surrounding fields, taking his time over it. After a moment he barked a command at one of his sergeants and a troop of four riders galloped ahead, reining in a few feet from the bloodied refugees, both of whom were too pretty to kill outright.

Frentis took a firm grip on his bow and stood up, their small company of archers following suit. The volley was inexpert but enough arrows were launched to bring down all four riders in an instant. Davoka leapt to her feet and sprinted towards the road, Frentis leading his twenty archers towards the caravan at a dead run.

The Volarian captain was clearly experienced, stringing his lead company out in skirmish formation before launching the charge, thirty or so riders bearing down on them at full gallop, long swords levelled.

Frentis stopped, notching another arrow and raising his hand, eyes fixed on the large pale boulder he had placed on the roadside earlier. When the first rider came level with the marker he dropped his hand.

They erupted from the grass on both sides of the road, more than twenty snarling, bounding monsters, voicing barks that were more like roars as they bore down on the charging cavalry. Horses and men alike shrieked in panic and fear as teeth rent flesh, the monsters leaping to tear riders from saddles, jaws clamping down and shaking their flailing prey. Swords hacked and slashed amidst the turmoil in brief but hopeless flickers of resistance.

Frentis waited for the screams to stop before venturing closer. So much blood had been spilled so quickly it seemed a red mist hung over the carnage, several of the archers gagging and turning away at the various horrors littering the road.

The beast sat on the remnants of the Volarian captain, licking its reddened paw. Seeing Frentis, it gave a small whine and dropped to low crawl, slinking forward to lick at his hand. "Slasher," Frentis said, kneeling down to hug his old companion. "Who's a good old pup, eh? Who's a really good old pup?"

There had been a short but ugly fight around the wagons, the mercenary guards and cavalry rear-guard put up stiff resistance but nothing Davoka and the other fighters couldn't overcome, though they lost five more of their number in doing so. He found Davoka restraining Illian, the girl flailing in her arms as she kicked and spat at the body of an overseer, a knife buried in his chest. The profanity flowing from the girl's mouth made Frentis suspect her upbringing hadn't been as sheltered as he imagined. Eventually she exhausted herself, sagging in the Lonak woman's arms, sobbing as she cradled her. "Sorry," she whispered. "He touched me, you see? He shouldn't have touched me."

Arendil was at work on the road-side, unlocking the shackles from a line of captives. He had a small cut on his forehead but was otherwise unscathed. Frentis surveyed the freed folk, finding the usual mix of mostly young men and women, picked for beauty or strength. Volarian enslavement standards had the paradoxical effect of providing him the most suitable recruits for his growing army.

"Ermund!" Arendil stared at a figure amongst the milling captives, a broad-shouldered man with a scarred nose and the marks of a recent whipping on his back. The man stared at the boy in confusion as he approached.

"Arendil? Am I dreaming?"

"No dream, good sir. How do you come to be here? My mother, grandfather . . . ?"

The man staggered a little and Frentis helped the boy support him as they propped him against a wagon wheel, Frentis handing him a canteen.

"This is Ermund Lewen," Arendil told Frentis. "First of my grandfather's knights."

"Darnel's dogs came to the estate," the knight said, having drunk his fill. "Five hundred or more. Too many to fight. At my urging your grandfather took your mother and fled. My men and I . . . We held them for a time, it was a grand thing to see . . ." The knight's head began to sag, his eyes drooping with exhaustion.

"I'll find a horse for him," Frentis said, touching Arendil on the shoulder and moving on.

A few horses had survived the dogs and the battle. Frentis ordered them all rounded up and taken back to camp as Master Rensial was sorely in need of a distraction. When not simply staring into space the mad master would relate the name of every horse he had ever trained to anyone in earshot. Recalling Frentis's name, however, seemed to be beyond him; he was always just "the boy."

He took the reins of one of the horses, a fine stallion with a silky black coat, nostrils flaring at the scent of the dogs still busily feeding on the corpses a short distance away. He soothed the animal with the whisper and led it towards the unconscious knight, pausing at the sight of Janril Norin pacing along a line of six Volarian survivors, idly swinging his sword as he addressed them. "Can anyone here sing, at all? We've a lack of music in our camp and I should like some entertainment of an evening." He stopped, turning to face them, sword point lowering to jab a cut into the cheek of the first in line. "Sing!"

Frentis moved closer as the man stared up at Janril in bafflement, tears streaming from terror-filled eyes.

"I said sing, you poxed son of a whore," Janril whispered, placing his sword against the man's ear. "I used to sing and my wife would dance . . ."

"Sergeant," Frentis said.

Janril turned to him, a faint look of irritation on his face. "Brother?"

"We've no time for this." He nodded at the third captive in line. "That one's an ensign, he may know something. Take him back for questioning. Kill the others, and be quick."

Janril stared at him for a second, face as expressionless as usual, then gave a slow nod. "As you wish, brother."

"We had no notion why Darnel chose to move when he did," Ermund said, the firelight painting his face a pale red. Arendil sat beside him, his brows furrowed in worry. Next to him Illian patted the head of the dog resting in her lap. The girl had betrayed some initial nervousness when Slasher and the rest of the pack had come to join them at the fire and a young bitch, only slightly less huge than the others, placed her head on her knees, eyes raised in expectation of petting.

"She likes you," Frentis explained. Slasher sat on his left, one of his many offspring on his right. The dogs, named by fallen Master Chekril as faith-hounds according to Grealin, were only a little smaller than Scratch, their long-lost forebear, with longer legs and a narrower snout. However, the unnerving loyalty and obedience of the slave-hound still remained strong in the bloodline, though they were somewhat easier to control.

"Only heard about the invasion after I'd been captured," Ermund went on. "Saw some ugly sights on the road I can tell you. Darnel's been quick to settle accounts with those who crossed him."

"Do his people join him in this treachery?" Master Grealin asked.

"Difficult to tell from the back of a wagon, brother," Ermund replied. "His own knights will be loyal, he tends to pick men of like mind, vicious dullards driven by greed rather than honour. But I know the temper of our folk. Darnel has never been well liked. Can't imagine throwing his lot in with foreign invaders will endear him any."

"My grandfather," Arendil said. "Do you have any notion where he may have gone?"

"None, my boy. Though, if I were him I'd head north to the Skellan Pass, seek refuge with the Order."

"The garrison in the pass is not what it was," Grealin said. "Aspect Arlyn was obliged to reduce their number in recent years. We can expect no great reinforcement from Brother Sollis."

"We fight alone," Davoka commented.

"Not alone," Frentis said. "The Tower Lord of the Northern Reaches will come. And when he does we'll retake this Realm."

Davoka frowned at the murmur of assent from the others at the fire. "The northern wastes are far. And this Tower Lord cannot have more men than the Volarians."

Illian voiced a small laugh. "Lord Vaelin could come to us with no men and this war will still be won in a day."

Davoka merely raised her eyebrows, letting the matter drop.

"We must endure," Frentis said. "Keep the flame of defiance alight in this Realm until he comes."

"And kill as many as we can," Janril commented. He stood outside the circle, face only half-lit by the firelight, fixing an intent gaze on Frentis. "Right, brother?"

Slasher raised his head, sensing some vestige of threat in the minstrel's tone, a low growl beginning in his throat. Frentis calmed the dog with a scratch to his ears. "Quite right, Sergeant."

Thirty-Four appeared out of the darkness, making Illian jump. The torturer had an uncanny ability for seeming to materialise out of nowhere. He was yet to choose a name, something that caused little trouble since so few in the camp were able, or willing, to talk to him. "The ensign was stubborn," he reported. "But not overly so, the damage was minimal."

"What intelligence do you have?" Frentis asked, gesturing for him to sit.

Thirty-Four chose a place between Davoka and Frentis, seemingly oblivious to the Lonak woman's palpable discomfort at such proximity. "They know about you, this group. The Free Swords call you the Red Brother. Plans are being drawn to drive you from this forest. The general offers ten thousand squares for your head."

"Hardly unexpected," Frentis said. "What else?"

"Taking the city and defeating your army proved more costly than they planned. They await fresh troops from Volaria. The bulk of the army moves south. The lord of the southern province has refused to treat with them and they besiege his city."

"Darnel sells himself whilst Mustor stands defiant," Master Grealin commented when Frentis had translated the news. "War always turns the world upside down."

Frentis caught Davoka's insistent expression. "Anything about the queen?" he asked Thirty-Four.

"He believes the King and his family all slain. There are no orders to hunt for the queen."

"That's all?"

"He misses his wife, their first child was born in the winter."

"How very sad." Frentis turned to Janril. "He's finished with the prisoner."

The minstrel's face betrayed a slight grin before disappearing into the darkness. Frentis ruffled the fur around Slasher's neck, feeling the thick slabs of muscle beneath. *We were made monstrous, old pup,* he thought. *But what am I making them?*

CHAPTER NINE
Reva

T he bodies lay thick on the causeway, a carpet of unmoving black forms reminding Reva of a field of dead sparrows near the barn, left in the wake of the villagers' yearly hunt. Ladders lay amongst the bodies, none closer to the wall than twenty yards. She counted some four hundred dead, all fallen to Lord Antesh's archers the day after the Volarian vanguard arrived. Since then they had held off making another direct assault, contenting themselves with raising earthworks and patrolling the surrounding country.

"They're waiting," her uncle had said, seated by the fire in the library, a thick blanket covering his knees, the blue bottle and the redflower within easy reach. "And why would they not? We're not going anywhere."

As Brother Harin had predicted, he grew worse every day, cheeks more sunken, skin ever more pale, every bone and vein in his hands seemingly laid bare beneath a wrapping of bleached skin. *His eyes though,* Reva thought. *Still so very bright.*

Until now she had kept her promise, staying at his side and ignoring the desperate desire to run for the wall when the horns sounded the alarm the second day, roaming the manor like a caged wild cat until news came of an easy repulse. But today he had relented, for now the Volarians came in force and he had not the strength to view them with his own eyes.

"My lords," she greeted Antesh and Arentes as they bowed to her and Veliss atop the gatehouse battlements.

"Do we have a count?" Veliss asked.

"I thought it best not to, my lady," Antesh said. "Large numbers may unnerve the men when constantly bandied about."

Reva stepped closer to the battlements, taking in the sight of the Volarian host. Their tents stretched away into the morning haze, more a city than a camp. At least two thousand infantry were marching across the plain, more descending the hill to the west in a ceaseless parade. However, what drew her gaze most was the sight of the tall wooden frames being constructed behind their earthworks.

"Are those their engines?" she asked.

"We've seen no sign of such devices, my lady," Lord Arentes replied. "Those are towers. They'll trundle them up to the walls on great wheels."

"I've prepared fire arrows," Antesh said. "And a plentiful supply of oil pots."

"They seem to be building a lot of them," Arken observed. He had taken to wearing a leather jerkin like Antesh, and carried his own longbow and quiver of arrows.

"Then we'll have plenty of targets, young sir," Antesh told him. Despite his apparent confidence Reva detected a tightness to his tone. *He's not a fool,* Reva thought, suspecting the Lord of Archers had in fact been scrupulous in counting the Volarian numbers.

"When can we expect the attack?" she asked.

"I suspect as soon as the towers are ready," Antesh replied. "I doubt they'll want to prolong this siege. They have a whole realm to conquer and won't want so many men tied down here for any longer than necessary."

She returned her gaze to the frames, fancying they had actually risen in height in the few moments since she ascended the gatehouse. She removed her cloak, revealing the light mail shirt she had found in the manse's mostly depleted armoury, and buckled her sword belt about her chest, the weapon worn across her back, the handle jutting over her right shoulder for a quick draw, as Al Sorna had taught her. She held out her hand to Arken and he passed her the wych-elm bow and quiver of iron-heads.

"Reva . . ." Veliss began.

"You should return to my uncle," Reva told her. "My place is here now."

Veliss looked at the Volarian host then back at her. "You promised him . . ."

"He will understand." Watching Veliss hug herself, Reva sensed she was fighting tears. She stepped closer to clasp the lady counsellor's hand. "Stay close to him. I'll return when the walls are secured."

Veliss took a deep breath and raised her head, eyes bright as she forced a smile. "Another promise?"

"This one I'll keep."

Veliss returned her clasp, the grip tight as she held it to her lips. A soft warm kiss and she was gone, turning and descending the steps without a backward glance.

"My lords." Reva turned back to Antesh and Arentes. "I should like to tour the walls once more."

They came that night, perhaps gambling the darkness would afford some cover from their arrows. If so, it proved a false hope. Antesh had prepared bales of pitch-soaked wicker, now cast from the walls and lit with fire arrows, the flames rising high and providing a clear view of the towers as they crawled along the causeway. Each tower had a long canopy extending from the rear under which men laboured to push them forward, their feet moving in time to an unheard rhythm. Antesh held the volley until the first came within fifty yards of the gate. At his order the clay pots were thrown, dozens shattering on the front of the tower, followed by a volley of fire arrows, the lamp oil catching immediately.

The tower continued on for several yards, Reva craning her neck for a clear view of the canopy at the rear of the monster where the legs continued their rhythmic plodding. She unlimbered her bow and notched an arrow, drawing with careful aim. The arrow flew into the mass of legs at the rear of the canopy and she had the satisfaction of seeing a prone figure emerge a few seconds later. He rolled clutching at his leg before several arrows pinned him to the ground. The surrounding archers were quick to follow her example and soon the tower was trailing a line of wounded men as the flames engulfed its upper half. It came to a halt a good twenty yards from the wall, close enough to hear the screams of men burning inside, then seemed to convulse like some great wounded beast, bleeding men as they tried to flee, most falling victim to the longbows before they could run more than a few yards. A cheer arose from the walls as the tower died, the flames eating away the framework and sending the upper half tumbling to the ground, wreathed in fire.

"Cheer later!" Antesh barked, pointing to the next tower as it attempted to manoeuvre around the flaming corpse of its brother. "Get some pots on that thing."

The second tower fared no better than the first, burned and gutted before it reached the wall, the crew falling under the arrow storm. Reva saw a few men jump into the river in an attempt to evade the rain of iron-tipped shafts. The third tower got closer, only ten yards short before fire and arrows halted its progress.

"Ladders!" a shout went up from somewhere to the left. Reva looked to the causeway, seeing several hundred men running past the line of towers, ladders raised above their heads. On reaching the end of the causeway they split into two groups, scores falling to the archers as they ran parallel to the walls for a hundred paces then turned and charged forward with their ladders raised. There was a strange disregard for safety to these men, barely seeming to notice so many of their comrades dying around them or tumbling from the ladders. *Varitai*, Reva recalled Veliss's words. *Slave soldiers with no will of their own.*

A faint groan of disturbed air gave enough warning for her to duck as an arrow flew overhead. A nearby archer wasn't so lucky, pitching back from the wall with a shaft embedded in his cheek. Reva risked a glance over the wall, seeing a thick knot of men with strongbows clustered at the end of the causeway, loosing arrows up at the defenders with mechanical speed and precision. Like the men on the ladders they betrayed little sign of fear.

Lord Antesh gathered several dozen archers into a tight group, having them duck down with arrows notched, then rise up and loose as one, swarms of iron-heads sweeping down on the Volarian archers in successive volleys until none remained standing. The Varitai were also dispatched in short order, none climbing more than halfway up their ladders before being brought down, the ladders pushed away from the walls to lie atop the piles of bodies below.

The remaining four towers came on, blundering through the corpse-strewn ground, trying to force their way past the burning remnants of their brothers, but finding their progress blocked and grinding to a halt. "Slow and steady now, lads!" Lord Antesh called as the fire arrows flew. "Let's not be wasteful."

Within an hour all four towers were burning and their surviving crew running back along the causeway. The walls erupted in celebration, Reva finding herself pummelled with back slaps as men raised their bows, yelling in exultation or shouting foul-mouthed taunts at the Volarians.

"Wasn't so difficult, was it?" Arken commented. His face was grimy with mingled smoke and sweat, his quiver empty of arrows. Reva moved to the wall and looked down at the many bodies cluttering the narrow road that circled the city, seeing a few wounded crawling about, their groans lost amidst the tumult of joy. *Slaves,* she thought. *Spent like a few coppers on a long-odds bet.* She raised her gaze to the uncountable fires of the Volarian camp, knowing somewhere amongst them whoever had commanded this hopeless spectacle would be staring back at the carnage and calculating a fresh stratagem for the following day.

She noticed that her hand tingled, just where Veliss had kissed it. In fact it had been tingling ever since, though she only realised it now. "I'll be at the manse," she told Arken. "Find me when they come again."

◆ ◆ ◆

Uncle Sentes was in a foul mood when she arrived, though she suspected it had more to do with the broken-nosed priest who stood before him in the Lord's chamber than her broken promise. "What's this supposed to mean?" the Fief Lord demanded in a rasp, waving a piece of parchment. Veliss placed a calming hand on his shoulder as he glowered at the priest.

"The Holy Reader's words are perfectly clear, my lord," the priest said, casting a wary eye at Reva as she strode to stand at her uncle's side. "His insight, gifted by the Father himself, has allowed him to divine the cause of our current plight. Our innumerable sins have incurred His anger, the godless beasts outside our walls are His punishment."

"'The World Father sees all, knows all and forgives all,'" Reva quoted. "'Denying yourself His love is His only punishment.'"

The priest didn't look at her, addressing the Fief Lord. "Our way is clear, my lord. To secure the Father's forgiveness we must divest ourselves of our sins." He gave a pointed glance at Veliss. "All of our sins. This city was built in honour of the Father's greatest prophet, but we allow the stain of godless souls within its walls . . ."

"Your Reader," Uncle Sentes broke in, a small line of drool dangling from his lower lip, "sits in his cathedral scribbling nonsense and refusing all entreaties to aid the people of this city as they defend themselves from slavery and slaughter!" He choked off, wincing as a fresh bout of pain coursed through him. Reva smoothed a hand over his back and gently took the parchment from his shaking hand.

"'All heretics within the city must be gathered for the Father's judgement,'" she read, walking slowly towards the priest. "'The Holy Reader himself will adduce their acceptance of the Father's love. Any found to be unable or unwilling to abandon their heresy will be given over to their fellow heretics outside the walls.'"

She looked up at the priest, finding his gaze averted, his misshapen nose slightly upturned. "This is going to save us, is it?" she asked.

"The Reader's words are for the Fief Lord . . ."

He trailed off as she ripped the parchment in half and let it drop to the floor. "Get out of here," she said. "And if you bother my uncle with any more of your old fool's prattle, we'll see what the heretics outside the walls will do to two such godly souls as you."

He bit down an unwise retort and turned to go.

"And tell him," she said to his retreating back, "that when this is over he'd better cough up the name of that bastard who raised me. Tell him that."

"Was it horrible?" Veliss asked. They sat in the library, her uncle asleep upstairs. The priest's visit had sent him into a rant that left him exhausted and gulping redflower. Veliss stayed at his side until sleep came.

Reva had taken off her mail shirt, marvelling at how it could manage to smell so bad after only a few hours. She lay on a couch beside the fire, Veliss seated opposite, her gaze intent, as if searching for signs of injury. "We held them off," Reva replied. "Cost them a lot of men. But they'll be back tomorrow."

"Seen plenty of blood," Veliss said. "Spilled a bit too in my time. But I've never seen war."

Reva thought of the wounded Varitai crawling about as thousands cheered their deaths. "It's horrible."

"You don't have to fight, Reva. These people need you, and the risk . . ."

"I do have to. And I will." She studied Veliss's downcast face for a moment, finding she preferred it when she smiled. "I have said things to you," she said. "Unkind things . . ."

"I've heard worse, believe me. Bitch, whore, liar . . . spy. And they've all been true. So don't worry over my feelings, love."

"Why did you stay? You could be far away by now, and rich into the bargain."

"I couldn't leave him, not now."

Reva sat up, massaging the ache in her arm. Drawing the wych elm was taxing but she only felt the strain now as the excitement of battle faded. "How long have you been with him?" she asked Veliss.

"We met years ago in Varinshold, when he was a guest of the King's court. He was a regular and generous customer so I was sad to see him called back to sit in the Chair. A couple of years later, when I had a . . . pressing reason to leave Varinshold, I thought I might find a welcome here, or at least enough coin for passage to foreign climes. He proved more welcoming than I hoped, and open to some sage advice."

"Will you do the same for me, when the time comes?"

Veliss met her gaze, speaking softly. "I think you know I'd do just about anything you asked, love."

Reva looked away, concentrating on working her fingers into her bicep.

"Your uncle and I," Veliss said. "We don't . . . We haven't, not for a long time. The drink took its toll on more than just his liver, and my, ah, non-professional interests have always lain elsewhere, interests he allows me to pursue, with due discretion. There would be no betrayal, if that's the issue."

Filthy, Fatherless sinner . . . "The Book of Reason," Reva said. "Relates how the Father made men and women to love each other as a reflection of his own love for all humanity. The Book of Laws decrees marriage as a union of man and woman. The Book of Judgement prescribes any desecration of that bond a sin against the Father's love."

"Just words, love," Veliss said. "Just a lot of old words. I see you, Reva, I see where your eyes linger, though you try to hide it."

Reva rubbed the back of her hand, trying to erase the tingle that suddenly seemed to have sprung to life once more. "He tried to beat it from me," she whispered, closing her eyes. "But it's too deeply buried, like a stain that won't wash."

"A stain?" She felt Veliss move to sit next to her, felt her hand take hers, the tingle burning now. "It's no stain. It's beautiful, it's a gift." Her breath drifted over the skin of Reva's neck, soft and warm, her lips leaving another tingle on her flesh.

The sound of crashing doors reached her and she stood up, slipping from Veliss's embrace and turning as Arken burst into the room. "They're back!"

They used shields this time, large boards of nailed-together wood held aloft with poles at each corner, wide enough for ten Varitai to shelter under as they trotted towards the walls with their unnaturally uniform step. The sun was rising, revealing the full order of the Volarian battle, Reva guessing the strength of their first assault wave at over three thousand men. Antesh had the archers assail them from the sides rather than waste arrows loosing directly down onto the shields. At least a fifth of the attacking force was lost on the causeway, men tumbling to the ground or into the river as the archers found their marks with dread precision.

On reaching the walls they tried attacking in three places, hauling their ladders up, the shields constantly pummelled by the heavy rocks heaved from above. Reva kept bobbing up to loose at any attackers who strayed from cover, shifting her aim to the men on the ladders when they began to climb. She would wait until they were a good twenty feet off the ground before sending them tumbling back, hopefully onto the heads of their comrades. She stopped counting at six.

"My lord!" a man called to Antesh, running from the wall's west-facing section. "The river!"

Reva and Arken followed Antesh as he ran to view the danger. The western defenders were staring and pointing at the spectacle of fifty or so large rafts making their way across the dark waters of the Coldiron, each laden with shield-bearing Volarians and propelled forward with long poles. From the constant movement of the rafts' occupants Reva judged these free men rather than Varitai. *Soon to be free corpses,* she thought grimly.

"Spread your men out," Antesh told the House Guard sergeant who had command of this section of wall. "Squads of ten. Each one goes for a different raft, tell them to aim at the polemen."

He ordered them to loose as soon as the rafts came within

range, arrows arcing down into the shifting mass of Free Swords, forcing them to keep their shields raised.

"Got the bastard!" Arken exclaimed as his arrow claimed a poleman on the lead raft, Reva's shaft taking the man who stepped forward to replace him.

The pitch of the arrow storm increased as the rafts drew closer and the archers could pick out gaps in their shield roofs, the raft in the lead soon drifting out of control and twisting in the current, scattering bodies from its deck that the river carried away. Another two rafts suffered the same fate, but the remainder managed to make the bank, although they all showed sizeable gaps in their ranks.

The Free Swords scrambled ashore and ran to preassigned points to begin their assault, losing ever more men to the archers, but there were too many to kill and soon their ladders were reaching up to the battlements. The Free Swords had archers mixed into their ranks, keeping up a steady stream of arrows at the point where the ladders crested the wall. Reva saw two archers fall as they stepped up to push a ladder away.

"Get your spearmen up," Antesh told the House Guard sergeant as the Volarians began to scale the ladders.

Reva loosed a final arrow at a climber, ducking back before she could gauge the result and moving to stand with the sergeant as he arranged his spearmen into tightly bunched groups. Arken stood at her side, hefting the axe he had chosen from the armoury. She never had enjoyed much success teaching him the sword.

Antesh kept his archers at the wall as long as he could, exacting a fearful toll on the climbers, but losing several more to the Volarian bowmen below. "All right, move back!" he shouted, walking to Reva's side and placing his bow carefully on the top of the inner wall. "Time to dance, my lady," he said to her, drawing his sword.

She placed the wych elm next to his longbow. "I still have questions about this," she said, tapping a finger to the carvings.

"Ask me tomorrow," he said with a faint grin.

The first Volarian to reach the battlements was a large fellow with swarthy, brutish features under a thick iron helmet, shouting in rage and terror as he pulled himself over the wall. Reva darted forward, ducked and rolled under the Volarian's wild slash, drawing her sword as she came to her feet and stabbing upwards, under the man's chin, forcing the blade through tongue and bone into the brain. She withdrew the sword, turning and slashing at the face of the next climber trying to haul himself onto the battlements. He fell screaming and blind onto the men on the ladder below, taking them with him as he plummeted to his death.

More Volarians appeared on either side of her and the spearmen charged forward with a yell, stabbing and killing in a frenzy, the battlements transformed into a confused jumble of thrashing men. One of the Volarians commanded Reva's instant attention as he cut down the spearman who came for him then began hacking through the melee with a short sword in each hand, three men falling to him in quick succession. He was clad in different armour to the others, less bulky with his arms left bare apart from greaves on his wrists, and no helmet on his head which was shaved bald. His face betrayed scant emotion as he fought, side-stepping thrusts and delivering killing blows with cool precision, moving with a speed that bordered on the unnatural.

Arken gave a yell and charged at the man, axe raised, deaf to Reva's warning. The skilled man brought both swords up in a crossed parry as Arken's axe came down, then extended a kick into the boy's midriff, sending him flat onto his back, the axe flying from his grip. Reva ran forward as the Volarian moved in with the killing stroke, flicking her sword at his eyes and forcing him back. There was no surprise on his face as he stood regarding her, blood trickling from the fresh cut below his eye, and barely any pause before he attacked, one sword slashing at her head, the other thrusting at her belly. She twisted, deflecting both blades with a vertical parry, continuing the spin but descending to one knee, bringing the blade round to cleave his leg above the ankle. He wore thick greaves on his calves so the cut wasn't enough to cripple him, and he registered little pain or shock as he stabbed down at her, the tip of his short sword shattering on stone as she spun again, rising to thrust the sword into the base of his skull.

The twin swords clattered onto the stone as the skilled man sank to his knees, spasming as Reva pulled her sword free, falling onto his face and lying still.

She drew breath and looked for Arken, finding him standing with the other defenders clutching his chest and staring at her. The Volarians seemed to have vanished. She went to the wall to watch them flee, some huddled behind shields as they attempted to shuffle to the causeway, others just running blindly towards safety, many falling to longbows as they did so.

"We may have a little respite . . ." she began turning back, falling silent at the sight of them all kneeling with their heads lowered. She looked around, ready to berate her uncle for coming to the wall, then realised he wasn't there. They were kneeling for her, even Antesh and Arken.

"Don't do that," she said in a small voice.

Reva spent the rest of the morning helping carry the wounded to the makeshift healing house Brother Harin had established in an inn near the gate. The brother and his two fellow healers from the Fifth Order, an elderly woman and a man of middle years, worked tirelessly stitching cuts and setting bones, whilst occasionally managing to save men from what Reva assumed would be fatal wounds.

"This may interest you, my lady." Harin held up an instrument and moved to the archer she had seen take an arrow in the cheek the night before. The shaft had been removed but the head was firmly lodged in the bones of his face. The brother had given him a hefty dose of redflower but he still whimpered in pain, staring up at the instrument in Harin's hand with fearful eyes. "This is called the Mustorian lance, in honour of your late father."

The archer shrank back as Harin crouched down to inspect

his wound, a deep gash in his cheek, recently cleaned but still leaking blood. Reva took the man's hand and squeezed it, forcing an encouraging smile. "My father?" she asked Harin.

"Yes, his famous arrow wound was pretty much identical to this unfortunate fellow's. The head so deeply buried that trying to cut it out would have been fatal. The healer who treated him was obliged to design a new instrument." He held the long probe up for her inspection. "See the way the point is shaped? Narrow enough to fit into the base of an arrowhead and when it does"— he pushed his thumb along the centre of the probe and it split in two—"I extend it and grip the head, allowing swift and easy removal."

"And painless?" she asked.

"Oh, Faith no," he said, leaning over the wounded archer and starting to guide the probe into the wound. "It's exquisitely agonising, so I'm told. Hold this fellow's arms for me would you?"

She found Arken in the inn's tap room, the elderly healer wrapping bandages about his chest. "Cracked ribs," he told her with a rueful grin. "Only two though."

"That was foolish," she said. "Choose an easier kill next time."

"None of them are easy, except for you."

"All done," the healer said, tying off the bandages. "I'd normally give you a vial of redflower for the pain, but we're having to ration it."

"There are a few extra bottles at the manse," Reva said. "I'll have them brought here."

"Your uncle's care requires redflower, my lady."

He won't last long enough to need it all, she thought then winced at the coldness of it. "He . . . wouldn't wish to see his people in pain." She turned to Arken, clasping his hand. "Get some rest."

She sought out Lord Antesh, finding him in a room in the gate-house arguing with Lord Arentes about how best to distribute the men. "They'll know by now that concentrating against one or two points will avail them nothing," he said with an air of forced patience. "Next time they'll try to test us in several places at once. The Father knows they have the strength to do it."

"We must make a stand," Arentes replied with a sniff. "Keep our best men concentrated for a counterstroke should they break through."

"Should they break through, this city is lost in any case, my lord."

They both fell silent as she approached, Antesh betraying the same odd expression as when he and the other men had bowed to her. Arentes was more guarded, perhaps not willing to believe the wild stories circling the walls, something she found she liked him for. "Is there a problem, my lords?"

"The Lord Archer seeks to exert control over my men, my lady," Arentes said. "Command of the House Guard and the City Guard was given to me. Already too many of my best men have been hived off to bolster the . . . amateur elements of the defence. Further weakening will reduce our ability to contain a serious assault."

"And the assaults we've faced already haven't been serious?" Antesh scoffed, his patience clearly running thin. "My lady, this city stands or falls on the strength we can place on the walls. If we are attacked at several points at once . . ."

She held up a hand. "My lords, in truth I see merit in both your arguments." She stepped closer to the map spread out on the table between them. *Why did this place have to be so big?* "If I may make a suggestion." She pointed to the barracks near the centre of the city. "Keeping so many men here seems pointless. If the Volarians do manage to seize a section of the wall, it'll take them too long to get there and drive them back. However, if the force is split into four, one for each quarter of the city, they can rush to wherever the threat is greatest in their sector. I suggest the House Guard be quartered here, just back from the gate. The City Guard divided into three and placed according to Lord Arentes's discretion."

Antesh considered the map for a moment then raised his eyebrows at Arentes. The old commander stroked his pointed beard then gave a slow nod. "There . . . may be some value to such a stratagem." He lifted his helmet from the table and gave a short bow. "I'd best be about it, my lord, my lady."

"I think he likes you," Antesh said when Arentes had gone. "Bit of a twinkle in his eye when you're around."

"Watch your tongue, my lord," Reva told him without much conviction. "How many did we lose today?"

"Thirty-five dead, twenty more wounded. Not a bad rate of exchange considering how many bodies lie on the other side of these walls."

"These slavers waste their men like cheap corn. How does such indifference breed loyalty?"

"Loyalty and fear are often the same thing, especially in war." He paused, expression guarded. "May I enquire as to the health of the Fief Lord?"

Reva saw little point in concealment. "He's dying. With the Father's grace he may last another month."

"I see. I'm sorry, my lady. He . . . proved a better man than most in the end."

"The end is not yet come." She held up her wych-elm bow. "You owe me a story."

"Arren was the finest bowsmith known to Cumbraelin history," Antesh said. They were on the battlements, touring the eastern section, Reva forcing polite nods at the reverent greetings, tolerating the stares and whispered awe. "Possibly the finest in the world. So great was his skill and so impressive were his bows that some have claimed there was a touch of the Dark to their fashioning. In truth, I think he was just a highly skilled man who saw great art in an ancient craft. From an early age he was crafting bows of great power but also beauty."

Antesh held up his own bow, displaying the thick stave, smoothed by years of use. "The longbow is powerful, and there's a pleasing aspect to its simplicity, but Arren brought an elegance to it, somehow managing to decorate the stave without diminishing its power. Naturally his bows carried a high price, though when the Lord of Cumbrael came calling he was wise enough to work for free." His eyes moved to her own bow.

"He made this for my great-grandfather?"

"That he did, and four more like it, all decorated differently to reflect the lord's various interests, literature, music and so on. Yours appears to be the hunting bow. The lord decreed they were his gift to future generations of the Mustor family. But, within a few short years, they were all lost when Janus set about forcing us into his new Realm. Arren himself died in a raid on his village, though there's a story Janus had wanted to take him alive and had the men responsible executed, but who can say?"

He halted, resting his back against the wall, regarding her with the same troubled expression from before, when he had named the bow. "And now here you are, lost daughter of House Mustor, making an art of battle the way Arren made an art of the bow, carrying one of your family's greatest treasures found by pure chance. A life of war, sustained by mere luck, has given me occasion to doubt the sight of the Father. But you, my lady, do give me pause."

She moved next to him, looking at the far bank. There was a caravan making its way towards the Volarian camp, bulky wagons drawn by oxen, men in black riding escort. After a moment they came to a halt, one of the riders dismounting and moving to the last wagon. He disappeared inside for a moment then emerged pulling a young man behind him. The man had something binding his wrists, making it seem as if he begged as the rider forced him to his knees. Something glittered in the rider's hand and the young man fell forward, a faint plume of red trailing from his neck. The rider bent down to remove his chains then remounted his horse, the caravan continuing on at a sedate pace leaving the corpse behind on the bank.

"I too have doubted the sight of the Father," Reva confessed. "I have seen ugliness, cruelty, lies . . . betrayal. But I've also seen beauty, kindness and friendship. If this city falls, I'll never see any of it again, nor will any of us. And I have a sense the Father's sight does fall here. I can't explain it, but I know it."

She watched the caravan until it came to a halt on the fringes of the Volarian camp, not fully within the picket line.

"They haven't fortified the eastern bank," she observed to Antesh. "We have boats don't we?"

Antesh refused to countenance her going, to the point that he threatened to give up his Lordship and become a common archer if she didn't agree. He sent thirty picked men in a dozen boats, launched from the north shore of the city shortly past midnight. The Volarians had left them in peace this night so all was quiet until they returned, pulling hard on the oars towards the eastern wall, the slavers' camp burning behind them and each boat laden with freed captives. The tide was friendly at this hour and they didn't have to fight the current, but the Volarians provided plenty of danger in the sheets of arrows they launched in pursuit. Most boats pulled free but the last fell victim to the iron rain. They had freed over forty people, about half Realm Guard, the others Cumbraelin, mostly younger folk, signs of recent mistreatment obvious in the pale-faced stares of the women.

The picked men had also contrived to bring her a gift. He was a tall man in a black leather jerkin with large hands that would plainly have preferred to be holding a whip rather than confined by his own manacles.

He drew back from the sight of Reva as the picked men dragged him ashore, eyes wide in fear, his lips forming a tremulous whisper. *"Elverah!"*

"What do you want done, my lady?" asked the raid leader, a hard-eyed veteran Antesh knew from the desert war.

"Put him on top of the gatehouse," she said. "Wait until midmorning to be sure they're all awake to see it, then cut his throat."

PART IV

You will know him by the blade he carries and the Dark-born skill with which he wields it, for none who know the love of the Father may defeat the Darkblade yet all must stand against him.

—THE TEN BOOKS, BOOK 4:
PROPHECY, VOL. 7: DREAMS OF THE MAIDEN

VERNIERS' ACCOUNT

Another interminable day and still it hadn't fallen. More smoke, more wounded straggling back, more rage from the general. It has caused me guilt since, but I must confess I began to hate these Cumbraelins as much as he did, for if they would just succumb to their inevitable defeat, then there would be no more reason for me to be there on that hateful ship suffering his inventive cruelties.

I had come to understand that the general was not a truly intelligent man, he was cunning and manipulative with a keen eye for opportunity, but so are many children. No, I am ever more convinced he was in fact a stupid man, but privilege had contrived to provide him an education, and an educated sadist knows well how to punish a scholar. I was commanded to learn by heart the complete poems of Kirval Draken, easily the worst poet in Volarian, or any language for that matter, and guilty of inflicting the most sentimental, unmetred drivel on the human ear. I was given an hour to learn all forty poems and recite them perfectly for the general's entertainment, standing on the prow of the ship, calling forth the doggerel as sweat streamed down my face and back, for he had promised instant death if I stumbled but once.

"My lady's lips bud like roses, and burn like fire upon mine own, I weep my tears of joy then grief, for now our love has flown."

"Excellent!" the general applauded, lifting his wine cup in appreciation. "More!"

"A hero comes with sword laid bare, his steel shines bright and true . . ."

He waved me to silence as a messenger approached from the shore, climbing aboard and handing over a scroll. "A breakthrough, eh?" he said to the messenger. "About time."

"Yes, Honoured General. My commander advises that with sufficient reinforcement the city will be ours by nightfall."

"No. The reserve must be husbanded to secure the rest of this rain-sodden dung pile. Tell him to hold off the attacks in other sectors and concentrate on the breakthrough. And tell him if this city isn't mine by nightfall, I'll expect him to have secured a sufficiently heroic death, because he'll get none from me."

He waved the messenger away and turned back to me. "Do you know, slave, I believe I've forgotten where we left off. Let's start from the beginning shall we?"

He had me recite it all three times over, every dreadful line penned by that talentless Volarian dullard. Even now, so many years later, I can still recite Draken at will. Not quite the worst of my scars, but still a painful reminder.

I was released come the afternoon, sent below to my cabin whilst he occupied himself with another pleasure slave until word of victory came. I sank onto my bunk, shaking with exhaustion and fear, and would have vomited if my stomach had anything to give. However, even this mean respite was to be cut short. The door opened and one of the mistress's slaves beckoned to me. "You're wanted."

She was in her own cabin, a cavernous space of silk drapery and cushioned comfort in comparison to my narrow prison. She wore a white gown with a neckline plunging to the soft curve of her belly, the skirts transparent and revealing as she walked towards me, a little unsteady on her feet and a wine cup raised to her lips. "You've heard, no doubt?" she asked in slow deliberate tones. "The great siege is almost over? My honoured husband's triumph nearly complete?"

"I have, Mistress. A great day."

She sputtered into her wine, stumbling as she laughed. "A great day! Yes, an ancient child wins a new toy. A great day indeed." She frowned, blinking and grimacing. "I haven't been drunk for over fifty years. I think I'm remembering why."

Fifty years? She saw my confusion and laughed again, just a small giggle, like a little girl with a secret. "Older than I look, my lord. How much older do you think?" She moved closer, making me fight the urge to step away. "Honestly now, how old would you say I am?" She pushed an insistent finger into my chest. "And I command you to speak the truth!"

I took a breath, wondering how a man could feel so much fear and still keep his mind. "I cannot believe my mistress is more than thirty years old."

"Thirty?" She stepped back, pretending offence. "I'll have you know I was no more than twenty-eight when I made my bargain, and that was over three hundred years ago."

She stood regarding me in silence, drinking more wine, eyes narrowed and causing me to consider if she was as drunk as she appeared. "Nothing to say?" she asked after a moment.

"Forgive me, Mistress, but that is impossible."

"Yes," she murmured, moving closer again, pressing herself against me, her head resting on my chest. "And yet here I stand, with so many memories. And I am still beautiful am I not? Do you not desire me, my lord? Or is your mind still so full of your dead poetess?"

The anger returned and I forced it down, knowing it to be a traitor. "My mistress is very beautiful."

"I am. But you do not desire me, I feel it. And I know why." She raised her gaze, searching my face. "You see it, don't you? You feel it?"

"Mistress?"

"The weariness. Who would have thought that I should grow so tired? So utterly weary. You would not believe how many have been drained to give me so many years, so much life wasted to keep a tired old woman on this earth, cursed to marry a murderous fool and witness his slaughters. That was the bargain we made, you see? Power for years, though only for those who wear the red of course, and even then only a select few. It made us the true power, the Council a convenient fiction. We, the endlessly young, and ever more weary, are the real power, for now they clamour for our favour. All those red-clad idiots, begging for a chance at the same bargain. We think we are slave owners, we are fools. We are the slaves. The great gift we bargained for was the greatest of chains."

Her hand came up, swift and smooth, and I felt the chill of a steel blade against my neck. "You spurn me," she said in a wounded tone. "Lusting after some book-loving corpse when you could have me. Do you know how many lovers I've had? How many men have begged just to plant a single kiss on my foot?"

"I will happily kiss my mistress's foot," I said, words softly spoken for the knife blade was pressed hard into my flesh and I felt a single drop of blood trickle down my neck.

"But you don't want to. You want your Alpiran bitch back. Maybe I'll send you to meet her. Would you like that?"

I never understood why, and I have tried very hard for many years to comprehend it, but at that moment all the fear fled and I felt what she felt, a great and terrible weariness. I do recall that I knew my death was now unavoidable. Her husband's anger or the overseer's whip would see me dead tomorrow or, if I was extremely fortunate, the day after.

I stepped back from her, opening my arms as the blood seeped from the shallow cut she had given me. "There was no poetess," I said. "No woman. But I did love, and the man I loved died, killed by the man who I hope with all my heart comes here now to kill you and that vile wretch you call your husband. You offer me a gift, Mistress. I welcome it, for it means I will no longer have to stomach the thought of sharing the same air as you."

She stared at me for a long moment as I marvelled at the steady beat of my heart. Is this courage? I wondered. Is this what the Hope Killer feels when he rides to battle? This strange calm.

"I often look for distraction amongst the slaves," she said. "I find it dispels the weariness, for a time. And you are so very talented." She tossed the knife away, sending it clattering across the floor. "Go and write some more flattering nonsense," she said, slumping onto the cushions with a tired wave of her hand. "It'll probably buy you a few more days."

I was summoned back to the upper deck barely two hours later, by which time my newly discovered calm had evaporated. Fornella sat next to her husband, apparently sober now, and dressed more appropriately in an elegant gown of red-and-black chiffon. She gave me the barest glance and turned back to the general. "The overseers are properly educated, I assume?"

The general seemed pensive, his time with the pleasure slave having done little to ease his temper. "Leave the practicalities to me, true-heart," he muttered. "Your family will get its share of any we find, as it always does." His gaze fixed on me and the scroll in my hand. "Your latest account, scribbling slave?"

"Yes, Master."

"Well give it here, let's see if you continue to earn my indulgence." He was unrolling the scroll when a guard called out the approach of another messenger. "Finally." He tossed the scroll onto the map table, standing with a studied air of stoic reflection, the dignified commander accepting news of his hard-won victory.

"Has the witch been captured?" he asked the messenger, looking off into the middle distance and speaking in an almost wistful tone. "Or did she die fighting? I expect she did. Strange that I should find room in my heart to admire such a creature . . ."

"Forgive me, Honoured General!" the messenger blurted. He wore the armour of an officer in the Free Cavalry, his face tense and slicked with sweat. "I come with graver tidings. A rider was found by one of our scout troops this morning, the only survivor of the Twelfth Free Sword Battalion. It seems he was captured and then set free. He brings word of an army marching towards us with great haste."

The general stared at him. "An army? What army?"

"Their number is estimated at over fifty thousand." The officer took a folded piece of parchment from his belt and held it out to the general. "The man was also given a message for you, Honoured General."

The general flicked a hand at me. "Read it. I don't speak their babble."

I took the parchment from the officer and unfolded it. "The message is in Volarian, Master," I said.

"Just read it."

I briefly scanned the contents and felt my already speeding heart increase the pitch of its hammering. I cast a furtive glance at the scroll I had given him earlier, wondering if I could contrive to retrieve it in the confusion that would doubtless follow my reading of this message.

"To the commander of Volarian forces currently besieging the city of Alltor," I began, hoping he hadn't noticed the slight hesitation. "You are hereby ordered to disarm, surrender all captives and stand ready to receive justice for your many crimes. If you comply with this order, your men will be spared. You will not. Signed under the King's Word, Tower Lord of the Northern Reaches, Vaelin Al Sorna."

CHAPTER ONE
Vaelin

The beauty of the forest was revealed in daylight, the sun painting an ever-changing canvas of dappled clearings and great old trees, gently flowing streams tracking to shallow waterfalls and pools of clear water. Vaelin felt the army's fears abate somewhat as they marched, won over by the unspoiled majesty of the forest, even giving voice to a few marching songs, though the often profane content seemed out of place amongst the trees, like a curse whispered in an Alpiran temple. The blood-song had never lifted from the moment he entered the trees, soft and melodious but also carrying a graver note, not in warning but respect. *So old,* he wondered. *Far older than the people who worship it.*

Four days in and Hera Drakil advised they were about halfway through, this being the narrowest stretch of forest between the Realm and the Reaches. Vaelin had given up trying to judge just how many Seordah travelled with them, and asking their guide proved pointless as the Seordah saw little meaning in numbers. "Many," the hawk-faced man had said with a shrug. "Many and many."

Although his soldiers may have been growing accustomed to the forest, his other recruits proved less than enamoured. "How much longer?" demanded Lorkan, forgetting his usual effusive courtesies. There was a deep line in the centre of his youthful brow and his eyes had the sunken look brought on by constant pain. Marken and Cara seemed only marginally less discomfited, both fidgeting and restless as they sat eating their cold breakfast. Weaver alone seemed unconcerned, hands busy with the hemp the Seordah had provided. For some reason he had abandoned baskets for a tightly bound length of strong rope, already ten feet long and growing every day.

"Four days only," Vaelin assured Lorkan.

"Faith, I don't know if I can stand it." He rubbed his fingers against his temples. "Can't you feel it, my lord?"

"Feel what?"

"The weight," Cara said, breaking her usual silence. "The weight of such a great gift."

"Whose gift?" Vaelin asked.

The look on her face told him she wondered if any awe she may have felt might have been misplaced. "The forest, Lord Vaelin. The forest has a gift all its own, covering every tree, branch and leaf." She clasped her hands together, forcing a faint smile. "I daresay we'll get used to it. The Seordah seem to cope well enough."

Why them and not me? he thought later. *Why do I feel nothing but welcome?*

"Because it welcomes you," Dahrena told him that night after their reading lesson. "It knows you, sees your soul."

"You talk as if it's alive."

The look she gave him was a harsher echo of Cara's. "Of course it's alive. Ancient life surrounds us on all sides, for hundreds of miles, nothing but life, breathing, feeling and seeing. It sees you and likes what it sees."

"Did it see you? When you first came here."

"I was a child then, when father found me. I thought it was a dream, the wolf, the forest's welcome." She fell silent, returning to binding a fletching to one of her arrows. Like the Seordah, she made her own, hands moving with unconscious skill and precision. Drakil had given her a bow some days before, much the same as his own but with pictograms etched into the stave, at first glance crude representations of the beasts of the forest but possessing an elegant clarity on closer inspection. From her reverent expression as she accepted the weapon he deduced it held some great significance for them both.

"Do you remember a time before?" he asked. "Your childhood amongst your people?"

"The Lonak are not my people. I can remember no more than a few words of their language. I recall a village, somewhere in the mountains. A number of women, harsh and quick with the back of their hands, but also kind sometimes. I recall a night of flames and screams and blood, I think they died that night. There was a man with a knife, walking slowly towards me, black against the flames . . . then there was the wolf. I think he killed the man with the knife, though I have no memory of it. He came and crouched down before me and I felt an urging to climb onto his back.

"We ran for such a long time, me clinging to his fur, the air cold on my face. I wasn't afraid, I was joyful, and sad when it ended somewhere dark and surrounded by trees. I got down from his back and he blessed me, his tongue covering my face, banishing fear. Then he was gone. Father found me in the morning, the first time the Seordah had ever allowed a Marelim Sil to walk the forest, and I was almost the first thing he saw."

From her tone he deduced she had long reconciled herself to the conclusion he had just drawn. *This was no accident. We are both children of the wolf.*

"How many times have you seen it?" he asked.

"Just twice, including the day we came here. And you?"

"Four." *Though there may have been one other time, when it was living in a statue . . .* "Every time it has saved me, as it saved you."

Her fingers became still and he saw her fear, the same tension he had seen when they first confronted Wise Bear. "For what?"

"I don't know. For this perhaps, a war that needed us to fight it."

"I was so young when he blessed me it's only now I come to

realise how it felt, the sense of a being so old I could never truly comprehend it. He must have seen countless petty feuds between the strange two-legged furless things that run around the earth, countless wars. Why is this one different?"

He recalled Aspect Arlyn's words on the fate of the Realm when he had questioned the wisdom of supporting Janus's mad war: *It will certainly fall. Not to warring fiefs once more but to utter ruin, the earth scorched, the forests burned to cinder and all the people, Realm Folk, Seordah and Lonak dead. What else would you have us do?*

"Because this one will claim his world as well as ours," he said. "I think we both know we face other enemies than the Volarians."

"Hence the good brother's continued presence." She glanced over at Brother Harlick, engaged in an animated conversation with Alornis. His sister seemed to find the scholar's inexhaustible knowledge fascinating and could spend hours assailing him with questions in the as-yet-vain hope she could stump him.

"He knows far more than he shares," Dahrena said.

"He'll share it," Vaelin assured her. "If I have to, I'll wring every ounce of knowledge from him until he has no more breath to speak it."

He spent the next morning travelling with the Eorhil, the horse-people leading their mounts through the trees and displaying almost as much discomfort as the gifted. "Horses can't see the sky," Sanesh Poltar said, smoothing a hand over his stallion's head, the animal's ears constantly twitching and his eyes wide. "Don't like it. Neither do I."

"The Eorhil are not welcome in the forest?" Vaelin asked.

Wisdom gave a soft laugh as she walked alongside the war chief. "We never have reason to come here. Eorhil and Seordah speak much the same tongue and trade for skins and weapons, but we are not the same people. They are of the forest, we are of the plains."

"Do the Eorhil have stories," Vaelin asked, "of the time before the plains, before the Marelim Sil came?"

Sanesh and Wisdom exchanged an amused glance. "Never a time before the plains," Sanesh explained. "Eorhil always ride the plains. Always will. There was a time the Seordah were not so many in the forest, so it's said by the grandfathers who speak of their grandfathers. But we had no knowledge of the Marelim Sil until they came to dig for stones in the hills."

"But you do know of the blind woman?" Vaelin said to Wisdom.

Both Eorhil instantly became subdued, Sanesh striding on a ways and tugging his horse along.

Wisdom walked in silence for several moments, face set and closed. When she spoke again her tone was heavy with reluctance. "There's a city, a ruin on the fringes of the Lonak Dominion. The Eorhil do not like the place and stay away, the grandfathers tell of troubled dreams and madness for any who venture there. But as a girl I was ever curious, for curiosity breeds wisdom, although I was yet to earn my name. So I journeyed there, alone, finding just the remnants of something that may have been wondrous in its time. I made my camp amongst the ruins and a woman came to my fire, a Seordah woman with empty eyes, although they could see me. I was not overly afraid for the Seordah are known to birth more gifted than the Eorhil. She said she also had journeyed far to view these ruins and we spent the night exchanging what little knowledge we had about the place. She pointed me to a certain stone amongst the rubble, very small, small enough to carry in both hands in fact, but also perfectly square, the surface smooth and undamaged. I asked her if she wanted it but she just shook her head, 'This is for you,' she said. So I picked it up."

"It took you somewhere," Vaelin prompted when the old woman fell silent once again.

Wisdom shook her head. "No. It gave me . . . knowledge. So much knowledge, all at once. Your language, the Lonak tongue, even the words spoken by the people we go to fight, and many more besides. I can recite every catechism of your Faith and every word in the Ten Books of the World Father, name all the Alpiran gods and relate every legend told by the Lonak. There was no insight to it, no context, just knowledge. It . . . hurt. So much that I fainted. When I woke the blind woman had gone, but the knowledge hadn't."

"So you are gifted?"

She shook her head with a small sigh. "Cursed, some might say. More puzzled than anything. That stone, that small perfect stone, filled with knowledge about the people of this world, but it was so old, crafted long before any of those languages were spoken as they are now. Who made it? And why?"

"Do you still have it?"

She raised her head, eyes searching for a gap in the canopy, no doubt hoping for a glimpse of sky. "No," she said, smiling a little as a small patch of blue appeared above. "I found a heavier stone and smashed it to dust."

The forest began to thin the next day, there was a noticeable widening of ground between the trees and clearings grew more numerous, although it remained dense in comparison to the Urlish. The mood of the men lightened further, the availability of open ground enabling more regiments to camp together, bringing a welcome sense of security. The forest's charms may have won many hearts, but the basic fear of it remained, the ever-present knowledge that they didn't belong here. The comparatively open ground also enabled Vaelin to gain a better appreciation for the Seordah's numbers as he moved from clearing to clearing.

"Has to be well over eight thousand of them," Nortah opined that evening at the council of captains.

"Ten thousand, eight hundred and seventy-two," Brother Hollun reported. "Those that have remained within sight long enough to count that is. Bringing the total strength of the army to just over thirty thousand men."

"I was wondering if we shouldn't give the army a name," Nortah said. "The Army of the North or something."

Vaelin glanced at Captain Adal, who gave a nod. "Binding the men under a single name couldn't hurt morale, my lord."

"Very well," Vaelin said. "I'll ask my sister to design a banner, something suitably fierce." His eyes tracked over the map. "The Seordah advise we are but one day's march from Nilsael. Captain Orven, take your men and scout east. Captain Adal, send a company of North Guard west and take another south yourself. Any Volarian forces of appreciable size within thirty miles are to be reported to me as soon as possible." He looked at Dahrena. "We will, of course, require deeper reconnaissance."

"You'll have it tonight, my lord."

"My thanks, my lady." He moved back from the table, addressing them all. "In the morning a full inspection of kit and weapons will be conducted and we will march into the Realm in battle order. Make sure every man under your command understands that we are now marching to war and like to find it in short order. If any were thinking of desertion, this is their last chance, though I wouldn't advise making the return journey through the forest."

"Good country," Sanesh Poltar commented, on horseback once again and clearly happier for it. Northern Nilsael was indeed well suited to cavalry, rolling fields of grass and low hills stretching off towards the south. "How many elk roam here?"

"None that I know of," Vaelin replied. "But you'll find deer and wild goats as we travel south."

"Goat," Sanesh said with distaste. "Takes ten of them to skin one shelter. One elk will give you two."

The army trooped from the forest in close order, well-dressed ranks moving with accustomed uniformity, though not quite in step. The ten regiments of infantry moved in a thick column, two regiments wide, the Eorhil on both flanks and the Seordah bringing up the rear in a mass of warriors, the various clans clustering together but giving only the vaguest impression of military organisation. The new banner of the Army of the North fluttered at the head of the infantry column, borne by Foreman Ultin himself, who had been fierce in warding off other hands when Vaelin handed it to him in the morning. Alornis had enlisted the help of the army's tailors in realising her design, a great white hawk fringed with an Eorhil lance on one side and a Seordah war club on the other. Below the hawk was the bright azure oval of a bluestone.

"A little simplistic, perhaps," she had said when showing him her sketch.

"When it comes to soldiers," he told her with a hug, "you can never be too simplistic."

He waited until the last Seordah had emerged from the forest and spent a while scanning the dark mass of trees, wondering if perhaps he would find a bright pair of green eyes staring back. There was nothing, just the trees and the deepening shadows, but there was a murmur from the blood-song, a forlorn note, uncertain but with enough ancient strength to carry a sense of hope.

"Good luck to you too," Vaelin replied in a whisper before turning Flame's head towards the south.

He marched them south for fifteen miles then called a halt, setting out pickets three times the usual strength. The Eorhil galloped off unbidden, some whooping with joy at the release from the forest's strictures, the war-bands returning one by one as night fell, some bearing a few deer they had managed to bring down. The Seordah had encamped on the northern fringe of the army, remaining as close to the forest as they could. They were quiet as they sat about their fires, Vaelin seeing just grim acceptance on the faces of the men and women as they mended their arrows and sharpened their knives.

He found Dahrena seated outside Hera Drakil's shelter, eyes closed and face immobile. The Seordah chief sat beside her, the concern on his face no doubt a mirror of Vaelin's own.

"Once a child was lost," he said when Vaelin sat down at the fire. "We feared he had been taken by a wild cat. Adra Dural sat like this for a whole night then took me to where he could be found. He had slipped on a rock in the river and hit his head. He lived but now has trouble remembering his name."

"Adra Dural?" Vaelin asked.

"Flying Spirit. What else could we name her?"

Dahrena gave a soft groan and opened her eyes, face tensing with sudden cold. Vaelin pulled a fur over her shoulders as she shuffled closer to the fire. "You were gone too long," he said.

"There was a lot to see," she replied in a gasp. "You were right, about Alltor. It still holds, and a very bright soul burns atop its walls."

"And between them and us?"

"Volarians move in large groups across Asrael and Cumbrael. Fewer in Nilsael but I saw more moving out from Varinshold. There are other souls in the forest to the north of the city, burning bright but also dark, some darker than the Volarians. I had a sense much killing was being done there." She paused to gulp water from her canteen. "What remains of the Realm Guard is moving north of the Greypeaks, trying for the Nilsaelin border. I guessed their strength at perhaps three thousand men. Their souls are dark with fear and the burden of defeat. I caught a glimpse of a large body of men approaching from western Nilsael, but I couldn't linger any further to discern their identity or intent."

"You have done more than I could ask, my lady."

Off the eastern perimeter a horn sounded the approach of mounted men. Vaelin rose as Captain Adal galloped into the camp, reining in and offering a salute, his face grave. "My lord, we found a village."

The bodies had been piled in the village square, stripped naked and bleached white, the limbs already stiffening in the morning air. Most had had their throats cut but some showed signs of having died fighting.

"Old people and children," Nortah observed. "For the most part."

"They kill what they can't sell," Dahrena said. She spoke in an even voice but tears streamed from her eyes as she viewed the carcasses. "Like a cattleman weeding out poor stock."

The village itself had been ransacked, valuables taken but the buildings left standing. It had been a pretty place of wattle-and-daub-walled cottages, thatched roofs and a tall windmill standing atop a nearby hill, the blades still turning, oblivious to the fate of those who had built it. "Build a fire," Vaelin told Adal. "Have Brother Kehlan say the words."

"Snowdance has the scent," Nortah said, pointing to the war-cat as she crouched with ears flat, staring eastwards at the wagon tracks leading away from the village.

"They'll have a day's lead on us," Adal pointed out.

"I'll only need a day," Nortah replied with a questioning look at Vaelin.

"What do you require?"

"A company of North Guard should do, plus Lorkan."

"And me, brother." Vaelin reached for Flame's reins, hauling himself into the saddle. "I should like to see the man who can't be seen."

"I don't know if I can." Lorkan's hands were shaking as he held the knife, eyes bright in the predawn gloom. "I've never . . ."

Vaelin saw Nortah's head slump a little, knowing he was wrestling with his own reluctance. "Have we ever asked you for anything?" he said to the gifted youth. "In all the years you have been sheltered, fed, educated *and* tolerated, has any price ever been asked?"

"Teacher, I . . ."

"Here." Vaelin took the knife from him and returned it to his sheath, holding it out blade first. "Hold it like this, hit them with the pommel, as hard as you can just below the ear. If they don't go down first time, hit them again."

Lorkan hesitated then reached for the knife, turning and walking towards the fires of the Volarian camp. He paused after a few steps and turned back to Nortah. "Teacher, if I fall tell Cara . . ." He trailed off then forced a grin. "Tell her I was a hero. She won't believe it, but it may make her laugh, finally."

He resumed walking, his slender form black against the pale orange horizon, moving without any attempt at stealth or conceal-ment. After he had gone about fifty paces Vaelin heard Adal and the other North Guard utter soft gasps of surprise and bafflement. Vaelin frowned, seeing only a young man walking across a field.

"Shouldn't be long now." Nortah notched an arrow to his bow and started after Lorkan. "We'll secure the slaves. Come on fast when you hear the commotion."

"He'll be seen," Vaelin said, nodding at Lorkan's retreating shadow.

"Really?" Nortah smiled over his shoulder. "I can't see him." He moved off in a low crouch, Snowdance slipping into the grass at his side.

"He's right, my lord," Adal said in a whisper. "The boy just . . . vanished."

They waited as the horizon faded to black and the stars were revealed in a cloudless void, the half-moon adding a pale blue tint to the swaying grass.

"Erm, my lord?" Vaelin turned to see Adal holding out a sword, handle first, the blade resting on his forearm.

"No thank you, Captain." The canvas bundle was tied to his saddle, the knots still firmly unpicked. "I have a feeling I shan't need it tonight."

The screams began shortly after, choked off by Snowdance's wailing growls. Vaelin spurred Flame into a gallop, the North Guard following instantly as they covered the ground to the Volarian camp in the space of a few heartbeats. He pulled up in the centre of the camp, seeing a slave-hound sail through the air, trailing blood from a torn throat as Snowdance tossed it aside and sought another victim. Bodies lay between the wagons, several pierced with arrows, most clearly the result of the war-cat's atten-tions. A few Volarians tried to assail the North Guard with whips and short swords but were swiftly cut down, some throwing their weapons aside and raising arms in a plea for mercy; however, the sights in the village had left the men of the Reaches with no inclination to show it.

He found Nortah helping Lorkan free the slaves from the wagons. They numbered at least a hundred people, evidence that the slavers had visited more than one village. On being unshackled some of them went wild, attacking any Volarians they could find, the living and the dead, but most just stumbled about in shock. One of the freed men recognised Vaelin and immediately sank to his knees, shouting gratitude with tears streaming from his eyes, soon joined by a dozen or more ragged people. He dismounted and went to them, raising his hands to call for silence.

"They answered us," the man who had recognised him said, still kneeling. "We called to the Departed to send you and they did."

Vaelin reached down and pulled the man to his feet. "No-one sent me . . ." he began then stopped at the sight of the naked devotion in the man's eyes. Most of the other freed captives had gathered round now, all staring with unnerving intensity, as if he were something that had stepped from a dream. "I come in answer to the Realm's need," he told them. "I offer only war and struggle for any who wish to join with me. Those who don't are free to go."

"We go nowhere but with you, my lord," the weeping man said, immediately echoed by the others. His hands clutched at Vaelin's arms, frenzied and desperate. "I was with you at Linesh. I knew you would never forsake us." The other captives closed in around him, voices raised in an awed babble. "You will lead us to freedom . . . The Tower Lord is blessed by the Departed . . . Give us justice, my lord . . . They murdered my children . . ."

"All right!" Nortah moved through the crowd, pushing them back with his bow. "Give His mighty Lordship some room, you fawning fools you."

Eventually the North Guard had to intervene to release Vaelin from the mob's adoration, Captain Adal leading Flame to his side so he could mount and ride free. "Escort them back to camp," he told the captain. "Weapons for any who want them."

"Even the women, my lord?"

Vaelin recalled the murderous hate in the eyes of a woman he had seen repeatedly lashing a Volarian corpse with her chains. "Even the women. Those unwilling or unsuited to fighting can cook or help Brother Kehlan."

He started back for the camp in company with Nortah and Lorkan, Snowdance bounding on ahead, her tail whipping about as she rolled and leapt in the grass. "She's always like that after a hunt," Nortah explained.

"You are . . . well, brother?" Vaelin ventured, noting a familiar haunted look in his brother's eyes.

"Thought it might have gotten easier," Nortah replied with the faintest of grins. "But even with scum like that, it still hurts as much as it ever did."

"Wasn't so bad," Lorkan said, drinking from a liberated flask of wine. From the slur of his words Vaelin suspected it wasn't his first. "Hit the last bugger like you said, m'lord. Bam bam behind the ear. 'Cept he didn't fall like the others, just staggered about a bit and reached for his sword." Vaelin noted the red-brown stain on Lorkan's hands as he drank some more. "He saw me. They always do when you touch them."

"But only those not gifted," Vaelin said. "We can see you regardless. To others it's as if you vanish."

"Well deduced, my lord." Lorkan bowed in his saddle. "But I don't vanish, not really. It's more like I slip beneath their notice, like the buzz of a fly or the shadow of a bird on the ground. As a child I walked the streets of South Tower for years, stealing at will. They see me but don't see me, so I can steal from them, unless I touch them, then these days it seems I have to kill them." He raised the wine flask to his lips again, gulping and nearly tipping over until Nortah reached out to steady him. "Don't tell Cara, Teacher," the young man said. "What I did. I don't want her to know."

◆ ◆ ◆

They marched on in the morning, halting at midday when Captain Orven rode in with confirmation of Dahrena's warning about a large host approaching from the west. "Twelve miles distant as of this morning, my lord," the guardsman reported. "We only saw the dust and a few outriders so I can't say for sure how many."

Vaelin ordered the regiments into a battle line astride a low hill, facing west with the Eorhil on both flanks and Nortah's archers strung out in a loose skirmish line a hundred paces in front. The Seordah had accepted the role of rear-guard without demur, clustering about the baggage train in their clans, an arrow notched to every bow. Vaelin placed himself in the centre, the North Guard on his left and Orven's men on his right, positioned just to the rear of Foreman Ultin's miners. Dahrena was at his side, patently ignoring Adal's scowl of disapproval.

There was little talk in the ranks, Vaelin recalled that the still-ness before battle had a tendency to calm the tongue. He sat astride Flame, watching the dust-cloud rise above the western hills as the blood-song sang a placid tune lacking any warning. He waited as they came on, loosely ordered companies of light infantry resolving out of the dust, a few troops of cavalry fanning out to cover the flanks. They strung out in a somewhat uneven line some three hundred paces distant, a banner showing an axe within a six-spoked wheel fluttering over the centre of their line.

"Lower weapons!" Vaelin ordered. "Stand easy in the ranks."

The miners stepped aside as he walked Flame forward then spurred to a trot, raising his hand to the man who rode from the Nilsaelin line to greet him, a lean-faced fellow with a muti-lated left ear and close-cropped hair. "I hope you brought more, my lord," Count Marven said. "As I fear this is nowhere near enough."

Fief Lord Darvus Ezua was possibly the oldest human being Vaelin could remember meeting, sitting in his high-backed Lord's Chair, bony hands clutching the rests and regarding Vaelin with a deep scrutiny that reminded him of Janus's owlish gaze. Vaelin and

Dahrena stood before him in a large tent in the centre of the Nilsaelin camp, the old lord flanked by his twin grandsons, both of whom seemed to have made efforts to distinguish themselves from one another with differing armour and mismatched capes. They were, however, both uniformly tall and blond with mirrored faces and, Vaelin noticed, a disconcerting tendency to blink in unison. Count Marven stood in a corner of the tent, his expression one of studied neutrality.

"This little jaunt nearly killed me, you know," Fief Lord Darvus said, his voice marked by a noticeable croak but still strong and clear. "And the poor buggers who had to carry my litter."

"War was ever a demanding master, my lord," Vaelin replied.

"War, is it?" The old man gave a brief cackle. "What makes you think I'm here for that?"

"We are invaded. Why else would you bring your host?"

"A show of strength is important when negotiating. Did the same thing when I bent my knee to Janus, though it was stiff as a board even then. Still made me do it though, the Asraelin bastard."

"Am I to understand, my lord, you intend to treat with the Volarians?"

Vaelin felt Dahrena stiffen at his side and gave her a placating pat on the arm. His meetings with Janus had given him ample experience with scheming old men. *This one makes a show before striking his real bargain.*

"Why shouldn't I?" Darvus returned. "Darnel did and his fief remains unmolested."

Vaelin tried to contain his shock. *The Fief Lord of Renfael a traitor?*

"Didn't know that, eh?" the old lord said with another cackle, easily reading his face. "You've been away too long, boy. Darnel led his knights against the Realm Guard. My agents tell me he's been given half of Asrael in return and lords it over Varinshold as we speak."

"A traitor's example is a poor one to follow, my lord," Vaelin replied.

A genuine anger coloured Darvus's wrinkled face. "My people look to me for protection and I've grown old providing it, swallowing every insult and humiliation heaped upon me by your kings along the way."

"The Volarians will bring no insult or humiliation, it's true. All they bring is death and slavery. We found one of your own villages yesterday, old people and children killed, the others taken in chains. We freed them and they joined us, all willing to fight and die to secure the freedom of this fief and this Realm. If you require an example, I suggest you look no further."

He saw the twins exchange a uniform glance as he described the fate of the village, hands tightening on their sword hilts. *Not their idea,* Vaelin realised. *They think the old man's words genuine.*

"My lord grandfather," the twin on the left said. "In reference to our discussion this morning . . ."

"Shut up, Maeser," the old man snapped. "And you, Kaeser. Your dear departed mother always had wise counsel for me, but all you two ever bleat about is war and swords and horses." He stared at the young lord until he looked away. "Their mother married a Renfaelin knight of great renown," he explained to Vaelin. "Had a son of my own in those days so I didn't see the harm, then the fool manages to pox himself into an early grave without issue and I'm left with these two."

"If I might enquire, my lord," Vaelin said. "What it is you want? I think we both know you have no intention of throwing your lot in with our enemy, and I have little time for elaborate bargaining."

Darvus reclined in his chair, a small pink tongue appearing between his lips for a moment. *Janus was an owl,* Vaelin thought. *Seems this one's a snake.*

"Out!" the Fief Lord barked at his grandsons who both bowed and exited the tent with such synchronised precision it seemed like a rehearsed dance step. "Not you, Marven," Darvus added as the count started for the exit. "I'd like a reliable witness to this little accommodation."

The old lord's gaze swung to Dahrena before he continued. "One of my agents had occasion to meet a fellow from the Reaches recently. A factor from some frost-bitten mining town, seemed to think he'd been poorly treated during a recent difficulty."

Vaelin heard Dahrena utter a soft sigh. *Idiss.*

"Sadly the fellow contrived to get drunk and fall into Frostport harbour," Darvus went on. "But not before he related an interesting story."

"As I said, my lord," Vaelin said. "I have little time."

"Gold," the old man said slowly, his gaze still fixed on Dahrena. "You have been keeping secrets, my lady." He leaned forward, small tongue darting over his lips once more. "One of the lessons taught by a long life is that the opportunity for enrichment comes and goes like an unpredictable tide, and Nilsael is always the last to catch a wave. Not this time. This time we get our share."

"There are sound reasons for keeping such information secret," Dahrena said. "For your fief as well as the Reaches."

"Not any more," the Fief Lord returned. "Not with so many wolves at our door, and Lord Vaelin so badly in need of troops."

"What do you want?" Vaelin asked, his patience reaching its limit.

"My dear departed daughter, keen-minded mother to idiot twins, used to say that gold was like water, it slips through one's fingers with such ease. It's not the man who digs the gold that gets rich, it's the man who sells him the pick." The bony fingers drummed on the armrests for a moment. "All gold mined in the Northern Reaches must be landed and sold in a Nilsaelin port."

"That's all?" Dahrena asked.

The old man smiled and inclined his head. "Quite all my lady."

Every ounce of gold sold within his own borders, Vaelin thought. *Any merchant seeking to buy it will have to come here, along with all their clerks and ships, no doubt laden with goods to trade in kind. The snake will make his fief the richest in the Realm within a generation. Janus would have been impressed.*

"Your terms are acceptable, my lord," he told Darvus. "Subject to ratification by the Crown."

"Crown, is it?" The old man gave another cackle, raising a skeletal hand to point a finger at Vaelin with no sign of any tremble. "There's only one head left fit to wear it and it stands before me right now."

CHAPTER TWO
Lyrna

Captain Belorath was a fine Keschet player, demonstrating a fundamental understanding of the game's many nuances whilst employing the more subtle strategies that set the skilled opponent apart. Lyrna beat him in twenty moves. It would have been fifteen but she thought it best to allow him some dignity in front of his crew.

He glowered at her from across the board, hands moving in a blur as he removed the remaining pieces. "We go again."

"As you wish," Lyrna said, removing her own pieces. For all his skill the captain laboured against a basic misunderstanding of the most important element of Keschet: the placement of the pieces. Every move flowed from this seeming formality. She had already won when he failed to place sufficient spearmen on the left side of the board to counter the lancers she would launch six moves in. *The game starts when you place your first piece,* her father had instructed all those years ago when he first taught a five-year-old a game that baffled most adults. Within a year she had beaten him in an epic battle of one hundred and twenty-three moves that would have made a salient entry in the history of the game, if anyone else had been there to bear witness. They never played again and the board and pieces disappeared from her room soon after.

The captain slammed his emperor onto the third square from the left in the first row, a standard placement if one intended an aggressive strategy, or sought to conceal defence with offence. She responded by placing one of her archers in the middle of the second row, continuing to build a standard formation in response to his seemingly complex arrangement. *The Emperor's Gambit,* she thought with an inward sigh as crewmen and Realm folk wagered around them. The odds seemed to be in her favour. *Thirteen moves this time.*

In the event she managed to string it out to seventeen, any more generosity would have been obvious.

"The Dark," one of the crew whispered as she plucked the captain's emperor from the board.

"Dark or not," Harvin replied with a laugh. "You owe me two cups of rum, my friend."

Lyrna cast her gaze at the placid sea as the increasingly red-faced captain set about removing his pieces once more. *Three days and not a whisper of wind,* she thought, straightening as a familiar sight came into view, the huge fin leaving an impressive wake in the becalmed waters before slipping under.

The captain had ordered the crew to the oars when the wind died, but the heat of these climes forced frequent halts lest the crew collapse from exhaustion. The Realm folk had taken their turn at the oars, Lyrna included, though their inexpert lack of rhythm often proved more of a hindrance. It was during the latest break from rowing that the captain had produced a Keschet board and commanded his first mate to play, beating him in only forty moves, apparently something of a record on the ship.

"Our lady can beat that," Benten had said, his tone one of complete confidence.

"Is that the case?" The captain's bushy brows knitted together as his gaze found her, rubbing her aching arms as she rested on her oar.

Lyrna gave the young fisherman a hard look. She hadn't shared a single word with him about the game yet instinct seemed to tell him a great deal.

"I can play," she replied with a shrug.

His third try was more impressive, abandoning long-established set attacks for a complex series of feints on the left, seemingly careless of losses, but masking the gradual approach of all three thieves towards the centre.

"Congratulations, Captain," she said with a bow some thirty moves later.

"For what?" he growled, staring at the emperor in her hand.

"For providing me with a unique game." She raised her head as a gentle breeze tickled the still-sensitive burns on her upper cheek. *Strange to feel the wind and not have it tousle one's hair,* she mused. "I believe we're about to resume our voyage."

The breeze built into a strong westerly wind, known to the Meldeneans as the Fruitful Vine as well-laden merchantmen were often to be found following its course. Now though the ocean seemed empty.

"Nothing makes for a clear sea like war," the captain said, joining her at the prow during her customary evening vigil.

"I thought we might see some Alpiran ships at least," she replied.

"They'll all be in port for a good while yet, if they're smart. War makes pirates of all sailors." He moved to the figurehead carved into the prow, a snarling woman with improbably large breasts, extended fangs and clawlike hands reaching out towards the oncoming waves. "Know who this is?"

"I would guess it's Skerva, stealer of souls, in her true form. She was sent by Margentis the Orca god to punish men for their crimes against the sea. It's said she walks amongst us in the guise of a comely maiden, seeking out the most valiant of men so she can feast on their souls."

He traced a hand over Skerva's wooden shoulder. "Have you ever forgotten anything?"

"Not to my knowledge."

"You make my crew nervous, the more fanciful wonder if you aren't her, trapped somehow between your two forms, waiting for the moment to strike."

"Wouldn't that require the presence of valiant men upon whom to slake my unnatural hunger?"

She saw him conceal a smile beneath his beard before he looked out to sea. "Your friend doesn't help."

The swell was high but she could still make out the shark's fin knifing through the waves off the port bow. "That is truly something I can't explain," she said honestly.

"The crew bring word of what those other land-bound whisper in the hold. They talk of a beast charmer."

Fermin's smile before the waters claimed him . . . Remember your promise, my Queen. "He died to free us," she said. "Called the shark somehow. Perhaps that's why it follows, an echo of that calling. Such things are outside my knowledge."

The captain snorted. "Finally, a flaw." His mirth subsided quickly, his expression completely serious. "The Isles are less than a week away."

"Where the Ship Lords await. I'll keep my bargain. They'll find me very convincing, I promise."

"The Ship Lords are one thing, the Shield is another."

The Shield of the Isles. Her brother's spies had brought ample word of him, famed swordsman and pirate, given charge of the defence of the Isles. "He's unlikely to believe me?"

"It's not whether he believes that matters, it's whether he cares." He gestured at the deck and the rigging. "The *Sea Sabre* is his. He oversaw her birth in the yards. Every plank, nail and rope has his hand upon it, and there's plenty of his blood in the deck too. For years we hunted the waves with her, took more gold and cargo than any ship ever born in the Isles. Yet here I am in command of her whilst he skulks on a wave-blasted rock. If his hand had been on her tiller we should have been home by now. And I doubt you'd've taken him in twenty moves."

"Fifteen, I was being kind. Why does he skulk, this great captain of yours?"

Belorath turned back to the sea, voice soft with regret. "Because it's a hard thing for a great man to fail, even when the failure is in securing his own death."

"'The predicted slave yield is estimated at twenty-five thousand,'" Lyrna recited. "'This is low in ratio to the overall population, but the expected high cull rate must be considered. The true value of the Serpent's Den lies in its ports and any ships our forces can capture, the islanders being uncivilised savages with surprisingly well developed skills in this area.'"

The assembled Ship Lords sat in silence as she spoke, most staring in dumb shock. Others, like the man seated in the middle of their line, with growing rage. A wiry man with the aspect of a fox, his gloved hands clenched repeatedly as she spoke on.

"'The Serpent's Den is known to retain a fleet in home waters for defensive purposes and resistance from this quarter can be expected to be fierce. A feinting strategy is therefore recommended, one division engaging the enemy to draw them away from the islands whilst another lands the invasion force. See table seven for suggestions on the makeup of the land forces . . .'"

The wiry man held up a hand and Lyrna fell silent. "Belorath," the Ship Lord said to the captain. "You vouch for this woman's veracity?"

"I do, Lord Ell-Nurin."

The Ship Lord turned back to Lyrna. "You have prepared a full translation, I believe?"

"I have, my lord." She came forward and handed him the bundle of parchment.

"What an accomplished hand you have," Ell-Nurin observed, scanning the first page. "For a merchant's daughter."

"My father relied on me to pen his correspondence, his own hands being victim to the bone ague."

"I am well acquainted with the merchants of Varinshold. Unlike most of my countrymen I was never a pirate and always found a welcome there, provided my hold was full of fresh tea of course. Tell me, what was your father's name? Perhaps I knew him."

"Traver Hultin, my lord. He dealt mostly in silks." A real merchant with a real daughter, one of many to beg her father's favour over the years.

"I've heard the name," Ell-Nurin said. "And yours, lady?"

"Corla, my lord. Merely a mistress, not a lady."

"Quite so. You wish to return to the Realm, I believe?"

"I do, my lord. As do those with whom I escaped."

"The Isles has never welshed on a bargain." He nodded at the captain. "See to it when we're done here. For now, Mistress, please leave us to discuss these matters in private."

She bowed and went to the chamber door, catching only a few words before they closed behind her. "You sent word to him?" Ell-Nurin asked.

"A boat was sent as soon as I arrived, my lord . . ."

The others were waiting on the quay, all dressed in a mismatched variety of Meldenean clothing and looking much like the pirates who had brought them here. They all rose as she approached, hope and wary expectation bright in their eyes.

"The captain will arrange a ship for us," she said. "We should be on our way come the next tide."

Harvin gave a whoop of relief, hugging Benten about the shoulders whilst Orena gave the first smile Lyrna had seen on her lips. Even Iltis seemed on the verge of a grin.

"Why?" said a small voice, and Lyrna turned to find Murel standing apart from the group, eyes downcast.

"What?" Orena asked her.

"Why go back?"

"It's our home," Harvin said.

"My home burned down with my parents inside," Murel responded. "What's there for me now?"

"The Realm is invaded," Lyrna said. "Our people need our help."

"What help can I give?" the girl asked. "I can't fight, have no skills beyond needlework, and I was never even much good at that."

"I saw you claw a man's eyes out on the ship," Harvin pointed out. "Seems to me you fight well enough."

"She has a point," Orena said. "All that awaits us in the Realm is war and death, and I've seen more than enough of both."

"So now what?" Iltis replied. "You'll just wait here for the Volarian fleet to arrive?"

"There are other ports," Murel said. "The Alpiran Empire, the Far West."

"You forget something," Iltis said in a harsh tone, his expression bordering on anger. "We owe this woman a debt. All of us would now be resting in the shark's belly but for her."

"And I'm grateful," Murel said, voice slightly choked as she reached for Lyrna's hand. "I really am. But I'm just a girl, and I've been hurt enough."

Queen of the Unified Realm, Lyrna thought. *Unable to persuade five beggared subjects to risk themselves in her service.* Watching Murel's sniffling, she remembered her first sight of her, the veil of hair over her face as they led her aloft, her whimpered sobs. "I'm sorry," she said, squeezing the girl's hand. "I will not ask any of you to come, you must all make your own choice. But I will sail for the Realm, alone or not."

"Not without me," Iltis stated. "I've not killed enough Volarians yet. Not by far."

"I'm with you, my lady," Benten said. "My father will be expecting me. Can't handle the nets so well by himself any more." From the catch in his voice she knew he was talking about a dead man.

Iltis turned to Harvin. "What about you, outlaw? Got guts enough to fight as well as steal?"

"You saw my guts on the ship, brother," Harvin replied with a dark glower before turning to Lyrna with apologetic eyes, reaching for Orena's hand. "But I have . . . a responsibility now."

Seems I don't see everything after all, Lyrna thought.

"You don't have to go," Murel said, still clutching Lyrna's hand. "Come with us. With you we could do anything, go anywhere . . ." She trailed off, eyes widening as she noticed something over Lyrna's shoulder.

She turned, seeing Ship Lord Ell-Nurin approaching along the wharf with a purposeful stride, flanked by at least twenty armed sailors. He stopped a few yards short as the sailors fanned out on either side and the three men closed in protectively about the women.

"Belorath was slow in relating all details of your voyage," the Ship Lord said. "Including your remarkable facility for Keschet. Traver Hultin liked Keschet too and he did deal mostly in silks, but he smuggled tea and his daughter was fat. Also he rarely shut up about his single visit to the palace, how he had met the King's daughter and been greatly impressed with her knowledge of his favourite game, though he was a rather poor player as I recall."

Ell-Nurin dropped to one knee, keeping his gaze fixed on her face. "On behalf of the Ship Lords' Council, I bid you welcome to the Meldenean Isles, Highness."

They put her in a well-appointed room on the topmost floor of a tall building overlooking the harbour. Iltis had stepped forward to prevent her being taken, Harvin and Benten close behind, but she put a firm hand on his chest. "No, brother."

"Is it true?" he asked her in a whisper, eyes tracking over her face. "Highness?"

She patted his broad chest and smiled. "Don't linger here. Take the others and go, far away like Murel said. Think of it as my first and last royal command."

They left her alone for four days. Servants brought food, bowing and leaving without a word. Later, equally silent maids brought dresses. They were fine but simple, the colours muted. *Suitable for an execution?* she wondered.

Ship Lord Ell-Nurin arrived on the evening of the fourth day as the harbour lights came to life below her, the multiple god-crowned towers of the city fading to dim grey spear-points. The Ship Lord came alone, bowing low once again, face absent of humour or false respect, something she found stirred her gratitude.

"You have everything you require, Highness?" he asked.

"Save my freedom."

"A salient matter we'll get to shortly. I thought you might like to know your subjects refused to leave. They were offered passage to the Realm in accordance with our agreement but steadfastly declined to take it."

"They are unharmed I trust."

"We quartered them downstairs, quite unmolested I assure you." He rose and went to the veranda, standing aside and indicating for her to join him. They stood regarding the darkening city for a time, Ell-Nurin's eyes frequently returning to her face. After a moment she took the scarf from her head and stepped closer to him, angling her head to display the full spectacle. "Please, my lord. Feel free to take a good long look."

"My . . . apologies," he said as she stepped back, tying the scarf back into place. "I merely wished to confirm . . ." He paused, grimacing in discomfort. "I saw you once. It was after the war, you came to the Varinshold docks to present rewards to one of your brother's ships, returned from a long exploration of some kind."

"The *Swift Wing*," she recalled. "The first Realm vessel to sail as far as the southern ice wall, though it took them five years to do it."

"An impressive feat, but one accomplished by Meldenean sailors near twenty years ago." He turned back to the city as more and more lights appeared in the blocky mass of shadows. "How do you like the view?"

"A pretty place." She gave him a sidelong glance. "You're about to tell me about my father's terrible crime and the greatness displayed by your people in building beauty from the ashes of destruction."

"Tales of your perception are clearly not exaggerated. However, I was also going to ask if you could offer any reasonable explanation as to why he did it."

"Your raids were becoming more than a nuisance," Lyrna said simply. "He couldn't afford the Realm's trade to be adversely affected, not with a long-dreamt-of war to plan."

"So he was planning it even then? Our city was burned to the ground in service to a war not destined to take place for over a decade?"

"I suspect he had it planned before he even finished building the Realm. It was the glorious summit of his reign."

"Utter defeat was glorious?"

Utter defeat was the point. "A young man's dream turned into an old man's desperate gamble. Perhaps, my lord, you would do me the courtesy of answering a question of mine. Just how did he persuade the Ship Lords to carry his army to the empire's shores?"

"A lot of gold, a ship-load of bluestone and a promise: Untesh was to be ours when the war was won. One of the richest ports in the Erinean given over to the Isles. The Council thought it worth the risk, plus if it failed, they would have the pleasure of witnessing the ruin of the army that destroyed this city. All decisions taken before I secured my own Lordship, I hasten to add."

He remained silent for a time, his foxlike face drawn with a mix of sadness and worry. "Will you fight?" Lyrna asked.

"What choice do we have?"

"Several. The Isles are rich in ships. Gather your people and flee, find refuge in Alpiran lands. The Emperor may be willing to forgive past indiscretions in return for such a sizeable and capable fleet. Or sail far away to a new land. The crew of the *Swift Wing* spoke of vast tracts of empty coastline in southern waters. It was one of my brother's more lofty ambitions to send settlers there, if ever the treasury could yield enough coin to fund it."

"Is that what you'll tell your people when you return home? Leave the land of your fathers and just run away?"

"Does that mean you intend to release me?"

"The time when we could be select in our allies is past. Since your father's crime we have not been idle, knowing that sound intelligence is the best defence, we sent spies to every port in the known world."

"Hence Captain Belorath's mission to capture the encoded book."

"Quite. It was not easy placing an agent so close to the Council-man's son. Luckily his greed worked to our advantage. We've also long maintained spies in your Realm, though I'm sure this is no surprise to you. They tell us the Volarian campaign is far from complete. Alltor still holds out against siege, slavers are afraid to journey beyond Varinshold's walls and their armies find burnt crops, dead livestock and spoiled wells everywhere they tread. It seems you may still have some kind of Realm to return to, Highness. Though I can't say for how much longer."

"Then return me there. When I've won back my Realm our strength is yours. You have my word."

"And I believe it, but it seems time is our enemy." He took a small roll of thin paper from his sleeve, holding it out to her. Another code, simpler than the Volarian cypher.

"VF sailed from Varinshold," she read.

"A pigeon brought it this afternoon. We have spies, as I said. It was dispatched two days ago."

VF: Volarian Fleet. "How long until they arrive?" she asked.

"With a fair wind, two weeks."

"My lord, if there was anything I could do . . ."

"There is, Highness." His gaze was fierce with conviction. "You can redeem your father's crime and give these islands its Shield back."

"So that's the Wensel Isle," Harvin said, peering at the small outcrop of rock rising from the waves a half mile distant. "Doesn't look like much."

"Show some respect," Iltis snapped. "You are privileged to look upon the birthplace of the Faith."

"Not quite, brother," Lyrna said. "Merely the site where the first catechisms were penned."

Iltis bowed in contrition. "Quite so. Forgive me, my Queen."

Stop doing that, she wanted to say, finding she much preferred his less-awed self. They had all begun to act much the same way since her identity became known. Murel was the worst, so stuttering and tongue-tied Lyrna felt tempted to slap her.

"I can't see anything," the girl said, leaning against the rail and peering at the rock.

"The Order House is carved into the rock," Iltis explained. "The oldest in the Faith's history and vault of the original catechisms. Even the Meldeneans respect its sacredness and leave the brothers in peace."

The *Sea Sabre* had weighed anchor after a two-day voyage from the Isles, the seas had been kind up until this morning when the waves began to rise as they approached the Wensel Isle. Captain Belorath had advised that the waters surrounding the Isle were ever troubled, so many hidden reefs and conflicting currents making it a notoriously difficult channel to navigate. *Is that why he chose it?* Lyrna wondered, watching the waves crash against the rocky mound. *Less chance of visitors.*

Belorath strode up to her and bowed. "The boat is ready, Highness."

"Thank you, Captain. The other matter we discussed?"

He nodded and beckoned to one of the crew who brought a canvas bundle and a small wooden chest, placing them at Lyrna's feet with a clumsy attempt at a bow. Lyrna raised her gaze to the five people with whom she had suffered so much, realising any chance of friendship was lost for good. It had always been this way. *Such things are not for us, Lyrna,* her father had said as she watched the other children of the court run and play and laugh. *We are not them and they are not us. They serve, we command and in commanding serve them in turn.*

She crouched down and undid the bundle, revealing three

swords of the Asraelin pattern. She stood and gestured for the men to take them. "This ceremony is normally more elaborate, and perhaps at a later date we can arrange a more formal occasion. But for now, good sirs, I merely ask you a question. Your answer is your own to make, to be made without regard to prior obligation or fear of recrimination. Will you pledge yourselves and these swords in service to the Unified Realm?"

They were already dropping to one knee before she finished speaking. She was startled to see Iltis's sword was shaking a little as held it up before his bowed head. "I will, Highness," he said, quickly echoed by Benten and Harvin.

"You honour me," she told them. "I hereby name you Swords of the Realm. All previous crimes and indiscretions are pardoned by the Queen's Word." She moved to Iltis. "Stand up, brother," she told him as he continued to kneel.

He rose, standing at rigid attention and swallowing. "Lord Iltis . . ." She paused, realising she didn't know his family name.

"Adral, Highness," the big man said.

"Thank you. Lord Iltis Al Adral, I name you Protector of the Queen's Person, until such time as you wish to return to your Order, of course."

"That time will never come, Highness."

She smiled and moved on to Harvin. "Don't have a family name, y'Highness," he said. "None that I know of anyways."

"I see. In that case it'll be Lord Harvin of the Broken Chain, until you find a name more to you liking."

"Think I like that one just fine, y'Highness."

"It's just Highness, my lord."

"Grey Gull, Highness," Benten said when she moved to him. "Fisher folk take the name of their family's boat. Boat might sink or get scrapped, but the name never changes."

"Lord Benten Al Grey Gull it is. You and Lord Harvin will answer to Lord Iltis from now on. Your sole concern will be my protection. The Realm needs a head to wear the crown, you will ensure I keep mine."

She lifted the small chest from the deck and turned to the women, both of whom were already on their knees. Lyrna opened the chest and held it out to them. "Not the style I would have chosen, but they'll do for now." The rings were both identical, simple silver bands inset with small bluestones, the best the Meldenean jewellers could offer at short notice. "A queen needs her ladies. But the choice is yours and the road ahead long and fraught with danger. So think well before you answer, will you stay at my side?"

Murel took the ring immediately whilst Orena was more hesitant. "My Queen," she said. "My life before . . . It was not noble. I shouldn't wish to besmirch your patronage with my reputation."

"I think such trivia is behind us now, my lady," Lyrna said.

Orena blinked away tears and took the ring. "Dunsa was my husband's name. I should like to use my own, Vardrian."

"Lady Orena Al Vardrian. Rise and take your place."

Lyrna extended her hand to Murel, who took it and pressed a kiss to the fingers, weeping openly. "H-Harten, my Queen."

"Lady Murel Al Harten." Lyrna took the girl by the arms and gently pulled her to her feet, pushing the hair back from her face and pressing a kiss to her forehead. "You really have to stop crying."

The warden of the Wensel Isle greeted them on the flat section of carved rock that served as the island's dock. He was an elderly brother of the First Order, wearing a once-white robe now grey with age and use, matching the extensive beard that swung from his chin like frayed rope.

"Grave news indeed, Highness," he said when Lyrna had related her reason for coming. The sight of her face and word of the Realm's troubles seemed to concern him no more than a bad turn in the weather.

He introduced himself as Brother Lirken as he led her up the carved steps to the Order House, hewn from this rock some seven hundred years ago. A few other brothers waited there, greeting her with bows but no sign of particular interest. Most soon returned to reading their scrolls or sitting in silent meditation. They were all of a similar age to Brother Lirken, making her wonder how they managed to subsist in such a harsh place.

"The rock pools supply crabs and mussels aplenty," Lirken said in answer to her question. "And we gather seaweed at low tide. It's surprisingly hearty if cooked properly. I can bring some if you are in need of nourishment."

"I'm afraid I must decline, brother." She cast her gaze around the chamber of elderly brothers. "Is he here?"

"Atheran Ell-Nestra does not live amongst us, Highness. In the months since he came here we've had no more than a few moments in his company. Come, I'll take you to him."

She followed the old brother through the Order House and out onto an uneven track leading along a narrow ridge to a promontory some two hundred paces away. "You would be well advised to keep low, Highness," Lirken suggested. "The waves sometimes sweep over the ridge."

Iltis stepped forward, the only escort she had chosen to bring. "This route is too treacherous, Highness. I'll go and fetch him back."

"No, my lord." Lyrna stepped onto the track, finding the rock more damp than she would have liked. "This is something best done myself, I think. Wait here for me. I believe Brother Lirken can show you the original parchments of the first catechisms."

"Indeed I can," Lirken said, suddenly enthused. "You are a scholar, my lord?"

Iltis's face was as hard as the surrounding granite. "I was a brother of the Fifth Order. Now I'm not. I shall wait here for my queen's return."

Lyrna suppressed a grin at the old brother's discomfort and started along the ridge, keeping low as he advised. She was halfway across when the first wave came, smashing into the rocks and raising a tall cascade of spume, crashing down on her with considerable force as she sank to all fours, clinging to the stone. She got to her feet when it subsided, thoroughly drenched, and stumbled on. She was obliged to suffer two more near drownings before reaching the promontory.

There was a narrow ascending path carved into the irregular pillar of granite, leading to a cave from which a thin column of smoke could be seen rising. The path was sloppy with moss and she stumbled several times before reaching the cave. The view of the surrounding ocean was impressive at this height, the curve of the earth discernible through the occasional break in the weather. Below her the *Sea Sabre* bobbed on the waves like a toy. Sunlight broke through the clouds to bathe the small plateau and she wrung out the headscarf she had been obliged to remove on the ridge, tying it back into place to ward against the paining heat. A noise caused her to turn to the cave, making out a shadowed figure against the dim firelight inside.

"You have chosen an uncomfortable perch, my lord Shield," she said. "But a fine view."

The man who emerged from the cave was tall and broad across the shoulders, long blond hair trailing in the wind as he stood regarding her in silence.

Just as pretty as the spies said, Lyrna thought, noting the handsome features beneath the beard.

"You know who I am," the Shield said after a long moment. "Who are you?"

"Queen Lyrna Al Nieren, of the Unified Realm." She bowed. "At your service, my lord."

Pale blue eyes searched her face for a moment before he turned away, returning to the cave without a word. Lyrna hesitated, wondering if she should follow him inside; however, he re-emerged soon enough bearing a steaming earthenware cup. "I just brewed some tea," he said, holding it out to her. "The only luxury I find I can't do without."

"My thanks." She sipped the beverage, raising her hairless brows in appreciation. "Very nice. From the southern Alpiran provinces is it not?"

"Indeed. One of the few lands whose ships always enjoyed immunity during my pirate days. In return they would deliver a year's supply to the Isles, just for me." He watched her sip more tea, arms crossed, the brisk sea wind ruffling his threadbare shirt. "I had the brothers send the Ship Lords' messenger away," he said. "Now they send you. Or have you usurped your brother and seized the Isles, I wonder?"

"My brother is dead. Killed by a Volarian assassin the night my Realm was invaded. She burned me with Dark-born fire, as you can see."

"A terrible thing. My condolences."

"Your own people will need your condolences soon, for the Volarian fleet sails to seize their islands as we speak."

"They are fierce and well supplied with ships. I'm sure the battle will be a grand sight to see."

"Ship Lord Ell-Nurin seems convinced of their defeat if you are not there to lead them. Captain Belorath also. He sailed the *Sea Sabre* across the entire Boraelin faster than any ship before to bring warning of the invasion."

"My first mate always was the finest of sailors. Please send him my regards."

She saw the hardness of his gaze then, the anger simmering away inside. "Lord Al Sorna is renowned as the finest warrior ever born to the Unified Realm," she said. "Defeat at his hands carries no dishonour."

"Defeat implies there was some form of contest," he replied in a quiet tone, turning back to the cave. "Enjoy the tea. Leave the cup when you go, I only have the one."

The cup shattered on the lip of the cave as he ducked his head to enter, turning to look upon her furious visage with narrowed eyes.

"It seems," Lyrna said, "I have suffered many trials to come here and beg aid from a man who has suffered no more than humiliation, wallowing in self-pity whilst his people face ruin and enslavement."

"Humiliation?" he asked, then began to laugh. "That's why you think I'm here? Did your own people ever shun you, Highness? Did they turn their gaze from you at every opportunity, teach their children insults they were too craven to hurl themselves? Watch men you sailed with for years spit on your shadow? All because you failed in a murder they had lusted after for a generation. I did not exile myself, I *was* exiled. I am here because I can go nowhere else. My face is known in every port from here to Volaria, and I'll find a well-earned noose waiting in every one."

"Not in my ports," she said. "I'll pardon every ship you ever ransomed, every scrap of treasure you ever stole. Even every murder."

"I never murdered. Never killed a man save in a fair fight." He drew up short as something drew his gaze out to sea. Lyrna turned to see a familiar sight. The red shark was back, it's full size revealed for the first time as it circled the *Sea Sabre* with slow flicks of its tail.

"Never seen one come that close to a ship and not attack," the Shield said.

"If you come with me, I promise an interesting tale that might explain it."

They stood side by side, watching the shark for a while, the Shield's face unreadable. "Belorath says you blame yourself for not dying," she said when the shark dived down into the murky depths. "That's why you're here. Waiting for the death you were cheated of."

"I wasn't cheated of anything. I was punished. Al Sorna knew well leaving me alive was a far worse fate than merely killing me."

"I know Lord Al Sorna and he is not cruel. He spared a helpless man, that is all."

Ell-Nestra gave the faintest of laughs. "I saw his eyes, Highness, heard his words. He saw my soul and he knew I deserved death."

"Come with me and perhaps you'll find it. Live and I'll have the South Tower yards craft you the finest vessel you could dream of, the hold filled with bluestone from end to end."

"Keep the bluestone, and the ship. I'll trade it."

"For what?"

He was too fast, grasping her arms and pulling her close,

pressing his lips to hers. She shouted, feeling his tongue probing as her lips parted. Fury gripped her and she bit down. He released her, laughing and spitting blood on the stone. Lyrna glared at him, her heart thumping as she wished the throwing knife still hung about her neck. Instead all she could do was rasp at him, "And you said Al Sorna was cruel."

"Not cruelty, Highness," he replied, lisping a little as his tongue continued to leak blood. "Curiosity. And not yet satisfied." He gave a practised and elegant bow. "Allow me to fetch my meagre belongings and I'll join you forthwith."

CHAPTER THREE
Frentis

Illian proved a far better archer than she had a cook. Her arms lacked the muscle for a bow so Davoka had given her a crossbow, the camp's cook-pots soon benefiting from her new-found skill as she returned from the daily hunt with braces of wood pigeon, pheasant or rabbit. The faith-hound bitch had rarely strayed from her side since that first night around the fire and she named her Blacktooth for the permanently discoloured fang she displayed whenever she growled.

"Thin pickings today," she said, dumping a single pheasant next to the fire. "I think this part of the forest is running out of game." She turned an imperious eye on Arendil. "Pluck that for me, will you, boy?"

"Pluck it yourself, snotnose."

"Peasant!"

"Brat!"

Frentis got up and wandered away as they continued to bicker, eyes tracking over the camp as he moved. Janril Norin was teaching the basics of the sword to some younger recruits, mostly boys no more than fifteen. Davoka sparred with Ermund, something she did most days now as the young knight recovered his strength. They fought with quarterstaffs, the clearing echoing with the sound of colliding wood as they whirled and danced around each other.

Frentis knew a little of Lonak customs and wondered if she wasn't auditioning a new husband judging by the intensity of her expression as they sparred.

Grealin sat with Thirty-Four, the torturer carefully enunciating every Realm Tongue phrase the master taught him. "My name is Karvil," he said in his odd lilting tones, the Realm words barely coloured by an accent. The days following his abandonment of the pain drug had been hard, seeing him shivering and sweating in his shelter, sometimes clamping a stick in his mouth to stop his screams. At night he rarely slept for more than an hour, Frentis remaining at his side as he writhed and whimpered, often convulsing as he voiced desperate pleas in Volarian. Frentis wondered if they were his own or his victims'.

"That's the name you've chosen?" Frentis asked the former slave.

"For now," he replied. "I am having difficulty in choosing. You may continue to call me Thirty-Four if you wish."

He moved on, finding Master Rensial with their small but growing stable of horses. He had them tethered in a narrow clearing away from the main camp where he spent all his time now, pausing only to sleep or eat the food Arendil or Illian brought him, proving no more capable of remembering their names than he was Frentis's.

"Need corn, boy," he told him, checking the hooves of a mare they had taken a few days before, a tall hunter ridden by a finely dressed Volarian who had unwisely decided to go in search of boar in company with only a handful of guards. Thirty-Four's questioning had revealed him as the son of some minor Imperial luminary with only one useful morsel of intelligence: Lord Darnel was now in command of Varinshold.

"This could play to our advantage," Master Grealin had said. "The Fief Lord is not famed for his intelligence."

"Best not to underestimate him, brother," Ermund responded. "A wild cat can't argue philosophy but it'll kill you just the same."

Frentis gave Rensial the same answer he had given several times before. "Corn is in short supply, Master."

"Corn builds muscle," the mad master went on blithely, moving to the next horse, a veteran stallion taken from the Free Cavalry. It had a greying muzzle but retained considerable power in its muscle-thick limbs and neck. "Warhorse needs corn. Grass is too thin."

"I'll make every effort to secure some, Master," Frentis said, as he usually did. "Is there anything else you need?"

"Ask Master Jestin if he can see his way to forging more shoes. Three of these have thrown them already. When you've done that the tack needs cleaning."

Frentis watched him brush the stallion's coat, seeing the blank devotion in his eyes. "Yes, master."

He toured the pickets next, pausing to converse with the former City Guard corporal who had charge of the south-facing watch. "No sign?"

"None, brother. Been at least half a day now."

Draker and Ratter had gone on a reconnaissance that morning, at their own insistence which was unusual. Frentis suspected they had gone to retrieve some long-buried loot concealed close to the city and surmised they had little intention of returning. It was a source of considerable surprise that they had lingered so long already, as was their failure to shirk danger when brought on a raid.

Good luck to them, he decided, having waited until dusk with no sign of the thieves' return. *Be halfway to Nilsael by now.*

"We've some brandy left from last week's raid," he told the corporal, rising from the concealed watch-post. "Come get your share when your shift's done."

A short whistle sounded, signalling possible danger and he immediately sank down again, eyes peering into the dim tree-line. After a few seconds the sound of laboured breathing could be heard, Draker stumbling into view shortly after. The weeks of meagre rations and hard living had denuded much of the outlaw's weight but he still had difficulty maintaining a decent lick of speed for any distance. He duly collapsed on seeing Frentis emerge from hiding, falling to all fours and gasping for breath.

"Ambush," he breathed as Frentis held out a canteen. The big man took it and poured the water over his face before taking several large gulps. "We got took. Those slave-soldier bastards and a couple of Renfaelins, hunters to trade by the look of them."

"Where's the rat?" the corporal asked.

"Killed him, didn't they? Took their time about it too. They left me to stew over it but I got free."

"Got free how?" asked Frentis.

"Worked me bonds loose, didn't I? Every outlaw knows that trick."

"Bonds? They didn't chain you?"

Draker shook his head dumbly.

Frentis raised his head, ears alive to the song of the forest, straining for the faintest sign . . . There, faint but clear, barking. *Renfaelin wolfhounds, not slave-hounds.*

"Back to the camp!" he ordered, pulling Draker to his feet. "Form up on the southern flank. We've no time to run."

"You fucking dullard!" the corporal snarled at Draker as he stumbled in their wake. "Led them right to us."

Frentis ran through the camp, shouting orders, calling the fighting groups to their positions. He had rehearsed this but never fully expected it to happen, always hoping they would have sufficient warning to flee before the storm descended. The fighters moved quickly after the initial shock, gathering weapons and running to form their uneven ranks.

"Arendil! Lady Illian!" They came running, Arendil with his long sword drawn, Illian with her crossbow and quiver. "There will be skilled fighters amongst them," Frentis told her. "Men who fight well but show no rage or fear. Get yourself in a tree and kill as many as you can. Arendil, keep her safe."

The boy lingered a second to argue but was forced to follow when Illian instantly scampered off.

"Best if you linger in the rear, Master," Frentis told Grealin as the bulky brother strode to his side, sword drawn. "Provide a rally point if they break through."

Grealin just raised an amused eyebrow and stayed where he was, soon joined by Ermund and Davoka. "The children?" she asked.

"As safe as I could make them," he replied. "Look for the Kuritai and stay close to me. We need to even the odds."

Draker came huffing up, his heavy cudgel in hand, deep contrition etched into his face. "Sorry, brother . . ." he began.

"Had to happen sometime," Frentis told him. "Did you find your loot?"

Draker gave a rueful shrug. "That's how they caught us. They'd staked out our stash. Ten full skins of redflower juice. We thought the healers could use it."

Frentis saw no trace of a lie on the thief's face. *Not a thief now,* he realised. *A soldier.* "Watch my back, will you?" he said.

Draker raised his cudgel in a salute. "An honour, brother."

Frentis unlimbered his bow and notched an arrow as a thick silence fell on the camp, all eyes fixed on the wall of trees. "Maybe they missed us," Draker whispered.

Frentis suppressed a laugh and kept his eyes on the trees. They weren't long in coming, moving forward at a steady run, no bugles or war cries, just a hundred or so silent expressionless men running to battle with a sword in each hand. *Expensive,* Frentis thought. *Gathering so many just for us.*

"Archers up!" he shouted and the bowmen rose from their hiding places to loose their volley. The Kuritai rolled, dodged and leapt as the shafts flew, no more than half a dozen falling before they closed on the fighters. Frentis managed to bring down two before tossing his bow aside and charging forward with sword drawn.

He saw a Kuritai hack his way into a knot of fighters, swords blurring as they tried vainly to fend him off. He leapt a fallen fighter, parried the Kuritai's left-hand sword and jabbed his longer blade into his eye, too fast for the counter. Another came for him, swords coming together like scissor blades as he attempted a decapitating blow, then doubling over as Davoka's spear took him in the side, Ermund stepping forward to finish him with a two-handed sword stroke.

A shout drew his gaze to the rear, finding Draker swinging his cudgel at a Kuritai who ducked and lunged forward, short sword jabbing. Master Grealin moved faster than Frentis thought possible, the Order blade taking the slave in the thigh, sending him to the ground. Draker yelled in fury and fell on the man, cudgel rising and falling in a cloud of blood.

Frentis surveyed the battle, seeing far too many bodies on the ground and too many Kuritai still standing. He looked for the hardest-pressed group, finding a dense knot of men and women near the centre of the camp, assailed on all sides.

"With me!" he shouted to Davoka, palming a throwing knife and casting it at the nearest enemy. The man staggered as the knife sank into his bare upper arm, reaching to retrieve it with a hand that was hacked off before his eyes. Frentis killed two more in quick succession, his sword like a steel whip as he parried and slashed his way through their line. The fighters rallied to him, screaming and hacking with their mismatched weapons, Davoka and Ermund joining the fray, fighting back-to-back, spear and sword stabbing and slashing in a tireless frenzy.

Not enough, Frentis realised as the fighters closed in around him, Kuritai moving in on all sides. *Didn't free enough for a real army.*

The thunder of hooves dragged his attention to the rear of the camp and he saw Master Rensial charging through the trees on the veteran stallion, leaning low in the saddle, sword extended. He speared a Kuritai through the back, pulling the blade clear as he galloped past the falling corpse, killing another with a slash through the shoulder and riding down one more, the stallion stamping and voicing a shrill whinny as the Kuritai rolled beneath its hooves.

A Kuritai ran forward to kneel in front of the rearing horse, another running and planting both feet on his back, vaulting towards the mad horse-master, both swords raised above his head. Rensial's face remained as blank as always as he danced the horse to the side, the Kuritai flying past, his slashing swords missing by inches. He landed, rolling and turning to renew his attack, then falling dead as a crossbow bolt flew from above to spear him through the neck, Davoka and Ermund charging in to cut down his companion in a coordinated dance of spear and sword.

Master Rensial's empty gaze found Frentis for a moment, then he was off again, charging towards the densest knot of Kuritai, his sword moving in the kind of perfect silver arcs Frentis had never quite managed to match on the practice ground. He saw three more Kuritai fall before the master disappeared from view.

His charge bought a brief respite as the Kuritai regrouped, the surviving fighters running to Frentis's side. *So few,* he thought as they clustered around him, eyeing the neatly ordered troops of Kuritai now moving to encircle them once more. *I shouldn't have waited so long.* He put his fingers in his mouth and whistled, loud and shrill. The answer was almost immediate, the snarling, roaring barks of the faith-hounds filling the forest as their handlers let them loose, hurtling through the trees towards the Kuritai. They saw the danger and fell into a defensive formation, forming into a single company with their impossible precision, one rank kneeling in front and the other standing behind, short swords held at full extension. A formidable, perhaps unassailable fortress of flesh and steel.

Slasher bounded towards them and leapt, turning in midair as he sailed over their heads and landed in the centre of the circle. A gap appeared in their ranks barely a second later, the hound tearing through flesh and bone as his pack raced towards the hole he had carved. Frentis raised his sword and charged in their wake, the fighters following as the Kuritai's cohesion shattered. He hacked a man's legs from under him, reversed the blade and stabbed down through his chest, the fighters racing past to join in the slaughter. The Kuritai fought to the end of course, no sign of panic or fear as they were hacked down or torn apart by fang and claw, claiming ever more fighters and hounds before the last finally disappeared under a dozen slashing blades.

Frentis did a count as the fighters staggered around in the aftermath of the carnage. *No more than fifty left,* he surmised. *At least a third of those wounded.*

Janril was still amongst the living, hacking at something concealed beneath the ferns with slow methodical strokes of his sword. He stopped and bent down to retrieve his prize, holding it up as blood gushed from the stump of its neck. The former minstrel laughed as he shook the head up and down, the mouth opening and closing in a grotesque parody of speech. Frentis found himself shamed by the realisation he had hoped Janril would have found his end today. *There will never be peace for one such as him.*

A high-pitched yell came from the rear, Davoka instantly hefting her spear and running towards it. *Illian.*

Frentis followed, seeing Master Grealin up ahead, the big man moving with surprising speed once more as he raced through the undergrowth. Beyond him Frentis could see Arendil battling two Kuritai, his long sword moving in fluid arcs as he turned aside their short swords, twisting and ducking as they tried to close. He could see Illian standing amidst the branches of an oak above the fight, hands spread helplessly. *No more bolts.*

Arendil was forced to back away at speed as the Kuritai redoubled their efforts, one slashing low the other high. The boy's feet found a tree root and he stumbled, falling flat on his back, the Kuritai closing, swords raised.

Master Grealin stopped twenty yards short, lowering his sword and raising his free hand, fingers spread wide . . . And the Kuritai flew.

It was as if some great invisible fist swept down to batter them from their feet. One colliding with the trunk of the oak, wrapping around it with enough force to shatter his spine. The other glanced off the branch where Illian was perched, the girl uttering a yelp as he spun from the impact to land some ten yards away.

Davoka paused to stare at Grealin for an instant, a palpable fear and distaste on her face. *"Rova kha ertah Mahlessa,"* she said in a low voice before running on to check on the young folk.

Frentis walked to Grealin's side, seeing an expression of sombre regret on his face, his skin clammy and pale, as if he had suffered a great pain. "I thought I had imagined it," Frentis said. "The Volarian impaled on the branch. A feverish vision. Any other surprises for me, Master?"

Grealin gave a slight smile. "Actually, my correct title is Aspect."

He sent Janril after the Renfaelin hunters along with ten of their most capable remaining fighters. As instructed, they killed the dogs to erase the memory of their scent and kept one of the hunters alive for questioning. His defiance didn't last long, a few moments in Thirty-Four's company proving sufficient persuasion to fully loosen his tongue.

"Our lord is convinced his son resides in this forest," the man said, a lean fellow of middling years with the weathered look of a professional tracker. The fingers of his left hand dripped blood continually from where Thirty-Four had thrust rose thorns under his nails. "We were promised ten golds to bring him back, twenty if he was still alive. He paid for the slaves out of his own pocket, bought them from the Volarian general."

"You hunt your own people for gold?" Janril asked him in an expressionless tone.

"I do as I'm told," the man whined, staring up at them from the tree root to which he had been bound. "Always have. Fief Lord Darnel is not a man to cross, not if you want to stay healthy."

"Neither am I," Frentis said. "Tell him that when you see him."

"You're letting him go?" Janril asked, following as he walked towards where Arendil was helping with the wounded.

"Leave him bound where he is when we move the camp," Frentis said. "I assume Lord Darnel will have a just reward for his failure."

"He deserves a traitor's death, brother," Janril insisted, an uncharacteristic heat colouring his tone.

"Not seen enough death for one day, Sergeant?"

"When it comes to scum like him, I'll never have seen enough."

Frentis paused, meeting Janril's gaze squarely. "Does it help? All the killing and the torture, does it take away the sight of her death?"

Janril's eyes were bright and pale beneath his lowered brow. "Nothing will ever do that. What I do I do in her name, I honour her with blood."

"Her name? What was it? I've yet to hear you speak it."

The sergeant just stared at him, only a faint uncertainty in his eyes, barely glimpsed beneath the burgeoning madness. "Leave the hunter where he is and get ready to move," Frentis ordered. "If you can't follow my commands, then take yourself off and do all the killing you want out of my sight."

Arendil was helping Davoka bind a bandage around Draker's arm. The Lonak woman was the only one amongst them with any appreciable healing skill. "Thought I'd clubbed the life from the bugger then he stabs me," the big man said through gritted teeth. "Finished him then though. Didn't stop till I saw his brains."

Davoka tied off the bandage and they moved away, speaking softly. "Ten will die tonight. The rest will heal with enough time."

"Time is not something we have," he replied. "We move within the hour."

She gave a sombre nod then cast a wary glance at where Grealin sat alone beside a small fire, huddling in his cloak as if chilled to the bone. "He comes too?"

"He's an Aspect of my Faith and leader of this group. Can't very well leave him behind."

She raised an eyebrow. "Leader?"

Frentis chose to ignore her and turned to Arendil, beckoning the boy over. "So, how well do you know your father?"

"Twenty golds?" Arendil pursed his lips in surprise. "And Grandfather always said the Fief Lord was too cheap to pay a tavern whore."

"What does he want you for?" Frentis asked.

"I'm his heir. The only issue of his filthy seed." The boy's discomfort was obvious, his gaze averted as he shifted from foot to foot. "I've never even met him but I feel as if he's always been there, a hateful shadow. And I know his mind, his need to claim me has become something beyond reason or sense. Sometimes I would see Mother looking at me with a strange frown and I knew she wasn't seeing me, she was seeing him." He stopped shuffling, raising his head to meet Frentis's eye. "I won't be taken by him, brother. I will die first."

Cut off a finger and send it to the Fief Lord with the hunter. Provoke him into even rasher action. It was not his thought, he knew that. It was *her.* The stain of their union went deep, all the way into his soul. "I swear to you that won't happen," he told Arendil, putting a hand on his shoulder. "You fought well today. Go help her ladyship with gathering the weapons, will you?"

There was a brief flash of pride on the boy's face before he ran off to find Illian.

"Did Vaelin know?" Frentis asked, sitting down opposite the Aspect of the Seventh Order.

"Not until his brief visit before he went to the Reaches," the Aspect replied. "We had an . . . interesting discussion." Grealin's pallor was still somewhat grey but a pinkness was creeping back into his ample cheeks. Frentis recalled the blood and exhaustion that always accompanied the woman's use of her stolen gift.

"Your ability. It pains you to use it?" he asked.

"It's more that it drains me. So much power released all at once has consequences. I remain fat for a reason, brother. It makes the aftermath more palatable."

"Where do we find the House of your Order?"

"The Seventh Order has no House. And hasn't for the past four centuries. We are woven like a gossamer thread through the fabric of the Faith and the Realm, our work always hidden."

"As you were hidden in our Order?"

"Quite. It seemed the most secure hidey hole." Grealin's tired features formed into a sardonic smirk. "How spectacularly are the wise proved foolish."

"The brothers I found that day, Aspect Arlyn sent them with you, as protection."

"Yes. And they died following his order."

"Where would you have gone?"

"North, to the Pass. If the way was blocked, west to Nilsael and on to the Reaches. Instead I found myself here with you and our heroic band of rebels. It'll make a fine story one day, don't you think? If there's anyone left to tell it."

This is a defeated man, Frentis realised, eyeing the sag of Grealin's features and the dullness in his eyes. "These people look to us for leadership," he said. "For hope. As an Aspect of the Faith you can give them that."

"My only gift to them is fear. They see what I am and they fear it. The Lonak woman is just more honest than the others. To carry a gift is to know fear and isolation. We do not belong in the daylight, we belong in the shadows. That is where we can best serve the Faith. The hardest lesson my Order ever learned."

"The time for old ways is gone, Aspect. Everything is changed. They came and broke it all apart. How we put it back together is for us to decide."

"Seeking to remake the world, brother? Looking for a noble quest to wash away all the blood you spilled?"

"It won't wash away. But that doesn't mean I have to wallow in it."

"Then what are we doing here? Why continue to fight this hopeless war? These people are all going to die. There is no victory to be had in this forest." His gaze dropped, becoming distant. "No victory anywhere. We thought we had won, you see? Turned aside the avalanche when Al Sorna revealed the One Who Waits. But all we did was allow our gaze to be drawn to one threat whilst another grew unseen. An entire army sent across the ocean to crush us. Who would have thought he would be so unsubtle after centuries of guile?"

"He?"

Grealin raised his gaze. "Your dead lady friend called him the Ally I believe. The Volarians do like to indulge their delusions. They may have divested themselves of gods and faith long ago, but they replaced reason with servitude in so doing."

"Who is he?"

"Who he was might be a more pertinent question, for once he must have been a man. A man with a name, a people, perhaps even a family he loved. All lost, of course, hidden even from the most gifted scryers in my Order. We have no name for him, just a purpose."

"Which is?"

"Destruction. Specifically our destruction, as it seems there is something about this land that stirs his hatred. He tried once before, when the great cities rose and a people far wiser than us crafted wonders. Somehow he managed to tumble it all into ruin, but not quite enough, something escaped him. And now he wants it gone."

Grealin lapsed into silence, eyes dulling once more as a wave of fatigue swept over his features.

Frentis got to his feet. "My thanks for saving the boy, I know it has cost you. We move in an hour. I should be grateful if you would come with us."

The Aspect's bulk shifted in a shrug. "Where else would I go?"

CHAPTER FOUR
Reva

"It means 'witch,'" Veliss said, peering at the open book in her hand. "Female derivation of the old Volarian for 'sorcerer.'"

"Elverah," Reva said, tasting the word. "Has a nice sound to it."

"They think you're a witch?" Arken said.

"Godless heretics," Lord Arentes sniffed. "Mistaking the Father's blessing for the Dark."

Reva stifled a groan. *Not him too.*

"It's good," Uncle Sentes said from his place by the fire, his voice a wheezing rasp. "Means they're afraid."

"Well they might," Arentes said, smiling at Reva. "My lady brings the Father's justice down upon them every time they assault our walls."

"The Realm Guard we freed?" Reva asked him, keen to change the subject.

"Joined them with the hundred or so others already on the walls, my lady," the guard commander replied. "Got them reinforcing the southern section. We're still thin there."

"Good." She turned to Veliss. "Supplies?"

"About two-thirds remaining," she replied. "But that's only because we're rationing so severely. There have been complaints, women mainly. Not an easy thing to see your children cry from hunger."

"Double the ration for women with children," Reva said. "I don't like to hear them cry either."

"Hunger is the enemy's best weapon, my lady," Lord Antesh pointed out. "Every mouthful we eat brings them a step closer to cresting the walls."

"Winter is no more than a month away," her uncle said from the fire. "And they have scant pickings for forage. We'll see who starves first." He fell to coughing and gave an irritated wave. "Enough of this," he choked when the fit subsided. "Leave me with my niece."

The others bowed and moved to the door, Veliss's hand brushing Reva's as she followed. She went to sit opposite her uncle, noting the shake in his hands as they rested on the blanket. "You know it'll only get worse," he said. "Crying children will be the least of it."

"I know, Uncle."

"This"—he waved his hand vaguely—"wasn't my plan. I'd hoped your tenure would be free of war."

"Not your doing."

"I had a dream last night. It was very strange. Your father was there, and mine, and your grandmother. All here in the library. Very strange since my parents could hardly stand to be in the same room . . ." He trailed off, blinking as his gaze drifted.

"Uncle?"

His eyes fluttered closed and she went to pull the blanket over his arms. His head jerked up as she came close, eyes bright with joy. "They said they were proud of me," he breathed. "Because of you, Reva. Seems I finally did something right."

She sat at his side, head resting on his knees as his frail hands played through her hair. "Too long," she heard him murmur. "Cumbraelin women don't wear it so long."

They came again the following night, attacking in several places at once as Antesh predicted. The battalions came trooping over the causeway in close order, shielded on all sides, Varitai in front marching with their unnatural rhythm, Free Swords behind, ranks not so tightly formed but careful to keep behind their shields. Antesh ordered all bows lowered as they reached the end of the causeway, opting not to waste arrows. The Volarian column split into two, the battalions inching along with slow deliberation to encircle the city, not a gap appearing in their protective walls.

"Buggers learn too quickly for my liking," Lord Arentes commented. He gave Reva a smart salute. "I shall take command of the western section, my lady. With your permission."

"Of course, my lord. Be safe."

The old commander gave a stiff bow and strode off. Reva watched the slow approach of the battalions for a moment then notched an arrow to her bow and vaulted onto the gatehouse roof.

"My lady!" Antesh reached out to her but she curtly waved him away.

"I want to see how much they fear me," she said.

The battalions kept marching, moving into position in accordance with a well-rehearsed scheme, seemingly oblivious to the hated witch staring down at them with bow in hand. It was the Free Swords who took the bait, as she expected. A small chink appearing in the shield roof of a battalion as it trooped off the causeway and wheeled to the left. Reva waited for the glint of metal to appear in the black triangle then stepped to the side, the arrow leaving a harsh whisper in her ear as it flew past. She drew and released in an instant, her shaft finding the chink. The Free Sword battalion convulsed like a wounded beast, the discord rippling through the ranks as sergeants shouted for order, but not before more gaps had appeared in the shield wall.

"Archers up!" Antesh barked and a hundred bowmen rushed to the wall, arrows descending in a furious iron-tipped rain. The battalion struggled on as the arrows continued to fly, trailing bodies and attempting to re-form ranks but the damage was done. A few more seconds and it convulsed again, flying apart as panic took the remaining men. Some ran for the causeway, others to neighbouring battalions seeking shelter. Most were cut down within seconds but perhaps a few of the more fleet-footed made it to safety.

Reva notched another arrow and continued to stand atop the battlement, eyes scanning the Volarian ranks below for another opportunity. She wondered if hatred was in fact a physical force because she could feel it now, rising towards her like a wave.

The last Volarian battalion trooped into place directly opposite the gatehouse. Smaller than the others, perhaps three hundred men, the ranks moving with greater precision than even the Varitai. *Kuritai,* Reva decided.

She raised her bow above her head, laughing and thinking about her dying uncle. *It seems I finally did something right.* "Well come on!" she called to the silent ranks below. "I'm waiting."

Antesh sent out parties in the morning to retrieve arrows and gather weapons from the dead. Reva chose to go with them, not wanting to be thought of as shirking the more odious duties.

"Lord Arentes puts the count at well over a thousand Volarians killed," Arken commented. He paused to tug an arrow from the corpse of a Varitai lying half-submerged on the bank, also taking his short sword and dagger.

"They kept us busy enough," Reva agreed. The night had been a blur of successive crises, seeing her rush from one section of the wall to the other as the Volarians sought to gain a claw hold. They had come close only twice, once on the western section where Varitai had used grapples to scale the wall whilst the main force of Free Swords tried vainly to climb their ladders. Lord Arentes had already contained the assault by the time she got there, the old commander bleeding from a cut on his forehead as he shouted orders to the City Guard. A single charge with lowered halberds had been enough to dislodge the Volarians, heralding another arrow-lashed flight to the causeway.

The incursion on the southern section proved the most

serious. Reva had dealt with the Kuritai assault on the gatehouse by the simple expedient of having them soaked in lamp oil when they abandoned their shields to sprint for the wall, grappling hooks whirling. Successive volleys of fire arrows saw most plummeting to the ground in flames but a few made it to the top of the wall, some still alight as they did their deadly two-sworded dance, killing many defenders before being cut down. She was ordering the bodies tipped over the battlements when a messenger came running with news more Kuritai were atop the southern wall.

She sent word ordering the House Guards to reinforce the sector and ran there with Arken in tow. The Kuritai had been hidden amongst the main force of Free Swords, an annoyingly clever tactic she would have to watch for in future. They had formed a tight defensive knot on the southern wall, bodies piled up on either side as the Realm Guard defenders rallied for another counterattack. Their commander was a young sergeant already showing numerous cuts on his bare arms and face.

"One more try, lads!" he called to his men. "We'll get the bastards this time."

"Hold," Reva ordered, eyeing the close ranks of Kuritai, crouched with typically blank expressions as Free Swords struggled over the battlements behind.

"Stand ready," she told the Realm Guard, stepping forward and unslinging the wych elm. She stood aiming with careful deliberation, barely twelve feet from the nearest enemy, killing one, then another, the Kuritai ranks closing the gaps with an unconscious lack of hesitancy. She killed two more before one of the Kuritai barked a command and they came for her. She tossed the wych elm aside and reached over her shoulder to draw her sword as the Realm Guard charged.

She had difficulty recalling the exact train of events after that. She remembered leaping and whirling, a Kuritai falling with a half-severed neck, but mostly it was all a red-tinged confusion of clashing blades and rending flesh. It ended with the arrival of the House Guards, charging in with halberds to finish the remaining Kuritai and push the Free Swords from the wall.

She found herself hailed once more, the Realm Guard pummelling her with slaps to the back. She was too tired to push them away and Arken had to pull her free from the press. She was gratified to see him unharmed, though his face had the pale aspect of one who has killed at close quarters for the first time.

She paused at the sight of the young Realm-Guard sergeant dragging a wounded Free Sword to his feet, the man clutching his forearm, the bone gleaming white from the gaping wound. "Where's your whip now, you fucking filth?" He drew a dagger and jammed it into the wound, twisting the blade as the man screamed. "Where's your whip now, eh?"

"Just kill him and have done!" Reva ordered. "Re-form your ranks. This night's not over."

They kept at it for nearly four hours until the first glimmer of dawn broke over the broad river, ever more battalions trooping over the causeway to try their luck, more and more bodies littering the ground as every assault failed. It was costly, Arentes reporting losses of over three hundred killed and another two hundred wounded, but they held. Finally the surviving Volarians pulled back, the Varitai re-forming ranks and reclaiming their shields, the Free Swords forgetting discipline and running as the arrow storm descended once more, burgeoning daylight increasing the toll exacted by the longbows.

Excited shouts brought her back to the present and she saw a live Volarian being dragged from the river. A Free Sword, judging by his evident fear, turning to abject terror when he saw her approach.

"Yes," she said. "The elverah's here."

The man just stared at her in frozen horror, only the faintest glimmer of reason in his eyes. *This one will never fight again.*

"My lady?" one of the archers asked, his dagger already drawn. "Does anyone here speak his language?"

Only Veliss had enough knowledge of Volarian to communicate with the man, and even then just in written form. She referred to her books to translate Reva's message and had him recite it back. Sending a note may have been easier but she wanted his comrades to hear the fear in his voice as he related her words.

"The elverah has much power and will kill all who come against this city. But she is merciful. Your commanders waste your lives in fruitless attacks whilst they sit safe in their tents. Any who throw down their arms and depart this place will be spared the elverah's vengeance. Only death awaits those who stay."

"Is he saying it right?" she asked Veliss as the man stumbled through the words held in front of his eyes.

"As far as I can tell."

Reva turned to Antesh. "Have him read it out ten times then let him go. I'll be with my uncle."

They didn't come the next night, or the night after that. The Volarian camp went about its martial business with no sign of preparing another assault. If any more towers or rafts were being constructed, it was done out of their sight. Otherwise they drilled, sent out cavalry patrols and made no further effort to cross the causeway.

"Seems they intend to starve us out after all," Antesh commented.

"Bloody cowards," Lord Arentes said. "A few more assaults like the other night and we'd have won this siege."

"Hence the starving us out." The Lord of Archers stepped to Reva's side. "We could sally forth, my lady. Launch a raid or two. Might provoke another unwise attack."

"As you wish," she said. "But keep it small, and volunteers only. Preferably men without families."

"I'll see to it, my lady."

The succeeding days saw her settle into an irksome routine of daily inspections, training the defenders to ensure they didn't slacken and going over Veliss's reports of ever-more-diminishing supplies.

"We're down to half already?" she asked one evening. "How is that possible?"

"People seem to eat more when they're afraid," Veliss replied. "Plus we went through the fresh meat and livestock in the first few weeks. Now it's just bread and a little salted meat. I'm sorry, love, but the ration must be cut again. And not just the people, the soldiers too. That's if we're going to last the winter."

Reva stared down at the neatly inscribed figures on Veliss's parchment. "Did you learn this somewhere?" she asked. "The pen work?"

"My old dadda was the village scribe. Taught me the trade, but the, ah, distractions of womanhood led me to Varinshold before I could be properly apprenticed."

"Did he beat you? Is that why you left?"

Veliss laughed. "Faith no. Doubt he ever lifted a hand to anyone, even my mother, though the cheating cow certainly deserved it. He was just a kindly, dull little man with no desire to see what lay beyond his village. I wanted more."

Over by the fire her uncle stirred again, mumbling something in his sleep. "He dreams a lot these days," Veliss said. "Rambles on about his family for hours when he's awake." Despite the caustic tone Reva could see the concern in her face, the onset of grief for a man not yet dead. She fought the impulse to reach for her hand and rose from the desk.

"Set aside enough wine for his needs," she said. "And empty the cellar, the bottles will be given to the people. Might sweeten the pill of cutting the rations."

"Or fill the streets with riotous drunks."

"Dole it out a little at a time. Any more visits from the Reader's dog?"

"No, the old man seems content to rave away in his cathedral. The services are well-attended though and my sources tell me his rhetoric is becoming more bizarre and doom-laden by the day.

The Father's judgement descends upon us, and so forth. Could be a problem as things get worse." Reva detected a certain weight of meaning in Veliss's words.

She glanced at Uncle Sentes. "Did he have any design to constrain the old man's power?"

"He preferred the slow game. Gather intelligence, evidence of hypocrisy or corruption, and wait for a time to use it, either as leverage or to have the Reader replaced with a more tractable cleric. With you we finally had something that might give us an advantage."

"But only if we could find the priest."

"Quite so."

Reva went to the window, gazing up at the twin spires. *He's not here*, she thought. *Not in the city. I'd smell it if he was.* "Tell your watchful friends to keep watching," she said. "For now."

She was woken in the early hours of the morning by Arken's insistent shaking. She had taken to sleeping on the couch in the library between shifts on the wall, not wishing to stray too far from her uncle's side. It seemed Veliss had decided to share it with her sometime in the night. The woman lay against her side, arm draped over her waist and head resting on her shoulder, thick dark brown curls partly covering Reva's face. They smelt like strawberry.

Reva disentangled herself quickly, reaching for her weapons and avoiding Arken's gaze. If he found anything untoward in the scene however, it was absent from his voice. "Something's happening on the river."

"What are they?" she asked, gazing out at the strange contraptions perched on the deck of the ships anchored in the river. They were hard to make out in the morning haze hanging over the Coldiron, large blocky shapes with round shoulders and stubby arms, crouching like malformed giants in the mist.

Lord Antesh stared at the ships in grim silence and it was Arentes who spoke up. "Engines, my lady. But not like any I have ever seen."

The faint echo of shouted orders drifted across the river as a long line of boats materialised out of the haze covering the far bank, each laden with something large and round.

"There's a quarry barely ten miles south," Antesh commented in a reflective tone. "Not a thing you can burn, a quarry." He hefted his thick-staved bow, notched an arrow and raised it at a high angle, drawing the string a good six inches past his ear before releasing. The arrow arced high over the river and fell into the swift-flowing current ten yards short of the nearest ship.

"What engine can sling a stone farther than an arrow?" Arentes wondered.

"It seems these can," Antesh replied. His gaze tracked from the engines to the wall. "The stones will likely fall somewhere between the gatehouse and the western bastion. If they're smart, they'll try for multiple breaches."

"Clear the battlements there," Reva said and Arentes immediately strode off shouting orders, the defenders on the wall breaking off from gaping at the engines to run for the stairways.

"We should prepare defences back from the wall," Antesh said. "It'll mean pulling down some houses to create a killing ground."

"Then get to it," Reva said. "Have Lady Veliss issue receipts for any loss of property. Oh, and give any dispossessed householders the best wine from the Fief Lord's cellar."

He bowed and marched off. Reva watched the boats as they made their way to the three anchored ships, hearing the crack of several whips as slaves laboured to haul the stones onto the decks. A faint clinking sound could be heard as the arms of the engines were drawn back, dim figures moving on the deck as the stones were hauled into place. Then silence, the engines primed but unmoving. *What are they waiting for?*

One of the archers straightened and pointed to something upriver. Reva moved to his side and peered into the mist, seeing only a faint shadow at first, a tall square sail ascending out of the haze. Soon however the full size of the ship was revealed, the largest she could recall seeing, the great dark hull displacing a wake that washed onto the shore like a wave at high tide. The ship's sides rose from the water at least twenty feet high, numerous figures moving about on deck in the centre of which stood a white awning. Reva strained her eyes and fancied she saw the outline of a tall figure standing beneath the canvas. *Come to watch the show, have you?* She gripped her bow and wondered if Arren's wondrous work would give an arrow enough flight to reach him from here, but knew it would be an empty gesture of defiance and the mood of the defenders was already plummeting before her eyes.

There came a rattling of chains then a splash as the huge ship weighed anchor, positioned some twenty yards to the rear of the three ships with their slumbering giants. A single flaming arrow arced up from the deck of the great ship, trailing smoke as it fell into the water, and the giants spoke, the stubby arms springing forward with a great thrum, the stones they cast at first too fast to follow as they ascended high enough to make them appear like pebbles thrown by an angry child. They seemed to hang there against the sky for an age, as if frozen by the World Father in answer to the thousand prayers now ascending from the walls. But if so, His hand reached down for no more than an instant.

The first stone fell short, impacting on the bank with sufficient force to shake the wall beneath her feet and raising a waterspout high enough to bring rain to the battlements. The second flew over the wall, gouging some stonework from the inner battlement before crashing into the houses beyond, raising screams and the sound of hundreds of bricks falling onto cobbled streets.

The engineers servicing the third giant, however, clearly knew their business all too well. The massive stone sphere struck just below the rim of the west-facing wall, the force of it sending her reeling as rubble exploded from the impact. The stone rolled down the outer wall to thump into the bank below. Reva stared at the point of impact, expecting the cracks she could see in the stone to immediately widen and the whole section collapse. Instead the dust settled and the wall held.

She got to her feet, watching the giants pulling their arms back in readiness for the next throw, engineers busy around the contraptions as they adjusted their aim. *Well,* she thought. *They have to go.*

This time she stood firm against Antesh's threats of resignation, and also Veliss's damp-eyed imprecations. "It has to be me," she said simply, leaving the reason unsaid. *No-one else can do it. He didn't send anyone else against the Alpiran engines during the desert war—neither will I.*

The boats were readied in the narrow channel through the north wall that provided access to river traffic. Fifty picked men in ten boats, piled high with oil pots and fire arrows. Like her, all were dressed in black with soot smeared over every inch of exposed skin and all blades tarnished to conceal their gleam. She found Arken at the prow of her own boat, sitting silently with his axe clamped in a two-handed grip. From the set of his shoulders it was clear removing him from the boat would require some considerable force.

"Hope you've kept it sharp," Reva said, sitting down next to him and nodding at his axe.

"Doesn't seem to matter," he said. "Hit them hard enough and they fall over regardless."

She pressed a kiss to his cheek, finding she couldn't help but enjoy the flush that crept over his skin despite a pang of guilt. *Don't make a promise you can't keep.* "Stay close to me."

The boats were launched a short while after midnight. The sky was cloudy, sparing them any betraying moonlight as they struggled against the current, working the oars in heavily greased cleats to conceal the sound. They ploughed downriver for a hundred yards before angling towards the west and shipping the oars, letting the current do the work as they hunkered low in the boats. The engines continued their bombardment even at night, well lit with torches to allow the engineers to service their monsters. The low crump of stone striking stone a slow drumbeat as the helmsmen brought them ever closer.

Reva stood as the nearest ship came within range, arrow notched as she sought a target, finding a stocky man on the port side, pounding a mallet into some fixture on the engine. It was a poor attempt, the bob of the current and the forward movement of the boat throwing off her aim, but she did manage to sink the arrow into the engineer's thigh. He gave a shout, falling to the deck as his comrades straightened from their work, frozen in surprise and easily made out in the torchlight.

"Up!" Reva shouted, notching and loosing once again. The other archers rose and loosed as one, the volley sweeping the engineers from the deck in an instant. The helmsman steered the boat to the ship's side, three more crowding alongside as Reva gripped a rope and hauled herself aboard. The deck was covered in corpses and wounded, some severely, others not.

"Finish them all!" she barked, pointing the men with oil towards the engine. "Burn it!"

They got to work as she went to the starboard rail to watch the other boats assail the remaining engines. The archers were standing with bows drawn when the blasts of multiple horns arose from the surrounding water. The great shadow of the Volarian warship suddenly blazed with light, torches sparking to life from bow to stern, revealing a dense mass of archers crowding the deck and the rigging.

"Down!" she shouted, reaching for Arken. He gaped at the swarm of arrows now rising from the warship's deck then dived to mask her with his greater bulk. The Volarian shafts sounded like a hailstorm as they covered the ship, Arken giving a shout of pain and collapsing onto her, bearing her down to the deck. She stared out from beneath his elbow to see four of her men pinned to the boards, pierced from head to toe. Arken grunted and tried to rise.

"The river!" Reva hissed.

Arken gripped her tight and rolled them both towards the port rail. He tumbled over as another volley descended, plunging straight into the river but she held on, wincing as the arrows smacked into the woodwork around her, one less than an inch from her left hand as it held to the rail. She paused to survey the deck, seeing no survivors amongst the men who had followed her to this ship, or the engineers they had come to kill. The engine, however, stood undamaged, gleaming from the oil with which it had been liberally spattered before the arrows fell.

Reva glanced down at the bow in her right hand, her thumb briefly tracing over the fine carvings. *Sorry, Master Arren.* She dropped it into the Coldiron and vaulted back onto the deck, snatched a torch from a stanchion and tossed it onto the engine, the lamp oil flaring immediately. She turned and dived over the rail, ears filled with the buzz of multiple arrows before the river's chill claimed her. She kept under as long as she dared, feeling the warmth of her body seeping away as she struggled towards the city, surfacing to gulp air then diving under again. It seemed an age before she felt the reeds close around her, gripping the stems to haul herself from the water. She lay gasping on the bank for a long time, raising her head to watch the ship and the engine burning, its two brothers, however, stood undamaged. She could see bodies floating in the water, borne upstream by the current.

"Arken!" She forced herself to her feet, stumbling along the bank. "Arken!"

As if in mockery the two surviving engines both launched at once, their stones sailing out of the black void to crash into the wall above her head, forcing her to dodge the falling masonry. It fell onto the pile of rubble below the increasingly deep rent in the wall. It was not a huge barrier, but now it seemed like a mountain.

"She's here!" came a shout from above. "Blessed Lady Reva lives!"

She looked up to see numerous pale faces staring down at her from the battlements, a growing chorus of adulation rising from the walls as word of her survival spread.

They think it a victory, she realised, casting her gaze at the river once more. The lights on the warship were blinking out one by one, the flaming engine still burning, but not so brightly, a phrase from the Book of Wisdom looming large in her mind: *War makes fools of us all.*

Arken had been found close to the causeway, an arrow jutting from his back and senseless from cold and blood loss. She rushed to the healing house on being hauled onto the battlement by means of a long rope. The defenders had crowded round, voicing awed appreciation, sinking to their knees, some praying openly to the Father, most just staring. Suddenly she hated them, finding their desperate belief a disgusting betrayal of the sacrifice she had just witnessed. *The Father did nothing!* she wanted to rail at them. *I am preserved by dumb luck. I hold no blessing. Look at the corpses floating in the river, I did that.*

None of it could be voiced of course. They needed her to be blessed, needed to know the Father's sight rested on this city.

Brother Harin was washing the blood from his hands when she got to the healing house. Arken lay face down on a table, his bare flesh bone-white save for the red rivulets streaming from the partly bandaged wound on his back. His eyes were closed, but she could see a soft flutter beneath his eyelids.

"Will he live?" she asked the healer.

"I expect so," Harin replied. "Being young and strong as an ox."

Reva collapsed in relief, slumping against the wall and sinking to the floor. *No more tears,* she reminded herself as she felt them welling.

Harin came to her with a blanket, gently pulling her upright and wrapping it around her shoulders. "Not good, my lady," he commented, pressing a hand to her forehead. "Not good at all."

He sat her by the fire, blanket about her shoulders, clutching a cup of something dark and steaming as he stitched Arken's wound. "The city's all abuzz with it," he said, eyes fixed on his work. "Bringing the Father's fiery justice to the heretics' dread engines."

"I doubt such sentiments are shared by you, brother," she replied and sipped her drink, face wrinkling with instant distaste. "What is this?"

"Brother's Friend. Always good for banishing a chill if warmed over the fire for a few minutes."

She recalled how Alornis's drunken poet had lapped up this concoction like buttermilk and could only shake her head in wonder as she forced down another mouthful. "Is it supposed to make you dizzy?" she asked after a moment.

"Oh yes."

"That's all right then." She sat, feeling the warmth spread as she sipped, her tongue numbed against the liquor's bitterness. Brother Harin's hands moved with a curious deftness for such a large man as he worked the catgut through the lips of Arken's wound with two tweezers. "You are very skilled, brother."

"Why thank you, my lady."

"He told me about you lot, y'know." She paused to drink some more. "Fifth Order. Besht healers in the world, he said."

"He?"

"Al Sorna. Darkblade. Who elsh?" She raised the cup to her lips, wondering how it had contrived to empty itself so quickly. "Thought I could do it, y'see? Do what he did. Just got everyone killed instead. Not me though. I've got the Father's blessing."

"I don't know about the Father's blessing, my lady," the big healer said in a soft tone. "But I do know this city continues to stand because of you. Never forget that."

There was commotion at the door and Veliss burst into the room, sighing in explosive relief at the sight of Reva. She came to her, hands soft on her cheeks, eyes wide with delight.

Reva hiccuped and gave a small burp.

"She's drunk," Veliss accused Harin.

"And considerably warmer," the brother replied.

Veliss's eyes went to Arken's unmoving form. "Just the two of them?"

"Sadly, yes. Lord Antesh had the banks searched, without luck."

"Fifty men," Reva slurred, wondering why the room was

suddenly so much darker. "Never killed so many at once before."

"Did what you had to, love." Veliss put an arm around her shoulders and tugged her to her feet. "Let's go home. Your uncle's been asking for you."

"Fifty men," Reva whispered as all sensation began to fade and her eyelids fell shut like lead weights. "Blessed by the Father . . ."

Her head hurt worse than she thought possible, making her wonder if the Father had placed an invisible axe in her skull as punishment for her sinful doubts. The ceaseless thump of the engines' stones did nothing to help. She went to view the breach first thing in the morning, flanked by four House Guards to keep the more ardent townsfolk at bay. Many voices were raised as she moved through the streets, calls of thanks and simple wonder, some kneeling as she passed, much as they knelt for the Reader in the square. It was too much.

"Stop that!" she said, halting by an elderly couple who knelt outside a wool shop. They both continued to stare up at her with baffled awe.

"The Father sent you to us, my lady," the old woman said. "You bring His sight upon us."

"I bring a sword and a bow, one of which I lost last night." She bent down, taking the woman's elbow and lifting her up. "Do not kneel to me. For that matter, don't kneel to anyone." She was aware of other people crowding round, the many eyes boring into her face as they stood in rapt attention. "This city will not be held by kneelers. Kneel now and the walls will fall, and the people who brought them down will ensure you'll be kneeling for the rest of your lives."

The crowd remained silent around her, reverence on every face . . . save one.

A young woman stood, cradling an infant, towards the rear of the crowd, her face sullen with despair, cheekbones sunken from lack of food. The baby in her arms pawed at her face with tiny hands. Reva moved through the throng, the people parting with bowed heads.

"May I see?" Reva asked, placing a hand on the baby's swaddling. The young woman gave a slight nod and pulled the blanket aside revealing a pink and happy face, cheeks plump and dimpled as the child smiled up at Reva. "He's well-fed," she said. "You're not."

"No sense both of us going hungry," the young woman replied in an Asraelin accent, which explained the lack of reverence.

"His father?"

"Went to the wall, didn't come back. They told me he was brave, which is something, I suppose."

Reva winced at the thunder-crack impact of another stone on the wall. The deepening breach was visible from here, a jagged upturned triangle above the rooftops. *When it's done this won't be a siege any more,* she realised. *It'll be a battle.*

"The rations will be doubled tomorrow," she told the young woman. "My word on it. In the meantime, go to the manor and ask for Lady Veliss. Tell her I sent you to help in the kitchens."

Lord Antesh was overseeing the construction of a stout defensive wall twenty yards back from the breach. The surrounding houses were gone, their stone used for the new wall. Masons were hard at work with mortar and trowels to build a barrier some ten feet high, curving around the breach site in a semicircle complete with a parapet.

"My lady," Antesh greeted her with a bow. "Two more days and we'll be done here. Of course we'll need more when they start on their second breach, as they're bound to do."

"Was half hoping they'd risk it all on this one," Reva replied, knowing that the previous night had provided ample evidence their opposing commander was done making mistakes.

"I have a surprise for you," Antesh said, moving to a nearby cart. "One of my men found it this morning when we were searching the bank." The wych-elm bow had lost its string but otherwise seemed undamaged, the wood still gleaming, no nicks or scars to mar the carvings. "Seems the Father doesn't want you to be parted from it," Antesh observed.

Reva suppressed a sigh. It would be all over the city within hours. *The Father returns the charmed bow to the Blessed Lady.* More evidence of His benevolent sight.

She was appalled to find an echo of the townsfolk's reverence in the Lord Archer's gaze as he handed her the bow. *Even him,* she thought. *Is that where the Father's sight truly resides? In the gaze of those who cling to him for hope and deliverance.* "Thank you, my lord," she said. "I'll be on the wall if you need anything."

It took another ten days, the unending crunch of the stones on the wall a constant reminder that the sand in their glass was running low. Reva took to sitting cross-legged on the battlements some fifty paces short of the breach, watching the great globes come rushing down. It was a strangely compelling sight to see them descend in a blur, dust and stone exploding upwards as they found their mark. She entertained a faint hope she would be spotted by the Volarian commander and he would waste a few stones trying to crush her, but if he had seen her, it appeared he was in no mood for distractions.

Afternoons were usually spent in the healing house helping Brother Harin or visiting with Arken, still recovering from his arrow wound. Despite the brother's best efforts the wound had contrived to fester, necessitating some deft work with the scalpel and a liberal application of corr-tree oil. "You stink," Reva told him the following day, wrinkling her nose at the acrid aroma.

"The smell I can get used to," he said. "The sting's the worst of it."

"From Veliss." She placed a bag of sugared nuts next to his bed. "Make them last, there won't be any more."

"Promise me," he said, reaching for her hand, eyes dark with serious intent. "You'll call for me when they come. Don't let me die in this bed."

You've a lot of years ahead, she wanted to say, but stopped herself. *He may be young but he's no fool.* "I promise," she said.

For all their apparent devotion, and despite the increase in rations, the mood of the people darkened as the breach widened. There were fewer shouts of adulation as she walked the streets, and she often saw people weeping openly, one old man surrendering to despair and collapsing to the cobbles, hands clamped over his ears against the slow drumbeat of the engines' labour. And the Reader kept preaching.

Veliss's reports told of the old man's increasingly deranged sermons. He would often speak for hours with no reference to the Ten Books, the words "heretic" and "judgement" most prominent in his rantings. "A mad old man screaming in a hall," Reva had said in answer to Veliss's worried frown.

"True," she replied. "But the hall isn't empty. In fact it's more full than ever."

A stone crashed into the breach, raising another cloud of dust and shattered masonry. Reva turned her gaze to the ships and found them busier than usual, the engineers rushing to and fro as they hauled ropes and worked levers, the engines swivelling on their mounts with slow deliberation.

She walked to the lip of the breach, staring down at the dust-shrouded wreckage below. Stones that had stood for centuries reduced to rubble in a few weeks. A familiar thrum sounded from the engines as they launched in unison, the stones describing their lazy arcs against a clear sky, smashing into the wall some two hundred paces north of where she stood.

She raised her gaze to the Volarian warship. The awning cast a dark shadow but she could just see him, a tall figure staring back. It may have been her imagination, or a trick of the light, but she fancied she saw him offer a bow.

"My lady . . ." A faint call behind her. She turned to find a woman hurrying up the steps to the battlements, a wailing bundle in her arms. The young Asraelin mother from the other day, face pale and drawn in fear. Reva rushed to her, reaching out a steadying hand as she swayed a little, her breath laboured, the words barely audible above the child's cries.

"They took her," she gasped. "Lady Veliss hid us but they took her, and all the other Faithful."

"Who did? Where?"

"A great many people, shouting about the Father's judgement." She paused, hugging the child to her. "They said they were taking them to the Reader."

CHAPTER FIVE
Vaelin

"Another two hundred today," Nortah said, putting his bow aside and collapsing onto a chair. "Mostly men this time. All raring for revenge, which is nice. Their women and daughters all got taken by another caravan. Poltar's off looking for them now."

"How many does that make?" Vaelin asked Brother Hollun.

"We have freed fifteen hundred and seventy-two people since crossing into Nilsael, my lord," the brother replied without pause. "Just over half are of fighting age. Almost all have opted to join our ranks. Though I should point out our continued lack of weapons."

"We've got the slavers' swords," Nortah pointed out. "Plus any axes and bill-hooks we can scavenge from all the corpse-strewn villages we keep finding."

Vaelin looked out over the camp, the tents clustered around a bend in the river which changed its name from the Brinewash to the Vellen when it crossed the Nilsaelin border. The camp grew larger every day, home to over forty-five thousand men now they had Marven's Nilsaelins to swell the ranks. Soon after Brother Harlick penned their agreement, their Fief Lord had taken himself off to his capital, pressing his seal into the wax with a customary cackle and waving at his litter bearers to get moving.

"You can have the idiot twins," he said to Vaelin, bobbing in his chair as they bore him away. "Been lusting for a war all their lives. Don't be too surprised if they piss their breeches at the first whiff of blood though. I'll conscript all the men I can and send them on after. Try not to lose too many. Fields don't plough themselves, y'know."

Alornis had been busy sketching during the sealing ceremony, beginning a new canvas depicting the event shortly after. Unlike Master Benril she felt no need for additional drama or embellishment. Although still roughly worked, her painting conveyed her gift for uncanny realism in its rendering of a grinning old man leaning over a scroll whilst the captains of the army looked on, varying depths of unease or suspicion on every face.

"Did I really look that angry?" Vaelin asked.

"I do not flatter, lord brother," she replied, flicking pigment at him with her brush. "I see and I paint. That is all."

Vaelin scanned the line of scowling or frowning faces, finding one exception. Nortah stood near the back of the assembly, a faint wry smile on his lips.

"They'll need training," he said to his brother now, moving to the table and reaching for parchment. He dipped his quill and began to write, the letters formed with slow precision. "Nortah Al Sendahl is hereby appointed Captain of the Free Company of the Army of the North." He signed the parchment and held it out to Nortah. "You can have Sergeant Davern as second."

"That blowhard?" Nortah scoffed. "Can't I have one of the North Guard?"

"He's good with the sword and he knows how to teach it. And I can't denude the North Guard any further. We can linger here only two more days, so train them hard."

"As you wish, mighty Tower Lord." Nortah went to the tent flap then paused. "We're really marching all the way to Alltor?"

The song's insistence had deepened the further south they marched, the tone ever more urgent. *She fights*, he knew. *They come to tear the walls down and she fights.* "Yes, brother," he said. "We really are."

Two days later they were on the march once again, Vaelin setting a punishing pace of thirty miles a day and letting it be known that he would be less than forgiving to stragglers. As in any army however, there were shirkers and deserters. The former he left to the sergeants, the latter were pursued by the North Guard and brought back to be stripped of weapons, coin and shoes before they were flogged and set loose. It was no more than a handful of men, and he hated the need for it, but this was far from a professional army and the leeway he had allowed the Wolfrunners would be a dangerous indulgence now.

They forded the Vellen on the fifth day, keeping a southward course until the jagged outline of the Greypeaks came into view and he ordered a halt for a day's rest and reconnaissance. As expected, Sanesh Poltar brought grim tidings come the evening.

"Many horsemen," he said to the council of captains. "South-east of here. Riding hard after Marelim Sil soldiers, on foot and only a third as many. They hurry to the mountains, seeking shelter." His expression was grave as he shook his head. "Won't reach them."

"Is there enough time for our horse to get there?" Vaelin asked.

The Eorhil war chief shrugged. "We will, can't speak for others."

Vaelin reached for his cloak. "Captain Adal, Captain Orven, muster your men. We ride immediately. Count Marven, send the Nilsaelin horse to screen the south and west. The Army of the North is in your hands until I return."

Flame reminded him somewhat of Spit in his love of the run, tossing his head and snorting in appreciation as they galloped south, the mass of horses around them raising thunder from the earth. Dahrena rode at his side, having snapped a curt rebuke at Adal when he suggested she stay with the army. They managed to keep up with the Eorhil, though the North Guard and Orven's men were obliged to trail in their wake by a half mile or so. The onset of darkness forced a halt after they had covered some twenty miles.

No fires were lit, the horsemen simply sitting or standing with their mounts, waiting for daylight. Dahrena had immediately slipped from her saddle and wrapped a cloak tightly about her shoulders as she sat on the grass. "Shan't be long," she said to Vaelin with a small smile before closing her eyes.

"Is this really necessary, my lord?" Adal asked, worry etched into his face as he stared at Dahrena's unmoving form.

"I do not command her, Captain." The blood-song gave a soft murmur, a note of anger and resentment, but also something else, something that now appeared obvious in the intensity of the captain's gaze. *All the years at her side and he's never told her,* Vaelin wondered.

Dahrena gave a soft gasp, opening her eyes and blinking rapidly. "They've stopped," she breathed, slumping forward a little. Adal stepped closer to steady her but she waved him away, climbing to her feet with a groan.

"The Volarians?" Vaelin asked.

"The Realm Guard. Stopped on a hill some sixty miles directly south of here."

My brother makes a stand, Vaelin thought. The song was quite clear, Caenis had command of the Realm Guard's remnants, and they were tired of running.

"Remount!" Vaelin called, striding to Flame and vaulting into the saddle. "We ride through the night!"

They kept to a trot until the sun rose then spurred to a full gallop, Vaelin driving Flame hard although the horse's flesh seemed to sing with joy as he struck out ahead of the Eorhil. After an hour's ride the ground flattened out into rolling plains, a low hill visible on the horizon and a large dust-cloud rising in the east. Sanesh Poltar managed to urge yet more speed for his mount, pulling ahead of Vaelin and raising his strongbow over his head then waving it towards the east. A third of the Eorhil host immediately peeled away from the main body, striking out in a parallel course to the approaching dust-cloud.

Vaelin could see the Realm Guard on the hill now, standing three ranks deep, a few banners waving. They were too distant to make out the sigils but he knew the one in the centre bore a wolf running above a tower.

The Volarian cavalry came into view shortly after, dark-armoured figures riding tall warhorses, charging with lances levelled. Sanesh Poltar waved his bow again and another contingent of Eorhil separated from the host to charge directly at the Volarian flank. Vaelin followed the war chief as he led the remainder into the ground between the Realm Guard and the oncoming Volarians. On either side of him Eorhil warriors all notched an arrow to their bows with smooth unconscious precision, still at full gallop. They rode to within a hundred paces of the Volarians and loosed as one, no commands had been given. The arrows descended onto the leading companies in a dense cloud, horses screaming and falling as they struck home, men tumbling from the saddles to be trampled by their onrushing comrades. The Volarian charge faltered as the Eorhil continued to loose from the saddle, skirting their ranks and sending arrow after arrow into the mass of men and horses.

Vaelin reined in and watched the unfolding spectacle. Whoever had command of the Volarian horse was evidently quick in recognising a hopeless cause; assailed on three sides by horse archers and outnumbered into the bargain. Trumpets sounded amidst the roiling companies and they drew back, striking out for the only open ground to the south. The Eorhil, however, were not done.

Sanesh Poltar kept his contingent on the Volarian right flank whilst the two other wings continued to assail their rear and left, the arrows falling in a continuous rain, claiming ever more cavalrymen and horses. Vaelin watched the mobile battle fade towards the south as the North Guard and Orven's men galloped past to join in the deathblow.

He turned Flame and trotted towards the hill where the Realm Guard were still standing in ranks. Their discipline held until his face came into view, whereupon they broke, running towards him with a great cheer, clustering around, joy and relief on every face. He nodded to them, smiling tightly at the babble of acclaim, nudging Flame forward until they came to the hill where a lone figure stood below a tall banner. He broke free from the clustering soldiers and guided Flame up the slope.

"Sorry, brother," he said, dismounting at Caenis's side. "I had hoped to get here sooner . . ."

He fell silent at the look on his brother's face, eyes glaring amidst the dirt-covered visage of a man who had known nothing but battle and torment for weeks. "This all happened," he said, the words spoken in a coarse echo of the voice Vaelin had known since childhood, "because you left us."

Adal's scouts brought news of three battalions of Volarian infantry to the west. It seemed the Volarian commander had split his force in his eagerness to finish the Realm Guard. Vaelin ordered the Eorhil to cut off their line of retreat and sent word to Count Marven ordering him to crush the enemy force with all dispatch. *Time they were blooded.*

"Five regiments," Caenis reported in a clipped voice, the tones used by a subordinate to a superior, lacking familiarity or affection. "Or what remains of them. The Thirty-fifth is the most numerous with a third of its men still standing."

"Is it true?" Vaelin asked. "About Darnel?"

Caenis gave a short nod. "We were drawn up for battle, the Volarians coming on in strength. When Darnel's knights appeared we thought it a deliverance. There was no warning, they just trotted within a few hundred paces of the left flank and charged, smashing it to pieces. As of that moment we were undone. The men stood though, every regiment stood and fought, most to the death. I don't have the words to do them justice. Lord Verniers might, if he still lives."

"Verniers?" Vaelin asked. "The Alpiran Emperor's chronicler. He was there?"

"At the King's command. Grist for his history of the Realm." Caenis met his gaze for the first time since their meeting on the hill. "He had an interesting story to tell and many questions, especially about our time in the Order."

"What did you tell him?"

"No more than you did, I suspect."

"How did you get away?"

"We rallied, launched a counter at the Volarian centre. I gambled their general would be careful enough of his own person to halt the advance and gather forces to his defence. As luck had it, I was right."

"Your men are alive thanks to you, brother."

"Not all, we lost many on the march."

"Gallis? Krelnik?"

"Krelnik during the countercharge. Gallis in the retreat."

Vaelin wanted to offer some words of commiseration, share memories of the grizzled veteran and the former climbing outlaw, but Caenis had taken his gaze away, staring rigidly ahead once more. "I regret asking you to march again so soon," Vaelin said. "But we have business at Alltor."

His brother's expression didn't change. "As my lord commands."

Is this how it will be from now on? Vaelin wondered. *Brotherhood turned to hate by lost Faith?*

His gaze was drawn by the sound of drumming hooves as Nortah rode into their makeshift camp at the gallop, Snowdance loping in his wake. *Perhaps this will lighten his mood,* Vaelin thought as Nortah leapt from the saddle, striding towards Caenis with a broad grin.

"*You* are dead," Caenis greeted him with a smile, his lack of surprise confirming Vaelin's long-held suspicion his tale of Nortah's supposed demise had never been believed by his brothers.

Nortah just laughed and enfolded Caenis in a warm embrace. "It's a great thing to see you, brother. Your niece and nephew have long wanted to meet you."

Caenis drew back a little as Snowdance padded closer, sniffing curiously. "Don't mind her," Nortah said. "We found some more slavers today so she's well-fed."

"We've solved your weapon-supply problem," Vaelin told him, pointing towards the dark mound of bodies to the south. The Eorhil didn't understand the concept of prisoners, war was a matter of absolutes to them, shorn of restraint or misplaced compassion, though they had been careful to spare as many horses as possible.

"Might be an idea if they left some alive in future," Nortah commented. "Dead men have no stories to tell."

"I'd hazard we'll have a few storytellers in hand tomorrow."

Count Marven had taken no chances with the Volarian infantry, sealing the flanks with his cavalry whilst the archers weakened them with successive volleys. The full army was unleashed when he judged the enemy sufficiently decimated. The Volarian host consisted of one battalion of Free Swords and two of Varitai. Predictably, the Free Swords were the most keen to surrender whilst the Varitai had to be slaughtered to a man. Even then there were only a handful of prisoners, most of them wounded.

"No officers," the count reported to Vaelin. "Highest rank amongst them seems to be a sergeant, or whatever they call a sergeant."

He gave an irritated glance over at Fief Lord Darvus's twin grandsons as one of them shouted in pain, his brother attempting to stitch a cut on his forearm.

"Didn't piss their breeches then?" Vaelin asked quietly.

"Hardly. No holding those two, my lord. Bravery they have in abundance." He dropped his voice. "Brains, however . . ."

"My lords," Vaelin called to the twins. "Best take yourselves off to Brother Kehlan's tent."

The two lords rose and bowed with their customary uniformity, the one on the left voicing their response. Vaelin had noted he was the only one who spoke, possibly in order to prevent them speaking in unison. "More grievously injured men require the healer's attentions, my lord. A true knight would not trouble him over a trifle."

"Clearly, your experience with true knights is limited. Your grandfather won't thank me if you return having lost limbs to festered stitching." He nodded at the tent flap. "Get you gone."

"We collected more than enough weapons for the Free Company, my lord," Brother Hollun reported when the twins had left. "In fact, we should have enough for six such companies."

"Our losses?" Vaelin asked.

"Thirty-five killed, sixty wounded," the brother responded with his usual lack of hesitancy.

"Would've been less if the freed folk hadn't joined in," Count Marven said. "Hate makes people careless of their lives, I suppose."

"Nevertheless it was well done, my lord," Vaelin told him. "Brother Harlick has been drawing up maps of Alltor and the surrounding country. I should like you to take a look, judge our best line of approach."

The Nilsaelin gave a hesitant bow of assent. Their time in Linesh had made the man wary of him, Vaelin knew, and in his turn he had distrusted the count's obvious desire for martial distinction. Now though, circumstance made such concerns seem trifling. "I . . . am pleased to enjoy your trust, my lord," Marven replied.

The prisoners were no different from any other group of defeated men Vaelin had seen over the years. Eyes full of fear, gaze downcast and wary of drawing attention as they shuffled under his scrutiny.

"They're all fairly ignorant and barely literate," Harlick reported. "Volarian education is notoriously poor. People are expected to teach themselves whatever they need to know. This lot know how to fight and follow orders. How to rape and murder too, no doubt. But they're somewhat close-lipped about their prior exploits in the Realm, as you might expect."

"Do they know the name of the man who commands their army?" Vaelin asked.

Like Brother Hollun, Harlick had no need to consult notes or pause before providing a response. "General Reklar Tokrev. A red-clad, as they usually are. Distinguished veteran of several border clashes with the Alpirans and renowned commander of numerous expeditions against the northern tribes. I have to say, I find the list of his achievements a little improbable since one of the campaigns he supposedly led took place over seventy years ago."

"Any news of Alltor?"

"They've never heard of the place. Seems they were sent after the Realm Guard before the general marched on Cumbrael. I . . . doubt they have anything else to offer, my lord."

Vaelin watched the wretched men fidget, some unable to keep the terrorised tremble from their limbs. The song rose as he saw their fear, a familiar complex note that denoted the birth of a stratagem. He turned to Orven, captain of the only company he could trust with this duty. "They're coming with us," he said. "Make sure they're suitably fed and watered. And keep them well away from Captain Nortah's people."

Crossing into Cumbrael brought sights of an even greater level of destruction and murder than those already witnessed. The succession of ruined villages along their line of march seemed endless, littered with so many rotting corpses Vaelin was forced to order them left where they lay as they couldn't afford the time needed to give them all to the fire. Unlike the Nilsaelin villages, these were extensively vandalised, mills and chapels burned, many bodies mutilated and showing signs of torture. Also the surrounding fields were often black from burning, the crops turned to ash and every well they found spoiled with a sheep or goat carcass.

"Doesn't make any sense," Adal said as they rode through a ruined cornfield. "All armies need to be fed."

"The Volarians didn't do this," Vaelin replied. "I suspect the Cumbraelin Fief Lord was keen to deny them any succour from his own lands. May explain their viciousness towards the people."

They came upon a macabre sight in the evening, ten men hanging from a large yew, eyes and tongues removed and the first two fingers of their hands severed and stuffed into their mouths. Vaelin saw his sister pale at the sight, swaying in her saddle a little.

"We'll see to them," he said, pressing his hand to her shoulder. "You don't have to linger here."

"Yes," she replied, dismounting and extracting parchment and charcoal from her saddlebags. "I do. Leave them there a moment, please."

She walked stiffly to a nearby tree stump and sat down, fixing her eyes on the scene and starting to draw.

"Must be archers," Nortah commented. "Taking their fingers like that. Saw our own men do something similar in the Martishe."

Vaelin saw that Alornis was crying as she sketched, tears streaming from her eyes as they constantly shifted from the hanging men to the image forming on the parchment. Dahrena went to her side as she finished, hunching over and weeping softly. "People will need to know," he heard her whisper as Dahrena pulled her close. "They'll need to remember."

The town had been named Two Forks for the branching streams that surrounded it. Vaelin had once passed through it with the Wolfrunners during one of their fanatic-hunting expeditions prior to the Alpiran war. He recalled a bustling place of winepresses and merchants bartering for the best price on the latest casks. The people had been guarded but not so hostile towards him as most Cumbraelins, their priest a hearty fellow of broad girth and rosy cheeks who happily offered Vaelin a prayer of the Father's forgiveness, wine cup in hand as he quoted the Ninth Book.

His church was a ruin now, the only sign of him some anonymous blackened bones in the scorched wreckage. The Seordah had found the place, the warriors standing in the streets and staring at the various horrors, more baffled than enraged. The town hadn't been easily taken, barricades had been constructed across the roads and the surrounding waterways made for effective defensive barriers. Vaelin judged it had taken several days to fall from the bodies in the factor's house, all lying in a row, bandages visible on the putrefying flesh. *Fought it out long enough to have a care for the wounded,* he thought.

"Children all in one place," Hera Drakil said, his face like stone. "No sign of wounds, but smelling of poison."

"Killed by their parents to spare them the torments of enraged men," Vaelin said. It seemed the Volarians had been obliged to visit their frustrations on the few surviving adults. A pile of disconstituted corpses lay in the centre of the town, not one left whole. The limbs were arranged in a circle about a central mass of severed heads, a thick cloud of flies buzzing amidst the miasma of decomposition. Vaelin was glad Alornis wasn't here to feel compelled to draw the scene.

"I would be grateful if you could bury them," Vaelin said to Hera Drakil, deciding this was worth the delay.

"We shall."

He nodded and went to where Flame was tethered, pausing as the Seordah called after him. "We were right."

Vaelin turned back with a questioning look.

"To heed the wolf's call," Hera Drakil said. "A people that would do this need to die."

"I once had occasion," Vaelin told the Volarian captive, "to meet the Alpiran Emperor. He presided over my trial, of course, but he came to my cell afterwards to talk to me alone. Just once."

The captive stared at him with bright but uncomprehending eyes. Vaelin had chosen him for his youth and the greater pitch of his terror. His fellow captives were hanging from the branches of a willow tree on the riverbank south of Two Forks, the ropes creaking as they swung in the breeze.

"It's not widely known," Vaelin went on, "but the Emperor is a very frail man. Victim of a bone disease since childhood. He's very small, very thin, and has to be carried about on a litter as his legs will break if he attempts to walk. But there's a great strength to him, I could feel it burning away inside when he looked at me. It's a very humbling thing to look into a man's eyes and know yourself his inferior.

"They brought him to my cell after the trial, servants placing him before me and leaving us alone, even though I was unchained and he must have known I could crush the life from him in an instant. I bowed and he told me to get up. I had been taught Alpiran at his instruction, for a man should understand every word spoken at his trial according to Imperial law. He asked if I had any complaints about my treatment, I said no. He asked if I felt any guilt over the death of the Hope and again, I said no. He asked why. I told him I was a warrior in service to the Faith and the Realm. He shook his thin, bony head and called me a liar. 'The song tells you,' he said. 'That you did no wrong.'

"He knew, you see. Somehow he knew, though I could hear only the slightest murmur of a gift within him. He said those chosen to sit in the Emperor's chair share the same gift, the ability to discern potential. Not greatness, not compassion or wisdom. Just potential, and the nature of that potential would only be revealed over time, sometimes with unfortunate consequences. Shortly before the war he had begun to discern the temper of the Hope's potential and found it worried him greatly. Also there was another within his court who offered a far brighter prospect, though choosing them would invite accusations of favouritism, a serious charge in a land where anyone may ascend to the throne with the favour of the gods, a mystical force for which the Emperor is merely a conduit. My actions had solved his dilemma, and so I would be allowed my life and suffer no torments. However, he loved his people and their suffering at the hands of our army made such mercy his own torment. 'If I have any claim to greatness,' he told me. 'It will lie in the victory I won over the hatred you tried to place in my heart. An Emperor can allow no such luxury.'

"As I said, I knew myself as his inferior, even more so now. I should like you to know I have tried to follow his example, to act without hatred in prosecuting this war. Sadly, your people have contrived to defeat me in this ambition."

Vaelin took a leather satchel containing the message he had dictated to Brother Harlick and lifted the strap over the captive's head, making him flinch and utter a whimper, calming a little when Vaelin smiled. "For the general," he said, recalling Harlick's words. "Tokrev," he repeated, patting the satchel.

The captive just stared back in unblinking terror. Vaelin took a moment to study his face, feeling the song swell as he committed it to memory.

"Put him on a horse," Vaelin told Orven, "and let him go."

Chapter Six
Lyrna

*S*o *many ships.* The harbour was jammed with them, the masts resembling a gently swaying forest, the crews crawling over deck and rigging like ants as she looked on from her balcony.

"Must be over a thousand by now," Iltis surmised.

"I make it twelve hundred," Orena said. "If you put them end to end, maybe we could walk home."

"Right now I'd rather swim," Harvin muttered, straightening as he caught Lyrna's glance. "Not that I would, Highness."

Lyrna turned back to the harbour without reply. Her decision to accompany the Meldenean fleet when it sailed forth had not been well received, Iltis protesting about the obvious dangers whilst Harvin had the additional worry of Orena who, along with Murel, refused to be left behind.

"My queen needs her ladies," she had stated. "She said so herself."

She had expected some obstruction from the Shield but he had just frowned and said, "Of course, Highness. I would have you nowhere else but at my side if the choice were mine." His dazzling smile was almost enough to order Iltis to strike him down there and then.

She could see him now, striding along the quay, exchanging words with various captains and sailors. Whereas he was all charm with her, his countenance when dealing with his own people was one of grim toleration, for all their obvious respect and relief at his presence. *They disappointed him,* she concluded. *He wonders whether they were truly worth the sacrifice he was prepared to make.*

"I realise it may be too early in my service to ask a boon, Highness," Harvin said. "But when this is over, I formally request never to be sent to sea again. I've seen enough rat-infested bilge tubs for this life."

Lyrna allowed herself a smile. "Your request is granted, my lord."

She watched the Shield as he strode closer, face upraised as he found her on the balcony, bowing deeply and extending an arm to where the *Sea Sabre* was moored.

"My ladies and lords," she said. "Our vessel awaits."

"The best way to avoid a trap," the Shield said, "is to kill the bastard who made it before he gets a chance to set it."

"As long as you can find him first," Ship Lord Ell-Nurin pointed out.

They stood around a map table set up in the *Sea Sabre*'s hold, an extensive chart of the Isles and surrounding waters spread out before them. There were eight other senior captains present along with Belorath, now happily returned to his role as first mate. Ell-Nurin was the sole Ship Lord present, apparently the only member of the council Ell-Nestra could stomach for any length of time.

"Thanks to Her Highness we know the Volarians intend a feint," he went on, finger pointing to the southern approaches. "Probably here, the most direct route to the capital aided by favourable winds. Whilst we can most likely expect them to send their troop ships to the beaches here." He tapped at three bays on the northern shore of the largest islands. "Where the wind will be against them, but since they expect us to be fully occupied to the south, it won't matter."

"What does that tell you?" Lyrna enquired.

"That they'll have to separate here." His finger picked out a small speck some eighty-odd miles to the east.

"The Teeth of Moesis," Ell-Nurin said. "A prophetic place for a battle."

"The gods are bound to smile on us there," Belorath put in. "If they smile on us anywhere."

"You intend to attack as they separate?" Lyrna asked.

"Indeed, Highness," the Shield replied. "We tack from the north-west with the wind in our favour, sink the troop-ships first. Without them their invasion is a pointless endeavour after all."

"What's to stop them simply joining forces again when they see our sails on the horizon?"

Ell-Nestra's finger tapped a point just to the south of the Teeth of Moesis. "The Serpent's Tail. The god left more than just his teeth behind."

"A great stone reef, Highness," Ell-Nurin explained. "Their southern division will have to navigate it to join up with the troop-ships. Not an easy task at the best of times."

"All dependent on whether they stick to the plan outlined in the book," Lyrna said. "A plan they may never have received."

"There was more than one book," Ell-Nurin said. "Safely received in Varinshold according to our sources. We are also advised the Volarian general wrote to the Council-man expressing his condolences at the loss of his son, presumably to a storm since no trace of his ship has been found."

"We sail with the tide," the Shield said, moving back from the table.

"The fleet is not fully gathered," Ell-Nurin said. "Another two days will give us fifty more ships."

"And hand the Volarians the Isles. We've tarried too long as it is, every scrap of sail will be needed to get the fleet to the Teeth in time." He looked at Lyrna with one of his hateful smiles. "My first mate tells me Your Highness is a great exponent of Keschet.

Perhaps you would honour me with a game once we're under way?"

He was a much better player than Belorath, relying on his own tactical acumen rather than learned strategies, improvising with considerable flair and imagination. But he was also overly aggressive and inflexible in the long game. But at least she didn't have to string it out.

"Fifty-eight moves," she said, plucking his emperor from the board. "Very impressive."

"It must have been hard," he said, reclining on his stool, his smile now genuine.

"Hard, my lord Shield? Keschet is very simple in essence . . ."

"Not the game. Pretending all those years. Not being you. After all, who wants the keenest mind in the room to be the princess in the corner? Did you do needlework whilst your father held his councils? I expect you're very good at that too."

"Actually I never learned needlework. Nor felt the need to sit through my father's meetings, since I could usually anticipate every word likely to be spoken. But yes, it was hard to pretend stupidity to the stupid."

"Now there is no need. The whole world can see your . . ." He faltered and fell silent, turning his gaze out to sea and the great host of ships surrounding them.

"My true face?" she asked, finding considerable enjoyment in his discomfort.

"I misspoke, and crave your forgiveness."

She busied herself removing her pieces from the board. "I'm sure I'll hear worse when I return to the Realm."

"You think they'll accept you?" he asked. "As you are?"

"You talk as if they have a choice. I am queen by right of blood. That's all they need to know."

"And you expect their instant servile obedience?"

"I am returned from the dead, bearing the scars of my suffering in service to the Realm's need at this time of greatest peril. Surely the Departed must favour me." She smiled and gestured at the board. "Another game, my lord?"

"I don't think there's much point, do you?" He leaned forward, all trace of a smile gone from his lips. "Why did you come? You could have stayed in the isles, sailed safely away if the battle went against us."

"Perhaps I wanted to see you perform."

His eyes flicked to the Keschet board. "You told me more than you intended, Highness. With you, seemingly simple moves always conceal complex intent."

"My intent is not so complex. Win your battle and I'll happily share it."

"I intend to." He rose and bowed before striding off towards the helm.

A night and a day brought the Teeth in sight, a black nub on the horizon occasionally obscured by crashing waves. The Shield ordered the fleet to strip sails and took the *Sea Sabre* on ahead, dropping anchor barely a half mile away from the Teeth. They were an impressive sight at this distance, great slabs of stone rising from the sea, swirling currents bringing wave after wave to batter their flanks.

"A great serpent's teeth?" Murel said when Benten had related the story of the Teeth's origins. She gave a scornful laugh. "All gods are a lie, but that's a gem." She fell silent at Lyrna's glare, the crewmen within earshot bristling with indignation.

"My apologies," Lyrna told them. "My lady is young and knows very little."

"Sorry, Highness," Murel murmured, gaze downcast as the crew resumed their tasks.

"Gods are real to those that hold to them," Lyrna told her, patting her hand, leaning close to add in a whisper, "But a lie is still a lie, no matter how big."

The Shield climbed aloft with his spyglass, standing on the mainmast and scanning the horizon, hair whipping in the wind. Lyrna saw Murel staring in open admiration then looking away with a flush on her cheeks when she caught Lyrna's eye. The hours stretched as Ell-Nestra maintained his vigil, the afternoon sun eventually burning through the haze and the sea calming in the warmer air.

He may very well be wrong, Lyrna thought, gazing at the empty sea to the east. *The Volarian fleet could have passed by in the night and we would never know.* She had never been a great believer in intuition, preferring reason and evidence to instinct and guess-work. But there was something in his certainty that told her they were in the right place, a lifetime at sea had to be worth some-thing.

She occupied herself searching the waves for sign of the shark but finding no trace of the fin. Perhaps the echo of Fermin's call had finally faded, or maybe it had sensed the coming battle and gone in search of easier prey. It was strange, but she found she missed it, the constancy of its presence had become a talisman for their continued survival. *I should have given you a name,* she thought. *One should always name a pet.*

"Hoist the black!" the Shield's order sounded from above as he descended to the deck, sliding down a rope to drop at the helm. "Raise anchor! Archers to the rigging!" He took the wheel and spun it as the anchor was hauled from the sea, the ship's prow pitching as they turned north. A large rectangular banner was raised to the top of the mainmast, completely black with no decoration. The signal for an enemy in sight.

Lyrna watched Ell-Nestra at the wheel, finding his expression graver than expected, the gaze he turned on her speaking of grim tidings. *Something is very wrong.*

They sailed north for a mile or so, turning and trimming canvas as the Meldenean fleet hurried in answer to the black banner's call. The Shield gave the wheel to the helmsman and went to the prow, eyes narrowed as he stared ahead. Lyrna went to his side, remaining silent as he continued to stare, face rigid with suppressed anger.

"I," he said after a moment, "am a fool."

"They did not split their fleet?"

"Oh they split it all right. Their feint sails south as we speak. Five hundred ships."

Five hundred. "The spies said their fleet was no more than twelve hundred ships. That would mean we sail towards only six hundred."

"The fleet that landed in Varinshold was twelve hundred strong, the fleet in front of us nigh on two thousand. They have been reinforced whilst at sea." He closed his eyes, cheeks bunching and fists balled on Skerva's wooden shoulder. "Why did I not see this?"

"What do we do?" Lyrna asked.

He straightened, unclenching his fists and breathing out slowly then turning to her with a grin. "We do what we came to do, Highness. The wind is at our backs and there are many prizes to claim this day." He turned back to the deck, pausing to brush his fingers over her hand, breath soft on her ear. "And I am so keen to hear of your true intent."

The Volarian battle line came into view all too soon, a long parade of dark-hulled ships all following the same southward course. "Trying to get some wind in their sails," Belorath explained. "Probably want to hook round and have at our arses."

"Watch your tongue in front of the queen," Iltis growled but Belorath just laughed and tossed him a broad leather-bound shield.

"You and your fellow lordships can keep the arrows off the women. Best leave the fighting to us, eh?"

"Pirate dog," Iltis grumbled, fixing the shield's strap over his arm, Benten and Harvin doing the same, as the first mate strode away. They wore much the same kit as the Meldeneans, a broad helm with leather chin-straps and mail shirts, though Iltis had been forced to stitch two together to fully cover his chest. Lyrna and her ladies had donned specially tailored mail of smaller dimensions which proved remarkably uncomfortable with a tendency to produce large amounts of unladylike sweat. However, she felt it preferable to a stray arrow in the chest. She also had a small dagger strapped to her forearm, the blade a little longer than she was used to but she had practised and found she could still throw it with reasonable accuracy. She doubted it would be much use in the coming maelstrom but drew some reassurance from the feel of it against her skin. *Never be without it.*

The Meldenean fleet were strung out in two roughly equal divisions, one following the *Sea Sabre* the other a narrow-hulled vessel commanded by Ship Lord Ell-Nurin. "The *Red Falcon*," Belorath had said. "Fastest ship afloat, some say."

The lead Ell-Nurin's ship was building over the *Sea Sabre* gave truth to his words, the prow cutting through the waves like a sword blade, sails seeming to strain against their lines from the wind that filled them.

"The bugger wants them all to himself!" the Shield called from the helm, raising a laugh amongst the crew. "Tighten those lines, I'll not be beaten to first blood!"

At his insistence Lyrna had positioned herself close to the entrance to the hold, ready to retreat below if the deck became too dangerous.

"What's that for?" Murel asked, seeing a sailor tossing sand from a bucket over the deck as the Volarians drew ever nearer.

"Blood," Benten said. "It's like to get slippery underfoot when it starts. Do the same thing on my father's boat when we do the gutting."

"Oh," the girl said in a small voice.

"My lady," Lyrna said. "You may go below."

"Thank you, Highness, but I prefer to stay."

No tears now, Lyrna saw as Murel straightened her back and drew a calming breath. *No longer just a girl.*

"Mangonels ready!" the Shield shouted and crewmen ran to pull the coverings from two bulky contraptions in the centre of the deck, others bringing baskets filled with projectiles and buckets of pitch.

The engines consisted of a single throwing arm fastened to a crossbeam around which thick lengths of rope had been wound. The ropes twisted as a crewman worked a lever to draw the arm back level with the deck. Their munitions were melon-sized balls of hemp, the rope wrapped tight around an iron core. Two were placed in the bowl at the end of the arm and soaked in pitch, a man with a torch standing by. One engine was positioned to cast its projectiles to the port side, the other starboard.

"I thought we'd be ramming them," Harvin said. "Then jumping on board to kill the crew."

"Most sea battles are won with flame," Lyrna said. *Though I'd hazard you'll see all manner of death this day.*

The Shield steered them towards the middle of the Volarian line, the *Red Falcon* heading for their rear. The archers began to loose before they were in range, tiny waterspouts appearing in the sea between the closing ships, the faint hiss of the falling shafts soon joined by the hard thunk of arrowheads on wood.

Lyrna could see the Volarians now, dark figures clustered at the starboard rail of a broad-beamed vessel, swords drawn and grapples ready.

"Loose!" Belorath barked and the torch-bearer lit the hemp balls in the mangonel bowl, standing back as his comrade kicked the release lever and the arm sprang forward, casting its flaming contents at the Volarian ship. The two fireballs described a lazy arc, trailing smoke as they fell amongst the Volarian soldiery, a cheer rising from the Meldeneans as the battle claimed its first victims, a few flaming men jumping into the sea.

The Shield put them alongside the opposing ship at a distance of no more than fifty paces, the air between them now thick with arrows.

"Down, Highness!" Iltis raised his shield as Lyrna and the two women crouched, Orena wincing at the hard rain. A cry came from above and Lyrna glanced up to see a crewman fall to the deck with a bone-snapping thump, an arrow jutting from his chest as he gasped out his final breaths from a bloody mouth.

The starboard mangonel loosed again, the fireballs flying into the Volarian rigging this time, their mainsail catching light and sending burning debris onto the men below, their arrow storm faltering as fire took hold. The ship lurched towards them in a last desperate attempt to board, grapples flying from the deck to fasten on the *Sea Sabre*'s rail. The Shield spun the wheel and the prow swung to port, the crew hacking away the grappling ropes but not before a small group of Volarians had managed to scramble across. They were lightly armoured men with twin short swords on their backs, moving along the ropes with an unnatural speed and sure-handed grace. A few fell to the Meldenean archers in the rigging but four of them managed to make the deck, vaulting over the rail and drawing swords to hack down the nearest crewmen. They charged for the mangonels, parrying the slashing sabres of the crew with ease, killing the men servicing the engines in a matter of seconds.

Then the Shield was amongst them, his sabre moving in a blur, killing one then ducking under the thrust of another to hack through his lower leg. The other two launched a coordinated attack, one slashing at Ell-Nestra's face whilst the other sought to deliver a killing blow to the chest. He backed away, parrying and twisting as they forced him against the starboard rail.

Iltis gave a roar and charged forward with his sword levelled, Harvin and Benten on either side. The Volarian managed to turn aside the big man's thrust but had no defence against the overhand slash delivered by Harvin, the sword cleaving through his shoulder. Benten hacked at the remaining Volarian as he continued to battle the Shield, earning a cut on his arm as the man easily side-stepped the blow and delivered a counter, only to fall dead a second later as Ell-Nestra's sabre speared him through the neck.

Lyrna saw that the Volarian ship was adrift now, her deck covered in flame and her sails burning rags. All around, the sea was full of battling vessels, many already fully aflame. Through the smoke she could see a Meldenean ship jammed between two enemy vessels, her deck a seething mass of combat.

She called to the Shield and pointed. He went to the rail, sabre dripping blood across the deck. "We'll need those mangonels working," he said.

She nodded and beckoned her lords over to the engines, dragging the bodies clear and gathering the remaining ammunition. "Can't say as I know how to work such a thing," Harvin said.

"It's easy," Benten said, grimacing a little as Murel tied a bandage about his arm wound. "This lever draws back the arm, that one releases it."

They managed to have it readied by the time the Shield had steered them within range of one of the Volarian ships. Lyrna touched a torch to the pitch-covered hemp and Benten kicked the lever, the fireballs sailing into the centre of the enemy ship without any obvious effect. They repeated the process two more times as the *Sea Sabre* closed, their efforts rewarded by the sight of a decent-sized blaze rising from the Volarian ship's deck but also drawing the ire of her archers.

"Faith!" Iltis grunted as they huddled under his shield, an arrowhead appearing through the leather binding just above his arm.

"Grapples out!" Belorath yelled as the *Sea Sabre* scraped against the Volarians' hull. Crewmen ran to cast their three-pronged hooks across the gap, one falling to an arrow and plunging over the side. However, the thickening smoke offered some protection as the rest of the crew clustered around and hauled on the ropes, pulling the two ships together then throwing boarding planks across the divide.

"They don't come with mercy!" the Shield yelled, standing at the rail with his sabre held aloft. "Don't show them any!"

The crew responded with snarling assent as they followed him across the planks, sabres and spears raised high, the sight of the ensuing battle lost to the smoke now billowing about the Volarian deck.

"Um, Highness?" Lyrna turned to see Murel standing at the starboard rail and beyond her a very large Volarian ship ploughing directly towards them.

"Reload the engines!" She went to the starboard mangonel, working the lever as fast as she could, casting glances at the approaching monster. *A few fireballs won't stop this one.*

"Murel!" she shouted. "Get the pitch!"

The lady didn't respond, still staring out to sea, but not at the Volarian ship, at something moving towards it at great speed, its fin leaving a wake like a streak of white fire.

The shark rose from the sea, tail whipping and jaws agape, falling onto the Volarian deck in an explosion of splintered wood. It thrashed, scattering men and rigging like chaff, bodies and wreckage cast into the air, some men leaping into the sea in terror. The Volarian ship listed under the weight of the shark, the upper deck collapsing as she keeled over and the sea washed across her hull. Dozens of men thrashed in the water, the sea roiling as the great ship sank into the depths, then turning red as the shark's head rose amongst the survivors, jaws snapping. Within a few seconds they were gone, the only sign of their ship a few splintered planks and barrels bobbing on the swell.

Very good, Lyrna thought, catching sight of the shark's red stripes beneath the waves. *Do it again.*

By the onset of evening what remained of the Volarian fleet clustered together for protection like bison facing a wolf pack as the Meldeneans circled, casting forth an unending rain of fireballs. Occasionally a Volarian captain would try to strike out at the tormentors, but the sight of the shark was usually enough to turn them back. Three times it had leapt from the sea to destroy any ship coming close to the *Sea Sabre*, spreading terror amongst the Volarian fleet and sapping their crews' courage with every shattered hull and blood slick. After the destruction of the third ship, a huge troop carrier which had gone down accompanied by the screams of the hundreds of men trapped belowdecks, many Volarian vessels had simply turned about and sailed off towards the east with every sail hoisted. By the time the sun began to wane Lyrna counted only some two hundred ships bunched together as the fireballs fell. The pirates' skill and the shark had tipped the balance, but at a cost. She estimated at least half the Meldenean fleet was gone, numerous vessels adrift on the surrounding sea, their decks thick with corpses.

The last Volarian ships attempted to break out as night descended, the flaming hulls of their sisters robbing them of concealment as the Meldeneans closed for the kill. She saw a troop ship assailed by three pirate vessels at once, the crews swarming aboard with spear and sabre, sounds of battle soon replaced by screams of slaughter and torment. By midnight it was over, the Shield ordering sails trimmed and a south-easterly course set.

"We still have five hundred more to sink," he said. "You'd best rest, Highness."

He had given her his cabin to share with her ladies. They were both already abed, lying fully clothed side by side, hands dark with dried blood after hours spent tending the wounded. Lyrna settled next to Orena, provoking a fearful whimper. She began to stir but relaxed as Lyrna stroked a hand over her hair. "Shhh, all over now."

Lyrna relaxed into the bed, bone-weary and hoping sleep would come soon, but knowing it was likely to elude her for some hours. She had seen too much today, the wondrous and the terrible, all crowding into her mind and making her long for the ability to forget. But when her memory brought forth a vision it was not of battle or screaming men snapped in half by a shark's maw, it was an old man on a bed . . . *so old, so sunken into age and regret, barely recognisable as her father, barely believable as a king.*

She looked down at her hands and found they held no scroll . . . It's different. *Her hands went to her face, finding the burns, the fingers tracing over a scalp of stubble and ruined flesh.*

"You are not my daughter," said the old man on the bed. *"She was beautiful."*

"Yes," Lyrna replied. "She was."

He coughed, a trickle of blood appearing in the corner of his mouth, his voice weak, pleading. "Where did she go? I have things to say to her."

"She went to speak with the Alpiran ambassador." Lyrna moved to sit on the edge of the bed, taking the old man's hand. "But she did give me a message."

His tired but still-shrewd eyes narrowed. "I trust it's an apology. I'll not have a lifetime's planning ruined by her weakness now."

Lyrna laughed, realising she still missed this dreadful old schemer. "Yes, an apology. She said she was sorry for beating you at Keschet all those years ago. But she was too young to realise how galling it would be."

"Hah." He grunted, pulling his hands from hers. "Every chance taken for a jibe. Her mother was the same. Took the board away for her protection. Couldn't have it known she was so . . . special. But that day I knew I had an heir."

Lyrna felt a tear trace down her cheek, smiling at the old man's scowl. "She didn't do what you ordered. You must know that. She agreed to the Emperor's terms and Malcius returned to take the throne. Your grand design was all for nothing."

"And is he a good king?"

Lyrna stifled a sob. "He's dead, Father. He was killed before my eyes, with his queen and his children. Your wish is finally fulfilled, I am queen now, and I rule a land of ruin and death."

His scowl transformed into a wry grimace, a bony hand coming up to lift her chin. "After the Red Hand it was all ruin and death too. But it rose again, because I made it. Grabbed it and dragged it to its feet in the space of a generation."

"The people may not accept me as I am . . ."

"Then make them."

"Our enemies are many . . ."

"Then kill them."

Lyrna felt a sudden chill on her scalp, turning to find the windows open, drapery tumbling in wind and rain. She turned back to the *old man, pressing a kiss to his cheek. "I wish you had been a better man, Father."*

"A better man would have left no realm for you to inherit, ruined or not." He smiled at her as the wind built, filling the room, the air cold enough to make her gasp . . .

She woke to find Orena and Murel battling to close the shutter on the window in the face of gale-driven rain, a dim lamp jerking about on the ceiling above. "Sorry, Highness," Orena said, forcing the shutter in place. "We'd hoped not to wake you."

Lyrna rose to be sent sprawling against the bulkhead by the pitching deck. "A storm?"

"It started about an hour ago," Murel said, hunching her shoulders as a thunderclap reverberated through the ship, wincing in fear. "After today I thought I'd never be afraid again. Now this."

Lyrna put a comforting arm about her shoulders and they sat on the bed, the howl and crash of the storm banishing all chance of sleep. "The crew think you're touched by their gods, Highness," Murel whispered. "Calling the shark from the depths. Odonor's Hand they call you."

"Udonor," Lyrna corrected. *God of the winds, the greatest of gods. If so, I wish he'd end this bloody storm.*

The storm raged all night and for much of the following day, Lyrna venturing from the cabin only once to find the deck repeatedly swept by tall waves and the Shield alone at the wheel, gesturing for her to go back inside although his smile blazed as white as ever through the rain. She provided a welcome distraction for her ladies with a tutorial in the basics of court etiquette, meaningless frippery for the most part but it might offer some uses when they returned to the Realm; people did like their petty rituals. Orena proved the best student, mastering the curtsy and the mysteries of the bow with a fluid grace that made Lyrna suspect she may have found occupation as a dancer in the years before landing her fat but rich husband. Murel, however, quickly grew flustered by her own clumsiness, not aided by the ceaseless pitching of the deck.

"Mother always said there was an invisible rope about my feet," she grumbled after stumbling through the correct greeting for a foreign ambassador.

The storm abated come evening and they emerged from the cabin to find the *Sea Sabre* alone on the ocean, save for the shark, its fin tracing a winding course through the waves some distance ahead. Belorath was at the tiller and the Shield at the prow.

"Where is the fleet?" Lyrna asked, moving to his side.

"Heading for the Teeth like us, I hope. Those still afloat that is." His eyes remained fixed on the shark. "You truly have no notion why that thing does your bidding?"

"None. And I'm not sure it's my bidding. What it did . . . Animals don't hate, they just feed. It *hates*."

"Or carries the hate of your dead beast charmer."

"And he seemed such an affable young man."

The first Meldenean ship came into view an hour later, soon joined by four more, the crews hailing them with cheers and waving sabres, increasing in volume when Lyrna moved to the prow. *Udonor's Hand,* she thought, finding the phrase had a certain ring to it. Although she doubted the Aspects would appreciate having it added to her list of queenly titles, if any were still alive to object.

By the time the Teeth came in sight there were over a hundred ships following the *Sea Sabre*, and perhaps another three hundred at anchor in the shallows to the west of the rocks. The *Red Falcon* was there, albeit bearing the scars of battle, the clean lines of her hull dark with scorch marks and her figurehead smashed beyond recognition.

The Shield put the *Sea Sabre* alongside and Ell-Nurin took a boat across to confer.

"No." Ell-Nestra shook his head, voice firm. "No more delay."

"More ships arrive by the hour," Ell-Nurin protested. "We'll need strength to move against their southern division."

"Udonor gave it to us last night," the Shield insisted. "Can you recall a storm of such power sweeping the Erinean at this time of year? He sends us a gift and I'll not waste it. One more turn of the glass, my lord, then we sail to end this."

The Serpent's Tail was well named, a twisting submerged snake of rock extending over twenty miles south of the Teeth, its course laid bare by the succession of wrecked Volarian vessels driven onto it by the storm.

The crew became oddly subdued at the sight, ship after ship blasted by waves, tattered sails tossed by the wind. Lyrna noted the guarded glances they cast in her direction, reverence and no small amount of fear on every face. *Udonor's Hand is not merciful,* Lyrna surmised surveying the line of wrecks. *For which I am grateful.*

"I count over two hundred, my lord," Belorath reported to Ell-Nestra. "There'll be more already sunk or smashed to splinters."

"A battle won without a single sabre bared or arrow loosed," the Shield mused. "Seems your shark will have to wait a while to feed his hate, Highness."

A shout came from aloft, the look-out pointing off to the south. The Shield took his spyglass to the prow, scanning the waves for a moment before ordering sails to full and changing course. "Or perhaps not."

There were some twenty ships moving south at a slow crawl, close together with scant canvas to catch the wind. On seeing the danger they clustered even closer, trimming sails as their ragged crews crowded the decks, weapons ready.

"Don't these bastards ever give up?" Harvin groaned.

The *Sea Sabre* overtook the Volarians in short order, circling with the rest of the fleet, edging closer as the mangonels were readied and archers climbed the rigging.

"Reckon we can hit 'em from here," Harvin surmised, standing at the rail. "Crave the honour of the first throw, Highness."

"Granted, my lord."

He grinned, slapping his hands together and stepping forward. The ballista bolt caught him square in the back, punching through the mail shirt as if it were paper. He staggered for a moment, staring at the bolt's steel head sticking from his chest with raised eyebrows and an odd grin, then falling flat on his face.

"Harvin!" Orena rushed to the body, pulling it over, hands fluttering over his face, desperate pleas coming from her lips in a torrent. "Love, come back to me love, come back to me . . ."

"Bastards!" Iltis lit the hemp and slammed his boot onto the release, running to the rail and shouting into the fireball's wake. "Don't you know when to fucking die!?"

Lyrna crouched at Orena's side as she cradled Harvin's head in her lap, whispering now. "Come back to me . . ."

Lyrna looked at the former outlaw's empty eyes, his teeth bared in the same odd grin. *He was the most likely of us to die laughing.*

She joined Iltis at the rail, watching a hundred fireballs descend on the Volarian ships in an inverted fountain of blazing teardrops. "I seek pardon for my language, Highness," her Lord Protector said in a soft voice.

Lyrna wrapped herself around his thick arm, hugging the rigid muscle tight, her head resting in his shoulder. The flames grew quickly in the midst of the cluster, a tall column of smoke rising, screams drifting across the water. Soon swimming men came splashing out of the smoke, a hundred or more desperate enough to hope for rescue from their enemy, all destined to perish as soon as they came within bowshot.

I know you're here, Lyrna thought, scanning the waves. *Who will you find to hate now?*

A great crash erupted from the burning ships, flaming splinters bursting into the sky as the shark ascended from the inferno. It rose free of the wreckage, twisting in the air, tail whipping upwards before it dived back down into the carnage, jaws wide and hungry.

Somehow Lyrna knew she would never see it again.

They gave the dead to the sea at twilight, the Meldeneans standing in silent regard for their fallen crew-mates, more than twenty canvas-wrapped bodies weighted and lowered into the waves. As each corpse was readied to be carried to the rail crewmen would come

forward to choose an item from the belongings laid out on a cloth
at their feet. Any coin or valuables had already been collected by
Belorath who would see them safely to the bereaved families, the
trinkets left behind were merely tokens of remembrance: a die, a
Keschet piece kept as a lucky charm, a favoured knife. The only
words spoken were the names of the fallen men, enunciated clearly
by the Shield to be crossed off the ship's roll by his first mate.

The ship's carpenter had fashioned a basic raft for Harvin, his
body placed on a bed of pitch-soaked rope and rags, the sword
Lyrna had given him resting under his crossed arms. Benten and
Iltis lowered him over the side and the former brother said the
words at his queen's behest. Orena stood between Lyrna and
Murel, clasping their hands in a tremulous grip, her cheeks dry
now as she seemed to have exhausted her tears.

"We stand in witness to the end of the vessel that carried this
man through his life," Iltis said. "We know there are those in the
Realm who would remember him without kindness or high regard.
But we knew him as a friend and a comrade in a time of great
trial, and he never failed us. An outlaw he may have been, but
he died a Sword of the Realm, beloved by his woman, his friends
and his queen. We give thanks for his deeds of kindness and
courage and forgiveness for his moments of weakness. He is with
the Departed now, his spirit will join with them to guide us in
life and our service to the Faith."

He let go of the rope holding the raft and it drifted away on
the swell. Benten raised a bow notched with a flaming arrow and
let it fly, the raft soon a fiery square on the broad ocean, carried
towards the horizon and lost to view before the hour was gone.

The Shield found her as night fell, keeping company with Skerva
once again. The sky was clear now, all trace of the storm gone
from a sky lit with numberless stars, the air cool and pleasing on
her skin.

"Your Highness owes me an answer," Ell-Nestra said, resting
against the figurehead's arm. "Your true intent."

She nodded, eyes still rapt on the sky. "When I was little, I tried to count them all. It proved very difficult, so I devised a plan. I would study just one section of sky seen through a window in the palace roof, count all the stars visible within it then multiply the result with the sky's overall area."

"Did it work?"

Lyrna breathed a soft laugh. "The number was so large there is no name for it. But that's not the interesting thing. You see when I came to check my figures, for a good scholar always checks their figures, the number of stars in the window had changed. It was the exact same date a year later, but there were two more stars in my count. Two distant suns that simply hadn't been there a year before."

"And what did this tell you?"

"That if the stars in the sky are not fixed, then nothing is fixed. Nothing is eternal, all is temporary and ever-changing." She turned away from the stars, meeting his gaze. "Nothing is fixed, my lord. No course is so set it cannot be changed."

He gave a wry smile. "You would have us change course."

"I would."

"Might I ask in what direction?"

"I understand the Coldiron River is navigable to oceangoing vessels at this time of year, all the way to Alltor."

"Which stands besieged and in dire need of relief."

"Quite so."

"And you command this in return for the debt we owe you?"

"You owe me nothing. My father tipped the scales and I tipped them back. I speak only sound strategy. You must know the Volarians will not just swallow this defeat and leave you in peace. This has been but one battle in a war that will end only with their utter ruin. And that ruin will start at Alltor."

He moved closer, no smile on his lips and just honest appeal in his gaze. "I offer a counterproposal, Highness." He nodded towards the west. "We have a fine ship, a loyal crew and all the world's oceans to sail. The Merchant Kings have large fleets, I hear."

Lyrna laughed, shaking her head. "You would make me a pirate queen?"

"I would seek to preserve your life. For I find it has great value to me."

"A queen does not live, she reigns, and my reign has begun. Will you take me to Alltor?"

He moved closer still, looming above her, brows creased and eyes lost to shadow as he stared down at her. "May the gods save me, but you know I'd take you anywhere."

CHAPTER SEVEN
Frentis

He woke to find Illian and Arendil sharing breakfast, a watery porridge of oats from their diminishing supplies. Repeated movement left no time for hunting and hunger was becoming a constant companion. However, neither of them had voiced a single complaint and even their tireless bickering seemed to have abated following the battle with the Kuritai.

They had moved twice in the space of a week. Fief Lord Darnel proved tenacious in his pursuit, sending more hunters with slave-hounds and Varitai in escort, seemingly having exhausted his supply of slave elite. Frentis ordered false trails laid and traps set. At night he led small bands of the more stealthy fighters forth to cut throats and sow confusion in the ranks of their pursuers. Varitai were easier to kill than Kuritai, but they could still be formidable, especially if allowed to form ranks. He would strike in the small hours of the morning, seeking to kill as many dogs and hunters as possible, then withdrawing at speed to a pre-prepared ambush. It worked the first few times, the Varitai marching blindly into arrow storms and spiked pits. But whoever had command of the hunt soon became wise to the tactic, keeping his men together in four solid groups each numbering more than three hundred, whilst Frentis lost people every time they launched another attack and there were no more caravans to raid for recruits.

Their pursuers had evolved an unpleasant tactic of their own, loosing packs of slave-hounds at the slightest hint of a scent, thirty or more of the beasts running unfettered through the forest killing anything they could catch. Yesterday had brought them close enough to the camp to force a battle, the faith-hounds meeting their relatives headlong in a morass of tearing claws and flashing teeth. Frentis led half the fighters against their rear whilst Davoka took the others into their flank. She seemed to have a particular hatred of the slave-hounds, killing without restraint or fatigue as she cut a bloody trail through their swirling ranks. Frentis found her finishing the pack leader with a thrust through the rib cage, an ugly grimace of distaste on her face as she turned the spear to find the heart.

"Twisted," she said in answer to his frown. "Made wrong and smell wrong."

"We saved some for you, brother," Illian said, offering him a bowl of the porridge.

He resisted the urge to ask if she had made it and accepted the bowl. "Thank you, my lady." He ate the gruel and surveyed the camp. Aspect Grealin sat alone, as he usually did these days, seemingly lost in thought. Davoka and Ermund were practising again, hand-to-hand combat this time. He noticed her occasional grin as they tumbled together and wondered if he should offer some warning to Ermund, then noticed the knight's own grin and decided it was probably redundant. *Where did they find the time?*

Thirty-Four, still undecided on a name, sat practising his Realm Tongue with Draker, although much of the lesson seemed to consist of the correct use of profanity. "No," the big man shook his shaggy head. "Pig-fucker not fuck-pigger."

Janril Norin was sharpening his sword, face impassive and eyes empty as he worked the stone along the edge. Beyond him Master Rensial tended their two remaining horses, the veteran stallion and the mare. Recently he had expressed his desire to breed them, providing a new blood-line for the Order's stables, the state of which drew his constant criticism. "Too much straw on the floor," he tutted. "Walls haven't been whitewashed in months."

"We were wondering, brother," Arendil said, breaking into his reverie. "About the Volarians."

"What about them?"

"Where they come from. Davoka says you've been there. Her ladyship thinks they all come from the same huge city, whilst my grandfather said their empire covered half the world."

"It's a big place," Frentis said. "And Volar is said to be the greatest city in the world, though I've never seen it."

"But you saw their empire?" Illian asked. "You saw what makes them into these beasts."

"I saw cities, and roads of marvellous construction. I saw cruelty and greed, but I've seen them here too. I saw a people live a life that was strange in many ways, but also much the same as anywhere else."

"Then why are they so cruel?" There was an earnestness to the girl's face, an honest desire to know.

"Cruelty is in all of us," he said. "But they made it a virtue."

He returned his gaze to the camp, forcing himself to count every soul in sight. *Forty-three, and eight hounds. This is not an army, and I am not a Battle Lord.*

He stood up, hefting his sword and bow. "We're leaving," he said, loud enough to draw Davoka's attention.

"Moving camp again, brother?" Arendil asked with a note of weary reluctance.

"No. We're leaving the forest. There is no victory to be won here. It's time to flee."

Janril stood with the old Renfaelin sword resting on his shoulder. He carried no pack or canteen, nothing that would sustain him.

"You don't have to do this," Frentis told him. "I would hear you sing again, my friend. This land was always richer for it."

The one-time minstrel just cast an impassive glance over his face then turned to walk away. He went a few yards before pausing to turn back. "Her name was Ellora," he said. "She died with my child inside her."

He resumed walking, soon lost from sight in the trees.

It wasn't easy, the master's eyes seemed about to birth tears as Frentis explained, but eventually he managed to persuade him to loose the horses, sending them north in the hope the hunters would follow the trail. "Too easily tracked, Master," he said. "They have horses at the Pass, and I'm sure Master Sollis will have need of the finest stable master in the Realm."

He ordered a westward course, intending to hook north having left more false trails for their pursuers. Frentis and Davoka brought up the rear whilst Ermund scouted ahead with Arendil and Illian, the girl's ear now as well tuned to the song of the forest as any brother or huntsman. They covered at least twenty miles by nightfall, a good day's march in the Urlish.

They made a silent and fireless camp, huddling together for warmth. "Stop fidgeting!" Illian hissed at Arendil as they lay side by side next to a fallen birch trunk.

"Your bloody dog keeps licking my face," the boy returned in a sullen whisper.

Frentis sat watch beside Grealin, eyes and ears alive to the forest's song. *The forest appears black at night,* Master Hutril had said years ago. *An endless void. But it's more alive in the dark than the daylight. Still your fears and know it as a friend, for it's the best watchman you ever met.*

In the tree tops an owl hooted at its neighbour with trustworthy regularity. The wind brought only the scents of the forest, free of man's sweat or the sweeter tang of dog. The void was empty of any telltale gleam of metal in moonlight.

"Open country to the north, brother," Grealin said in the softest whisper. "And near a hundred and fifty miles of Renfael to traverse before we reach the pass. The risk is great."

"I know, Aspect. But it's greater here."

They kept a westward course for the next day, Frentis ordering a turn north come evening. He spent an hour continuing west alone but for Slasher and Ermund, laying a trail of broken branches and conspicuous boot and paw prints. They kept at it until nightfall then moved north to find the river, following the bank to a shallow ford. The others were waiting on the other side, Davoka stepping from the shadows with spear ready and Illian rising from a bush, crossbow in hand.

"We move on at dawn," Frentis said, slumping at the foot of a pine trunk and letting sleep claim him for the few hours left until daylight.

Morning brought a new scent on the wind, musty and acrid. Frentis called to Illian and nodded at the pine trunk. The girl handed Arendil her crossbow and began to climb, scampering from branch to branch until she had reached the highest point.

"Fire," she reported on returning to earth. "Lots of fire."

"Where?" Davoka asked.

"Everywhere. All around. The largest one is burning to the south of us though, just a little ways from the city."

Frentis exchanged a glance with Grealin. *Darnel burns the Urlish just for us?*

"What do we do?" Draker asked, unable to keep the old whine from his voice.

"What every other living thing is this forest is doing." Frentis slung his bow across his back and began to throw away anything that might slow him down. "We run."

He ran them for an hour at a time, taking the lead and setting a punishing pace. Some of the fighters flagged, collapsing from the strain, but he allowed no lingering, setting Davoka to haul them along, promising direst punishment if they fell out again. All the time the smell of smoke grew thicker, the first columns rising to stain the sky through breaks in tree cover. Predictably,

Grealin found the pace the hardest to bear, huffing along behind with sweat streaming over his fleshy face. But he voiced no complaint and kept on his feet until nightfall.

Illian climbed another tree as the sun waned, her slight form black against an orange sky as she surveyed the forest. "It's just one big fire to the south now," she said. "You can't see the city for it, the flames are so high. There's another one almost as big to the west."

"Ahead of us?" Frentis asked.

She gave a grim nod. "Still patchy. But it's growing."

"Then we can't linger. Move in a line and stay together. When the smoke gets thick join hands."

They felt the heat build after the first mile, a pall of cinder-rich smoke descending soon after, bringing coughs and retching as they stumbled forward hand in hand. Frentis had hold of Illian whilst she held to Arendil. He was forced to stop frequently to peer ahead, looking for a path free from the orange glow of flame. Occasionally a deer or wild boar would come racing through the haze, lost to view before he could discern any escape route their senses may have revealed.

They were following a narrow trail when a great crack told of a falling tree, a tall pine descending to block their path, wreathed in flame from end to end. Frentis looked about for another path, seeing only the orange glow on all sides. He pulled Illian closer, obliged to shout into her ear against the fire's roar. "Tell the Aspect to come to the head of the line!"

Grealin appeared shortly after, the sweat now a constant slick over his face. Frentis pointed at the blazing pine trunk with a questioning glance. The Aspect stared at it for a moment then stepped forward with a resigned grimace. He raised both hands, fingers spread wide, his shoulders hunched as if straining against an invisible wall.

For a second nothing happened, then the pine trunk trembled, shuddered and burst apart, scattering burning splinters in all directions. Grealin fell to his knees, gasping and retching in the smoke, blood pouring from his nose. He waved away Frentis's helping hand and gestured impatiently for him to move on.

"I will not leave you, you fat old fool!" Frentis yelled, hooking his free arm under the Aspect's meaty limb and pulling him upright. "Now walk! Walk!"

The smoke soon became so thick all vision was lost and they were forced to crawl, seeking cleaner air closer to the ground. All around trees snapped and tumbled in the flames, the oak and yew falling with mighty groans. *It's dying,* Frentis thought. *Between us, we killed the Urlish.*

A sudden breeze dispelled the smoke enough for him to gauge their surroundings, finding a broad clearing with widely spaced trees ahead as yet untouched by flame.

"Up!" he shouted, dragging Grealin to his feet. "We're nearly out. Run!"

The line fragmented as they ran, stumbling and coughing, feeling the ever-rising heat on their backs. Frentis collapsed to a halt when he realised he was running through long grass with a clear sky above. He lay on his back, gulping air and wondering if he had ever tasted anything so sweet.

"Never seen," he heard Grealin muttering, sitting up to find the Aspect staring at the burning forest. It seemed to be on fire from end to end now, the sky above the trees filled with roiling black smoke, banishing the sun and leaving them in a cold shadow.

"Aspect?" Frentis asked.

"This was never seen." Grealin shook his head, deep confusion on his face as he continued to stare at the dying forest. "Not by any scrying. We are beyond prophecy now."

They had lost five people to the fire, vanished somewhere in the smoke. Frentis had thought the faith-hounds lost too but Slasher appeared as they marched north, bounding out of the long grass with Blacktooth and six of his pack loping behind. He knocked Frentis onto his back and covered his face with licks, voicing one of his rasping whuffs. "You're a good old pup," Frentis told him, running a weary hand through his fur.

They kept a wary eye out for Volarian cavalry but the wind proved a friend, calling the smoke from the Urlish down around them in a concealing fog. Frentis heard distant bugle calls and drumming hooves but none came close enough to pose a threat. The land north of the Urlish turned from rolling hills to gullies and crags after twenty miles or so, well remembered from his Test of the Wild and providing welcome cover. He sought out an overhanging cliff he recalled from the three days before One Eye's men had come for him, a tall sandstone edifice with an eroded notch in its base large enough to accommodate the whole group. The rushing stream outside also masked any sound they made though they dared not risk a fire.

"I've seen enough fire for one day," Illian said, forcing a laugh, but Frentis saw how she shivered and the gauntness of her cheeks. They had no food and only the clothes they stood in to guard against the night's chill. *I should have spared them this,* he knew. *Too many weeks spent drunk on blood.*

Her voice sounded in his mind again, as he found it often did in moments of doubt. *But didn't it taste so good, beloved?*

She was there again in his dreams that night, on the beach once more, the surf crashing under a red sky. But this time there was no child. She stood as she had before, not turning as he approached, regarding the spectacle before her with statuelike stillness and wind-tangled hair. He moved to her side, taking in her sombre profile. "So many," she said, without turning. "More than we ever managed, beloved."

He looked at the shoreline, seeing the corpses tossed by the waves. The beach stretched away on either side as far as he could see, thick with dead at every step.

"Did we do this?" he asked.

"We?" A small grin came to her lips, a glimmer of the old cruelty in her eyes as she angled her head to regard him, her hand reaching for his. "No. You did this, when you killed me."

It wasn't just the shoreline, he could see that now. The sea was crowded with corpses from beach to horizon. All the world's dead within his gaze. "How?"

"I would have been terrible," she replied. "My reign one of boundless greed and lust, a bitter queen visiting her lonely spite on the whole world. For you would have left me by then, fallen in the last hopeless battle against my Horde. But terrible as fate would make me, I am not *him*. This would not have been my doing. I was the one chance this world had for salvation."

He let her take his hand, feeling the warmth of her flesh, not cold like before. He knew then in a chilled rush of certainty that if she had agreed to his bargain, they would have been together for the rest of their days. All hatreds and crimes forgotten in this distant place where they would have raised their child as the world fell to ruin beyond their sight. The guilt of it choked him, made him want to enfold her in his arms once more, snap her bones and feel her shudder as death took her.

She smiled, the cruelty gone as she clasped his hand tighter, her voice catching as she said the final words. "I'm sorry, my love. But we both need to wake up now."

"Brother!" Arendil's voice was low but urgent as he shook him from sleep with a hard tug on his arm. "Riders coming."

He led them up a narrow track in the cliff's side, lying down atop it and peering over the edge as the riders came into view. A battalion of Free Cavalry headed by a troop of Renfaelin knights, a tall figure in blue-enamelled armour riding in front. Frentis felt Arendil stiffen at his side as the figure came closer.

"Your father?"

The boy's face was grim with hate, knuckles white on the handle of his long sword. "He always wears blue armour. Spends half the fief's treasury on it, so they say."

The riders halted about three hundred paces off, hunters and dogs coming to the head of the column. It wasn't long before one pointed directly at the gully.

"We run while they look for us here," Davoka said. "Be miles gone before they find our trail."

Grealin spoke the words already forming in Frentis's mind. "And when they do they'll be on us before nightfall." He met Frentis's gaze. "I'm very tired of running, brother."

The fat man stood outside the overhang, hands clasped over his extensive belly as the riders galloped into the gully. The tall knight in the blue armour raised a hand, halting the battalion and trotting forward with a bow to greet the fat man, although he felt no impulse to dismount. Their conversation could be only half heard from Frentis's hiding place at the head of the gully, crouching behind a rock with Arendil at his side, but he discerned the words "Red Brother" and "son." Grealin spoke his replies with an easy smile and an affable nod, neither of which seemed to hold much sway with the knight who soon drew his sword, nudging his mount forward until the tip was a few inches from the Aspect's chest. "Enough, brother," Frentis heard him say. "Where are they? No more games."

Frentis raised his eyebrows at Arendil. The boy's face was bleached white but still determined as he replied with a nod.

"Darnel!" Frentis called, stepping free of cover, bow in hand with arrow notched, Arendil at his side, long sword drawn.

The knight wheeled his horse towards them, eyes unseen behind his visor but the triumph of the moment clear in the shouted orders he cast at his retainers. They spurred forward in an instant gallop, forgetting Grealin in what proved a singular misjudgement.

The Aspect allowed the knights and a dozen Free Swords to gallop past before stepping away from the cliff face, turning and raising his arms as he backed away, splayed fingers pointing at the worn notch of the overhang. A sound like a thunderclap echoed through the gully, red dust exploding to envelop the Volarian cavalry, horses rearing in the billowing cloud.

Grealin continued to back away as another thunderclap sounded, the knights' charge faltering at the force of the concussion shaking the earth, making their mounts draw up in alarm. The man in the blue armour whipped his reins against his horse's flank to stop it rearing, turning in time to see a spiderweb of cracks spread through the sandstone cliff in the space of a heartbeat. Frentis put an arrow in his leg as he sat staring, the steel-headed barb finding the thinly shielded knee joint. The knight twisted in the saddle, clutching at the shaft then tumbling to the ground as another shaft took him in the gap between breastplate and shoulder.

He lay on the ground, his shouts lost as the cliff continued to fragment behind him, breaking apart in a blast of sound that sent Frentis and Arendil reeling. The sandstone slabs tumbled into the gully below, shrieks of men and horses drowned by the crescendo of falling stone.

More dust rose in a tall plume, swallowing Grealin's slumped form as the surviving cavalrymen and knights wheeled in confusion. Frentis got to his feet and felled a cavalryman with an arrow to the back as the fighters appeared on both sides of the gully's edge, loosing arrows and crossbow bolts in a volley that did credit to their weeks of hard-won experience. Frentis saw about half the horsemen fall as he cast his bow aside and charged forward with sword drawn, the fighters running in from both sides.

It was done quickly, the knights and cavalrymen speared or hacked down in short order. He saw Arendil leap and bring his long sword down to cleave through a cavalryman's arm as he tried to slash at Davoka. Ermund stood in front of a charging knight, sword held level with his head, stepping aside at the last instant to deliver an expert upward slash, finding the knight's unarmoured throat and sending him from the saddle in a spiral of blood.

Frentis found Grealin lying on his side, eyes half-closed and a thick stream of blood seeping from every opening. He crouched next to him, laying a hand on his broad arm. The Aspect's eyes fluttered open, still weeping red tears. They regarded Frentis for a silent moment, bright and clear, the flesh around them creasing as Grealin smiled. He sputtered, blood spurting from his mouth as he tried to speak. Frentis leaned close to hear him rasp, "I think . . . I prefer life . . . without prophecy."

"Aspect?"

But there were no more words from the Aspect of the Seventh Order. Nor would there ever be.

Frentis walked towards the prostrate form of the man in the blue armour. He was struggling to rise, a torrent of pained profanity issuing from his masked lips. Frentis put his sword point under the visor, the knight becoming instantly still as the other fighters crowded round.

"Don't we have to try him first?" Draker asked. "Since he's a Fief Lord and all."

"Just kill the bastard, brother," Ermund said. "Or let me have the honour."

Frentis flipped the visor up, revealing a thin face with bloodied lips and terror-filled eyes.

"Wenders!" Ermund said in disdain, stepping forward to deliver a kick to the man's skewered knee, drawing an agonised howl. "We want the master, not the dog. Let you out to play in his armour did he? Where is he?" He kicked again. "Where?"

"Enough," Frentis said. "You know this man?"

"Rekus Wenders, Darnel's chief retainer and lick-spittle. Led the knights who came for the baron, handed me and my men to the Volarians. Those he hadn't slaughtered."

"I-I follow my Fief Lord," Wenders stammered. "I am bound to him by oath . . ."

"Fuck your oath." Ermund stamped his boot onto Wenders's neck and began to push down hard. "My cousins died that day, you filth!"

Davoka stepped forward, laying her hand on Ermund's chest, her face fierce with disapproval. The knight stared at her in fury then turned away with a shout of frustration, leaving Wenders gasping on the ground.

Frentis beckoned to Thirty-Four. The former slave left off from cleaning his short sword and came to stand at his side, regarding Wenders with his customary incurious stare.

"This man was a numbered slave with a particular skill set," Frentis told Wenders. "I assume you've seen enough of the Volarians to know what that means."

The knight's face became rigid with fear and a sharp smell arose from his armour.

"Faith!" Draker said, turning away in disgust. "Watching the knight kill him would've been easier to bear." He walked off to rifle the corpses for valuables; an outlaw's habits were hard to break.

"Good," Frentis said to Wenders, sinking to his haunches. "We have little time for my friend's usual subtlety, so you'll understand the importance of brief but honest answers."

The knight's head began a vigorous nodding in the confines of his helmet.

"You will tell me all you know of Lord Darnel's dispositions in Varinshold," Frentis informed him. "How many men he has, where he sleeps, what he eats. And you will also tell me where he keeps the Aspect of my order."

They built a fire for Grealin, having no time for more than the briefest of words, Frentis stumbling through them as best he could. *How do you do justice to a man like this in a few phrases?* he thought. He faltered to a halt in trying to recite the Catechism of Faith and Davoka stepped forward as the others exchanged uncertain glances.

"My people fear those like him," she said, voice ringing in the confines of the gully. "We think they steal what belongs to the Mahlessa and the gods, becoming twisted with the theft, unworthy of trust or clan. This man taught me that we are wrong."

Arendil came forward, smiling sadly at Grealin's shrouded bulk. "He used to tell me stories about the Order sometimes, at night when the others were asleep. Every one was different, carrying a new lesson. I hope I listened as well as I should."

Illian went to his side as her face bunched in anticipation of tears, grasping his hand before raising her own voice. "He said blood made me a lady, but life had made me a huntress. He thought it suited me better."

Frentis moved forward with the torch, touching it to the kindling and stepping back. "Good-bye Master," he whispered as the flames rose.

Davoka stripped Wenders of his armour and removed the arrows before binding his wounds. She wasn't gentle and the knight's yelps were enough to make Ermund clamp a hand over his mouth and hold a dagger to his throat as she completed her work. They propped him against a fallen section of cliff with a canteen within easy reach.

"When your lord asks," Frentis said, "tell him the Red Brother offers his compliments and will return shortly to settle our business. If you're smart, you'll forget to tell him how helpful you've been."

"You're all fools," the knight replied, finding some vestige of courage now it was clear they didn't intend to kill him. "This land belongs to the Volarians now. If you want to live, you have to join with them. Think me a coward if you want, but I'll still be breathing twenty years from now whilst you'll all be long de—"

Illian's crossbow bolt made a loud metallic ping as it punched through Wender's eye to connect with the rock behind his head. Incredibly he managed to gasp out a few final words, whatever wisdom they held lost in a babble of spittle before he slumped forward, lifeless and silent.

"Sorry, brother," Illian told Frentis with an expression of sincere contrition. "My finger slipped."

They trekked north for three days. There had been only two surviving horses from the carnage in the gully, tall Renfaelin steeds now pressed into service as pack animals under Master Rensial's care. The Volarian dead had yielded a decent supply of food, strips of dried beef and a hard biscuit of wheat and barley that turned into a surprisingly appetising porridge when placed in boiling water.

On the third day the crags and vales of northern Asrael gave way to the tall downs of the Renfaelin border, the grassy mounds rising from pasture largely devoid of forest or sheltering rocks.

"We could turn east," Draker suggested. "Make for the coast. Country's more broken up there. Remember it well from my smuggling days."

"We can't afford the time," Frentis replied, though he shared the big man's reluctance. *Perfect place for cavalry, but there's nothing else for it.*

They kept to the low country as much as possible, steering clear of roads or villages, climbing the downs only to make camp come evening. Two more days' march brought them within sight of the River Andur, beyond which Arendil assured them lay forest aplenty.

"Thanks to the Departed," Illian said. "I feel naked out here."

They covered five miles the following morning before they heard it, a distant thunder accompanied by a faint tremble in the earth. By now there was none amongst them so naïve as to mistake it for an approaching storm.

"Moving south," Davoka reported, lying down with her ear to the ground. "Ahead of us." She got to her feet with a grave expression. "Be here very soon."

"Illian! Arendil!" Frentis beckoned them over to the two horses, Master Rensial swiftly removing the packs and handing them the reins. "Ride west," Frentis told them. "Push hard. A week's journey will take you to Nilsael . . ." He trailed off at the sight of Illian releasing the reins and stepping back, arms crossed. Arendil stood at her side, also empty-handed.

"This is not a game . . ." he began.

"I know it's not a game, brother," Illian broke in. "And I am not a child, neither is Arendil. You can't do what we have done and remain children. We're staying."

Frentis stared at them helplessly, guilt threatening to force a scream from his breast. *If you die here, it's my fault!*

"Always was a long bet, brother," Arendil said with a grim smile.

Frentis breathed out slowly, letting the scream die, casting his gaze about their bedraggled company and finding no fear on any face. They all looked at him in silent respect, waiting for orders. *I was made monstrous, they made me better. They brought me back. I came home.*

He could feel the rumble in the ground beneath his feet now, building steadily. *Must be a thousand or more.* "Form a circle," he said, pointing to a slight rise in the ground twenty paces off. "Master Rensial, please mount up and stand with me in the centre."

He hauled himself onto one of the warhorses, trotting over to the rise and standing with Rensial alongside as the others closed in around them, forming a spiked hedge of drawn swords and raised bows.

The first riders came into view only minutes later, dim figures in the lingering morning mist, twenty men riding hard. *No armour,* Frentis saw. *Volarian scouts . . .* All thought fled as he caught sight of the face of the lead rider. A lean man of middling years with close-cropped hair and pale eyes, his dark blue cloak billowing behind.

"Lower weapons," Frentis said, dismounting and walking forward on unsteady legs as the blue-cloaked man reined in a short distance away.

"Brother," Master Sollis greeted him, his voice even more hoarse than Frentis remembered. "You seem to be marching in the wrong direction."

CHAPTER EIGHT
Reva

R eva could hear the Reader's voice before she reached the square, making her wonder how such an old man could shout so loud.

". . . the Father's Sight is taken from us, stolen by these wretched Heretics . . ."

She sprinted into the square, finding it full of people from end to end, crowding around with eyes fixed on the centre, rapt by the Reader's words.

". . . this city is the Father's gift! The jewel given unto the Loved and named for his greatest servant! But we have allowed the corruption of unbelief to fester here . . ."

"Move aside!" Reva began shoving her way through the crowd, most onlookers making way when they saw her face, others proving more reluctant and she was in no mood to be gentle. "Move I said!" she snarled, the man who reached out to grasp her arm staggering back with a bloody nose. Her passage was a little easier after that.

". . . cleanse this city! Those are the Father's words to me, revealed in the Ten Books, though I have laboured long to find another course. 'Make my city pure again and my Sight will fall on you once more . . .'"

She struggled free of the crowd, emerging to find the square filled with kneeling people, all bound with rope and surrounded by men with swords. She noticed a few of the sword-bearers were priests whilst others were mostly men of middling years, some a little too old to have seen service on the walls. At the sight of her a few grew visibly discomforted, but there were plenty who stared at her with stern-faced defiance, one even stepping forward to block her path as she moved towards the Reader.

Her sword came free of the scabbard in a blur and the man drew up short. With a shock Reva recognised him as the fruit seller who had sold her an apple that first day on the cathedral steps. "Get out my way," she instructed him, voice soft and full of dire promise. The fruit seller paled and stepped back.

"She comes!" the Reader intoned from the cathedral steps. "As I foretold. The whore's bastard pupil, the falsely blessed."

Reva's gaze took in the sight of Brother Harin, kneeling with a bloodied face in the front row of captives. Veliss knelt beside the healer, arms tied behind her back and a wooden gag secured in her mouth. Arken knelt at her side, hardly able to keep upright, his skin pale and head sagging.

"I have a blessing for you," Reva told the Reader, breaking into a run, a red haze clouding her vision. "It's made of steel, not words."

The Reader's pet priest tried to stop her, casting an inexpert thrust at her chest with a rapier. It clattered to the tiles along with two of his fingers. The Reader was flanked by his bishops and she found it significant that none came forward to shield him from her charge, most staring in shock or deciding to avert their gaze, although she was sure she glimpsed a smile or two. The old man fell like a bundle of rags as she grasped his robe, forcing him to the steps, sword drawn back.

"The priest!" she said. "Who is he? I know he answers to you."

"Such sin." The old man shook his head, madness and wonder in his eyes. "Such corruption of holy flesh. You, the one promised as our salvation, vile with unnatural lust . . ."

"Just tell me!" She forced him lower, the sword point pressing through his robe.

"The bright light of your sacrifice would unite us. It was promised to him by the Father's own messenger . . ."

"REVA!"

It was the only voice that could have stopped her. She turned to see her uncle hobbling through the crowd, people backing away with heads lowered. He made a pathetic sight, a wasted, dying man shuffling along, using an old sword as a walking stick. But there was dignity there too, a command in the unwavering gaze he cast about him, a few of the sword-bearers lowering their weapons as he made his slow progress to the steps.

Reva let go of the Reader, stepping back as her uncle came to a wheezing halt a few steps below. "I think," he said in a thin gasp, "our people should like to hear your news."

"News, uncle?" she asked, chest heaving with repressed rage.

"Yes. The Father's revelation. It's time we shared it."

Revelation? Reva's gaze tracked over the crowd, seeing a confusion of expression on the assembled faces; fear and hope but mostly just great uncertainty. *That's what he offers,* she realised, glancing down at the Reader. *Certainty. The lie of a great truth. Killing him won't disprove it.*

"Lord Vaelin Al Sorna rides to our relief!" she told them, casting her voice as wide as she could. "He rides towards us now with a great and powerful army!"

"Lies!" the Reader hissed, getting slowly to his feet. "She seeks to usurp the Father's words with lies! Invoking the name of the Darkblade no less!"

"Al Sorna is not the Darkblade!" she shouted as the crowd began to murmur. "He comes to save us. I am Lady Reva Mustor, heir to the Chair of this fief and daughter to the Trueblade. You call me blessed, you believe the Father's Sight rests upon me. I say it rests upon all of us. And the Father does not reward murder."

"They shun the Father's love!" The Reader cast a bony hand at the kneeling captives. "Their presence within these walls weakens us!"

"Weakens us?" Reva picked out the fruit seller who had

confronted her earlier. "You! You have a sword. Why haven't I seen you on the wall?"

The man shuffled and looked around warily. "I have a daughter and three grandchildren, my lady . . ."

"And they'll die unless we hold this city." She turned on a priest standing near the steps, a portly man with a thin-bladed sword dangling from his plump hand like a wet twig. "You, servant of the Father, I haven't seen you either. But this man"—she pointed at Arken—"him I've seen, fighting and shedding blood in your defence. Whilst this man"—she pointed at Brother Harin—"works tirelessly to tend our wounded. And this woman . . . " Veliss's eyes were wide above the gag, shining bright. ". . . this woman has served this fief faithfully and well for years, and worked without pause or rest to secure this city and ensure all are fed."

Her gaze blazed at the crowd. "They do not weaken us. You do! You are the weakness here! You come here like the slaves our enemy would make us, bowing down to this lying old man, filling your hearts with easy hate when you know the Father only ever spoke of love!"

She looked at the portly priest once more. "Put that down before you hurt yourself." He stared at her, his sword falling from his grasp to clatter onto the tiles. She cast her gaze over the other sword-bearers, each dropping his blade as her eyes met their faces, looking away in shame or staring back in wonder.

There was a commotion off to the right as Antesh and Arentes forced their way through the throng, the entire House Guard behind them along with dozens of archers and Realm Guard. Reva held up a hand as they advanced towards the disarmed men, then pointed at the captives. "Free these people, my lords, if you would."

She glanced over her shoulder at the Reader, his face white with either rage or disbelief. "The cathedral is closed until further notice. Don't show your face outside it again." She sheathed her sword and descended the steps towards the Fief Lord, reaching out to him. "I think you need a nap, Uncle."

He nodded wearily, smiling then blinking in shock, eyes widening in alarm at something behind her. She turned to find the Reader flying towards her, a dagger raised high in his bony hand, yellowed teeth bared in a hate-filled grimace, too fast and too close to side-step or parry. Something blurred in the corner of her eye and the Reader doubled over before her, the dagger scraping a shallow cut on her arm as he collapsed onto the cathedral steps, her grandfather's sword buried in his belly. He coughed, twitched and died.

She caught her uncle as he fell, cradling his head on her lap, her hand on his chest, feeling the beat of his heart slowing. "Never . . . killed anyone . . . before," he said. "Glad it . . . turned out to be . . . him." His hand fluttered to her cheek and she held it there. "Don't . . . doubt the Father's love . . . my wonderful niece. Promise me."

"I won't, Uncle. Not now, not ever."

He smiled, his red eyes dimming. "Brahdor," he whispered.

"Uncle?"

"The man the priest called lord . . . His name . . . Brahdor . . ." The bony hand went limp in her grasp. His eyes still stared up at her but she knew they saw nothing.

Fief Lord Sentes Mustor was laid to rest in the family crypt within the manor walls. By Reva's order only she and the coffin bearers were present. She had wanted Veliss at her side but the lady was too stricken by the day's events to attend, stumbling back to the manor white-faced and locking herself in her room. Reva sent the bearers away and sat by the coffin until nightfall. It was a plain pine box, incongruous next to the ornately carved marble of her forebears, something she would have to fix in time. Outside, the faint thump of engine-cast stones could be heard as they ate another breach into her wall. Antesh reported that it was only another two weeks away from completion.

She had hoped sitting here with the bones of her ancestors might provoke some vision or insight, a cunning stratagem to win the day when the final stone fell. But all she earned was a cold behind and a sense of loss so great it felt as if some invisible hand had scooped out her insides.

She rose and went to the coffin, touching her fingers to the unvarnished wood. "Good-bye, Uncle."

Veliss opened the door at the seventh knock, red-eyed and pale. A ghost of a smile played on her lips before she turned back, leaving the door open. Reva closed it behind her, watching Veliss sit at her desk where a piece of parchment waited, half-covered in her fine script. "My formal letter of resignation," she said, picking up the quill. "I think I'll take you up on that horse, and the gold. When this is all over, naturally. I hear the Far West offers many opportunities . . ."

She fell silent as Reva came to place her hands on her shoulders, eyes raising to meet hers in the mirror as they lingered. "I thought it was a stain."

Reva bent to press a kiss to her neck, exulting in the thrill of delight as she provoked a gasp. "It washed." She took Veliss's hands and drew her towards the bed. "Now it's a gift."

Is it wrong? she wondered the following morning. *To feel so good at a time such as this?* She had been fighting to keep the smile from her face all through the council with her captains, scrupulously avoiding catching Veliss's eye for fear of a betraying grin or blush. Her uncle dead, the Reader slain on the steps of his own cathedral and the city on the verge of destruction, but all she could think about was the wondrous night before.

"It's just not enough," Antesh was insisting to Arentes, his knuckles thumping onto the map on the library table. "We'll hold them at the breaches for no more than a few hours, and all the time you can bet they'll be making a fresh assault on the walls to draw off our strength."

"What else can we do?" the old guard commander asked. "This city's defence rests on its walls. There is no provision, no plan for anything else. My lady"—he turned to Reva—"it might help if we had some notion of how long the Dar—, Lord Al Sorna will take in getting his army here."

Reva stopped the amused frown before it reached her brow. *He believed me.* Seeing the intent gaze of Lord Antesh she realised the old guardsman was not alone. *They actually think the Father has sent me some holy vision.* "Such . . . details were not revealed to me, my lord," she replied. "We must plan on holding this city as long as possible."

Antesh sighed, returning his gaze to the map. "Perhaps if we build towers here and here, just behind the new walls. Pack them with archers to loose down at them as they rush through . . ."

Reva surveyed the map as he went on, noting how circular it was, the empty space of the square in the centre like the bull's-eye of an archer's target, the surrounding streets ordered in a circular pattern radiating outwards. She reached for a charcoal stub and began to draw on the map. "We have been thinking on too small a scale," she told the two lords, tracing a series of black circles through the streets, each one smaller than the last. "Not two inner walls, six. Each to be held for as long as possible. Archers on every rooftop. The streets are narrow so their numbers won't matter so much. When one wall is breached, we fall back to the next."

Arentes looked at her plan for a good while before commenting, "It'll mean tearing down a quarter of the city."

"The city can be remade, its people can't." She looked at Antesh. "My lord?"

The Lord of Archers gave a slow nod. "It seems the Father's blessing is not misplaced. But it'll take a mighty effort to have it all done by the time the breach is complete."

"Then let's be about it. Besides I think the people will welcome any distraction from the sound of those bloody stones."

Veliss organised work gangs based on neighbourhood allegiance, putting a skilled builder in charge of each one. They worked in seven-hour shifts, no-one was hungry now as rationing had been abandoned in the face of more pressing need. They worked through the night pulling down houses that had stood for centuries, their bricks moulded into the new barricades which had quickly been dubbed the Blessed Lady's Rings. The taller houses were turned into miniature fortresses with wooden platforms added to the rooftops to accommodate additional archers, each one well-stocked with arrows and weapons. A series of walkways was also constructed across the rooftops, allowing reinforcements to be rushed from one point to another.

Reva spent the time rehearsing the House and City Guard in their response to the coming Volarian assault. "Is this really necessary now?" Veliss asked, watching the soldiers running from the wall for the tenth time as Reva counted down the seconds.

"Every one we kill on the wall or in the breaches is one we don't have to kill in the streets," Reva replied. She strode over to where the House Guard sergeant stood wheezing with his men. "Better than last time, but still too slow. Do it again."

"You're lucky they love you," Veliss observed as the guardsmen trooped back to the stairs.

"I'm discovering the Father's Blessing can do wonders, real or imagined."

Veliss nodded, pursing her lips. "I, ah, thought I'd take another look at the stocks in the cellar. Should take an hour, perhaps longer."

She gave a precisely formal bow and strode away, Reva hoping the guardsmen would ascribe the flush on her cheeks to the recent exertions. This was how it had been since that first glorious night, hurried but delightful fumblings in dark corners, the sense of stealing private pleasures adding a wicked charm to every encounter.

"Working hard?"

She turned to find Arken walking towards her with a stiff gait, his face tense with suppressed pain. "Go back to bed," Reva instructed him flatly.

"Another minute of the healing house and I'll go mad," he replied. "Brother Harin is a good man, but his stories never end.

This is his fifth war, you know? He'll tell you all about the others in great detail, if you let him."

She saw the determination in his gaze and let it drop. "Lord Antesh requires help in the eastern quarter," she said. "There's an old wine-shop with unusually deep foundations."

He nodded, hesitating. "We're never going to the Reaches, are we? Even if we win this."

Looking at his broad, honest face she saw the boy he had been replaced by the good and brave man he now was. It hurt, because she knew he couldn't stay with her now. She might want a brother but he already had a sister. "I've decided on Lady Governess of Cumbrael," she said. "As my formal title. As you said, Fief Lady didn't sound right."

"Lady Governess," he repeated with a grin. "Suits you." He gave an overly florid bow, wincing and rubbing his back as he straightened then walked off towards the eastern quarter.

She was with Veliss when the stones stopped falling, lying entwined on a pile of furs in a shadowed corner of the manor cellar, sweat-covered and panting. "I love your hands," Veliss said, entwining their fingers together, nuzzling at her neck.

"They're rough, callused and the nails are horrible," Reva replied. "Though my feet are worse."

"You're mad." Veliss raised herself up to kiss her, lips lingering, tongue probing. "There isn't an inch of you that isn't gorgeous."

Reva giggled as her lips moved lower, her hands bunching in Veliss's rich, strawberry-flavoured hair . . .

"Wait!" she said as it came to her.

"What?" Veliss raised her head, pouting in annoyance.

"They've stopped." After so long the absence of the stones on the wall was like an endless shout of silence. Reva disentangled herself and reached for her clothes.

"I thought I'd help Brother Harin with the wounded," Veliss said as they dressed. "Not much else I can do now, is there?"

She stared at Reva with wide eyes, a frown of desperate hope on her brow. Reva strapped her sword across her back and paused to plant a kiss on her lips. "Stay safe." She brushed the tousled hair back from Veliss's forehead. "I love you."

The Kuritai gave a soft grunt as the sword slashed across his eyes, the only time she had witnessed one express any pain. She leapt and planted both feet on his chest as he slashed the air, blind but still deadly. The kick propelled him to the wall, sending him tumbling over onto the heads of his comrades. Reva rolled to her feet, dodging sword thrusts from three directions, the House Guards closing around her, halberds stabbing and slashing.

She did a quick head count, finding she had lost half her command already. She glanced over at the inner wall around the first breach, noting the piles of Volarian dead and the constant rain of arrows delivered by the archers on the rooftops. But there was a cohesion to the attackers now, a hard knot of shielded men inching forward with more crowding in behind. *It's time.*

"Break!" she shouted, lunging forward to spear the exposed neck of a Kuritai, then turning and running with the guards. They were faster than any practice, sprinting down the steps and vaulting the first of the rings without losing any more to the pursuing enemy. The Kuritai didn't pause in their charge, coming on at a run to scale the new wall but falling by the dozen to the archers on the rooftops above. Those that did make it over were hopelessly outnumbered and soon hacked down.

"Remember the signal," she told Sergeant Laklin. "Three blasts of the horn and you break for the next ring."

"I remember, my lady." Laklin wiped his sweat-streaked brow and gave a grin. "Made them pay for it, didn't we?"

"That we did. Let's see if we can exact the full price."

She ran for the western section where Antesh was assembling his companies after breaking from the breach defences. She was forced to duck as one of the Volarian fireballs came crashing down a few yards ahead, scattering bricks and embers in a blast of heat and smoke. Antesh had anticipated this tactic, forming firefighting companies to safeguard the streets between the rings. They came running now with buckets in hand, older people mostly with a few youngsters. They attacked the blaze with all the ferocity of a company of guardsmen, sand and water quelling the flames in a few minutes. It had been surprisingly small considering the size of the fireball.

"Pays to live in a city of stone, my lady," the fire-company leader said, a brawny woman of middling years Reva recognised from the line of petitioners the day she had intruded into the manor. Despite her words Reva could see half a dozen columns of smoke rising from the surrounding streets, evidence that some parts of the city were not so immune to fire.

"No let-up, lads!" Antesh was on the rooftop overlooking the western section. He had placed his command post atop the home of the masons guild, the most sturdily built structure in the city, the walls thick and the windows narrow, perfect for bowmen. Below them the Volarians clustered about the wall with shields raised, more pouring through the breach behind. The Volarians seemed to be assaulting the wall itself rather than attempting to climb it, the occasional flash of short swords through the shields told of a concerted effort to hammer their way through the recently finished brickwork.

Reva took a clay pot of lamp oil and threw it at the knot of shields, the liquid exploding across them as it shattered. She followed it with a fire arrow, the Volarians soon forced to abandon their flaming shields, most perishing under the instant volley from the archers above. But there were more trooping through the breaches, always more.

From the right came the sound of two horn blasts, the signal for an imminent breach. "Keep holding here!" she told Antesh and sprinted for the nearest walkway.

Two battalions of Free Swords were attacking at different points along the north-facing ring, one was being held but the other had managed to force a toehold on the other side, a small but growing cluster of shields constantly assailed from above by a rain of arrows and other missiles. The defenders here were mostly townsfolk stiffened with a few archers and guardsmen, their lack of expertise remedied in some part by their ferocity. She saw a large, elderly man in the leather smock of a carpenter charge at the Volarian cluster with an axe in hand, several young apprentices close behind. On the surrounding rooftops people hurled rocks and bottles at the enemy along with a torrent of abuse.

"Die, you heretic fuckers!" a young woman screamed, lifting a large piece of masonry over her head and hurling it at the Volarians. It landed in the middle of their shields, leaving a hole. Reva saw her chance, sprinted to the edge of the roof and leapt. She landed on the Free Sword who tried to lift his shield to plug the gap, breaking her fall and forcing him to the cobbles. The sword plunged through his open mouth and into his brain. She leapt again as the short swords came for her, spinning and twisting, the sword a flicker of silver, finding eyes and throats with terrible precision. Seeing her intervention, the townsfolk redoubled their efforts, the old carpenter laying about with his axe and voicing a roar as his apprentices hacked away with hatchets and hammers. Others came running from the surrounding houses, armed with knives and cleavers. Some had no weapons at all, running and leaping onto the Free Swords, hurling punches and gouging eyes.

The Volarian cluster soon broke apart under the assault, some trying to scramble back over the wall only to pitch over with arrows in their backs. Others fought to the end, one man managing to hold the townsfolk back as he stood over a fallen comrade, his sword moving with the expert economy and effect of a veteran as he forced the townsfolk to hold off. He snarled at them, shouting curses in his own language as they steeled themselves for the final rush, then stiffened at the sight of Reva.

"You're very brave," she observed, attacking without a pause. It was over quickly, the brave veteran coughing his last as her sword found the inch-wide gap below his breastplate.

"May I?" Reva asked the carpenter, gesturing for his axe. He handed it over in wordless awe.

"This man," she told them, standing astride the veteran's corpse and reaching down to remove his helmet. "Is probably a hero to our enemies. They need to know what happens to heroes in this city."

She could hear the shouted orders on the other side of the wall, sergeants and officers marshalling their men for another try. The voices stilled to silence after she cast the veteran's head over the wall.

"You fought well," she told the townsfolk with a smile, keeping the annoyance from her voice as they all knelt before her. "Gather these weapons and stand ready. This is far from over."

They held the outer ring until nightfall. The breakthrough came in the east-facing wall, a slave-soldier battalion suffering fearful casualties to bring down a section of wall with a battering ram, Kuritai rushing through to consolidate the success. Lord Arentes had ordered three horn blasts sounded and the pre-rehearsed withdrawal commenced. Archers covered the retreat from the rooftops, loosing five arrows then retreating twenty paces to pause and loose five more. In the streets below, people hauled carts and furniture to bar the path of the onrushing Volarians for a few precious seconds before running to the next ring.

Reva took her bow and stood on the tallest rooftop behind the second ring, watching the last of the defenders running across the fifty yards of flattened city that formed the killing ground. Fortunately the Volarians' blood was up; this was the fruit of their labours after all, slaughter and rape the inevitable reward for those who take a city. So they came streaming into the killing ground, swords raised, blood-crazed and shieldless.

Later, Antesh called it the finest hour in Cumbraelin archery and it had certainly been a spectacular sight. So many arrows crowded the air it was difficult to see the effect, like peering through smoke to glimpse the fire beyond. Reva loosed six arrows in as many seconds, Arken straining to match her as he stood at her side, grimacing in pain with every draw of his longbow. The storm continued for a full minute, not a single Volarian soldier making it to the second ring. Antesh called a halt and the air cleared, revealing a carpet of bodies covering the killing ground, none closer than a dozen yards to the wall. The survivors could be seen hovering in the shelter of the streets beyond, a few men stumbling about in the open with arrows protruding from their limbs, Varitai from their oddly calm expressions.

Reva finished them herself, one arrow each, an ugly growl rising from the defenders when the last fell, soon building to a prolonged roar of hate-filled defiance.

There was no respite that night, the Volarians trying fire in place of massed assaults, throwing oil pots over the ring followed by fire arrows. Once again the stones of the city came to their aid and most of the fires were swiftly quelled. But whilst stone couldn't burn, people could and Brother Harin soon had dozens of burnt souls crowding the cathedral. She had given it over to him as a healing house, the pews transformed into beds, becoming ever more full by the hour. Only one of the bishops had had the temerity to object, a wizened old cleric who held on to his staff with gnarled and trembling hands, scowling at her as he quoted the Ninth Book: "'Only peace and love can reside in a house blessed by the Father's sight.'"

"'Turn not your gaze from those in need,'" she countered, calling on the Second Book. "'For the Father never will.' Get out of the way, old man."

The burnt people were a pitiable sight, hair singed away, flesh turned black and red, given to terrible screams that only abated with large doses of redflower. "Another day like this and it'll all be gone," Veliss advised. She wore a plain dress covered in bloodstains and sundry dirt, sleeves rolled up and hair tied back, soot and sweat mingling on her face. Reva wanted very badly to kiss her, here and now in full view of the scowling old bishop and the Father, if in fact He ever cared to spare a glance for this place, which she doubted.

"Careful, love," Veliss said quietly, reading her gaze. "Turns out they'll tolerate a lot, more than ever I thought they would. But not us."

"I don't care," Reva said, reaching for her hand.

"Just win the battle, Reva." Veliss's thumb traced over her hand for a moment before she released it. "Then we'll decide what we care most about."

The second ring held through the night but by morning a fire had taken hold in a building near the south-facing wall. It was a storehouse for the weavers guild, packed with linens. The fire was too fierce to be contained, the heat soon proving unbearable to the defenders and Reva ordered a withdrawal to the next ring. It was more costly this time, the Volarians quicker to take advantage of the confusion, swarming over the wall whilst their own archers engaged the men on the rooftops, many falling into the struggling mass of bodies choking the streets below. Pockets of defenders were cut off, holding out in fortified houses and exacting a fearful toll on those sent to root them out.

Reva watched from a rooftop as Varitai tried repeatedly to storm a chapel a few streets away, squads attempting to scale the walls or force their way through the windows, their bodies soon flung out again. Eventually they surrounded the building and assailed it with a hundred or more oil pots before an officer threw a torch. The flames took hold quickly and the defenders came streaming from the chapel, not in panic but fury, throwing themselves at the Varitai with no trace of fear. Reva straightened in surprise at the sight of the man leading the defenders, portly and dressed in a priest's robes, hacking at the Volarians with a thin-bladed sword. *The priest from the square*. He died of course, along with the others, hacked down and butchered in the street, but not before they had felled at least twice their number.

Reva was turning away when something impacted on the roof-tiles with a wet smack. It rolled along the roof to rest at her feet, slack leathery features and empty eyes staring up at her. She looked around as more impacts sounded, the heads raining down around her. She heard a woman screaming in the street below, perhaps in recognition of one of the disembodied missiles.

She went to the manor where Arentes and Antesh were conferring over a map. "Do we have any prisoners?"

There were a little over two dozen men herded into a corner of the manor grounds under close guard, most wounded and all mute with the expectation of death. They were all Free Swords— Kuritai and Varitai didn't surrender and none of the defenders felt inclined to care for any too wounded to keep fighting. "All officers or sergeants," Antesh explained. "Thought they might have something to tell us."

"We're in here, they're out there," Reva replied. "That's all we need to know." She turned to the House Guard sergeant in charge of the prisoners. "Any problem with this? If so, I'll see to it myself."

The sergeant gave a stern shake of the head and hefted his pole-axe. "Spread them around a bit," Reva told him. "Throw them over where the Free Swords are thickest."

She forced herself to stay and watch, finding it curious that so few of them begged or tried to run. They had to know there was no refuge for them here, that surrender had only delayed the inevitable. Most were too cowed and fearful to do any more than stumble weeping to the block, eyes closed or vomiting in terror as the axe fell, but one man was straight-backed and defiant, staring at Reva with hard eyes as he was forced to his knees. "Elverah," he said.

Reva gave a slight nod in response.

"No better," he said in thickly accented Realm Tongue. "No better than us."

"No," she replied. "I'm much worse."

Somehow she had managed to sleep, waking on a rooftop near the square with Arken sitting on the edge. He had found a blanket to cover her though the chilled night air still left her shivering. "Might have bought us some respite," he said. "The thing with the prisoners.

There hasn't been an attack for nigh on two hours." There was no reproach or judgement in his voice, just tired acceptance.

"They'll be back," she replied, standing and working the stiffness from her limbs. "Lord Arentes had good things to say about the help you gave the Realm Guard yesterday. Seems they want to adopt you."

"Not a decent archer amongst them," he said with a shrug. "Easy to stand out."

She pulled the blanket tighter over her shoulders, surveying the half-ruined city before her, the fires burning in the streets taken by the Volarians, watching them scurry from doorway to doorway having learned not to linger in sight of the defenders' archers. Below her, people huddled together in the cramped streets behind the third ring, sitting around cook fires or just slumped in exhaustion. There was little talk, just the occasional infant's cry or a sergeant's shouted rebuke to a weary guard.

"I lied, Arken," she said.

"What about?"

"Al Sorna. There was no vision, no gift of the Father's Sight. For all I know he's still in the Reaches. Perhaps he never had any intention of coming to our aid. Why would he? This land is filled with those who curse his name."

She heard him rise and soon felt his arms close around her, strong and warm. "Is that what you think?"

I came back to this land to find a sister, instead I found two. "No," she breathed, stifling a groan at the sight of a column of Varitai mustering in the streets opposite the south-facing wall. "No. He's coming."

It began again in the small hours of the morning and continued all day, the Volarians attacking in strength at four separate points, each fresh assault preceded by a rain of engine-launched gifts. Not just captive defenders now, women and youths amongst the severed heads smacking into the cobbles as they steeled themselves for the next rush. Inevitably some broke at the sight, a townsman running from his company and vaulting over the wall when a girl's head landed amidst their ranks, screaming with a meat cleaver in hand as he charged the Free Swords approaching the wall, soon disappearing under a mass of stabbing short swords.

Reva rushed to wherever the need was greatest, killing with bow or sword to restore the position. Sometimes just the sight of her was enough, people gathering courage and rejoining the fight as she appeared on the rooftops or leapt into their midst. But as the noon sun rose she knew the time had come and ordered the three blasts sounded.

She was running with Arken across a walkway towards the fourth ring when she saw Lord Arentes in the street below, fighting together with a small band of surrounded guardsmen, Varitai assailing them on all sides. "Steady now!" the old commander intoned as they slowly inched their way towards the safety of the third ring. "One step back."

Reva unslung her bow and took down three Varitai in quick succession, but it wasn't enough. A tight formation of Free Swords came charging in, crashing into the guardsman and shattering their ranks. She saw Arentes parry a sword thrust and deliver an overhand slash to his opponent, cutting him down but leaving his sword embedded in his shoulder. Reva re-slung the bow and leapt from the walkway, landing in the swirling battle with sword drawn, cutting down a Volarian lunging at Arentes. Another came for her but was crushed under Arken's boots as he dropped from the walkway, hacking wildly with his axe.

"The wall my lord!" she told Arentes and they ran, scrambling over with the help of many defenders as the archers above drove the Volarians back.

She looked up to see Arken cresting the wall, a large silhouette against a clear blue sky, tumbling to a heap on the street before her. "Arken?"

His face was pressed into the cobbles, the flesh bunched, eyes dim and unseeing. A Volarian short sword protruded from his back.

◆ ◆ ◆

The third ring held for no more than an hour, despite the killing she did around Arken's corpse as the Free Swords came over the wall. All sense of time lost in the fury of it, no weariness could touch her. They came and she killed them until hands grabbed her and dragged her away. Her senses returned then, a red slick covering her sword arm from blade to shoulder, eyes fixed on Arken's body lying amidst the Volarian dead, lost to sight as they rounded a corner and she was borne over the fifth ring.

"My lady?" Antesh stared into her face, hand rough on her shoulder. "Please, my lady."

She blinked at him and got slowly to her feet. "How many left?"

"Half at most. We lost too many when the last ring fell."

Arken . . . "Yes, we lost too many."

She looked down at the sword in her hand, finding half the blade sheared off. She couldn't remember breaking it. She tossed it to the cobbles and found a trough, sinking her head into the water to get the blood out of her hair. "We can't hold here," she told Antesh, raising her head from the water. "Fall back to the last ring. The killing ground is wider."

Reva went to the manor as Antesh and Arentes organised the final defence. The sword was where she had left it, propped beside the fireplace in her uncle's memory. She hefted it, finding it lighter than she remembered. The edge keen and bright, all trace of the Reader's blood cleaned away. "You're not what I came for," she told the sword. "But you'll do."

The sixth and final ring was constructed around the cathedral square, every foot of it sheltering at least one defender. Those too old, injured or young to fight were crammed into the cathedral. The remaining guardsmen were arrayed in the square itself, ready to counter any breakthrough. They were weary, she could tell, but all stood straight as she approached, her grandfather's sword resting on her shoulder.

"I thought it was time," she said. "That I thanked you for your service. You are hereby dismissed with full honours and may depart at your leave."

The laugh was surprisingly loud, if short-lived thanks to Lord Arentes's glower of disapproval. "It can be said," Reva went on, "that my family has not always deserved such great service. Nor in truth, have I. For I am not blessed, you see. I . . . am a liar . . ." She paused as a drop of rain fell onto her hand, strange, as the sky had been so clear for so long. She looked up to find the sky darkening, clouds forming with uncanny speed. Soon the rain was falling, driven by a hard wind, the fires on the other side of the ring dying under the deluge.

"My lady!" Antesh called from the walkway above, standing and pointing towards the south. "Something's happening!"

CHAPTER NINE
Vaelin

Cara swayed a little as the clouds began to move in the sky, thin wisps of cotton coalescing into dark spidery tendrils, forming into a slowly spinning spiral a mile wide.

"Are you all right?" Vaelin asked, reaching out to steady her as she stumbled.

"Just a little light-headed, my lord," she replied with a forced smile. "Haven't done this for such a long time." She took a breath and raised her gaze to the sky once more, a fresh breeze stirring the grass on the hilltop. The spiral twisted in the sky, darkening with every passing second, the tendrils thickening into roiling mountains of grey and black. Cara gritted her teeth and gave a pained grunt, the swirling mass of cloud starting to drift towards the smoke-shrouded city some six miles away, its course heralded by a rumble of thunder and lit by the occasional flash of lightning.

Cara sank to her knees, face pale and eyes dim with exhaustion. Lorkan and Marken rushed to her side, the young gifted casting a resentful glare at Vaelin which he chose to ignore. Weaver stood a little way off, his usually placid features now drawn in confusion as he paced back and forth, his ever-growing rope grasped tight in both hands. As far as Vaelin knew he hadn't used his gift throughout the entirety of the march, though he was often seen carrying wounded from the field in the aftermath of battle. The song sounded a clear note of frustration as Vaelin watched Weaver turn his gaze from Cara, wincing in discomfort before straightening into a determined stance. *He waits for something,* Vaelin realised. *Or someone.*

He turned to watch the mass of cloud rumble towards Alltor, pregnant with menace and hopefully enough rain to quench the fires raging within the walls. North Guard scouts had reported in the day before bringing news of the city's dire straits and he had ordered the army's pace quickened. He drove them hard, riding along the columns of trotting men with a grim visage and sincere threats for any who seemed likely to fall out. They continued through the night, covering fifty miles before he called a halt. In the morning Nortah had brought Cara to his tent with a suggestion.

"I have to stress, my lord," the girl said. "I cannot predict the consequences if I do this. I can bring the rain down on the city, but what happens next . . ." She gave a helpless shrug. "When I was a girl a drought blighted our village, the crops withered and my mother said we were like to starve come the winter. I had some knowledge of my gift by then, making little whirlwinds and such, sometimes forming the clouds into pretty shapes. So I made a big cloud, called all the other clouds to join it, and it rained. For three days it rained and people rejoiced. Then the rain stopped and the duck pond froze over. It was the middle of summer. Erlin found me shortly after, telling my parents of a place in the north where I would be safe."

"You don't have to do this," Vaelin cautioned her. "I know well the price our gifts exact."

"I didn't come all this way just to watch, my lord."

He waited until the clouds were over Alltor, glimpsing the curtain of shifting grey that told of heavy rain. The song was strong now, singing Reva's tune with a note of pride but also foreboding. Time was short.

"Odds of at least two to one," Count Marven told the council of captains. "Lengthening by the hour as they draw more troops from Alltor to face us. Given the enemy's strength, my lord, I am bound to suggest a feinting strategy." He pointed to the centre of the map Harlick had drawn, showing the Volarian camp now no more than a few hundred paces distant, lines of Free Swords and Varitai drawn up to bar the route to Alltor, cavalry in large numbers on both flanks. "Keep our infantry where it is and send the Eorhil to the western bank to draw their gaze. At the same time the Nilsaelin horse and the North Guard go west. The enemy will be forced to reorder their ranks, allowing for an assault around here." His finger moved to a section on the right of the Volarian line. "We hit them hard then veer off to the west to join up with the cavalry whilst the Eorhil threaten their eastern flank. It should draw off enough of their forces to buy the city some time. We can then pull back to the forest where I'm sure our Seordah friends can make great play with their infantry. We tie them up in small battles, ambushes and the like. It won't be quick, a matter of weeks rather than days, but I think this is a battle we can win."

"Alltor doesn't have weeks," Nortah said. "Or even days."

"And we do not have the numbers, good Captain," Marven returned, the strain of the past week telling in his voice. "We need an army twice the size to break their line."

"So we've come all this way to run around the woods whilst the city perishes?" Nortah gave a disgusted snort.

"What about the river?" Adal put in. "We could build boats. There are plenty in our ranks who know how. Send reinforcements to the city that way."

"By the time we get across there won't be anyone to reinforce," Nortah said. "That's if we can make it past that monster they've got moored in the river."

Vaelin glanced up at the tent roof as a thunderclap sounded overhead. Cara's storm was gathering force and soon the ground would be too sodden for cavalry. He went to the rear of the tent where the canvas bundle lay on his bunk, the captains' dispute continuing as he undid the knots, pulling back the wrapping to reveal the sword. The blood-song swelled in welcome as he grasped the scabbard, the heft of it so comfortable in his hand. He was aware their voices had stilled as he strapped on the sword, the scabbard resting against his back with a familiar weight.

"My lord?" Dahrena asked as he walked from the tent. He went to where Flame had been tethered, hauling the saddle onto his back and tying it in place, then leading him towards the ranks of assembled infantry.

"What are you going to do?" Dahrena stood in his path, a little breathless, eyes bright with fearful suspicion. Behind her the captains all stood, most looking on in bafflement but Nortah and Caenis wearing expressions of grim understanding. They exchanged a glance then moved off in opposite directions, Caenis calling to his sergeant, Nortah running to his company, with Snowdance padding along in his wake.

"My lord?" Dahrena said.

"You see the souls of others when you fly," he said. "But do you ever see your own?"

She gave a wordless shake of her head.

"That is a great pity." He reached out to cup her face, thumb tracing over her cheek. "Because I can see it, and I find it shines very bright indeed. I should be grateful if you would have a care for my sister. She will not understand this."

He turned away and mounted up, trotting to the front rank of the army, finding the miners' banner and reining in. "Break ranks!" he called to the surrounding regiments. "Gather round."

There was some hesitation amongst the officers before they repeated the order and a few minutes delay before they stood around him a loose circle, the bulk of the infantry with the Seordah crowding behind.

"We have reached a point," he told them, "where I can no longer command your obedience through duty alone. Now every man and woman in this army must choose their own course. For my own part"—he turned in the saddle, pointing to the rain-lashed city beyond the Volarian line—"I intend to ride to the centre of this city. For my friend is there, and I would very much like to see her again."

He reached behind his shoulder and drew the sword, raising it high. The light was meagre under the darkening sky but still it caught enough sun to gleam. He cast his gaze over their faces, pale and rapt in the rain as he spoke again, "And I will kill any man who raises a hand to stop me. Those who wish to come with me are welcome."

He turned Flame about, moving forward at a slow walk, hearing the commotion build behind him, Marven's and Adal's voices audible above the multitude of shouted orders. He called on the song and let the voices fade, scanning the Volarian ranks and waiting for the note of recognition. *Perhaps they executed him for cowardice.* But then it rose, a clear note of pure fear as his gaze fell on a battalion positioned just to the left of the Volarian centre.

Well, he thought. *At least I got to know Alornis.*

He kicked his heels into Flame's flanks and the stallion reared before spurring into a gallop.

Time seemed to slow as they sped towards the Volarian line, the spectacle of it all filling his gaze. Fireballs fell in a low arc, cast by the ballista-ships in the river, the city's fires now smouldering under the rain, the clouds above thick and black save for the occasional flicker of lightning.

Arrows came for him as he charged, easily avoided thanks to the song, its music louder than he had ever known it. He waited until it picked out the former captive, his fear a high-pitched scream in the second rank of his battalion, then began to sing, forcing every vestige of anger and bloodlust into the song he cast forth. He felt it strike home, the Free Sword's last hold on sanity breaking like glass as he beheld the charging figure on the horse, coming straight towards him with sword levelled. The ranks of the battalion rippled as the youth began to claw his way towards the rear, lashing out at restraining hands with his short sword, screaming in terror, a few soldiers in the front rank turning to look on the commotion.

In truth it wasn't much, just a small flaw in an otherwise impressively disciplined line, but today it was enough.

Flame struck home with the fearless charge of a born warhorse, smashing men aside and trampling the slow-footed into the earth as Vaelin's sword began its own song. He cleaved a man's face apart from chin to skull with an upward slash, his helmet parting with the force of it, then spurred Flame onward, the sword slashing in an unceasing, unstoppable blur. Men rolled limbless in their wake, screams adding to those of the former captive, still fighting his maddened way towards safety.

A hard-faced veteran loomed out of the throng, short sword raised in a swift thrust, but the song saw all today and blared a warning, the veteran sinking to his knees a second later, eyes and mouth agape at the jetting stump of his wrist. Another Free Sword tried to hack at Flame's legs, earning a sweep of the sword that left him headless.

They burst through the rear of the Volarian line, Vaelin hauling Flame to a halt in a fountain of churned sod. The terrorised Free Sword was kneeling in the open ground beyond, eyes wide and unblinking, all trace of sanity having fled. Vaelin turned the horse about, finding the Volarians moving to encircle him, blades levelled as they edged closer, fear on every face.

Vaelin heard laughter somewhere and realised it was his own. He also felt the trickle of blood from his nose that told him he had sung long enough. He ignored it and charged again, riding down the nearest Free Sword and killing the men on either side of him, wheeling to the right and hacking down a man shouting orders, then another who stood frozen in fear.

But not all were so fearful, a dozen men or more leaping and slashing in an attempt to bring him down, but the song warned of every attack. He parried, ducked and killed in a whirl of song and blood until Flame gave a loud pain-filled whinny and reared, an arrow buried in his flank. The horse stayed upright for a few more seconds, rearing and lashing out with his hooves, but a spasm of pain brought him to his knees, Vaelin rolling free of the saddle, coming to his feet to parry a thrust and punch his sword point through the breastplate of the man who delivered it, the star-silver blade penetrating the armour with ease.

He wrenched the blade free and stood beside his dying horse, Free Swords on all sides, creeping closer as officers hounded them with curses. The song birthed a new note, something discordant, touched by wildness but also a fierce and boundless loyalty. He laughed again and the Free Swords paused.

"I'm sorry your general didn't take my offer," he told them.

Snowdance landed in their midst in a blaze of teeth and claws, pinning two men to the ground, her great jaws fixing on each head in turn and ripping them free. Her gaze fell on Vaelin for a moment, the song rising in warm regard, then she was gone, charging into the thickest knot of Volarians, blood and limbs scattering in her wake.

The Volarian line was torn apart now, a gaping rent some twenty yards wide proving an irresistible target for the North Guard and Captain Orven's guardsmen. They came streaming through with swords flashing, the gap widening further until the entire Free Sword battalion broke apart. Captain Adal hacked down a running Volarian and pulled up as he caught sight of Vaelin standing beside Flame's corpse. "You're hurt, my lord."

Vaelin touched a hand to the blood streaming from his nose and shook his head. "It's nothing. Rally your men and wheel to the left, engage the cavalry on their flank."

"You're dismounted . . ." the captain protested as Vaelin walked towards the nearest Volarian battalion.

"I'll be all right," he replied with a wave, not turning.

The song was an unquenchable fire now, fuelling his charge through their ranks as he killed and killed again, parrying or side-stepping blows that should have brought death. He attacked the next battalion from the rear, finding them Varitai immune to any terror he might spread but lacking the instinct needed to counter his song-born skill. He hacked his way into their midst to cut down their commander who, unlike them, was entirely capable of feeling fear, whipping his horse bloody and laying about with a whip as he tried to fight free of their ranks. It didn't help.

The battalion disintegrated around him as Foreman Ultin led his miners in a headlong charge against their front, the men of the Reaches giving full vent to their rage, born of the terrible sights witnessed on the march. The Varitai responded with automatic precision, forming densely packed defensive knots as they fought to the end.

"Re-form!" Foreman Ultin was shouting, having planted his banner to the rear of the Volarian line. "Form on me!"

"Take them left," Vaelin told him, frowning at the man's appalled expression.

"You . . ." Ultin gulped, eyes staring into Vaelin's for a moment, then blinked and looked away. "Yes, my lord!"

Vaelin felt a dampness on his cheeks and touched a hand to his eyelids, the fingers coming away bloody. He paused and tried to quiet the song, but a new note of warning made it flare again. He turned to the right where Count Marven's infantry were engaged in a furious struggle with a smaller number of lightly armoured men. Vaelin saw how they moved with a remarkable fluency as he ran towards the fight, most armed with a sword in each hand as they did their terrible dance, the Nilsaelins falling by the dozen as they pressed around them. *The famed Kuritai*, he realised, ducking under a slashing sword, rolling into a kneeling position and hacking back to hamstring the swordsman. The Nilsaelins roared and fell on the wounded Kuritai in a mass, swords and daggers flashing.

The song flared again and Vaelin looked up to see three Kuritai coming for him, one in the lead and two moving to his flanks. He removed all restraint from the song and suddenly the Kuritai were moving through air made of clay, their coordinated attack clumsy and sluggish, leaving so many openings. The song faded a little as the three Kuritai tumbled to the earth around him, splashing mud in the unending rain, blood gushing from near-identical wounds to the throat.

He straightened, seeing a Kuritai regarding him with his head tilted, face blank like a child seeing a puzzling trick for the first time, an expression also worn by many of the onlooking Nilsaelins. A bowstring snapped and the curious Kuritai fell with an arrow in his chest, his brothers turning to face a new threat as Hera Drakil led his Seordah into the fray. The Nilsaelins were brave but could only prevail through weight of numbers. The Seordah, it transpired, needed no such advantage.

Vaelin watched the Seordah chief slide under a slashing short sword and bring his war club round as he sprang to his feet, the back of the Kuritai's head exploding from the impact. The other Seordah dealt with the remainder, war clubs and knives whirling, Kuritai falling in a matter of seconds.

"I see why the forest remains untouched," Vaelin commented as the war chief crouched at his side.

"You need the healing man, Beral Shak Ur," he said, pulling him to his feet.

Vaelin staggered a little as the song flared again, fighting down a shout of pain as fresh blood rose in his mouth. *Reva!* He turned to the city, eyes tracking along the causeway to find the gates lying wrecked and open. "I need a horse," he said.

The Seordah was clearly reluctant but Count Marven pulled up beside them, dismounting and offering Vaelin the reins. "Fight better on foot in any case," he said, blood flowing freely from a cut on his cheek.

"Form your men up," Vaelin told him, hauling himself into the saddle. The new vantage point gave him a clearer view of the battle. He could see every section of the Volarian line now engaged, broken here and on the right where Nortah's company gave full vent to their rage as they tore apart a Free Sword battalion twice their number to join up with Ultin's miners. The left still seemed to be holding despite a furious assault by Caenis's Realm Guard. Beyond them the swirling mass of horses just visible through the rain told him the Eorhil were in the process of mastering the Volarian cavalry.

"Push through their rear opposite the Realm Guard," he told Marven, finding he had to keep hold of the pommel to stop from falling. "Hera Drakil," he addressed the Seordah, "I should like you to meet a friend of mine in the city."

He tugged Marven's horse around and set off at the gallop. He saw something near the causeway that made him pause for a moment. The captive Free Sword, lying dead with his throat cut, a bloody knife in his hand, his face frozen in the same mad rictus born of the song.

He knew from Harlick's reports that this causeway was almost exactly three hundred yards long, so it was strange to find it seemed to have grown by several miles. His breath was laboured now, he could feel the blood seeping through his shirt under the light mail as it flowed from his nose, mouth and eyes. He spat it out every few yards and forced Marven's mount to a faster pace.

He was obliged to jump the horse over the remnants of the gate, clattering through the cobbled streets beyond, finding bodies and destruction everywhere. Blood ran in rivers along the rain-soaked gutters, streaming in red streaks from the corpses he found at every turn. Some Volarians were stumbling about but offering no threat, madness plain on their faces. The defenders had constructed walls within the city, forcing him to find the breaches made by the Volarians before proceeding further, the delay making him seethe in frustration as the song rose ever higher.

He was compelled to dismount a short distance from the cathedral, the streets so choked with bodies even Marven's veteran warhorse shied from going further. He moved on, his vision clouding as he tripped over bodies, stumbling to his knees beside a young man with a short sword buried in his back and an axe resting under his pale hand. *Little more than a boy.*

He forced himself upright and staggered on, the sounds of

battle reaching his ears. He emerged into an avenue of flattened buildings, finding five thousand or more Volarians assailing another wall. They had managed to batter a breach through it, bodies piling up as a furious fight raged just within the wall. Another shout from the song confirmed it, she was there, in the thick of it. *Where else would she be?*

"We do this," Hera Drakil said, appearing at his side, his many many warriors running from the surrounding streets.

"I should appreciate it very much," Vaelin replied.

The Volarian host made a curious sound as the Seordah charge struck home, a great sighing groan of absolute despair. Days of torment suffered within these walls only to earn a swift death at the hands of warriors they had no hope of matching.

He closed his eyes as the sounds of battle faded. *Stop now,* he told the song, but he was so weary and so very cold.

"You don't need to kneel for me."

She stood over him, looking down with a warm smile, a sword of Renfaelin design resting on her shoulder, the blade bloody from end to end.

"Is that it?" he asked.

She shook her head. "I never found it."

His vision dimmed, blackness descending for a moment. When it faded he found he was on his back, her face only inches away, tears falling onto his bloody face. "I always knew you would come."

He managed to raise a hand and trace his fingers through her hair. *Kept it long I see.* "What sort of brother would I be if I hadn't?" He coughed, a plume of blood erupting from his mouth, staining her face.

"DON'T!" she screamed as his vision dimmed again. "DON'T! Please don't . . ."

Cold. Absolute, inescapable cold. Cutting through skin and bone to clutch at his heart. Yet there was no tremble to his limbs, no mist to his breath. He blinked as his vision cleared, seeing a wall.

He turned and his boots raised an echo, very loud and very long. No echo was ever so long.

The room was a simple cube of roughly worked stone, a single window in the wall to his right. In the centre stood a plain table fashioned from some dark wood, the surface gleaming even though he could see no lamp or light from the window. A woman sat on the opposite side of the table, regarding him with an expression that was equal parts fury and scrutiny. An empty chair waited before him.

"I know who you are," the woman said, her voice birthing another echo of unnatural length.

Vaelin moved towards the chair, pausing as a faint sound came to him, a soft plaintive call. *Did someone call my name?*

"Was it Tokrev, I wonder?" The woman angled her head, eyes narrowing. "No, I don't think so."

She was dark-haired, young and beautiful, her eyes bright with intelligence and a greater depth of malice than he had seen before. It reminded him of the thing that had lived in Barkus, but he saw now that had been a spiteful child compared to her.

"You know who I am," he said. "Who are you?"

She gave a mirthless smile. "I'm a songbird in a cage. And now so are you."

He tried to summon the blood-song, searching for some guiding note but finding nothing.

"No songs here, my lord," the woman told him. "No gifts. Only those he brings and they are rarely welcome."

"He?"

A spasm of fury passed over her face and her hand slammed onto the table. "Don't play with me! Do not act the fool! You know very well where you are and who holds you here."

"As he holds you."

The woman reclined, relaxing with a soft laugh. "His punishments are cruel but unimaginative, for the most part. This room, the cold, no other distraction save memory, and I have many of those." Her hand moved to her chest, massaging the flesh between her breasts, eyes growing distant. "Did you ever love anyone, my lord?"

The sound came again, louder this time and he was certain it was a voice speaking his name, distant but familiar.

He ignored her question and went to the window, looking out on a shifting landscape, the sky a rapidly swirling canvas of cloud above tall mountains. He watched as they slowly descended, the slopes become less steep, richer in grass until he looked upon a land of gently rolling hills.

"It changes by the hour," the woman told him. "Mountains, oceans, jungles. Places he knew once I suspect."

"Why did he put you here?" Vaelin asked. "What was your crime?"

Her hand stopped moving on her chest and she returned it to the table. "Loving and not being loved in return. That was my crime."

"I've met your kind before. There's no love in you."

"Trust me, my lord. You have never met my kind." She nodded at the table.

The flute hadn't been there before but now it sat on the gleaming wooden surface. It was a simple instrument, fashioned from bone, the surface stained with age and use, but somehow he knew if he picked it up and put it to his lips the tune it birthed would be very strong.

"*VAELIN!*"

There was no mistaking it now, a voice beyond this room was calling his name with enough power to shake the stones.

"He'll give it back to you," the woman said, inclining her head at the flute. "It's a hard thing for those like us to live without a song."

The room shuddered, the bricks beginning to break apart as something assailed them from outside, mortar and stone fragmenting and warm white light breaking through the cracks.

"Just pick it up," the woman said. "We'll sing together when he sends us back. And what a song we'll make."

He looked at the flute, hating himself for how much he wanted it. "Do you have a name?" he asked the woman.

"A hundred or more, probably. But my favourite was the one I earned before I accepted the Ally's kind bargain. At my father's behest I once laid waste to a land in the south where the local savages were proving troublesome. A superstitious folk, they thought me a witch. Elverah, they called me."

"Elverah." He looked again at the flute as the wall behind him gave a loud crack of shattered stone. He met her gaze and gave a smile before turning his back on her and the flute. "I'll remember."

He heard her shouting as the wall exploded, light flooding the room and banishing the cold. "Tell your brother!" she cried. "He could kill me a thousand times and it would change nothing!"

The light came for him, embracing him with its blessed warmth, drawing him from the room. It seemed to seep into him as he was pulled away, bringing visions of a face he knew. "You shine brightly too," Dahrena told him. "So easy to find."

Light filled his gaze, the last vestiges of cold banishing . . . but then a final shiver as another voice reached him. Not the woman this time, something far older, the voice free of all expression save certainty. "We will make an ending, you and I."

He woke with a shout, convulsing and shivering, as cold and weary as it was possible to be and still live. He felt a weight on his chest, finding his hands tangled in long silken tresses. Dahrena groaned and raised her head, her face pale and eyes dim with exhaustion. "So easy to find," she said softly.

"Vaelin!" Reva was kneeling at his side, smiling and weeping. Behind her he could see Hera Drakil standing with his warriors, a deep disquiet on his hawk face.

"I thought it was Darkblade," he replied.

She laughed and pressed a kiss to his forehead, tears flowing freely. "There is no Darkblade. It's a story for children."

He put an arm around her shoulders as she wept, searching inside himself and knowing what he would find. *It's gone. The song is gone.*

PART V

My father has never been a man to indulge in deep reflection or wise pronouncements. His few writings and typically terse correspondence make dry reading indeed, riven as they are with the mundane inanities of military life. But there was one occasion that has stayed at the forefront of my memory, something he said the night Marbellis fell. We stood on a hilltop watching the flames rise above the walls, hearing the screams of the townsfolk as the Realm Guard gave vent to bestial vengeance, and I felt the need to ask him why his mood was so sombre, had he not just secured a victory worthy of glorious celebration for all the ages? I was, you may understand, quite drunk.

My father's gaze never lifted from the tormented city and I heard him say, "All victory is an illusion."

—ALUCIUS AL HESTIAN, *COLLECTED WRITINGS*,
GREAT LIBRARY OF THE UNIFIED REALM

VERNIERS' ACCOUNT

"Set sail!" the general was shouting at the ship's captain, voice pitched just below a scream. "Set sail I said! Get this hulk moving!"

I went to the rail as the slave-sailors rushed in answer to the captain's orders. The remnants of the army were being herded towards the river now, Varitai fighting to the end in dumb obedience, Free Swords taking to the water in panic. A half mile to the south the Free Cavalry seemed to be making a stand against the men in green cloaks, whoever had command of them rallying his men with admirable coolness as they attempted to break out. It proved a vain ambition however, as a great host of horsemen appeared to their rear, launching a cloud of arrows from the saddle before driving their charge home. Within seconds all vestige of organised resistance had vanished from the Volarian army, leaving only a terrorised mob with no chance of escape.

I turned my gaze from the ugly spectacle and saw a lone rider galloping along the causeway, followed by what seemed to be thousands of men and women with clubs and bows, not a scrap of armour amongst them. The distance was too great to make out the face of the rider but I had no doubt as to his identity.

"Faster!" the general was shouting amidst the racket of the anchor's chain. "If this ship isn't at sea within the day, I'll see the backbone of every slave aboard!"

"Are you sure?" Fornella asked, standing near the map table, wine cup in hand. "Returning home with such impressive tidings is not something I would recommend."

"We're not going home," he snapped back. "We return to Varinshold to await the next wave. When they get here I will build an army that will leave this land barren. Write this down, slave!" he snarled at me. "I, General Reklar Tokrev hereby decree the extermination of all denizens of this province . . ."

I was reaching for parchment when something caught my eye. The ship had finally begun to pull away as the sails unfurled and the prevailing wind took us downriver, the crew deaf to the entreaties of the Free Swords struggling in the water. I squinted at the sight of a new sail appearing above a bend in the river little under a mile ahead. I had seen enough of ships by now to recognise the Meldenean pennant fluttering from the mainmast, a large black flag signifying the sighting of an enemy. A shout from the rigging confirmed I was not labouring under a fear-born delusion.

"Archers up!" the ship's captain ordered. "Ready the ballistas! Kuritai to the prow!"

I watched as another sail appeared behind the Meldenean vessel, and two more after that. I glanced over at the general and was surprised to find myself regarding the visage of a coward. All trace of bluster and poise had disappeared, replaced by sweat-soaked features and limbs twitching with unrestrained fear. I knew then that this man had never actually been in a battle. He had seen them, commanded men to die in them, but never fought in one. The thought raised a laugh in my breast which I managed to contain. Coward or not, he had charge of my life whilst this ship still floated.

However, whilst I was able to restrain my mirth, his wife was not. His fevered gaze swung to her as she stood by the map table, holding the scroll I had handed him earlier, laughing heartily at the contents.

"What is it!" he demanded. "What causes you so much amusement, honoured wife?"

She waved a hand at me, still laughing. "Oh, just the pleasure of money well spent."

The general's eyes swung towards me, anger adding some colour to his pale features. "Really? How so?"

"Allow me to recite quite possibly the last work by renowned scholar and poet Lord Verniers Alishe Someren, entitled An Ode to General Reklar Tokrev, after Draken." She paused for a theatrical cough, stifling a giggle. "A man of vice and misplaced pride, Rightly detested by his bride, He drank and whored whilst safe afloat, Penning lies for his scribe to quote . . ."

"Shut up," the general told her in a quiet tone but she went on without pause.

"Sent his men to die in flame, Whilst he dreamt of unearned fame . . ."

"Shut your mouth, you venomous bitch!" He rushed towards her, a hard blow of his fist sending her reeling, delivering a kick to her stomach as she tried to rise. "Year after year of your bile!" He kicked her again, making her retch and writhe on the deck. "A century in your company, true-heart!" Another kick, blood appearing in her mouth. "After the first week I knew I would kill you—"

The knife my mistress had tossed aside in her cabin had a short blade, but it was very sharp, sinking into the base of the general's skull with ease. He gave a strange high-pitched groan, a little like a tearful child drawing breath for another sob, then fell forward, his nose making a loud crack as it smashed into the planking. It has always been a matter of great regret to me that his death was so brief, and that he never knew who had delivered the killing blow. However, I have long had occasion to ponder the unpalatable fact that so few of us receive the end we deserve.

Fornella heaved a red stain onto the deck, casting a weary gaze of acceptance at me. "I . . . suppose a . . . final kiss is . . . out of the question?"

I turned at the sound of running feet, seeing two Kuritai charging with twin swords drawn. I was about to run for the rail and take *my chances in the river but drew up short as an arrow thumped into the planking beside me, quickly followed by many more. I dived for the table, rolling under as the arrows sent the Kuritai tumbling to a lifeless halt. I looked at Fornella as she uttered a frightened whimper, an arrow pinning her gown to the deck. I would like to relate how there was some chivalrous motivation behind my next action, that I acted on nothing more than courageous impulse in grabbing her arms and pulling her under the table as the arrows continued to rain down. However, that would be a lie. I knew she would be valuable to the Meldeneans and thought they might regard me with some favour if I delivered her to them unharmed.*

We huddled together as the arrows fell, soon followed by the whoosh of something large and heavy that brought a blast of heat and an instant pall of smoke. More arrows, more whooshes, Fornella pressing herself against my side, though what reassurance she felt I could offer escapes me. Soon the deck pitched at an alarming angle, the hail-like pattering of the arrows replaced by the shouts and metallic clashes of men in combat. A slave-sailor fell dead a foot away from the table, blood still gushing from the wound in his neck as shouts of anger and challenge gave way to screams and pleas for mercy.

Silence fell for what seemed an age, eventually broken by a voice speaking the Meldenean dialect of Realm Tongue. "Get those fires out!" it called with peerless authority. "Belorath, get below and finish any still in arms. And check the hull for breaches. Be a shame not to claim her as a prize."

A pair of boots strode across the deck to stand before the table, polished and gleaming despite the blood that stained them. Fornella coughed, clutching at her belly, and the boots shifted, a familiar face appearing below the table edge, bearded and handsome with golden hair hanging over his blue eyes.

"Well, my lord," the Shield said. "You must have a tale to tell."

The fires were quickly extinguished as per his order, his first mate returning from below to report the hull intact. "Excellent!" the

Shield enthused, running a hand over the finely carved woodwork on the starboard rail. "Have you ever seen the like, Belorath? A ship to sail all the world."

"She's called the Stormspite," Fornella said in her heavily accented Realm Tongue.

The Shield turned to her with an expression of dark promise. "She's called what I choose to name her. And you don't speak until told to." He brightened at the sight of something behind us. "In fact, her namesake comes to bless her now." He strode forward greeting an odd group of people climbing aboard from the Meldenean vessel tied alongside.

Two men were first on deck, one large with a brutish aspect, the other much younger but clearly no stranger to the sights of battle. They both surveyed the carnage with drawn swords and little sign of alarm. The large man turned and bowed to the three women who followed them aboard, one of whom instantly captured the attention of all in sight. She stood straight and slender in a plain gown and a shirt of light mail, a silk scarf tied around her head, walking across the deck with a sureness of step and innate confidence that gave the lie to the dead general's pretensions to greatness.

"Welcome, Highness," the Shield greeted her, bowing low, "to the Queen Lyrna. My gift to you."

The woman gave a slight nod, looking around with keen eyes. "My brother's fleet had a ship called the Lyrna. I wonder what became of her." She paused as her gaze fell on me and I saw her scars plainly for the first time, the waxy mottled flesh that covered the upper half of her face, the mutilated ear only partially hidden by the scarf.

I lowered my gaze as she approached, falling to one knee with head bowed, as I had in her brother's throne room a few short months before. "Highness," I said.

"Do get up, my lord," she told me and I raised my gaze to find her smiling. "We have an appointment I believe."

CHAPTER ONE
Lyrna

There were perhaps fifty people waiting on the riverbank as the boat brought her to shore. There was no sign of any ceremony, just a cluster of hard-eyed, somewhat bedraggled people watching the boat approach with either distrust or puzzlement, many curious eyes lingering on the burnt-faced woman in the headscarf. The Shield stood at the prow, eyes fixed on the tall figure in the centre of the group. *He seems so pale,* Lyrna thought, unable to slow the sudden thump of her heart. At Vaelin's side stood an athletic young woman with a sword strapped across her back, long auburn hair tied back from a face of near-flawless porcelain, provoking an unwelcome stirring of jealous regret in Lyrna's breast.

Stop that! she commanded herself. *A queen is above envy.*

But it was hard to watch the way the young woman kept close to him, eyes on him constantly, brows furrowed in concern. She recognised some faces amongst them; Brother Caenis, stern-faced and standing slightly apart from the others. Al Melna, the young captain from the Mounted Guard, holding the hand of a woman with long dark braids and a fresh scar above her eye. Also, the late Tower Lord's adopted daughter, another who seemed keen to stay close to Vaelin.

The keel scraped through the reeds at the bank's edge and Ell-Nestra stepped ashore, offering a typically accomplished bow to the assembly. "Atheran Ell-Nestra, Shield of the Isles," he said, straightening to offer a humourless smile to the tall man. "Although, I believe I know one of you, at least . . ."

Vaelin barely glanced at him, moving forward with an expression of blank amazement as Lyrna stepped from the boat flanked by Iltis and Benten. He halted a few feet away, staring in unabashed wonder as she tried not to shrink from his gaze.

After a moment he blinked and sank to both knees. "Highness," he said in a voice so thin and strained she wondered if it was truly his, the expression on his face one of overwhelming relief. "Welcome home."

The Fief Lord's manor seemed to be the only building in Alltor to have escaped the siege untouched. Lyrna's passage through the city had been marked by the destruction she saw at every turn. Most of the bodies had been cleared away and numerous fires were burning outside the walls alongside the many graves dug by the Cumbraelins. The Volarian dead were being carted a few miles to the south and heaped into a quarry to be covered with earth and no words spoken to mark their passing. It seems the Volarian general's wife was one of only five hundred survivors from their entire army.

She stood before her now, face tensed with suppressed pain, hands clasped in front of the belly where her unmourned husband had kicked her. The assembled captains of the army stood behind her along with Lady Reva's court. They were a disparate bunch: a bewhiskered old guardsman who had somehow contrived to survive the siege, a veteran archer apparently of Vaelin's prior acquaintance and an Asraelin woman with a falsely cultured accent who seemed keen not to meet Lyrna's gaze for any longer than necessary. Whatever their differences, their fervent loyalty to their new Lady Governess matched the sentiment of the entire city. *I'll have to watch her,* Lyrna decided with a note of regret, smiling at the young woman standing to her left. *A realm can't have two queens.*

She was seated in an ornate chair on the dais in the Lord's chamber. Lady Reva had offered the use of the Lord's Chair but Lyrna wouldn't hear of it. "That belongs to you, my Lady Governess."

On her right stood Vaelin, arms crossed and his too-pale face drawn with a weariness that made her worry he might collapse at any moment. But throughout the petitions and judgements that had occupied the preceding hours he stood straight and still with no word of complaint or request for a chair.

"We'll speak in Realm Tongue," Lyrna told the general's wife. "For the benefit of all present."

The Volarian woman inclined her head. "As you wish."

Iltis stepped forward with a fierce glower. "The prisoner will address the queen as Highness," he stated.

The woman winced in discomfort, hand spasming over her midriff. "As you wish, Highness."

"State your name," Lyrna told her.

"Fornella Av Tokrev Av Entril . . . Highness."

"You are hereby judged as an aggressor to this Realm, having made war upon us without just cause, employing such means as to befoul the very name of humanity. The sentence is death." She watched the woman's face carefully, finding some fear, but less than she'd hoped for. *Could it be true?* she wondered, recalling Verniers' tale. *Has she really lived so long death holds little threat?*

"However," Lyrna went on, "Lord Verniers has spoken in your favour. He tells me you are a woman of considerable practicality and, whilst you were happy to profit from the many horrors visited upon this Realm, you took no direct part in it. For this reason I am minded to be merciful, but only on the condition that you answer all questions put to you without hesitation or deceit." She leaned forward, her gaze boring into the woman's eyes as she added in Volarian, "And believe me, honoured lady, we have those amongst us who can hear a lie as if it were a scream, and pull the secrets from your head after we hack it from your shoulders."

The woman's fear deepened slightly and she gave a nod, making Iltis stamp his foot. "I agree to your terms, Highness," she said quickly.

"Very well." Lyrna reclined in the chair, fingers gripping the sides for a moment. "There will be a more detailed questioning in private later. However, Lord Verniers tells me your husband spoke of returning to Varinshold to await the next wave. What did he mean?"

"The next wave of reinforcements, Highness," Fornella replied with a gratifying lack of hesitation. "The forces that were to occupy this land and prepare for the next stage."

"Stage?" Lyrna frowned. "If your invasion was complete, what next stage could there be?"

The Volarian woman shifted, suppressing a shudder of pain. "The seizure of this realm was but a first step in a larger design, Highness. This land offered certain geographical advantages for the fulfilment of the ultimate objective."

Lyrna sensed Vaelin straighten beside her, turning to find him frowning at the woman in intense concentration before breathing a sigh of frustration.

"My lord?" Lyrna asked him in concern.

"Forgive me, Highness." He offered a wan smile. "I am . . . very tired."

She surveyed his face, taking in the reddened eyes, the hollow cheeks and the great sadness that clouded his gaze. She knew what he had done the day before, in time she expected the whole world would know, and wondered if it was the killing that brought this malaise. She had always thought of him as immune to such pettiness as guilt or despair, his actions always being so far above reproach. But now . . . *Can he really be just a man after all?*

"Speak plainly," she said, turning back to the prisoner. "What exactly is this ultimate objective?"

"The Alpiran Empire, Highness." Fornella seemed puzzled she hadn't already divined such an obvious answer. "The invasion of this realm was a precursor to the seizure of the Alpiran Empire.

By the summer of the next year an army will be launched from this realm's ports to land on the empire's northern coast. A second force of similar strength will launch a simultaneous attack across the southern border. And so the long-held dream of the Volarian people will be fulfilled." The woman's smile was barely noticeable. "Your pardon, Highness, but I must tell you this invasion was never more than an opening move in a much larger game."

"Yes," Lyrna replied after a moment's consideration. "A game I'll finish when I watch Volar burn."

That evening there was a banquet of sorts. Despite the siege the Cumbraelin capital seemed to be well stocked with supplies and the manse's long dining table was piled high with food as well as numerous wine bottles of impressive vintage. "My uncle's collection," Lady Reva explained. "I've already given most of it away to the townsfolk."

They stood together in the grounds of the manor a short distance from the open dining-room windows, Iltis and Benten standing no more than a dozen paces away on either side. The Asraelin woman, apparently Honoured Counsel to the former and current holder of the Lord's Chair, stood just outside the windows, her stance and expression rigidly neutral but her gaze bright and unwavering as she surveyed their meeting.

"My lady does not like wine?" Lyrna asked the Lady Governess, turning her back on the counsellor's scrutiny.

"Can't stand the stuff." Reva smiled in discomfort, hands clasped together and head slightly lowered. It was plain she had only a scant knowledge of etiquette and kept forgetting the necessary honorifics, something Lyrna found irked her royal person not at all.

"Your uncle was something of an expert, as I recall," she said. "I remember he could take a single sniff of a glass and tell the year of bottling, the vineyard and even the direction of the slope on which the grapes had been grown."

"He was a drunk. But he was my uncle and I miss him greatly."

"Especially tonight, I'd guess."

Reva gave a short laugh. "It's . . . not what I'm used to." She frowned in annoyance before adding, "Erm, Highness. Sorry."

Lyrna just smiled and glanced back at the banquet. It was a subdued affair, the conversation muted, the guests preoccupied with the horrors they had witnessed or the friends they had lost. However, the wine was going down well, especially with Nortah Al Sendahl who sat on the manor steps, arm draped over Brother Caenis's shoulders as he held forth, wine sloshing from his glass with every expansive gesture. "Iss beautiful, brother. Big open spaces, fine view of the sea and"—he nudged the Lord Marshal with a wink—"I go to bed with a beautiful woman every night. Every night, brother! And you'd still rather stay in the Order."

"That man is very annoying," Lady Reva said. "Even when sober."

"He's certainly talkative for a corpse," Lyrna replied. She looked at the other guests, noting one significant absence. He had taken himself off to his army's camp after the first hour of the banquet, pleading tiredness which certainly could not be questioned. Lady Dahrena had left with him, causing Lyrna to realise her unwelcome pang of jealousy towards the Lady Governess may well have been misdirected.

"What happened to Lord Vaelin?" she asked her.

There was an evident reluctance in Lady Reva's expression, a tenseness to the porcelain mask of her face. "He saved us."

"I know. But I can't help but recognise the manner of saving has left its mark. My lady, please tell me what happened to him."

A thin hiss of breath came from Reva's lips, her mouth twitching at an unwelcome memory. "He led the forest folk into the city and they killed the Volarians. All of them, in the space of a few moments. By the Father, I wish we'd had them with us during the siege. I found him when it was done. He . . . was bleeding, a lot. We spoke and he fell. It seemed . . ." She trailed off, raising her gaze to meet Lyrna's. "It seemed that he'd died. Then the Lady Dahrena came. The way she moved was very strange, her eyes were closed but she walked straight to him without a stumble.

Her skin was so pale . . . She fell onto him and I thought they had both perished. I prayed, Highness. I prayed to the Father in a scream, for it was so unfair. And then . . ." She shivered, hugging herself tight. "Then they were alive again."

"Did anyone else see this?"

"Only the forest people. I could tell they didn't like it at all."

"It would be best if it was kept between us, for now."

"As you wish, Highness."

Lyrna touched her on the arm and started back to the manor. "Did you mean it?" Reva asked. "About burning their city?"

Lyrna paused and nodded. "Every word."

"Before all of this I was so certain, so convinced of the rightness of my course. I had a mission, a holy quest blessed by the World Father himself. Now . . ." The young Lady Governess frowned in consternation, suddenly seeming so much older than her years. "I have . . . done things here. In defending this city I have done things . . . I thought them right and just as I did them, now I don't know. Now I wonder if I mistook rage for right and murder for justice."

"In war they are the same thing, my lady." She returned and clasped Reva's hand. "I have done things too and every one I would do again."

"I should like to take a stroll, my lords," she told Benten and Iltis a short while later. "To view my new army."

Iltis gave a typically prompt bow whilst Benten was preoccupied with stifling a yawn. "Feeling the lateness of the hour, my lord?" she asked him.

"Apologies, Highness," he stammered, straightening up. "I am at your . . ."

She waved him to silence. "Go to bed, Benten."

Like many of the other guests, Orena seemed to appreciate the late Fief Lord's taste in wine. "We'll come too, Highness," she said, slurring a little, her eyes somewhat unfocused. "I like soldiers."

"I'll put her to bed, Highness," Murel said, taking the lady's hand and tugging her towards the manor despite her plaintive whine, "Wanna see the soldiers."

"Her mourning period didn't last long," Iltis noted, watching them go.

"We all grieve in different ways, my lord. Shall we?"

"I believe there is something I have to tell you, Highness," the big man said after they had traversed the causeway. "Concerning Lord Al Sorna."

"Really? And what is that?"

"I've made his acquaintance before. Twice in fact. Once at Linesh where he gave me this"—he touched his misshapen nose—"and once some months ago when I . . ."

Lyrna stopped, regarding him with a raised eyebrow.

"I tried to kill him," her Lord Protector finished. "With a crossbow."

Her laugh pealed out across the river as Iltis stood in stoic silence. "That's why you were in the vaults with Fermin," she said. "It was a singular misjudgement. One I assure you I'll not make again. My attachment to the Faith was fierce, unquestioning. I . . . have different loyalties now."

"I should hope you do." They resumed walking, following the bank where some corpses still floated in the reeds, bloated and rich with the odour of rotting flesh. In the aftermath of the rains, the air had taken on an unseasonal chill, misting her breath as she walked, even forming a thin layer of ice around the bodies in the river.

"Ice in summer," she said, pausing to peer closer. "Late summer, granted. But still, very strange."

"Never seen the like, Highness," Iltis agreed, stooping to get a better view. "Not in all my d—"

The arrow took him in the shoulder, spinning him to the ground with a shout. Lyrna dropped as battle-won instinct seized her, the second arrow streaking overhead to punch through the thin ice on the river. *They're close*, she surmised, judging the angle of the arrow's flight. Iltis was lying a few feet away, teeth gritted as he fumbled for his sword. Lyrna shook her head, holding up a hand, eyes scanning the long grass. Iltis stopped moving, biting the cloth of his cloak to keep from voicing his pain.

Never be without it. She had strapped the dagger to her calf before the banquet, unseemly for a queen to carry a weapon. She drew it and reversed the blade, hiding the moonlit gleam under her forearm. Waiting.

Two figures rose from the grass a little over twenty paces away, one tall the other stocky. The tall man carried a longbow, arrow notched and half-drawn, the stocky man an axe. They advanced slowly, the stocky man issuing a laugh. "You should trust my word more, my holy friend. I told you the Father would guide us to her." She could see him now, broad-bearded features and a bald head, teeth bared as he raised his voice, the tone rich with mirth. "Show yourself, Highness. We only want to offer our respects."

A little closer. She lowered her arm, letting the blade fall into her palm.

"Oh, don't be difficult," the bearded man groaned. "We're doing you a service. Do you really want to go through life with a face like that?"

Iltis sprang to his feet with a roar, sword scraping free of his scabbard, the tall man swivelling towards him, bow fully drawn. Lyrna glimpsed a narrow handsome face, drawn in hate.

It was her finest throw, the knife tumbling in a perfect arc to take him in the throat, the bowstring snapping as he fell, the arrow lost to the grass. Iltis charged towards the stocky man but could only manage a few steps before stumbling to the ground with a yell of agonised frustration. Lyrna rushed towards him as the stocky man closed, taking the sword from his limp grasp and swinging it two-handed. The steel rang against the axe blade and something smacked across her face, sending her sprawling.

"What a hard head you have, Highness," the stocky man

observed, flexing his fingers and stepping closer. "Perhaps I'll have it mounted."

He grinned as he hefted his axe, then blanched as something looped over his head and tightened about his neck. His shout choked to a crack as he was jerked from his feet, eyes bulging, the axe falling from his grasp as he clutched at the rope. Lyrna got to her feet, spitting blood, seeing a muscular, curly-haired young man dragging the stocky assassin away. The young man gathered the rope with quick, skilful jerks of his brawny arms, the stocky man's feet drumming the earth as he was drawn backwards. When he had the assassin at his feet the young man placed a boot on his neck and tightened the rope further, his face like a mask the whole while. The stocky man's choking rasps faded after a few seconds.

Lyrna went to Iltis, finding him pale from blood loss and barely conscious. "My thanks, soldier," she told the muscular young man as he approached. "Please, my lord needs a healer . . ."

She frowned when he didn't respond, moving towards her without pause, his face still absent any expression. "What . . . ?"

He moved too fast for her to dodge away, large powerful hands gripping her shoulders and drawing her close. She stared into his eyes as they roamed over her scars, seeing only a blank sense of purpose. "Hurt," he said and enfolded her in his arms, crushing her against the hard muscle of his chest.

And she burned.

Appendix I

Dramatis Personae

The Unified Realm

The Royal House of Al Nieren
Malcius Al Nieren—King of the Unified Realm
Lyrna Al Nieren—sister to Malcius, Princess of the Realm
Ordella Al Nieren—wife to Malcius, Queen of the Realm
Janus Al Nieren—son to Malcius, heir to the throne
Dirna Al Nieren—daughter to Malcius, Princess of the Realm

The Noble House of Al Sorna
Vaelin Al Sorna—former brother of the Sixth Order, Sword of the Realm and Tower Lord of the Northern Reaches
Alornis Al Sorna—artist and sister to Vaelin

The Northern Reaches
Dahrena Al Myrna—First Counsel to the North Tower
Adal Zenu—captain of the North Guard
Kehlan—healer and brother of the Fifth Order
Hollun—record keeper and brother of the Fourth Order
Orven Al Melna—captain of the Third Company, King's Mounted Guard

Harlick—librarian and brother of the Seventh Order, Archivist of the North Tower

Nortah Al Sendahl—teacher and former brother of the Sixth Order, friend to Vaelin

Sella Al Sendahl—wife to Nortah

Artis Al Sendahl—son to Sella and Nortah

Lohren Al Sendahl—daughter to Sella and Nortah

Snowdance—war-cat

Wise Bear—shaman to the Bear People

Sanesh Poltar—war chief to the Eorhil Sil

Wisdom—sage elder to the Eorhil Sil

Insha ka Forna (Steel in Moonlight)—Eorhil warrior

Ultin—mine foreman at Reaver's Gulch, later captain of the First Battalion of the Army of the North

Davern—shipwright, later sergeant in the Army of the North

Cara—resident of Nehrin's Point

Lorkan—resident of Nehrin's Point

Marken—resident of Nehrin's Point

Weaver—resident of Nehrin's Point

The Sixth Order of the Faith

Sollis—sword-master and Brother Commander of the Skellan Pass

Caenis Al Nysa—brother of the Sixth Order, Sword of the Realm and Lord Marshal of the Thirty-fifth Regiment of Foot

Frentis—brother of the Sixth Order, friend to Vaelin

Grealin—Master of Stores and brother of the Sixth Order

Rensial—horse-master and brother of the Sixth Order

Ivern—brother of the Sixth Order, stationed at the Skellan Pass

Hervil—brother of the Sixth Order, stationed at the Skellan Pass

Alltor

Sentes Mustor—Fief Lord of Cumbrael

Reva Mustor—niece to Sentes

Veliss—Honoured Counsel to the Fief Lord of Cumbrael
Arentes Varnor—Lord Commander of the City Guard
Bren Antesh—Lord Commander of Archers
Harin—healer and brother of the Fifth Order, Master of Bone Lore
Arken—Asraelin youth, friend to Reva
The Reader—leader of the Church of the World Father

Renfael

Darnel Linel—Fief Lord of Renfael
Hughlin Banders—knight and Baron of Renfael
Ulice—illegitimate daughter to Banders
Arendil—son to Ulice
Ermund Lewen—knight and chief retainer to Banders
Rekus Wenders—knight and chief retainer to Darnel

The Urlish Forest

Ratter—outlaw
Draker—outlaw, comrade to Ratter
Illian Al Jervin—escaped slave, friend to Davoka
Thirty-Four—former numbered slave and torturer
Slasher—faith-hound and friend to Frentis
Blacktooth—faith-hound and friend to Illian

Others

Alucius Al Hestian—poet, friend to Alornis and Vaelin
Nirka Al Smolen—Lord Marshal of the King's Mounted Guard
Tendris Al Forne—Aspect of the Fourth Order
Benril Lenial—renowned artist and brother of the Third Order
Janril Norin—minstrel and former standard-bearer in the Thirty-fifth Regiment of Foot
Ellora—dancer and wife to Janril
Count Marven—commander of the Nilsaelin contingent of the Army of the North
Jehrid Al Bera—Tower Lord of the Southern Shore

LONAK DOMINION

The Mahlessa—High Priestess and leader of the Lonakhim
Davoka—warrior of the Black River Clan, Servant of the
  Mountain, friend to Lyrna
Kiral—huntress of the Black River Clan and sister to Davoka
Alturk—Tahlessa of the Grey Hawk Clan
Mastek—warrior of the Grey Hawk Clan

THE ALPIRAN EMPIRE

Aluran Maxtor Selsus—Emperor
Emeren Nasur Ailers—former ward to the Emperor
Verniers Alishe Someren—Imperial Chronicler
Neliesen Nester Hevren—captain in the Imperial Guard

THE VOLARIAN EMPIRE

Arklev Entril—member of the Volarian Ruling Council
Reklar Tokrev—general of the Twentieth Corps of the Volarian
  Imperial Host
Fornella Av Entril Av Tokrev—sister to Arklev, wife to Reklar
Vastir—overseer of the pits, in the employ of Arklev

MELDENEAN ISLANDS

Atheran Ell-Nestra—Meldenean sea captain and Shield of the
  Isles
Carval Ell-Nurin—Ship Lord and captain of the *Red Falcon*
Belorath—captain of the *Sea Sabre*

SEORDAH SIL

Nersus Sil Nin (Song of the Wind)—seer of ancient legend

Hera Drakil (Red Hawk)—elder and war chief

Appendix II

The Rules of Warrior's Bluff

A standard Asraelin deck holds the following cards, listed in order of rank:

King of Wolves (value: 12)
Queen of Roses (value: 11)
Prince of Snakes (value: 10)
Lord of Blades (value: 9)
Lady of Crows (value: 8)
Red Captain (value: 7)
Black Sergeant (value: 7)
Golden Guard (value: 7)
Green Archer (value: 7)
White Swordsman (value: 7)
Blind Blacksmith (value: 6)
Smiling Mason (value: 6)
Lovelorn Miller (value: 6)
Happy Weaver (value: 6)
Weeping Maid (value: 6)
Howling Wolf (value: 5)
Soaring Hawk (value: 5)
Feasting Crow (value: 5)

Rearing Horse (value: 5)
Coiled Snake (value: 5)
Palace (value: 4)
Throne (value: 4)
Castle (value: 4)
Crown (value: 4)
Scroll (value: 4)
Crossed Swords (value: 3)
Poisoned Cup (value: 3)
Bloody Dagger (value: 3)
Drawn Bow (value: 3)
Shining Axe (value: 3)
Candle (value: 2)
Book (value: 2)
Spyglass (value: 2)
Pestle (value: 2)
Quill (value: 2)
Grey Ship (value: 1)
Merry Sailor (value: 1)
Rising Storm (value: 1)
Darkening Sea (value: 1)
Drowned Man (value: 1)

Warrior's Bluff may be played by up to five players. At the start of the game the dealer shuffles the cards and deals six cards to each player. Each player may choose two cards from his hand to be substituted for two from the deck.

The player to the dealer's left will make the first bet or fold his hand and so on until each player has either placed a bet or folded. During the next round the players have the option of raising or sticking with their previous bets. If all players opt to stick, the cards will be shown and the player with the highest-value hand wins the pot. If one or more players opt to raise, each player must match the highest bet to stay in the game. Betting continues until all remaining players stick in the same round, after which all cards are shown and the player with the highest-value hand wins.

Any player drawing the Lord of Blades plus the five cards in the Martial Suit (Red Captain, Black Sergeant, Golden Guard, Green Archer and White Swordsman) has drawn the Warrior's Bluff and wins the hand. All other hands are won by virtue of the total value of all five cards held by each player. Where the value of two or more hands is identical, the player with the highest-ranking card wins, e.g. a player holding the King of Wolves and five other cards with a total value of thirty will win over a player with a Queen of Roses and five other cards also with a value of thirty.

ACKNOWLEDGMENTS

Once again thanks to Susan Allison, my editor at Ace, for her continued support and advice. Repeated appreciation to Paul Field for all the proofing. Thanks to Michael J. Sullivan for his early and ongoing support. But most of all thanks to everyone who took a chance on *Blood Song* and liked what they saw enough to allow me to write another one.

extras

www.orbitbooks.net

about the author

Anthony Ryan lives in London and is a writer of fantasy, science fiction and non-fiction. He previously worked in a variety of roles for the UK government but now writes full time. Anthony maintains an active blog at www.anthonystuff.wordpress.com.

Find out more about Anthony Ryan and other Orbit authors by registering for the free monthly newsletter at www.orbitbooks.net.

interview

Blood Song is an epic fantasy in every sense of the word – particularly in that it took you six years to write! Why did it take so long and what was the spark that started it all?

Working a full-time job whilst studying part-time for a history degree had a lot to do with the time taken to write *Blood Song*. Also, although I had a one-page synopsis, I wasn't working to a detailed plan, something I've subsequently learned is very useful in speeding up the writing process. It's always difficult to pin down the genesis of an idea but I recall the basis of *Blood Song* germinating for a few years but not really coming together until I started my history studies. The themes of religious conflict and political intrigue were also at the forefront of my thinking in the aftermath of 9/11 which probably had an influence.

You were influenced initially by Lloyd Alexander's Prydain Chronicles, and then later by legendary British fantasy author David Gemmell. What was so special to you about the works of these two writers, and how do you think they influenced your own writing?

Although I was aware of Tolkien as a kid, my first foray into fantasy began with Lloyd Alexander, who was writing YA fantasy long before it had a name. The Prydain Chronicles are essentially a coming of age tale mixing Welsh legend and epic fantasy, completely capturing my ten-year-old imagination from the moment I picked up *The Book of Three*. There are echoes of my main character Vaelin in Alexander's Taran, orphan and apprentice pig keeper continually beset with questions over his past and doubts about his future. Whilst Lloyd Alexander began my love of fantasy, David Gemmell ensured it continued into adulthood with the wonderful *Wolf in Shadow*, an action-packed but also sublimely sombre tale mixing the western with fantasy. Gemmell is primarily remembered for the pace and action of his books but I also think his characterisation is excellent; his characters are flawed, conflicted and, most importantly, consistent whilst also being capable of change, all elements I've tried to include in my own work.

What is it about epic fantasy as a genre that attracted you to it, from a writing perspective? Given that you studied medieval history, did you ever consider writing a purely historical novel?
I've read plenty of historical novels but not yet had the yen to write one – though I do have a germ of an idea for a historical detective story, so who knows? However, at the moment I think I would find it too restricting: you have to spend a long time on research and are stuck with recorded events that can't be changed. Epic fantasy gives the writer the room to create the history of their imaginary world allowing a great amount of scope for drama, spectacle and a combination of themes that would be denied the historical novelist.

You originally self-published *Blood Song* and achieved considerable success, so why did you decide to sign with a traditional publisher?
Simply put, I weighed up the pros and cons and decided it was the best decision for me. Although I think self-publishing is a great

thing, and continue to self-publish my Slab City Blues sci-fi novellas, I wanted the Raven's Shadow trilogy to have the widest possible audience, including foreign sales and access to bookshops. A traditional publishing deal still seems the best way of achieving that.

Blood Song eschews the multi-viewpoint format used by so many current epic fantasies, focusing instead on telling the story from Vaelin's point of view. What are the advantages and limitations of this more singular approach?

The primary advantage is that it enables a more thorough exploration of character over the course of a fairly lengthy narrative: we see Vaelin's journey into adulthood with all the many tribulations on the way, which hopefully adds a greater emotional resonance to the ending. Also, for a fantasy author, a single point of view begun in childhood enables a more narrative-driven approach to world-building; we learn about the politics and history of Vaelin's world as he does, avoiding the dreaded info dump in the process. The disadvantage is that a lot has to happen off-camera, which is why the sequel has four point of view characters instead of one, as the scope of the overall story has expanded greatly. If I ever got lucky enough to write the whole trilogy I had always intended to open out the narrative, a device I found particularly effective in David Eddings' Belgariad which features just one POV until halfway through the third book.

One of my favourite characters from the book is Master Sollis: grim and steely on the outside, but perhaps a _little_ softer on the inside – if you can get past his stern façade. Was there any particular inspiration behind this character – an old school-teacher perhaps?

I had some great teachers as a kid (and some not so great), but I can't recall any even vaguely resembling Sollis. He's kind of the ultimate PE teacher meets the ultimate Sergeant Major. He came about because I needed Vaelin to have an unyielding mentor, someone even more single minded and devoted to the Order than he is, but also never needlessly cruel (at least in his own head).

You've made the jump to becoming a full-time writer – how has this changed your writing routine and lifestyle? Do you find you're a lot more productive, now that you don't have to fit the writing in around your work?

The main difference is that I'm a lot less tired these days. My decision to go full time was motivated by the experience of writing Book 2; producing two thousand words a day whilst commuting to a full-time job was not something I wanted to repeat. Oddly, my word count hasn't gone up all that much despite my heroic efforts to resist the lures of daytime telly (actually, that's pretty easy because it's uniformly awful).

You're a big film fan, so which actor would you like to see playing Vaelin in any film adaptation of *Blood Song*?

To be honest I've yet to see an actor that matches my vision of Vaelin. Also, he's never fully described in the book because I wanted the reader to conjure their own image of him, something I'm loath to spoil (at least until those nice Hollywood people cough up some option money). Writers are usually pretty bad at casting anyway; I read somewhere that Ian Fleming thought Cary Grant would make the perfect Bond, a good indication why casting directors are paid so much.

You've already finished the second novel in the Raven's Shadow trilogy, and are well into writing the third. Have you always had an overall plan in mind for how the trilogy would pan

out, or have you generally been making it up as you went along?

As I said earlier, I had only a one-page outline for the first book. The outlines for Books 2 and 3 are much more extensive, running to over four thousand words each. That being said, I do frequently deviate from them as I find actually writing the book the best way to develop plot and character. However, unlike the writers of *Lost*, I always had the general shape of the story in my head and know how it all ends.

if you enjoyed
TOWER LORD

look out for

PROMISE OF BLOOD
Powder Mage: Book 1

by

Brian McClellan

CHAPTER

1

Adamat wore his coat tight, top buttons fastened against a wet night air that seemed to want to drown him. He tugged at his sleeves, trying to coax more length, and picked at the front of the jacket where it was too close by far around the waist. It'd been half a decade since he'd even seen this jacket, but when summons came from the king at this hour, there was no time to get his good one from the tailor. Yet this summer coat provided no defense against the chill snaking through the carriage window.

The morning was not far off but dawn would have a hard time scattering the fog. Adamat could feel it. It was humid even for early spring in Adopest, and chillier than Novi's frozen toes. The soothsayers in Noman's Alley said it was a bad omen. Yet who listened to soothsayers these days? Adamat reasoned it would give him a cold and wondered why he had been summoned out on a pit-made night like this.

The carriage approached the front gate of Skyline and moved on without a stop. Adamat clutched at his pantlegs and peered out the window. The guards were not at their posts. Odder still, as they continued along the wide path amid the fountains, there were no lights. Skyline had so many lanterns, it could be seen all the way from the city even on the cloudiest night. Tonight the gardens were dark.

Adamat was fine with this. Manhouch used enough of their taxes for his personal amusement. Adamat stared out into the gardens at the black maws where the hedge mazes began and imagined shapes flitting back and forth in the lawn. What was...ah, just a sculpture. Adamat sat back, took a deep breath. He could hear his heart beating, thumping, frightened, his stomach tightening. Perhaps they *should* light the garden lanterns...

A little part of him, the part that had once been a police inspector, prowling nights such as these for the thieves and pickpockets in dark alleys, laughed out from inside. *Still your heart, old man*, he said to himself. *You were once the eyes staring back from the darkness.*

The carriage jerked to a stop. Adamat waited for the coachman to open the door. He might have waited all night. The driver rapped on the roof. "You're here," a gruff voice said.

Rude.

Adamat stepped from the coach, just having time to snatch his hat and cane before the driver flicked the reins and was off, clattering into the night. Adamat uttered a quiet curse after the man and turned around, looking up at Skyline.

The nobility called Skyline Palace "the Jewel of Adro." It rested on a high hill east of Adopest so that the sun rose above it every morning. One particularly bold newspaper had compared it to a starving pauper wearing a diamond ring. It was an apt comparison in these lean times. A king's pride doesn't fill the people's bellies.

He was at the main entrance. By day, it was a grand avenue of marbled walks and fountains, all leading to a pair of giant, silver-plated doors, themselves dwarfed by the sheer façade of the biggest single building in Adro. Adamat listened for the soft footfalls of patrolling Hielmen. It was said the king's personal guard were everywhere in these gardens, watching every secluded corner, muskets always loaded, bayonets fixed, their gray-and-white sashes somber among the green-and-gold splendor. But there were no footfalls, nor were the fountains running. He'd heard once that the fountains only stopped for the death of the king. Surely he'd not have been summoned here if Manhouch were dead. He smoothed the front of his jacket. Here, next to the building, a few of the lanterns were lit.

A figure emerged from the darkness. Adamat tightened his grip on his cane, ready to draw the hidden sword inside at a moment's notice.

It was a man in uniform, but little could be discerned in such ill light. He held a rifle or a musket, trained loosely on Adamat, and wore a flat-topped forage cap with a stiff visor. Only one thing could be certain...he was not a Hielman. Their tall, plumed hats were easy to recognize, and they never went without them.

"You're alone?" a voice asked.

"Yes," Adamat said. He held up both hands and turned around.

"All right. Come on."

The soldier edged forward and yanked on one of the mighty silver doors. It rolled outward slowly, ponderously, despite the man putting his weight into it. Adamat moved closer and examined the soldier's jacket. It was dark blue with silver braiding. Adran military. In theory, the military reported to the king. In practice, one man held their leash: Field Marshal Tamas.

"Step back, friend," the soldier said. There was a note of impatience in his voice, some unseen stress—but that could have been the weight of the door. Adamat did as he was told, only coming forward again to slip through the entrance when the soldier gestured.

"Go ahead," the soldier directed. "Take a right at the diadem and head through the Diamond Hall. Keep walking until you find yourself in the Answering Room." The door inched shut behind him and closed with a muffled thump.

Adamat was alone in the palace vestibule. Adran military, he mused. Why would a soldier be here, on the grounds, without any sign of the Hielmen? The most frightening answer sprang to mind first. A power struggle. Had the military been called in to deal with a rebellion? There were a number of powerful factions within Adro: the Wings of Adom mercenaries, the royal cabal, the Mountain-watch, and the great noble families. Any one of them could have been giving Manhouch trouble. None of it made sense, though. If there had been a power struggle, the palace grounds would be a battlefield, or destroyed outright by the royal cabal.

Adamat passed the diadem—a giant facsimile of the Adran crown—and noted it was in as bad taste as rumor had it. He entered the Diamond Hall, where the walls and floor were of scarlet, accented in gold leaf, and thousands of tiny gems, which gave the room its name, glittered from the ceiling in the light of a single lit candelabra. The tiny flames of the candelabra flickered as if in the wind, and the room was cold.

Adamat's sense of unease deepened as he neared the far end of the gallery. Not a sign of life, and the only sound came from his own echoing footfalls on the marble floor. A window had been shattered, explaining the chill. The result of one of the king's famous temper tantrums? Or something else? He could hear his heart beating in his ears. There. Behind a curtain, a pair of boots? Adamat passed his hand before his eyes. A trick of the light. He stepped over to reassure himself and pulled back the curtain.

A body lay in the shadows. Adamat bent over it, touched the skin. It was warm, but the man was most certainly dead. He wore gray pants with a white stripe down the side and a matching jacket.

A tall hat with a white plume lay on the floor some ways away. A Hielman. The shadows played on a young, clean-shaven face, peaceful except for a single hole in the side of his skull and the dark, wet stain on the floor.

He'd been right. A struggle of some kind. Had the Hielmen rebelled, and the military been brought in to deal with them? Again, it didn't make any sense. The Hielmen were fanatically loyal to the king, and any matters within Skyline Palace would have been dealt with by the royal cabal.

Adamat cursed silently. Every question compounded itself. He suspected he'd find some answers soon enough.

Adamat left the body behind the curtain. He lifted his cane and twisted, bared a few inches of steel, and approached a tall doorway flanked by two hooded, scepter-wielding sculptures. He paused between the ancient statues and took a deep breath, letting his eyes wander over a set of arcane script scrawled into the portal. He entered.

The Answering Room made the Hall of Diamonds look small. A pair of staircases, one to either side of him and each as wide across as three coaches, led to a high gallery that ran the length of the room on both sides. Few outside the king and his cabal of Privileged sorcerers ever entered this room.

In the center of the room was a single chair, on a dais a handbreadth off the floor, facing a collection of knee pillows, where the cabal acknowledged their liege. The room was well lit, though from no discernible source of light.

A man sat on the stairs to Adamat's right. He was older than Adamat, just into his sixtieth year with silver hair and a neatly trimmed mustache that still retained a hint of black. He had a strong but not overly large jaw and his cheekbones were well defined. His skin was darkened by the sun, and there were deep lines at the corners of his mouth and eyes. He wore a dark-blue soldier's uniform with a silver representation of a powder keg pinned above the heart and nine gold service stripes sewn on the right breast, one for every five years in the Adran military. His uniform lacked an officer's epaulettes, but the weary experience in the man's brown eyes left no question that he'd led armies on the battlefield. There was a single pistol, hammer cocked, on the stair next to him. He leaned on a sheathed small sword and watched as a stream of blood slowly trickled down each step, a dark line on the yellow-and-white marble.

"Field Marshal Tamas," Adamat said. He sheathed his cane sword and twisted until it clicked shut.

The man looked up. "I don't believe we've ever met."

"We have," Adamat said. "Fourteen years ago. A charity ball thrown by Lord Aumen."

"I have a terrible time with faces," the field marshal said. "I apologize."

Adamat couldn't take his eyes off the rivulet of blood. "Sir. I was summoned here. I wasn't told by whom, or for what reason."

"Yes," Tamas said. "I summoned you. On the recommendation of one of my Marked. Cenka. He said you served together on the police force in the twelfth district."

Adamat pictured Cenka in his mind. He was a short man with an unruly beard and a penchant for wines and fine food. He'd seen him last seven years ago. "I didn't know he was a powder mage."

"We try to find anyone with an affinity for it as soon as possible," Tamas said, "but Cenka was a late bloomer. In any case"— he waved a hand—"we've come upon a problem."

Adamat blinked. "You...want my help?"

The field marshal raised an eyebrow. "Is that such an unusual request? You were once a fine police investigator, a good servant of Adro, and Cenka tells me that you have a perfect memory."

"Still, sir."

"Eh?"

"I'm still an investigator. Not with the police, sir, but I still take jobs."

"Excellent. Then it's not so odd for me to seek your services?"

"Well, no," Adamat said, "but sir, this is Skyline Palace. There's a dead Hielman in the Diamond Hall and..." He pointed at the stream of blood on the stairs. "Where's the king?"

Tamas tilted his head to the side. "He's locked himself in the chapel."

"You've staged a coup," Adamat said. He caught a glimpse of movement with the corner of his eye, saw a soldier appear at the top of the stairs. The man was a Deliv, a dark-skinned northerner. He wore the same uniform as Tamas, with eight golden stripes on the right breast. The left breast of his uniform displayed a silver powder keg, the sign of a Marked. Another powder mage.

"We have a lot of bodies to move," the Deliv said.

Tamas gave his subordinate a glance. "I know, Sabon."

"Who's this?" Sabon asked.

"The inspector that Cenka requested."

"I don't like him being here," Sabon said. "It could compromise everything."

"Cenka trusted him."

"You've staged a coup," Adamat said again with certainty.

"I'll help with the bodies in a moment," Tamas said. "I'm old, I need some rest now and then." The Deliv gave a sharp nod and disappeared.

"Sir!" Adamat said. "What have you done?" He tightened his grip on his cane sword.

Tamas pursed his lips. "Some say the Adran royal cabal had the most powerful Privileged sorcerers in all the Nine Nations, second only to Kez," he said quietly. "Yet I've just slaughtered every one of them. Do you think I'd have trouble with an old inspector and his cane sword?"

Adamat loosened his grip. He felt ill. "I suppose not."

"Cenka led me to believe that you were pragmatic. If that is the case, I would like to employ your services. If not, I'll kill you now and look for a solution elsewhere."

"You've staged a coup," Adamat said again.

Tamas sighed. "Must we keep coming back to that? Is it so shocking? Tell me, can you think of any fewer than a dozen factions within Adro with reason to dethrone the king?"

"I didn't think any of them had the skill," Adamat said. "Or the daring." His eyes returned to the blood on the stairs, before his mind traveled to his wife and children, asleep in their beds. He looked at the field marshal. His hair was tousled; there were drops of blood on his jacket—a lot, now that he thought to look. Tamas might as well have been sprayed with it. There were dark circles under his eyes and a weariness that spoke of more than just age.

"I will not agree to a job blindly," Adamat said. "Tell me what you want."

"We killed them in their sleep," Tamas said without preamble. "There's no easy way to kill a Privileged, but that's the best. A mistake was made and we had a fight on our hands." Tamas looked pained for a moment, and Adamat suspected that the fight had not gone as well as Tamas would have liked. "We prevailed. Yet upon the lips of the dying was one phrase."

Adamat waited.

"'You can't break Kresimir's Promise,'" Tamas said. "That's what the dying sorcerers said to me. Does it mean anything to you?"

Adamat smoothed the front of his coat and sought to recall old memories. "No. 'Kresimir's Promise'...'Break'...'Broken'... Wait—'Kresimir's Broken Promise.'" He looked up. "It was the name of a street gang. Twenty...twenty-two years ago. Cenka couldn't remember that?"

Tamas continued. "Cenka thought it sounded familiar. He was certain you'd remember it."

"I don't forget things," Adamat said. "Kresimir's Broken Promise was a street gang with forty-three members. They were all young, some of them no more than children, the oldest not yet twenty. We were trying to round up some of the leaders to put a stop to a string of thefts. They were an odd lot—they broke into churches and robbed priests."

"What happened to them?"

Adamat couldn't help but look at the blood on the stairs. "One day they disappeared, every one of them—including our informants. We found the whole lot a few days later, forty-three bodies jammed into a drain culvert like pickled pigs' feet. They'd been massacred by powerful sorceries, with excessive brutality. The marks of the king's royal cabal. The investigation ended there." Adamat suppressed a shiver. He'd not once seen a thing like that, not before or since. He'd witnessed executions and riots and murder scenes that filled him with less dread.

The Deliv soldier appeared again at the top of the stairs. "We need you," he said to Tamas.

"Find out why these mages would utter those words with their final breath," Tamas said. "It may be connected to your street gang. Maybe not. Either way, find me an answer. I don't like the riddles of the dead." He got to his feet quickly, moving like a man twenty years younger, and jogged up the stairs after the Deliv. His boot splashed in the blood, leaving behind red prints. "Also," he called over his shoulder, "keep silent about what you have seen here until the execution. It will begin at noon."

"But..." Adamat said. "Where do I start? Can I speak with Cenka?"

Tamas paused near the top of the stairs and turned. "If you can speak with the dead, you're welcome to."

Adamat ground his teeth. "How did they say the words?" he said. "Was it a command, or a statement, or...?"

Tamas frowned. "An entreaty. As if the blood draining from their bodies was not their primary concern. I must go now."

"One more thing," Adamat said.

Tamas looked to be near the end of his patience.

"If I'm to help you, tell me why all of this?" He gestured to the blood on the stairs.

"I have things that require my attention," Tamas warned.

Adamat felt his jaw tighten. "Did you do this for power?"

"I did this for me," Tamas said. "And I did this for Adro. So that Manhouch wouldn't sign us all into slavery to the Kez with the Accords. I did it because those grumbling students of philosophy at the university only play at rebellion. The age of kings is dead, Adamat, and I have killed it."

Adamat examined Tamas's face. The Accords was a treaty to be signed with the king of Kez that would absolve all Adran debt but impose strict tax and regulation on Adro, making it little more than a Kez vassal. The field marshal had been outspoken about the Accords. But then, that was expected. The Kez had executed Tamas's late wife.

"It is," Adamat said.

"Then get me some bloody answers." The field marshal whirled and disappeared into the hallway above.

Adamat remembered the bodies of that street gang as they were being pulled from the drain in the wet and mud, remembered the horror etched upon their dead faces. *The answers may very well be bloody.*

CHAPTER

2

Lajos is dying," Sabon said.

Tamas entered the apartments of the Privileged who'd been Zakary the Beadle. He swept through the salon and entered the bedchamber—a room bigger than most merchants' houses. The walls were indigo and covered with colorful paintings that displayed various Beadles in the history of Adro's royal cabal. Doors led off to auxiliary rooms, such as the privy and Beadle's kitchens. The door to the Beadle's private brothel had been ripped apart, splinters no bigger than a finger scattered across the room.

The Beadle's bed had been stripped of sheets, the Beadle's body tossed aside for a wounded powder mage.

"How do you feel?" Tamas said.

Lajos managed a weak cough. Marked were tougher than most, and with the gunpowder Lajos had ingested, now coursing through his blood, he would feel little pain. It was little consolation as Tamas gazed on his friend. Half of Lajos's right arm was gone—lengthwise—and a hole the size of a melon had been torn through his abdomen. It was a miracle he'd lived this long. They'd given him half a horn's worth of powder. That alone should have killed him.

"I've felt better," Lajos said. He coughed again, blood leaking from the corner of his mouth.

Tamas drew his handkerchief and dabbed the blood away. "It won't be much longer," he said.

"I know," Lajos said.

Tamas squeezed his friend's hand.

Lajos mouthed the words, "Thank you."

Tamas took a deep breath. It was suddenly hard to see. He blinked his eyes clear. Lajos's breathing came to a rasping stop. Tamas made to pull his hand away when Lajos gripped it suddenly. Lajos's eyes opened.

"It's all right, my friend," Lajos said. "You've done what needed to be done. Have peace." His eyes focused elsewhere and then stilled. He was dead.

Tamas closed his friend's eyes with the tips of his fingers and turned to Sabon. The Deliv stood on the other side of the room, examining what was left of the door to the harem where it hung on the frame by one hinge. Tamas joined him and looked inside. The women had been corralled away an hour ago by his soldiers, taken to some other part of the palace with the rest of the Privilegeds' whores.

"The fury of a woman," Sabon murmured.

"Indeed," Tamas said.

"There's no way we could have planned for this."

"Tell that to them," Tamas said. He jerked his head at the row of four bodies on the floor, and the fifth that would soon be joining them. Five powder mages. Five friends. All because of one Privileged that had been unaccounted for. Tamas had just put a bullet in the Beadle's head—a man who he'd shaken hands with and spoken to on a regular basis. Tamas's Marked stood around him, ready in case the old man had some fight in him. They were not ready for the other Privileged, the one hiding in the brothel. She'd sliced through that door like a guillotine blade through a melon, Privileged's gloves on her hands, fingers dancing as her sorcery tore Tamas's powder mages to shreds.

A powder mage could float a bullet over a mile and hit the bull's-eye every time. He could angle a bullet around corners with the power of his mind, and ingest black powder to make himself stronger and faster than other men. But he could do little to contest Privileged sorcery at close range.

Tamas, Sabon, and Lajos had been the only men with time to react, and they'd barely fought her off. She'd fled, echoes of sorcerous destruction following her through the palace as she went— probably nothing more than a show to keep them from following. Her parting shot had been Lajos's mortal wound, but it had been randomly flung. It very well could have been Sabon, or even Tamas himself, who'd died there on the bed a moment ago. The thought chilled Tamas's blood.

Tamas looked away from the door. "We'll have to follow her. Find her and kill her. She's dangerous on the loose."

"A job for the magebreaker?" Sabon said. "I wondered why you've kept him around."

"A contingency I didn't want to use," Tamas said. "I wish I had a mage to send with him."

"His partner is a Privileged," Sabon said. "A magebreaker and a Privileged should be more than a match for a single cabal Privileged." He gestured at the wrecked door.

"I don't like to fight fair when it comes to the royal cabal," Tamas said. "And remember, there's a difference between a member of the royal cabal and a hired thug."

"Who was she?" Sabon asked. There was a note in his voice, perhaps reproach.

"I have no idea," Tamas snapped. "I knew every one of the king's cabal. I've met them, dined with them. She was a stranger."

Sabon took Tamas's anger without comment. "A spy for another cabal?"

"Not likely. The brothel girls are all checked. She didn't look like a whore. She was strong, weathered. The Beadle's lover, maybe. I've never seen her before in my life."

"Could the Beadle have been training someone in secret?"

"Apprentices are never secret," Tamas said. "Privileged are too suspicious to allow that."

"Their suspicions are often well founded," Sabon said. "There has to be a reason for her presence."

"I know. We'll deal with her in good time."

"If the others had been here…" Sabon said.

"More of us would be dead," Tamas said. He counted the bodies again, as if there might be fewer this time. Five. Out of seventeen of his mages. "We split into two groups for precisely this reason." He turned away from the bodies. "Any word from Taniel?"

"He's in the city," Sabon said.

"Perfect. I'll send him with the magebreaker."

"Are you sure?" Sabon said. "He just got back from Fatrasta. He needs time to rest, to see his fiancée…"

"Is Vlora with him?"

Sabon shrugged.

"Let's hope she gets here soon. Our work is not yet done." He raised a hand to forestall protests. "And Taniel can rest when the coup's over."

"What must be done will be done," Sabon said quietly.

They both fell silent, regarding their fallen comrades. Moments passed before Tamas saw a smile spread on Sabon's wrinkled black face. The Deliv was tired and haggard, but with a hint of restrained joy. "We succeeded."

Tamas eyed the bodies of his friends—his soldiers—again. "Yes," he said. "We did." He forced himself to look away.

A painting stood in the corner, a monstrosity with a gilded frame on a silver tripod befitting a herald of the royal cabal. Tamas studied the painting briefly. It showed Zakary in his prime as a strong young man with broad shoulders and a stern frown.

A far cry from the old, bent body in the corner. The bullet had entered his brain in such a way as to kill him instantly, yet his lifeless throat had gasped the same words as the others: "You can't break Kresimir's Promise."

Cenka was white as a mummer's painted face after the first of the Privileged cried out as they died. He'd demanded that Tamas summon Adamat here, to the heart of their crime. Tamas hoped that Cenka was wrong. He hoped that the investigator found nothing.

Tamas left the cabal's wing of the palace, Sabon following close behind.

"I'll need a new bodyguard," Tamas said as they walked. It pained him to speak of it, with Lajos's body still cooling.

"A Marked?" Sabon asked.

"I can't spare one. Not now."

"I've had my eye on a Knacked," Sabon said. "A man named Olem."

"He's a soldier?" Tamas asked. He thought he knew the name. He held his hand just slightly below his eyes. "About this tall? Sandy hair?"

"Yes."

"What's his Knack?"

"He doesn't need sleep. Ever."

"That's useful," Tamas said.

"Quite. He has a strong third eye as well, so he can watch for Privileged. I'll have him briefed and by your side for the execution."

A Knacked wouldn't be as useful as a powder mage. Knacked were more common, and their abilities were more like a talent than a sorcerous power. But if he could use his third eye to see sorcery, he would be of some benefit.

Tamas approached the barred doors of the chapel. A pair of Tamas's soldiers emerged from the shadows by the wall, muskets at the ready. Tamas nodded to them and gestured at the door.

One of the soldiers removed a long knife from his belt and slid it between the doors to the chapels. "He flipped the Diocel's latch," said the soldier fiddling with the knife, "but he didn't even bother to stack anything in front of the door. Not very enterprising, if you ask me." He flipped up the lock and he and his companion pushed the doors open.

The chapel was large, as were all the rooms in the palace. Unlike the rest of the palace, however, it had been spared the seasonal remodeling customary of the king's whims and remained close to what it must have looked like two hundred years ago. The ceiling was vaulted impossibly high, with boxes for the royalty and high nobles set about halfway up the walls in between columns as wide across as an oxcart. The floor was tiled in marble designed in intricate mosaics of various shapes and sizes, while the ceiling contained paneled depictions of the saints as they founded the Nine Nations under the god Kresimir's fatherly gaze.

Two altars sat at the front of the chapel, raised slightly above the benches, next to a pulpit of blackwood. The first altar, smaller, closer to the people, was dedicated to Adro's founding saint, Adom. The second, larger altar, sided by marble and covered with satin, was dedicated to Kresimir. Beside this altar huddled Manhouch XII, sovereign of Adro, and his wife Natalija, Duchess of Tarony. Natalija stared behind and above the altar, her lips moving in silent prayer to Kresimir's Rope. Manhouch was pale, his eyes red, lips drawn to a thin line. He spoke in a desperate whisper to the Diocel. He stopped as Tamas approached.

"Wait," the Diocel called, one hand rising as the king jogged down the steps from the altar and stormed toward Tamas with purpose. The Diocel's old face was fraught, his robes wrinkled from a hasty rush to the chapel.

Tamas watched Manhouch march toward him. He noted the one hand held behind his back, the fury of emotions playing across Manhouch's aristocratic young face. Manhouch looked barely seventeen thanks to the high sorceries of his royal cabal, though in reality he was well into his thirties. It was supposed to reflect the monarchy's agelessness, but Tamas had always found it hard to take such a young-looking man seriously. Tamas stopped and regarded the king, watched him falter before coming closer.

Five paces away, Manhouch revealed his pistol. It came up swiftly. His aim was sure at that range—after all, Tamas himself had taught the king to shoot. It was an unfortunate reflection on his detachment from the world, however, that Manhouch attempted it at all. He pulled the trigger.

Tamas reached out mentally and absorbed the power of the powder blast. He felt the energy course through him, warming his body like a sip of fine spirits. He redirected the power of the blast harmlessly into the floor, cracking a marble tile beneath the king. Manhouch danced away from the cracked tile. The ball rolled from the barrel of his pistol and clattered to the ground, stopping by Tamas's feet.

Tamas stepped forward, taking the pistol from the king by the barrel. He barely felt it burn his hand.

"How dare you," Manhouch said. His face was powdered, his cheeks blushed. His silk bedclothes were rumpled, soaked with sweat. "We trusted you to protect us." He trembled slightly.

Tamas looked past Manhouch to the Diocel still beside the altar. The old priest leaned against the wall, his tall, embroidered hat of office balanced precariously on his head. "I suppose," Tamas said, shaking the pistol, "he got this from you?"

"It wasn't meant for that," the Diocel wheezed. He stuck his chin up. "It was meant for the king. So he can take his life honorably and not be struck down by a godless traitor."